Ian Irvine was born in ~~~~~~~~~~~~~
educated at Chevalier ~~~~~~~~~~~~~~~~~~ of
Sydney, where he took ~~~~~~~~~~~~ine science.

After working as an environmental project manager,
Ian set up his own consultation firm in 1986, carrying
out environmental studies for clients in Australia and
overseas. He has worked in many countries in the Asia-
Pacific region. An expert in marine pollution, he has developed some of Australia's national guidelines for the
protection of the oceanic environment.

The international success of Ian Irvine's debut fantasy series, The View from the Mirror, immediately established him as one of the most popular new authors
in the fantasy genre. He is now a full-time writer and
lives in the mountains of northern New South Wales,
Australia, with his family.

Ian Irvine has his own website at www.ian-irvine.com
and can be contacted at ianirvine@ozemail.com.au

Find out more about Ian Irvine and other Orbit authors
by registering for the free monthly newsletter at
www.orbitbooks.net

By Ian Irvine

IAN IRVINE

A TALE OF THE THREE WORLDS

Geomancer

VOLUME ONE OF THE WELL OF ECHOES

www.orbitbooks.net

ORBIT

First published in Great Britain by Orbit 2002
This edition published by Orbit 2003
Reprinted 2011

A CIP catalogue record for this book
is available from the British Library.

ISBN 978-1-84149-137-0

Printed in the UK by CPI Mackays, Chatham ME5 8TD

Papers used by Orbit are from well-managed forests
and other responsible sources.

MIX
Paper from
responsible sources
FSC® C104740

Orbit
An imprint of
Little, Brown Book Group
100 Victoria Embankment
London EC4Y 0DY

An Hachette UK Company
www.hachette.co.uk

www.orbitbooks.net

To Simon

ACKNOWLEDGEMENTS

Thanks to Eric, Simon and Angus for their comments on the manuscript, to my agent Selwa Anthony, to Cathy Larsen, Janet Raunjak, Laura Harris and all the lovely sales and marketing people at Penguin Books, and to my tireless editor, Kay Ronai.

CONTENTS

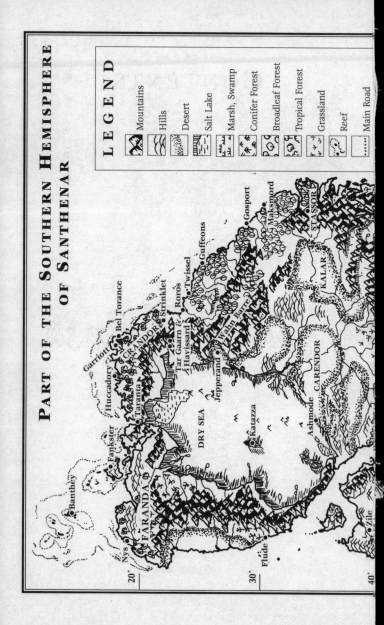

PART OF THE SOUTHERN HEMISPHERE OF SANTHENAR

LEGEND

- Mountains
- Hills
- Desert
- Salt Lake
- Marsh, Swamp
- Conifer Forest
- Broadleaf Forest
- Tropical Forest
- Grassland
- Reef
- Main Road

Banthey
Nys
Fankster
FARANDA
Flude
Zile

Garriott
Huccadory
Bel Torance
CR...OR
CRANDOR
Taranta
Strinklet
Roros
Twissel
Far Gaarn &
Havissard
Jepperand
Guffeons
Walin Barre
Gosport
Maksmord
STASSOR
KALAR
Ashmode
CARENDOR
Katazza

DRY SEA

20°
30°
40°

Maps by the author

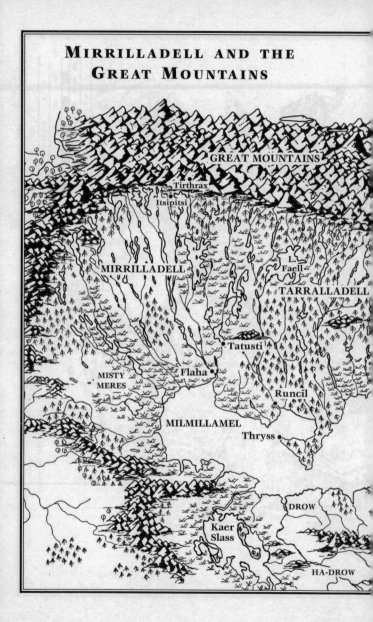

MIRRILLADELL AND THE GREAT MOUNTAINS

GREAT MOUNTAINS

Tirthrax

Itsipitsi

MIRRILLADELL

L. Faell

TARRALLADELL

Tatusti

MISTY MERES

Flaha

Runcil

MILMILLAMEL

Thryss

Kaer Slass

DROW

HA-DROW

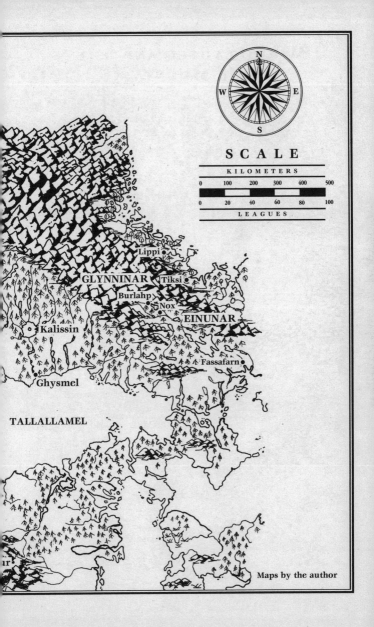

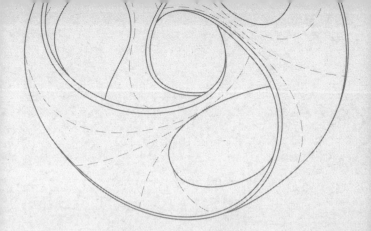

PART ONE

ARTISAN

ONE

Tiaan could hear her foreman's fury from halfway across the manufactory. Doors were kicked open, workers cursed out of the way, stools slapped aside with his sword. 'Where the blazes is Tiaan?' he roared. 'She's really cruelled it this time.'

The urge to hide was overwhelming; also futile. She busied herself at her bench. What had she done wrong? There had never been a problem with her work before.

The door of her cubicle slammed back and Foreman Gryste stood in the opening, his chest heaving. A huge, sweaty man, he reeked of cloves and garlic. Thickets of hair sprouted between the straining buttons of his shirt.

'What's the matter with you, Tiaan?' he bellowed. 'This hedron doesn't work!' He banged a crystal down on the bench. 'And that means the controller is useless, the clanker doesn't go *and more of our soldiers die!*' He shook a fist the size of a melon in her face.

Letting out a yelp, she sprang out of the way. Tiaan and the foreman did not get on, but she had never seen him in such a rage before. The war must be going worse than ever. She took up the hedron, a piece of crystalline quartz the size of her fist, shaped into twenty-four facets. 'It was working perfectly when I finished with it. Do you have the controller?'

Gryste set that down gently, for it was a psycho-mechanical

construction of some delicacy, a piece of precision craft work even the scrutator's watchmaker would have been proud of. The controller resembled a metal octopus, its twenty-four arms radiating from a basket of woven copper and layered glass.

Fitting the hedron into its basket, Tiaan unfurled the segmented arms. She clutched a pendant hanging at her throat and felt a little less overwhelmed. Visualising the required movement, she touched her jewelled probe to one metal arm. The arm flexed, retracted, then kicked like a frog.

'Ah,' sighed Gryste, leaning over. 'That's better.'

Tiaan moved backwards to escape the fumes. The foreman did not understand. This was not a hundredth of what the controller was supposed to do in working a battle armoped, or clanker as everyone called them. And the crystal had hardly any aura. Something was badly wrong. She visualised another movement. Again the spasmodic frog kick. Frowning, Tiaan tried a third. This time there was no reaction at all, nor could she gain any from the other arms. The aura faded to nothing.

'The hedron has gone dead.' She plucked anxiously at her pendant. A single facet sparkled in the lamplight. 'I don't understand. What have they been doing with the clanker? Trying to climb a cliff?'

'It died not fifteen leagues from Tiksi!' snapped Gryste, taking out a rusty sword and slapping it on his thigh. He took pleasure in intimidating. 'And the last two controllers you made also failed. *In the battle lines.*'

Her skin crawled. No controller from this manufactory had failed in twenty years. 'W-what happened?' Tiaan whispered.

'No one knows, but two precious clankers were lost and twenty soldiers are dead. Because of *your* sloppy work, artisan.'

Groping for her stool, Tiaan sat down. Twenty dead. She was numb from the horror of it. She never made mistakes in her work. What had gone wrong? 'I'll . . . have to talk to one of the clanker operators.'

'One was torn apart by a lyrinx, another drowned. Don't know what happened to the third. What the scrutator will do when he hears . . .'

4

Tiaan shivered inside. 'Do you have the other controllers?' she asked in a small voice.

'How could I?' he snarled. His tongue was stained yellow from chewing nigah, a drug the army used to combat cold and fatigue. That explained the spicy smell. Perhaps the garlic was an attempt to disguise it. 'The first clanker was taken by the enemy, the second swept down the river. This controller is from the third. We would have lost it too, had it ever reached the battlefront. Gi-Had has gone down to Tiksi to find out what went wrong. The whole manufactory is going to suffer for your incompetence.'

Gi-Had, the overseer of this manufactory, had complete power over the lives of the workers. If she let him down he could send her to labour in the pitch mine until the black dust rotted out her lungs. 'Is he . . . angry?'

'I've never seen him so furious!' said Gryste coldly. 'He said if the problem isn't fixed this week, you're finished! Which brings me to another matter . . .'

Tiaan knew what the foreman was going to say. Stolid-faced, she endured the lecture, the appeal to duty, the veiled threat.

'It is the duty of *every one of us* to mate, artisan. There can be no exceptions. Our country desperately needs more children. The whole world does.'

'So they can be killed in the war,' she said with a flash of bitterness.

'We did not start it, artisan. But without men to fight, without people to work and support them, without women having more children, we will certainly lose. You are clever, Tiaan, despite this failure. You must pass your talents on.'

'I know my duty, foreman,' Tiaan said, though she did not like to be reminded of it. There was a serious shortage of men at the manufactory. None of those available appealed to her and she was not inclined to share. 'I *will* take a partner, soon . . .'

How? Tiaan thought despairingly after he had gone. And who?

Why had her controllers failed? Tian went through the problem from the beginning. Controllers drew power from the *field*, a nebulous aura of force about naturally occurring *nodes*. The field dominated her life. Artisans made controllers and, more importantly, tuned them so they did not resist the field but drew power smoothly from it to power clankers. If a controller went out of tune, or had to be tuned to a different kind of field, artisans did that too. Their work was vital to the war.

Clankers were groaning mechanical monsters, covered in armour and propelled by eight iron legs. Hideously uncomfortable to ride in and a nightmare to the artificers who had to keep them going, they were humanity's main defence against the enemy. A clanker could carry ten soldiers and their gear, and defend them with catapult and javelard. But without power it was just dead metal, so a controller had to work perfectly, all the time.

Had she made a terrible blunder? Removing the hedron, Tiaan inspected it carefully. Dark needles of rutile formed a tangled mass inside the crystal. It seemed perfect. There were no visible flaws, nor had it been damaged, yet it had failed. She had no idea why.

There was no one to ask. The old master controller-maker, Crafter Barkus, had died last year. What notes he'd made on a lifetime's work were almost unintelligible, and the rest of his knowledge had died with him. Tiaan had learned everything he'd cared to teach her, and had made small but useful improvements to controllers, some of which had been adopted at other manufactories. However, at twenty she was too young to rise from artisan to crafter. The manufactory was sorely in need of someone with greater experience.

Through the door her fellow workers were talking among themselves, no doubt about her. Tiaan felt oppressed by their knowing looks, their unsubtle judgments and pointed jokes about not having done her duty. A twenty-year-old who had never been with a man – there had to be something wrong with her. It was not said meanly, more in puzzlement, but it hurt just the same.

There's nothing wrong with me! she thought angrily. I just haven't met the right one. And not likely to, among the misfits and halfwits here.

Two of the prentices sniggered, looked up at her cubicle then guiltily bent over their grinding wheels. Flushing, Tiaan hurried out of the workshop. She wove her way through the warren of clerks' benches, past the clusters of tiny offices, the library and the washing troughs, then between infirmary and refectory and out through the wall into the main part of the manufactory.

Out here the racket of metal being worked was deafening and everything stank of smoke and tar. She turned left toward the front gate, crossing a bleak yard paved in dolomite in which a warren of buildings had been thrown up as the need required. There were drifts of ash and dust everywhere; the sweepers could not keep up with it. Every surface was covered in a film of oily soot.

'I'm going down to the mine,' she said to Nod, gate attendant for the past thirty years.

The old fellow had a white beard so long that he could tuck the end into his belt, but not a hair on his head. He raised the iron grille. One tall gate stood open. Nod held out his hand. No one was supposed to go out without a chit from their foreman.

'Sorry, Nod,' she said. 'I forgot again.' Gryste always made a fuss so she was reluctant to ask, even though going to the mine was part of her job.

Nod looked over his shoulder then waved her on. 'I didn't see you. Good luck, Tee!' He patted her on the shoulder.

Tiaan found that rather ominous. He'd not wished her luck before. Shrugging on her overcoat, she went out into the wind. The path down to the mine was slushy, the snow on either side brown with soot from furnaces that burned night and day. At the first bend, just before the forest, she looked back.

The clanker manufactory carved an ugly scar across the hillside. From here it comprised a grimy series of scalloped walls ten spans tall, with slits high up and battlements above them. Guard towers hung over the corners, though they were seldom manned, the manufactory being hundreds of leagues from the enemy lines. From the rear a cluster of chimneys belched smoke of various hues – white, orange and greasy black.

7

Tiaan did not think of the place as ugly. It was just home, and work, the two concepts like joined twins. It had been home since her mother, the pre-eminent breeder in the breeding factory at Tiksi, had sold Tiaan's indenture to the manufactory at the age of six. She had been here ever since. She occasionally went to Tiksi, three or four hours' walk down a steep and stony path, but the rest of the world might not have existed.

There was no time for it. Life was regimented for war and everyone had their place in it. The work was tedious, the hours long, but crime was unheard of. No one was afraid to walk the streets at night.

To her left, another path tracked the snow under the aqueduct, then across the gash of the faultline before winding up the mountain to the tar mine. On rare hot days up there, tar oozed out of the shattered rocks and could be scraped into buckets. Mostly, though, the miners hacked solid tar from the drives or followed erratic seams of brittle pitch though the mountain. It was the worst job in the world, and few survived to old age, but someone had to do it. The furnaces of the manufactory must be fed. Its clankers were vital to the war. And the war was being lost.

Controllers were just as critical. Tiaan could imagine how the soldiers must have felt, attacked by ravening lyrinx and realising they had no protection because their clankers had stalled. She could not bear to think that it might have been her fault.

She hurried along the path to the lower mine, where the hedron crystals were found. It was twenty minutes' walk down a steep decline and Tiaan had plenty of time to fret, though she was no closer to a solution when she reached the main adit.

'Mornin', Tiaan!' Lex, the day guard, nodded at her from his cavern like a statue in a temple. His ill-fitting false teeth sat on the counter, as usual. Sometimes the miners hid them, sparking a frantic search and emotional outbursts.

'Morning, Lex. Where's Joe today, do you know?'

'Down on fif' level,' Lex mumbled. Without his teeth it was hard to make out what he was saying. 'Take six' tunnel on right an' follow to end.'

'Thanks!' Selecting a lantern from the shelf, she lit it at Lex's

8

illegal blaze, a brazier full of fuming pitch shards, and set off. The sides of the tunnel were strewn with broken wheels off ore carts, cracked lifting buckets, tattered strands of rope and all the other equipment that accumulated in a mine as old as this one.

When Tiaan reached the lifting wheel she found it unattended. She rang the bell but it was not answered so she got into a basket, eased off the brake and wound herself down. Level one, level two, level three. The shafts ran deep and dark and old here. It had been a mine for hundreds of years before the value of the crystals was recognised. As she passed the fourth level a blast of air set the basket rocking, almost blowing out her lantern. At least the ventilation system was working. There had been bad air down here the last time she'd come. One of the miners had nearly died.

Cranking herself down to the fifth level, Tiaan stepped into the tunnel and made sure the brake was off, otherwise no one could use the lift and the attendant would have to come down on a rope to free it.

It was pleasantly warm on this level, a nice contrast to outside and to the manufactory itself. It was always cold there unless you worked near the furnaces, and then it was unpleasantly hot. However, the artisans' workshop was right up the other end of the manufactory, on the frigid south side. Tiaan had been cold for most of her life.

She trudged on. Every chunk of waste rock had to be carried up and out, so the tunnels were no bigger than necessary to gain access to the ore and the veins of crystal. Often she had to go on hands and knees, or slip through a gap sideways with the uneven edges scraping her ribs. The rock here was pink granite, impregnated with veins that writhed like blood vessels in a drunkard's eyeball. The miners came for gold, platinum, copper, tin and silver, though her old friend Joeyn delved for something much more precious – the crystals from which the magical hedrons were made. Some were as big as her fist, and it was these Joeyn especially sought. Only certain crystals could be used for making hedrons. Few other miners could tell which ones to take and which, apparently identical, to leave behind.

Wriggling around a knob of layered granite glinting with

mica, Tiaan saw a light ahead. An old man sat in an egg-shaped space, his lantern, pick and hammer beside him.

'Joe!' she yelled. 'I've found you at last.'

'Didn't know I was lost,' grinned the miner, climbing to his feet with many a groan and a clicking of aged joints. Joeyn was a small, wizened, skinny man, at least seventy, with a long sharp face and skin impregnated with mine dust. He was Tiaan's only true friend. He gave her a hug that made her ribs creak.

They sat down together. Joe offered her a swig from his bottle but Tiaan knew better than to accept. Distilled from fermented turnips and parsnips, the spirit was strong enough to knock out a bear.

'Have you eaten today, Tiaan?'

'Only a crust.'

He passed her a cloth-wrapped bundle, inside which she found three baked sweet potatoes, a boiled egg, a stalk of celery and a ball of sticky rice flavoured with wild saffron and pieces of mountain date. Her mouth watered. She was usually too busy to eat.

Tiaan selected the smallest of the sweet potatoes. 'Are you sure it's all right?'

'Stand up, Tiaan. Let me look you over.'

She did so, potato in hand. Tiaan was average in height but slender. She had jet-black hair, raggedly hacked off halfway down her neck, almond-shaped eyes of a deep purple-brown, a broad, thoughtful brow and a small though full-lipped mouth. Her skin was like freshly rubbed amber, her eyes a darker shade. She had long-fingered, elegant hands, which she liked, and large feet, which she did not.

'You're thinner than when I saw you a month ago.'

'I only get paid when my controllers go into service, and . . .'

'But you're the hardest worker in the entire manufactory, Tiaan, and the cleverest.'

She looked down at her boots, unable to reply to the compliment. 'My last three controllers failed after they left the manufactory, Joe. Two clankers were lost, and their operators. *Twenty* soldiers are dead.' Her chest was heaving in agitation.

He regarded her steadily. 'Doesn't mean it's your fault.'

'They were *my* controllers. Of course it's my fault.'

'Then you'd better find out what's gone wrong.'

'I don't even know where to start.'

'Well, you still have to eat.'

'I only take the basic ration,' she muttered. 'I'm saving to buy out my indenture. I'll have enough in two more years.'

'But you'll stay at the manufactory after you do. It's not going to change your life. What's the hurry?'

'I want to be free! I want to *choose* to be at the manufactory, rather than being forced to work here because my mother signed my life away when I was six!' There was a stubborn set to her jaw, an angry light in her eye.

Tiaan was indentured until the age of twenty-five, and until then was the property of the manufactory. If she failed at her work, or for any other fit and proper reason, the overseer could sell her indenture to whomever he chose, and there was nothing Tiaan could do about it. Gi-Had was neither cruel nor vindictive, but he was a hard man. He had to be.

The only way out was for her to become crafter, effectively the master controller-maker. In that case her indenture would be cancelled and she would be part of the committee of the manufactory, a position of honour and influence. But that was just a dream. The crafter had to do much more than be good at her trade. Artisans were notoriously tricky to manage and she was not good with people.

'What's the matter with your controllers?'

'I've no idea. I've only just found out that they'd failed. They were perfect when I finished them.'

'How long since you've been paid?' he asked sternly.

'Six weeks.'

'Sit down; eat your lunch!'

'It's your lunch,' she said stubbornly, wanting the food but not the charity.

'It's yours and I expect you to eat it all.'

'But . . .'

Joeyn patted the bottle. 'This'll do me. I'm going home shortly. I've already met my quota for the day.'

'Quota of what? Illegal drink?' she asked cheekily.

'Do what you're told!' He tilted the bottle up again.

Tiaan consumed the sweet potatoes and began peeling the shell off the egg. She felt better already.

'So why the visit, Tiaan? Not that you aren't welcome any time.'

'Does there have to be a reason?'

'No, but I bet there is. And I'm wondering if it's not about my old stones.' Even if he had just mined the most perfect crystals in the world, Joeyn still referred to them as 'my old stones'.

'It is,' she said. 'The last three you gave me seemed perfect, but failed after a few weeks in their clankers.'

'They were a bit different,' he admitted over another healthy swig. 'But not unusually so.'

'Can I see where you got them from?' she asked, her mouth full of egg. Her belly felt wonderfully full.

'Back this way!' He headed off in the direction she'd come from, lantern swinging.

She followed, nibbling on the sticky rice ball. Tiaan was saving the celery stick till last, to freshen her mouth. Beyond the squeeze, Joeyn went down on hands and knees beneath a bulge of shattered granite held together with tiny white veins, and through into a cavern higher than their heads. In the lamplight Tiaan saw threads of native silver shining in the wall, and across the other side, a vein of massive crystals.

'I love it down here,' Joeyn said, patting the wall. 'The wonders of stone. Ever the same yet always different.'

'You talk as though the rock is your best friend.'

'It is.'

'Is this a new area?'

'The miners dug it out last year. One day they'll be back to follow these seams as far as they go.'

'Why didn't they keep going while they were here?'

'Because they found some interesting old stones and had to call me in to check them. Woe to any miner who smashes up good crystal in search of base silver or gold.'

'The bloody damn war! Is it ever going to end?'

Joe prised at a vein with the point of his pick. 'Been going for a hundred and fifty years, and the lyrinx came well before that, when the Forbidding was broken and wicked Faelamor opened the void into our world. I don't see it stopping anytime soon.'

Tiaan knew that story by heart. The twenty-seventh Great Tale, written by the chronicler Garthas, was the most important of the recent Histories, and taught to every child in the civilised world. It was based on the final part of the twenty-third Great Tale, *The Tale of the Mirror*, but that tale was no longer allowed to be told.

Many creatures had invaded Santhenar at the time of the Forbidding, two hundred and six years ago, though only one had thrived: the winged lyrinx. Intelligent predators with a taste for human flesh and a burning desire for their own world, they had been at war with humanity ever since.

'We're never going to defeat the lyrinx, are we, Joe?'

'I'd say not. They're too big, too smart and too damn tough. I hear that Thurkad has finally fallen.'

She had heard that too, and that there were a million refugees on the road. Thurkad was the fabulous, ancient city that had dominated the island of Meldorin, and indeed half the known world, for thousands of years. Tiksi was about as far as one could get from Thurkad and lyrinx-infested Meldorin, but the Histories had told Tiaan all about it. If such a powerful place had been overcome, what hope did they have?

Joeyn withdrew a chisel from a loop of his belt, placed it carefully in the vein and gave a gentle tap, then another. Tiaan watched him work, nibbling her celery. She felt more at home here than anywhere, but only because of him. 'How do you tell which are the right crystals?'

'Don't know! When I touch one I get a warm, flowering feeling above my eyes, like a waterlily opening in a pond.'

She wondered where he got that image from. It was too cold here for waterlilies, or even down the mountain at Tiksi. 'Were you always like that?'

'Nope! Happened about ten years ago. I'd just turned sixty-six. Got sick one night after dinner; nearly died. Turned out it was the

13

pork. Been eating it all my life, but since then, even if I just touch a bit of bacon rind, throat swells up and I can hardly breathe. Next time I was down here, mining the silver, I touched a crystal and a flower opened inside my head. Happened every time I touched that crystal, so I took it home and kept it beside my bed.'

'Why?'

'I liked the feeling it gave me; sort of warm and comforting. Both my boys were killed in the war, and my wife died of grief . . .'

'I'm sorry. I didn't know.'

'Why would you? She's been dead thirty-one years, and the boys more than that. Such a long time ago. Life was so lonely.'

'Why didn't you take another wife? I would have thought . . . Well, I'm in trouble because I haven't mated . . .'

'Never met a woman I liked enough.'

Tiaan considered the old man thoughtfully. They had been friends from the day they'd met. 'I don't suppose you'd consider – '

'Don't be silly, Tiaan,' he said gruffly. 'Anyway, as I was saying, my crystal came along and I wasn't so lonely after all. Felt I was a bit special. One day I happened to mention it to old Crafter Barkus. He was a widower too; we used to share a jar or two some evenings. He came and looked at it. Next I knew, I wasn't a silver miner any more – I was paid twice as much to sense out crystal and send the good ones to him. Been doing it ever since.'

'I wish I knew how,' she said.

'I wish I could teach you.'

He had been tapping away with hammer and chisel while he was talking. Now he laid them aside, inserted the point of his pick into the cavity and levered carefully. A crystal wobbled. 'Want to catch that for me?'

It fell into her hands. 'You can take it, if you like,' said the miner.

'Thanks. But what if it turns out like the others? Have you found a new vein?'

'No, though there are some promising ones down on the sixth level.'

'Are you going down there next?' She looked hopeful.

'Not if I can help it.'

'Why not?'

'Rock's rotten there. Roof used to cave in all the time, before we sealed it off. A shear zone cuts right through the best area.'

'Oh well, I dare say you'll find your old stones somewhere else.'

'Dare say I will.' Joeyn stretched and yawned. 'Time to go. Air's not as good as it should be, down this end.'

Tiaan felt drowsy, now that he'd mentioned it, and saw that the lantern flame had burned low. She followed him to the lift, stepped into the basket and allowed him to wind them to the surface.

Out in the cold and the blustery wind that blew her drowsiness away, she said goodbye.

'Bye.' Joe turned down the track to the miners' village and his lonely hut. 'Now, you call me if that crystal don't work,' he said over his shoulder. 'I'm sure I can find a better one, with a bit more time.'

'Thanks! I will.' Pulling her thin coat around her shoulders, she set off up the slushy path.

Tiaan shaped the crystal and, taking great care, began to wake it into a hedron. This was done with the pendant at her throat, her personal *pliance*, which enabled her to see the field. Without it she would be psychically blind. The pliance was the badge, almost the soul, of every artisan; making it had proved her worthy of being one. A small hedron of yellow tiger's-eye quartz, set in swirls of laminated glass and silver metal, it hung from a white-gold chain. Tiaan had used her pliance every day for the past three years and knew its every idiosyncrasy.

A crystal had to be woken before it could draw power from the field, and not even Tiaan could describe how that was done. It was a psychic tuning of mind and matter, a talent you either had instinctively or not at all. It could be trained but not taught. And it was hazardous; it could bring on the hallucinations, and eventually the madness, of crystal fever. Prentice artisans had years of practice with the master, using the merest chips of a crystal, before they were ready to do it themselves. Yet accidents still happened, and the reckless attempted what was forbidden, often with unpleasant results.

Every crystal was different and waking this one proved unusually hard work; it seemed to resist her. She could barely sense its structure through swirling fog. Tiaan concentrated until her head hurt, and slowly something began to resolve. It was a tiny pyramid, vibrating in a blur. Others, identical, lay all around, linked into hexagons that extended to infinity. She lost herself in the pattern, drifting on a sea of regularity. Drifting . . .

The current was whipping her along now. A long time must have passed. Tiaan had no idea how long she had been lost inside, but she did know that some artisans never came out. However, she had learned how to wake this crystal.

Tearing herself free of its spell, she took a mental step backwards, focussing not on the regularity of the crystal but on the tendrils chaotically drifting through it. Selecting just one, she forced it to take the straight path. It resisted but she pressed harder, using the strength of her pliance, and it moved. The first was always the most difficult. First one, then dozens, then thousands of tendrils aligned and began to stream the same way. Suddenly they vanished, she was looking at the crystal from outside and its aura floated around it like the southern aurora in the night sky. It was *awake* and meshing beautifully with the field.

Though exhausted, she kept working. There was so much to do. By ten o'clock that night Tiaan knew that the new crystal had the same properties as the last three. Would it fail the same way? Her body felt all hot and cold, her arms twitchy. Such were the effects of working with hedrons, and they were not always benign. Artisans had been known to die at their benches, burnt black inside or their brains boiled in their heads. It was called anthracism and everyone lived in terror of it. Tiaan's head was throbbing. Time to stop.

Depressed and hungry, she blew out her lantern and trudged off through the labyrinth of the manufactory, with its hundreds of compartmentalised work spaces. Each was crammed with workers, mostly women, making the individual pieces of the clankers that were so vital to the war. Such colossal labour it was that in a year the manufactory, with its thousand workers, its tar-fired furnaces going non-stop, could turn out only twelve clankers. The enemy could destroy a clanker in a few minutes.

Tiaan's room was tiny, but at least she had one. Most of the workers slept in dormitories where privacy was unknown. She climbed into bed but could not stop thinking. The war was delicately poised; it could go either way. Or so they were told. The failure of a few clankers could lose an entire army, and that could lose the war. And *everything* depended on controllers and the hedrons that were the core of them, the only way a human mind could shape and focus the power of the field to control such a massive object as a clanker.

The lyrinx were more than the equal of humans, in every respect. Only clankers could make the difference. Without them, humanity was doomed . . .

Tiaan slept badly and not for long. Her head was full of brilliant, chopped-up images – crystal dreams. She always had them after work. These ones were about dead soldiers all lying in a row, covered in sheets to conceal their horrible mutilation. Long before a weak autumnal sun skidded over the mountains to blink at the fog and furnace fume, she was back at her bench.

Hunger nipped at her belly. She kept it at bay with sips of tar-flavoured water. The manufactory grew crowded. The artisans worked in their own little building on the cold, southern side, walled away with all the other clean occupations. The workshop had double doors to keep out ash and fumes, but they could not keep out the noise. She closed her door, unable to think with the racket of metal being shaped on a hundred anvils, the shouted conversations, the roars of a score of foremen, and always in the background, the hissing of the bellows and the blast of the furnaces.

The failed hedron was still dead, not a spark left of its

potential when shaped by her hands. It was as if it had been drained dry, all that psychic promise withdrawn. Now it was no more than a blank piece of quartz.

Tiaan took her mug to refill it at the barrel outside. On opening the door she was confronted by a dark, wiry man with an eagle beak of a nose. He threw out one arm as if to block her way. His hands were enormous, sinewy, though the rest of him was compact.

'Overseer Gi-Had!' She stepped back involuntarily. Though she had been expecting him, his sudden appearance came as a shock.

'Artisan Tiaan, what progress have you to report?' Gi-Had's brows squirmed over those sunken eyes like a pair of hairy grubs. He had a wooden case in his other hand.

'I – ' she turned back to her bench, where the hedron lay with its spread-out controller apparatus like a disassembled birthday toy. 'I haven't found the problem yet. They worked perfectly when I delivered them.'

'Well, they don't work now and soldiers are dying.'

'I know that,' she said softly, 'but I can't tell why. I've got to talk to one of the clanker operators.'

'Ky-Ara is the only one still alive. He should be here to-morrow. He's been putting a new controller into his clanker. He's not happy!'

He wouldn't be, Tiaan thought. The bond between operator and machine was intimate. To have a controller fail on him would be like losing a brother. To then train himself to the idio-syncrasies of a different controller would be gruelling, physically, mentally and emotionally.

'What have you come up with?' Gi-Had persisted.

'There are ... t-two possibilities. Either the crystals have invisible flaws or the field has somehow burnt them out ...' She broke off as a third, more alarming possibility occurred to her.

'Or?' grated Gi-Had. His heavy-lidded eyes narrowed to slits. 'Or what, artisan?'

'Or the enemy has found a way to disable the hedrons,' she whispered.

'Better hope they haven't, or we'll all end up in the belly of a lyrinx.'

'I'm working as hard as I can.'

'But are you working as *smart* as you can?'

'I –'

'I've got my orders. Now I'm passing them on to you. If you can't do the job I'll have to find someone who can, even if I have to bring them a hundred leagues. You've got a week to fix this problem, artisan.'

Opening the wooden case, he placed two controllers on her bench, next to the one she'd been working on. 'Twenty soldiers died because these failed. Another three died recovering them. A *week*, Tiaan.'

'And if I fail?' she said slowly.

'Have you given any thought to your *other* responsibility?'

She stared at him, white-faced. Tiaan could not think what he meant.

'Your responsibility to mate!' he said testily. 'Your foreman spoke to you about it yesterday.'

Was every single person going to remind her of it? 'N-not yet!' she stammered. Just the thought of it made her heart race. 'But I will soon, I promise.'

'You've been saying that for three years, artisan. I'm sorry, but the scrutator is giving me hell and I can't defend you any longer. If you can't do your job, and you won't do your duty –'

'What?' she cried.

'I might have to send you to the breeding factory.'

TWO

It reminded Tiaan that she had not seen her mother for nearly a month. She did not look forward to it, but it was another sacred obligation. Besides, after Gi-Had's threat she could hardly think straight so she might as well visit Marnie, who did not think at all.

'I'm going down to Tiksi,' she said to Nod at the gate. 'To see my mother.'

This time he did not ask for her permission chit. 'I hope you're coming back, Tee?' Nod tucked his beard into his belt anxiously, then took it out again.

Nod still held to the old view that men and women were equal, but not everyone did these days. In olden times a woman could do whatever she was capable of, the same as a man. However, the war had taken a heavy toll of humanity. The population was falling and, before anything else, fertile women were expected to breed. Tiaan's mother was a champion. In twenty-one years she had produced fifteen healthy and surprisingly talented children.

Tiaan did not want to think about that. 'I'll be back, don't worry.' She buckled her coat, pulled a cloak around her and set off on the long walk down the mountain to Tiksi, thinking about Gi-Had's words.

The scrutator of Einunar, the great province that included

this land, was a shadowy figure, spymaster, head of the provincial secret marshals, adviser to and, word had it, power behind the governor. He was one of a dozen on the Council of Scrutators, which was said to run the affairs of the eastern world. No one knew how the council had come into being, or if it answered to a higher power. Certainly it knew too much ever to be disbanded. That was all she knew, and more than she cared to. No one wanted to come to the notice of the scrutator. Tiaan shivered and walked harder.

The manufactory lay in rugged Glynninar, a minor state of Einunar at the end of an eastern spur of the Great Mountains. That chain of unclimbable peaks ran from beyond Ha-Drow in the icy south, encircling Mirrilladell and Faralladell and disgorging glaciers to the points of the compass, then on to the tip of the fiord-bound peninsula of Einunar, a length of eight hundred leagues. Northward, a mountain chain almost as large ran up the eastern side of the continent of Lauralin to fabled, wealthy and gloriously subtropical Crandor.

With a sigh at the thought of warmth, she trudged on. This was poor, granitic country, no good for anything but growing trees. From spring to autumn it drizzled, when it was not pouring. Cold mists sprang up from nowhere overnight, while the rare warm days ended in clinging fogs that blew up the range from the sea. From autumn to spring it froze – gales, snow and sleet for week after week.

She passed quite a few people on the track, for Tiksi supplied most of the manufactory's needs. Though Tiaan knew many of the travellers she did not stop to chat. No one had time these days. The best anyone got was a friendly hello, the worst a curt nod. The land bred dour folk hereabouts; the war had made them even more taciturn.

Tiaan was shy and uncomfortable with people. She found it hard to make friends, for she never knew what to say and felt that people judged her, not for what she was, but because she had no father and had been born in the breeding factory. Not all the propaganda of the war could erase that stain, least of all from her own mind. She felt alone in the world.

It began to drizzle. After an hour or two Tiaan sat down, just for a minute. Any longer and the cold would creep into flesh and bones. She contemplated the sombre pines, wreathed in moss and trailing lichens that stood out like banners in the wind. They had a certain stark beauty. Taking up a piece of decaying granite, she crumbled it in her fingers, allowing the grains to spill onto the slush of last night's snow. Better go. No point putting it off.

Another hour and more passed before Tiksi began to emerge from the grey, a collection of tall but narrow buildings capped by yellow tiled roofs. The doors and window frames were faded blue. Everyone thought alike in Tiksi. With twenty thousand inhabitants, it was the largest city for a hundred leagues.

Even from here she could pick out the breeding factory. The official name was The Mothers' Palace, but 'the breeding factory' was what everyone called it, and the others like it that had sprung up along the coast over the past thirty years. Its yellow stone walls contrasted sharply with the dingy grey of the sur-rounding buildings. In a hard world it was supposed to symbol-ise reward for a job well done, the most important work of all. For Tiaan, who had lived there until she was six, the place had a rather different meaning. It epitomised a world that was trying to take away her rights.

Beyond and below Tiksi she caught occasional glimpses of the steel-coloured ocean. Out to sea an iceberg squatted in the water like a snowy plateau. More dotted the surface all the way to the horizon. This year there were more than usual.

There was a fuss at the gates because she had forgotten to bring her manufactory pass. The guard allowed her through, after much debate, though Tiaan knew it would go on her record, *again*. Inside the city gates, she checked passers-by, as always, looking for one particular face, her father's. Without knowing what he looked like, or even his name, Tiaan was sure that she would recognise him instantly.

As she wove through the markets an elderly matron hissed at her, 'Go home and do your duty!' Others cast accusing glances at her slender waist, her ringless fingers. Flushing, Tiaan tried to ignore them. She *was* prepared to do her duty, but not just yet.

Turning in at the gates of the breeding factory, she passed through the front door, nodding to the guard. Inside, the place was luxurious, even decadent. Ornately corniced ceilings were painted in a dozen colours. The walls were beautifully papered, while costly paintings and fabrics, and gleaming furniture, were everywhere. A tray of pastries sat neglected on a table. It would probably be thrown out, uneaten. She salivated.

The breeding factory was the most visible propaganda of all, a sign of a future when women might be valued only because they produced the next generation of fodder for the battlefields and maternity wards.

With a heavy sigh she pushed open the door of her mother's rooms and went in. As one of the best breeders in the history of the place, Marnie had the largest suite with the most luxurious furnishings.

Her bed was larger than Tiaan's living cubicle in the manufactory. The silk sheets were crimson, the cushions velvet. Marnie lay asprawl on the tangled sheets, a sleeping baby on her belly. A satin nightgown, which to Tiaan's prudish mind looked positively indecent, was hitched up to the top of her plump thighs. One enormous breast, milky from the baby's attentions, was fully exposed.

Marnie opened her eyes. 'Tiaan, my darling!' she beamed. 'Where have you been? I haven't seen you in ages.'

Tiaan bent down to kiss her mother's cheek. She looked like a pig in a wallow, and neither covered her breast nor drew down her gown. Tiaan could smell her lover on her and was disgusted. Pulling the chair away from the bed, she sat down.

'I'm sorry, mother. We've all been working seven days a week.'

'Don't call me mother, call me Marnie! What are you doing way over there? Come closer. I can't see you.'

'Sorry, Marnie. I just don't get any time to myself.'

Marnie's eyes raked over her. 'You look awful, Tiaan. Positively *thin*! Why won't you listen to me? It's no life for you, working day and night in that horrible manufactory. Come home. Any daughter of mine can have a position here tomorrow.

We'll fatten you up nicely. You can lie in bed all day if you like. You'll need never work again.'

'I like to work! I'm good at it and I feel that I'm doing something worthwhile.' As always, Tiaan could feel her temper going. She tried to rein it in.

'Any fool can do what you do, fiddling about with dirty bits of machinery!' One chubby hand found a box of sweetmeats on the bedside cupboard. Tipping the contents onto her ample belly, Marnie sorted through them irritably. One disappeared into her navel. 'Damn it! All the best ones are gone. Would you like one, darling?'

'No thanks!' Tiaan said, though she was starving. Her temper began to flood. Marnie, despite her image as the wonderful earth mother, was as selfish a person as ever lived. She loved her children only while they were infants. Once off the breast she sent them to the creche, and at six indentured them to whoever offered the most for their labour. Marnie was one of the wealthiest women in Tiksi, but her children saw none of it.

Tiaan changed the subject. 'Marnie, there's something I've always wondered . . .'

Marnie bristled. 'If it's about your wretched father . . .'

'It's not!' Tiaan said hastily. 'It's about me, and you.'

'What about me, darling?' Marnie picked fluff off a chocolate-coloured delicacy and tasted it with the point of her tongue. She settled back on her cushions. No subject was dearer to her than herself.

'It's about where I got my special talent from – of thinking in pictures. When I think about something I see it in my mind as clearly as if I was looking at it through a window.'

'You got it from me, of course! And I got it from my mother. The fights we had when I wanted to come here.'

Tiaan could well imagine them. Marnie's mother had been a court philosopher, a proud and feisty woman. *Her* mother had been scribe to the governor, her sister an illusionist of national repute. How Marnie had let the family down!

Marnie, of course, did not think so. She closed her eyes, smiling at some particular memory. 'Ah, Thom,' she whispered,

'I remember every one of our times together, as if you lay beside me now . . .'

Tiaan rose hastily. In this mood Marnie was prone to go into raptures about past lovers, describing intimacies Tiaan had never experienced and certainly did not want to hear from her mother's lips. Whoever Thom was, *he* definitely wasn't her father.

'I have to go, Marnie.'

'You only just got here,' Marnie said petulantly. 'You care more about your stupid work than about me.'

Tiaan had had enough. 'Any fool can do what you do, mother,' she cried in a passion. 'You're like a sow at the trough!'

Marnie rolled over abruptly, scattering sweetmeats across the carpet. The baby began to cry. She put it to the breast in reflex. 'I'm doing my duty the best way I know!' she screeched. 'I've produced fifteen children, all living, all healthy, all clever and hardworking.'

Tiaan's anger faded. 'I never see them,' she said wistfully. She longed for a proper family, like other people had.

'That's because they're out doing their duty, and not whinge-ing about it either. I've done all I could for you. You have the best craft I could find, and don't think that was easy.'

'Ha!' Tiaan muttered. Her mother twisted everything. Not only had she *not* gotten Tiaan her prenticeship, Marnie had fought against it.

'Maybe you do love your work, Tiaan, but it doesn't feed you.'

'Better hungry freedom than pampered slavery!'

'You're free, are you?' Marnie shouted. 'I can leave this place today and be honoured wherever I go. You can't even scratch yourself without getting permission from the overseer. I hear your work isn't going so well, either. Don't come whining to me when they cast you out! I won't let you in the door.'

That was too close to the bone. 'I'd sooner die than live the way you do!' Tiaan yelled.

'You wouldn't have the choice! No man would want to lie with such an ugly, scrawny creature as you.'

Tiaan rushed out and slammed the door. Every visit ended in tears or tantrums, though it had never been as bad as this before.

The people hurrying by gave her knowing looks or, occasionally, friendly smiles. Everyone knew how it was between her and her mother. Had something else upset Marnie?

Tiaan sat on the front step, trembling. She was not ugly or scrawny, just hungry and afraid. The rest of the insult passed over her head. Repelled by Marnie's greedy sensuality, Tiaan could not imagine lying with a man, even to aid the war. *Never!* she thought with a shudder. I'd rather die a virgin.

Unfortunately, she was hungry for love. Brought up on a diet of her grandmother's romantic bedtime stories, she dreamed of little else. The women in the manufactory all had husbands or lovers, mostly gone to the war, and talked of them constantly. Tiaan did so yearn for someone to love *her*. She had no friend but old Joeyn.

Realising that she was shaking with hunger, Tiaan felt a copper coin out of her purse and trudged down to a barrow boy. There she bought a long spicy sausage baked in pastry and set off for home, nibbling as she walked. The sausage was delicious, hot and with a strong peppery flavour. Just half of it filled her stomach and made her feel better.

It was a slow, slippery climb back up the mountain in the rain. Darkness, which at this time of the year came before five o'clock, was already falling before she saw the lights of the manufactory high above. Tiaan toiled up the last distance, went inside and sat down in her cubicle. The hedron lay there accusingly on the bench. Since she was no closer to a solution than before, Tiaan went looking for Overseer Gi-Had.

'He's gone up the mountain,' said Nod the gateman. 'Trouble in the tar mine. Poisoned air, I think.'

'Then he won't be back today,' said Tiaan. It was four hours' walk to the tar mine, each way. 'Have you seen Gryste?'

'He's unblocking the waste drains.'

Going left out the gate, Tiaan followed the earth track around the outside of the manufactory wall. She turned the corner, taking a shortcut between huge stone cisterns excavated into the rock to prevent them freezing solid in the four-month winter.

In the space between them she glimpsed a couple locked in passionate embrace. There were so many people in the manufactory, and so little privacy, that even the most inhospitable places were in demand.

The discharge flume from the aqueduct had a curtain of icicles hanging from the lip. In the distance a creche-mother was instructing twenty or thirty of her young charges in the use of a sling. They were firing pebbles at the outline of a winged lyrinx, painted on one of the pillars of the aqueduct.

The path wound past stockyards, barns, slaughterhouses and a butchery. The smell was frightful. Tiaan hurried by a cluster of outbuildings where the weavers and other non-essential tradespeople worked. Around the back, piles of furnace ash were eroding into a gully. A series of stonework pipes dripped noxious fluid over the edge.

She found the foreman by a stand of blazing torches, shouting at a group of blackened navvies hacking tar from one of the pipes. They could only work for a few minutes before the fumes drove them out. Their hands and arms were blistered, their red noses dripping.

'Excuse me?' she said hesitantly.

'Yes?' snapped Gryste, smacking his sword on his thigh.

'I need to talk to you. About the cont – '

'Not here!' He hauled Tiaan away.

Pulling free, she rubbed her throbbing wrist.

'You can't talk in front of the navvies, artisan!'

'Why not?'

'Morale is bad enough as it is. They'll get it wrong, and gossip. Where were you this morning?'

'I had to go to Tiksi to see my mother.'

'You did not seek my permission.'

'I – I'm sorry.' He would not have given it so Tiaan had not asked, though she was due the time off.

'I've had it with your slacking and your refusal to obey the rules. I'm adding a month to your indenture. If it happens again, *six months*,' he growled. 'What do you want?'

Tiaan could not speak. The punishment was all out of

proportion to the crime. It did not occur to her to challenge him; to ask if he had that power.

'Well, artisan? Don't waste my time.'

'I need to know how the controllers failed,' she said in a rush. 'Did they go suddenly? What other signs were there? Did anything unusual happen at the same time?'

'I've had a report from the battlefield but it doesn't say much. The controllers started acting erratically. The field came and went. Some of the clankers' legs had power, the others not. Then the field failed completely.'

'Has it happened with clankers built by other manufactories?'

'No idea. They're scattered across half a thousand leagues and we don't have enough skeets to send messages back and forth. The armies have priority.' With a curt nod, he went back to the drains.

Feeling obstructed at every turn, Tiaan went inside and unlocked the old crafter's rooms. Everything was exactly as it had been the day Barkus died. The new crafter, when appointed, would take over his offices, but though Tiaan was the senior artisan she had no right to use these rooms. The hierarchy must be maintained. She still laboured in the cubicle she'd had as a prentice.

Tiaan spent hours going through the crafter's journals, trying to find out if controllers had ever failed this way. Barkus turned out to be the least methodical of men, which was surprising since he'd checked her workbooks and journals every day of her eight-year prenticeship. Nothing was organised, much less indexed or catalogued. The only way to find out if he'd worked on a particular problem was to read everything he'd ever written. That was frustrating too, for he often broke off in the middle of an investigation and never resumed it, or continued in the blank spaces of whatever journal he'd happened to lay his hands on at the time.

She went through the bookshelves, cupboards and pigeon-holes crammed with scrolls, but found not a mention of her problem. The desk contained nothing of interest – everything secret had been locked away after Barkus's death. However, as she pulled out the lowest drawer, it stuck.

It took some time to free it, after which Tiaan removed the drawer to see what was the matter. She was used to fixing things. Probably the runners needed waxing. As she was rubbing them with the stub of a candle, she noticed that the drawer was shallower than its external dimensions indicated. That could only mean one thing.

It did not take her long to find the secret compartment. Inside lay a slim book made of rice paper, with soft leather covers. She picked it up. The title page simply said: Runcible Nunar – *The Mancer's Art*.

No wonder Barkus had hidden it. The penalty for having an illegal copy of any book on mancing would be horrific. Nunar's treatise was justly famous and many copies had been made, though such books were guarded jealously. Why had Barkus, a humble crafter in an obscure manufactory, obtained an illegal copy?

At a footfall outside the door, Tiaan thrust the book into her coat and pushed the drawer in. A cold voice broke into her thoughts.

'Just what do you think you're doing?'

'I beg your pardon?' Tiaan said. The intruder was Irisis Stirm, a fellow artisan slightly Tiaan's junior, although Irisis did not think so.

She stood in the doorway, tapping an elegant foot. Irisis knew *her* worth. Tall and lavishly endowed, with corn-yellow hair and brilliant blue eyes, she stood out in the manufactory like a beacon. Tiaan had never met anyone with hair that colour, and no one around here had blue eyes, though the old crafter's may have been when he was young.

'You have no right to come in here. These are the crafter's rooms. He was my uncle!' Irisis pointed that out at every opportunity.

'I answer to Gi-Had, not you! Look to the quality of your own work!'

That was a mistake. Irisis was much better at managing the other artisans than Tiaan was. Moreover, she made controllers of rare perfection and extraordinary beauty – works of art.

Her use of crystals, though, was timid, and she was peculiarly sensitive to criticism about it.

'At least my controllers work!' Irisis sneered.

'Only because we all help you tune them.'

'How dare you!' Irisis cried. 'If Uncle Barkus was still alive he'd put you in your place.'

'He did! He put me above you. Now he's dead and I am responsible for your work.'

'Unless,' Irisis said reflectively, 'you're sent to the breeding factory to do your duty.'

Tiaan had no comeback. Irisis did *her* duty enthusiastically and often, though so far with no sign of success. Perhaps she used a preventative. That was a serious crime, though not an uncommon one. Heading for the door, Tiaan laughed nervously. 'I think I'm more valuable here than there!'

Irisis's blue eyes flashed. 'You couldn't manage a dung fight in a pigsty! I'll be crafter here one day, *over you*! Then you'll know it.' She stood by the door as Tiaan went out. There was no chance to put the book back.

Returning to her bench, Tiaan watched Irisis across the room as she donned goggles and mask and sat down at her grinding wheel. It began to whine and the artisan took up a crystal. Soon the air was full of drifting specks.

Tiaan worked fruitlessly for hours, until her head drooped. She laid it on the bench, then realised that the manufactory was silent. It must be midnight. Plodding to her room, she washed in a basin of cold water and fell onto her straw-stuffed pallet.

As soon as her head hit the pillow, Tiaan's worries returned and, though exhausted, she found herself wide awake. She went over her problems again and again, quite uselessly. Finally, knowing she was never going to get to sleep, she lit a candle, locked her door and took out the forbidden book.

She did not open it immediately. Tiaan was not sure she should look at it at all, but if she took it back to the crafter's workshop, Irisis's spies would tell her at once. If she handed it in to the overseer after this delay there would be suspicion that she'd read it first. The scrutator had watchers in the manufactory and little escaped their attention. She would be marked for life.

She considered hurling it into one of the furnaces when no one was looking. However, if the book was protected by a spell, as such things often were, anything might happen. Besides, books were precious, sacred things and Tiaan could not imagine burning one. She could hide it, but what if someone unsuitable found it? What if it fell into the hands of the enemy?

Tiaan opened the book. The paper had a lovely silky feel. The text was written in a number of different hands, no doubt a copy. The language was the common speech spoken throughout the south-east, so she could read the words, though they made little sense. That was not surprising. Her day book, which contained details of her work on controllers, would be equally incomprehensible to most people. Then, as she was flipping through, a heading caught her eye.

Application of the *Special Theory* to the Powering of Mechanical Contrivances

My *Special Theory of Power* describes the diffuse force, or field, that surrounds and permeates the fabric of nodes. It is this force that mancers have drawn upon since the Secret Art was first used, at least seven millennia ago. However, mancing has always been restricted by our inability to understand the field: where it comes from, how it changes over time and how it can safely be used.

Furthermore, all drawn power must pass through the mancer first, which causes aftersickness, and the greater the power the worse the effects. Too great a drain of power will be, and has proven many times, horribly fatal.

The traditional solution has been to enchant an artefact, such as a mirror, ring or jewel, and simply trigger the device when needed. This also has problems: artefacts are notoriously difficult to control, may become corrupted over time (witness the Mirror of Aachan) and once discharged are useless until they can be recharged.

31

Yet we know the ancients used devices with the capacity to replenish themselves. We do not know how that was done, but how else can we explain such long-lived devices as the Mirror, Yalkara's protected fortress of Havissard, or contrivances that used such prodigious quantities of power as Rulke's legendary construct?

The field, the weakest of the five elemental forces, is the only one we mancers have ever been able to tap. Nonetheless, much can be done with it. My *Special Theory* enables us to understand the diffuse force, and perhaps create a *controller* apparatus to tap it safely. Instead of all power being drawn through the mancer, with its limitations of frail flesh, the mancer simply senses the field and draws just enough power to channel the flow, via the ultradimensional ethyr, directly into the controller. The controller can then transmit it to power the contrivance, whether this be a mechanical cart, a pump or any other mechanism required.

Being a humble theoretician, I will leave the design of such devices to those with the aptitude and interest in such things. Suffice it to say that any such device should comprise the following components . . .

Tiaan knew all about such devices; that was her work. She skipped forward a few paragraphs.

The process may generate a shifting aura about the crystal powering the controller, perhaps mimicking the aurora-like field about the node from which the power was drawn. A nearby sensitive might be able to detect this aura, though in normal use it is expected to be insignificant . . .

Tiaan put the book down. This was the very document wherein Nunar first set down the principles of controllers, nearly a hundred years ago. Her theory had enabled the construction of clankers and certain other secret devices, without which the war would have been lost long ago.

She ploughed on. Nunar went on to speculate about a *General*

Theory of Power, which would deal with nodes themselves, the several different *strong* forces they were expected to be made of, how they related to each other and, finally, how such prodigious forces might be tapped. Nunar noted, however, that nodal forces might never be tapped safely. She also mentioned the holy grail of theoretical mancers, the *Unified Power Theory*, which would reconcile all the forces mancers knew of, weak and strong, in terms of a single field. Nunar closed the section by stating that such a theory seemed as far off as ever.

Tiaan hid the book behind a loose brick in the wall, under her bed. It seemed no use at all.

She dozed briefly, her head crackling with fractured crystal dreams, to wake with the answer in her mind. She must design a device to test the faulty hedrons and read what had happened to them. Only then could she find a way to solve the problem. Sitting up in bed, Tiaan reached for slate and chalk and began sketching.

She had just completed a rough sketch, and blown out her candle, when Tiaan heard the rattle and groan of a clanker coming up the road. It had to be Ky-Ara returning. Since it was practically dawn, she dressed and went out.

A sleepy attendant with a lantern was opening the side gate as she arrived. Gi-Had was there too. He must have returned in the night. Tiaan watched the monster emerge from the dark. The clanker had covered lanterns on the front, a broad, segmented body made of overlapping plates of armour, and four pairs of mechanical legs driven by ingenious gearing. It was large enough to carry ten people and all their gear, though in bone-shaking discomfort. The shooter's platform on top, with its mechanical catapult and javelard, was empty.

The clanker clumped into the shed and stopped. The mechanism creaked and groaned, then there was silence save for the whine of the twin iron flywheels that stored power in case the field was interrupted momentarily. The flywheels would still be going at dinnertime, slowly running down.

The back hatch opened. A slim young man climbed out, pack in one hand, a satchel in the other. He stretched, gave the machine an anxious pat on the flank and turned around.

Ky-Ara was not overly tall. His lean, handsome face was marred by a weak jaw. A shock of wiry hair stood out in all directions. His dark eyes were red-rimmed. There was a smudge of black grease across one cheek. Despite all that, Tiaan rather liked the look of him.

'It's good to have her whole again,' Ky-Ara said to Gi-Had, avoiding Tiaan's eye. 'After the controller *died* . . . I thought I'd never drive her again.'

His face crumbled. The bond between clanker and operator was intense, almost like that between lovers, and a threat to it had been known to cause mental breakdown. Ky-Ara looked close to one now. Tiaan felt for him.

'It's been hard work getting used to the new controller,' he continued. 'I've got a shocking headache. Despatch for you, surr!' He handed the satchel to Gi-Had.

'Thank you.' The overseer turned away to open it. He began to read a document, frowning as he did.

'What happened when it failed?' Tiaan asked Ky-Ara.

The operator's top lip quivered but he mastered himself. 'We were heading up the coast from Tiksi. Everything had gone perfectly. We were passing out of the aura of the Lippi node towards the Xanpt node. That's a really strong one . . .'

'So I believe,' said Tiaan. She liked the shape of Ky-Ara's mouth. A wonder she hadn't noticed him before.

'I had the controller helm on, sensing out the Xanpt field in advance. Sometimes it can be tricky shifting from one to another, and I didn't want to get stuck between fields. The flywheels won't drive her weight for *that* long.'

He looked sideways at Tiaan. She nodded.

'The Lippi field began shifting wildly: sometimes strong, at other times hardly there at all. The fields grew harder and harder to visualise; I couldn't tune either of them in.' His voice cracked as he relived the awful scene. 'I began to think that the Lippi field was going, though the two clankers ahead of me seemed to be having no trouble.' Ky-Ara went pale and had to sit down.

'What happened then?' Gi-Had prompted after a long silence.

'I lost it. Both fields were gone! The hedron was dead and there was nothing I could do about it. If it had happened in battle . . .' He shivered. 'I took the controller out, got a lift back to Tiksi on a cart and sent the controller up the mountain.'

'I have it in my workshop,' said Tiaan. 'I can't work out what's happened. The crystal is completely dead.'

Ky-Ara looked distressed, like a lost boy. 'If that's all,' he said, cradling the controller in his arms, 'I'll go to my quarters. I haven't slept for two nights.'

'Yes, thank you, Ky-Ara,' said Gi-Had. 'I know you've done your best. It must have been difficult for you.'

The young man went out. Tiaan's dark eyes followed him thoughtfully.

'You're wondering if he might be the one?' Gi-Had's rumble broke into her thoughts, startling her.

Tiaan flushed. She had been thinking exactly that. Also thinking that, if she must mate, why not with a clanker operator? There were many similarities in their lives and work, and if they did not get on, he would be away most of the time. If nothing came of it, no one could say that she had not done her duty.

'Yes,' she said softly.

'Strange folk, clanker operators. Their machines always come first – you know that.'

It didn't require an answer. He shook out the rolled despatch, scowling ferociously. 'Bad news?' she asked.

'Another problem. A worse one.'

'Oh?' said Tiaan warily.

'More clankers wiped out, on the coast well north of Xanpt. Each time, the enemy knew just where to find them.'

'Clankers are pretty noisy,' said Tiaan.

'Not these ones.' Gi-Had looked over his shoulder. The attendant was a long way away but the overseer lowered his voice anyway. 'They were using a new development, a Sound Cloaker! You can't hear them move. And no one knew where they were going.'

'But that means,' said Tiaan, 'the enemy has a way of finding them. Using the Secret Art – '

Gi-Had spun around. 'Oy, you, clear out, *now*!'

A large bald man touched his brow then slouched off. It was Eiryn Muss, a halfwit who had a lowly place at the manufactory. He was always shambling about, peering over people's shoulders.

Gi-Had turned back to Tiaan. 'And if they can do that, they will destroy them all. *And us!* Find out how they do it, Tiaan.'

'Is this more important than finding out why the hedrons failed? Or making replacement controllers?'

'They're all important,' he growled.

'I can't do everything. I'm always exhausted as it is.'

'Leave controller-making to the others for the time being. The best artisans from every manufactory have been ordered to work on these two problems.'

Her head jerked up. 'So it's not just *my* controllers that have failed?'

'Not according to this. But that doesn't mean you're in the clear.'

'Are *you* happy with my work, overseer?'

'Let's just say that I'm keeping an eye on you. Better get on with it.' Nodding distractedly, Gi-Had hurried off.

THREE

Cryl-Nish Hlar looked up from his bench as Tiaan went by. He desired her, and had ever since arriving at the manufactory three years ago. Unfortunately, Tiaan was oblivious to him. That hurt Nish, as he was mockingly known. In the local dialect the word meant pipsqueak.

Nish was short and it was the bane of his life. He came from a long line of short people and despised every one of them for it. He was not unhandsome, in a brooding sort of way, with his cap of dark hair that showed the contours of his skull, and bright eyes that could be as green as the ocean, or as grey. Unfortunately his sallow skin was spotty, which was a torment, and his downy chin incited sneers of 'bum fluff'.

He had a strong body though – broad, square shoulders, a stomach as hard and flat as a paving stone, jutting buttocks which excited ribald comments from the women he worked with, and heavy thighs. He was also, he liked to think, sturdily equipped for breeding.

Not that, Nish thought gloomily, he got any chance for that. Despite the severe shortage of males the women of the manufactory, like those of the mining village nearby, were not enamoured of him. He felt sure it was because he was short and spotty, and had no beard. How he hated his body.

That had nothing to do with it, of course. In these times even hideous men had their choice of partners. Moreover, he had other appealing characteristics – he was clever and of good family. Unfortunately he had one handicap fatal to intimacy. With women younger than his mother, Nish was so anxious that he became mortifyingly inarticulate.

Though not particularly skilled with his hands, Nish had a lively, restless intelligence and learned quickly. He also had a brilliant memory – for names, faces, things seen and conversations overheard. That was of great benefit to him in his other, unmentioned occupation.

Both his father, Jal-Nish Hlar, and his mother, Ranii Mhel, had been examiners. All the more incomprehensible that they could have made such a mistake with him. Every child in the east, and possibly the entire world, was taken before the examiners at age six, where every talent, creative or intellectual, manual, mechanical or psychic, was identified. On that basis children were assigned their occupations for life – labourer, miner, scribe, artisan, merchant, soldier, *breeder*! There was no room for childhood; the war with the lyrinx was a hundred and fifty years old. The soldiers, and the other dead, had to be made up. Children must work. The entire world was regimented for one thing – survival.

The examiners came again at the age of eleven, and for the third and final time at sixteen, to make sure. Some promising talents withered early, while others blossomed late.

Nish had been happy in his prenticeship as a scribe for one of the great merchants of Fassafarn, a trading city on the south coast of Einunar. Fassafarn was an ice-free port through which much of the wealth of the south was shipped to markets as far away as Crandor, and even Thurkad before its fall. He had been learning the principal languages and scripts of the known world, and was ideally suited for such work. Nish liked meeting powerful people and being trusted to translate their documents. He'd planned to become a merchant himself, one day, and make so much money that he could buy anything he wanted.

Then, aged sixteen, came the catastrophe. After his examination there had been hurried conferences and, with no more than an hour's notice, his parents had shipped him across the mountains to become a prentice artificer at this godforsaken manufactory. Nish was devastated. It did not occur to him that the move might have saved him from the army. Their only instruction had been to 'Keep your eyes and ears open, and write about what you see and hear, every day'. Nish was a dutiful son. He still wrote every day, and once a month his bulky letter would go out with the other mail.

His first year at the manufactory had been a nightmare. All the other prentices, male and female, had been taller. His skin erupted into hideous spots. Worse, he knew less about being an artificer – the design, constructing, operating and repairing of machines of warfare – than even the six-year-old factory kids. But worst of all, rumour spread that he had failed disastrously as a scribe and had been sent here as a last resort. If he failed again he would become a pit labourer, as good as a slave.

Nish could not bear that. It was the most powerful motivation of all. He was determined to succeed at being an artificer, no matter what it took. Though he had little aptitude for the craft, he would master it.

What he lacked in ability and experience, Nish made up with hard work and sheer, directed intelligence. He worked night and day until he was so exhausted that he could have slept standing. He drove his supervisors mad with questions, had them show him the workings of the war engines over and again, and invented ways of teaching his reluctant fingers what the other prentices learned easily.

At the end of his first year he was ranked among the lowest of the prentices, along with the stupid and the chronically lazy. But he was not *the* lowest, and to Nish that was a major achievement. If his parents were impressed, they did not say so in their infrequent letters. Nish was hurt, but planned to try even harder next year.

After two years, he was around the middle of the group. That earned grudging praise from his mother and a call to come home to celebrate his eighteenth birthday. He worried in case they had another change of profession for him, perhaps sending him to the army. His imagination and his wide reading told him exactly what war was like. He did not want to experience it – at least, not on the battlefield.

When he got home Nish discovered that his father was the one who'd changed profession. Jal-Nish was now a perquisitor, charged with rooting out troublemakers, subversives and traitors wherever he might find them. It was an important, lavishly paid position, answering only to the scrutator for Einunar. One day he might even *be* scrutator.

At the end of his third year Nish had moved above the middle of the prentices, but there, to his intense chagrin, he stayed. Sheer intelligence and hard work, no matter how well directed, could raise him no further, for he simply lacked the aptitude for artificing. It galled him, but Nish was nothing if not self-aware and wrote to his father telling him so, and expressing the wish that he might go back to being a merchant's scribe.

His father showed neither surprise nor disappointment. Jal-Nish merely wrote, 'You're doing well. Don't forget to write, every day.'

Nish bent his head to the clanker parts he had been wrestling with all morning. They formed the lower half of a mechanical-leg assembly, and putting it together was a job he particularly hated. The parts had been made in a dozen different sections of the manufactory and if any one was infinitesimally out of toler-ance the assembly became a nightmare. Sometimes he spent days on the most tedious work only to find that one part had to be machined again, and all his labour undone.

He banged the housing with a dirty fist. He was covered in grease, as always. Nish hated that – he liked to look his best. The women of the manufactory tended to sneer at artificers, mere 'fitters' as they called them, because it was such a filthy job. Many of the fitters were women, and they were friendly enough, but Nish disdained them. Artificers were beneath him, though he was one himself. He looked to the top of the heap, where he belonged.

At that moment Tiaan walked by. Most respected in this

manufactory were the artisans. They worked with their hands, but only with precious things: gold and silver, platinum and quicksilver, copper, amber and crystal. They never got dirty doing it and the best were brilliant, lateral-thinking designers. More importantly, artisans worked with their *senses*. They had special talents, akin to the Secret Art that was the province of mages and mancers.

Nish could never hope to be an artisan; he lacked the vital talent. But prestige was everything to him and he wanted one of them for his woman. There were four artisans here, though only two were available. Of those, Irisis went by the fitters with her nose in the air, for she was of the House of Stirm, a crafter's daughter and a crafter's niece, made for better things than a lowly artificer. Nish hated her for it, but he understood her too. She was much like him.

Tiaan was a different matter. He felt that he might be in love with her. Now he looked up to see Tiaan on her way back. Putting down his wrench, he stared at her. She was above him, and yet beneath, for she came from the breeding factory and did not know her father. To lose a father was commonplace, in these times. Not to know his identity was a major failing in a world obsessed with family and Histories.

Tiaan carried her head high, though not aloof as Irisis did. Tiaan seemed oblivious to her surroundings, as if the only world that mattered was inside her head. The Ice Virgin, some called her, but Nish knew better. He felt he understood her too. She had the reputation as the hardest worker in the manufactory, and the cleverest. She was trying to make up for something. Was it her unfortunate birth? Her lack of a father?

She wore loose trousers and a blouse of grey flax, with old but well-cared-for grey boots. More was not tolerable here, just across from the furnaces. Her breasts bobbed with her light step, a sight that liquefied his middle. Desire made him forget everything.

Do it now! She's a quiet little thing. She will listen and be flattered. He hesitated too long. Without a glance, without even knowing he was there, Tiaan went by. She wore a faint, internal smile. Her glossy black hair bounced against the back of her neck.

Soon she would turn the corner and be gone, down to her own workroom in the cold part of the manufactory. Go on, you fool! Today you have something to offer. Not even the Ice Virgin will refuse you now. She has the breeding factory in her blood and her belly. She's just holding out for the best offer, and no one can best you.

Dropping his tools on the bench, Nish wiped his greasy hands on a rag and ran after her, up the aisle and round the corner to the section where the artisans and all the other clean crafts worked. Inside, the artisans' workshop was sealed off by double doors designed to exclude all dust and dross.

Tiaan was already out of sight. He burst through the doors without putting on a clean overall or taking off his filthy boots. Everyone stared. He did not notice.

'Tiaan!' he cried. 'Artisan Tiaan!'

She was going through the door into her own cubicle, but turned at his wild cry. 'Yes?'

He ran up to her, froze, then forced the words out.

'Tiaan, I admire your work tremendously. I . . . I think you are the most brilliant woman I've ever met.'

For an instant he saw panic in her eyes. Anger covered it up. 'If you admire it so much,' she said frostily, 'why are you dropping your filth and grease everywhere?'

Recalling the state of his clothes, he flushed. Sheer desperation propelled him on. 'I'm sorry, I'll clean it up.'

'Don't bother. What do you want, artificer?'

'Just to talk to you. You're brilliant, Tiaan.'

'You already said that.'

'Would you . . . Would . . .?' He faltered under her astonished stare. Her lips were the reddish-purple colour of pulped blackberries. He wanted to crush his mouth against them.

'What?' she snapped.

'I thought . . . perhaps dinner . . . or a walk along the path to the lookout . . . and then . . .' He couldn't get it out, with the prentices sniggering and rolling their eyes at each other. Artisan Fistila Tyr, who was heavily pregnant, set to with her grinding wheel to cover it up.

Tiaan turned those unusual eyes on him, scanning Nish from smoky cheeks to grease-stained hands and filthy boots. He felt sure he knew what she was thinking. *Not only is he dirty and spotty and inarticulate, but he's a runt!*

'Yes?' she said in a low voice that had the prentices bending over their work. Nish recognised the danger, but if he did not speak now he would never be able to.

'We both have our duty to perform. I thought we might share your bed!' he burst out. 'Or mine, if you prefer. I have . . .'

Her honey skin flushed red-brown. For a full minute she could not meet his eye; then Tiaan drew herself up. 'How dare you!' she hissed. 'How can you imagine that I would give myself to a dirty little artificer, and not a very good one either? The thought makes me sick. Get out!'

Nish flushed beneath the dirt. Across the room, Irisis was watching the show with open mouth. This afternoon he would be the laughing-stock of the manufactory. There was only one way to recover.

'I don't think you realise who my father is, Artisan Tiaan,' he said coldly. 'He is Perquisitor Jal-Nish Hlar, one of the most important people in the land. He is a high inquisitor! He can make you, Tiaan, or he can break you. And my mother is a chief examiner, nearly as important.' Looking over his shoulder, he softened his voice. 'I know you and Irisis are rivals, Tiaan. Think what you can achieve with a perquisitor's patronage. You need never fear her again.'

He gave an uncertain smile, for Nish was new to this game. He'd not tried to use influence before and wasn't quite sure how to go about it, despite having often seen it done in his scribing days. He lacked the authority, and the easy arrogance that told him he deserved whatever he desired.

'What do you say, Tiaan? We can take pleasure from each other and your career will blossom. Do you want to work in this dungheap of a manufactory forever? Come – '

'I would sooner mate with a lyrinx!' she shouted. 'I don't care who your father is. I will never lie with you. Now get your squalid self out of my workroom!'

'Why won't you do your duty, artisan? What are you afraid of?'

Tiaan paled. 'Go away, little man.'

Nish's fury was barely controllable, but he made one last effort. 'If you knew who I really am,' he hissed, 'you would not be so – '

'Get out!' she roared and, seizing a pair of red-hot tongs resting in a brazier, Tiaan brandished them before his face.

Nish broke. Bursting through the double doors, he raced past the infirmary, out through the wall and down towards the furnaces. He could not go back to his own bench, for everyone would see the tears of rage streaming down his face. Creeping around the back of the furnaces, he hauled a recalcitrant sweeper boy out of a warm niche, clipped the lad over the ear for neglecting his work and crept in to lick his wounds. He would ruin Tiaan, somehow. Then he would bed her and cast her off.

Shortly he heard soft footsteps and to his astonishment Irisis appeared. She squatted down before him, offering a snowy handkerchief.

'Artificer Cryl-Nish,' she said softly, winning his undying gratitude for using his name and not the detested nickname. 'Would you like to learn how to pleasure a *real* woman?'

Nish could have fainted with astonishment. Irisis was not known for her kindness. Surely she was playing a cruel joke. He did not know what to say.

Bending forward, she gave him a savage kiss on the mouth. His body responded instantly. She laughed and took his hand, though she wrapped the handkerchief around it first. 'Come to my room.' Then she wrinkled her pretty nose. 'No, to the bath-house first, I think. We'll neither of us be missed for an hour or two. Time for a couple of lessons.' Her eyes met his. 'And after that, we'll find plenty to talk about on our pillows.'

'Talk about?' he said dazedly.

'About who our friends are. *And our enemies!*'

FOUR

Irisis propped herself up on an elbow, inspecting the youth who lay dozing in post-coital bliss beside her. She was not attracted to Nish at all, though she had to admit he had been vigorous, not insensitive, and displayed an admirable willingness to learn what pleased her. That was more than could be said for her previous lover. Her interest had been stirred by what he'd said to Tiaan, her rival here since childhood.

Irisis ran a hand down his chest. Nish was the least hairy man she had ever seen. She liked that, and the way their bodies touched. He smiled in his sleep. She slid her hand lower, tangling her fingers in the downy hair and tugging. He snapped awake.

'Cryl-Nish, lover,' she whispered, her breath tickling his ear. She wanted him capable of thinking just one thing.

He rolled over, pressing himself against her. Irisis kept him away with her hip. He froze. There was a message in the movement, though clearly he had no idea what it was. Good.

Irisis inspected him, the sheet up around her throat. As if by accident she let it fall, revealing one heavy breast swaying above his face. His eye followed it and she knew she had him.

'We know what you want, Cryl-Nish.' He reached for her. She moved back, saying thoughtfully, 'I hear your father is no longer an examiner.'

'He is chief perquisitor for the entire Einunar region,' he said importantly.

'Oh?' Irisis was impressed but did not want to show it. She allowed him to bask in reflected glory for just a moment. 'But what about the scrutator?'

His chest deflated. She had caught him trying to make his father seem more important than he was. He looked down at the rumpled bed, perhaps thinking that she was trying to make a fool of him.

'Anyway,' Irisis waved a hand, knowing it made other parts of her oscillate delightfully, 'who cares about all that stuff? I'm *much* more interested in you.'

'Me? Why?' Nish was staring at her dark, puckered nipple. He would do anything to have more of her.

'I've always had my eye on you, Cryl-Nish.' That was a lie, of course. 'Tell me about yourself.'

He began on the story of his life, suitably edited to impress. He had not gone far when she interrupted. 'I know all that. But there's one thing I don't understand . . .'

'What's that?'

'Why you're here at all. You're not an artificer, Cryl-Nish.'

'I am!' He sat up angrily. 'And I've worked damned hard to become one.'

She pushed him down. 'I'm sorry. I didn't mean to offend you. Of course you're an artificer, and a good one too . . .'

'Don't patronise me!' Rolling out of bed, he reached for his trousers.

The sheet slid away, exposing the other breast and her artisan's pliance hanging between them. He swallowed. Putting out her arms, she pulled his face against her bosom. Nish resisted, but not for very long.

'What I meant to say was . . . Your father sent you here for another reason, surely? A more important one than becoming an artificer. You would be much more valuable as a scribe, an assistant to a merchant, or even, one day, secretary to the scrutator.'

'Yes,' he said thickly, intoxicated by her. He lacked the experience to put her body out of mind.

'What is it?' Irisis stroked his chest with two fingertips.

'I'm also a prober,' he said rashly. That meant a prentice inquisitor, lowest on the rank that ran prober, querist, perquisitor and, unthinkably powerful, scrutator.

'A spy!' she exclaimed, tucking the sheet across her front.

He reached for it, more confidently now. She allowed him to caress her through the fabric before drawing away again. He hastened to reassure her.

'Not a spy. A watcher, helping to maintain order. This is a vital manufactory . . .'

'Is it?' she said. 'But there are hundreds. Why is ours so important?' Irisis leaned forward.

'We build the best clankers, because we make the finest controllers of all.'

'Why is that?' she whispered, taking his hand and sliding it inside the sheet.

Nish's eyes bulged. Sweat broke out on his forehead. 'Because,' he said hoarsely, 'we have the most perfect hedrons and the best artisans anywhere. The scrutator wants to know why, to protect us from harm and make sure no one steals our secrets.'

'Someone has to be the best. And if we have the best crystals, it stands to reason we would make the best controllers . . .'

She looked at him sideways. He hesitated, knowing he'd said more than he should. She slipped her hand lower. He groaned.

'It's something about this place!' Nish burst out. 'Our artisans are *much* better than others, even when they use inferior, imported crystals. It must be the node here.'

She resumed her caresses. 'A lowly prober isn't sent to solve *those* kinds of problems. That's mancer's work.'

Nish looked chagrined, as if he'd revealed too much already.

'How long have you been a prober, Nish?'

He flushed. 'Just since my father's letter came, a week ago.'

'And perhaps if he knew what you've told me, you'd be a prober no longer.'

He went still. She considered him, head tilted so that the glossy hair stroked his shoulder. Her eyes ran up and down

47

before settling about his middle. 'I know something else you may like.' She bent over him.

Now he moaned when she stopped prematurely. 'What are you really probing for, my little spy?'

'I can't tell you,' he gasped. 'A prober who talks is no prober at all, and likely to end up a slave. Or dead!'

'Or in the front rank of the army, which amounts to the same thing. Let's see if I can guess. This place is full of rumours but who can tell truth from falsehood? What does a prober do? He stays alert for people who aren't doing their job, those who have unfortunate ideas, and those who think someone else could run the world better than our leaders. None of that here, though. This is a well-run, happy manufactory.

'But there's one other thing that probers do.' She paused, gave him a long look, then bent her head again. He choked. She looked him fair in the eye. 'They hunt spies!'

The expression on his face almost made her laugh. He could not think straight. How she loved this power she had over men. Few women did these days.

'Please,' he whimpered.

She just stared at him. He put his hands around the back of her head, trying to pull her down. She went with him a little way then stopped, and when he tried to use his strength she bared her teeth. They were alarmingly sharp.

There was only one way to get what he wanted. Nish licked dry lips. 'There is a spy, father is sure of it. Twice now, secrets of clankers made here, and only here, have been discovered far away.'

'Who is the spy?'

'We don't know. Whoever he is, he's too clever.'

'Or she!'

'Or she,' he repeated.

'I'll help you. People will be wary of you, since your father is known to be perquisitor. But why would they suspect me?'

He looked uncertain.

'You're worried that I'll take the credit,' she said with a lazy smile. 'You need not – spycatcher is the last thing I want put to my name.'

'What *do* you want, Irisis?'

'What you offered Tiaan. What is mine by right. I want to be crafter, in charge of the entire controller works, and, one day, chanic of the province.'

'But you're only an artisan, and it's not long since you were prentice.'

'Crafter!' she said coldly. 'Then chanic.'

'Most artisans never become crafter, and few – very few crafters will rise to be chanic.'

'I have the talent for it; and the heritage. My father, my uncle, my grandfather, my great-grandmother and her mother before that, all were crafters or better. For four generations my family has held the position here. I'm going to be the fifth.'

'You're not old enough.'

'That rule can be broken, in an emergency.'

'Not by me.'

'A chief examiner can. You promised it to Tiaan. I heard you.'

'You didn't want me at all!' Nish cried. 'All you wanted was what you could get out of me.'

'Are you unhappy with what I've given you?'

'N-no!'

'Good, because I can't stand whiners. Were you lying to Tiaan? I hate liars more than anything, *Nish*. I hope you never lie to me.'

The fury of his thoughts showed on his face. 'I . . . I might be able to do something for you. I have . . . some influence with my father, and more with my mother. I think I can sway them, as long as there is something in it for them.'

Irisis did not believe him, though she had not expected much. 'There will be. Now, how shall we seal the deal?'

She looked down and he up. He put his hands around her head, drawing her down, and this time she went willingly.

Irisis rolled over and shook Nish awake. He struggled out of deep slumber into listless lethargy.

She leaned on one elbow, gazing at him. 'While you were snoring, I've been thinking.'

'Oh?' he said dully.

'I have an idea who the spy might be.'

He sat up abruptly. 'Really?' He clutched at her arm, staring into her eyes. 'Who?'

She smiled, showing those teeth again. 'I think it's Tiaan.'

He burst out laughing. 'Tiaan? You'd never make a prober, Irisis.'

She hurled herself off the bed, flinging the sheet around her with a gesture simple yet elegant. She looked like a marble statue carved by one of the masters of old, though her face spoiled the pose. 'No? What was she up to yesterday?'

'Visiting her mother. She goes down every month.'

'Tiaan was a long time away.'

'Maybe she had shopping to do.'

'And maybe she was meeting an accomplice to hand over our secrets.'

'Probers require proof,' he said loftily. 'Not idle speculation born out of malice.'

'I'll prove it to you!' she hissed. 'And now, Nish dear, *get out!*'

Nish left Irisis's rooms physically sated but more anxious than before. If she betrayed his confidence, he would suffer. No prober's position then. No future at all, just the front-line until a lyrinx tore him apart.

Irisis was wrong. He'd had his eye on Tiaan for months. There had been nothing suspicious about her behaviour. Tiaan worked night and day, talked to her solitary friend, the old miner, and occasionally visited her mother in Tiksi. That was her entire life.

If there *was* a spy or a saboteur, and it seemed there must be, it had to be someone else. Possibly Irisis, unlikely as that seemed. With a thousand workers in the manufactory it would not be easy to find out.

Better patch things up with her. He could not afford to make enemies, especially of someone so well connected. And as he returned to his bench the image of her long, lush body grew in his mind. Nish knew he'd struck gold with Irisis. He might never find a better lover and he wanted more of her lessons. Better humour her, take her suspicions seriously, offer to help with her career and, if necessary, hint at a subtle prober's threat behind it.

But if he found the least scrap of evidence against Irisis, he would destroy her. Not without regret, but without hesitation.

FIVE

Gi-Had's news came as a great relief to Tiaan. She had begun to doubt her own competence, but if hedrons from other manufactories were also failing there must be more to it than bad workmanship. Did the enemy have a way of disabling them from afar, or were they being sabotaged here? How could a crystal be sabotaged yet look unmarked? She had never heard of such a thing, nor had the other artisans. She was not out of trouble yet.

While everyone was at lunch, Tiaan scoured the crafter's rooms for anything he might have written on the topic. She found nothing, but did not return *The Mancer's Art* to its hiding place. She was not ready to give it up.

As she locked the door, Irisis appeared. 'What are you doing?' she said furiously.

'I'm trying to find out how a hedron could be sabotaged and leave no trace,' Tiaan replied, and passed by.

Something woke in the artisan's eyes. Irisis stared after Tiaan for a very long time.

Tiaan could think of only one approach – to probe deeper into the faulty hedrons, even if she destroyed them in the process. Slipping her pliance over her head, she reached for the first crystal, but stopped. What if the damage spread back? Her throat went tight at the thought of losing her pliance. She dared not risk it. Instead she got out the rough design she had done in the night and set to work.

After three days of dawn-to-midnight toil Tiaan had put together a hedron probe, in two parts. The first was a globe constructed of copper wires following longitudes, latitudes and diagonals, on which were set a number of movable beads, like a model of the moons and planets in their orbits. The beads, each different, were made of carefully layered strips of metal, ceramic and glass. The other part was a helm of enamelled silver and copper lacework in delicate filigrees, designed to fit over her head. A series of springy wires went down through her hair, their flattened ends pressing against the sides and back of her head, unnervingly like a wire spider. At the front, a setting the size of a grape was designed to hold a shaped piece of crystal.

Tiaan opened the two halves of the globe and placed one of the failed hedrons inside. Inserting a piece of crystal into the setting on the helm, she put it on her head. The wires were chilly. Closing her eyes, she slid her hands around the globe and pressed her fingers in through the wires until her fingertips touched the faces of the hedron.

At once she sensed something in its heart – a tiny, shifting aura, all fuzzy and smeared out, like a comet's tail. Her fingers moved the beads one way and then another. The aura was stronger in some positions, almost non-existent in others. Once or twice it disappeared. She tried rotating various wires, then flipping them north to south. That did not help either. Her apparatus was not powerful enough to read the aura, though while viewing it she had the uncomfortable feeling that someone was looking for her. She opened her door but found the workshop empty.

Tiaan examined the small crystal in the helm. It was not a particularly strong one, just the first she'd picked up. She searched through her offcuts but found nothing better, and the basket of waste crystals was empty.

'Gol?' She looked around for the sweeper boy. He did not answer. Tiaan found him sleeping in one of the nooks behind the furnaces, his head pillowed on a burlap sack. These hidey-holes had been the favourite haunt of factory kids since the manufactory had been built. She had used this nook herself once or twice, when she was little.

Tiaan looked down at the sleeping boy. He was an angelic-looking lad – olive skin, a cheerful oval face, red lips and a noble brow capped by black curls.

'Gol!' She shook him by the shoulders.

He woke slowly, smiling before he opened his eyes, as if from a pleasant dream. When he saw her standing there, his eyes went wide.

'Artisan Tiaan!' He fell out of the niche in a comical attempt to look alert and hardworking. 'What can I do for you?'

With an effort she kept a straight face. Gol was always willing, but his work never came up to expectation. Slapdash as well as lazy, he did not know the difference between a job well done and an entirely inadequate one. A harder master would have beaten that out of him but Tiaan could not bring herself to do it.

'Where did you put the waste crystals from my workbench?'

'Around the back of the manufactory,' he said brightly. 'On the ash pile. Would you like me to show you?'

'I told you to put them in the basket in my storeroom!' she said sharply. 'If this happens again, Gol, I'll send you back to your mother.' As if she could. The poor woman was a halfwit with seven children, none good for anything but lyrinx fodder.

'I'm sorry!' He assumed an expression of profound mortification.

Gol's emotions tended to the extreme. Tiaan wondered if there was a brain in his head at all. 'Come on! I'm in a hurry!'

They went past the smithies, where a bevy of half-naked lads wielded long-handled hammers. Eiryn Muss leaned against an anvil, ogling the youths and grinning loutishly. A pair of prentices mocked the halfwit behind his back, slouching about with their tongues out, drooling. Tiaan wondered if men like Muss were required to mate.

As she went past the artificers' workshops, Nish gave her a smouldering stare. He had been watching her ever since

54

the incident in her workshop. She hurried by, looking straight ahead, and opened the back gate.

The rear of the manufactory was a dismal place. The open drains steamed and reeked, a mixture of foetid human waste, tarry effluent and brimstone that had killed every plant in sight. Furnace ash and slag were piled all around the ravine, the most recent deposits steaming gently in the drizzle. A thousand times as much had clotted in the valley below. The river ran acid for two and a half leagues, a series of poisoned pools, stained iron-red or tarry black, in which nothing lived.

Gol led her through the reeking piles then stopped abruptly. 'It's not there!' He began to bawl.

Tiaan went to the brink of the ravine. Ammonia fumes brought tears to her eyes. Most of the ash mountain, saturated after weeks of rain and sleet, had slumped over the edge. Running down in a thick blurt to the water's edge, it looked exactly like a cowdung mudslide. There was no chance of recovering the precious offcuts.

Tiaan wiped her dripping nose. 'Oh, stop whining, Gol! Why can't you ever do what you're told.' The lad wailed loudly. 'Go! Get on with your work! And if this happens again I *will* have you whipped!'

He ran sobbing up the path. Tiaan leaned against a fragment of wall, all that remained of the monastery that had stood here for a thousand years. Before that, for another thousand, pilgrims had come to worship at the holy well, now buried under piles of slag. Had that been related to the node here?

Returning to the workshop, she checked the benches of the artisans. They had been cleared of their crystal waste as well. There were fresh crystals in the storeroom but she did not want to cut one down. She needed one that was the right size to start with. First thing in the morning she would have to go back down the mine.

'Morning, Lex, I'm looking for old Joe. Is he still working on the fifth level?'

Lex came out of his cavity. A little globe of a man, he looked like one of those smiling dolls that, after being knocked over, always came upright again.

'I haven't seen him, Tiaan,' he said clearly, evidently having his teeth in today. 'I don't think he's here.'

'Oh! I hope he's not sick.'

'Old Joe? He's as tough as miner's underpants. Naw, probably gone down to Tiksi.'

'I'll try his cottage, just in case. Thanks, Lex!'

She headed for the village, a third of a league down the mountain. A cluster of fifty or sixty stone cottages had been built in terraces on either side of the path, though Joeyn's place stood uphill among the trees. An oblong granite structure of two rooms, it had a mossy thatched roof and was surrounded by a fence of woven wattles.

The sun was just coming up as Tiaan pushed open the gate. A path of crushed granite led to a north-facing porch, unfurnished except for a rude chair. A scatter of white daisies grew beside the porch. Clumps of autumn crocuses were in flower here and there. On the other side of the path a vegetable garden contained onions, garlic, leeks and a few red cabbages.

The door was closed. A wisp of smoke came from the chimney. She knocked at the door. No answer. She knocked again and thought she heard a faint reply. Tiaan pushed open the door, afraid something had happened to him.

It was dark inside, the windowless hut lit only by the glow from an open fire. At first her eyes could make out nothing.

'If it isn't Tiaan!' came a hoarse voice from beside the fire. 'Come in, my dear.'

Tiaan made out a seated figure at a bench beside the fire. Joeyn started to get up but broke into a coughing fit.

'Are you all right, Joe?' She ran to him.

He wiped his eyes on his sleeve. 'Miner's lungs!' he gasped, clearing his throat and spitting into the fire. 'It's always like this in the morning.'

'I was worried. I thought something must have happened to you.'

'I've made my quota. I didn't feel like going to work today.'

'But . . .'

'I'm seventy-six, Tiaan. I only keep going because there would be nothing to do if I stopped. But some days I just don't feel like working.'

'Can I get you anything?'

'I'm not an invalid,' he said with a smile. 'But I wouldn't mind a cup of ghill, if you feel like waiting on me. It's in the jar on the mantel.'

Taking down the jar, she picked out several curling strips of ghi wood and moved the pot over the coals. 'Strong or weak?'

'Like tar. Put in about five strips and leave it a good while. Let's sit on the porch.'

He carried his chair out. Tiaan settled into the other. They watched the mist drifting between the pines. The wind sighed through the wattle fence. Finally Joeyn spoke. 'It's always nice to see you, Tiaan, though I'm sure you didn't come to pass the time of day.'

'What am I going to do about a partner, Joe?'

Looking her over, he smiled to himself. 'I don't see any problem.'

'I'm afraid . . .'

'It's not such an onerous duty, Tiaan.'

'I didn't mean *that*. I'll get the ghill.' She rose abruptly, coming back with two wooden mugs. The steam smelt like peppery cinnamon.

While they sipped their ghill, she went over her problem with the crystal.

Joeyn sat ruminating. 'So, you need me to find you another.'

'The most powerful one you can. The last wasn't strong enough.'

'And I suppose it's urgent?'

'Gi-Had threatened to send me to the breeding factory if I didn't solve the problem by the end of the week.'

'As if he would! You're too valuable to him, Tiaan.'

'Why would he say that if he didn't mean it?' Tiaan was not good at reading people and could not separate idle words from serious ones. 'He's in trouble because of the failed clankers, and

57

Foreman Gryste is whispering in his ear about me. He doesn't like me.'

'Gryste doesn't like anyone, Tiaan. Especially since . . .'

'What?'

Joeyn sniffed his drink. 'He was passed over for overseer when Gi-Had came back from the war a hero. Then Gryste did his own service, was blamed for a defeat that wasn't his fault and broken to a common soldier. He's been at odds with the world ever since. And his habit doesn't help.'

'The nigah leaf?'

'Yes. Makes a man angry. And it's expensive.'

'I'm afraid of him. The war is going really badly, Joe. Desperate people do stupid things.'

'It's been going badly since I was a boy. You stop believing everything you're told after a while. I'm so old that I've seen the Histories rewritten.'

'The Histories are truth!' she cried. More than that, they were the foundation of the world. To challenge them bordered on blasphemy.

'No doubt of it,' he replied, 'but whose?'

'I don't know what you're talking about.'

'Not many people do. Hardly anyone lives to my age any more. Have you ever heard of the *Tale of the Mirror*?'

'Only as a monstrous lie.'

'It wasn't when I was a little boy. It was one of the Great Tales, and Llian of Chanthed one of the greatest chroniclers. Now he's Llian the Liar, the man who debased the Histories. Why?'

'I supposed someone proved – '

'The greatest people of the age were there when he told the Great Tale – Nadiril the Librarian, Yggur, Shand, Malien the Aachim. No one said a word against the tale for a hundred and thirty years, then suddenly the Council of Scrutators had it rewritten. Why, Tiaan?'

'I don't know.'

'This war has destroyed everything we once held sacred.'

She squirmed on her chair. 'I don't like that kind of talk, Joe.'

He went back to the previous topic. 'I don't imagine the

breeding factory would suit you very well.' He gave her a sly grin. 'Though it is a life of luxury and pleasure . . .'

'Don't joke about it, Joe! I'm not going to be treated like a brood sow.' Her face had gone brick-red. 'I love my work, and I can do it better than anyone else. I just want to do my job and live my life.'

'That's all any of us want. Unfortunately the war . . .'

'The cursed war!'

'Still, I don't suppose Gi-Had *would* send you down, Tiaan. You're his best artisan.'

'I do seem to have an unusual talent,' she said thoughtfully.

'So I've heard. Do you know where it came from?'

'From my mother, according to her, though she tried to cover *my* talent up.'

'Is that so?'

'I first realised I was special at the examination, when I was six. In one of the tests they held up a picture, just for a second, then asked me questions about it. I knew all the answers. They were astounded, but it wasn't hard at all – in my mind's eye I could see the picture perfectly. I can still see it now, a family playing games on a green lawn. A mother, a father, a girl, two boys and a dog!' She sighed heavily.

'After that they showed me all sorts of images. There were maps of places I'd never heard of, the workings of a clock, a tapestry of the Histories. My answers were perfect, because every image stayed in my mind.'

'What else did they ask you?' Joeyn looked fascinated. 'I never had the examination. It hadn't started when I was a kid.'

'Hadn't it?' Tiaan said, surprised. 'Oh, all sorts of things. Reading, spelling, remembering, aiming and throwing, number puzzles.' She smiled at a memory. 'One didn't seem like a test at all. The examiners put a little piece of honeycomb in front of me and said that if I didn't touch it until they came back, I could have a really big piece.'

'Did you eat it?' Joeyn asked.

'No, though I wanted to. Other tests involved making things out of gears and wheels and metal parts. I did badly on those.'

'That's odd, for a controller-maker.'

'I never had those kinds of toys when I was a kid. Mother sneered at people who worked with their hands. Her daughter was certainly not going to.

'The examiners seemed disappointed, as if that lack had cancelled out my other talent. I remember them talking in the corner, looking back at me and shaking their heads.'

'So how *did* you end up at the manufactory?' Taking another sip from his mug, Joeyn settled back in the chair.

'The last test involved a collection of crystals; kinds of hedrons, I suppose. At least, some were. The others must have been dummies. They put the first in my hand. It was dark-green. A mask went over my face and they asked me to describe what I saw.' She paused for a pull at her mug.

'What did you see?'

'I didn't see anything. I felt as if I'd failed another important test. Someone took the crystal away and gave me another. I concentrated hard, but had no idea what I was supposed to see.'

Joeyn was leaning against the wall with his eyes closed. Tiaan continued.

'They gave me the third crystal. It was really cold. I started to say, "I can't see anything with this one either . . ." when a pink wave moved through my inner eye. It disappeared and I must have cried out. I tried really hard to get it back. Someone called, "What did you see, child?"

'The crystal warmed in my hand and suddenly it was like looking down on a pond with oil on it. I watched the patterns and time stood still. There were layers of colours, all going up and down, back and forth and passing in and out of each other. In places they twisted into swirls like water going down a plughole, then came out the other side of nowhere and joined up again. It was so beautiful! Then it vanished. The examiners had taken the crystal. I'd been using it for an hour!

'I looked for it, frantically. I had to have it back. I kicked and screamed, something I'd never done in my life. It was *withdrawal*, the first time I'd ever felt it. Nothing mattered but that I got the crystal back.

60

'I told them what I'd seen and I could see the excitement in their eyes. I wanted to try the other crystals but they put them away and sent me back to my mother. A few weeks later, after an indenture was drawn up, I was sent to the manufactory. Marnie was furious. She'd planned a different prenticeship for me, one worth a lot more to her, but the examiners had made their decision.'

'For you to become a prentice controller-maker?' asked Joeyn.

'Well, yes, though for two years all I did was sweep, clean and empty out the waste. I wasn't clever little Tiaan any more, I was the brat from the breeding factory. In a way I'm still that kid. I've never been able to make friends here.'

'The cat that walked by herself,' Joeyn murmured. 'You're too different, Tiaan.'

'What?'

'You give the impression that you don't need anyone else. It must be rather off-putting to the people you work with.'

'I suppose I want ... different things. Anyway, old Crafter Barkus started me on my prenticeship when I was eight. I felt *really* useless then. Everyone else was good with their hands and I had a hand full of thumbs. It took ages before I could do the simplest things.'

'So what did you do?' he asked with a bit of a grin, as if he already knew. Perhaps he did: it had created quite a stir at the time.

'I couldn't stop thinking about the crystal and what I'd seen with it. I wanted it desperately. There were plenty of hedrons in the artisans' workshops but I wasn't allowed near them. Prentices don't get to touch hedrons until they're twelve. I emptied the waste but those offcuts were from crystals before they'd been *woken* into hedrons. I tried them all but saw nothing.

'Then one day, a few months after I began my prenticeship, a hedron offcut was thrown out by mistake. I'd given up looking by then so I just scooped the contents of the basket onto the slag heap. As I did, I felt a flash of light and colour.

'It took hours to find the one chip of hedron in that mass of crystal and slag, but as soon as my fingers touched it I *saw*. I saw things no one else could see, beautiful colours and patterns, forever in motion. I couldn't make sense of them so I began sneaking into Crafter Barkus's lectures. I'm sure he knew. He never said anything, but every so often would break off from some abstruse theory to deliver a piece of instruction so basic that the prentices scratched their heads and wondered if he was going senile. I learned enough that way.'

'What did you learn?' Joeyn asked idly.

'What hedrons were for. I became obsessed. My crystal was like the friend I'd never had. I spent the whole day holding it. The nights too. I learned how to read the shifting field around the node here, better than anyone in the manufactory. When I was nine I made a series of paintings showing how it changed every day for a month. The field wasn't random, as everyone thought. There was a pattern to it, though no one had seen the field clearly enough to realise the pattern was there.

'I went running into the crafter's rooms with my paintings . . .' She broke off, giving a little shiver. 'I burst in on a meeting with the old overseer and a *perquisitor*!'

Joeyn chuckled.

'There was a deathly silence, then the perquisitor turned my paintings to the wall. The room was sealed, a guard put on the door and I was questioned by the sternest old man I'd ever met. Where had I got the pictures from? I was terrified that he would flog me. He did, too, but it wasn't the worst he could have done. He took my hedron away. I had not been separated from it for months and had the most terrifying withdrawal. I thought I was going to die. I was in a fever for four days.

'The perquisitor could not believe that I'd mapped the field myself, not until every artisan and operator in the manufactory had been interrogated. I'd made a better map than the army had. It was priceless information, especially to the enemy.

'Then, when I told him that I could actually change the pattern of the field, the perquisitor went silent. That's how adepts draw power, you see, and it's a vital secret. He was afraid I'd let something slip in my childish chatter. He also worried

62

that I would draw power without realising it and end up killing people, or myself. There was only one thing he could do.

'My true prenticeship began that day, three years early, although it did not end any sooner. Barkus started me with hedrons straight away but my talent did not make it easier. Well, using the hedron was easy but nothing else was. Learning to make the tiny parts of controllers was a nightmare. I was the worst of all the prentices at any kind of craft work. I tried really hard but it didn't seem to make any difference.'

'But you mastered the craft in the end.'

'Yes. My controllers aren't beautiful, like Irisis's, but they work better.' She bent down to sniff the autumn crocuses. 'The other part was nearly as much trouble.'

He waited for her to go on.

'Seeing things with a hedron is easy. Tuning the wretched controller to its hedron, and then to the field, was the hardest thing I've ever tried to do.'

He took another sip and made a face. 'Brew tastes a bit mouldy.'

'Sorry,' she said at once. 'I – '

'It's the ghi, Tiaan, not the making. Go on.'

'As students we did not have our own hedrons. We had to use ones made for the prentices years ago. They never *fitted*, and I used to see strange after-echoes from all the different wills that had used and abused them, the way students do. Anyway, they were flawed to begin with.'

'You wouldn't give a good one to a bunch of prentices,' said Joeyn. 'They'd ruin it.'

'No doubt.' Walking to the wicket gate, she stared into the woods.

'You were talking about tuning the controller,' he prompted after a while.

She came back. 'Oh yes. Nearly all hedrons have flaws and a hundred parts of the controller have to be adjusted to take account of them. Sometimes you don't know how. Move one part too far and it throws everything else out. It might take a day just to get back to where you started from, even if you knew what you'd done wrong. But when you're a prentice you never do know, and the beatings just make it worse.'

'I never thought old Barkus was a beater,' Joeyn frowned.

'He was a gentle old man. It was the older prentices. They resented me. Anyway, that's a long time ago. It took ages to learn, but once I did it was easy. I didn't even have to think about tuning a controller, especially after I made my own pliance. Suddenly I could see the field perfectly. It was . . .'

'Like having your own eyeglasses,' said Joeyn, 'instead of using someone else's.'

'Exactly. I don't know what I'd do if I ever lost my pliance.' Tiaan clutched at her throat where it normally hung, before realising that she'd left it back on her bench. She felt anxious about that; not that anyone would dare touch it.

'I suppose we should be going.' Joeyn drained his mug.

She stayed where she was. 'I'm worried, Joe. Irisis tries to take the credit for my good work and blames me for everything that goes wrong. She hates me because I'm better than she is. She's afraid I'll be made crafter. Just because her uncle had the position . . .'

'And her father and grandfather before that. Birth *is* right, to a lot of people.'

'And I'm not one of them. Especially since I have *no* father.'

'Well, what you lack in heritage you must make up for in sweat and cleverness. Let's go up to the mine and see what we can find.'

Inside, in the lift basket, Joeyn kept winding down after they reached the fifth opening.

'I thought this part was closed off,' Tiaan said as the basket shuddered to a stop at the sixth level.

'It is.'

'Isn't it dangerous?'

'Parts are very dangerous. Fortunately I know which parts.'

She looked down. The shaft continued. 'What's below this?'

'Levels seven, eight and nine. Don't *ever* go down there.'

'Is the rock all rotten?'

'Yes, and some parts are flooded. Pity, because there's more ore down there, and richer, than ever was taken from the higher levels.'

'What about crystal?'

'Don't know. That's before my time. No one was interested in crystal in them days. Leastways, not here. It would have all been tossed on the mullock heaps, unless a pretty bit caught someone's fancy.'

'Maybe I should try there,' Tiaan said.

'Too late. I had a look after Barkus first asked me for crystal. I couldn't sense anything at all. They must need to be freshly mined.'

'I wonder if that could be the problem?' she said thoughtfully. 'Maybe the operators had the controllers out in the sun, and the last crystals were really sensitive to it.'

'Perhaps. Could also be heat, or frost, or wet. Coming?'

The tunnel snaked this way and that, following the seams. There were many dead ends where seams pinched out or were truncated by faults or shear zones full of crumbled rock and greasy clay. After some hard walking they reached a low mound of rubble. Joeyn surveyed it carefully, holding his lantern up to check the roof.

'See the cracks up there? An old fracture zone runs right through. Rocks are all shattered to bits; just a few seams of quartz holding it together.'

Her eye followed his battered finger. A web of cracks ran across the roof. Another, larger crack snaked down the side of the tunnel as far as she could see. 'What if . . .?'

'If we're under it when it comes down, we're dead! If beyond, we can probably move enough rubble to get out. Depending how much falls. Still want to go?'

'Can we find the crystal I need anywhere else?'

'Not quickly.' He raised an eyebrow, which already had rock dust clinging to it.

'I'll do whatever you say.'

'There's a lot of dead miners who thought the roof would stay up. Still, I think this one is good for a while. We'll go carefully.

No loud noises. Follow ten paces behind, so if I set something off . . .'

Tiaan shivered, feeling the roof twitch above her. He patted her shoulder. 'I started in the mines when I was eight. You develop a nose for danger, if you survive.'

She stayed well back, anxious as she walked under the fractures. Grit trickled down her neck. The place turned out to be a long way in. They went under several more unstable areas before Joeyn stopped where the tunnel terminated in triple dead ends like the stumps of amputated fingers.

'Up there!' He pointed with a chisel.

Tiaan lifted up her lantern. A massive vein, hollow in the centre, slashed across the middle end of the tunnel. It was bristling with crystals fist-sized or bigger, more perfect than any she had seen. She could feel something too – the field. She wished she had her pliance so she could sense it properly. If she closed her eyes she could almost see it as coloured curls and billows, like tendrils of chromatic fog moving in and out of the three dimensions. All her senses seemed more acute, as if the field was amplifying them. She wanted those crystals. Tiaan darted forward.

Joeyn caught her by the collar as she went past. 'Stop!'

The shock jerked her off her feet. Tiaan rubbed her throat, which was bruised from the collar. He steadied her.

'Sorry. Didn't mean to hurt you. It isn't safe there.'

The roof above the vein contained a series of concentric fractures as well as cracks radiating from the centre. The pattern was rather like a spider's web.

Her skin crept. 'I don't know why I ran, Joe. I just felt drawn to it.'

'I can feel it too. I often have, down here, though I was never tempted. I don't see how we can get to the vein, Tiaan. The roof is much worse than I remember. It's going to fall. Soon!'

'Is there no way we could hold it up?'

He eyed the rock. 'Wouldn't be easy. Could take days to get enough plates and props in here, and it'd probably come down on us while we were putting them up.'

'What about making it fall?'

He stroked his jaw. 'You don't know what else will come with it. The entire roof could collapse.'

'Oh!' She felt her last hope disappearing.

He paced back and forth, examining the roof from various vantage points. 'Don't give up yet.'

Sitting on the floor, Joeyn withdrew a roll of cord from his pack and tied a slipknot in one end. Laying the knot over the end of his pick handle, he ran the cord down the handle and crept around the wall until he was as close as he could get to the vein without going under the cracked roof.

He reached up with the pick, as high as he could, but not high enough. He edged forward a bit, just under the shattered zone. Still he could not reach. Going right under, and lifting the pick high, Joeyn eased the handle up to a single crystal, trying to slip the knot over the end. The cord fell down.

Creeping back to the safe area, Joeyn replaced the knot and tried again with the same result. He tried a third time. The cord slipped over the crystal. Putting down the pick he pulled the cord tight and gave it a jerk. The crystal did not move. A harder jerk and the cord broke.

Joeyn cursed, which brought on a fit of coughing. He bent double, gasping and choking.

'Don't stand there, please. Get out of the way!' She imagined the roof thundering down on him. No crystal was worth that risk.

The fit ended. He wiped his mouth, gave her a weak kind of a grin and looked up. 'It's not my day yet, Tiaan.'

'How many dead miners have said that?' she murmured.

'Thousands.' A better grin.

Tossing the cord aside, he slipped along the wall, reached up with the handle of the pick and with a single blow snapped off the small crystal. Unfortunately it fell back among the others. Dust filtered down from the roof. Tiaan caught her breath. Joeyn flipped the pick end for end, caught the handle, stood on tiptoe and flicked the crystal out. He caught it in his other hand, creaked backwards and landed in the safe area. Chips of stone fell from the roof.

As he came across, there was a spring in his step she had never seen before. 'My lady!' Holding out the crystal, he bowed.

'Thank you.' She embraced him, the hand holding the crystal touched her ear and she went rigid against him.

'Something the matter?' he asked, stepping back.

She rubbed her ear. 'It felt as if something stung me.' Tiaan took the crystal. It was smaller than the ones she normally worked with, not much thicker than her thumb. It might not do for a hedron but it looked perfect for her sensor helm. Unlike the other crystals it was perfectly clear, save for a hexagon of tiny bubbles midway along its length.

It did not sting her hand but Tiaan could feel the potential in it – stronger than any crystal she'd ever had.

Six

'Nish!' Irisis wailed, right in his ear. 'Get up, *quick*!'

Rolling over, he blinked at the bright lantern and tried to pull the pillow over his head. 'Later,' he moaned. 'I'm too tired.'

She poured icy water onto the back of his neck.

Nish shrieked and leapt out of bed. 'What the hell do you think you're doing?'

'Look what Tiaan's done now!' she said savagely.

He rubbed sleep from his eyes. She was holding out a controller, the most beautiful piece of work he'd ever seen. At least it had been. Several arms were broken off and the others twisted as if someone had jumped on them.

'What happened to it?'

'Tiaan smashed it, the vicious little cow.'

'Why would she do that?' Nish could not believe anyone would wantonly destroy such a precious thing, least of all Tiaan.

Irisis sat on the bed, holding the controller against her breast. Its broken arms dangled uselessly. 'I only finished it yesterday!' Her lip trembled and she turned away, as if ashamed at that loss of control. 'It's taken me a month to make and it's the best one I've ever done. I came in early to fit the hedron but the controller was gone. It was behind the door of Tiaan's cubicle, like this.'

'There's a guard down at the offices, night and day.' Nish rubbed the back of his neck, still throbbing from the ice water. 'Better speak to him.'

'I have! The only artisan who's been in the workshop since I left was Tiaan. She's in the pay of the enemy. You've got to stop her, Nish.' She moved up close behind him.

Her warm breath aroused distracting thoughts. He turned away. 'It could be just an accident.'

'Don't be stupid! It was in her cubicle, Nish. It didn't float there. She destroyed my controller, just as she sabotaged the others.'

'That's hard to believe.'

'What does it take to convince you?' she raged. 'Will you let her destroy the manufactory?'

'It takes evidence!' he said vehemently. He longed to get back at Tiaan but probers must follow the rules. His father would never trust him again if he accused someone who subsequently turned out to be innocent. Especially the best artisan in the manufactory.

'Go and talk to the guards,' she said icily.

'I will.'

'Bah!' she snorted. 'You're secretly in love with her. You don't want to find her out.'

Nish went looking for the guards who had been on duty outside the offices overnight. Their post was close to the artisans' workshop. He found the midnight guard in the refectory and explained what had happened.

'No one went near the workshop on *my* shift,' she said, pointedly turning her shoulder to him. He was a lowly artificer, after all.

Nish had to take her word, though the damage could have been done in a few minutes while she was at the privy, or gossiping to another guard, or warming herself by the furnaces. After all, there had been no one watching the guard.

The day guard, who was talking to Foreman Gryste, had seen no one go into the workshop except Tiaan and, sometime after that, Irisis.

'My door was open,' said Gryste. 'If anyone else came past I would have seen them.'

'Where's Tiaan now?' Nish asked Irisis, who was coming out of the workshop.

'She's gone out again. Come on!'

Nish followed her towards the front gate. 'Where did she go?'

'How would I know?'

They asked old Nod at the gate. 'She went down to the mine,' Nod said.

'She goes there all the time,' said Irisis as they walked out into the wind.

'She has to select the best crystals.'

'You're a fool, Nish! She's selling our secrets to someone there. She's going to meet him.'

'Don't call me a fool,' he said coldly. 'And don't ever call me Nish again. My name is Cryl-Nish.'

His anger made her step backwards. Bowing her head, she took his hand. 'I'm sorry,' she said breathlessly. 'I didn't mean to offend you, Cryl-Nish. Please come and see for yourself.'

As they emerged from the forest Tiaan came out of the adit and took the path to the village. Irisis and Nish followed, keeping at a safe distance.

'Where's she going?' Nish asked.

'To old Joeyn's place, I'd say.'

They tracked her to a hut above the village. Tiaan went inside, then she and the miner came out and sat on the porch.

'What are they doing?' Irisis whispered.

'Drinking tea.'

After some time, Tiaan and Joeyn headed back up the path to the mine.

'Come on!' said Irisis.

Nish went with her to the hut. She slipped inside. 'Quickly!' she said as he lingered on the path.

Nish thought it unlikely that there was anything to be found, but humoured her. Shortly, however, feeling under the old man's blankets, his hand touched a folded piece of paper. He carried it to the doorway.

71

Both sides of the page were covered in writing in a tiny hand. It was a description of the preparation of a hedron. 'That's Tiaan's writing,' Irisis said, coming up behind him. 'The traitorous slut!'

Nish examined the paper, which was rough-cut on three sides, razor smooth on the fourth. 'Looks as if it's been taken from a book.'

'It must be from her day journal.'

They found nothing else. Without saying a word Nish went back to the manufactory, searching Tiaan's room and then her work cubicle. Her room revealed nothing. Her day journal had a leaf missing, neatly razored out.

He locked the cubicle, put the key in his pocket and went to see Overseer Gi-Had. There he explained that he was a prober, working secretly on his father's behalf, showed his letter of appointment and told Gi-Had about the ruined controller and the missing leaf.

'I don't believe it!' said the overseer, though he looked worried.

'Anyone can be corrupted by the enemy.'

'Not Tiaan. She has no vices, no secrets, no life apart from her work.'

'Perhaps one of her brothers or sisters is in trouble and she needs money desperately.'

Gi-Had consulted a ledger. 'She has forty-nine silver drams to her account, more than almost anyone in the manufactory. Twenty-six more and she could pay off her indenture. Unheard of!'

Nish whistled. It was a small fortune. 'There you are – it's her wages as a spy.'

'It's her pay over the past fourteen years! She's spent virtually nothing in that time. You can check the entries, prober. Every copper nyd is accounted for.'

Nish did, and found all to be exactly as Gi-Had had said. It shook him. 'Perhaps you'd better come and see the journal.'

'I will,' said Gi-Had, and his face grew even blacker as he matched the leaf to the cut. 'Anyone could have done this! Why would she cut a leaf from her own journal, incriminating herself, when she could simply copy it?'

Nish was forced to consider the unpalatable alternative, that

Irisis had smashed her own controller and planted the evidence to discredit her rival.

'Do you have anyone in mind?' Gi-Had rasped. It was clear that *he* did.

'Me?' Nish said hoarsely.

'You *are* supposed to be the prober.'

'I'm thinking on it.'

'Then think fast! I want a report today. Tiaan is working on a special project for me and suddenly this happens. It's damned suspicious! If someone is trying to bring down my best artisan, I'll hang their head over the front gate and their guts from the flagpole. *Whoever their family is!*' His eyes flashed. 'I'm putting a guard on the workshop, night and day! No, two guards.' He stamped out.

Nish sat down on Tiaan's stool, shaken. What was he supposed to do now? He was almost sure Irisis had cut the page from the ledger. If she was behind the sabotage too, she must be denounced. She was a liability he could not afford.

The door opened and Irisis came in, smiling. The smile vanished when she saw the expression on his face.

'It was you!' he said through gritted teeth. He jumped up, knocking over the stool. 'Gi-Had knows Tiaan was set up and he suspects you. I should call him back right now.'

'Go ahead. He's my cousin.'

'I can't believe you would smash your own controller!' he said coldly.

Irisis stared at him in incredulity, then spun on her heel and stalked out. He ran after her, grabbing her by the arm.

She whirled. 'You *do* believe it, Nish! You think more of her than you do of me.'

'You manipulating bitch! How dare you use me?'

'You love her,' she sneered. 'Your brain is addled by the little cow.'

'I despise her, but not as much as I despise you. Don't ever lie to me, Irisis. Do you deny that you did it?'

She said nothing at all. He held her gaze but she did not look away. 'You can't deny it, can you, Irisis?'

'I don't have to justify myself to you, Nish.'

'You *did* do it!'

'I have nothing to say.'

'In that case I must do my prober's duty and take my evidence to Gi-Had.'

She pulled her arm free. 'If you do,' she said coldly, 'don't think I'll go without a fuss. Your father the perquisitor will be told that you talk on your lover's pillow, and that I bribed you to bring Tiaan down and make me crafter. It'll be the end of your career too, *Ex-Prober* Cryl-Nish.'

He knew she would. He might lie his way out of it but his prospects would be badly damaged. His liaison with her was already the talk of the manufactory and she could turn his collaboration into treason. It would be a disaster for them both.

Nish had everything to lose if she went down, much to gain if she did not. Her family was nearly the equal of his own. It would be a good alliance, to say nothing of the pleasures of her glorious body. But if she was behind the sabotage he must denounce her.

He faced up to his duty. 'I don't care! I hate Tiaan, but I'll go to my doom before I help the enemy . . .' He tried to look implacable.

'Very well,' she said. 'I admit that I cut the page from her book and hid it, but only because of what she'd done to me.'

Nish took a deep breath. It did not make things any easier. 'And the sabotage of your controller?'

'Don't be absurd!' She met his eye, unflinching.

Irisis looked convincing, though Nish knew what a gifted liar she was. 'Swear it!'

'I swear,' she said evenly, 'on my sacred family Histories, that I had nothing to do with the sabotages. Any of them!'

He was still not absolutely convinced, though he had no option but to take her word. 'In that case, who did?'

'Tiaan did!' she grated. 'Why won't you look at the evidence? Nothing I've said changes the facts. You heard the guards – there's no one else it could be.'

'I still have to tell Gi-Had that you cut out the page.'

Irisis looked as if she'd been slapped across the face. Her big eyes were on him, a single tear quivering on one lash. She took a tentative step toward him, a gliding movement, then up on her toes at the end. Her bosom heaved. The buttons seemed to have come undone. It was the oldest trick of all and he wasn't going to be taken in by it.

'Please, Cryl-Nish!' She held out her arms.

He folded his across his chest, desperately trying to control his body. With an insignificant movement at her waist, her trousers fell to her ankles. She stepped out of them. Ah, but her body was magnificent!

'Would you let them kill me so cruelly? They would disembowel me, hang up my entrails for the world to see and cut my body into quarters to feed the scavengers.' With another movement she stood naked before him. 'Would you do that, to this!' She held out her breasts, one in each hand.

Nish flung himself on her and they copulated on the floor of Tiaan's cubicle like beasts. After it was over and they lay panting, slicked with sweat, Irisis opened her eyes. They were so very blue. 'I think I see a solution to both our problems.'

'Oh?' he said.

'Do you believe Tiaan is innocent or guilty?'

'I don't know,' he said heavily.

'What do you think?'

'I think, on the balance of the evidence, that she probably is guilty.'

'Then help me stop her. If something were to happen to Tiaan . . .'

He pushed her away roughly. 'What are you talking about? It had better not be what I'm thinking.' Though for more of what he'd just had, there was little he would not do, if he could get away with it.

Irisis pulled him back, and he relented. 'She has betrayed her country, and you, and me! Soldiers have died; clankers have been lost. I know my duty too, Nish. We've got to be rid of her for the good of the war.'

She was moving too fast for him. 'But . . . the manufactory can't do without her.'

75

'Do you know how many artisans there are, just in this province?'

'I have no idea.'

'More than a thousand! If something happened to her, or to me for that matter, either of us could be replaced tomorrow.'

'I hadn't thought there could be so many,' Nish said.

'Well, there are.'

'Do you deny she is a good artisan?' Nish expected her to.

'Tiaan is very talented. Since I'm being honest with you, she's better than I am. But she's using those talents against us, Nish. She's helping the enemy.'

'I don't like it.'

'That's because you're in love with her.'

'I'm not! But . . .'

'After what she said to you the other day? No *real* man would put up with that kind of abuse.'

Still he hesitated.

Irisis stood up. 'Make up your mind, Nish. Support her and you'll get no more of me, *ever*! Which is it?'

'I hate Tiaan for what she did to me,' he said. 'If proof against her can be found – proper proof – I'll help you destroy her.'

'And you won't tell Gi-Had that I cut out the page?' Those big blue eyes were all over him again.

'No,' he said softly.

Nish spent the rest of the day agonising about what he had got himself into. Concealing evidence was a serious crime, and if he was wrong about Irisis, it would mean his doom.

SEVEN

Tiaan returned from the mine, still puzzling over Joeyn's observation that crystals exposed on the mullock heaps were useless. Oblivious to the furore, she collected a handful of hedron chips and put them at various locations inside and outside the manufactory, to test the effects of exposure. She did not need to hide them since they looked like any other fragments of quartz.

On the way back to her cubicle Tiaan ducked into the library and went to the section where the Great Tales were kept. These books, of which there were twenty-nine, were the highest achievement of the Histories and every child was taught them. The manufactory's copies were bound in red leather reinforced with brass, and fixed to the shelves with brass chains. She lifted them down, one by one. All of the Great Tales were there save one, the twenty-third. *The Tale of the Mirror*.

She went to the librarian, an old, old man as bald as a marble, with thin blotched hands and perpetually moist eyes.

'Hello, Gurleys,' she said. 'I'm looking for one of the Great Tales.'

'They're all on the shelf.' He did not take his eyes from his catalogue.

'No, one is missing. *The Tale of the Mirror*.'

He looked up sharply, opened his mouth and closed it again.

He seemed to be in pain. Moisture leaked from his eyes.

'There is no *Tale of the Mirror*!'

'But . . . it's the twenty-third tale. There must – '

'There is not!' he hissed, 'and if you keep on about it I will have to enter your name in the scrutator's log.'

'I beg your pardon.' Tiaan thanked him and went out. So Joeyn had been right. But why *had* the tale been withdrawn?

Just outside the door, Tiaan was called to Gi-Had's office. The overseer was sitting behind his table. He said nothing as she came in and shut the door, though he held himself as straight as a poker. He indicated a chair. She sat down.

'What did you want to see me about, overseer?'

He pinned her with those deeply sunken eyes. 'This!' Gi-Had threw a controller onto the table.

Tiaan started. It was the one Irisis had been working on for the past month, though so battered that it could not be repaired. She picked it up. 'How did this happen?'

'Irisis accuses you,' Gi-Had said without expression.

'Me?' Tiaan swallowed. 'Why would I do such a wicked thing?'

'Because you and Irisis are feuding? Because you hate her? Perhaps because you are in the pay of the enemy?' He held his hands out as if offering her a choice rather than accusing her, but all at once she felt desperately afraid. The breeding factory could be the least of her worries. Gi-Had looked every bit as ferocious as that perquisitor of her childhood. And after all, Irisis was his second cousin. Blood was thick in these parts.

It was hard to control her voice. 'I – I don't like Irisis, but I don't hate her. I'm just trying to do my job and my best for the war.'

'The guards say you're the only one who went in there this morning.'

'The night guard spends most of her shift gossiping by the furnaces. She's never around when I finish work.'

'The day guard says the same thing. And Irisis's controller has been smashed *in your cubicle*.'

'Maybe someone is trying to get rid of me,' she said simply.

'Are you accusing Irisis?'

'I don't believe she would wreck her controller, even to be rid of me. She loves her work too much.'

'Then who?' Gi-Had cried.

'I don't know, overseer.'

'I suggest you try very hard to find out! Once Perquisitor Jal-Nish hears of this outrage he may decide to pay us a visit. He's not as trusting as I am, Tiaan, and he's quick to jump to conclusions. If he decides against you, *nothing* I say will change his mind. That's all!'

She went out, a black chill settling over her. She had heard all about the new perquisitor. Before she reached her cubicle Tiaan found another reason to be afraid. The perquisitor was Nish's father. She had spurned the little artificer and now he was Irisis's lover. There was no doubt whose word Jal-Nish would take.

Her only refuge was work, though it could not stop her cycling thoughts. The new crystal needed no shaping; it was perfect as it was. After waking it with her pliance, Tiaan merely cleaned up a few sharp edges, then reconstructed the mounting on the front of her helm to fit. At dinnertime she slipped the crystal into place. It fitted perfectly. Pushing the clasps down, she sat back. It was a fine piece of work, as good as she could do, but it gave her no pleasure. And again, as she put her devices down, Tiaan had the feeling that someone, in some distant place, was trying to find her.

Uncomfortable with that thought, she closed her eyes and lay her head on the bench. The door opened. Irisis stood there, the last person she wanted to see. 'I heard about your controller – ' Tiaan began.

Such fury passed across Irisis's face that Tiaan froze. 'Don't say another word!' Irisis snarled.

Tiaan looked down at her helm, wondering what it was that Irisis wanted.

'Have you found the answer yet?' Irisis picked up one of the failed hedrons.

'No, but I'm making progress. What about you?'

'It's not *my* controllers that failed.'

'I thought you'd want to help, for the sake of the war,' Tiaan said acidly. A tiny victory but it made her feel better.

Irisis's eyes darted to the globe and helm. 'What's that? Another toy for your bastard brothers and sisters?'

As little as twenty years ago that would not have been an insult, in the days when women could choose to take a partner, or not. Tiaan clenched her fists. Irisis laughed openly. 'You came from the breeding factory and that's where you'll end up. It's all you're good for anyway, lying on your back with your legs over your shoulders.'

Tiaan gritted her teeth and said nothing, since that would annoy Irisis more than any reply she could think of.

'Well, what is it?' Irisis burst out.

'I should have thought someone with your great crafter heritage would know at a glance.'

'Just tell me!'

'It's a probe,' Tiaan said, 'to read the history of the faulty controllers and find out why they failed.'

A spark lit in Irisis's eyes. 'It'll never work.' Picking up the helm, she weighed it in her hands and then put it on her head, where it sat like a pancake. 'Doesn't even fit.'

'My head is smaller than yours.'

Irisis rotated the helm, pushing its spidery legs down hard. She reached for the globe that still held the faulty hedron, but as she touched it the crystal in the helm flared white. There came a snapping sound, accompanied by a sizzle. Irisis screamed, tore the helm off and hurled it at the bench.

'Are you all right?' Tiaan could not comprehend what had happened.

Irisis staggered drunkenly about, her eyes crossed. Her fingers rubbed furiously at her temple. Tiaan got her into a chair. The skin beneath where the crystal had sat was blistered and several strands of yellow hair had frizzled up.

Irisis's eyes uncrossed and she slapped Tiaan across the face with the full weight of arm and shoulder. It knocked Tiaan sideways. 'You rotten little cow, you did that deliberately. Stay away from me, do you hear?'

Tiaan backed away, rubbing her cheek.

Irisis rose out of her chair as if propelled by a spring. She looked frightened, not a common expression on her face. What had the device done to her?

'That thing's corrupt, like you, Tiaan. You'll never get anything out of it.'

'You just don't understand it,' said Tiaan as Irisis made for the door. She could not resist a taunt, for she seldom got the last word with Irisis. 'Maybe it's you who'll be going to the breeding factory.'

'People like *me* don't go to the breeding factory!' she spat. She was peculiarly sensitive to slights against her ability as an artisan. 'We marry well and live in luxury. Enjoy it while it lasts, Tiaan. You won't be here much longer.'

Tiaan, who before her mother's decline had come from a long line of proud, independent women, wanted to fling herself on Irisis, clawing and screaming. But restraining herself, she slammed the door in her rival's face. In a few days she had made two mortal enemies. And despite the shortage of men, she had no doubt that Irisis would make a good match. Her kind usually did.

These controllers would decide Tiaan's fate. If she found out why they had failed, and could solve the problem, she should be secure. If not, she was surely doomed.

Tiaan could never submit to the breeding factory. It was a propaganda weapon, but also a way of using women who had failed in other areas of life, and those who could never find a mate because so many men had been killed in the war. Whole generations of youths had gone away and not come back.

It was impossible to work now. As she was locking her door, Tiaan saw Nish across the way, leaning against the wall of the offices. No doubt he was gathering evidence for the perquisitor. Her life was collapsing around her.

In her room, too shaken to eat or wash, Tiaan tossed her clothes into the basket, crawled in between the freezing sheets and curled up into a ball. Using a hedron always gave her fantastic dreams, as if it left her mind close to the ethyr that was the carrier of power. She hoped her dreams would be romantic ones tonight. Dreams were a refuge and an escape. She had never needed one more desperately.

Tiaan dreamed about an unknown world, a gloomy land lit by a brooding orange moon, nothing like *the* moon. Black grass bent under a hissing wind. Oily, suppurating bogs were scattered across the landscape, around which grew blue and black and purple flowers, luminous in the darkness.

She was standing on a balcony, staring toward broken-glass mountains in the west. Tiaan could feel her heart thudding against her ribs, the prickly rush of fear in the backs of her hands. Her fingers gripped the rail so hard that it hurt. Her jaw was clenched. She could feel her teeth grinding together. Why was she so afraid?

A low rumbling began in the distance, like thunder but more earthy, as if transmitted through the ground. The breeze was whipping mist past her face, but it had the pungent reek of sulphur. Her eyes watered.

She wiped the tears away. Staring at the jagged range, Tiaan realised that she was holding her breath, waiting for something to happen. She counted her heartbeats: one, two, three, four, five, six, seven, eight, nine, ten. Then backwards. She was still counting when there came a colossal explosion from the middle of the distant range, a flash that lit up the sky. Yellow glowing objects described parabolic trajectories through the air, slowly changing to orange and red as they fell.

More explosions illuminated belching clouds that rose higher and higher, forming shapes like clenched fists, like anvils, like black mushrooms. Lightning rent the clouds. There was no thunder, no sound at all but the wind hissing over the grass.

The explosions spread along the range from one horizon to the other until it looked as if the whole world was splitting apart, blowing its molten insides out. The clouds grew so thick that the wheeling fireballs could scarcely be seen. As Tiaan stared, a glowing paste made its way down the side of the mountain where the first explosion had occurred, like a red slug down the side of a pot. More streams followed until the dark mass of the mountain was woven with them. Tiaan felt another trickle of fear.

The lava was flooding everywhere, issuing from every peak of that horizon-spanning chain, oozing toward her as if, in its inexorable progress, it would overwhelm the whole world.

Her viewpoint shifted. Tiaan stared at the figure on the balcony, realising that it was not her at all, but a young, handsome man, tall and broad-shouldered, with glossy dark-brown hair, a trim beard, a full, sensuous mouth. He resembled the bold prince of her grandmother's romantic tales.

He seemed just as afraid as she had been, and she knew his doom was written in those red glyphs running down the mountains. He threw out his arms, looking around frantically as if seeking someone in the darkness. *Help!* She saw him mouth the words. *Please help me!*

Before the sound reached her, there came a boom and roar like all the thunder in the world going off together. A solid wall of wind bent the grass, the scanty trees, the young man on the balcony. He looked directly at her and froze. His tentative, almost pleading smile cracked her soft heart. She smiled back, he cried out *Help!* then man and balcony were blown away. The earth moved, tossing her off her feet. Tiaan lost the dream.

But later that night she dreamed that the young man lay beside her. Disturbing dreams they were – sensual, almost erotic. They made her hideously uncomfortable, yet she did not want them to stop.

Tiaan woke with a headache and a faint memory of the first dream – the explosions, the stench of sulphur, the wild wind. She remembered that glorious face and the young man crying out. How strange! It was almost as if he had been begging *her* for help. But after all, it was just another hedron-induced fancy. She threw herself out of bed and hurried off to work.

The first experiments with the device had gone well. She was beginning to read the history of the crystal, as if the letters that made up its story were stored in layers of light trapped within it. It had a strange, hot sense, which was odd. Hedrons usually seemed cool. So far, though, she had not learned what had gone wrong.

At mid-morning her head began to ache and it grew rapidly worse. It seemed to be burning, like the image of the crystal. Don't push too hard; anthracism is a horrible way to die . . .

Tiaan went outside, collected her little chips of crystal and laid them in a line across the back of the bench. She put the helm on but a piercing pain made her whip it off again. She was hunched over, head in hands, when Gi-Had appeared with Gryste, the foreman, who reeked of spice.

'You won't make any progress that way, Artisan Tiaan!' said Gryste.

She squinted up at him. 'I'm working eighteen hours a day.'

'We're all working hard,' said the overseer.

'I'm working harder than anyone!' she snapped. Then, more softly, 'My head feels as if it's on fire, Gi-Had. I'm afraid . . .'

He blanched. 'Then stop. I'll have no boiled brains in my manufactory.'

'But I am making progress. I made this device to read the hedrons.' She held it out.

Gi-Had took up the helm, turning it in his fingers, and touched the crystal with a fingertip. Tiaan held her breath in case it stung him too, but nothing happened. That was not surprising. Psychically speaking, his mind was no more active than a piece of mutton.

She put a hedron inside the globe and demonstrated how it was meant to work. The overseer and foreman listened carefully but probably did not understand much. That did not matter. Neither knew how controllers worked either, but they understood their value to the war.

'What have you discovered?' Gryste barked, like a general to a raw recruit.

'All three hedrons show the same pattern. They worked perfectly when first installed. I have our log books here if you'd care to check them . . .'

Gi-Had waved them away. 'We trust your word.'

'I don't trust anyone who doesn't obey my rules,' said Gryste, 'and she's always going out without permission.'

The overseer gestured him to silence. Tiaan described Joeyn's observation about the effects of exposure on crystals, and her own experiments. She went through the series of numbered pieces on the bench, one by one. 'I left these eight outside: two in sun, two in shade, two in wet, two in dry. And these eight inside: two right next to the furnace, two a little further away though still hot, these two where it was only warm, and these two against the cold south wall.'

Gi-Had looked impressed. 'What have you discovered?'

'Nothing yet. I only just brought them in.'

'Bah!' said Gryste. 'I told you she was a waste of time.'

'Be quiet, *junior* foreman!' Gi-Had snapped.

Gryste's face froze and Tiaan knew she had made another enemy.

'Read them now, artisan,' Gi-Had said.

Tiaan prayed she was not going to disappoint the overseer. Donning the helm, she gritted her teeth against the pain and put the first chip in the globe. 'There's hardly any aura left.' She took it out and began on the others, one by one.

The overseer tossed the first chip in his big hands. 'Number one,' he read. 'This one was left in sunlight?'

'That's right.'

They watched in silence as she read the crystals. 'The two in sunlight have some aura left, though not much. The four heated by the furnace are completely dead. All the others are unchanged.'

Gi-Had looked confused.

Tiaan explained. 'Their ability to draw power from the field can be destroyed by putting them out in the sun, though that must take quite a while. Days or weeks for a big hedron, I'd think.'

'That can't be why yours failed,' said Gryste. 'They're well looked after.'

'No, but . . . I have an idea!' Taking another handful of chips from her basket, she checked that they all had a strong aura. 'Come with me to the furnaces.'

They followed her, Gryste not trying to hide his irritation. 'I've got work to do, even if no one else has,' he grumbled.

Tiaan put two chips against the wall of the furnace where it was practically red-hot, and two more where it was just hot enough to burn a fingertip. She left them there for five minutes then retrieved them with a pair of tongs.

Back in her cubicle she read their auras. 'The first two are completely dead. The others have a faint aura, though it's fading. You see!' she said triumphantly. 'Make them really hot and they won't work at all. Less hot, they work for a while, then fail.'

'You're saying that your hedrons were sabotaged,' Gi-Had exclaimed. He exchanged glances with the foreman, whose face had gone stubbornly blank.

'I don't see how it could be anything else,' Tiaan said. 'The crystals never see sunlight from when they're mined to when they reach our workshops, and once the operators receive the controllers no one could guard them more jealously. But put them against the wall of the furnace for five minutes and they're useless. Anyone could have done that.'

'Can you tell who?'

'I've picked up strange traces in the little bit of aura that was left, but I can't read them. I would need a really strong crystal to do that. Or perhaps with my pliance . . .'

'Haahhh!' Gi-Had let his breath out in a hissing sigh. Going to the door, he looked out and closed it. 'Then we do have a spy among us.'

'So it would seem.'

'You'd better find out before the perquisitor does.' He looked irritable again.

'I'm trying, but . . .'

'No excuses now!' Gi-Had snapped. 'Our soldiers are dying every minute for want of clankers to protect them. If I can't produce our quota, I'm likely to end up in the front-lines. At my age!'

'I can only work for ten minutes before I get the headaches.'

'Then get someone to help you. Irisis doesn't look too busy today.'

'She tried it yesterday,' Tiaan said. 'It hurt her badly.'

'She accuses you of trying to kill her,' said the overseer.

'I did not ask her to touch my helm.'

'Well, find someone else.'

'No one else has the experience, or the control.'

'There must be someone. There's a thousand people in this manufactory, dammit!'

'Would you ask a blacksmith to make your wife a necklace?

86

Or a librarian to work the foundry? No one else here can do it, Overseer Gi-Had.'

'Then go see the apothek, have him mix a potion for the headaches, and get to work! Everything is resting on you, Tiaan.'

'And the spy?' she said quietly.

'Gryste will make that his first priority.'

'I'll begin on it right away,' said the foreman sourly. 'As if I don't already have enough on my plate.'

Gi-Had scribbled Tiaan an authorisation for the apothek. 'Come on, foreman, we've work to do.' They hurried off. The overseer was at home with ores and furnaces and metal, all things mechanical, but the work done here was well beyond his comprehension. He did not like that.

Tiaan came back from the dispensary without the balm, which would require some time to prepare. Taking several glasses of tarry water, she rubbed her temples and went to see what the prentices were doing. Darya was head-down at her grinding wheel. Vyns and Ru-Dan were adjusting a set of clamps over another crystal, careful not to damage it. The other prentices were busy at their benches.

'Where's Gol?' Tiaan asked.

Ru-Dan looked up and said something to Vyns, who steadied the crystal while she strolled over, taking off goggles and dust mask. Ru-Dan was short and plump, with a cheerful round face marked (though not marred) by a round pox scar just above the corner of her mouth.

'I beg your pardon?' Ru-Dan smoothed back chestnut hair with a hand glittering with powdered crystal.

'I was looking for Gol.'

'Haven't seen him for an hour or two.'

'What was he doing then?'

The prentice hesitated, not wanting to get Gol into trouble.

'Nothing, I'll bet!' said Tiaan. 'When you see him, tell him I want to see him *immediately*.'

Ru-Dan nodded. 'Did you want anything else? Vyns and I are mounting a crystal right now.'

'That was all.' Then, as Ru-Dan walked back, 'Have you seen Irisis?'

'She was in your workroom a while ago.'

Tiaan felt a twinge of unease. 'Oh, thanks!'

Some hours later, Irisis appeared at Tiaan's cubicle with a small jar in her hand. 'I was going past the apothek and he asked me to give you this,' she said frostily.

'Thank you.' The label said to rub a small amount on her temples every four hours, or more frequently if the headache did not go away.

Pulling off the lid, Tiaan took a smear of balm on her fingertip and began to massage it into her forehead. The skin grew warm. Her headache, which had been a dull throb for the past hour, faded slightly. Putting the jar to one side, she drew the wire globe toward her and looked around for the helm.

She could not see it anywhere. Tiaan rifled through the clutter on the bench. Surely Irisis wouldn't have taken it? Could she be the saboteur? It hardly seemed possible. But she had nothing to lose by undermining Tiaan, and everything to gain.

Tiaan dismissed that as a fancy brought on by overwork and not enough in her belly. Heading out the door to the refectory, she saw something bright lying hard up against the wall. Her helm! It was bent out of shape, though nothing she couldn't fix. How had it got there? She'd left it up the other end of the bench.

It would not have been so deformed from falling off the bench. It must have been thrown, or struck! With a growing feeling of alarm she checked the crystal and immediately saw the crack, which went right across the hexagon of bubbles. Small curving cracks radiated away from one point, as if it had been struck with a hammer.

Tiaan put the helm on her head, already knowing what she was going to find. It was completely dead. The crystal was ruined.

EIGHT

After reporting the damage to Gi-Had, who had roared 'Gryste, get in here!' Tiaan returned to the workshop. There was only one solution, reluctant though she was. She would have to ask old Joe to find her another crystal.

She did not want to. Tiaan even toyed with the idea of going to the sixth level by herself to avoid troubling him, but that would be irresponsible. Joe would be furious, and what if she had an accident? No, what he could do in safety would be fool-hardy for her to attempt.

Joeyn was back on the fifth level in the place he had been working earlier in the week. He looked pleased to see her, even when, with some reluctance, she explained why she had come. She showed him the damaged crystal.

'I thought we might need to go down again.' He pressed his lunch on her.

Tiaan took one of the spicy meal cakes. It was delicious, though hot; sweat broke out on her forehead. 'I didn't want to ask you.'

'Why not?'

'I hate asking people for favours. And you've done so much already.'

'I hope you weren't thinking of going to the sixth level by yourself,' he said with a steely glint.

Tiaan looked down at her boots. One lace had come undone. She tied it.

'This is my work, Tiaan. My life. If I had to go to the sixth level a hundred times I'd do it cheerfully. Especially for you.'

She could think of no answer to that.

'Besides, I carried a bit of formwork in yesterday,' he went on. 'Not much, just a beam and a couple of props, but it'll be safer than before.'

He sketched the arrangement on the floor with his knife. 'Want to go?'

'Might as well.'

This time, the trip did not seem quite so doom-laden. In the cavern she stood well back while Joeyn gauged the height with a folding ruler.

He measured the props, sawing a handspan off one, the thickness of a finger off the other. 'Now we come to the danger-ous part. If you're a believer, say your prayers now.'

Tiaan was not but she uttered a sincere prayer anyhow.

'This is what we're going to do,' the old miner said. 'We'll each hold our props at an angle to the vertical, like this.' He demon-strated. 'Then, we lift the timber plate on top, like a lintel over a doorway. Finally we move under the cracked area, just in front of the vein, and bring our props upright, forcing the plate hard against the roof. Hard enough to hold it, but not hard enough to bring it down on us, of course.' He grinned.

'Of course!'

She bent down to lift the prop, which was a span and a half long and half as big round as her waist. It proved to be incred-ibly heavy. Heaving and gasping, Tiaan managed to get one end as high as her shoulder. The prop was not made from the light local pine but from a dense, wavy-grained hardwood with a rank odour, like wet socks.

'Lean it against the wall,' said Joeyn. 'They're buggers to lift!' He rested his own a couple of spans from hers. 'Have a breather.'

They lifted the beam, which was even heavier, and laid it on top of the props, lying flat. 'Ready?' said Joeyn. 'It's going to be bloody hard work!'

Moving the prop away from the wall was the easy part. Keeping the plate on it was murder. The split edge cut into her shoulder; splinters needled her fingers. But that was nothing compared to the sheer agony of lifting prop and beam and walking with them. One step and she was exhausted; two, bone weary; three, and every muscle in her body was shrieking.

'Rest it!' said Joeyn, who seemed to be bearing his load easily enough. No doubt he was used to it. 'I'd have brought a couple of pit labourers in, but they've got families, and this level is forbidden . . .'

'I think I can manage,' she said stoutly. 'It's just, well, I'm used to working with my fingers, not carrying heavy loads.'

'We'll take it one step at a time. As soon as it starts to hurt, ground your pole.'

She gave a weak smile. It hurt before she'd even got it off the floor. After two steps her prop began to shake. Tiaan grounded it hastily.

Another step. Now they were going under the cracked area. The pole wobbled; she let it down, expecting the beam to fall on her head. Joeyn's hand flew up, steadying it.

Parts of the roof rock, segments bounded by fractures, looked ready to fall. She closed her eyes and instantly saw that final image from last night's dream – the handsome young man on the balcony, begging for help as volcanoes erupted fire and ash all around.

Tiaan snapped her eyes open. The scene vanished. 'Are you all right?' Joeyn asked.

'Yes,' she said dazedly. She lifted her prop. They moved another two steps, rested, then one more.

'Just a half step to your left now, Tiaan.'

Finally they were ready. 'This is the difficult part,' he said. 'We slowly raise our poles to the vertical, pushing the plate up against the roof. When it's in position I'll wedge the props so they're tight and we'll be done. Carefully now. You go first; I'll match it.'

Tiaan began to push her prop up. Slowly, ever so slowly. The tip wobbled. She steadied it with her shoulder.

'Easy does it,' said Joeyn. 'Take all the time you need.'

Up again, and again. 'Just one more lift.'

Up they went. Half the prop was above her shoulder now, and harder to steady. The tip wobbled. She threw her weight against it but the base skidded on a pebble and the pole tilted. The plate began to slide off.

'Up hard!' Joeyn cried, but it was too late.

Tiaan dropped the prop and crouched with her arms over her head. The plate struck the floor with a tremendous clatter. Her prop hit the wall. Joeyn remained where he was, still holding his pole, staring up at the roof.

Grit rained down on Tiaan's back. A chip of granite bounced off the plate. She stood up, gasping. 'I'm sorry, Joeyn.'

'No – my fault. It wasn't such a good idea after all.'

'Let's try again. One last effort.'

'Are you sure?'

'I think so.'

The second time was harder than the first, if that was possible. Tiaan's back was throbbing, low down, and her arms had lost the best of their strength. But she knew how to balance the plate now, and the tiny movements needed to keep it there. This time they got it almost to the roof with no fatal wobbles.

'The last bit is always the hardest to control,' he said.

'I'm ready.' She had to succeed this time. Tiaan could not make another attempt. She eased the pole until it was nearly upright. It wobbled and she could barely hold it.

Joeyn thrust his prop up hard, jamming the plate against the roof. That steadied it enough for Tiaan to raise her end the last distance. They'd done it!

'Keep it steady.' He nudged a wedge under the prop with the toe of his boot and tapped it in. After wedging the other side, he shook the pole. It did not budge. He did the same with hers. 'You can let go, Tiaan.'

Now that the strain was off, Tiaan could not stand up. She crawled across to the far wall, laid her burning cheek on the cold floor and watched while Joeyn tightened the wedges, one by one, with his hammer.

He sat beside her. Tiaan began picking splinters out of her palms. 'That'll hold against a minor fall,' he said.

'But not a major one?'

Joeyn eyed the erection. 'No, but it'll only take a few minutes to get the crystal.' He offered her his flask of turnip brandy.

This time she took a sip. The liquor tasted revolting, but it warmed her all the way down. Tiaan felt better, though she was not tempted to take a second.

Joeyn was back at the vein, staring up. 'Come here. Pick the one you want.'

He linked his hands, making a step. She put her foot in it and was boosted up to shoulder height.

'Oh, Joe, they're the most perfect ones I've ever seen. They feel strong, too – even better than the crystal you got the other day.' She exclaimed over one, then another. It was impossible to decide. Had she brought her pliance she might have tested them, to see which was most suited to her. Tiaan felt a pang of withdrawal. 'But which are the good ones, Joeyn? No point me picking one out if it's just ordinary crystal.'

'I think they're all good. I had a bit of a look at them when I brought the timbers in.'

'You mean . . .?'

'Yes. This vein is worth as much as the rest of the mine put together.'

Unimaginable wealth. If she owned one of these crystals, she could buy out her indenture ten times over. Tiaan edged a bit higher, searching for a crystal just a bit more perfect than the others. 'Joe, look!'

'What is it?'

'The hollow goes in for ages, and it's all lined with crystals. There must be hundreds of them.' She gazed in wonderment. 'Maybe thousands.'

'I hate to disturb you,' said he. 'I know you're only a slip of a woman, after all, but I can't hold you up forever.'

'Sorry.' She had quite forgotten. 'Do you need a rest?'

'Not if you've found what you're looking for.'

She selected a perfect hexagonal prism terminated by a

pyramid. It was a delicate ruby-pink colour, almost transparent. 'I've got one.'

'Put your feet on my shoulders and I'll pass up the hammer and chisel.'

Taking the tools, with a single, well-placed tap she knocked the quartz crystal off at the base. It fell back into the cavity. She reached in to recover the crystal. 'Aah!'

'What's the matter?'

'It felt like a hundred hot needles touching my skin at once. It's all right; it's gone now. Hello?' She stood up on tiptoe. 'What's *that*?'

'What?'

'Way up at the end, a crystal seems to be glowing by itself.'

'How far in?'

'A long way. Seven or eight arm lengths, I'd say. It's the most perfect one I've ever seen. A bipyramid.'

'Well, you can't have it. There's no way of getting it out.'

'I don't suppose . . .' she looked down at him, 'from the other side?'

'That'd be weeks of tunnelling, even supposing the roof stayed up. Sorry, Tiaan.'

'Oh, well,' she said regretfully. 'A pity. It looks so perfect.' She jumped down.

'They all look perfect from that distance.' He began to tap one of the wedges out from under his prop.

'Maybe you should leave that there for a while. In case something happens to this crystal too.'

'Irisis?'

'Or the saboteur, *if they are different.*'

'Maybe I will.' He kicked the wedge back in.

The new crystal proved much more difficult to wake, and even more draining. She had now woken three in a few days, which would have exhausted the greatest crafter in the east. After it was done, Tiaan did not don the helm at once. The way forward was no longer clear. Because of the headaches, she felt anxious about using her device. But then, everything about her life made her anxious.

Tiaan kept thinking about the strange crystal. She had never heard of one that glowed. She also wondered about her vision in the mine, that fragment of dream about the young man. Crystal dreams usually vanished when she woke up but she could remember his face perfectly. He had been so desperate. She recalled the sensual dreams that had followed. They made her hot in the face.

Don't be stupid. *They were just dreams!* Cramming the helm on her head, Tiaan set to work, trying to trace the residues of use and purpose, the history of the failed hedron since she had made its controller weeks ago. She found nothing, but then had a brilliant idea. What if she *forced* the hedron to wake, then read its induced aura? It required her to use her pliance in a dangerous way but Tiaan could not see any other choice.

Taking it from around her neck, she unhooked the pliance from the chain and put it in the globe so it touched the failed hedron. She felt a moment's anxiety. Anything might happen.

With gentle touches of her fingertips, Tiaan began sensing out the field. The familiar aurora flowed into her mind. It was particularly strong today, the billows and eddies tinged deep purple. Locating a suitable vortex, she drew power into her pliance just as she had done a thousand times before.

Pressing pliance and hedron together, she directed a flow of power into the failed crystal. It created no aura at all. The power vanished as if it had passed straight back into the field.

That was odd. Even a dead hedron should produce *some* aura after such a flow. She drew more power, with the same result. The hedron felt warm now. More than odd, it was downright peculiar.

Taking deep, slow breaths, she relaxed until her arms hung limp, her head lolled. Tiaan did not consciously try to visualise the field, but just allowed it to wash over and through her.

Her view drifted. She was looking for something greater than she had used before, a vortex so potent that it was tinged blue-white. Finding one, she traced the sub-ethyric path from it into the pliance and steadied herself. This could be quite dangerous. It might contain more power than she could safely handle. She allowed the vortex to drift towards the pathway. *Now!*

The vortex coloured down through purple, blues, reds, yellows and finally turned black. Pain stabbed through her head, the pliance flared and for an instant an aura appeared inside the crystal. Tiaan locked the image in her memory, then something crackled and both field and aura disappeared.

'I've done it!' she exulted, feeling the special thrill of having tried something new and, against all the odds, succeeded. She examined the image frozen in her mind. There was something at its core. Rotating the image, Tiaan picked up an echo of power like none she'd ever come across. It felt intelligent: organic yet alien.

Her head began to throb. Tiaan pushed up the helm, rubbed balm onto her temples, and let it fall again. Another image flashed into her mind. An armoured, crested head; enormous yellow eyes; a mouth big enough to take in her own head; hundreds of teeth. The folded wings made it certain. A lyrinx! It seemed to be talking to someone human, probably a man. There was something familiar about the shape of the head, the set of the shoulders. The image began to fade and she could not hang on to it. Could it be the spy?

Tiaan rubbed her eyes. Feeling unaccountably tired and weak, she went on unsteady legs to the door.

'Have you seen Gol?' she asked Irisis, who was walking by with a coil of silver wire in one hand.

'No!' she snapped. 'Why?'

'I wanted him to fetch Gi-Had.' Tiaan's legs folded up under her and she slid down against the wall.

'What's the matter with you?'

'Just working too hard,' Tiaan croaked, wishing Irisis would go away.

'On what?' Her blue eyes scanned the room. Irisis picked up the globe, gave it a gentle shake and laid it down. 'I'll tell Gi-Had.' Irisis looked back at the globe. 'I was going that way anyway.'

Tiaan was too exhausted to wonder why she was being cooperative. 'Thank you,' she whispered, putting her head between her knees.

*

A rough hand shook her by the shoulder. 'What the blazes is going on, Artisan Tiaan?'

'O-Overseer Gi-Had,' she said dazedly. 'I wanted to see you.'

The man looked as if every drop of blood had been drained from his veins. What was the matter now?

Irisis came in behind him, to stand beside the door.

'What are you doing down there?' He lifted her to her feet.

'I don't know what happened.' Tiaan was having trouble thinking straight. It was as if she was drunk.

'Artisan Irisis has made a serious allegation about you,' said the overseer.

Tiaan had no idea what he was talking about. 'I've been sensing out what happened to the hedrons.'

'She's lying,' Irisis said coldly. 'The apparatus nearly killed me when I tried it last night. Maybe that was her intention. That's why she broke her crystal and implied that I'd done it. *And now she's broken her pliance, too!*'

Tiaan caught her breath. Irisis would say anything to get rid of her. 'No artisan would ever break her own pliance!' she said scornfully. 'It would be like cutting off her arm.'

'No *sane* artisan would,' said Irisis. 'But you're suffering from delusions, Tiaan. Either you're the spy or . . . you've got crystal fever.'

'What are you talking about?' cried Tiaan. 'Overseer, she's making up stories. She hates me.'

'Am I?' Irisis thrust one elegantly manicured finger in the direction of the globe. 'Take a look at that!'

Tiaan threw herself on the globe, fumbling with the catch. It came open and the failed hedron rolled out. Its insides had gone milky.

'Now she's destroyed it as well,' Irisis said. 'You must be rid of her, overseer, for the good of the manufactory.'

Gi-Had fretted a scrap of paper to pieces. 'There had better be a good explanation for this, artisan.'

'I was reading the hedron,' Tiaan said lamely. She snatched her pliance and its crystal fell to pieces in her hand. Tiaan stared at the fragments, uncomprehending. Her pliance was ruined. It would take weeks to make another. She wanted to scream.

'Well,' cried Gi-Had. 'What do I tell the perquisitor?'

Tiaan fell to her knees and wept.

'It's crystal fever!' Irisis repeated. 'She doesn't know what she's doing. She can't do her job, overseer.'

'Shut up!' Squatting before Tiaan, Gi-Had offered her a cloth. 'You must help me, artisan.'

Tiaan mopped her face. 'I was reading one of the failed hedrons,' she sniffled. 'I woke it anew and forced it to reveal its aura. I saw something there.'

'She's a liar!' said Irisis. 'She hasn't been here all day.'

Gi-Had looked from one to the other, not knowing whom to believe.

'I've been down the mine with Joeyn,' said Tiaan, 'risking my life on the sixth level to find a suitable crystal.'

'You've done what?' Gi-Had said.

'It's the only place I can find crystals of sufficient power. The others are no good at all.'

'That level is forbidden! How dare you risk your life down there? What would the manufactory do if you were killed?'

'Would it matter? You'd still have Artisan Irisis,' Tiaan said with heavy sarcasm.

His lack of response gave Tiaan heart. He must have reservations about Irisis too. 'My discovery might save hundreds of soldiers. And if these new crystals turn out as I suspect . . .'

'What?' he cried.

'They're much stronger, and there's a lot of them. They might drive a clanker twice as fast as the other hedrons. And that might win the war.'

He softened. 'Indeed, it was a brave and noble thing you did today. *Do not do it again!* If lives must be put at risk, let it be those that we can do without. What did you see in the hedron, Tiaan?'

Tiaan placed the helm over Gi-Had's square head, put his fingers on the wire globe and, holding the milky crystal, recalled the image seen in its aura. He looked annoyed, then mulishly stubborn, then frustrated, as if what he was looking for lay forever beyond his reach. Suddenly he went rigid. Gi-Had stood up like a mechanical man unfolding, and his eyes were staring. 'I saw!' he said, turning to Tiaan. 'I saw the face of a beast.'

'A lyrinx?'

'Yes!' He gave a great shudder of horror. 'It was crouched over a round thing on a stalk, like a luminous mushroom, as if it was spying on us. Then it looked up and it was talking to a man. The spy! The enemy knows our every plan. They'll cut off our clankers one by one.'

Irisis could not contain herself. 'She lies! She put the image in your mind. She knows nothing; she's only worth the breeding – '

Gi-Had struck her across the face with his open hand. 'Shut up, second cousin! We're fighting for our lives. How dare you bring your petty jealousies into my manufactory!'

Irisis touched her cheek. 'But I – Look at the evidence against her.'

'I have,' he said grimly. 'And I see your hand in most of it.'

'But . . . Uncle promised that I would follow him as crafter. She doesn't even have a father. She comes from – '

'And that's where you'll be going, artisan, if you cause any more trouble. Tiaan has just proved what a brilliant artisan she is. I can't do without her.'

The fingermarks stood out red and purple on Irisis's blanched face. 'You wouldn't!'

'Desperate times, artisan. Someone's been sabotaging the hedrons, the enemy can see our clankers, and now . . .!' Gi-Had went white, began to shake and had to be helped onto a stool.

'What is it, cousin?' cried Irisis. It was the first time Tiaan had seen her show concern for anyone. But then, he *was* family.

Tiaan offered the overseer a mug of water. 'You said there was a disaster?'

He took a small sip, then looked to them both. 'You might as well know,' he said hoarsely. 'It concerns us all, but especially artisans.'

'What?' Irisis took his hand.

'Word came in a despatch this morning. It happened way up the coast, two hundred leagues north of here. A vital node has gone dead.'

'Dead?' Irisis echoed.

'Well, of course the node is still there but its field faded to nothing, stalling fifty clankers on the plain of Minnien. The enemy destroyed the lot, then advanced fifteen leagues in a week. If the lyrinx can keep it up they'll be at the gates of Tiksi by mid-winter.'

No one spoke. They were going to lose the war, and against the lyrinx, losers were eaten.

'Does anyone know why it happened?' Tiaan asked, forcing calm on herself. 'Is it like what's happened to the controllers, only larger?'

'We don't know. There seem to be two possibilities, one nearly as bad as the other,' said Gi-Had. 'The first is that the enemy has found a way to block the field, or destroy it.'

Tiaan digested that. 'And the other?'

'That clankers take too much power from the field. With so many of them drawing on it at once, they've drained it dry, like pumping too much water from a well.'

No one said anything. Gi-Had got up. 'A state of emergency has been declared. I have authority to do whatever is necessary to produce clankers. Survival takes precedence over everything. And everybody!' He waved a dismissing hand. 'Though what is the use if we cannot power them . . .?'

'If the enemy can detect our controllers by the aura,' Tiaan said thoughtfully, 'what we need is some kind of shield to render it invisible to their senses.'

'A shield?' He looked doubtful. 'Is such a thing possible?'

'It might be. I have an idea I'd like to try, surr.'

'Very well. Leave your other work. Spend two days on this task, no more, then report to me. What ideas do *you* have, cousin?'

'I was thinking the same thing,' said Irisis.

'Good,' said Gi-Had. 'When can I see your work?'

Irisis looked shocked but recovered quickly. 'It'll take a day. Or two.' Giving Tiaan a look of purest malice, she went out.

With his hand on the latch, Gi-Had turned back. 'The failed hedron, and your pliance, contain evidence of the traitor. Is there any way of telling who it is?'

'Not without a new pliance.'

'Do you mind if I take them? In case we find someone who *can* tell?'

'They're no use to me.'

Gi-Had wrapped the evidence in a piece of cloth. Tiaan choked as he carried the ruined pliance away. Incapable of thinking coherently, she went to bed. This time she locked the door and took the globe, helm and crystal with her.

She was still agonising two hours later. How were the enemy sensing the hedrons? Maybe lyrinx had senses that humans did not have. She had no idea, and with her pliance gone, how could she find out?

The loss hurt, physically and emotionally. Withdrawal was going to be worse, and for that nothing could be done except to replace the device as soon as possible. Weeks of misery lay ahead of her.

As she drifted off to sleep Tiaan found herself thinking about that glowing crystal in the mine again. She coveted it more than ever.

Help! Please help me! It was a scream inside her head, a cry of absolute terror.

Tiaan could see nothing but smoke and yellow sulphur fumes that stung her nose. The manufactory must be on fire. She groped in the darkness for her clothes but could feel only coarse vegetation, like bracken or heath. Her toe caught on a root and she went sprawling among the shrubbery.

Something bright and hot curved across the sky, an irregular glowing object that rotated, *whoosh-thump*, as it went. It slammed into the ground not far away, the shockwave knocking her off her feet. The heath exploded into flame that flared high on a mist of leaf oils. A breeze drove it toward her.

She ran, sharp leaves tearing at her naked thighs, branches twisting themselves around her ankles. Over and again she fell. The last time, too exhausted to get up, she simply lay there as the flames rushed up and over. She screamed but once.

Tiaan woke gasping in her bed, scarce able to comprehend

that she had not been burned alive. She fumbled for the lantern, clicking the flint striker over and over, even after the wick had lit. The room looked normal.

Feeling a growing pressure in her temples, she dug a finger into the jar of balm and slathered it across her forehead.

Someone started hammering on the door. 'What's going on in there?'

Wrapping a blanket around herself, Tiaan went to the door. Half a dozen of her fellow workers stood outside. 'Sorry!' she said. 'A nightmare. Must have been working too hard. I'm all right now.'

Muttering to themselves, they went back to their beds. Tiaan locked her door and was just tucking the blanket in when she was flung back into that crystal dream, wide awake. This time she was standing on an island in the middle of a broad river. Behind was a pavilion with seven columns surmounted by a dome of beaten copper.

She was reaching into a basket of fruit when there came an explosion of steam and a wavefront of boiling water thundered down the river. She smelt cooked fish. The water divided on either side of the island before roaring past.

The level sank. Tiaan sighed, but a heart-stopping grinding noise came from upstream, followed by a blast of superheated air. Inexorably, around the bend rumbled a wall of lava – the red viscous ooze continually breaking through the blackened crust. On it came, and on, and nothing was going to stop it.

Tiaan ran back and forth across the island. Boiling water surrounded her. There was nowhere to go. She stood back, watching the lava crackle toward her. 'Help!' she cried uselessly.

Help! echoed that handsome face on the balcony, the young man from her dreams. He looked her way, started, and gave a sweet, sad smile that brought tears to her eyes. He put out his arms. He cares for me, she thought, amazed. She began to run, then a wave of lava swept him away.

Again she screamed, again woke; again she reassured the increasingly angry crowd at the door.

Tiaan tried to sleep but was plunged back into the nightmare, running down the corridors of a palace as volcanic bombs fell everywhere, crashing through the ceilings, exploding and setting fire to the magnificent building. 'Help!'

There was no answer.

NINE

By the time a drizzling morning broke against Tiaan's solitary window, the dormitory was in uproar and she could no longer distinguish between being awake and dreaming. A nurse checked her symptoms and called the healer, who shouted for the apothek. Between them they decided that Tiaan had gone mad and were about to put her in a straitjacket when Overseer Gi-Had came running.

'What the blazes are you doing?' He hurled them out of the way.

'It's crystal fever,' pronounced Healer Tul-Kin gloomily. He reeked of parsnip brandy. 'Her mind's broken and will never recover. Might as well send her to the breeding factory.'

'In a straitjacket?'

The healer shrugged. 'It only goes to her waist. The business can still be done.'

'My arse! We can't do without her. Find out what's wrong and *fix it*!'

They took Tiaan to the infirmary, where a nurse bathed her face and forehead, and fed her tea and barley broth. The waking nightmares continued until noon, when she suddenly sat up, saying, 'What am I doing here?'

She remembered the mad episodes, but only as dreams that were rapidly fading. In an hour or so the details were gone.

All that remained was the young man on the balcony and a world exploding. He *really* cared about her. She knew he did. It *was* more than a dream. He had been searching for her all this time. She had to find out who he was.

They let her go back to her workroom in the mid-afternoon. The prentices gathered round, delighted that she had recovered. They liked Tiaan, even if they weren't her friends.

Irisis stood in the background, her face unreadable. Tiaan vaguely remembered the artisan's face at the door, the pleasure her rival could not entirely conceal. She wondered about that. The whole episode was so strange, and becoming more unreal every second, that she could find no sense in it. Had it been crystal fever? She could not bring herself to believe it. It did not fit the pattern she'd been taught. But then, those with the fever could never be convinced that they had it.

Tiaan sent Gol to fetch the globe, crystal and helm from her room and got back to work. While she was waiting for him to return, old Joeyn came in, covered in dust from the mine. On seeing her, he beamed from ear to ear.

'I was afraid,' he said when the prentices had gone back to their benches. 'Such rumours I heard! I was preparing to break down the doors and carry you away.'

Tiaan was so touched that tears sprang to her eyes. 'You would condemn yourself to save me?' She embraced him.

'Life has already condemned me. What do I care how I die? But you have so much to live for, Tiaan. So much to give; and receive!'

She felt quite overcome. Gol came running with her globe and helm. 'Did you bring the headache balm?' she asked the boy.

'You didn't ask me to. Shall I get it?'

'Never mind. Thank you, Gol. I'd like you to empty the baskets around the prentices' benches.'

The lad raced out. Joeyn hefted the wire globe in his scarred fingers. 'I'd better go. Take care, Tiaan. I'm afraid for you.'

'I'll be all right. I've just been working too hard.'

'There's more to it than that. There's malice behind this, Tiaan, and we both know where it's coming from.' He looked over his shoulder. Irisis, at her bench, gave him a glare of cold ferocity. 'If you're ever in trouble, no matter what it is, *come to me*.'

He was gone. Overwhelmed by all the work she had to do, Tiaan bent to her globe again. She felt awful, hot and cold at once, as if she had a bad dose of the flu. It was withdrawal from her ruined pliance and there was only one thing to be done about it – work herself so hard that there was no room for anything else. But what if it *was* crystal fever? Overwork was just the way to bring it back, permanently. Tiaan tried to put that out of mind. She had to prove herself to Gi-Had. Tomorrow might be too late. She needed a breakthrough.

As Tiaan was puzzling over the problem, a few lines from Nunar's book, *The Mancer's Art*, came to her mind. *The process may generate a shifting aura about the crystal powering the controller . . . A nearby sensitive might be able to detect this aura, though in normal use it is expected to be insignificant.*

What had Nunar meant by *normal use*? Surely she'd had in mind small devices that used small amounts of power. At the time, more than ninety years ago, no one had conceived of such mechanical monsters as clankers, or the immense amount of power they would use. To completely empty the field around the node at Minnien the power drain must have been immense, and such power would create an enormous aura. That must be what that shadowy lyrinx had been doing, using some kind of device to pick up the aura of a controller from far away. Yes, that was why clankers could no longer move in secret! It was all connected.

Somehow the hedrons had to be shielded. What did Nunar have to say about that? Going back to her room, Tiaan went through the book, but learned nothing. Nunar had not foreseen the rapid development of controllers, much less that such things would be used by ordinary people instead of mancers, who had their own ways of protecting their work from the prying mind. Controllers had a fatal flaw: their aura – obvious in hindsight. Putting the book back in its hiding place, she returned to the workshop.

The problem was to prevent the hedron leaking an aura that could be sensed, while at the same time allowing it to trickle power to the controller. She tried various coatings – tar, wax, clay, paper, leather – but none had any effect.

Perhaps metal was the answer. Having a sheet of beaten copper to hand, Tiaan wrapped the hedron in it, wondering if it would work at all. If the metal blocked the aura it might stop the hedron drawing on the field as well. However, the hedron worked perfectly, and of course it would. Power was not drawn from the field through the material world, but via a sub-ethyric pathway. That was the very basis of mancing as set out in Nunar's *Special Theory*.

She encountered another problem. The copper sheet stopped the aura but it also prevented power flowing from hedron to controller. Tiaan folded the copper back so that it was not touching the metal connectors. Now the signal came through, but the aura leaked as well.

She tried silver foil instead of copper. That was better, because the silver was softer, but she still could not stop the aura leaking. Tiaan fixed the controller-arm stubs onto the hedron facets with dabs of hot pitch. The arms worked as well as before; maybe better. What about gold leaf? Gold was more malleable than silver. Perhaps she could beat the layers together to a tight seal.

Going to the old crafter's workshop she unlocked the door of the storeroom and took a small bead of gold from a bottle. Tiaan beat it out until it would have covered a bound book. Holding it up to the light, she checked for holes. None.

She carefully wrapped the hedron, with its pitch-covered connectors, in gold leaf. After tapping it down until there was not the least sign of join or crinkle, she tested it again. Just a trace of aura leaked from around one connector. After fixing that, the hedron was undetectable.

Covering the entire object in warmed pitch, being careful that it was not too warm, she smoothed it down with a spatula and made sure she got rid of all the air bubbles. Finally she pressed her personal seal all over the soft pitch. No one could tamper with the coating now without it being obvious. Nor could anyone expose the hedron to heat or sunlight without it being detected. She had solved both problems at once.

When the pitch had set she tested the controller, which worked perfectly. There was not a trace of aura. The problem *was* solved. She wrote up her journal, then a report to Gi-Had, describing exactly what she had done, and why.

Putting the report in her pocket, she yawned. Her head felt awful. Time to catch up on the sleep she'd missed last night. Time to dream about the young man. That brought a smile to her face. Tiaan set the controller to keep working overnight, to make sure it did not run down as the others had, locked the door and went to bed.

As Tiaan lay on her bed, waiting for sleep that would not come, the headache grew worse. She was thirsty but too tired to trot down the hall and fill her jug. Instead she rubbed a double dose of balm on her forehead and worked it in with her fingertips. It did not seem to help. The pain throbbed away, beating time to her heartbeat.

Slathering more on for good measure she sat up, listening to the wind blowing rain against her window. It was a cold night – much colder than any this autumn. The winter blizzards could not be far away.

She fell back on the pillow, sliding instantly into sleep. The dreams began at once: more intense, more prolonged, more terrible. A whole world was exploding, twenty thousand volcanoes erupting at once. The air was thick with ash, dust and fumes that made the lungs ooze yellow foam, like a snail crawling across a bed of lime. Burning clouds of ash, so hot that it was almost molten, rolled down the mountainsides, obliterating fields, forests and villages, entombing them in smoking mounds.

The young man stood on the balcony, screaming for someone to come to the aid of his world. No one came, and finally he bent his head and wept. The heat dried the tears before they touched his cheeks. He watched the flow grinding toward him.

In the darkest part of the night Tiaan's door opened. A figure entered, closed the door and lit the candle by the bed. The room was frigid but Tiaan lay naked on top of the covers, bathed in sweat.

Putting on a rubber glove, the figure scooped out the contents of the jar of balm and rubbed it all over Tiaan – face, hands, breasts, belly, thighs, buttocks, back. Tiaan kicked once or twice then went still. When every speck of skin was gleaming with unguent, the intruder left the room as silently as he or she had come.

Not long afterwards the dreams resumed. Nothing remained of Tiaan's logical mind to keep them at bay. Plunging off a precipice into a pool of lava, she began to scream aloud. Four hours later she was still screaming. And eight hours after that she was trying to, though she had no voice left. Her throat was a raw, red wound. When she opened her mouth, blood dribbled out. At midnight she finally ceased. Her cries rang inside her skull for hours more until reason fled. Her mouth was wide open, and her eyes, but nothing registered.

Irisis had been watching Tiaan for days and, after spying on her latest experiment, went to bed thoughtfully. Woken in the night by the artisan's screams, she went down to see what the matter was. She stood in the background as the healers talked. Clearly Tiaan was mad with crystal fever. Irisis knew that her chance had come.

Using a master key, Irisis entered Tiaan's cubicle. The journal told Irisis all she needed to know. She cut out the last page, destroyed it and took the completed controller, as well as another two as yet unfinished. In the workshop she found all the materials she needed. Locking the door, Irisis prepared to work for as long as it took.

Gi-Had had been to see Tiaan five times. He was not satisfied that she had gone mad. Crystal fever was not uncommon among artisans, but no one from this manufactory had had it in twenty years. He sat with the healer, the nurses, and even brought back the old healer, Ruzia, who had retired a decade ago.

'She's quite insane,' Healer Tul-Kin said. His words were slurred, for he had been drinking all day. 'If she does recover, she'll never be an artisan again. Not one you can rely on.'

Gi-Had turned to the old healer. She was nearly blind and her head rolled from side to side, but her mind was still keen. 'I'm afraid he's right,' she said in a reedy voice. 'I don't see any hope. Once their minds go in this way, they seldom recover.'

'Curse you all to hell!' Gi-Had cried. 'I can't do without her.'

'You'll have to,' said Ruzia.

They debated the matter for another hour, and finally Gi-Had was swayed. If Tiaan was no use here, she must go where she could still contribute in some way.

At that moment Irisis reappeared and showed him how she had brilliantly solved the problem of the faulty controllers. He examined them carefully, and at last he smiled. One small ray of light in a disastrous day.

'Thank you, cousin. I'm sorry I doubted you.'

Despite her youth, he offered Irisis the position she so coveted, that of acting crafter at the manufactory. Then Gi-Had signed Tiaan's indenture over to the breeding factory.

TEN

A week and a half went by, during which Tiaan experienced only fleeting moments of lucidity. She saw her mother's face several times, a mixture of concern and irritation. She vaguely recognised several other women, as well as Tobey, a boy of five, one of her half-brothers. And Joeyn. Twice she woke to find him sitting by her bed, but Tiaan lacked the strength to keep her eyes open. She woke again and found the chair was empty. A woman and a man were talking but she could not turn her head to see who they were.

'I don't like it,' said the man. 'She's not supposed to be here.'

'Crystal fever happens! The papers are in order,' said the woman. 'Besides, she's a virgin. There's good money to be made and it all goes into our pockets.'

'But what if . . .?'

'Oh, stop whining! She won't be on the books anyway.'

The voices faded away and Tiaan slept. Sometime later she woke and Joeyn was there.

'Joeyn?' she whispered. Her throat burned terribly. 'What happened?' She did not recognise the room at all. 'Did I have another fit?'

'They say you screamed for twelve hours, as if you were being burned alive.'

'I don't remember anything.' It was all gone, including the dreams. The last she recalled was solving the riddle of the controller and going to bed. Her voice sounded hoarse. 'I've got to get up. There's work to do.' Tiaan sat up, realised that she had nothing on, and hastily slid under the covers again.

'You have to rest and get better.'

'But I've two controllers to fix. No one else can do it. The war . . .'

'They've been fixed and sent to the front a long time ago.'

'What?' She stared at him, uncomprehending. The world seemed to have gone mad.

'Irisis fixed the controllers while you were . . . sick,' Joeyn said as gently as he could.

She clutched at his hand. 'It can't be so!'

'It is so, Tiaan.'

'Joe, *I* fixed the first controller before I went to bed last night. If Irisis has done the others, she's just copied me.'

'Are you sure?' He gave her a look that said he doubted her sanity.

'Of course I'm sure!' She told him exactly how she had shielded the controller. 'Irisis hates me. She's always trying to take the credit. She'd love to see me sent down.'

A spasm crossed his face, one that alarmed her.

'Where am I?' She looked around at the unfamiliar room. 'This isn't the infirmary.'

'It's the sickroom in the breeding factory.'

'I hadn't realised that I was *that* sick . . .' She broke off, staring at his craggy face. His eyes shifted as if he could not face her. 'No!' she gasped. The very air was choking her. She opened her mouth wide, to scream.

Joeyn slapped her face, just hard enough to bring her to her senses. She broke off.

'Don't!' he said. 'Or *I'll* think you're mad too.'

'*That's* why I've been sold to the breeding factory? I'm not mad. Yesterday I solved . . .'

'Tiaan,' he said gently, 'you've been here for more than a week, delirious the whole time. Before that, you screamed for

112

half a day without stopping. Little wonder the healers thought your mind had gone. Gi-Had had no choice. The manufactory must have reliable artisans.'

'Irisis has replaced *me*?' Her voice rose dangerously.

'Hush! She's done better than that. By special decree she has been made acting crafter, though she is only twenty-one.'

How Irisis must be gloating. Tiaan wanted to die.

'I won't stay here! I'll never submit to this place. If I can only get to Gi-Had, I'm sure I can convince him . . .'

'The deed is done, Tiaan. It can't be undone. Twice you have had mad fits and two healers have diagnosed you with incurable crystal fever. Gi-Had could not keep you on, even if he wanted to. A mad artisan is worse than none.'

'But I'm not mad.'

'People with crystal fever always say that. It's no use. You are indentured to the breeding factory.'

'But Gi-Had is a fair man . . .'

'He has a manufactory to run and clankers to produce. There's been a disaster up north, a whole cluster of clankers destroyed in a day.'

'I heard that . . .' Tiaan broke off. She had been going to say 'yesterday'.

'You're a breeding-factory woman now, Tiaan. Artisan Tiaan is gone forever. I'm so sorry.' There were tears in his eyes.

The door opened. A big woman who could only have been the matron hurried in. 'Visiting time is over. Say your goodbyes. Tiaan needs her rest. *Her first day is coming up!*' She hurried out again.

Only then did the horror fully strike Tiaan. Her work, her life, her very existence had been taken away. All that was left was the profession she despised most in the world. The urge to scream was almost irresistible. She opened her mouth, saw the look on Joeyn's face and quickly closed it again. 'I won't be a woman of the breeding factory, *ever*!' she hissed. Only her rage stopped her from collapsing.

'I don't see . . .' he said doubtfully.

'I'm not mad. I'll run away.'

'In time of war, refusing to do your appointed job is treason.'

'*Men* don't get sent to breeding factories!'

'And women aren't sent to the front-lines to be slaughtered, like my sons,' he said softly. 'I did not say it was fair, Tiaan, just that there's nothing can be done about it.'

'I won't stay here. This place disgusts me.'

'A runaway on the road has no place, no rights. Anyone can enslave you or strike you down without penalty.'

'I don't care!' she raged. 'I will give myself to no man save of my own choosing.'

'Times change. The war . . .'

'Curse the damned war! It's just an excuse to take our rights away. Joeyn, you said you would help me if ever I needed it. I've never needed it more.'

He looked anxious. For her, she knew, not himself. 'Of course I'll help you, if you have truly made up your mind. What do you want me to do?'

'Go to my room in the manufactory and, if it has not been cleared, bring away my clothes, journal and tool bag, and my wire globe and helm. And there's a book!' She explained where she had hidden the copy of Nunar's treatise. 'Keep it hidden. I'm not supposed to have it.'

'Tiaan, the crystal was the source of your madness. If you ever touch one again . . .'

'I'm not mad!' she said vehemently.

The door opened, the matron again. 'Time for visitors to go. *Now!*'

'Please, Joeyn,' Tiaan said.

He nodded and went out.

'Disgusting old man!' said Matron. 'We'd certainly not use *him* here. Out of bed!' She hauled Tiaan out by the arm. 'Stand there. Let me look at you.'

Matron inspected Tiaan like a carcass in a butcher's shop, prodding and poking her mercilessly.

'Hmn! Beautiful hair, though a terrible cut. Looks like it was done with an axe. Nice eyes – unusual colour. Good skin, apart from a few minor blemishes, though we'll soon fix them. Nose,

114

not as broad as they like, but it'll do. Ears . . .'

She brushed back Tiaan's hair. 'Oh yes, very neat.'

'Such dark lips – they'll go for that. Open your mouth. Teeth's where they mostly fall down. Hmn, not too bad, at least they're all there. Those two could be a bit straighter but nobody's perfect.' She checked Tiaan's gums, her tongue, her throat, muttering to herself all the while.

'Good, good! No disease, no sores.' She moved Tiaan's head from side to side and made some marks on a slate. 'Head, eight out of ten. Or should that be seven and a half? Smile for me, please?'

Tiaan felt like biting Matron's hand off, but at the same time, inexplicably, she wanted to do well on the test. She smiled.

'Oh, very good. Dimples, too. Definitely an eight!'

Matron continued. 'Shoulders a bit narrow. Still, many like them that way. No accounting for folk!' Her own shoulders were almost an axe-handle across and heavily larded. 'Hmn! You're scrawny, girl. Not much demand for that look around here. We'll soon fatten you up, though.' She rattled a knuckle down Tiaan's ribs, weighed her breasts in big, damp hands. 'Not bad; not bad at all. Could be bigger, especially the left one, but I can't see too many complaints.' She flicked a nipple with her fingertip until it stood up, then moved on.

Her belly was not full enough, her pubic hair too coarse and curly, her thighs too slender, her feet definitely too big. And last was the worst. 'Oh dear, just look at these hands! What have you been doing, girl? Your hands are as rough as a navvy's, and there's a festering splinter in your finger.'

Her figure only rated six and a half, though Matron supposed she could bring that up a point with some proper feeding and grooming. 'Overall, better than I expected. Especially after – well, let's not go into that. I think we've made a good buy after all. Come along now, there's a lot of work to do.'

'Work?' said Tiaan, feeling dazed.

'Bath, manicure, haircut, skin-polishing – we'll be lucky to be finished by dinnertime.'

Two attendants bathed Tiaan in a tub so large that a horse

could have comfortably stood in the middle, and it was full of *hot* water. Tiaan was staggered at the extravagance. At the manufactory, being too shy to use the communal bathhouse, she washed with cold water in a dish and yellow, caustic soap that stung her eyes. Tiaan could not remember ever having a hot bath.

They kept her in until she felt dizzy and her fingers and toes were wrinkled. The attendants fed her in the bath – spicy pastries, sweetmeats soaked in honey and cream, bowls of preserved fruit covered in sweet yoghurt – and kept urging more on her long after she was full. To lie in the hot water was one of the strangest feelings she'd ever had. It felt sinfully lazy and wicked. The attendants got in too, scrubbing her until her skin throbbed.

After that she was helped to a low table covered with a cloth, where they rubbed perfumed creams into her skin, massaging her until her muscles felt as loose as jelly. They plucked out every body-hair, sanded her hands with pumice, trimmed her nails, brushed her teeth and gently shaped her hair. At the end they made up her face with the lightest of touches.

One attendant held a mirror out. Tiaan was stunned. She looked transformed; almost beautiful. She wondered if, just possibly, she could endure the breeding factory after all.

Matron reappeared. 'Not bad!' she said, head cocked to one side. 'Better than I expected. We'll do well out of you, my girl. Show me your hands.'

Tiaan held them out. Matron frowned. 'Better, but still a long way to go. We'll have dim lights for your first time, and a bold tapestry at the head of the bed. And a low-cut gown. How long ago was she fed?'

'Two hours,' said the little, sandy-haired attendant.

'Feed her again.' Matron turned to go. 'No, first we must see to the formalities. Come with me.'

'Where are we going?' Tiaan asked anxiously.

'To my office. There's nothing to worry about.'

Tiaan *was* worried. Matron's grip on her wrist was unshakeable. They went along the corridor, up a flight of stairs, around a corner and through a heavy door. The small room contained a desk piled with papers, documents, a large tray of biscuits and several mugs, partly full of some dark, oily brew.

'Sit down!' Matron slumped into a chair on the other side of the table. Taking a biscuit, she pushed the tray towards Tiaan. 'Have a handful. They'll do you good.' She turned to a cupboard which she unlocked with a small key. There were a number of books and ledgers inside, though evidently not the one she was looking for. 'Where is the damn thing?' she muttered, sorting distractedly through the piles on the table.

Her excavations uncovered another ledger which she picked up, frowned at, then put down as someone rapped on the door. An aged attendant put his head around. 'Yes?' she snapped.

'It's . . . one of the clients is making rather a fuss, matron. Too much to drink. And little Zizza is quite hysterical. You'd better come quickly.'

Matron looked furious, but heaved her bulk out of the chair, glancing at Tiaan. 'I'll just take her back . . .'

A scream came echoing down the corridor, followed by drunken roars and the sound of breaking glass being smashed. Matron was through the door in an instant. 'Wait here, Tiaan. Don't touch anything.' She disappeared.

Tiaan sat for a while, then bored, began to flip through the papers on the table. They were all tedious administrative or financial documents. She put them back as she had found them, uncovering the ledger. On the front it said *Bloodline Register 4102, Tiksi*.

Inside she found a list of women's names with numbers after them. Page numbers, presumably. Tiaan turned the first page. The name at the top was Numini Tisde, a woman she had met here once. The page was ruled into columns, with dates, notes on her monthly cycle, health, male names with descriptions as well as lists of abilities, talents and ancestral details, baldly intimate details about sexual congress, and a variety of symbols and abbreviations that meant nothing to Tiaan. Occasional rows contained details related to pregnancy – weight changes, complications, miscarriages and births: six in eleven years, though only four were still living.

She turned the page. A different name was at the top, though the same kinds of entries were present. Tiaan closed the cover, appalled. It was a *stud book*!

It had just occurred to her to look up her mother's entry when she heard Matron's voice outside. Tiaan sat back in the chair and tried to assume a bored air.

Matron thrust the door open, red-faced and breathing heavily. Stamping across the room, she fell into her chair. 'Some people just aren't worth feeding!' Her eyes raked Tiaan. 'I hope you're not one of them.'

Tiaan lowered her eyes in what she hoped was modest incomprehension.

Matron went through the litter again. 'What the blazes was I doing?' She pulled out a stamped and sealed parchment, stared at it for a moment then tossed it aside. 'Ah, I remember.' With an air of triumph she withdrew a set of documents pinned together at one corner. 'Your indenture.' Turning to the back page, she said, 'Sign here!'

Tiaan took the sheets and began to read.

'Just sign!' Matron snarled.

'I'm not signing anything I haven't read,' Tiaan said. 'I know my rights.'

'Give me back the indenture.' Matron looked ferocious.

Tiaan passed it to her, quaking.

Matron placed it carefully on the cabinet behind her and stood up. Tiaan did too, wondering what was going to happen. Matron came around the desk and lashed out with her left fist. Tiaan ducked out of the way only to be clouted over the side of the head by the other hand. It knocked her sideways onto hands and knees.

Matron loomed over her. 'Will you sign?' she panted, her cheeks like slices of bloody liver.

'No!' Tiaan scrabbled out of the way, expecting more blows.

Matron's anger disappeared just as quickly. 'No matter!' She now seemed grimly indifferent.

'You can't keep me here without my signature. I'm not a child.'

Matron looked irritated. 'You have been certified insane by your own healers. I have the record here. It's properly drawn up and witnessed by the manufactory legalist, Chicanist Runne, and our own, Shyster Dusin. I don't need your signature.'

'I'm not insane!' Tiaan said vehemently.

'Do you have a certificate to prove your sanity?'

'No one does,' said Tiaan.

'Then you're still insane. It says so right here.' Matron was growing bored with the business. She rang a bell on her desk. The attendant appeared. 'Take Virgin Tiaan to her room. And keep a firm hold on her, just in case.'

Tiaan went scarlet. The title was mortifying.

'Please,' she said plaintively. 'I'd like to see my mother.' She felt lost. She needed the familiarity of Marnie.

'Good idea! She's an absolute corker is Marnie. Almost past it, but she still pulls in her regulars, and punches out a child every year. Nothing like old Marnie for convincing reluctant virgins. Take her dinner down there.'

Marnie was on her bed, as always, leafing through an illuminated book. As soon as Tiaan was ushered in, her mother tossed it aside with a bored frown. She always looked bored, unless she was eating or preening.

'Tiaan!' she exclaimed. 'What trouble you've caused me. I had no end of work to get you in here.'

Tiaan doubted if her mother had anything to do with it, but let that pass. 'You're looking well, mother.'

'I'm not! The effort it takes to maintain my position is incredible. But somehow I manage it. There's a dozen begging for my favours tonight. Not many women can say that, at my age.'

Vain cow, Tiaan thought. Her mother had probably not been outside the breeding factory in twenty years. Her skin was so pale that she looked like a fat slug crawling across the bedcovers.

'Mother . . .?'

'Marnie, dear. Call me Marnie, I do so loathe the word *mother*.'

That was odd, since *mother* was the very description of her life. 'Marnie, I need to ask you a few questions about this place.'

Marnie waved a plump hand. 'Ask me anything, daughter. Oh, I'm so happy you've come. We'll have such times together.'

'It's just that – what do I do?'

'You mate, and you have babies.'

'And the rest of the time?'

'Bathe, eat, be pampered. Talk to the baby. Read. You can do anything you want.'

'What else?' Tiaan felt rather alarmed.

'You don't have to do anything. That's what's so wonderful.'

'What about work? I can't do nothing, Marnie. I'll turn into a mindless idiot . . .' She broke off, not quickly enough.

'How dare you!' Marnie flung a vase of flowers at her.

Tiaan ducked and the vase shattered against the wall. She began mopping up the water with a hand towel.

'Leave it!' Marnie screeched. 'That's not work fit for one of us.'

Tiaan did it anyway. 'I'm sorry, Marnie, I didn't mean to sound rude.'

Marnie sniffed and turned her vast back. Tiaan went round the other side, got down on her knees and stroked her mother's hand. She knew how to placate her.

'I'm sorry. I do appreciate how hard you've worked for me,' she said untruthfully. 'I – I'm afraid, mother. About what happens . . . with a client.'

'You don't know?' Marnie's eyebrows danced in astonishment.

'Of course I know. It's just that I've never done anything with a man.'

'But you're . . .' Marnie calculated, using her fingers, 'you're *twenty*!' She said it accusingly.

Nice of you to remember your firstborn! 'There's always more work than I can get done.'

'And to think I was worried about your virtue up at that horrible place. No wonder you had a breakdown.' Marnie sniffed. 'You have to *live*, child. You can't just work. Women can't do without it any more than men can. Of course you went mad, holding it in like that. Now, this is what's going to happen for your first time. You lie on the bed, open your legs, then the man . . .'

'I know how it's done, mother!' Tiaan snapped. 'I'm not a complete idiot. I want to know what's expected of me. How often do we mate? Once a year? Once a month? How long does it take to get a baby?'

Marnie burst out laughing, which sent ripples along her belly and flanks. 'Dear me, child, you have no idea, do you?'

Tiaan gritted her teeth. 'That's why I'm asking, Marnie.'

'You have only one client for the month, and you do it every day, except during your courses. That's how The Mothers' Palace survives and prospers.'

The light suddenly dawned. 'You mean this place is a . . . brothel? And we're just common harlots?' Harlotry was not a dishonourable profession, well above seamstress or washerwoman or nurse in status, but it was a long way below artisan.

'Certainly not!' Marnie rose off the bed in her wrath. 'What do you take me for? We're doing a vital job here, setting an example to the women of the world. No work can compare to that of breeding. Without what we do, humanity would disappear.'

'We don't need a breeding factory for that.'

'Yes we do! Too many women have become selfish, like you. They prefer to work rather than doing what's required. We're showing them how wrong they are.'

'Ordinary men and women . . .'

'Half the men are dead; there aren't enough to go around. Besides, the men *we* mate with are carefully chosen.'

That reminded Tiaan of the stud book upstairs, and her own longing. 'Who was my father, Marnie?'

'Don't start that again!' Marnie said coldly.

'I've got to know my father's family Histories; surely you can see that? Not knowing them is like only having half a life.'

'You'll not get them from me!' Marnie snapped. 'The Histories are a waste of time. Your father's aren't worth having.'

'Mother!' Tiaan cried out, aghast. 'How can you say such a wicked thing?' The Histories were everything. People often tried to censor their past, but never to ignore it or wipe it away

121

completely. To have no past was worse than having an evil one.

'Well, it's true. We should be thinking about the future. I wish I'd never met your father. If I hadn't been so young and stupid I'd have refused him.'

'What was he like? At least tell me that,' Tiaan pleaded. 'Can't you see how hard it is not to know my own Histories? I hardly know who I am.'

'He was selfish, dominating and cruel. He thought he knew better than I did. He wanted to carry me away from here – the only place I've ever been happy. And the fuss he made when you were born.'

'What fuss?' Tiaan asked eagerly.

'He seemed to think he had rights over you. He wanted to take you home. Stupid man. They're all stupid! They lie with you a few times and then think they have rights. They're just tools to get children.'

'What happened?'

'Matron put guards at the door. He fought to get in. I had to speak to one of my other clients, an influential man. Your father was sent to the front-lines.'

'Was he a soldier?'

'Of course not!' Marnie sneered. 'What do you take me for?'

Tiaan gritted her teeth. She felt like telling her mother exactly what she took her for. 'What happened to him?'

'He never came back,' said Marnie. 'I suppose the enemy ate him.'

It was like a blow in the belly. 'You killed him,' cried Tiaan. 'You killed my father!'

'The enemy killed him. Why should he live when so many others were dying?'

'Why should *you* live?' Tiaan snapped.

'Because I create the future!'

'Only as long as you can have children,' Tiaan said frigidly.

Marnie stiffened, drawing in a deep, gasping breath. So that's what the matter was, thought Tiaan. Her life here was practically over and Marnie was terrified.

'I'm sorry, mother. Please.'

122

Marnie turned her face to the wall and Tiaan knew she would get no more from her on that topic.

There was a long silence. 'Our partners are selected carefully, you said?'

'They're prime specimens,' her mother enunciated, 'chosen for the qualities they bring to our children.'

'But they pay?' Tiaan persisted.

'Of course they pay! Where do you think all this comes from?' She swept an arm around the room.

'Thank you, mother. You've told me all I need to know.' Tiaan went to the door, which opened and an attendant came through, bearing a loaded tray – her dinner. 'I'll take that in my room,' she said grandly, and sailed out.

Tiaan hugged her thoughts all the way back to her room. Her father *had* cared for her. He'd tried to take her away from this ghastly place. It made her feel warm inside.

Logic told her that the poor man must be dead, though she clung to the hope that he had survived, perhaps trapped in a foreign land. All the more important that she find out who he had been and learn his Histories. When she had children they must know. It was practically a crime to bring up a child without its family Histories. She wondered what qualities her father had given to her. Well, she was unlike her mother in practically every respect, so she must be a lot like her father. If Marnie would not tell her, there was only one way to find out. She would have to take another look in the bloodline register.

Tiaan sampled the pastries on her tray. They were delicious, though they left a fatty taste in her mouth and she was still overfull from her previous meal. She had to get away. She would go mad here. That thought made her smile wryly. *Or end up like my mother.*

She went out again, walking the halls, acutely conscious that she was naked under her gown. No one gave it a second glance – the other women wore more or less flamboyant versions of the same article.

Tiaan came down a staircase into the colonnaded marble

foyer, whereupon she was stopped by an elderly man in maroon and grey livery.

'Tiaan Liise-Mar,' he said. 'Where are you going?'

'To the markets. I have some shopping to do.'

'You may not go out unescorted. Your indenture has not been cleared.'

She whirled and stormed up the stairs, back to her mother's room. 'They won't let me go out!' she cried.

Marnie looked up irritably. 'Of course you can't go out. You might run away.'

'You mean I have to stay trapped in this hideous place until I die?'

Her mother pursed her lips. 'You are permitted to go shopping once a month with an attendant. You will, of course, wear a discreet wrist manacle.'

'What, forever?'

'Until your indenture is paid off.'

'But that's two years away, even with what I've got saved.'

'The old indenture was paid out when you came here, and a new one written. All this has to be paid for,' Marnie said. 'Your gowns, food, attendants . . .'

'Not forgetting the manacle. I suppose I have to pay for that too?'

'Well, of course you do. Money doesn't float in the air like butterflies.'

'I didn't ask for any of this.'

'It comes with the position.'

'How long?' Tiaan cried hoarsely.

'Depends on how many clients you service, how many children you bear, and how many of them survive. Some women have done it in five years, some ten or twelve, and some . . .'

'Twelve years!' Tiaan sank down on the bed in despair.

'Tiaan, daughter. It's a wonderful life here. You'll soon come to love it.'

'If it's so wonderful, how come we have to be chained to a guard when we go out?'

ELEVEN

Tiaan had two more days of eating, sleeping and being waited upon. Her attendants appeared three times a day, doing more work on hands, skin and nails. She hardly noticed. Tiaan had not stopped thinking about her father. It sounded as if he'd been a young man of good family. Clearly he'd loved his daughter, and Marnie had repaid him by sending him off to be killed. Every time she thought about it, tears streamed down Tiaan's cheeks. How could she find out? There was no one to ask. Her grandmother had died nine years ago and Tiaan had no other relatives. She was never alone, even for the few minutes it would take to sneak into Matron's office and check the register.

On her third lucid evening, Tiaan sat in silence until the attendants finished working on her hands, trying and failing to work out a plan. Tomorrow was to be her first time with a client, so she had to escape tonight. No way was she going to give herself to a man for money. There were too many of her grand-mother's romantic stories in her head. Too many dreams. As she had that thought, her first dream came back – the young man on the balcony, crying out for help. The later dreams she had had of him followed.

But *were* they dreams? They were different from crystal-induced ones, which were like chopped-up nightmares that vanished on waking. The young man had been much more vivid. She could remember every incident perfectly, as if they had actually happened. He must be real. And he had cried out to *her* for help. Her soft heart was touched. She had to find out who he was. But how could she, except through her dreams?

Maybe her artisan's life *was* over, but never would she work in this disgusting place. They had no right over her, no matter what the law said. She would break out and make a new life for herself, far away. At that thought, Tiaan felt the terror of the unknown. Her whole existence had been organised for her. In the manufactory everything was taken care of and all she had to do was work. Here it would be the same. But if she fled, how would she survive? A runaway would not be welcome anywhere. Did she have the courage? She was no longer sure.

The moon was rising through her barred window. There had been gales and snow all day but they had passed, leaving clear skies. It was late, past ten o'clock. Tiaan was not tired – she'd slept for a week. How to escape? She'd gained the impression, from the chatter of the attendants, that the work of the breeding factory went on until the early hours of the morning.

Sitting by the window, she ran various schemes through her mind. The window bars were set solidly into the mortar and it would take days to dig them out. She must have money and warm clothes, for winter was coming and even down on the coast the nights would be bitter. But first she had to recover her artisan's toolkit, her most precious possession. If only she still had her pliance. Just the thought of it set off a flood of withdrawal. Deprived artisans had committed the most degrading acts to get their pliances back.

The door opened. It was Matron. 'Your first contract begins at one tomorrow afternoon. The attendants will wake you at nine with breakfast. They will take you to your bath at eleven, then make you ready. Go to sleep now.'

Matron pulled the door closed. A key turned in the lock.

Tiaan was left with her despair. Would the fits start again, the next time she used a hedron? What if she had an attack out in the snow where there was no one to look after her? Tiaan knew little about the world and how to survive in it. She'd never had

126

to and was not sure she could. Maybe she was more like her mother than she'd thought.

The moon, shining on her face, roused Tiaan. It was bright for a crescent – the bright face of the moon, not the dark. It must be well after midnight. She lit the lamp and tiptoed to the door to examine the lock. It was an old-fashioned one, enough to keep in any ordinary prisoner, but not an artisan with her skills.

Bending one of the tines of her dinner fork over, Tiaan picked the lock in a minute. The corridor was dark but for a night lamp down the far end. She went back, grabbed the knife and headed up the hall. She had to find clothes and shoes; but first, the register.

Tiaan opened Matron's office easily enough – the lock was similar to the first. She felt around until she found a lamp and got it going. The bloodline register was no longer among the mess on the table. The cupboard was locked and her probe would not fit through the tiny keyhole.

She looked around for something to break in with. Her eye lighted on a climbing vine in a pot in the corner, which spiralled up around a length of wrought metal. Pulling it free, she jammed the point between the doors and wrenched. The timber split from top to bottom with a loud squeal. She whipped out the register and frantically turned the pages.

Someone called out, down the hall. Better hurry. The book was arranged in date order. Unfortunately Tiaan did not know what year Marnie had come here. Matron's writing was hard to read in the dim light and it was not until Tiaan noticed a familiar name, Jaski, that she realised she was on her mother's page. Jaski was one of her half-sisters, only four years old. Tiaan looked to the top of the page. No name. Marnie had been here so long that she had several pages. She flipped back to the first, scanning the entries until she found her own name, details of her birth and her first years. A cryptic note was scrawled in the Comments column, 'Does she have it?' and below that, in another hand, 'Not possible to tell. Put her into a suitable job and see.'

Have *what*? Footsteps roused her. Someone was coming.

The name, quick! She checked the entry but could not make it out. The ink was faded, the handwriting abominable. Was the first name Omarti, or Amante, or even Arranti? The second name was a scrawl she could not decipher at all. It might have been Ullerdye, or Menodyn, or something quite different. She ran through the sounds in her mind. They did not seem to fit. Below the name, in different ink, it said simply 'Deceased'.

Tiaan let out an involuntary cry. He was gone. She would never know him.

She blew out the lantern, tucked the register under her arm, and slipped out. At the corner she edged around, then ducked back. A bulky shadow was moving about further down. It looked like the matron.

Darting to the night lamp, Tiaan blew it out. She flattened herself against the wall and edged down the corridor. Before she was halfway to the stairs she heard Matron slip-slopping along, muttering to herself.

'More trouble than she's worth, fat old cow! Time to put her out the door. She's got enough gold stacked away to pay for the wretched war, and then demands half of this new indenture. Skinny little thing won't survive a year. Hell, she'll probably go mad again in a month and then where'll I be? Clients won't pay a nyd for *that*.'

Tiaan went very still. Had Marnie, who was as rich as the legendary magister of Thurkad, extracted more coin after Tiaan was indentured here? She felt betrayed.

She held her breath as the old woman came shuffling past, wheezing. 'Useless maid! I told her to check the lamps.' She stopped just past Tiaan. 'That's funny. Is anyone there?'

Tiaan's heart was crashing around. Surely Matron must hear it. But she moved off again. Tiaan scuttled the other way, round the corner, heading for the stairs. Had she remembered to close her door? She did not think so. Too late now.

The top of the stair was dimly illuminated by a lamp in the foyer. Peering over the rail, she saw the door guard at the foot of the steps. There was no way to get past him.

Hurrying into the darkness she ran straight into a huge

potted jesmyn on a stand. It fell and the pot smashed with a noise that must have been heard throughout the building. The register went flying. She groped for it in the dark.

'What was that?' cried the guard, thumping up the steps.

Tiaan could not find the book. As he came to the top step she pulled the gown up around her hips and ran, her breasts bouncing painfully. At the end of the corridor a hall went in either direction. She turned left, only to bang into a wall in the darkness. She scampered back the other way, rubbing her nose. If only she had not dropped the book.

This corridor was not lit and once past the junction Tiaan had to slow down. The corridor narrowed. She crept forward, her foot went down a step, she stumbled and just caught the rail as she fell.

Tiaan lay on the step, getting her breath back, until she heard shouts and the guard pounding up the corridor. At the bottom of a narrow service stair was a warren of rooms which she identified by feel – laundries, linen presses, pantries, storerooms, then a vast kitchen lit by the glow of a pair of iron ranges that were never allowed to go out.

Dough was rising in covered bowls – Tiaan could smell it. The bakers would appear shortly to produce the fresh breads, cakes and pastries for the day. The door to the outside had a complicated lock she might not be able to pick. The pantries and storerooms offered no refuge – as soon as the cooks appeared they'd be in use. Tiaan felt panicky, like a criminal on the run.

Matron's voice bellowed orders, not far away. Tiaan ducked into the laundry, lit by moonlight through a high, barred window. It contained a row of coppers for boiling the washing and a vast rectangular bin full of dirty clothes, mostly scanty nightwear and bed linen. This door was also locked. Tiaan was probing it with her pick when someone ran into the kitchen. Cupboards were pulled open and slammed again. The laundry would be next. She dived into the clothes bin and burrowed down to the bottom.

It reeked of perfume, massage oil, sweat and other more offensive odours. One sheet was drenched in sickly sweet sherry. At the bottom, at least a span down, she encountered the tiled floor. Tiaan wormed into the corner furthest from the opening and waited.

It was hot; the bin backed onto the kitchen ranges. Sweat trickled down her back.

'Not yet!' a man's voice said sharply. 'Mathys, do the laundry. Hysso, check the pantries and cupboards. I'll go through the kitchen. Lock every door as you come out. Matron, put someone in every corridor. As soon as she moves, we'll find her. Mathys?'

'I'm working!' said a petulant young woman's voice.

The room search was a series of long silences punctuated by rattles and bangs. Tiaan wondered if the servant had gone or was waiting silently for her to emerge from some hiding place.

After one long interval there came a thud and the laundry pressed down on her. Mathys must have climbed into the bin. Was she pulling all the washing out? If she did, there was no chance of avoiding discovery. Tiaan would have to knock her out. She would do anything short of murder to get away.

The weight eased. Tiaan was not game to move – even under all these clothes the servant girl must feel it. It became brighter, as if she was inspecting the bin with a lantern. A sudden, heart-stopping panic. What if she dropped it? The filmy nightwear would catch fire instantly.

Tiaan felt her moving away, walking up the other end of the bin. The movements went on for ages, then a little thump as she jumped back out.

'Mathys!' came Matron's angry shout.

'In the laundry, Matron.'

'Haven't you finished yet? Lazy slut of a girl!' A slap, a cry broken off. 'Did you check the laundry bin?'

'Yes,' said the girl sullenly.

'You took all the washing out?'

'Yes,' Mathys lied. 'I was just putting it back in.'

'Leave it – there's still a hundred rooms to search. Come on, and lock that door behind you!'

The door slammed. The lock clicked. Tiaan waited in case it was a ruse. After five minutes, when there had been no further sound, she judged it safe to come out. Emerging as slowly as a butterfly from a cocoon, she found the room empty. Creeping to the back door, she attacked the lock. It proved more difficult than the other. The mechanism must not have been oiled in ages. She forced too hard and the prong of her fork broke off.

Easing it out with the other, Tiaan tried again. It was tense work; if she broke this prong she'd be finished. However, after some minutes, the lock clicked. She eased open the door, letting in a blast of frigid air. She had to have warm clothes, and food if she could possibly find any. She was cut off from both by the locked door. Was she game to pick it and go back in?

A distant angry shout convinced her not to try. She would have to go hungry. Tiaan hacked a woollen blanket in two, folded it over half a dozen times and bound it around her feet with strips torn from a sheet. She put on eight nightgowns, one over the top of another, hoping that enough layers would compensate for their individual flimsiness.

Tiaan hunted for another blanket but could not find one. She made do with three sheets wrapped around her, tying them at the waist with another strip of linen. A flint striker, on the shelf above the coppers, caught her eye. She tied it into her sash. It could well save her life. She took a handful of tinder too. Tiaan pulled the door closed and, mindful of her previous failure, bent to lock it.

That proved even harder, but finally the door clicked. She scurried away, gravel crunching underfoot. It was freezing outside – puddles from the earlier rain had iced over. Layers of filmy cloud hid the setting moon. It must be around four in the morning.

Daylight was around seven-thirty so she did not have long to get out of Tiksi. She crept up the side of the building, walking on the paved edges of the gardens, and out the carriage entrance. The front door was open, the doorman standing in the light talking to Matron. A carriage waited nearby. The horse's breath steamed, as did a pile of manure behind it. Slinking into the shadows, Tiaan made her way up the street.

There was no one about – even the rare drifters who spent

summer nights sleeping in doorways and under bridges would be in shelter on a night like this. Tiaan headed toward the western gate, avoiding the smoggy haloes surrounding occasional street lamps.

Not long after, a closed carriage clopped past. It looked like the one she'd seen outside the front door. Pressed back under a leafless bush, Tiaan doubted that she had been seen. The driver, swathed in greatcoat and fur hat, stared fixedly ahead, no doubt desperately wanting to get home.

It was strange being out alone at this hour. Everything had a misty, unreal air. Fog crept up the street, assuming shapes reminiscent of dream or nightmare. Shadows waxed and waned as the moon drifted in and out of hurrying clouds. The staid buildings of Tiksi joined together to form fairy castles or hellish dungeons.

Tiaan was not frightened. There was little crime in Tiksi, since everyone above the age of six worked at least twelve hours a day. The mist and shadows were her friends.

Approaching an intersection, she heard the clump of hobnailed boots. She ducked under a hedge, holding her breath as a watchman paced by. He walked like a man who had been on the beat too long, looking neither left nor right.

A sudden gust lifted her robes, replacing the layer of warmth with freezing air. Her exposed arms were aching. Tiaan hurried on. She had to get on the mountain road well before dawn. As soon as it was light, the carriers would move out with their daily loads. No doubt there'd be a reward for her and it would be difficult to escape a hunt up there. There were few paths and, at this time of year, little chance of survival off them. Dressed like this, no chance.

She made it to the western gate unnoticed. A sudden flurry of sleet caught her out in the open. It wetted only the outer layer of her clothing, and her hair, but ice water began to penetrate her blanket boots.

The gate, when she reached it, posed a greater challenge. The guard was pacing up and down. She could see no way to get past him.

TWELVE

Tiaan waited near a small well, across the way from the open guardhouse. Though a brazier glowed inside, it must have been freezing in there. No doubt that was why the guard was marching so vigorously. It gave her an idea.

The pattern of his movements did not vary. He walked fifty paces up the road inside the wall, striding furiously, turned, paced back, looked across to the gate and continued for another fifty paces. Each time, his back was turned for less than a minute, not enough to climb the gate.

Tiaan needed a diversion. Taking the bucket off its hook, she hid it in the shadows across the street. As soon as the watchman turned away she scampered to the guardhouse, her blanketed feet making no sound on the cobbles. Inside was no more than a cupboard, a row of hooks on which hung two oilskin coats, and a pair of boots below them. She spilled hot coals from the brazier into the pocket of one oilskin. It began to smoke. She knocked the other coat down, tipped the brazier onto it and was about to dash out when she heard the guard tramping back. *Thud-click*, *thud-click* as a metal heel-piece struck the cobbles.

It had taken too long. Tiaan crouched down, praying that he did not see the smoke rising from the oilskin, or come in to warm himself. If he did she was undone.

The footsteps stopped opposite the gate. Tiaan prepared to

defend herself, hopeless as that was. She held her breath. Silence.

The footsteps resumed, *thud-clicking* away. Tiaan blew on the spilled coals; the oilskin burst into flame. She dashed out, hid across the road in the shadows, then made a noise vaguely like a cat screaming.

The watchman checked, looked around, and continued his pacing. By the time he came opposite the gatehouse the oilskins were blazing as high as the ceiling. He ran inside, cried 'Bloody cat!' and raced for the well.

His curses when he could not find the bucket would have disturbed the corpses in the cemetery outside the wall. Pelting down the street, the guard hammered on the front door of the first house. 'Fire! Fire! I need a bucket, quick!'

Tiaan scuttled across to the gate, lifted the bar, rested it on its bracket and closed it behind her. She gave it a hard shake. The bar fell into place.

Outside, free at last, she ran up the track in the direction of the manufactory and did not stop until she had turned the corner, out of sight. Sitting on an ice-glazed rock she wept for joy. The moon glowed through the mist like a distant lamp through frosted glass. The trees were mere outlines, black as ink. A shooting star carved a fiery path across the sky before bursting into fragments that swiftly faded. It seemed to be pointing west. Was that an omen?

Knowing that her troubles were only beginning, she continued on.

The moon had fallen behind the mountains. Dawn was some way off. The stars, when visible through the racing mist, gave off just enough light for it not to be called pitch dark. Tiaan trudged up the path, following little more than instinct. She was freezing cold, dampness having seeped through the layers of clothing long ago. The wind stuck to her skin as if she wore a single layer of gauze. One blanket boot was already wearing through.

She kept on until the black sky was touched with the faintest blush in the north-east. The blankets were soaked, her feet in danger of freezing. Turning off the path, Tiaan went up the hill, avoiding places where she would leave tracks. The crest was bare save for a broken watch-tower of crumbling green slate and the moss-covered skeleton of a mountain pony. Down the other side she found shelter among up-jutting rocks and twisted trees. There was little risk of a fire being seen here.

The sun came up as she was gathering firewood, casting long conifer shadows that, low down, blurred into the mist. It was eerily beautiful. Tiaan warmed herself by the blaze until her foot coverings were dry. She was thinking about her father, wondering about his Histories, how he had lived and died and how he came to meet her mother. Had it just been a transaction in the breeding factory? She could not think so.

That set her puzzling about the bloodline register. Why did they need such a detailed record, if the idea was simply to produce as many children as possible? The mating details were clear – never more than one man in the same month. It did not seem to agree with what she knew about the place. But what if, she thought idly, the breeding factory was a place where children were bred *with particular talents*? Had her father been chosen on that basis? What a horrible thought!

It was lovely putting her hot boots back on. After heaping snow on the fire, she returned to the path. Another hour went by. It was nearly midday. The blankets were wearing thin again. Brushing wet ice off a log, she sat to remake her boots. Tiaan had just finished the first when she heard raised voices. A search party? She rolled off the other side of the log, hoping that the shadows would be enough to hide her.

Something cracked. She had broken the ice on a puddle and freezing water seared her side. She crouched behind the log, cursing her ill-luck.

Shortly a group of people ran past, as if fleeing for their lives. Since they were going downhill they could not be searching for her. They must have come from the manufactory or the mine. In the fog she did not recognise any of them, though one wore a carrier's cap and another an escort guard's uniform.

Tiaan ducked her head as they passed, though she need not

135

have. They looked neither right nor left. What could the matter be?

After a few minutes she judged it safe to come out. Her wet sheets had frozen. She cracked off the ice, re-bound her other foot and headed carefully up the track.

It wound around a buttress of crumbling granite, turned sharply into a chisel-shaped gully, crept across a shear zone where the rock had weathered to greasy clay speckled with quartz gravel, then carved out the other side again. In the gully the path was shaded by tall pines. She edged through the gloom. Whatever they had been running from, it could not be far away.

There were Hürn bears in these mountains, vast creatures ten times the weight of a man. Also wildcats of various types ranging from the panther-like carchous to the stubby-nosed and bewhiskered ghool. Wild dogs were a threat to solitary travellers, particularly the tigerish rahse and the pack-hunting mickle. However, attacks by any of those creatures were rare, especially in the autumn of a good year, when there was easier hunting than armed and vengeful humans.

On rare occasions there had been bandit raids near the coast, though never this high. On the other hand, the metal mine had been producing well lately, particularly the precious white gold, platinum, which was easily carried and easily hidden.

Tiaan had just come out of the forest into sunlight when she caught the tang of blood on the wind. It could be no further than the hairpin bend up ahead or she would not have smelt it. That area was exposed, for a recent landslip had carved most of the trees off the point. Ducking into the forest, she climbed the side of the ridge. At the crest, a good hundred spans above the path, she went right, following the ridgeline until she reached the top of the landslide.

Tiaan made sure that she was upwind. The point was concealed behind a large boulder. Tiaan crept down. On this barren rockslide even a dislodged pebble would give her away. Reaching the boulder in safety, she edged around the left-hand side until she had a clear view of the road.

None of her suppositions had been correct. It was neither

bears, beasts nor bandits. Far worse! A brand-new clanker, just completed by the manufactory, lay on its back with its metal legs in the air. The back half of the machine had been crushed under a boulder that had been rolled down the hill. No doubt the people inside were dead. She hoped Ky-Ara had not been the operator. Tiaan tried to recall his face but got the young man from her dreams instead. She put both firmly out of mind.

There were at least six bodies on the road. Pawing at one of them was what could only be a lyrinx. Her heart began to pound. Tiaan was shocked at the size and brutal power of the beast. It stood well over the height of a tall man, a massively muscular creature that seemed to be all claw, tooth and long, armoured body. Its wings were folded. It had a huge crested head, the crest jade-green, indicating a mature female. It could have taken on a Hürn bear and won. And, she reminded herself, they *ate* people.

At the same time, something seemed not quite right about the lyrinx – there was a slight awkwardness about it, as if it was not quite at home in its powerful body.

A pair of lyrinx were methodically tearing the armoured side out of the clanker, opening it up like a lobster at a dinner party. Armed with no more than metal bars they created an opening big enough to squeeze inside. Bags and boxes were tossed out, ripped open then abandoned.

Clankers were often used to deliver precious metal to Tiksi. Clearly that wasn't what the lyrinx were looking for, since Tiaan could see a scatter of golden rods on the ground from a broken bullion box. So what were they after?

A lyrinx pulled its head out of the opening, calling in a piping whistle to the third. Leaving off her gruesome business with the corpses, she joined the other two. With much heaving they rolled the boulder off the rear of the clanker, toppling it over the edge.

Tiaan took advantage of the racket to creep closer. The lyrinx tore the ruined clanker open from end to end. Splintered boxes and crushed bags were tossed to one side, and three sadly mangled bodies. With a shrill cry, the female held aloft an object that Tiaan recognised all too clearly.

It was one of the new controller apparatuses, with its pitch-coated hedron. Was that what they had come for? It must be, for they gathered around, their chatter emphasised by violent changes of skin colour.

Abruptly the discussion ended. The female with the green crest put the controller in a small chest pack, then the lyrinx touched crests and separated. The female went over the side; Tiaan heard her skidding down in the path of the boulder. The second lyrinx set off down the Tiksi path at a lope, perhaps going after those that had fled. The third tore a haunch from one of the corpses and, gnawing at the grisly article, scrambled up the hill toward Tiaan.

There was nothing she could do to avoid discovery. Tiaan simply crouched behind her rock and prayed. The lyrinx rattled its way across the scree, diverted round a boulder and headed up past her, not thirty paces away. She could smell the sweat on it, and the blood. What if it smelt her?

As it moved up, she edged back. About a hundred paces away the lyrinx checked and looked around, sniffing the air while Tiaan held her breath. It continued on. Soon it disappeared in the forest.

Tiaan did not move. Her legs had no more strength than the corpses down on the road. What were lyrinx doing *here*? The war must have taken a desperate turn for the worse, for she'd never heard of them coming so close to Tiksi. Unless the true state of the war was being kept from everyone. Clearly the creatures had come for the shielded controller. So there *was* a spy in the manu-factory.

The sun came out. Tiaan was glad of it, weak and wintry though it was. She felt frozen to the core. She'd have to take the dreadful news to the manufactory. How was she to do that without being seized as a runaway and sent back to the breeding factory?

She climbed down to the track in case there were any sur-vivors. There weren't – the bodies were torn apart. Perhaps others had escaped up the road. She could not tell; the rocky path held no tracks. None of the bodies belonged to Ky-Ara, thankfully.

Tiaan continued, creeping through a forest so silent that it was eerie. An hour later, when her much-repaired foot blankets were practically falling to pieces, Tiaan heard tramping. She ducked into the pines, watching a group of porters go by. Well, they could read the evidence as readily as she; no need to risk her freedom.

It was only a few minutes from there to the shortcut to the miners' village. Below the village she went off the path and up through the forest, circling around to come to Joeyn's front door without being seen, for she stood out like a ghost in her pale shrouds.

Pushing open the wattle gate, she ran down the path and hammered at the front door. Tiaan did not expect him to be there – he usually went to the mine at dawn. However, the door opened and Joeyn stood in the opening, blinking.

'Yes?' he said.

She smiled uncertainly. He did not seem pleased to see her. Then she realised that his old eyes were slow to adjust to the light.

'It's me, Tiaan.'

'What are you doing here? Get inside, quick!' Jerking her in by the wrist, he banged the door closed.

'I escaped,' she said softly. 'I was afraid you wouldn't be here.'

'I haven't been out for days. Didn't have the heart for it.'

Now he smiled, hugged her and stirred up the fire. 'What on earth are you wearing?'

'Half the dirty laundry. It was all I could find.'

'I suppose you're hungry.'

'Starving. And freezing.'

He pulled up a stool by the fire. 'Sit here. Take those rags off and put your feet on the hob.' He busied himself, carving slices of corned goat leg onto a wooden platter, adding a wrinkled apple and a large sweet rice ball. While she began on that he put the pot on the coals. 'You can't stay here. They'll come looking for you.'

'I don't think they'll be here for a while.' She told him about the lyrinx attack. 'No one will be walking the road now without a small army.'

'Lyrinx, *here*?' He paced across the hut and back.

'Perhaps something has drawn them to the manufactory; or the mine.'

'Who knows? What are you going to do now, Tiaan?'

She didn't answer at once. Tiaan was wondering if the manufactory might take her back, after this dreadful news. 'Do you think there's a chance for me?' she said wistfully. 'To work as an artisan again?'

'I suppose it might be possible . . . I've known Gi-Had since he was a little boy. His father was my younger sister's second husband. Would you like me to speak to him? In a roundabout sort of a way?'

She hesitated. The memories of her treatment, and the horror of the breeding factory, were strong. 'I'm afraid. I'll die before I go back down there.' She shivered.

He went to the fire, made mint tea with a sprig of dried herb from a hanging bunch, sweetened it with honey, and handed it to her.

'Thank you! Did you manage to get back my . . . things?'

'I picked them up on the way back from Tiksi. All except your journal. The new crafter has it.'

'Thank you. If you could see what I'm wearing under this.' She held up the muddy sheets at the back, allowing heat from the fire onto her bare skin.

He laughed. 'I'm too old for that sort of thing.'

Tiaan yawned. 'I'm so tired. I think I'll just curl up right here.'

THIRTEEN

Tiaan slept and did not dream, to be woken after dark by Joeyn carrying wood inside. She yawned, stretched and sat up.

'Going to be a cold night.' He stacked the fire. 'Lucky you're not sleeping out in those rags.'

'Where did you put my clothes?' she asked, warming herself at the blaze.

'They're in the pack under the bed.'

She fell on it, pulling out woollen trousers, shirts, undergarments, socks and boots, a heavy coat of waxed cloth with a fur lining, brushes for teeth and hair, a few other personal items, the copy of Nunar's book, and at the bottom, most precious of all, her artisan's toolkit. She unfolded the canvas with its dozens of pockets, each containing a special tool. Tiaan remembered the day she'd finished making them. It had been the day she graduated from prentice to artisan. Her fingers lingered on the tools of her trade. She might never use them again but there was no way she could leave them behind. All her self-worth was represented by that small roll of canvas.

'Was there anything else?' she asked.

'Oh, yes!' He took a leather bag from behind the door.

She loosened the drawstring and opened the mouth of the bag. Feeling inside, her fingers encountered the helm and she had an instantaneous flash of the young man on the balcony, crying, *'Help me!'*

She went still, looked up at Joeyn, began to say something then decided not to. Tiaan laid the helm on her lap, the globe beside it.

'Beautiful work,' said Joeyn. 'What are they for?'

'To sense out what was wrong with the controllers. The crystal we found the other day went in this bracket.' Just the thought of it set off her withdrawal cravings. She had to make another pliance. She was shaking with desire for it.

'There was no crystal in your room,' Joeyn said.

'Irisis would have taken it down to the workshop.'

'I wonder she didn't take these too.'

'They're made for me. She wouldn't want them.'

'There's something else.' Joeyn held a piece of cloth under her nose.

The smell made her step backwards. 'It's my headache balm.'

'Where did you get it?'

'From the apothek. The crystals gave me terrible headaches.'

'Are you sure that's where the headaches came from?'

'Yes. Why?'

'My grandmother used herbs and warned me against this one – calluna root. I could never forget the smell. It causes visions, fits, madness, and if you take enough of it, you can choke to death.'

'But why would the apothek put calluna in my ointment?'

'I don't know. He wasn't a lover of yours?' said Joeyn with a cheeky grin.

'I have never had a lover,' she reminded him primly. 'Anyway, I hardly know the man.'

'Perhaps he loves you secretly.'

'I doubt it. People say that he's . . . incapable.'

'Could anyone else have interfered with the balm?'

She wrinkled her brow. 'I was too busy to wait while he made it up. Hang on! Irisis brought it down. She wanted to be rid of me.'

'And now she has, and there's no way to prove she had anything to do with it. No way to unseat her either.'

'I thought . . .'

'She's your enemy, Tiaan. She'll never allow you to come back.'

Tears formed in her eyes. 'I don't know why I keep hoping. I'll go tomorrow, though I don't know where to go.'

'We can talk about that later. It's dinnertime.' He lifted the lid of the cauldron on the hob. A delicious spicy smell wafted out. Tiaan licked her lips.

Joeyn dug caked rice from another pot, shaped it into a raised doughnut on a wooden platter then ladled a good helping of stew into the centre. He handed it to her.

'I can't eat that much!'

'Of course you can. The only way to set out is with a full belly.'

'That's not till tomorrow.'

'It might be a long time until you get another meal as good as this one.'

True enough. She dipped her fork. It was a thick stew of meat and vegetables: rich, spicy and hot. Tiaan ate slowly, thinking about tomorrow. She was lost; just as lost as the young man of her crystal dreams.

Had they just been hallucinations brought on by calluna? Was the young man no more than the fantasy of a drug-addled brain? She could not believe that. The dreams were the only good things left in her life. Anyway, she had first dreamed of him the night *before* she got the balm.

Joeyn was gazing wistfully at her.

'What is it?' she asked.

'Oh, nothing really. It's good to have someone to eat with. I haven't, since my wife died.'

It was pleasant in his hut. Companionable. She felt at home here. 'I usually eat alone, too. I . . . don't know what to say to people, as a rule. They find me strange.'

'People *are* strange. Here we are, you just starting out in life, and me at the end of mine.'

'No!' she cried. 'You're my only friend, Joe.'

'Then you'd better make some more. Not many miners get to seventy-six. I won't see eighty, nor want to. What are your plans,

143

Tiaan? I know you've something in mind, for you keep going all dreamy and vague, and smiling to yourself as if thinking of a distant lover.'

'I'm going to go after my dream.' She left it at that. There was no way to explain the young man, even to Joeyn. 'There's only one problem . . .'

He scraped up the last of the stew with a rice ball and popped it in his mouth. 'What's that?'

'I need another crystal, Joe.'

'Why?' He stopped in mid-chew.

'The helm and the globe are useless without one. It's . . . I suppose it's like not being able to find your reading glasses. You can see the words on the page but you can't make out what they say.'

He gave Tiaan a keen glance. 'Well, my roof props are still there. It wouldn't be too dangerous to get another, I suppose.'

'Any old crystal would do.' Tiaan was already feeling guilty. 'It wouldn't have to be a specially good one . . .' The craving was back again – crystal, crystal, *crystal!* She had to have another, whatever it cost.

'I don't suppose so. But on the road *you'll* be travelling, you'll need the best you can get.' He broke off abruptly. 'I'm going for a walk. I like to settle my dinner before bed. You'll want to change, and wash, I suppose.'

'Thank you.'

After the door closed she washed the platters and leaned them against the fireplace to dry. Taking off her layers of rag and gown, she bathed as thoroughly as she could with a bucket of water and put on knickers and singlet. Lying beside the fire, she pulled the rags over her and was soon asleep.

In the night she dreamed of the young man on the balcony and the catastrophe that had befallen his world, but this time the images were fleeting, hopeless, as if he had given up hope. The dream shifted into one of her grandmother's tales, of a young woman going to the rescue of her lover, only the young woman was Tiaan. She shifted under her covers, sighed and slipped back into the wonderful dream.

Tiaan stirred when Joeyn came in around midnight. She sat up, gave him one of those faraway smiles, and went straight back to sleep.

Shaking his head, Joeyn took off his boots and turned to his own cold bed.

When she awoke just after dawn, his bed was empty. Tiaan dressed, glorying in her own clothes again rather than those hideous, confining gowns, and breakfasted on stew, rice and mint tea. Only then did she notice the chalk scrawl on a broken piece of slate near the door:

Gone down mine. Back by lunch. Keep a careful lookout, just in case. I left you a few old things. They were my wife's.

On the bed lay a jacket and overpants lined with fur and filled with down, and a sleeping pouch of the same material. They were better quality than anything she had. Tiaan thanked him silently.

The Tiksi watch could be looking for her right now. She packed, including one of the sheets. You never knew when a rag might come in handy. Knowing Joeyn would not have her set out on the road with nothing to eat, Tiaan wrapped a stale loaf, the partly used leg of corned goat, a handful of rice balls and a lump of cheese, and shoved them in as well.

Rubbing off his note she wrote her own, a simple *Thank you, Joe.* Her preparations completed, Tiaan checked outside and slipped into the forest. She climbed a tree that had a view of the path and the village, and waited.

It was a clear, windy morning and the wind intensified as the day wore on, shaking the walls of the hut. It was exposed in her tree; Tiaan was glad of her new clothing. Nothing happened, except for occasional people passing up and down the path. Noon came and went. Joeyn did not appear. Anxious now, she went back to the hut for bread, cheese and water, then resumed her watch.

A long time afterwards, when Tiaan was beginning to think she should go looking for Joeyn, a short man appeared, striding down the path as if he owned it. He wore the uniform of an artificer. It was the detestable Nish.

145

Could he be looking for her? News of her escape would have reached the manufactory by now. Her discarded garments were under Joeyn's bed but there was nothing she could do about them.

Joe had not appeared. She set off for the mine at a trot, trying to leave as few tracks as possible. There was no one in sight as she darted across the open ground and inside the adit. Lex was in his cavern, tallying quotas of ore on a slate. Crouching low, she made it past unseen, took a full lantern from the rack, lit it and hurried to the lift. She got into the basket and wound herself down to the sixth level.

Tiaan stepped out of the basket and took off the brake. If someone came after her, and thought to look, they might tell which level she'd gone to by the markings on the lift rope. Nothing she could do about that either.

Holding her lantern high, Tiaan made her way down the tunnel, praying that Joeyn was here. There was always the chance that she'd missed him, or he'd gone up to the manufactory first. Thus preoccupied, she did not give a thought to the unstable areas as she passed under them. What a change from her first time.

Not far now. She negotiated a tight squeeze, a gentle curve, and ahead were the triple dead ends. In her withdrawal Tiaan could sense the field strongly. She would tear crystal out of the rock with her teeth if there was no other way to get one. She ran forward, then stopped. The middle end was piled with rubble that had half-buried the props. Part of the roof had collapsed.

She moved forward slowly, hoping against hope. It could have fallen any time in the last two weeks. Then, as she swung the lantern, Tiaan saw a battered boot sticking out from under the rocks. She clutched at her heart.

'Joe?' she whispered. 'Joeyn?'

She ran around the pile. He lay on his face with one of the roof props across his back, weighed down with rubble the size of small boulders. Tiaan fell to her knees beside him. 'Joe?' She stroked the thin hair off his cheek. It was warm. Her heart leapt. A trickle of blood ran out of his nose. 'Joe?'

He gave the tiniest of groans, deep in his chest, and his eyes came open. 'Tiaan?'

'It's me!' She clutched his hand. 'What happened?'

'Want to send you off . . . best you could possibly have.'

She thought of that glowing crystal up the back of the cavity; the one she'd so coveted. He had dug out the vein at the front and dozens of crystals were piled against the wall. The craving urged her to throw herself on them, even with Joeyn dying here. She felt disgusted by her weakness.

'You shouldn't have, Joe. Any one of those would have done. How did you hope to get to it anyway?'

His eyes indicated a long pole with a wooden jaw on the end, closed by pulling on a string.

'Oh, Joe!' She stroked his brow. 'Let's get you out!' She began to toss the rocks to one side. Grit sifted down from the roof.

'Stop!' he gasped. 'There's more to come down, Tiaan. Maybe all of it.'

'I don't care! I'm not leaving you here.'

'Tiaan,' he gasped, breath bubbling in his chest. 'I can't feel anything from the waist down. My back is broken and I've burst something inside. I'm dying.'

'No!' she screamed. 'I won't let you.'

'This is the way it's meant to be. I'm a lonely old man. I've spent my whole life down here. Do you think I want to become a cripple who can't even wipe his bottom?'

'I want you to live,' she muttered.

'That's cruel. But I'd like you to do something for me.'

'Anything.'

'Take my belt off. I want you to have it.'

'I don't want your wretched belt.'

'Do as I ask, Tiaan.'

It was not easy, weighed down as he was, but at last she managed it. It was thick and rather heavy.

'It's a money belt,' he whispered. 'There's enough gold and silver in it to carry you a tidy stretch of your journey.'

'I'm not taking your gold,' she said stubbornly.

'I can't spend the gold where I'm going. I have no relatives left. Put the damn thing on, Tiaan!'

Shocked by his vehemence, she pulled it round her, found that it needed another hole to buckle at her small waist, and began to make one with the point of his knife.

'Take the knife too. It's a good one.'

Putting the belt on, she hung the knife from its loop. This was unbearable. Tiaan paced across the tunnel and back. Across again. Her eye lit on the pile of crystals he'd worked so hard to get. Picking out the best of them, she held it up. It did nothing for her craving, of course. It had to be woken first, and that would be a mighty job without her pliance. She squatted beside him. 'How are you feeling, Joe?'

'Not so good! I wouldn't mind a drink though.'

'I've got a bottle of water . . .'

'I don't want your bloody water. I'll *die* before I ever touch water again.'

Smiling sadly, she looked for his pack, which was propped against the far wall. She found the flask, lifted his head as best she could and held it to his mouth. He took in a small amount of the dreadful brandy.

'More!' He attempted a grin. 'It won't kill me, you know.'

'How can you joke about it?' She brushed tears out of her eyes.

'How can you not?'

She gave him a good-sized slug.

He gasped. 'That's better. This is the way I've always wanted to go, Tiaan. Would you bring my pick and hammer and chisel? I'd like them to hand.'

She laid them on the floor beside him.

'We've been together a long time, old friends,' he said. 'Let's go the last little step together, shall we?' His left hand extended to stroke the handle of his pick. 'You've served me well.' His eyes closed. He murmured a snatch of an old song, one that had been popular in his distant youth. 'Are you still there, Tiaan?'

'Yes,' she whispered, quite overcome. 'I'm not going anywhere.'

'Could I have another drop of brandy?'

She tilted the flask, although this time he seemed to have

trouble swallowing. 'Joe?' She clutched his hand.

'Yes?'

'Is there any other way out of this mine?'

'Why?'

'They're looking for me. Nish the artificer went down to the village just as I was leaving.'

He said nothing for so long that Tiaan thought he must have slipped away. His hand was a rigid claw, clutching hers. She squeezed it and he spoke.

'There used to be a way out from the ninth level. A long, long adit that ran south to the Bhu-Gil mine. Its entrance was blocked up a long time ago, though it could have been unblocked since. We miners are a greedy lot; the things we get up to in our spare time, no one knows.'

'Any other way?'

'Not that . . . I know of. Not good, too many entrances to a mine. Gold just turns to air.' He gave a quiet chuckle. 'Probably flooded. Long swim, my girl.'

'Oh!' She remembered him saying that the other day. 'No other way out?'

'Who knows? Some miners are thieves, and the thieves don't tell the honest ones.'

That was not much help. 'More brandy, Joe?'

'Just a taste, to wet my tongue.'

She dribbled a little more into his mouth. It ran out again. His fingers stroked the pick handle, then lay still.

'Joe!' she cried. There was no answer. 'Joe?'

'Something for you,' he said in a whisper no louder than a sigh. 'Help you on your way.'

'I've already got the money belt.'

'Something else . . .' He tried to smile but the breath whistled out of him; Joe gave a little shudder and lay still.

He was dead. Tears swelled under her eyelids. Poor Joe, such a gentle, kindly old man. She kissed him on the forehead, closed his eyes and put his hand on the pick. As she did, something slipped out of his other hand, something that glowed faintly in iridescent swirls, like oil on luminous water.

It was the crystal she'd lusted after when she saw it up the far end of the cavity the other day. It was a bipyramid of quartz, blushing the faintest rose, but inside each end was a radiating ball of needle crystals finer than human hair. The two balls were almost joined down the length of the prism by longer needles, but there was a gap in the middle, a tiny bubble of air partly filled with liquid.

She picked up the crystal and light exploded in her mind, rainbow streamers that went in all directions, coiling, looping and whorling back on themselves endlessly. It was as if she was *inside* the field, but one unlike any she had ever seen before. Rather, there was more to it than before. Curves and circles and spheres appeared out of nowhere to drift across her view, constantly changing shape and size, disappearing then re-forming differently, as if she was seeing fragments of structures that had the wrong dimensions for this world.

The crystal was already awake – it had to be! It was ecstasy, not least because the withdrawal was gone instantly. It was disturbing too. Her head spun with the effort of trying to make sense of it all.

She had often seen rutilated quartz. It was common in this mine and many of the best hedrons were made from such crystals. But she had never come across anything as perfect or symmetrical as this one. It made her hair stand on end to think what, as an artisan, she might have done with it.

Tiaan wrapped the hedron in a scrap of leather and put it safely in her pack. Kissing Joe's brow, she took the flask. There was some bread and cheese in his pack. She ate that, sharing one last meal with her old friend, and saluted him with a tot of the turnip brandy. Laying his pack beside him, she took her lantern, leaving his to burn down in its own time, and departed without a backward glance.

PART TWO

ARTIFICER

FOURTEEN

Nish wrote a long letter to his father on the day Tiaan's indenture was sold to the breeding factory. He told Jal-Nish everything, except for his dealings with Irisis. The perquisitor would expect a full report and he dared leave nothing out that could be heard from anyone else. Inquisitors were also watched. Probers, being no more than prentices in the spying art, were especially subject to surveillance.

Tiaan's madness and banishment gave Nish rather less pleasure than he had expected. Revenge was less sweet than he had been led to believe and he could not help worrying about Irisis's part in it. Had she done something to the artisan to bring on crystal fever? There was no way to find out. Irisis now avoided him, and on the rare occasions they did meet she refused to talk, much less lie with him. He'd risked everything and gained nothing. Moreover, he found that he missed Tiaan about the place, especially her trim figure and light step going past the artificers' workshops.

A couple of days later, on his monthly day off, Nish walked down to Tiksi, giving his letter and the news to Fyn-Mah, the querist there, chief of the city's intelligence bureau. Fyn-Mah reported directly to his father. A slight, small woman of no more than thirty years, she was young to have such responsibility. Judging by her black hair and dark eyes, her delicate features, not to mention her cool manner, she was Tiksi-born. The querist was an attractive woman, and wore no ring, but Nish did not consider her for an instant. Everything about her shrieked 'keep your distance'.

Fyn-Mah laid the letter aside. Her eyes met his and he had to look away. 'I already know about Tiaan,' she said without expression. 'A bad business.'

Nish looked down at the table, wondering what she knew.

The querist ran her fingers over the letter, then placed it in a grey satchel. 'I will send it with the courier this afternoon.' She nodded. He was dismissed.

Nish turned away from her door with a great sigh. The deed was done and it would take a couple of weeks for the courier to get to Fassafarn, where his father lived. Even if Jal-Nish was angry, as seemed probable, there could be no response in under a month.

On the way back Nish happened to pass the breeding factory. On impulse he went to the grand entrance, to enquire about the new woman, Tiaan. Several silver drams jingled in his pocket, his first wages as a prober, and he had the delicious thought of buying what he'd previously been refused.

'We don't do business with *boys*,' sneered the man at the door.

'I'm a man! I'm twenty. I have my rights.' As it happened he was only nineteen, but the lie could not hurt.

'The breeding factory is not a right, it's a privilege. We choose the seed carefully here, as well as the man. And the first thing we do is make sure it's ripe!'

'But I'm . . .'

'No, you're not!' said the guard. 'And if you were, the fee would be fifty drams. In any case, the woman you mention is ill. Be on your way now, before I call the watch.'

Nish hurried back to the manufactory, smouldering.

A week and a half later he was called to the overseer's office to receive an urgent package from his father. So urgent, in fact, that it had come by skeet. Nish knew how expensive that was, for the

154

big carrier birds were vicious, difficult to train and in great demand by the army. What could it be?

He unfastened the oilskin wrapper, anxious now. There were two letters inside, one addressed to him, the other to 'Probationary Overseer Gi-Had'. Nish handed that one to the overseer, wondering what it meant. Gi-Had had been overseer for ten years.

Gi-Had was staring at the envelope in uneasy bafflement. He slit the envelope and turned away. Nish went to the window and sat down. He did not open his own immediately. Something was badly wrong.

He was staring out the cobwebbed window when the overseer cried out. Nish tore open his own letter, which was not dated.

> Jal-Nish Hlar
> Perquisitor for Einunar
> The Cleftory
> Munning Har
> Fassafarn

> Artificer Cryl-Nish,
>
> I am most displeased. Your report so alarmed Fyn-Mah that she sent it to me by skeet. I cannot believe your incompetence. Artisan Tiaan has brilliantly solved two problems that have plagued our clankers in recent months, and we have great plans for her.

Nish put down the letter, thinking out aloud. 'But Irisis solved those problems.'

Gi-Had swung around, balling up a hairy fist. 'Irisis made one mistake,' he grated. 'Tiaan wrote a report on what she had done *before* she went mad. It was found in her pocket by your father's *other* prober. The one who *isn't* an incompetent fool. Thinking I was in on the conspiracy, he sent it straight down to the querist. Now Jal-Nish questions my loyalty. *My loyalty!*' he choked. Gi-Had tore a page off the back of his letter and thrust it in Nish's face.

Nish read Tiaan's report and blanched. There was no doubt

that it was genuine. Irisis must have been behind it all – the sabotages, the faked evidence, and Tiaan's crystal fever too. Nish knew he was undone. Doomed! Why had he been taken in by her? Why hadn't he listened to that inner voice? He went back to his own letter.

Tiaan's day journal reveals the development of an artisan of rare talent, unlike any in the sixty-seven manufactories in the south-east. Fortunately I have *competent* people reporting directly to me from your manufactory, though it took them a while to find out what had happened. This was no fit of crystal madness, idiot son of mine! It was brought on by tincture of calluna, a herb that causes hallucinations. Her bedclothes stank of it. Some traitor gave it to her, you thrice-cursed fool! Someone who cares only to see the enemy ruin us.

Clearly there is a conspiracy in this manufactory and I am coming personally to root it out. Everyone is under suspicion, particularly you and your *friend* Irisis. I have been told of threats you made against the artisan. Why, Cryl-Nish, why? As of this instant you are relieved of your position as prober and your whole future is at stake. I have instructed Gi-Had to punish you.

Immediately afterwards you will go to Tiksi, as assistant to Probationary Overseer Gi-Had. You will bring Tiaan back and ensure she is restored to health and to her position. I have ordered Querist Fyn-Mah to the manufactory. She will take charge of the investigation until I arrive. Make sure no evidence is tampered with or your head will swiftly leave your shoulders.

Do a good job and, if Tiaan recovers fully, you may in time be restored as prober. Fail, and you will be in the front-line as fast as you can be carried there. The scrutator has been informed and he is as displeased as I am.

Jal-Nish
Perquisitor

Nish's shaking hand dropped the letter. As he bent to pick it up he caught Gi-Had's eye. The overseer's dark face had gone as pale as paper. Casting Nish a look of purest fury, he screamed,

'Why did you do this, artificer? Guard!' He threw himself out the door, bellowing so loudly that it shook the flimsy wall of his office.

A brace of guards came running, and more behind them. 'Take this man to the whipping posts and strip him naked, ready for the lash. Bring *everyone* outside. The entire manufactory will watch!'

The guards dragged Nish away. The bellowing continued behind him. Gi-Had was a most frightened man. What had been in *his* letter?

Outside Nish was stripped and tied to the middle whipping post. Shortly he heard screams, scuffles, and a naked Irisis was bound to the post next to his. He cast her a furious glare. She stared him down. Her pale skin was covered in purple blotches, for it was well below freezing.

'I curse the day I met you!' he hissed.

She looked him up and down. 'I can't say that you were worth it either, *little Nish!*'

They stood there for an hour while the thousand people in the manufactory were assembled. Nish felt sure he had frostbite in his toes, which had lost all feeling. How could he have been such a fool? Irisis had been behind it the whole time. But why would she betray everything her life had stood for? It made no sense.

Finally Gi-Had appeared. 'When my father hears of this . . .' Nish blustered.

'He ordered it!' Gi-Had said savagely. Standing before the assembled workers, he read from the letter:

I, Perquisitor Jal-Nish Hlar, order Probationary Overseer Gi-Had to personally give twenty lashes to my incompetent son, Cryl-Nish, and to Artisan Irisis, for suspected complicity in the drugging of Artisan Tiaan and her banishment to the breeding factory, and for other crimes that I do not specify.

Tiaan will be restored to her position immediately. Once the investigation is completed, if their guilt is established, Cryl-Nish will go to the front-lines, Irisis to the breeding factory and . . .

He choked on the words.

> Gi-Had will clean out the drainage pipes for what remains of his
> miserable life.

While waiting for the lash, Nish looked across at Irisis, who
was still staring straight ahead. 'My father is coming,' he said
out of the corner of his mouth. 'What evidence is there against
us?'

'The word of one man,' she said grimly.

'Who, Irisis?'

Her lovely lips set in a hard line. 'Even if I knew I wouldn't
tell you.'

'Can he be blamed?'

'Only if he's dead!' She bared those carnivore's teeth.

The first lash fell on her creamy back. Irisis writhed, tossed
back her head and opened her mouth, but let forth no scream.
After that, as the knotted leather tore into his own back, Nish
was in too much agony to notice. And agony it was, the humiliation even worse than the pain.

Gi-Had wielded the whip as if he was trying to flay them
alive. Nish broke on stroke sixteen. He screamed, and again for
each of the remainder, not to mention afterwards when a tar-boy
painted the wounds with a bristle brush.

Only then did he realise what a strong woman Irisis was. She
had bitten through her lip, her back was a bloody ruin that
would be scarred for life, but she had not let out a whimper.

Nish watched, with a thrill of horror, the mixture of tar and
blood dribbling down her backside. His own must be the same.

'I can't do anything!' he gritted. 'I'm bidden to Tiksi with
Gi-Had.'

'Just as well!' she hissed back. Irisis stood up straight, thrusting out her chest, and at that moment he desired her more than
he ever had.

Nish and Gi-Had left for Tiksi immediately, but after an hour
were forced back by a blizzard so strong they were in danger of

being blown off the path. By the time they struggled through the gates, four hours later, it was growing dark.

The manufactory was abuzz. Apothek Mul-Lym was dead, having committed suicide with an extract of tar. It had been a horrible death that left his lips and mouth blistered, and his corpse with a pungent phenolic reek. There were no witnesses. It was assumed that he was Tiaan's poisoner, though many wondered why he had taken his life in such a painful way. His drug ledger was open at the next but last page. It showed a tiny vial of calluna to have been used, though no patient's name had been entered.

A rumour spread that he'd been spurned by Tiaan, had poisoned her in revenge, and then, knowing the deed would be traced to him, had taken his own life. Gi-Had questioned Irisis and Nish closely but of course Nish knew nothing about it. If Irisis did, she gave not a hint of it under a six-hour interrogation, and no witness could place her anywhere near the scene of the crime. Finally Gi-Had dismissed her. The apothek's death was the best solution for them all.

Nish ran into Irisis in the corridor in the middle of the night and asked her what had happened. 'I know nothing about it,' she said, and walked away.

Nish was more worried than ever. She must have murdered the man. Nish was in way over his head and sinking fast.

Querist Fyn-Mah had still not appeared when Gi-Had and Nish set out at dawn. Presumably she had also been delayed by the weather. The snow had stopped but the wind was scouring snow off the path as they hurried down the mountain.

They arrived in Tiksi with red, wind-blasted faces, reaching the breeding factory at midday. The door guard sneered when he caught sight of Nish, who trembled lest the man reveal the details of his previous visit. In Matron's office they received a most unpleasant surprise. Tiaan had escaped in the night.

Gi-Had let out a monumental groan and gripped his head in gnarled hands, as if trying to squeeze the pain out of it. 'Where has she gone?'

'How in the blazes should I know?' Matron replied. 'I wish I'd never set eyes on the wretch. The damage she's done to our reputation won't be undone in a hurry. I've a good mind to ask for the indenture money back, after the damaged goods you've sold me.'

'You knew what you were buying!' he cried, unwilling to let her get the better of him.

'You said she was incurably mad!'

'That was the advice my healers gave me,' Gi-Had said stiffly.

'She was sane and cunning when she woke up.'

'In which case you should have paid more for her, not less.' Nonetheless Gi-Had was delighted to hear that Tiaan had recovered. 'Where is she now?'

'No one knows. She led the entire household a dance for hours, then escaped.'

'The factory will buy her indenture back,' Gi-Had said, 'as soon as she's found.'

'Now just wait a minute . . .' she began.

'There'll be a bonus in it. And, I should warn you . . .'

'Yes,' she said, alerted by his smouldering temper.

'This comes at the orders of Jal-Nish Hlar, the perquisitor.'

'Of course we'll do everything in our power to cooperate,' she said quickly.

'Did she have any visitors?'

'Only a decrepit old miner. Should never have let him in the place.'

They questioned Tiaan's mother too, but all Marnie could do was complain – about the discomfort, the ingratitude of her daughter, but most of all that her client would not be coming. Next they went to the querist's house but Fyn-Mah had left Tiksi some days back. By the time they reached the fire-scarred city gate they were no better informed as to where Tiaan might have fled.

'She could not have gone far,' said Nish, 'with no money, clothes or friends.'

'Perhaps to the coast,' Gi-Had mused. 'She has half-brothers and sisters down there.'

At the gate they had their first piece of useful news, for among the guards was the fellow Tiaan had escaped from.

'Damn near burned the guardhouse down.' He indicated the charred timbers. 'And then she fixed the bar so it'd fall closed behind her. I'd never have known, had I not seen it fall.'

Nish was about to make a sarcastic remark about the intelligence of guards. He'd had an awful day and his back was in agony. But he caught Gi-Had's eye on him and, mindful of the trouble he was in, held his tongue.

'Do you have any idea which way she went?' he asked.

'Straight up the road.' The guard pointed.

'She might have doubled back,' Gi-Had said.

'I followed her tracks as soon as it became light,' said the guard. 'She was going up the path to the manufactory. It's a wonder you didn't run into her this morning.'

'She must have heard us coming.' Gi-Had gave the man a coin for his trouble.

About an hour later, rounding a hairpin bend in light snow, they came upon two porters and a guard, plodding along, heads down, in a state of exhaustion.

'Hoy!' Gi-Had roared.

Their heads jerked up. The guard broke and ran but the others called him back. Gi-Had jogged up to them, stepping high through the snow. Nish hurried after him, which hurt his back cruelly.

The woman cried out, 'It's Overseer Gi-Had. Gods be praised. Surr, surr, we've been attacked by lyrinx!'

She staggered and nearly fell. Gi-Had held her up. 'Porter Ell-Lin, is it not?'

'That's right, surr! Kind of you to remember.' Ell-Lin touched one shoulder and then the other, a sign of respect. She was a large, stocky woman with big shoulders and a thick neck. Jet-black hair had been cropped short around a broad, weatherbeaten but not unhandsome face. Her slanted black eyes were narrowed to slits.

'Tell us about the attack, Ell-Lin. You know Artificer Cryl-Nish, of course!'

'I saw him at the whipping.' She averted her gaze. Nish flushed nonetheless. 'We were coming down Ghyllies Pinch, ten of us and the new clanker. We'd left late because of a cracked

161

front strut. It was the last hour of the morning. As we rounded the corner a boulder rolled down the hill and smashed the clanker in. The beasts came out of the rocks; three, there were. Everyone else is dead. Were we not ahead they'd have got us too.' She shuddered at the memory. 'Lyrinx were eating Wal, and poor ole Yiddie . . .' She put her head in her hands. 'It ain't right, is it! Eating folk!'

'What about the clanker?' said Gi-Had. 'Could it not . . .?'

'It was destroyed, surr.'

'What, completely?'

'The back was crushed, and the people inside. Beasts got the other soldiers too. They fought bravely but it was useless. We dropped our loads and ran.'

'Cowards!' sneered Nish, forgetting himself.

'Shut up, *boy*!' Gi-Had roared. 'Or you'll join them. You did well, Ell-Lin. The goods we can replace, if they took them, but porters are vital to the war. Which way did they come?'

'Down the mountain,' muttered the man who had tried to run away.

'And you didn't see which way they went?'

'They were still there, trying to open up the clanker, when we turned the corner.'

'And you saw no one else? No sign of Artisan Tiaan?'

'No,' said Ell-Lin, and the men shook their heads.

'We'll go carefully.' Gi-Had eased the knife in his belt. The others were not armed. There had never been a need for it up here. 'I don't like this,' he muttered to Nish. 'Lyrinx in these mountains, attacking our caravans – there's something we're not being told. And what's become of Tiaan? We need her more desperately than ever.'

'Perhaps she came upon the caravan. The lyrinx may have eaten her too.'

'Better pray they haven't, *Nish*!' said Gi-Had.

It was late afternoon by the time they reached the scene; shadows slanted right across the road. A breeze carried the stench of blood and ordure. A snow eagle, its beak and breast feathers tinged red, flapped slowly off as they trudged up to the wreck. The bird went as far as the out-jutting branch of an ancient pine, where it perched, watching them with jealous eyes as if they wanted to share in its feast.

Gi-Had inspected the ruin gloomily. 'No chance of repairing it, artificer?'

Nish shook his head. 'Even if we could, you'd never get anyone to operate it. Death Clanker, they'd call it, and you'd have to force them at swordpoint. The hedron would probably pick up the taint of the lyrinx . . .'

'Maybe we could salvage some of the parts.'

'Perhaps.' Nish put his head in through the opening, but one look at the shambles inside and he hurriedly withdrew. Running to the edge of the road, he vomited up his breakfast. Then, thinking how far he had to go to rehabilitate himself, he hurried back. 'Sorry! I've not seen . . .'

'Just get it done,' Gi-Had said sharply. He seemed to be having trouble with his own stomach.

Nish held his breath this time. The operator and passengers must have died instantly, though the bodies had been further despoiled by the lyrinx. The inside looked like the floor of an abattoir. He finished his inspection and pulled away. The smell lingered in his nostrils.

'The controller's gone!' said Nish.

'I'm starting to see a story here. First they sabotage the crystals, then my best artisan, and now they're stealing the controllers. What's next? And why steal them? Are they planning to use them against us?'

'I don't know, surr,' said Nish.

'I don't like this at all. It's too big for me. For the first time since the letter, I'm wishing your father would hurry up.'

I'm not, thought Nish.

'Anything else missing?' said Gi-Had.

'I don't think so.'

'The porters' boxes have been torn open, but nothing else taken, as far as I can recall from the shipping manifests. Not even the white gold.'

'Maybe the beasts have no use for it,' Nish said.

163

'I wouldn't advise you to think of them as beasts. They're as smart as you or I. We'll take back what we can and send a salvage party for the rest. Any sign of Tiaan?' he said to Ell-Lin, who was standing up on the bank, well away from the gruesome scene.

'None here, surr.'

'Very well. Come down. Take what you can.'

They loaded up and began the trek, arriving at the manufactory without incident after dark. News of the attack had already reached them. Tiaan had not been seen.

'She was poorly dressed,' said Nish, consulting the inventory of clothing the matron had given him. 'Her feet were wrapped in rags. She's probably dead by now.'

'Neither you nor I can afford to think so,' said Gi-Had. 'I'll make up a search party and you'll be on it.'

Nish knew better than to complain, though his back was crucifying him. 'In that case I'll need – ' he began.

'You won't be leading it,' Gi-Had said coldly. 'Don't imagine I'll be giving you responsibility anytime soon. Gryste!' he bellowed.

The foreman came running. Within minutes a salvage party and a search party had been formed and sent out. They searched the road all night with blazing torches, and on into the following morning, but found nothing.

Returning bone weary and in great pain around noon, Nish looked up to see Querist Fyn-Mah standing by the great front doors, scowling fiercely at him.

FIFTEEN

Nish gaped at her. 'How . . . how did you get here?' As far as he knew there was only one road from Tiksi to here, and he'd been on it.

'I was already in the mountains. *Hunting!*' The word tolled like an execution bell. 'Did you find her?'

'Not a trace!'

Fyn-Mah caught him by the arm. He resisted momentarily, though only long enough to think better of it. She could be the means of his rehabilitation, or destruction. He went with her to the wall where it was sheltered from the driving snow, and from being overheard.

'Bloody damn fool!' she said in a low voice. 'What were you thinking, to do such a thing?'

'I was . . . Irisis said . . . I didn't . . !' Nish could think of nothing to say.

'Do you realise what you've done?' she hissed. 'Tiaan had just made a desperately needed breakthrough. We were eagerly awaiting her thoughts on the bigger problem . . .'

'What bigger problem?'

'You don't even know?' she exclaimed. 'The failure of the field at Minnien. Fifty clankers were destroyed in a few hours.'

'I had no idea.' The implications were horrifyingly clear.

'We've always thought Tiaan had potential, though only

recently has she begun to show it. In a few days she solved two controller problems. Two, artificer! She may have helped us with the third had she not been *conspired against*. Was that malice, or treachery of the highest order? Is that why the lyrinx are all around?'

'All around?' he gasped.

'The mountains are full of them. We're losing the war, Cryl-Nish. If more fields fail, *we're finished.*'

'I didn't know.' He was stricken with horror at his folly. 'I just didn't know. What is my father going to say?'

'I'd be more worried about what he will *do*. And all this for the sake of your – ' She broke off, jerking her knee up towards his groin.

He flinched. She let her knee fall again.

'I don't know what you're alluding to,' Nish lied.

The knee came up again, so fast that he had no chance of avoiding it, crushing his testicles. Pain shrieked through him as the blow toppled him backwards onto the frozen ground.

She stood over him, looking down. 'You dare lie to a querist? Clearly the whipping has taught you nothing, *boy*!

'Now you listen! Are you stupid as well as a liar? I had not thought it. We have special ways of finding out the truth. I've been here since yesterday morning and in that time I've questioned two hundred people. I know *everything*! Surely you realise that? I know you boasted about your family connections as you crudely tried to seduce Tiaan, and then threatened her. I know how Irisis seduced you, and every jerk and thrust of your little fornications.' Her voice rose higher. 'I know all about her lies, how you conspired to cover them up, and your betrayal of your prober's position. I suspect Irisis of being behind the sabotages and the poisoning of Tiaan. I suspect you connived at the death of Apothek Mul-Lym, Cryl-Nish, even if you did not actually hold the flask to his lips. If that turns out to be true *nothing* can save either of you.'

'No,' he cried. 'I don't know anything about *that.*'

She fixed him with her dark eyes, saying nothing. It was worse than her interrogation.

'I've been a fool,' he whispered. It was the only thing he could think of to say. 'An utter fool. I deserve the front-lines.' He hoped the admission would gain him some credit.

'You'll probably get them. Your father will be bitterly hurt by this stupidity, Cryl-Nish. If it is stupidity, and not collaborating with the enemy.'

'I would never do that, I swear it!'

'I'll leave that to your father. He can tell a liar just by looking at him.' She sighed. 'He had such hopes for you.'

'Then why did he send me to this awful place?'

'A test. Not such a hard one, for someone expected to rise high. But you failed, and for the crudest of reasons.'

'What can I do?' he whispered. Nish was not a coward; nor was he excessively brave. The thought of the front-lines was a nightmare.

'There's only one thing can save you, *if anything can*. Find Tiaan and bring her back unharmed.'

'She's probably dead,' he said despairingly.

'Then so are you!'

'How will I find her?' he said to himself.

'A true prober would not ask. And you won't solve it on your back!'

He got up, holding his bruised organs. After wandering through the manufactory he ended up near the artisans' workshops. Irisis was glowering at her bench. He ducked away. If she had murdered Mul-Lym the apothek, as seemed probable, he wanted no further contact with her.

Trudging through the dormitories, lost in his miserable thoughts, Nish noticed that he was passing the door of Tiaan's room. He'd never seen inside. He lifted the latch. The room was tiny, considerably smaller than Irisis's. Tiaan probably had not cared.

All it contained was a narrow bed, a chair, table and lamp. A rod set in the wall at both ends would have served for hanging clothes, while a small chest sat at the end of the bed, though it was empty. All trace of Tiaan was gone. Not surprising; she had been taken to the breeding factory more than two weeks ago. What had happened to her possessions?

He found nothing in her work cubicle and her fellow workers did not know either. Nish went to the ratifier's office, where the manufactory account books were kept. She was out, but her assistant, a slender, beautiful young clerk with red lips and a roving eye, smiled at him. Nish gave him the thinnest smile in return. He did not want to antagonise the fellow, nor encourage him.

'Hello, I'm Wickie. How may I help you?' Wickie stood up, holding out his hand.

Nish shook it – a rather firm hand for a clerk – but had trouble disengaging himself afterwards. Wickie stood too close and it made him uncomfortable.

'I'm on business for the querist,' he said sharply.

Wickie stepped smartly backwards. 'Oh!'

'What happened to Artisan Tiaan's possessions?'

'I don't know, but it'll be in the book.' Wickie turned the pages of a ledger as long as his arm. 'Here we are. Old Joeyn the miner came for them a few days back.' He frowned. 'Must have been when I was at lunch. It's all written up and he's signed for them. See here – and the ratifier herself has initialled it.'

Nish spun the ledger around and checked the entry. 'Thank you very much.' He turned to go.

'Cryl-Nish?' said Wickie softly.

'Yes?'

'Your poor back must be troubling you. If you should need someone to rub salve into it . . .'

'Thank you! It's healing well, but if it did need attention, I'd go to the healer.'

'Ah!' said Wickie.

Nish knew Joeyn, though not well. The old man had visited Tiaan twice down in Tiksi. She might be at his cottage now, waiting for the weather to improve.

He ran for the village. The day remained windy and cold, but by the time he reached the lookout perspiration was stinging his back. The last part of the steep path was icy. Nish crept towards Joeyn's hut and hid behind a tree, watching the door. He could not see anything; the fence blocked his view.

He eased through the gate and onto the veranda but heard nothing.

Pulling up the latch, he thrust the door open. The cottage was empty. The bed had been made, the table cleared. There were two plates on the hearth, two mugs, two spoons. A note on a slate by the door said *Thank you, Joe.* The writing could have been anyone's.

Nish scouted around the house for prints. There were none – the wind had scoured the loose snow away, exposing a crust from the last thaw. If Tiaan had been here, where could she have gone? He continued in a widening spiral that took him into the forest. There he found tracks leading to a tree, back toward the hut, and uphill in the direction of the mine and manufactory.

The tracks were the size of his own, but shallower and with a short stride. Someone light, and limping – one print seemed to favour the heel. Tiaan surely. Was she going to the mine or the manufactory? Nish followed her through the forest, several times losing the prints but always finding them again in the direction of the mine. As it was getting dark he emerged in the cleared area. There were no tracks on the crusted surface but she seemed to be heading toward the main adit.

At the entrance he stopped. Nish had never been down the mine. Moreover, he'd had, from birth, a tremendous fear of confined spaces. As a child, his sister and brothers had tormented him by bundling him up in the bedclothes. As soon as they closed over his head, panic had made him lash out.

Edging forward, he came to the recess occupied by Lex, the rotund day guard, who was shrugging into his coat.

'Hello,' Nish said tentatively, 'I'm Cryl-Nish Hlar . . .'

'I know!' Lex growled. 'Were it up to me, would have been a hundred lashes, not twenty! What do you want?'

Evidently more people liked Tiaan than he'd thought. 'I'm looking for Artisan Tiaan.'

Lex raised a gnarled fist. 'She's down in the . . . town, *thanks to you.*'

'She's escaped from the breeding factory!'

'Has she now?' Lex grinned from ear to ear. 'Glad I am to hear of it.'

'She came this way. In the last few hours, I think.'

'Haven't seen her,' said Lex. 'And if I had, I wouldn't tell you, you poxy little prick! Now get out of my way. I'm going home.'

Nish stood his ground, though it took an effort. 'I'm here in the service of the querist,' he said in a mild voice. No one would dare make that claim without authorisation. 'And if you won't cooperate . . .' There was no need to complete the threat.

'That's different,' Lex said hastily. 'I'll help Fyn-Mah in whatever way I can. I haven't seen Tiaan, though.'

'What about Joeyn?'

Lex looked up at the large sheet of slate at the back of his recess, on which were noted the miners' names, their hours, where they were working and the tally of ore each had produced. 'He came in at dawn.'

'And he's working on the fifth level.' Nish read it off the slate.

'Been there for months. Likes it by himself.'

Nish considered. 'If you were inside, working, could she have crept by without you noticing?'

'Could have, though I doubt it.'

'Where would she have gone?'

'Along to the bucket lifts. It's the only way down to the levels from here.'

Nish followed him to the great wheels, and every step into the darkness was a further descent into his nightmare. He had to force himself to go on. The roof seemed to be quivering above him, alive and malicious, aching to bury him.

Examining the lifts, Nish said, 'These would make rather a racket. Did you hear anything earlier on?'

'They go all the time. There's ninety miners in here. Usually it's someone going from one level to another. Or the ore buckets coming up.'

'But they're much heavier. And you'd hear the ore falling onto the pile.'

'True,' said Lex. 'Come to think of it, I did hear the miners' lift going an hour ago. It went all the way but no one came out.'

'It must have been her going down!' Nish exclaimed.

'Could have been,' Lex said grudgingly. 'Or someone else.'

'You've got to take me down. At once!'

'Not allowed,' said Lex. 'Got no miner's ticket.'

'I'm ordering you in the querist's name.'

Lex was unmoved. 'Can't do it, even on her authority.'

'Then find someone who can!' Nish snapped.

'Should've been two hundred lashes,' Lex said to his face. 'Obnoxious little turd!' Nonetheless, he ambled over to a board beside the lift and pulled a rope twice, then twice more. A bell rang faintly in the depths. Before too long the upper bell replied and the rope began to move. A basket appeared, and in it a small wizened figure, lethargically winding the handle.

He stopped below the floor with a jerk that made the basket wobble on the cable. 'Wassamatta?'

'Flyn, Artificer Nish-Nash needs to be taken down to the fifth level. He's looking for Joe and Tiaan.'

Nish ground his teeth. He hated that nickname more than anything.

'Is he now?' Flyn made a hawking sound in his throat and spat, the gob landing next to Nish's boot. 'Ain't seen 'em. Take him down to the ninth level, if you like.'

'What's on the ninth level?' Nish asked nervously.

'Water, mostly,' said Lex. 'He's on the querist's business, Flyn.'

The man's face closed, the hostility submerged. 'What about my quota?' he said in a nasal whine.

'I'm sure you'll get a credit from Gi-Had,' Nish said. He did not know if that was true, and did not care either. 'Shall we go?'

'Shall we go?' Flyn mimicked in a sing-song voice. 'Jump in then.'

Nish blanched. The basket was nearly a span below him, and the opening looked tiny compared to the yawning hole of the shaft. If he missed . . . Not even to save face could he do it.

'Bring it up,' he said, and the quaver in his voice made Flyn snigger. The miner exchanged glances with Lex, who was also grinning. Damn them both, if he ever had power over them. 'Come on. All the way!'

Lex fiddled with a lever as Flyn wound the bucket to the surface. Nish climbed in, hanging grimly onto the rope. 'Hurry up!' he snarled to conceal his unease. 'The querist's business can't wait.'

Flyn winked at Lex, very obviously, then lifted one hand, which held a miner's hammer. He swung it hard and low. Nish flinched, thinking the man was trying to cripple him, but the head whizzed by, knocking the brake right off. The bucket dropped, leaving Nish's stomach halfway up his throat.

He choked, drew a deep breath, and screamed his heart out. In the darkness he could hear Flyn's roars of laughter.

They flashed past lighted openings, one after another, going faster and faster. Nish was steeling himself for the shattering finale when the basket slowed. The fourth level went by, they slowed rapidly and drifted to a stop directly opposite the fifth level. Lex had put the brake on, up top. Nish had been taken in by a trick to terrorise apprentices and unwanted visitors.

A lighted lantern stood in the entrance. Nish gave Flyn a look of purest hatred, which was returned with bland indifference. Miners were a rebellious lot, contemptuous of any authority but their own. If I'm ever perquisitor, he thought, I'll put the curb on them.

Small chance of that. There was a long way to go to avoid the army, much less be reinstated as a lowly prober. Putting his dreams of power and revenge aside, Nish tried to conquer his claustrophobia and failed miserably. 'Where can we find Joeyn?'

Taking up the lantern, Flyn stumped off down the tunnel. He was even shorter than Nish. Most of the miners were small, wiry and old. Nish followed, shuddering at the weight of rock above.

Joeyn was not at the place he usually worked, nor in any of the other tunnels Flyn knew about. Nish studied the crystals in their veins and cavities, wondering how the old miner knew which ones to collect. They all looked the same to him.

They ended up searching the entire fifth level, which took many hours and several refillings of Flyn's lantern. There was no trace of Joeyn or Tiaan. Nish could tell that his guide was worried by the time they got back in the basket. Flyn rang the bell and wound them up to the main level.

Even after all this time, Nish was nowhere near conquering his claustrophobia, and it was with the greatest relief that he saw the wheel come into view, and the lighted entrance to the mine. It was morning. They'd searched all night.

A crowd near the entrance headed toward him as the basket stopped.

'No sign of him,' Flyn called.

'Nor in the higher levels,' a young miner said quietly. 'We'd better go down to six.'

Nish climbed onto the edge of the basket, caught his foot, and almost went head first down the shaft. A big man dragged him to safety. Nish's knees would no longer hold him up.

A dozen pairs of boots came toward him, then stopped. He looked up. The querist was there, Overseer Gi-Had, and many others he recognised. They parted and a short, round man came through. Nish's heart almost stopped. How could he have gotten here so quickly? He must have travelled night and day for two weeks.

'Get up!' said Perquisitor Jal-Nish, his father. His voice sounded like the ore-grinding mill in the manufactory.

Nish levered himself to his feet and stood before his father. Jal-Nish was no more than forty, a good-looking man, for all that he had short legs like hams and a belly as round as a ball. He was taller than Nish, the one thing his son could never forgive him for. The perquisitor had a proud, arching nose; a neatly trimmed beard thrust perkily forward from his chin. His dark hair was thick and his eyes had a twinkle for everyone except those he interrogated. He could be a charming man when things were going well, though he had a ruthless streak.

There was no twinkle as he examined his son. No allowances would be made, Nish knew. His father was not that kind of man.

'Well?' said Jal-Nish.

'We've searched the entire fifth level. There's not a trace of her.'

'What about her friend?'

'No sign of Joeyn either.'

Jal-Nish's wide mouth curved down in a bloodless slash. 'You moron, Nish! I'm going to be scrutator one day, and not even your stupidity will stand in my way. It's the front-line for you, son!'

SIXTEEN

Nish was interrogated by Jal-Nish and Fyn-Mah. It was like being whipped all over again, only worse. His father was coldly angry, Fyn-Mah reserved and efficient. Once, though, Nish noticed her staring out the window, clearly thinking about something else. She looked sad. What was it about her?

Later he was questioned together with Irisis, which he found even less comfortable. Twice she lied to his father with a completely straight face, then glared at Nish as if daring him to betray her. Irisis did not seem to care. It was as if she had a death wish.

She had admitted to harassing Tiaan, including planting the page from her journal and stealing her method of blocking the aura of controllers. Irisis flatly denied any of the other crimes with which she had been charged. Was she innocent, or would she, as before, only admit to a crime once it was proven against her? Nish rather suspected that she was guilty, and under interrogation he was forced to reveal that he doubted her. Irisis did not react to that either.

As the interrogation went on, Jal-Nish grew more and more frustrated. 'She must be the spy,' Nish overheard him whisper to Fyn-Mah during a break in the proceedings. 'I've a good mind to put her in the Irons, to be sure.'

He meant a form of torture so hideous that it was rarely used even on the most recalcitrant of prisoners. Nish was shocked. If it came to that, he could not stand by.

'I wouldn't advise it, unless you're *certain* she's guilty,' said Fyn-Mah. 'Her mother is an old friend of the scrutator.'

'No, no,' Jal-Nish said hurriedly. 'We won't go down *that* path.'

He kept Nish and Irisis up all night, then sent them to the mine to help with the search. Nish, staggering along behind Fyn in a lather of pain and claustrophobia, did not even think of escaping. One fate worse than the front-line, in this world where everyone had their place, was to become an outlaw with no hope of rehabilitation.

They went through the mine down to the eighth level, until Nish, who had not slept for days, was like the walking dead. Joeyn's body was found but not recovered, for the attempt brought down the rest of the roof, burying him, two miners and the fabulous vein of crystals under twenty wagonloads of rock.

Finding no trace of Tiaan, they began to question whether she had ever been in the mine. Two afternoons after Nish began it, the search was called off. The mine had to get back into production and every spare hand was needed to bolster the defences of the manufactory.

Nish humped stone until dark, when he had another blistering interview with his father.

'You've blackened me in the scrutator's eyes, boy!' Jal-Nish growled. 'I can't forgive that.'

'What are you going to tell my mother?' It was Nish's only trump.

The perquisitor, who had been pacing vigorously, stopped dead. The one thing he feared more than the scrutator's wrath was the fury of his spouse.

'Please give me another chance, father.'

'You've disgraced the family,' Jal-Nish said coldly. 'In ordinary times I might have been lenient but this time I can't, not even for your mother. You've turned Tiaan's triumph into a disaster. If I let you off, the scrutator will think I'm as big a knave as you are, and where will we be then? I know Ranii will agree with me on this.' He resumed his pacing, more anxiously than before.

Nish tried again but his father proved immovable. As soon as the weather cleared up enough to travel, Nish was to take ship to the front-lines, two hundred leagues north. There, in the unlikely event that he was not killed and eaten straight away, he would have an opportunity to rehabilitate himself.

Fortunately the weather showed no sign of abating its autumnal fury. Storms alternately lashed them with sleet, freezing rain, wet snow and frigid mist. For once Nish was grateful for it. He was lying awake on his pallet the following morning, listening to the wind rattle the roof slates as he waited for the gong to get up, when the whole wall shook. A second later there came a dull boom.

Earth tremblers were not uncommon here, and sometimes dangerous. Nish flew out of bed, scrambled into his boots and tore open the door. 'What was that?' he yelled to the guard standing outside.

'I don't – '

Another great smashing thud shook the manufactory. 'That's not an earth trembler,' Nish shouted. 'Something's attacking the front gate. Quickly, man, to your post!'

The guard, well drilled as was everyone in the manufactory, ran for the gate. Nish, whose station was up on the wall, took a shortcut through the women's dormitory, where scantily clad women (and occasional lovers) were falling over each other in their urgency to get dressed. The scene was much the same in the men's sleeping hall.

'Sleepers, wake!' he roared. 'The enemy is at the gates. Quick, quick!'

He continued up the other end, banging a stick on the doors of the workers important enough to have their own rooms. It amused him to see the condition of those who stumbled out, including his father.

Naked, still dazed from sleep, Jal-Nish was in no way the commanding figure he cut in his clothes. His belly quivered, and his lip. He kicked the door closed, though not before Nish saw Wickie, the young clerk from the bursar's office, standing mouth agape.

Nish was shocked, to say nothing of disgusted. His own

177

father! But there was no time for that now. Throwing the door open again he shouted, 'The gates are attacked, perquisitor!' deliberately using the title rather than his father's name. A spasm warped Jal-Nish's face, then Nish ran on.

Fyn-Mah hurried by, shepherding a gaggle of little children to safety. For the first time, her reserve had broken – she looked to be in pain.

A fascinating character study, had Nish the time to dwell on it, the way people dealt with the shock. Overseer Gi-Had looked as if he'd had to force courage on himself, yet he came running. There was no sign of Foreman Gryste at all, and two artificers, big men well known for their pride and their boasting, had to be shamed from their rooms.

Not so Irisis. Her door flew open as he reached it. She had a long knife in her hand, almost the length of a short sword, but wore only a pair of knee-length trousers. 'The enemy, you say?'

'At the gates.'

'Where's my blasted shirt?' She looked around for it, then spat, 'Ah, damn it,' and ran out, her magnificent breasts bare.

Nish followed, suspecting she had done it deliberately. With her hair streaming out, and her scarred back, she looked just like the paintings of Myssu, a great revolutionary hero of old.

They ran up the steps onto the wall. Hastily lit torches guttered in the wind. It was still dark outside. The light showed only mist and shadows.

The wall shook again, then a missile smashed one side of the great gate. Nish looked down to see a boulder, hurled by some mighty catapult, crack the steps before rolling onto the road.

'What is it?' he shouted to the nearest guard. Before the fellow could answer a smaller missile struck him in the chest, carrying him backwards over the edge to his death.

Irisis came sprinting along the wall, hair flying. 'It's lyrinx!' she screamed, ducked past him and raced to the watch-tower above the left gate, snatching a torch on the way. Several rocks followed her path though none went near. Flying up the steps, she hurled the torch high and straight, through the opening of the watchlight.

Tar-soaked straw, placed there for the purpose, burst into flames, illuminating the area between the gate and the forest, though leaving the defenders on the wall in shadow. Nish knocked down the other torch and ran up to the watch-tower, where Irisis was sighting a crossbow toward the forest. She fired. There came a single, truncated cry.

Another boulder hurtled out of the darkness, tearing the broken gate off its hinges. Instantly it was charged by three lyrinx and a violent skirmish took place on the steps.

Irisis stood barefoot in a drift of snow, calmly reloading the crossbow. She seemed oblivious to the cold, though her skin was purple. 'Damn you!' she screamed. The crossbow had jammed.

Nish quickly freed it, his artificer's skills proving some use after all, and handed it back.

Irisis leaned over the wall, sighted straight down, held the position and fired. A pulpy thud made her grunt with satisfaction. 'Got you!' She ducked out of the line of fire, looking around for more bolts.

Nish was struck by the change in her. He had never seen Irisis look so alive. He glanced over the side. Her target lay still, a bloody smear on the top of its crested skull. How could she be a traitor? It made no sense.

The other two lyrinx were at the gate. Nish ran to a rock pile, grabbed one as big as he could lift, sighted and dropped it. It missed, shattering on the steps. He hurled another, which struck an attacker on its plated shoulder. The lyrinx lurched around, shaking an arm which looked to be dislocated, then crashed through the gate into the manufactory. Screams and roars marked its passage.

Nish aimed another missile, but as he let it fall the second lyrinx hurled something up at him with a whip-like underarm flick. There came a blinding pain in the throat; the blow punched him onto his back. He cracked his head on the rock pile and sank into a daze where all he could feel was the agony in his neck, a creeping cold and the blood running out of him.

Shortly he was picked up and carried down. Irisis was one of the bearers, her breasts swaying above his face. Whoever had his feet was lost in fog that rose with every step.

He came to on a table in the refectory with a dozen people staring at him. One was his father, and his face bore a look of terror such as Nish had not seen before. Maybe Jal-Nish cared about him after all.

Beside him loomed the healer Tul-Kin, and Nish was not pleased to see *him*. Up close, the man's nose and cheeks were a mass of broken veins, while his breath reeked of the home-made rhubarb brandy that the miners distilled in the village. The manufactory was dry – only weak beer allowed – but the healer was permitted brandy for use in his surgery. An unfortunate exception.

'Come on, man!' cried Jal-Nish. 'Get the dart out and sew him up before he bleeds to death.'

Tul-Kin wrung his plump hands. 'I dursn't. It's lying between the arteries and bladed on three edges. One slip and he's dead.'

'Drunken fool,' roared Jal-Nish. 'Where the devil is Gi-Had?'

'Gone after the enemy, surr,' Nish heard someone say. 'One of the beasts has got into the offices.' Nish felt dizzy, though his mind was clear. He was going to die because the healer lacked the courage to try to save him.

'Is this wretch the only healer you have?' the perquisitor persisted.

'There's old Ruzia, surr,' said the unknown voice, 'but she's blind and has the shakes something severe. We also had Mul-Lym the apothek. He was a good hand with the bone saw, in emergencies, but . . .'

'But the damn fool is dead,' Jal-Nish grated. 'Killed himself, if someone else didn't do it for him.' He scowled down at his son. 'Could be a poetic kind of justice, I suppose.'

Nish could see the irony too, but he did not appreciate it.

A slap, a curse and Irisis's voice raged, 'Keep your hands to yourself or I'll spill your brains on the floor. Get out of my way.' The crowd parted before her. She had put on an undershirt, a clinging article that distracted the eye.

'What do you think you're doing?' screamed Jal-Nish.

'Saving your worthless son's life,' she replied softly. 'Or if not, putting him out of his suffering.' She had a piece of copper tubing in one hand, a small artisan's hammer in the other.

'Be damned! Tul-Kin, get back here!'

Tul-Kin was retrieved from the corner, gulping from a flask. When they took it away his arm twitched so hard he could not hold the knife they pressed upon him.

'Well?' said Irisis with magnificent arrogance.

Jal-Nish closed his eyes, opened them and wiped away a tear. 'He's going to die, isn't he?'

'At the rate he's losing blood,' said one of the nurses, 'I'd give him an hour.'

The perquisitor waved a hand. 'I don't suppose you can do any worse.'

Irisis pushed through, leaned over Nish and gauged the wound. 'The shard is a length of metal about as long as a small knife blade. It's triangular in cross-section and each edge is razor sharp. It's gone through the muscle of his neck. The point has come out the back, next to the spine. To pull it out, or push it through, risks cutting the vein, in which case he will die in a minute.'

She took the piece of copper tube, checked that the diameter was large enough, then wiggled it into the slit in Nish's neck. He screamed and fainted. 'Just as well,' Irisis muttered, and eased the tubing over the end of the shard. As she pushed, there came a gentle sucking sound. Blood began to drip from the tube.

Sweat was pouring down her face. There were a dozen people around the table but no one said a word. The entire room seemed to be holding its breath.

Irisis gently worked the tube back and forth, as if trying to get it over a snag in the metal. The least pressure and one of the blades would go through a vein. She eased the tube out, wiped the blood on her shirt, cleaned her fingers the same way, tilted the tube and slid it back in. This time it kept going.

'Lift his head!' she said harshly.

Jal-Nish did so. He looked stricken.

She moved his hand down to support Nish's neck. 'Hold him firmly.'

Taking a small cap from her pocket, she screwed it on the end of the tube. Irisis took up her hammer and, with a single sharp blow that drew a gasp from the watchers, drove the tube all the way in. Nish woke, screamed and convulsed.

'Hold him!' she roared, 'or we'll lose him.'

The watchers scurried to take hold of Nish. Irisis took a pair of pincers from her pocket, gripped the end of the tube protruding from the back of his neck and drew out tube and shard in a single clean movement. Nish shrieked.

Pent-up blood poured out, front and back. They waited for the telltale spurt from a severed artery.

'What's happening?' wailed Nish. 'I'm going to die, aren't I?'

Irisis stood back, panting. Her shirt and arms were coated with blood. Blood dribbled from the end of the tube. She was staring at his throat.

'What . . .?' said Nish.

'Shut up, Nish! You're not going to die, more's the damn pity.' Irisis looked around at the crowd. 'Can anyone sew?' The faces looked blank. 'Of course you can't, morons! Get me the healer's bag and bottle.'

Someone scurried off, returning with the items. Irisis found a needle and thread and calmly sewed up Nish's neck, then doused the wounds with brandy.

Finally she tossed needle, thread and flask onto the table, took up her tools and, without another glance, went back to her room.

Nish's mouth was dry, his head throbbed and his neck was so unbearably painful that he could not move his head. He had vague memories of someone sitting by the bed, stroking his brow, but only Irisis was there now.

'You saved my life,' he said, reaching for her hand.

'Don't think for a minute it's because I care for you, Little Nish-Nash,' she said in a gritty voice.

'Then why?'

'For your father's favour, of course! It was that or the breeding factory.'

'Oh!' He missed the strange look in her eye, being unable to turn his head. 'But if you'd killed me . . .'

'It was worth the gamble. I like gambling, especially when things can't get any worse.'

'Then hadn't you better go for your reward?' He put as much sarcasm into it as his awful neck would let him. 'That's exactly what I expected of you, after all.'

She shrugged it off. 'I've some broth. Wouldn't want you to die and spoil everything.'

'Of course not!'

She dipped the spoon, put it to his lips. 'Open up!'

He did so and found the broth delicious, nothing like the dishwater he'd expected from the cookhouse. Smacking his lips he said, 'That's good!'

'Of course it is. I made it myself. Specially.'

She fed him the rest, then went out without further word. Nish lay back, feeling the blood pounding in his ears. The small exertion had exhausted him.

Irisis was at her bench fitting together a controller when the door banged open and Jal-Nish came hurrying in. He hurried everywhere, though with his portly figure it made him look faintly ridiculous.

'Yes?' she said imperiously, afraid of what he could do to her. She had spent most of her life afraid, and concealing it. A word from the perquisitor and she could be any kind of drudge or slave he cared to name. Her pride would not allow that.

'I've come to thank you for saving my worthless son.'

'Worthless? I suppose so. He has certain talents.' She gave a mocking, pointed leer.

'I don't want to know,' he said hastily.

'I bet you *do*. I know all about *your* nocturnal activities.' She tossed back her yellow hair. 'Tell me my fate. Whatever it is, I would know it right away.'

He walked up and down, casting her sideways glances as if he did not know what to make of her.

'There's more to you than reports indicate.'

'What *does* Fyn-Mah say about me? Am I guilty of treachery, even murder, as my one-time lover believes?'

'There is now . . . room for doubt,' he said.

'Oh?'

'It's hard to imagine a traitor killing one of the enemy so brilliantly.'

'What did the lyrinx come for?'

'Just a wandering band.' Jal-Nish was a little too offhand. 'Who knows why they go where they do?'

'I heard that one beast fought its way into Gi-Had's office before it was killed. Sounds like they came with a purpose.'

He hesitated. 'It took a piece of evidence . . .'

'Are you saying Gi-Had is the traitor?'

'Don't be absurd. The lyrinx had Artisan Tiaan's broken pliance. We think it contains evidence of the traitor's identity, which seems to clear you of that particular charge.'

'But not the others?'

'You have admitted to serious crimes, and Fyn-Mah tells me – '

'Yes?' She clenched her fingers under the bench, out of sight.

'That you're vain, proud and have an overly high opinion of yourself. But it's a front you've been putting on all your life, to protect yourself from an abusive mother, an incompetent father and a family desperately trying to relive its past glory through you. That you're quite lacking in morals and would do anything to advance yourself and bring your rivals down. That you're bold, even foolhardy, yet dogged in pursuit of your ultimate goal. That you have a desperate craving for recognition . . .'

She could never argue, for that would lose face in her own eyes. 'All true!' She feigned boredom. 'I am what I am. Rather, what circumstances and my own wit have made me.'

'Indeed, and that is why I am here. I have a little job for you, one by which you may, just possibly, redeem yourself.'

'A job?'

'Of a sort.' He hesitated, then with swift strides went to the door, checked outside and closed it tight. Jal-Nish drew up a stool and sat down before her. 'Back in my own realm, certain, er . . . experimental procedures have been done in . . . how shall I call it in this tongue? *Farsensing*, or perhaps *tracking*.'

'What, people?'

'Indirectly. Really, it's tracking the use of power – the Secret Art.'

'I have no talent for the Secret Art.'

'I've brought with me a natural adept who can sense when power is used; and *where*! I hope she can help with a particular problem.'

'The failure of the field at Minnien,' Irisis guessed.

'Indeed. We don't know why it happened, or how. Is the field gone forever or will it suddenly come back?'

'Did we drain it dry,' said Irisis, 'or did the enemy learn to cut it off?'

'Precisely. You have a quick wit, artisan.'

She yawned, deliberately.

'We've had scores of crafters and mancers working on the problem but thus far they have failed,' said Jal-Nish.

'We need to see inside the node,' said Irisis.

He looked startled but recovered quickly. 'My thoughts exactly. And that's what I hope to do with my adept – the *seeker*.'

'Why are you telling me this?'

'The seeker's talent is not enough, for it is bound up with fatal weaknesses.'

'I have no idea what you're talking about.'

'I've not put it clearly. Come with me.'

She followed him through the manufactory, which was full of idling workers. So soon after the attack, no one could concentrate on their work. They passed by the overseer's door, which had been smashed to pieces, walked around the corner and down a long corridor where Jal-Nish stopped at a closed door. He took up a lantern, lit it, shuttered it nearly all the way and went in. She followed him. He pulled the door closed. The light fell on a small figure hunched up in the corner. It put its hands over its face, making a mewling noise.

'Ullii,' Jal-Nish said softly, 'this is Artisan Irisis. Please say hello.'

The figure writhed and then slowly unfolded. At first Irisis thought the seeker was a child, but when Ullii stood up, she turned out to be a young woman, well formed but small, with little hands and tiny, slender feet. She was naked, her clothes scattered across the floor as if she'd hurled them away. Everything about her was pale to the point of colourlessness. Her hair was so transparent that it could have been drawn from strands of water. Her eyelashes and brows were the same. Her skin had no colour at all, so that, even in this light, every blood vessel showed, and between them the pinkness of her flesh.

Ullii turned away from the light, dim though it was. Irisis wondered if she had some terrible deformity, but Jal-Nish faced the lantern into the corner and Ullii looked back. She appeared perfectly normal except for enormous eyes with no colour or visible structure. Was she a moron-savant?

'It hurts,' said Ullii in a voice as colourless as her hair. The light *had* hurt her though, for tears were dripping from her lower lashes.

'Say hello, Ullii,' said Jal-Nish.

'Hello, Irisis,' Ullii said in a voice that now reflected Jal-Nish's accent. She stared straight through Irisis as if she was not there at all. Or as if she herself was blind.

'What do you see, Ullii?' Jal-Nish spoke more sharply than he had intended.

She jerked as though his voice had hurt her, then began to curl up. 'Sorry,' he whispered soothingly. 'Don't be afraid, Ullii. No one's going to hurt you *ever again*. Tell Irisis what you see.'

It was no use. The young woman curled into a ball with her head tucked right under. Jal-Nish shrugged, indicated the door and took up the lantern.

'What's the matter with her?' Irisis said.

Closing the door, Jal-Nish led Irisis down the corridor. 'She's a strange little thing. All her senses are so acute that she can't exist in our world. She's practically blind in light, though she can see well enough in the dark. Noise is like physical pain to her –

186

a shout or a cry, everyday sounds to us, are to her like being trapped inside a tank with a banshee. Touch is just as bad – she cannot bear to wear clothes. Even silk she finds irritating. She is frightened of everything and everyone.'

'I wonder she was not put out of her misery long ago,' said Irisis. 'I would have, were she mine. She doesn't seem all there.'

'What a cold woman you are!' said Jal-Nish. 'She's not an idiot; just overwhelmed.'

Irisis suppressed her impatience, waiting for him to get to the point.

'Ullii sees things. In her mind,' he said at last.

'So do I.'

'You don't see the kinds of things *she* does. Let's try again. And keep your voice down.'

It was *you* who upset her last time, Irisis thought.

They went back in. 'Ullii, this is Artisan Irisis. Please say hello.'

She had unfolded. Turning toward Irisis, Ullii said, 'Hello, Irisis,' again mimicking the perquisitor's voice. 'I remember you from before.'

'Hello, Ullii,' Irisis said as quietly as she could. 'Tell me what you see.'

She stood up, staring at the air above Irisis's head. 'I see shapes not far away. They're all dark but they have crystals at their heart. Very weak crystals!' she said dismissively, now imitating Irisis's rather strident tones. Irisis wondered at the mimicry. Was it an attempt to deflect the words away from herself?

'Your controllers!' Jal-Nish said.

'I'd already worked that out!' Irisis hissed, though she had not.

Ullii started, began to curl up, then slowly unfolded again, like a ballet dancer imitating a flower. There was grace in her movements such as Irisis had never seen before. Her curiosity was aroused.

'I see other shapes, further away,' said Ullii. 'Some strong. No one is using them.'

187

The crystals in the mine? Irisis wondered.

'Go on,' said Jal-Nish 'Do you see anything else?'

She turned around, stiffened, and her owl eyes went wide. 'I see clawers, many of them. Hunting, hunting! Searching. Aaah!' She began to whimper. 'They're coming to eat me up! They're coming! They're coming!'

Irisis, uncharacteristically moved, would have thrown her arms about the young woman. Jal-Nish caught her sleeve, shook his head, and indicated the door. 'Leave her! She can't bear to be touched.'

Ullii was already curling up. They withdrew, this time for longer than before, and when they went back she took much coaxing before they could communicate with her at all.

The 'clawers', lyrinx presumably, were not far away. Ullii would say no more about them. She did not see them clearly, not in the way that she seemed to see the crystals.

'I don't like this,' said Jal-Nish under his breath. 'We can't withstand a major attack. What are so many doing, so near?'

Ullii's hearing must have been incredibly acute for she said, 'Hunting her!' now mimicking his voice.

'Hunting whom, Ullii?'

'The girl.'

'Which girl?'

'The girl with the bright crystal.'

'Who is she?' breathed Jal-Nish.

'Her crystal is as bright as the moon,' said Ullii.

'Tiaan!' Irisis cried, then quickly lowered her voice. 'Is that who they're hunting? Can she still be alive?'

'I don't know her name,' replied Ullii, staring through the ceiling. 'I can't see her clearly, only the crystal. But when she touches it, it blazes like a shooting star.'

'Where is she?' hissed Jal-Nish. 'Quick, girl. Which way?'

'This way.' Ullii pointed towards the door. 'Or maybe that way.' Down through the floor. 'All ways are the same.' Her eyes closed; she began to rock back and forth. 'Same, same, same, same, same, same, same, same, same, same, same, same, same, same . . .'

Jal-Nish led Irisis out and closed the door. 'Once she goes into that state it can be hours before she's any good. We'll come back later. I'll send out more search parties, in case it is Tiaan.'

'There's another possibility,' said Irisis.

'Oh?'

'That Ullii did not see her at all. She may just be parroting what she thinks we want to hear.'

'I was careful not to talk about it in front of her.'

'The whole manufactory has been talking about Tiaan. With Ullii's hearing she might have picked up what was said at the other end of the corridor.'

'Perhaps, but she's all we have.'

'I still don't see why you showed me,' Irisis remarked as they headed back to her workshop.

'Don't you? She can see forms of power, whether they be natural ones like nodes and crystals, or people who are working the Secret Art. No one has ever been able to do what she does. Think how she might help us on the battlefield, where the enemy uses the Art. To fly on our heavy world, lyrinx must use power to stay aloft. With her there, they won't be able to surprise us any more. But we need an artisan, like yourself, to give sight to her seeings. I didn't select you because you're so brilliant, if that's what you're thinking. I chose you because you're the best here, and because you've twice shown courage and initiative today. You will design and build a controller, specially to work with Ullii, so we can track down anyone using the Secret Art; *either lyrinx or human*! And when you've done that, you will find Tiaan.'

'Why is she so important?' asked Irisis. 'There are thousands of artisans . . .'

'Because the scrutator says so!' Jal-Nish snapped. 'It was your stupidity that drew her to his attention and now I'm ordered to get her back. As far as I'm concerned, what the scrutator wants, he gets! Succeed and this will be your reprieve! Fail and you're dead! So get to work.'

SEVENTEEN

It was hard to judge the passing of time in the unrelenting blackness. When her hunger pangs became severe, Tiaan judged ten hours had passed. She took a small slice of corned goat meat, some bread and a rice ball, and slept. There was nothing else to do.

On waking, she ate an equally meagre portion of breakfast and walked up and down the tunnel until she was bored witless. Her lantern had run out long ago. Tiaan did not miss it; she was used to walking in the dark and if she did want light, the crystal provided enough to see by.

She sat by the entrance with her legs dangling down the shaft, watching and listening. The silence was broken every so often by the rumbling of the great wheels carrying up filled ore buckets, or taking the miners up and down the shaft. There was a lot of activity the day after Joeyn died, while the search went on.

The day after that the normal routine of the mine resumed. The passenger wheel was busy twice a day, at around five in the morning and at the same time in the evening, as the miners came and went. Once, she heard the thunder of a roof fall, which created little avalanches of grit along her tunnel.

Occasional shouts or greetings echoed down the shaft. Conversations could be heard from top to bottom. They talked a lot of old Joe, and sometimes about the war. There had been lyrinx raids all along the coast, some not far north of Tiksi. Mostly, though, they yarned about mining, of this seam where the rock was brittle and difficult to work, or that place where the lode was unusually rich but hard to follow through the rock, or about the risk of the roof falling. It was tiresome and repetitive.

Tiaan often thought about that page from the bloodline register. She recalled the image perfectly but could not decipher her father's name. She would have to find someone who had known him. If she ever got out of here.

Her thoughts kept going back to the glowing crystal and the strange field it had shown her. Just touching the crystal had been exhilarating, though the patterns of the field had stretched her brain to bursting point. Dare she make her new pliance from it? She missed it terribly, but if she used *that* crystal, would she be strong enough to handle it? It might bring on crystal fever. Maybe she should use the ordinary crystal instead, but what a pallid thing it now seemed. It had a dozen imperfections that would have needed attention, had she been in the workshop.

A crystal usually required careful cutting, then hours or even days of delicately attuning one's mind, in a state almost trance-like, before it was ready to be woken into a hedron. The glowing crystal had not a single flaw; she might have used it in a controller as it was.

It felt as if it had already been woken. She desired it all the more, but feared it too. Surely the crystal was destined for a great mancer who had the strength to control it and the vision to see its true potential, not a humble artisan. Uneasy now, Tiaan put both crystals away.

On the third morning Tiaan heard nothing, which bothered her. The mine worked every day, apart from rare holidays, but there were none this month. Fashioning a hook from her toolkit, she tossed it up on a length of cord and pulled the nearest basket down. Carefully winding herself to the top, she peered over. There was daylight at the end of the tunnel and a crosswork pattern told her that the grid was down.

She edged to the entrance. It was a gloomy morning outside, blowing sleet. There was no one in sight. Something was wrong. It took her little time to pick the lock, ease up the grid and wriggle underneath. She headed through the forest up the steep slope to the manufactory.

It was hard walking in fresh snow. The path was unmarked, which was worrying. When she reached the edge of the shrubbery and saw the ugly walls of the manufactory ahead, Tiaan checked. The front wall was peppered with pale scars. Boulders clotted the road, while one of the great gates had been smashed off its hinges. Smoke curled up from inside the entrance.

The body of a lyrinx lay against the wall, one wing extended. Another made a dark blot to the left of the entrance. People milled about, keeping well away from the alien dead.

A lyrinx attack was the logical next step, she mused. Why wait until the clankers were complete? Controllers were easily concealed and conveyed elsewhere. Far easier to put the source out of action. No doubt the mine would be attacked next.

As she wondered whether she should declare herself, a tall, yellow-haired figure appeared. Irisis! Tiaan ducked into the bushes, but a branch snapped underfoot.

'What's that?' came a nervous cry from the gate.

'Lyrinx!' cried another. 'Kill it!'

Tiaan fled. Arrows whistled through the leaves. There were cries, crashes, then something shrieked through the branches above her. It was a 'screamer', a crossbow bolt with edges shaped so as to make an unearthly noise as it flew. The sound raised the hackles on her neck. This mob would shoot anything that moved and worry about what it was later; not that the death of a runaway breeder would worry anyone.

Her only chance was to outdistance them. Racing through the trees, she gained the track, skidded on a patch of ice, and raced on. Banners of fog wreathed across her path. It was getting gloomier by the minute. She hurtled around a bend and the cleared area appeared in front of her. Her pack was in the adit and she could not survive without it. The grid was barely visible through the mist. She ploughed through the snow, desperate to get to the entrance before they appeared. If she managed it, they might think the 'lyrinx' had gone to the miners' village. Tiaan jerked up the grid and rolled under.

As she slid it down, the mob burst out of the forest. Was she in time?

'There it goes!' It was Gi-Had's great bawling voice. 'It's got into the mine. Shoot it!'

Tiaan flattened herself against the wall. Arrows, bolts and screamers came through the grid, one striking sparks above her head. She grabbed the pack and, taking what shelter she could from the wall, ran back to the lift, leapt into the basket and wound herself down as far as it would go.

The basket slapped into water just below the ninth level. She threw her bag into the dark entrance. There came cries from above. A bolt plopped into the pool, followed by a rock that drenched her in stagnant water. If they pursued her down she was finished. Maybe they would not be so bold but she dared not take the chance.

Tiaan scrambled into the tunnel. Just as she put a foot on the shelf a rock went straight through the bottom of the basket. It began to wind back up. She rang the bell rope furiously. It stopped but jerked up again. Snatching out her knife, Tiaan hacked at the tough rope. She hung on with one hand, going up with the rope, but after sawing through three-quarters dared go no higher. She leapt free, onto the landing of the ninth level.

The rope moved, stopped, jerked again, then with a twang it broke. The short end whipped down, lashing the water into foam. The other end zipped up. Cries echoed down and she heard a threshing noise that must have been the wheel-housing stripping the baskets off. The rest of the rope, a couple of hundred spans, sizzled into the water. Silence came from above.

No way back. Tiaan gathered her pack, started to head up the tunnel, then realised that a length of rope might mean the difference between survival and death. She sawed off a length, looped the heavy stuff over her shoulder and set off down the tunnel to nowhere.

*

Tiaan walked all day, through the labyrinth of tunnels and cross-passages, many flooded, of the ninth level. Finally, when it must have been well after dark and she had heard no sign of pursuit, she could drag her weary feet no further. Probably she would starve down here. Missing Joeyn terribly, she spread out her coat, lay on the floor with her head pillowed on her pack and tried to sleep.

That did not work either. Her body was worn out but her mind kept turning on the possibilities, none of which were pleasant. The luminosity of the crystal swirled in front of her. Its brightness had not changed in the days she'd had it. Surely that energy could not be coming from within or it would have run dry by now. Not only was the crystal awake, it must be drawing power from the field without human intervention. If it was, it was different from any hedron she had ever heard of. Maybe stronger, too.

Placing the hedron inside her wire sphere, Tiaan adjusted the beads into a pattern that pleased her and put the helm on. She sensed nothing at all. She rotated the beads on their wires. Still nothing, which was strange. From *any* hedron she could pick up the field. With the power of this one, focussed by globe and helm, she should be able to hear the ticking of the earth.

Perhaps it was too strong; too raw. Or maybe it worked in a different way. How little she really knew about the forces she'd been tinkering with for the past eleven years.

Putting it away, she began on the other crystal, which required a good bit of work with her toolkit before it would fit the bracket. She snapped the crystal in, took it out again and inserted it the other way round, made sure the brackets were tight and lowered the helm onto her head. Brilliant colours exploded in her mind: swirling, twisting, running back on themselves, vanishing and reappearing. They became brighter, more lurid, until everything went a brilliant white in which she could see nothing at all. Tiaan lost the capacity to think, to see, to be.

The next thing she knew, she was picking herself up off the floor. The helm lay beside her. There were cramps in her belly. The glow of the hedron seemed brighter and a tiny spark now drifted down one of the central needles, vanishing as it came to the bubble.

What had happened? She could not think straight. Tiaan leaned against the tunnel wall. It took ages for the cramps to go away. Had the crystal always been that way? Had it lain in that rock cavity for a million years, *waiting*? She felt a deeper chill. How could she hope to control a device that had been its own master for so long? Those patterns would be crystallised into its very matrix. Such a thing was not for her.

Her stomach felt awful and it could only get worse. Freedom no longer seemed so precious. Freedom for what – to starve to death in the dark? Was this really better than being pampered in the breeding factory, pleasuring the clients and being pleasured by them in turn? Tiaan had overheard enough talk about the business from her workmates – they seemed to enjoy it.

Her life was out of control and she hated it. That was why she'd worked so hard at her craft. It offered control over her existence. As soon as she entered the world of emotions Tiaan floundered. Relationships were like a blueprint where the lines had faded, leaving only a jumble of meaningless symbols. Now Joeyn, the only person she'd really cared for, was gone.

The cramps faded. Leaning back against the wall, she slipped imperceptibly towards sleep. One hand groped across the floor until it found the helm. Tiaan slid it onto her head, where it perched rakishly over her ear. Her hand dragged the globe toward her. Clutching it against her chest, Tiaan's fingers moved the orbital beads on their wires. It felt good to be using a hedron again. Very good. She could never be parted from it.

Volcanoes exploded. Congealing lava bombs wheeled through an acid sky, slowly fading to nothing.

Her slender fingers found new positions, rattling the beads back and forth faster than a merchant's abacus. The scene flashed into view – a colossal lava fountain, achingly beautiful. It vanished too.

Again she worked the beads and all at once the scene locked in, tuned perfectly to the man of her dreams. The balcony was

195

white marble, stained ruddy red by flames not far off. His dark fingers gripped the rail and he stared at the distant mountains as if seeking an answer in eternity.

Help! he mouthed.

An age later the cry came to her, or its echo. *Help!*

'I'm coming!' she cried aloud, still in her dream.

His head snapped around. *Who are you? Where are you?*

'I'm Tiaan,' she said softly. 'I'm on the ninth level of the mine.'

Mine? He sounded uncomprehending. *What mine?* He spoke in a rough, attractive burr, though with a speech pattern she had never come across before. He articulated every letter – m-i-n-e; h-e-l-p.

'The one near the manufactory, not far from Tiksi.'

What is Tiksi?

In her dream, Tiaan wondered how intelligent this young man really was. But after all, it was only a dream. She knew that.

'Tiksi is a city on the south-east coast of Lauralin, on a spur of the Great Mountains.'

Lauralin? His astonishment could have been no greater if she'd said the surface of the sun. *Lauralin?* He let out a great roar that made her hair stand up. *Are you speaking to me from SANTHENAR?*

Goosepimples broke out all over her scalp. 'Yes, of course I'm on Santhenar. Where else could I be?'

Abruptly he disappeared from the balcony. She heard him say, *Be praised, uncle, an answer! From Santhenar!*

The dream ebbed away, to Tiaan's regret, and she did not get it back. She woke shortly afterwards, having tossed so hard that she'd cracked her head on the wall, leaving a painful bruise. She spent hours of frustrated wakefulness, turning the globe over and over in her hands, moving the beads into a thousand positions, but could not tune him in again. The young man was gone.

Tiaan slept, finally, and when she woke the dream was still there. It was definitely not a crystal dream for she could remember every instant of it, even replay it at will like one of her blueprints. It was seared into the fibres of her brain.

The young man *was* real, not some fevered hallucination. And that meant . . . Recalling her previous, sensual dreams, her cheeks grew hot. What if *her* dreams were also going to *him*? What would he think of her? Somehow that mattered more than anything.

EIGHTEEN

There was no point arguing so Irisis did not bother, though she had no idea how to do what the perquisitor wanted. How could she work with Ullii, who shied at light and sound and touch. Who knew not how to communicate what she saw?

Going into Tiaan's cubicle she sat, head in hands. Someone had lied to her. It was now clear that Tiaan had never been a spy or a saboteur. Irisis had allowed her feelings, and her ambitions, to blind her. She had wronged the other artisan and was going to pay for that folly. The existence she had so carefully constructed was being pulled down around her. After this it could not be put up again.

'What progress, artisan?'

Jal-Nish's voice roused Irisis from her despairing daze. She glanced across at the round figure filling the doorway.

'It's a different kind of problem,' she said stiffly. 'I have to think it through and then come up with a workable design.' To her ears the lie was unconvincing.

'It's urgent!' he said coldly.

'There are many problems to be solved: communicating with Ullii; finding how her talent works and how to tap it; making a type of device that has never been made before. These are not tasks that can be done in an afternoon. What you want may never be possible.'

'It had better be.'

Irisis let her forehead fall on the bench so hard that it raised a bruise. Worse than anything – death, even the breeding factory – would be to be exposed to her family for what she really was.

Irisis hated her family for what they had done to her, yet she craved their approval and desperately wanted to achieve their goals. This news would destroy her mother. Even more horrible, she, Irisis, would go down in the family Histories as the cheat and liar that she was. Her name would be black as long as the Histories endured, and on Santhenar that was a very long time indeed. The Histories were the core of civilisation and the root of everyone's life, great and humble.

Even illiterate peasants knew their Histories by heart, back ten generations or more. Minor families had written Histories. Those of the House of Stirm went back twenty-six generations; eight hundred and seventy-one years. Years of her childhood had been spent learning them by heart. The greatest families recorded as much as three thousand years and had a personal chronicler at their elbows all the time to remind them. Her family Histories defined who she was. They were, at once, an ocean she was drowning in, and a lifeline.

She went out, locking the door, and stumbled up to Nish's room. He was still sleeping soundly. Sitting on the edge of the bed, she watched him until the light began to fade. Even Nish, who only weeks ago had begged for her body, had cast her aside. She could not blame him but it had proven unexpectedly painful. She should leave before he rejected her again, but Irisis had nowhere to go.

Kicking off boots and socks, she slipped under the covers. Nish was warm. She pressed her cold body against him, took a little comfort there, and slept.

When she woke it was dark. Nish rolled over carefully, putting an arm across her back. She drew him to her, mindful of his wound.

'Irisis?' he whispered.

Feeling the tension in him, she steeled herself. 'Yes?' she said in his ear. 'If you want me to go away, just say so.'

He squeezed her hand, almost as if he cared. 'You saved my life.'

She did not answer.

'What are you doing here, Irisis?'

'It was this or killing myself.'

'*Irisis!*'

She let out a choked sob, which she tried unsuccessfully to turn into a cough. 'I'm undone, Nish. I'm going to be exposed for the fraud I am.'

'What are you talking about?'

She told him about the blind seeker, Ullii, and what Jal-Nish required of her.

'A seeker!' he exclaimed, but the cry turned into a moan and he fell back on his pillows.

She sat up. 'Are you all right?' It surprised her that she cared, for in his disgrace he could be no further use to her, but somehow she did care.

'My neck feels as if someone hacked into it with a sword.'

'It's a nasty wound.' She stared up at the ceiling, invisible in the darkness. 'You've come across seekers before?'

'I heard mention of them when I was a scribe, though I never met one. It may even have been Ullii that they were talking about.'

'What did you hear?'

'Wild theories and hope unsubstantiated, for the most part. My master held that they were the answer to our prayers. His friend, a damned lawyer, thought the whole idea a nonsense and a waste of precious time and money. Father was somewhere in the middle. If an idea works, he believes in it. From what I heard, seekers are strange people, highly unstable.'

'That's Ullii! She's even more flawed than I am.' Irisis gave a bitter snort.

'What are you talking about? You're still an artisan, and could well be crafter again, like your uncle. Some day you may even be chanic. And after your great deeds this morning, who could believe – '

'Nish!' She squeezed his arm hard and he broke off. He no

longer minded her calling him that. 'It's true; I do come from a long line of artisans and crafters. Two reached the very pinnacle of the art and were awarded the honour of chanic. I'm not one of them, Nish.

'The day my mother knew she was with child she began making plans for me. The first words I heard were not baby talk, but a map of my future, which was no more than a reflection of our past. You think my father and uncle were great achievers because they became crafters? In fact they let the family down. Once we were chanics, now we're reduced to crafters. What next? Labourers in the pit? It was up to me to restore the family.

'I was trapped in our Histories. Other children had toys; I was given a tiny set of tools, waste hedrons and old controller apparatuses that had been taken to pieces. I was putting them back together as soon as I could walk. Before I turned six I was making controller parts. By the age of twelve I could make anything: the tiniest part for a pocket chronometer, the most delicate jewellery, perfect lenses for a 'scope. I wanted to be a jeweller; I knew I had a rare skill for making beautiful things. Even my controllers are works of art.

'My family would not allow that for an instant. *A jeweller? A common craft worker!* I might as well have said a brothel madam, the way they reacted. I was to be the greatest artisan of all time, raising the House of Stirm back to the pinnacle it had fallen from. They told me that every day. You can have no idea how I suffocated under their ambition. There was only one problem.'

She stopped there. Nish did not say a word, and after some minutes she continued. 'I have no talent for tapping the field, Nish. None whatsoever! I'm a fraud.'

He sat up and lit the lantern. 'But, that's not possible, Irisis. You make the most perfect controllers I've ever seen.'

'I lie and cheat and manipulate others to do what I cannot do myself. I've been doing that since I was four and discovered that I'd lost the talent every member of my family has had for five generations.'

'What?' He stared into her eyes.

'It was my fourth birthday and I was in my party dress and

201

ribbons, the *prettiest* child there!' She spat the word out. 'Everyone else was doing tricks with the family talent, showing off, each trying to top the other.'

'What kind of tricks?'

'Oh, you know. The usual stuff.'

'I have no idea. My family doesn't have the talent, remember?'

'Sorry – I assume everyone knows. In our family, people did it as often as the washing up.'

'Did *what*, Irisis?' he said irritably.

'Pulled energy out of the field to play tricks. Like making snow fall in the house in mid-summer, or cooking the food on our plates at the dinner table. Silly little things that could only amuse silly little people! Anyway, on my birthday Uncle Barkus, the old crafter, put a hedron in my hands and told me to show them what I could do. He boasted that I would be the most brilliant of the lot, though I was the youngest. My brothers, sisters and cousins already hated me, having been told I would be better than all of them put together. You have no idea the pressure I felt, and how I strove to work some wonderful trick with the hedron.

'I tried too hard. I *knew* I was the best, for I had been doing tricks since I could walk. But I wanted it too much, and I was too anxious. I could feel the talent, deep down somewhere, but I just couldn't reach it. I began to think that I never would, and that was that. The harder I tried the further the talent receded. I lost it that day and never found it again. It taught me a good lesson,' she ended bitterly. 'Don't give yourself, and don't care too much. *About anything!*'

'I don't understand,' said Nish. 'What did you lose?'

'The ability to tap the field. I can see it as well as anyone. I can visualise how to draw power from it, and the precise sub-ethyric path it must take. But when I try, nothing happens.'

'What did you do?'

'The only thing a pretty little girl could do. I burst into tears. Mother yelled at uncle and there was a huge fuss, everyone blaming everyone else. My father gave me a special gift. Mother put the hedron in my hands and did a trick with it, saying it was me. She froze the flowers in the vase so hard that when she tapped them they shattered like glass. The adults clapped, my cousins scowled, my big sister punched me when no one was looking, and everyone went home. I learned two good lessons that day. To use my beauty, *and to lie*! My family would not hear the truth so I kept lying. I even learned to fool my mother. It wasn't hard; she wanted to be fooled.

'I got by here easily enough. It was easy to trick Uncle Barkus, and I was so good with my hands that no one considered I was incapable of drawing power. Lying and cheating served me well, as a workshop girl, then as a prentice. Once I became an artisan it was even easier. I had the other artisans and prentices do the work I could not, under the guise of teaching them their craft. I have a rare talent for teaching, born out of desperation. When that fails, I fly into a rage, or use my womanhood. I hate myself, Nish, but I can't go back. I live in terror that I'll be exposed.'

Nish put his arms around her but she pulled away.

'The examiner seduced me at my eleventh-year examination,' she continued. 'I allowed him to; I could see no other way to avoid discovery. At the examination when I was sixteen, *I* seduced the examiner for the same reason. I did it subtly though. I used my wiles to give the impression of vast ability, and a family destiny, tempered by a charming smallness of confidence.

'When all other avenues failed I was not afraid to humble myself. I would go to the crafter, or the examiner, and explain what it was I did not understand, or what I could not solve. I was quite brilliant at leading them through it step by step, with my bosom heaving and tears of frustration quivering on my lashes, so they thought they were drawing my knowledge out of me. I know it all, as well as Tiaan does, *but I just can't do it*!

'It worked perfectly until Uncle Barkus died, leaving me and Tiaan as the senior artisans, and not much in terms of experience between us. A problem came up that I could not solve. I tried to work Tiaan the way I had manipulated uncle, but she was too smart and too impatient. She simply told me what to do and waited for me to do it. I had the most agonising moment of humiliation, sitting there with the hedron in my hands and her staring at me expectantly. Of course I could not do it. I thanked her, made my face into a mask, and fled.

'Fortunately she went to see her mother and was snowed in for a week. By the time she returned I'd taught another artisan to do what I could not do myself. I never approached Tiaan again. She did not ask how I solved the problem, though I knew she hadn't forgotten. I was sure she suspected my incompetence and I've hated her ever since. That's why I had to get rid of her. I knew she would expose me, eventually. Horrible, aren't I?'

'How would you have survived as crafter?' said Nish.

'It would have been easy.' A smile crept into her voice. 'I'd have hired artisans with the skills I lacked, ones I could control. People who did not ask questions; who were creative but lacked ambition. I can manage people, and I know exactly what's required. I just can't do it.'

'Why not do that with the seeker?'

'Tracking the Secret Art is a new problem and it needs a brilliant, creative mind. I have no idea how to solve it and the other artisans won't either. If Tiaan was here I would simply turn it over to her . . .' She gave a hollow laugh. 'Ironic, isn't it?'

He did not reply. She blew out the lamp. He drifted into sleep, Irisis back to her despair. Why had she confessed? Nish was as much an opportunist as she was. He would denounce her to gain credit for himself. There was only one way out. She eased her feet to the floor, trying not to disturb him.

'Where are you going, Irisis?'

'Nowhere. For the rest of my life!'

His groping hand caught her wrist. Irisis jerked away but he did not let go, so her heave pulled him out of the bed. His head struck the corner of the cupboard and Nish let out a shriek.

Footsteps came running down the corridor. The door was thrust open. A lantern dazzled her eyes. She made out the portly figure of Jal-Nish. Other faces appeared.

'What's going on here?' snapped the perquisitor. 'What have you done to my son?' He seized her arm.

Nish rubbed his head. A trickle of blood seeped from under the bandage on his throat. She held her breath, waiting for him to betray her. She had no doubt that he would, for Irisis judged other people by her own standards. Nish was out for what he could get and she was in his way.

'Well?' raged Jal-Nish. 'Move, woman! Let me get to him.'

Nish got to his feet, shakily, and subsided on the edge of the bed. He gave Irisis an ambiguous glance. She steeled herself.

'I can solve my own problems, thank you, father.'

'You can't!' Jal-Nish said curtly. 'That's increasingly evident.'

Nish supported himself on the cupboard. Looking his father in the eye, he hardened his downy jaw. 'It was just a lovers' tiff and I don't need you to sort it out. Get out of my life, father!'

Jal-Nish looked as if he had been struck across the face. It was the first time any of his children defied him. Then he nodded, reached down and hauled Irisis to her feet. 'Get back to your workshop. Time's wasting.'

'She stays!' Nish snapped.

Irisis looked from one to the other. What was Nish up to?

'We are working together on your problem,' Nish said.

'It has nothing to do with you, Cryl-Nish,' said Jal-Nish.

'I am an artificer. I know how to make things; I know how to talk to people; I know many languages. Together Irisis and I will learn how to communicate with the seeker and solve your problem, father.'

The perquisitor's face became unreadable. He frowned, nodded and withdrew, pulling the door shut. Nish lit the lamp with trembling hands, but had to sit down. His face was covered in a sheen of sweat.

Irisis did not move. 'Why did you say that?'

'What did you expect me to do?'

'To tell him the truth,' she said simply. 'Let's not delude each other, Cryl-Nish. I'm not a nice person and neither are you.'

'Maybe so but if there's one lesson from *my* childhood I did take to heart, it's loyalty to my family, *and my friends*!'

Irisis choked, and tried to muffle it with her hand. Friendship had played little part in her life. Her dealings had always been 'use more than you are being used'. Friendship was a weakness other people were afflicted with. She had never understood it.

'Why, Nish? I mean, Cryl-Nish.'

'I know you lie and cheat and connive, and yes, maybe you did murder the apothek. But I saw you on the wall this morning. You showed courage that I don't have.'

'I was terrified! I had to kill it before it killed me. To be eaten by a lyrinx . . !' She shuddered.

'All the more courageous,' he said softly. 'You killed a lyrinx all by yourself, Irisis. Not many people can claim that.'

'A lucky shot,' she said, still wary.

'A clever shot! And your operation saved my life.'

'I might just as well have killed you. I might have been trying to, and make it look . . !'

'You didn't though, *did you*? No one else knew what to do, yet you knew in an instant. They would have let me die, too afraid to save me. You tried, knowing that if you failed you would be put to death. The perquisitor is not a forgiving man.'

'A rush of blood to the head. I did not stop to think.'

'You thought it through in an instant. Can it be that you . . . love me, Irisis?'

Irisis could not believe that Nish, or anyone, would care what happened to her. 'Don't flatter yourself, my spotty little Nish-Nash. Love makes fools of the cleverest of people. I was just trying to buy favour with your father.'

'And I with your family just now!' he snapped. 'If you don't mind, I'm tired and my neck hurts, and I'm going back to bed. *Good night!*'

She stood in the shadow cast by the half-shuttered lantern, unmoving. Irisis opened her mouth as if she wanted to speak, then closed it again.

'What is it?' he said irritably, holding his neck.

'Nothing!' she whispered. 'It's nothing.'

She went out, closing the door silently. Irisis returned to the workshop and sat in the dark, turning what had happened over and over in her mind, like stones on a barren plain. She expected to find something venomous underneath. She did not. All she found was cool shadow, and in it things she did not recognise at all.

NINETEEN

That night a despatch came from the scrutator, by skeet. What it contained was not revealed though it appeared to be more bad news about the war. Jal-Nish, pallid and uneasy, held a hasty conference with Fyn-Mah, after which she sent out search parties in all directions.

In the morning Nish learned that Gi-Had had taken a troop of armed men into the mine in pursuit of a lyrinx. Not even the bravest soldiers wanted to venture into the maze of shafts, drives and unstable tunnels, but duty must be done.

Irisis appeared at the door around eight in the morning. 'Nish, your father bids you come to meet the seeker.' She went out at once, her back very straight.

'Wait!' he called but she took no notice.

Nish dressed as quickly as he could. His neck was nicely scabbed over, front and back, though so painful that he could not turn his head. He felt utterly drained.

Going via the refectory, he collected a handful of millet cakes. Slabs of boiled pork lay on a platter, the thick layers of fat like grey jelly. The thought of eating it was nauseating.

He found Irisis standing outside the seeker's door. Jal-Nish was not there. 'Irisis . . .?'

She cut him off, briefly explaining what the seeker was like and how she must be treated. Nish followed her in. Irisis carried a lantern but kept it fully shuttered, so the room was lit only by scattered rays from under the door. There was no furniture apart from a wooden chair with high arms.

The seeker crouched in a corner. The light was too dim to see her clearly, only that she was hunched right over, enveloped in a shroud-like cloth and rocking back and forth. At Nish's footfall she started, then began to rock furiously.

Irisis plucked at Nish's sleeve, drawing him out and closing the door. They went looking for the perquisitor. He was not to be found, however Fyn-Mah was working at a table in the overseer's office. A pair of carpenters had the smashed door up on a trestle in the hall and were tapping new timbers into place.

'Jal-Nish has gone down to the mine,' Fyn-Mah said without looking up.

'Oh!' replied Irisis.

'There is a difficulty?'

'It's the seeker,' said Nish. 'She's just sitting in the corner, rocking.'

'You'll get nothing from her this morning then. *If ever!*'

'What do you mean?'

'I've seen it too many times!' With a sigh, Fyn-Mah laid down her quill. 'What you're trying to do is impossible. I told Jal-Nish that before he began.'

'Why impossible?'

'The poor child is too sensitive. A whisper is like a shout to her; silk feels like sandpaper; a candle flame hurts her eyes like the noon sun.'

Nish tried to imagine it but could not. 'A wonder she didn't go insane.'

'Her family tried to beat it out of her, then abandoned her to a cripples' asylum. The things that went on there – well, she doesn't trust anyone, now. You're wasting your time.'

'I might as well go straight to the breeding factory,' said Irisis.

'It's an important duty,' snapped the querist. 'Not a punishment.'

Irisis glanced at Fyn-Mah's ringless fingers. 'Really?' she sneered. 'That's not how the workers here see it!'

208

Fyn-Mah went rigid. 'How *do* they see it?'

'One rule for them, another for the powerful. People like you.'

A red flush crept up Fyn-Mah's face. She closed her eyes for the count of three but when she opened them she was icily calm. 'The scrutator is furious that Tiaan has not been found. He has a special job for her. Now, if you'll excuse me?'

They went out. 'Did you see how she reacted?' said Irisis to Nish. 'I was right. She must be taking a preventative.'

'To prevent children? But that's a crime.'

'And I'll use it against her if I have to.'

He stared up at her. 'You would dare attack a *querist*?'

'What have I got to lose?'

'Give me a hand,' he said before they had gone much further.

'Why?' she responded listlessly.

'I can't stand up any longer.'

She offered him her shoulder. Nish held on, she caught him about the waist, and they made their slow way down to the refectory, where they sat at a long bench furthest from the door. The room was empty, breakfast having finished long ago.

'It's not like you to give up so easily,' he said.

'This job is impossible, so I'm resigning myself to my new life in the breeding factory. Or a swift extinguishment, should it come to that.'

'No!' he cried.

She smiled sadly, touching him on the arm. 'Enough of that. If you like I could find you a replacement lover. It won't be easy, with the stigma you bear, but – '

'I don't want another lover, you stupid bitch!' He hurled himself off the bench, swayed, the blood ran from his face and he fell down. As she ran around to him, Nish regained his feet and staggered out like a drunken man, waving her away.

He got as far as one of the warm niches around behind the furnaces, dragged a sweeper lad out by the ear and fell into the deliciously warm space. Someone cried out. Beneath him, a girl frantically adjusted her garments. Nish cursed the pair of them, though he should have looked first. Such places offered the only privacy most lovers got.

Crawling out, he lurched back the way he had come. He made it as far as the door of Ullii's room, caught the handle and fell through the door as it opened. As it swung shut he swooned on the floor.

Opening his eyes Nish saw a shadow behind his head. What was Ullii doing? He tried to turn his head and felt such a stabbing pain in his neck that he groaned aloud. She backed away. He raised his hand to the bandage. It was wet with blood.

The seeker crouched nearby. She was curious about him. He watched her from slitted eyes, wondering if he might use the incident to his advantage. She might feel empathy. Or contempt that he groaned at what she had suffered in silence.

Ullii came creeping back, a little shadow from which, occasionally, those big eyes reflected a stray gleam of light coming under the door. She crouched not far away, hands on the floor but head in the air, sniffing like a dog. If she could smell as well as a dog there would be plenty to read off him: blood; tears; sweat; the scent of Irisis.

Nish lay so still that he could hear his heartbeat. She came closer, sniffing around the back of his head. Something touched his hair – a fingertip. He did not move, sensing that she was ready to spring away at any provocation. Fingers touched his hair, shaping his head as gently as a sigh.

Nish held his breath. The fingers traced his cheek and the other hand joined them: eyes, nose, mouth, ears, chin. At his infinitesimal movement she drew back. He heard the faintest sound, like an inrushing of air. And again. She was sniffing her fingers, imprinting his smell on her memory.

She edged forward and her fingers slid down the curve of his face from either side. Her hand struck the wound. Nish cried out; it was torment.

Ullii scurried to the corner and curled up into a ball. He came to his knees, enduring the shooting agony. She began rocking furiously, perhaps scared he would beat her. An interesting experiment, though it was over for the moment. When the pain became bearable Nish went out, as quietly as he could.

He walked between the furnaces, where stokers were shovelling slabs of pitch into the fire pits. The blast was so intense that they wore suits of woven rock fibre, with goggles of black glass to stop their eyes from drying out. The heat made him feel dizzy. Another worker was drawing out samples of molten metal with a cup on the end of a long rod. He was similarly garbed and goggled, and wore earmuffs, for the roar of the furnaces up close was deafening.

Nish went out the back gate, desperate for a gasp of clean, cold air. In the distance Irisis was walking along the edge of the ravine. He turned the other way, which led him to the slag and ash piles. Beyond he was brought up by the breath-snatching whiff of ammonia and a corrosive reek of phenol from the effluent drains. A group of workers, supervised by Foreman Gryste, were busy clearing tar-choked drains.

'It's no use,' said Gryste, tossing his spade-tipped probing pole to one side. 'We'll have to go up. Glyss, are you ready?'

Glyss was a large man, big in the upper body but with thin legs and a meagre bottom. He was clad head to foot in a waxed canvas suit, booties and cap. They greased his face, his hands and every speck of exposed skin. He donned goggles, slipped plugs up his nose and went down on hands and knees. Taking half a dozen deep breaths, he scuttled up the drain as fast as a cockroach. A rope unreeled behind him. Thumping went on for a couple of minutes then stopped.

'Pull!' Gryste roared. Two labourers, holding the rope, hauled Glyss out again.

He was gasping, and his hands and lips were blistered. Glyss plopped on the ground, spitting bloody sputum.

'Ready, Glyss?' Gryste said after a few minutes.

A look of terror crossed the man's face, then he gave a spasmodic jerk of the head. Nish resumed his walk. There were worse lives than being a soldier.

Nish paced back the way he had come. The air near the sewer drains reeked so badly that he wished for a pair of Glyss's nose-plugs. Further on, he diverted from the path that led to the front of the manufactory, not wanting to go inside. Instead he wandered along the edge of the gully, here a broken slope that plunged steeply into the gorge. Further along, the slope became a cliff.

Feeling faint, Nish sat near the edge, scowling at the leaden sky. The air was clean here but deathly cold and it was looking as though it would snow. How he hated the manufactory. It was the filthiest place he had ever been. Every plant back there was dead, while the river into which their wastes flowed was a reeking cesspit. Moreover, the place had the most miserable weather on Santhenar and it prevailed all three hundred and ninety-six days a year.

Weighing an egg-shaped pebble in his hand, Nish tossed it idly over the cliff.

'Aah!' came a cry from below.

Nish looked down to see a big man scowling up at him, rubbing a completely bald pate. It was Eiryn Muss. The halfwit eked out a living growing air-moss on a ramshackle structure of poles and withes on the upper edges of the ravine. Air-moss was a superlative wound dressing, though the war had used up all accessible natural supplies. It grew naturally only on tree trunks on the upper parts of escarpments near the coast, where up-draughts maintained the moist air it required. The trees here had been burned long ago, fuel for the insatiable furnaces, hence Muss's dangerous yet poorly paid occupation.

A touch of sulphur in the air resulted in premium-quality moss, but the growth rate was so low that no normal man could have survived on the earnings, even from such an extensive array of structures as Muss had built. Fortunately Muss was no ordinary man. He was happy to eat wood grubs and beetles if he could get no better, and after each sale rewarded himself with a flask of turnip brandy and an hour of watching the sweeper boys through a crack in the wall of the bathhouse.

But Muss had sold no moss in a month and someone had plastered over the peeping hole. He was desperate for turnip brandy, had no money to get any and wanted someone to suffer for it.

Catching sight of Nish, Muss growled and began to scramble up the slope.

'It wasn't me!' Nish lied instinctively.

'I'll kill you and eat your brains,' Muss roared, hurling a rock at him. Nish ducked. 'It's Little Nish, isn't it, the overseer's bum chum! Enjoy your flogging the other day, Nish-Nash?' Muss clawed his way up. 'I'll whip your fat little backside so hard . . .'

Nish fled up the path in the direction of the cliff, then darted off among the boulders. Peeking out, he saw the fellow come panting and gasping up over the edge. Muss looked around wildly, cursed and ran up the road toward the rocks, his great belly wobbling. He stopped, panting, baffled, then shambled back the other way, swearing blood-black oaths.

'Stupid old fart!' Nish squatted until his head steadied before continuing the other way. He had to rest every few minutes now. Must have lost more blood than he realised. He was leaning against a boulder, its frosting of wind-driven snow steadily melting, when someone appeared on the cliff edge several hundred paces further on. Yellow hair flew in the wind. It was Irisis. He thought it best to creep away, even at the risk of running into Muss again.

Something stopped him. It was the way she was standing right on the brink, staring down. Didn't she realise how danger-ous that was? What if the edge crumbled . . .?

Of course she realised! Maybe she was daring the cliff to hold her up. *Or fling her down!*

Irisis tensed, then went into a crouch. Nish's heart turned over. She was going to jump.

He began to run. It was so awful he could not contemplate it. Her beautiful body, her lovely face, smashed on the rocks. Not brave, bold, fearless Irisis. Not even Irisis the liar, cheat and possibly murderer. It must not happen.

He lost sight of her as he pounded down into a little dip in the path. Let her still be there, he agonised as he laboured up the other side. His legs felt like wet string. Her image shivered, body and legs seeming to move separately. Nish's neck wound pulsed; wetness ran down his chest. He felt faint. As he gained the top she was still there, trembling on the brink.

'No, Irisis!' he screamed. 'Don't jump!'

Wobbling down the slope, he hit an icy patch where the path was in shadow and his feet went from under him. 'No!' Nish said faintly, fell forward, landed on his knees and skidded over the edge. His head struck something and a black overcast blocked out the sky.

Irisis felt the rock slip beneath her left foot and had to steel herself not to move. Her heart was leaping from backbone to ribcage. Killing herself was not quite as easy as she'd thought. Three times now she'd gone into a crouch, preparing to fling herself over, but found after the crisis passed that she was still standing there.

It was the leap she feared. The fall would be an instant of bliss. She did not want to think what came after that or she would never do it. Inordinately proud of her looks, Irisis dared not contemplate the splattered ruin she would become. She prayed that her remains would be eaten quickly. For people to see her like that . . .

Again the rock cracked. She wanted it to do the job for her but it refused. Perhaps if she just toppled forward?

Irisis was about to when she heard Nish's frantic cry and saw him staggering toward her like a white-faced drunk. She tried to jump but her muscles refused. Vanity had beaten her – she especially did not want *him* to see the aftermath.

She spun on one foot, the rock broke under her and Irisis had to fling herself sideways to survive. She landed hard, just a breath away from oblivion. Before she could move Nish cried out, threw out his arms and skidded over the edge.

Irisis, who had not wept since her fourth birthday, let out a scream of anguish. Rolling to safety, she came to her feet and ran. It was easy to imagine *his* fate. She could not stop herself.

Where had he fallen from? The icy patch stretched along the curving path for twenty or thirty paces. It could have been anywhere along here. Walking carefully now, she peered over the edge. There was a fall of ten or fifteen spans onto blocky, broken boulders. She could not see him, nor any splash of red, but he might have gone into the shadows between the boulders.

'Nish?' she said softly, knowing how pointless that was. 'Nish?' Perhaps it had been further up around the point. It was really slippery here. She put her arms out, afraid of falling now. Also ironic.

Coming around the point she saw him, caught in Muss's air-moss farm. He'd landed on a coarsely woven withy mat, half collapsing the structure of poles and round cross-pieces supporting it. Now he was tangled up in the mat and the poles leaned crazily out over the lower cliff.

'Nish?' she whispered.

He groaned and she felt a pang of longing. 'Irisis? You're alive!' The joy in his voice was, somehow, alarming.

'Of course I'm alive!' she said sharply. 'Why wouldn't I be?'

'I thought you were going to jump . . .'

'Don't be stupid!' she lied.

Nish jerked around, trying to see her. One of the supporting poles lifted right out of its rock socket. 'Don't move!' she roared. 'You'll go right over. Stay perfectly still.'

She looked around. It was a long way to the manufactory – more than half a league. The best part of an hour by the time she got back here with help. If Nish lasted that long in his thin garments, she doubted that the structure would.

'Muss!' she roared, cupping her hands around her mouth. 'Eiryn Muss.'

'He won't help!' Nish said weakly.

'Oh?'

'I accidentally dropped a pebble on his head a while ago.' He had the grace to look ashamed.

'Bloody idiot! *Muss!*'

Some minutes later he came blundering up the path, brawny arms hanging loose. Irisis ran to meet him. 'Muss, help me! Nish has gone over the cliff.'

'Good,' said Muss. 'Very good!' His halfwit eyes gleaming, he turned away.

'Muss, please. He's fallen into your moss farm. He's breaking it.'

Muss followed her to the edge, looked down and gave an

215

incongruous, high-pitched giggle. 'Old one. No good now. Build new one.'

'Please, Muss. I will pay you well.'

His blank face strained to express some emotion. An idiot's leer appeared. What could she offer that would mean anything to him? 'Bottle of brandy.' Irisis held her hand out as if offering him one, then her other hand as well. 'Two bottles.'

His eyes shone. A trickle of saliva made its way down his bearded chin. He licked his lips. 'More!'

She could not imagine what he would value. He was some kind of pervert or peeping tom, she recalled.

'Would you like to see my breasts?' she said in desperation. She'd even sleep with him if there was no other way to save Nish, though it would be the most squalid transaction of her opportunistic life.

Such a look of disgust mixed with terror passed across Muss's face as she had never seen before. Nish let out a choked gasp, writhed and the brittle withies broke. He went through head first but a branch end caught in the waistband of his trousers, dragging them down to his ankles.

He stopped with a jerk, hanging upside down, bare bum pointing at them. His shirt fell down over his head, revealing the healing lash marks on his back.

Irisis eyed his stocky body, discovering that she liked the musculature, especially his smooth, pale backside. So, evidently, did Muss, who was giggling and snorting beside her.

No time to waste. As Nish swayed back and forth, several poles lifted from their sockets. It would take little for the whole tangled structure to go over.

'Come on!' she hissed, shaking Muss by the shoulder. 'Four bottles.'

Muss tore his eyes away from the glorious sight. They climbed down to the ledge. Irisis held the poles steady while Muss swung along the rickety frame and freed Nish. It took more time than it should have, but Irisis closed her mind to that. If Muss was taking liberties, she thought unsympathetically, it served Nish right for being so damn stupid.

Finally they were back at the top. Nish was white-faced and shivering. 'Carry him back,' Irisis said.

Muss threw Nish over his shoulder, steadied him with a paw on his backside and shambled off. Half an hour later the artificer was propped up on a bench in the refectory, next to the wall warmed by the great ovens, and warmed inside by a bowl of dried fishhead soup. Irisis went around the back and purchased four bottles of brandy from Flyn the miner, who kept an illegal stall behind the practice ground.

She gave them to Muss, who tore the cork from one bottle and poured half straight down his gullet. His eyes crossed, he reeled, giggled and said, 'Good luck with hunt for crystal lady.' Juggling his bottles, Muss wandered off.

She stood looking after him, wondering how the halfwit came to know that. Well, he was always snooping around, minding other people's business.

As she entered the refectory, Nish smiled at her, uncertainly.

'If you were my slave for the rest of your life you'd never repay what you owe me!' she said furiously. That he'd saved her from killing herself was another black mark against him.

He sat up straighter, giving a cheerful grin. 'Oh, I don't know. While I was hanging back there, and you were letting Muss fondle my bum, I had an idea that may just save us both.'

TWENTY

Ullii crouched in her corner, shivering. The room was cold but she had thrown off her clothes. Her pants and shirt were made of finest lamb's wool that a baby could have worn without difficulty, yet the fabric felt to be covered in tiny hooks that pulled at her skin with every movement.

She put her fingers in her ears. That kept out the cacophony which made it impossible to think. Even so, sound was everywhere. Ullii could hear the chomping of tiny borers in the floorboards. A mouse skittering in the ceiling was like a man walking in miner's boots. She could even hear the faint movements made by a spider's spinnerets, the clacking of its joints as it moved, the subtle twang of silken threads.

The smells were overpowering. Ullii knew when the furnace stokers changed from one pitch bin to another. The stokers did not notice, yet to her it was like the difference between apple and onion. She could even tell which way the wind was blowing from the smell of the air.

Easterlies carried the tang of salt, seaweed and fish smoking on the racks below Tiksi. Northerlies, a mixture of tar, ammonia and human waste from the drains. South brought the faint aroma of pine needles and resin, though only on warm days. Westerlies had no smell at all, for that way was only snow and ice and mountains forever.

Ullii knew everyone who had ever walked past her door, as a dog knows each creature by its smell. She could recognise at least a hundred people; some foul, some fair, some masking poor hygiene with sickly, cloying scent. One unfortunate wretch had teeth so rotten that she could smell him as soon as he came into the corridor.

Of all these she knew only the names of four. Jal-Nish had a sweetly foetid smell, with metallic overtones. She knew him well, having come all the way from Fassafarn with him. She shrank inwardly as soon as she detected the perquisitor. He pretended to care about her but she knew he did not. Jal-Nish wanted to be scrutator desperately and feared only two things – the wrath of his wife, Ranii Mhel, and displeasing the scrutator of Einunar, Xervish Flydd. His smell reminded Ullii of childhood memories better forgotten.

Ullii also knew Querist Fyn-Mah, soap-scented with rose petals. She must wash six times a day to have so thoroughly removed all trace of her own odour. Fyn-Mah spoke in soft tones, the least hurtful Ullii had encountered in years. She did care, in an efficient sort of a way, though not to the extent of inconveniencing herself. Fyn-Mah was wrapped up in her own torment.

The third person was Nyg-Gu, the woman who brought food and cleaned up Ullii's messes. She had a strong complex odour, such that Ullii wondered if she bathed from one year to the next. The last was Irisis, who also smelt of soap and flowers but her own scent was stronger – ripe womanhood. Ullii did not know what to make of her. Irisis's voice had harsh overtones, and she looked to have a temper, but Ullii saw warmth carefully hidden.

The scent that most intrigued her had no name. It was the young man who had appeared with Irisis, then returned to collapse on the floor. He had a musky, spicy aroma that warmed her in ways she did not understand. He also smelt of metal, oiled machinery and blood. She did not know his voice. And she had hurt him, which made him special in her eyes. Many people had made her suffer but she had not hurt anyone before. He had not struck back at her either. He was a very special man. Ullii wanted to see him again. She was waiting for him now.

Her mind wandered back to Fassafarn, where she had lived for most of her eighteen years. Ullii was not stupid, despite what people thought of her. Far from it. She could not read or write, but only because the glare from paper burned her eyes. Ullii's life had been shaped by her experiences, and she'd experienced life as no other person on Santhenar had.

She had first met Jal-Nish twelve years ago, when as a child of six she'd been put up before the examiner. In normal times Ullii would have been classified as a moron and cast out on the streets, or shut up in an institution if they'd felt like prolonging her torment. But Jal-Nish was no ordinary examiner and those were desperate times. The examiners had been ordered by the Council of Scrutators to keep watch for children with unusual talents, especially those related to the Secret Art. Humanity was fighting for its very survival and no one knew which abilities might prove vital in the struggle against an enemy unlike any this world had ever encountered.

Ullii was as unusual a child as Jal-Nish had met. Sight and hearing and touch being overwhelmed, she lived mainly through smell and through another sense long since atrophied, or perhaps never developed, in ordinary people. She sensed the structure of things, and the forces that held them together or acted to pull them apart. Ullii could stand outside with her eyes screwed shut and describe the wind. She could see it in three dimensions like waves all flowing, ebbing and billowing.

More importantly, she could see the Secret Art like knots in a lattice, though one whose structure fitted no pattern anyone else could comprehend.

Ullii had often heard Jal-Nish talk about her unique talent. In her worst moments the feeling of being special was all that kept her going. He had referred her to one mancer after another, to see if any use could come of her abilities. Nothing had, for no one had the patience, or the vision, to understand Ullii. She knew instantly when someone wanted to use her. Ullii would go into a catatonic state that no amount of punishment could bring her out of. They could hurt her, and many did. It made no difference.

Ullii had not run away, because she could not survive in the outside world. She simply withdrew. Finally old Flammas, the last mancer she had been given to, put her in one of his dungeon cells and forgot about her. She was fed once a day, like the other prisoners, and every few days given a bucket of cold water to wash in while the cell's filth was hosed into the drain.

It was the best thing that could have happened to her. Her cell was dark; little sound penetrated the heavy door. The smell was unpleasant but at least it was her own. And it was warm enough, so that she never had to wear the hated clothes. It suited her better than anywhere she had lived since she'd left her mother's womb and found the world to be a sensory nightmare.

Ullii spent five years in that cell, living a life entirely of the mind. She grew into a woman there and suddenly her abilities blossomed. To fulfil her need for order, she began to construct a three-dimensional lattice of all the world within range of her unique sense. Physical objects like tower, dungeon, land and rock were poorly defined, but some life-forms made tangled shapes in the lattice that she might, with much effort, unravel. Occasionally she could identify them and they always turned out to be mancers or other powerful adepts. If they were using the Secret Art, or a device driven by such magical power, that knot in the lattice flowered especially brightly.

One day, trying to unpick a difficult and unusual knot, she uncovered an alien – a *lyrinx*. Times before she had sensed natures that frightened her, but none like this. It was terrifyingly different.

She began to scream, and kept on until Mancer Flammas was called to what he had forgotten years ago. He had to be reminded of her name, found that nothing could be done with her, and called Jal-Nish. Ullii was then sixteen, so she was taken to her third examination.

Jal-Nish coaxed out of her what the matter was and realised that he had made the discovery of the age, if a way could be found of using her. It gained him the perilous honour of perquisitor, but two years later he was no further advanced when came the dreadful news about Tiaan. Unwilling to leave Ullii with people who might break her to get at her talent, and thinking that, just possibly, she could be able to help, Jal-Nish had bundled her up and brought her with him.

The journey had been a torment for Ullii. She'd spent all the daylight hours in a silken bag suspended from the roof of a wagon, held in place with guy ropes. Even so, she'd been in sensory overload from the instant they'd set out. Her screams made the trip a hideous experience for all and Jal-Nish had to post a guard over her bag lest someone tumble it, with her inside, over a precipice while no one was looking.

Shouts and roars outside the door brought Ullii back to the room where she crouched in the corner, rocking on her bare feet. Of necessity, her feet and hands were the only parts of her not hypersensitive.

It was Irisis, talking quietly. Ullii knew the fascinating young man was out there too. She wanted him to come in so she could learn about him, for he did not appear in her lattice. Irisis did, though as an impenetrable ball. The door opened but a tidal wave of light roared in, stabbing her in the eyes. She covered them with her hands and curled up in a hopeless attempt to block the world out.

Irisis entered, and the young man. His musky aroma unsettled her. They left the door open, flooding her with so many sensations that Ullii was helpless. Their feet thundered toward her; nothing could block the sound out.

Irisis bent over, her breath whooshing in and out, her heart like a great drum being pounded. Was Irisis going to torture her?

Irisis pounced, grabbing Ullii around the waist and lifting her easily. The seeker flailed her legs, letting out a shrill squeal, but could not take her hands away from her eyes to defend herself. The iron grip, the rough fabric pressed against her skin, were unbearable.

Irisis spoke to the man in booming notes that smashed together in Ullii's mind. She had spoken softly before. Why did she want to hurt, now? The man answered, less loud, but Ullii could not make out what he was saying either. He was not kind after all.

222

Turning Ullii's head to one side, Irisis said something in an urgent whisper. It sounded like 'Now!'

Ullii felt an uncomfortable, hot feeling in her ear. Awful crackles, booms and bubbles reverberated through her head. Whatever was in her ear slowly cooled until she could not feel it at all. She felt dizzy. Where was up? Where down? She tried to claw the stuff out of her ear. Irisis held her hands. The sensations built up in her brain, echoing back and forth, feeding on themselves. It was the worst feeling of all, for it cut off the lattice – the only place she had ever been able to escape to.

Without warning, Irisis turned her over while the man poured the hot substance in her other ear. More crackles and booms as the stuff cooled, then for the first time in her life Ullii experienced absolute, blissful silence. It was so unprecedented that she stopped screaming and hung limply from Irisis's arm with her hands over her eyes, exploring the sensation.

The man closed the door and unshuttered a lantern so it cast a faint light on the far wall. Irisis put Ullii down on her feet, holding her in an unbreakable grip. Ullii did not move. She no longer felt the desperate urge to curl up and rock. She stared at the pair through the cracks between her fingers, wondering.

'Now what?' said the man.

Ullii read his lips and turned to face him. Irisis must have spoken though Ullii did not see it.

'My name is Cryl-Nish!' said the man. 'You can call me Nish, if you like.' He was resigned to the nickname now.

'Nisssshh!' she whispered.

He reached out one hand, as she had done when he lay swooned on the floor. She did not withdraw. He grazed her hair with a fingertip, stroking down its length. The back of his hand came to her cheek, touching it gently. It felt rough, but kindly. A strange feeling, kindness. Something silky hung from his fingers. He stroked them up her face; the silk came with it. He put his hands over her hands. Aah, the smell of him; the touch! She drew her hands out. Her eyelashes fluttered against the palms of his hands. She felt that she might trust him after all, this unknown, nice-smelling man.

223

'You smell good, Nish.'

His fingers urged the silk up over her eyes. She allowed him to. The light seeping between his fingers was cut off. Glorious, absolute dark descended. Ullii, wondering, allowed him to tie the mask at the back of her head. Nish stroked her face with his fingertips then backed away. Irisis let go too.

Instinctively, Ullii bent down to go into her crouch, but discovered that she did not need it. There was no light, no sound, no feeling but her feet on the floor and the touch of the mask over her eyes. The sensations that for the whole of her life had flooded her were gone.

The lattice was so much clearer now. The knots, she felt, would be so much easier to untangle. Her brain could think what she chose. Ullii sat down on the floor. A tear formed in one eye, then the other. Soon she was weeping floods for what she had never dared hope. The war in her mind was over. She was free of her prison at last.

Nish and Irisis stood watching, not saying a word. Ullii wept for a long time, then drooped, tilting forward until her forehead touched her hands, which rested on the floor. And in that strange position, bottom in the air, completely naked, she slept.

Nish went to cover Ullii with her clothes but Irisis shook her head. 'Come outside. She's used to sleeping like that, strange as it seems. We'll come back later.'

Irisis closed the door and they went down to the refectory. 'Hungry work!' said Nish, selecting a bowl of lemon tea and another of pickled kumquats.

'That was a brilliant idea, to fill her ears with wax. How did you think of it?'

'I'm amazed no one else has. Lots of workers here wear goggles or earmuffs or gloves. It wasn't until I was upside down over the cliff, with my bum hanging out and you leering at it, that I realised what she needed.'

'It's not *my* leers you need to worry about,' she said cheerfully. 'You should have seen the looks Muss was giving you.'

'More than looks, as he was getting me down,' Nish said sourly. 'He felt me up something severe. You might have stopped him!'

'I was holding the pole,' she said.

'So was he!'

Irisis burst out laughing. 'Maybe that will teach you to mend your ways and treat the unfortunate more kindly. You know, I wonder about Muss.'

'What do you mean?'

'Something he said. I don't think he's as stupid as he seems.'

'He couldn't be.'

'Still, I'm going to keep an eye on him.'

'You can't think *he's* the spy?' She did not answer, so he went on, 'We'd better make something more permanent for Ullii.'

That took a day. It was simple work for an artificer to design and make a pair of lightweight goggles that completely covered her eyes. He had the glassblower tint glass until it was almost black and cut two round plates from it to fit the frames. Nish tested the goggles by looking at the sun, which became the faintest glowing disc. Every part that would touch her skin he padded with silk. He also made a pair of padded muffs to go over her ears, in case the wax irritated her.

Irisis was also busy, though she did not say what she was doing. Nish was conscious that the time was fleeting by, and of the sentence they both were under.

They checked on Ullii every few hours. She slept for most of the day. Later they found her walking back and forth talking to herself, wearing her silk shirt but not the trousers.

'She must have been cold,' Irisis said as they went out again. 'In an hour or two she'll throw it off again.'

That night he went to Irisis's workshop to see what she had been up to. She was holding a pair of trousers up to the light. They were made of a fine fabric with the faintest blue iridescence that swirled and shimmered as she moved it in the light.

'And to think I've been working,' he sniffed.

'And I haven't?'

'A bit small for you, I would have thought. Ah, the vanity of the woman!'

'They're for Ullii, fool!' She held them up. 'What do you think?'

She tossed them to him. They slipped through his fingers as if coated in oil.

'Careful, Nish!'

'They're beautiful!' He picked them up. They were made of the softest, silkiest fabric he'd ever felt. 'How did you make them?'

'Uncle Barkus had some reels of spider-silk in his storeroom. He'd got it for some project or other but never used it. I had the master weaver make cloth from it and I've made Ullii two complete sets of clothing. She can wear it next to her skin, and ordinary clothes on top.'

'Spider-silk?'

'From the deathwatch spider. It's the softest thread in the world, but many times stronger than silk. I defy anyone to tear it.'

'And you think Ullii will wear it?'

'She'll have to. She can't go marching across the mountains in the nuddy.'

'Who said she would be?'

'How else are we going to track Tiaan down?'

TWENTY-ONE

The following morning found them back at their starting point. Ullii had knocked off her mask while sleeping and was woken by Nyg-Gu slamming in with her breakfast, leaving the door wide open. Ullii let out a screech, whereupon Nyg-Gu, frightened, slapped her. The seeker went into a screaming fit in which she clawed out her earplugs. By the time Nish, who had heard the screaming from the other side of the manufactory, arrived, Ullii had gone catatonic. Nyg-Gu was shaking her and roaring abuse. Before he could drag the servant out, a hundred workers were crowded around the door, all talking loudly, staring and making rude remarks about the naked madwoman.

'Get them away from here,' Nish yelled as Irisis came running up.

'What are you going to do?' she said, breathless.

'I don't know!' Pushing the people away from the door, he closed and bolted it. As he stood there in the dark he heard his father's voice.

'*I've had this!*' said Jal-Nish. 'It's a damn waste of time. I knew you'd fail.'

'We haven't had the chance to show you what we've done,' came a honeyed voice, the one Irisis used to get her way with men. 'This time tomorrow you'll be amazed.'

'Oh, all right!' he said angrily. 'But . . .'

They moved away; Nish did not hear the rest. 'Ullii,' he said in the softest voice he was capable of. There was no reply but he could hear her rocking, humming to herself. He went back and forth across the floor until he found the mask. He discovered the earplugs when they crunched underfoot. The racket outside had stopped.

He could make her out now, right in the corner. Nish went forward, slowly but not creeping. He had the feeling that creeping might alarm her. 'Ullii,' he whispered. 'I have your mask. Do you want it?' He held it out.

She rocked faster than ever. Her eyes were tightly closed.

'Ullii, here!' Reaching out with exquisite care, he touched her cheek with the back of one finger.

Faster she rocked. He was amazed she did not topple over. As he touched her, she made a keening noise in her throat. He backed off.

'Ullii? Can you see me? In your mind's eye?'

She shook her head. Nish squatted back on his heels, rubbing his jaw. She stiffened. Having not shaved in several days, there was enough soft stubble to make a rasping noise.

'Can you smell me?'

The keening stopped. Nish was sure he saw a fleeting smile. Maybe that was the key. She'd mentioned his smell earlier.

'What do I smell like, Ullii?'

Again that smile. 'Nice!' she said softly, mimicking his voice. 'You smell like a kind man – musk and spice, metal and oil.'

He was flattered but knew he'd made a breakthrough. If she judged people by the way they smelt, it might be a way into her confidence. He found that he liked her. He also wanted to see what she looked like in the light. The brief glimpses he'd had were tantalising.

He rubbed the mask over his face, then inside his shirt in sweeping curves. Taking it out again, Nish sniffed it. It had no smell that he could detect.

He extended his arm, mask in hand, toward her face. She smiled, snatched it and brought it to her face, sniffing like a dog. A barely audible sigh escaped. Ullii put the mask over her eyes, gave another sigh, and tried to tie it at the back. The mask fell off. She tried again with the same result.

Ullii whimpered. Nish's fingers found hers, she drew them to her nose, sniffed deeply, then allowed him to tie on the mask. Her fingers followed every movement of his. When it was done she pushed his hands away, tore off the mask and tied it herself, giving a little chuckle when she succeeded at the first attempt.

Nish sat back on his haunches, wondering what she would do next. Had he made a lot of progress, or none at all? She squatted along the wall, just an arm's length away. He sensed her alertness, her curiosity, but also the barely suppressed terror of being hurt again. How could he convince her otherwise in time to save himself?

He thought about his own troubles, particularly the threat of being sent to the front-lines. Giving a little whimper, he began to rock back and forth. It was partly feigned, but only partly. The whimper expressed how he felt, alone in his personal darkness.

Ullii turned her head.

He kept rocking, sure she was investigating him with her strange senses. What would Ulli do now? That was all that mattered.

She reached out ever so tentatively, touched his cheek with a fingertip and swiftly withdrew it. He sighed. She went still, her head cocked to one side. Then Ullii rubbed her hands over her face, through her hair and across her breasts and belly. She extended her fingers toward him till they were cupped under his nose.

A tiny miracle. She was offering him her trust, that she had never offered to anyone. He sniffed her fingers. Ullii had barely any smell, for after the mancer's dungeon she'd developed a compulsion for washing and would do it as much as a dozen times a day. She just smelt pleasant, and faintly creamy. He pressed his nose into the cup of her hand.

Nish sighed, and smiled, and raised his head. She withdrew her hand, brought it back palm outward and urged him away. Taking the hint, he went softly to the door. There was a long way to go but at least they were on the road.

As he lifted the latch, but before the door opened, she said quietly, 'I will wear your mask, Nish. I will help you find her.'

'Thank you,' he whispered back.

In the artisans' workshop he told Irisis all that had happened, scarcely able to contain his glee. 'I've done it!' he concluded. 'She trusts me. She said she would help find Tiaan!'

Irisis was not quite as pleased as he'd expected, and she positively scowled at the sniffing episodes. 'Like a dog and bitch on heat!' she snapped. 'Let's get to work.'

They began with the goggles, which were as light a pair as Nish could manufacture, large oval lenses framed with wire and filled in all around with beaten silver. The arms hooked around Ulli's ears like a pair of spectacles.

She fitted them over her eyes, tentatively, walked across the room and back, then whipped them off again. 'Can't!' She rubbed her ears and the bridge of her nose.

The first setback. Nish tucked them under his arm, handing her the earmuffs instead. Putting them on, she adjusted the fit and smiled – the first true smile he'd seen from her, though it fleeted away.

He gave her the clothing. She ran her fingers over the blouse, a high-necked one, and frowned. Ullii pulled it over her head, settled it around her waist, arched her back and screamed.

'It's crawling! It's crawling all over me!' In a single movement she tore it off, flung it into her water bucket and held it under. She stood up, shuddering and rubbing furiously at her belly, breasts and shoulders.

Irisis flung the door open. 'What's the matter?'

Nish took the bucket, goggles and the rest of the clothing and went outside. 'Well, at least she likes the earmuffs.' He told her what had happened.

'I checked everything,' said Irisis, piqued. 'All the seams are concealed. There's not a single thread loose.'

'If she says it's crawling,' said Nish, 'it must be. Maybe if we talked to the weaver.'

'Good idea!' They turned out the gate, past the water cisterns and the slaughterers doing their bloody business, and down to a collection of smaller buildings occupied by craft workers not directly related to the making of clankers.

'Good morning, master weaver,' Irisis said, putting her head through the door. 'Are you busy?'

'I'm always busy!' A cadaverous-looking man with one twisted leg, he never smiled. He was untangling a mess of threads in one of the looms. 'Look at this. Damned prentices; if you put all their brains together it wouldn't fill the skull of a nit. What do you want?'

'It's this spider-silk.' She explained what had happened.

'Women!' he said under his breath, evidently being one of the new breed. 'Hold on! There was a bit left over.' Diving into a chest of reels, he pulled one out and wound some of the thread off, testing it with skeletal fingers. Nish thought he looked rather like a spider, the way his fingers worked. 'Did you wash the cloth first?' the weaver challenged.

'No!' said Irisis. 'I thought you'd already done that.'

'Not a bloody washerwoman!' He glared at her. 'There's your answer then. This is raw silk. It's still got the prints of the spider on it.'

'How do I get it off?'

'How would I know? I've never used spider-silk before. Nor will again, after the trouble it was to weave.' Scowling, he banged the loom with his fist. 'Warm water and mild soap. No lye! Definitely not hot water, or it'll only fit a mouse afterwards.'

'Thank you,' said Irisis.

'Bah!' he turned back to the loom, tossing a head like a fluffy skull.

'Charming fellow,' said Nish.

'He's all right. He does a good job, exactly the way he's asked. Just doesn't like women. And with some reason, I understand.'

Nish did not ask why and she did not elaborate. She left the garments at the laundry with many instructions. Nish returned to his workshop, where he replaced the arms of the goggles with a split strap that would buckle over the back of Ullii's head.

The padding he covered with scraps of spider-silk cloth, washed carefully beforehand.

He spent hours in Ullii's room that afternoon and evening, watching her walking about with the earmuffs and mask on. She tried the goggles several times, but each time took them off after some minutes. Evidently she preferred to see nothing rather than put up with the least discomfort.

Nish kept quiet. He wanted her to get used to him being there. The door was open now, lighting the room, though guards at either end of the corridor kept the curious away.

He liked watching her. Ullii was small but sweetly formed, her compact curves a contrast to Irisis's elongated form. Her skin, which had never seen the sun, was as soft as a baby's. As she walked back and forth, unselfconsciously naked, a germ of desire formed.

And why not, he thought. She is a grown woman. Perhaps it would help to cement her trust in me. Irisis need never know. His mind wandered on that delicious track until he realised that Ullii was pacing frantically, radiating anxiety.

Had she sensed the direction of his thoughts? Nish hastily adjusted his trousers and saw a tall figure at the door. He went across. 'She's better, though she still has trouble with the goggles.'

Irisis gave him a frosty, up-and-down glare as if she knew what he had been daydreaming about. 'Her clothes are dry!' she said curtly.

Nish held out his hand but Irisis brushed past and stalked straight up to Ullii. The seeker backed away until she hit the wall, holding her hands up as if to ward off some horror.

'It's crawling!' she said in a cracked voice.

Irisis looked irritated. Her frustration must soon burst out. That would ruin all the trust built up so far.

'Stop!' he hissed. 'Let me do it.'

Irisis raised her fist. Nish thought she was going to thump him. Well, let her, if that was what it took. It might lower another barrier between him and Ullii. He steeled himself against the blow.

A wild, bubbling hiss came from Ullii's throat and she went

into a crouch, her fingers hooked into claws, glaring through her mask at Irisis.

Irisis took a step backwards, then shrugged and tossed the garments to Nish. 'I wish I inspired that kind of loyalty.' She went to the door.

He wondered how to convince Ullii that the clothes were different now. Unbuttoning his shirt, Nish dropped it on the floor. Her face turned his way.

Irisis gave a disgusted snort. 'I don't believe this!'

'Just keep quiet!' The clothes were too small for Nish, of course. Taking up the spider-silk shirt, he smoothed it across his chest and rubbed it up and down, then pulled it over his head, burying his face in it. It felt sensual, like nothing he had ever worn before.

Tucking the garment under his arm, he did the same with the pants, socks and gloves, then held the shirt out to her. She took it by one finger and thumb, holding it away as if it was crawling with spiders. Slowly she brought it up to her face and sniffed. She sniffed it up and down, across and back, gave a little grunt and touched her face with it, gingerly. It seemed to be all right for she pulled open the neck hole, eased her head through and drew it on. At the level of her breasts she stopped, giving a little shudder of remembrance. She pulled it down and stood frozen, one foot in the air. Nish held his breath. Irisis, by the door, was doing the same.

Ullii gave a little, sensual chuckle that was, to Nish, like his lover blowing in his ear. In a single movement she stepped into the trousers, pulled them up to the waist and leapt high in the air, crying out for joy. She ran around the room skipping and dancing.

Coming up behind Nish, she threw her arms around him and put her hands over his nose. He sniffed her hands, evidently what was expected, for she resumed her dance. She was perfectly dexterous and graceful. Despite the mask, Ullii knew where everything in the room was. She did not once look like tipping over the water bucket or crashing into the walls.

Nish went to the door. 'Very good,' said Irisis. 'This afternoon we begin.'

TWENTY-TWO

Before long, Tiaan found herself at a dead end. She turned back and not far from the entrance to the ninth level crossed a passage that she must have stumbled by yesterday without noticing. Right or left? Going left, she soon encountered another cross-passage. Tiaan stopped, frowning. It would be easy to get lost in here. Returning to the entrance, she looked up the shaft. Hammering echoed down. They must be preparing to come after her.

She hurried back to the first cross-passage, noting the number of steps and wishing she had paper to make a map on. As a prentice artisan she'd often been required to memorise an entire blueprint and recreate it perfectly a week or even a year later. Could she still do it? As she paced, Tiaan began to create a map of the mine in her head. It would not be accurate, since she could only estimate directions, but better than none. Eventually, if she did not starve to death, or her pursuers didn't find her first, she hoped to locate the long passage Joeyn had mentioned, that led to the other mine.

She moved back and forth, building the map in her mind, a labyrinth of thread-like passages with herself just a speck at the centre. At one point Tiaan realised that she was humming a tune. She felt back in control.

A full day went by, judging by her stomach, before she had

mapped the entire level. Maintaining the relationships between wandering adits, shafts and pillars was hard work. Her skills were rusty. She enjoyed testing herself though; the harder the work, the better.

The lower sections were partly flooded. She wished she'd brought along Joeyn's grappling pole to probe the lifeless water. Without it, all she could do was wade in and hope it did not come up over her shoulders, for her gear was too heavy to swim with.

Most times the water only reached her thighs but it was damnably cold and not doing her boots any good. By the end of the day Tiaan was exhausted and the wet cloth had chafed the insides of her thighs.

She found a place to sleep for the night, took off her clothes and inspected the damage. She was red raw. Imagining what Matron would say to blemishes in such a strategic spot, she burst out laughing. It sounded strange, and more so after the pitch-shifted echoes came back. On edge; maniacal. That was not far off it, either.

Tiaan had been thinking about the glowing crystal all day. It was different from every hedron she'd come across. It had never been shaped, it just *was*, as it had crystallised half a billion years ago. She wanted it desperately, and that worried her. Could the bond have been established after only using it once? It took all her willpower to leave it in her pack.

That night she again dreamed about the young man, though this time it was different. They were on opposite sides of the room, gazing at each other. He began to run towards her. She ran too. He held out his arms, naked desire on his face. She froze. Her daydreams had always ended with the rescue. The reality of this dream was that he wanted something of her. What was it? Afraid to commit herself, she turned away. He let his arms fall and, with sunken shoulders, stumbled off.

Once Tiaan woke, she recalled the mortifying emotions all too well. Feelings of helplessness, of having no idea what was required of her, flooded her. That was the other reason she had not taken a partner. To share her life with another meant losing the control that she had worked so hard for. Afraid of those unplumbed emotions, she closed her eyes and groaned aloud. Then a thud echoed down the tunnel.

They were after her! Stripping off her dry clothes, Tiaan put back on the wet, which were clammily uncomfortable. With the pack on her back, the coil of rope over her shoulder, the glowing crystal in one hand and a crust in the other, she set off.

Only as she neared the first cross-passage did Tiaan realise that the map of the ninth level had vanished from her mind. She stopped dead, panic rising up from her stomach like bile. How could it have happened? Without that rational part of her controlling the world around, she was no more than an indenture breaker, a non-citizen who had no rights and belonged nowhere.

Thud-thud! Nearer this time. She stood still, pushing the panic down as she had so often done before a test of her prentice's skills. *Calm yourself. You can do it. This map is simple compared to the blueprints you've memorised. Take deep breaths, one after another. Empty your mind of everything else.*

Tiaan could not get the map back – she was too tired. Snatches of a soldiers' marching song drifted up the tunnel. Panic told her to run. She almost gave in to it.

She had to consciously lay out, step by step, what had long ago become automatic. 'Start from the beginning, girl!' the old crafter had told her many times. 'You're trying to do more than your mind can manage.'

This place could not beat her. Imagining her starting point at the entrance to the ninth level, Tiaan mentally went into the dark and began to make her map anew. She traced a path to the intersection where she now stood. As she passed it, the side passages marked themselves on her map, though only as far as the illumination from the hedron reached.

She walked forward, slowly mapping the labyrinth again, then one time she went through an intersection and the cross-passages of her mental map ran off through the darkness to link up with another tunnel. She refused to think about that, just kept going, and suddenly the map exploded into her mind, entire and complete. At that instant she understood where the long tunnel to the other mine had to be.

She zig-zagged through the maze for a couple of hours, twice through breast-deep sections of water. It was cold and uncomfortable but she did not mind – the water was an obstacle to her pursuers too, and one they could not track her across. They would have to search every passage.

Once on the long tunnel, Tiaan moved as fast as she could. She had to get well ahead or she'd never dare to rest, and already she was desperate for sleep. After going hard for another few hours, Tiaan calculated that she'd gone about five thousand paces: a league. She sat down for a brief rest and a swig from Joeyn's flask. It was only water; the brandy was gone long ago. A pity – she could have done with something to warm her up right now.

Hunger had become a constant ache, one she could do nothing about. But at least she had heard no further sound from behind. That was no comfort. Maybe they knew where she was headed and had sent people off another way to catch her. Or maybe they were just sneaking along, biding their time. After all, they thought they were hunting a lyrinx.

On and on and on. Step after weary step. Slower and slower. Everything hurt except her stomach, which was numb, though when she drank it throbbed. Tiaan snatched a few hours of restless sleep, afraid they would come on her in the darkness. She lost track of time. Had it been a day, or two, or even three she'd been marching? Her map was still extending eastwards. She'd gone nearly five leagues in this winding, up-and-down but otherwise featureless passage.

At some point along that endless scream of infinity, Tiaan became aware that she was being followed. She did not know how she knew. There had been no sound, no telltale glimmer of light. Her pursuers were a long way back, but they were there.

Tiaan came around a gentle curve in the tunnel, which dipped down and at the bottom contained water as far as the light extended. She moved into it, her legs so lethargic that it was like pushing through syrup. What if it was too deep to wade?

The water came up to her neck, her chin, her lips, then fell again. After ten minutes of splashing, the tunnel ended in smooth rock. Too smooth – it turned out to be a stone door and it took little searching to find the concealed lever that opened it. Tiaan was not surprised to find a door. There were many old tunnels in these mountains, and in the past whole villages had sheltered in them during the winter. She stood in the water, staring at the blank face. The tunnel walls were still granite but the door was pale grey stone. She ran the tip of the knife down it. Marble.

She heaved on the lever; the door rose vertically with much whining and grating, and when it reached its full height, an alarming *twang*. Water poured through, pulling at her trousers. Tiaan ducked under and took hold of the lever on the other side, wondering if she could seal the door against her pursuers. There was a louder *twang*, the slab fell, drenching her, and split down the middle.

Tiaan kept going, shortly to be confronted by a mound of blue clay and fragments of rock. A great shear cut across the tunnel, on the other side of which the pink granite changed to crystalline marble, streaked with blue and purple. Above, a ragged cavity extended into the darkness.

She passed through rock that was every colour and pattern she could imagine, eventually to emerge in a natural cavern about the size of the breeding factory. A ragged pool of clear water lay in the centre. The floor sloped up on all sides, though much higher to her left, where corrugated humps and hollows were reminiscent of theatre benches.

Tiaan drank from the pool, filled her flask, washed her face and hands, went up and heaved herself onto the highest hump. Down to her left, five passages led from the cavern, roughly like the ribs of a fan. Surely one of them was the exit she had been seeking for so long. Utterly exhausted, she made a bed between the humps and slept.

In a long dreaming of being hunted, several times Tiaan was roused by sharp rapping, a distant, echoing sound as of metal on stone. It sounded like a stonemason working on a carving, except that the blows were few and separated by long intervals of silence.

The sound was more intriguing than disturbing; each blow roused Tiaan momentarily before she slipped back into sleep. Soon she settled into a dreamless slumber, the like of which she had not had in weeks.

'There it is! Up top! Careful now!'

The cry frightened Tiaan awake. The cavern stank of burning tar. She sat up, rubbing sleep from her eyes.

Four tarred sticks blazed in a staggered line down below, near the tunnel through which she had entered. Another crept towards her. The light revealed soldiers, in uniforms she did not recognise.

'It moves! Shoot now!' roared a man in sergeant's colours.

Tiaan threw herself flat. Crossbow bolts smashed into bench and wall. 'Stop!' she screamed.

After a silence, the sergeant shouted, 'Who are you?'

'I'm from Tiksi!' She dared not say her name. 'Don't fire!'

'Show yourself. Hold your hands high.'

She did so, slowly and carefully. Five heavily armed soldiers trooped up. She did not know any of them.

'I'm Sergeant Numbl, of the Morrin garrison,' said the leader. He was a tall man, greatly scarred on the left cheek. 'What are you doing here?'

'Have you seen the lyrinx?' a dark, thickset soldier added.

'There is no lyrinx,' she said weakly.

'What is she talking about?' the soldiers cried. 'Where has it gone?'

'Maybe it's a shapechanger lyrinx, turned itself into this miserable girl,' said a thin bald man. 'Better kill it to make sure.' Thrusting his sword forward, he twisted it and made a squelching sound.

Sergeant Numbl clouted him out of the way. A dangerous light flashed in his eyes and, taking Tiaan by the collar, he shook her. 'It was *you*! We've been hunting *you*, all the time.'

'Yes!' she whispered, terrified of the man.

'Who is she?' asked another soldier, who had a chirping, over-the-mountains accent.

'It must be the runaway from the breeding factory,' said the thickset soldier. 'The mad woman!'

'Shut up!' the sergeant roared over his shoulder. His face had gone purple, except for the scars, which were bone-yellow. 'Do you realise what you have cost us?'

'You were shooting at me!' she cried.

'Stupid girl!' Numbl slapped her hard across the face.

The bald soldier raised his sword. Drops of saliva hung on his lower lip. 'Let me finish her,' he said eagerly.

'We might as well have the pleasure of her first,' said a broad-shouldered, good-looking man with a receding chin disguised by wisps of beard. He began to tear at her garments. Tiaan tried to protect herself, but another soldier caught her hands.

This could not be happening. 'You're scum!' she said, struggling furiously. 'I'd sooner be eaten by a lyrinx.'

'That's all you'll be good for when we've finished with you,' said the good-looking man.

'You would take a woman without her consent, Pelf?' said Numbl.

'She's a runaway,' said Pelf. 'If you don't like it, walk away.'

'Please, no!' Tiaan whispered.

'I'll take care of her,' cried the bald man with the bloodlust in his eye.

Seizing him by the arm, the sergeant walked down toward the tunnels. 'Oh, let them have their fun! We might all be dead tomorrow.'

The remaining three threw her down on the stone. Tiaan struggled but they were too strong. Someone bound her hands. She screamed at the top of her voice. A rough hand went over her mouth.

'Hoy?' came an echoing cry from below. The sergeant ran toward the left-most of the five lower passages, to listen at the entrance.

'Hoy?' came the cry, once more.

'Yes?' said Numbl cautiously. Before long Gi-Had appeared, followed by a troop of ten soldiers, and a guide.

'How did you get here?' said Numbl in amazement.

'I would ask the same of you?'

Tiaan bit the hand, which jerked out of the way. She gasped for air.

'What's going on?' roared Gi-Had. 'I heard a woman scream.'

The soldiers let Tiaan go. She stood up. There was a mutter of conversation down below.

'You damn fools!' Gi-Had roared. 'That's Artisan Tiaan! If you've harmed her you'll be quartered by the perquisitor himself! Get down here.'

The soldiers trotted down, looking everywhere but at him.

'How were we supposed to know?' said the sergeant. 'Nobody told us you wanted her.'

'Tiksi cretins!' Gi-Had raged. 'So you just go around molesting every woman you meet, do you?'

None of them met his eyes.

'Bah!' cried Gi-Had. 'Get out of my way! Tiaan, I must – '

Before he could move there again came that tapping sound she had heard in her dreams.

The overseer's head whipped around. 'What's that? Sergeant, go and see.'

The entire group went still. Tiaan could hear Gi-Had's breath whistling in and out. No one spoke. *Tap-tap-tap*.

Numbl tiptoed from one entrance to another, trying to work out where the noise was coming from.

'I heard it before,' Tiaan called down.

'When?' cried Gi-Had.

'Quite a few hours ago.'

'It could be someone in the mine,' said Pelf.

'This mine's been abandoned for twenty years,' said Gi-Had. 'It was worked out when my father was still alive.'

'Could still be a prospector in there,' said the bald man who had wanted to kill her.

'Or a bear,' the sergeant conjectured, 'cracking open a goat's thigh bone.'

'I said shut up!' hissed Gi-Had. 'Gull, Dom, Hants, Ven-Koy, Thrawn! Stand at the tunnel entrances and listen. Everyone else, ready your weapons and take cover.'

Five of his soldiers went to their positions. 'It's probably nothing,' said Gi-Had, pacing back and across. Another tap.

'It came from here,' said stocky, white-haired Hants, an ugly man with pox scars and a cast in his left eye. He was standing at the entrance to the middle tunnel. 'Will I go and see?'

'Yes!' said Gi-Had. 'Hey, what's your name?' he asked the good-looking soldier.

'Pelf, surr!'

'You're a *brave* man, Pelf. Go with him.'

The two headed off, pitch-coated torches flaring. Tiaan flexed her bound hands, began to go down, then stopped. Everyone was as tense as wire. Gi-Had jammed a torch in a crack in the floor and stared into the third tunnel, tapping one boot. There was no further sound.

'Can you see their torches?' he asked.

'No!' said tall Gull, beside him.

'Neither can I,' Gi-Had muttered.

A scream reverberated out of the tunnel.

'What was that?' whispered Gull.

'More torches!' yelled Gi-Had, gesturing behind him. The soldiers crowded around.

'We'd better go help them,' said Gull, making no attempt to do so.

There came a thud, a shriek, and feet pounded down the tunnel. Pelf burst from the entrance, running without sword or torch. A continuous moan came from his open mouth.

'What is it, man?' yelled the sergeant. 'What's the matter with you?'

Pelf kept going. Gi-Had caught him by the shoulder, twisting him around. He shook him. 'Speak, damn you!'

Pelf choked and a clot of slobber ran into his beard. 'A band of lyrinx. We walked right into them.'

'How many?' said Gi-Had.

'What's happened to Hants?' yelled Numbl.

'He's dead. It bit his head right off. He kept walking, like a slaughtered rooster. The brains squirted . . .' Pelf vomited on his boots.

Gi-Had blanched but stood his ground. 'There's fifteen of us, and the guide. How many of them, Pelf?'

'Three, that I saw.' His downy jaw quivered.

The soldiers moved uneasily. 'Not good odds,' said the sergeant. 'Reckon we'd best retreat while we can. And maybe send someone on ahead to warn the manufactory. Just in case,' he added in a low voice, 'if you take my meaning.'

'Good idea. Rusp, go with the guide. Run, and don't stop for anything.'

Rusp, a man as wide as he was high, said, 'Think I'd be more use here, surr.'

'Maybe you're right. Gull – '

'I'll go,' said Pelf. 'We can take the woman too. Get her out of the way.'

A chill ran all the way down Tiaan's back.

'Get to your post, Pelf!' said Gi-Had. 'I'll not leave her in *your* hands. I'll be looking to you to lead the defence, since you showed such courage with an unarmed woman.'

Gull and the guide, an ancient miner Tiaan had met once or twice, by the name of Hurny, hurried off. The soldiers moved into a semicircle around the mouth of the third tunnel.

Tiaan did not rate their chances highly, or her own. She began to rasp her bonds on an edge of stone, since she could not reach her knife. It was hard work, for the marble tended to wear away before the fibres did. She had not made much progress when a noise shocked the soldiers rigid. It was a sharp *clack*, like an armoured foot striking a pebble.

'They're coming!' hissed Gi-Had.

The soldiers jammed their torches into whatever crevices and hollows they could find. The advance guard presented their javelins. Those on the wings of the semicircle held out swords. They looked like a bunch of terrified youths. Two, armed with crossbows, moved back.

Another noise, like the skittering of a stone across the floor. The javelins wavered, dipped then firmed. Fourteen pairs of eyes stared at the black opening. Tiaan rasped her bonds furiously.

Without warning a dark creature erupted from the tunnel to the left of the middle one. Another lyrinx came out of the right tunnel. They hurled themselves through the swordsmen and attacked the javelin-armed soldiers from behind. Three were dead before they could get their weapons into position. The fourth impaled a lyrinx in its armoured thigh, then his spear was broken, and he with it.

'To me!' roared Gi-Had, standing at the front with the sergeant. 'Archers, *fire!*'

The crossbows fired over the heads of the soldiers. A green-crested lyrinx fell, shot through the eye. Another was pierced in one mighty shoulder, though it shrugged at the injury and kept fighting. The creature was powerfully armoured there.

Four swordsmen were still on their feet, and Gi-Had. They stood shoulder to shoulder, their swords weaving, while the archers struggled to reload their clumsy weapons. A third lyrinx hurtled out of the middle tunnel. The soldiers had their backs to him and three fell without ever knowing why. The sergeant and Gi-Had fought on.

One archer fired again. The third lyrinx, which was smaller than the others, clawed at the back of its neck. It recovered, bounded across the cavern and took out both archers with single blows. A bolt shot vertically from the other crossbow, shattering a stalactite to pieces and raining down shards of limestone on the creature. A large piece struck it on the head, felling it. The second lyrinx had disembowelled Numbl, but was skewered between the thigh plates by Gi-Had. Purple blood gurgled out. Gi-Had feinted, ducked, darted to one side and ran for the tunnel that led back to the hedron mine. The lyrinx went after him, limping badly.

In all her life Tiaan had never seen such bloodshed and brutality. Everywhere she looked, men were thrashing, moaning, dying. She gave a last rasp of her bonds and they parted. She crept down to the battlefield. Twelve soldiers lay on the floor. Ten were dead, no question of it, and the others had not long to live.

One was handsome Pelf, the man who had wanted to molest her. A slash of the lyrinx's claws had opened a rift between his ribs, from which pink foam oozed. Parts of one lung could be seen.

Despite everything, Tiaan could feel only pity for the man. She put a hand on his brow.

Pelf's eyes opened wide as he relived the horror of the last few minutes. They drifted as aimlessly as fireflies, before lighting on her face. She saw his self-revulsion. 'I knew I was doing the greatest wickedness of all,' he said. 'I brought all this down on us.'

Pelf twitched and a clot of pink foam shot from the chest cavity to land quivering on his trouser front. He watched it dribble down, then caught at her hand. 'Take this dagger, girl. Put out my eyes that lusted over what they had no right to. Tear out my tongue that urged foul rape on you. Sever my treacherous member . . .'

'Hush!' said Tiaan. 'You're dying, Pelf. Make your peace before it's too late.'

She ran to the other man. He was fatally wounded, blood pooling in the hollows of the floor beside him, and already unconscious.

She dared not go after Gi-Had, not with a live lyrinx between her and him. But she could not stay here with the mutilated dead, and maybe the lyrinx already on the way back. There had to be another way out. Perhaps that was what the tapping signified.

She'd need plenty of food if she was to venture outside, for it would take days to get back to the manufactory from here. Feeling in the unconscious man's pack, she found some cloth-wrapped rations. 'Have you food?' she said hoarsely to Pelf. She felt uncomfortable about robbing the dead and the dying.

'Take it all!' he gasped. 'I've gold in my wallet. Take that too!'

She took the provisions but not the gold, and rifled the sergeant's pack as well, until she had as much food as she could carry. The torches were burning low now. The scene was like a twisted, classical painting of hell. Tiaan heaved the bulging pack on her back and went down between the two dead lyrinx toward the middle tunnel.

As she passed by, the smaller lyrinx grabbed her by the forearm. She tried to reach her knife but with a swift movement the creature caught that arm too, holding both in a clawed hand that could have spanned her skull. As it drew her forward, leathery elephant skin parted on its face to reveal an eye. It was large and oval, yellow with tawny specks and a star-shaped pupil.

The head was enormous, the mouth as wide as her skull. Tiaan had heard awful tales about lyrinx. It would torment her just for the fun of it. The mouth opened, revealing a large quantity of grey teeth. Its breath was strangely sweet. Chameleon colours flickered across skin that had been dark-grey.

'Get it over with!' she said limply.

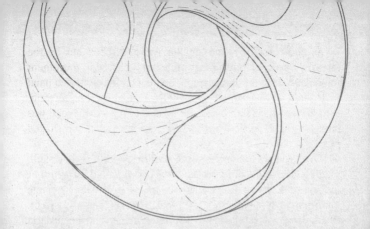

PART THREE

SEEKER

TWENTY-THREE

Irisis sat in a leather chair in the master crafter's old chambers, listening to the storm rage outside. The wind howled in the battlements and it was turning into a blizzard. The weather suited her mood. The experiment with Ullii was bound to fail. What was she to do then?

Another artisan might have fled to make a new life somewhere far away. Irisis could not. Her entire identity was tied up with her family and her trade. For all that she railed against them, for all that she neglected them, she would rather die, even in disgrace, than live without her family.

Nish brought the seeker down before dawn, when the manufactory was at its quietest. Even so, it was a trial for her. Ullii shied at every sound and whenever someone approached she shrank against the wall.

The crafter's chambers comprised two rooms. The larger one was a combined office and workshop with an enormous rosewood desk in the centre, surrounded by three leather chairs. Along the far wall a wide bench was still cluttered with the equipment Barkus had been using when he died. Another wall contained a library of several dozen bound volumes, plus scrolls and fan-folded books. The smaller room was stuffed with artisans' tools, charts and blueprints, mechanical devices complete and incomplete, and stores and materials of every kind. Irisis had found the reels of spider-silk there.

A tray beside the door contained food and drink. Irisis was tapping one foot when Nish came in, Ullii at his heels like a masked, earmuff-wearing dog. He closed the outer door and locked it, then the inner.

Ullii looked anxious. Irisis wondered if it was the unfamiliar surroundings, or what they expected of her. She stood against the inner door, head to one side, sniffing the air.

'Would you like something to eat, Ullii?' Irisis said loudly.

The earmuffs allowed some sound through and the seeker jumped, as if she'd not known the artisan was there. There were so many odours in the room that she had not picked Irisis out. It smelt of old books, mouldy carpet, the spicy bouquet of rosewood, oil and fuming acid from the bench, hot candle wax and an indescribable odour from the mounted swordfish over the fireplace. Irisis had half a dozen aromatic oil diffusers going over candle stubs: civet and rosemary and the sharp tang of cedar oil. She'd done it deliberately, to see if Ullii could be confused.

'No, thank you,' Ullii said, mimicking Irisis's voice. She went around the room step by step, once bumping into the desk, another time a stool, though only on her first circuit. Occasionally she touched things, or brought them to her nose.

Nish stayed close behind. He can't take his eyes off the little cow, Irisis thought. It made her angry. Could she be jealous of the seeker? Surely not.

'Tell us what you're doing, Ullii,' said Nish softly.

Perhaps too softly, for she looked around as if trying to make out a whisper in the dark. He repeated his words more loudly. Ulli looked at Nish, using her own voice now, which was as soft and colourless as her hair. 'The lattice is different here. It's all twisted up and there are new knots in it.'

'From the old crafter's artefacts, no doubt,' said Irisis. 'If you can see the Secret Art, you're in the right place. He had magical devices aplenty. He used to show them to me when I was little.'

'I can only see two,' said Ullii, in Irisis's voice. She no longer used Nish's. That irritated Irisis too. Ullii answered Nish's question. 'I am seeking out the lattice and trying to fit you into it.'

'What does it look like?' Irisis asked.

A stubborn expression crossed Ullii's face, then she seemed to think better of it. 'Did you make this?' She held out the front of the spider-silk blouse.

'Yes,' said Irisis. 'Do you like it?'

'It feels lovely. Other clothes make me itch and burn all over.' She shivered. 'The lattice looks just how I want it to. I change it, sometimes.'

'What does it look like now?' asked Nish.

She frowned, just visible above the mask. 'Fans.'

'Fans?' cried Irisis. 'What the hell does that mean?'

For once Ullii did not cringe or bridle, though she moved closer to Nish. 'I like fans!' she said defiantly. 'Mancer Flammas, who let me live in his dungeon, had hundreds of them. They were beautiful. All the colours; all the patterns. I used to peek through my fingers.'

'Ullii, our minds can't see what you see,' said Nish. 'We don't understand what you mean by fans.'

'My lattice is a fan. A great one comes out in front of me, folded in a hundred places.' She held out spread arms. 'It's turquoise now, but I can change the colour if you like – '

'I don't care what bloody – ' Shushed by Nish, Irisis broke off.

'Everything in front of me is on the fan, like a million scribbles. People look different to *things*. They're brighter, but tangled. Sometimes I can unravel their knots.'

'What people?' said Irisis, intrigued. 'You mean you can see everyone in the world?'

'Of course not! Only people with *talents*.' Her scorn was withering. 'Most are just little tiny spots and I can't see inside, but some people make bright tangles, especially ones who use the Secret Art. Jal-Nish taught me that.'

'Can you see me?' Nish asked eagerly.

'You don't have any talent.' She said it so baldly that he cringed.

'You can't see me either,' Irisis said in a dead voice.

'Oh, yes. I can see *you*! But you're not a knot, you're a hard black ball.'

251

After a pause Irisis spoke. 'You said *fans*.'

'Another fan goes behind me. It's azure now, much smaller. I can't see it so well. And fans go out to the sides.' She held her arms out. 'And up, and down. The one that goes down is brown but I can't see much on it.'

'Brilliant!' said Irisis. 'That's the talent we've been working so hard to tap? *She scribbles on fans?* We might as well ask the perquisitor to cut off our heads right now.'

Ullii froze with her arms out. Nish gave Irisis a furious glare.

Ullii slowly rotated, arms spread, until she faced Nish. 'Cut your head off?' she whispered.

'If we don't find Artisan Tiaan and get her back, that's what will happen to us,' said Nish. 'What we were hoping, Ullii, was to make a magic device that we could use with you, to see where Tiaan might be.'

'It doesn't have to be fans,' said Ullii. 'It can be anything I want it to be. Sometimes the world is like an egg floating in the air, full of coloured speckles. Or – '

Irisis gripped a handful of yellow hair as if to tear it out. She began grinding her teeth.

Nish squatted down in front of Ullii. 'The problem is, Ullii, that we don't understand how you see the world. We don't see in fans, or specks in eggs, and we don't know how to use your lattice to find Tiaan. We have to find her or we will lose the war and the lyrinx – ' He broke off as she shrank away.

'She has to know,' said Irisis.

'The lyrinx will eat us all,' Nish finished.

Ullii choked, scuttled into the storeroom and curled into a ball. They did not go after her.

Nish carried the platter of food to the desk, offering it to Irisis. She refused. He took a handful of dried figs, tearing their leathery skins open with his teeth and sucking the grainy insides out. Irisis found the sound particularly irritating.

'This isn't going well, Cryl-Nish!'

He looked up, startled. 'That's the first time you've used my proper name in ages.'

'Which should tell you how desperate I feel.'

'I can't believe *you'd* give up, Irisis.'

'We'll never do it. We'll never see what she sees, and even if we could, I can't make a device to hunt Tiaan down. You know why.'

'I'm beginning to,' said Nish.

'What are you going to tell your father?'

'That it's impossible to make a seeker device because it would take years to work out how Ullii does it. That's true enough, anyway.'

'Yes! No need to say that it's because I'm a useless, incompetent fraud!'

'No need,' Nish echoed. 'We're finished, then.'

He wandered the room, looking at the charts, books and scrolls, and the strange, half-finished devices on the bench. Irisis tore the end off a stick of cinnamon-flavoured sausage. She ate a small piece before laying it aside and staring gloomily at the dusty table.

Someone knocked on the outer door. Nish ignored it but the knocking continued.

'Will you answer the damned thing!' Irisis snapped.

He opened the inner door, unbolted the outer. It was the perquisitor, looking agitated. 'Well?' Jal-Nish cried.

'We're making progress,' lied Nish. 'I can't talk now; we're in the middle of something.'

Jal-Nish grabbed him by the shirt. 'You've got till dawn. Gi-Had's troops found Tiaan in the mine but a band of lyrinx attacked them. Gi-Had was the only one to survive. And Tiaan ... Tiaan ...' He choked on his own rage. 'This is going to ruin me.'

'What?' cried Nish. A cold foreboding came over him. 'What is it? Is she dead?'

'Her body wasn't among the others. Either she's dead and eaten, or they've taken her! If they torture our secrets out of her ...'

'Maybe she's escaped,' Irisis interrupted. 'She's good at it.'

'No one could escape a lyrinx. What am I going to tell the scrutator?'

Nish sank to his knees. 'What are we going to do?'

The perquisitor hauled him up. 'The scrutator wants Tiaan. We're going to find her, if she's alive, and get her back.'

He flung Nish backward to land hard on his bottom. 'You've got until dawn. Succeed or fail, you two are coming with us to finish your work, or to go up against the lyrinx as common soldiers.' He slammed the door in Nish's face.

'I feel sick,' said Nish. 'Like when my father asked me about my school work. Nothing was ever good enough.'

Selecting a piece of cheese, Irisis gnawed at a hard edge. Nish scratched his fingernails on the floorboards. The noise was so annoying that she wanted to smack him in the mouth.

'There's only one thing we can do,' said Nish, 'since making a seeker device is quite impossible. We'll have to take Ullii with us and try to use her directly.'

'She'll go mad!'

'Our necks depend on finding a way.'

Ullii came creeping over to Nish and touched his cheek. 'I want to help you, Nish.'

'I know you do.' He sat up. 'Can you see Tiaan?'

Ullii shrugged. 'I don't know what she looks like.'

Irisis leaned forward. 'The other day you said you could see a woman with a bright crystal. Can you still see her?'

'The crystal went out.'

'You mean she's dead?' cried Nish.

'I can't see her.'

'When was this?'

'Today. Yesterday.'

'Which, Ullii? It's important.'

'I don't know.'

Irisis put a controller on the table and unfolded its arms. 'This was made by Tiaan. It might help you sense her out.'

Ullii did not look at it. 'I don't need to sense her out. If the crystal wakes, I'll see it in my lattice.'

'Is the woman Tiaan?' Irisis demanded. 'Is her knot like this controller's?'

'No, but I can tell she made it.'

'So the woman was Tiaan?' Nish said urgently.

'Yes.'

'At last!' Irisis cried. 'And what is the crystal? Is it like the one in this?' She held the controller out.

'No,' said Ullii.

'What about this?' Irisis took the pliance from her neck and pressed it into the seeker's hands.

'No, it's *much* stronger.'

'What can it be?' said Nish.

Irisis's blue eyes positively gleamed. 'I wonder . . .?'

'What?'

'Doesn't matter.'

'Do you understand maps?' Nish said to Ullii.

'I know what they are. I've never looked at one. The bright light hurts my eyes.'

Pulling down one of the charts he had been looking at earlier, he unrolled it on the floor. 'This is a map of the manufactory. Here is the room where you live . . .' He broke off. 'Of course, you can't see it, and I can't describe it well enough.'

She stared at him through the mask. A long silence. She shivered. Finally, 'I will try with the . . . goggles. Just for a little while.'

He fetched them off the bench then eased the mask off her face. Her eyes were screwed shut. He fitted the goggles and buckled the straps.

Irisis, noting how his fingers grazed Ullii's nape, scowled.

Ullii looked down.

'Can you see the map?' Nish asked.

'Yes.' Her reply was faint.

He explained the symbols for walls, doors, windows and furniture. She seemed to catch on quickly. Ullii lived in a world of symbols. 'Your room is here. This is the way we walked today. This is where we are now.'

She traced the walls with a finger, so Nish knew she could see them.

'This symbol is the scale. You can use it to work out how far things are from each other – how many steps we walked.'

She understood the concept of measurement but could not apply it. Direction was another problem – she knew right and left, front and back, but the points of the compass meant nothing to her. Her lattice was not based on a fixed frame of reference.

Nish tried to explain north, south, east and west, but Ullii related them to right hand and left hand, becoming hopelessly confused when he turned the map around. He showed her another map, of the lands between Tiksi, the manufactory and her home town of Fassafarn. That meant nothing to her either – the journey here, inside her bag all the daylight hours, had been such a nightmare that she had blocked everything out. Ullii had no idea how far she'd gone, what lands she had crossed or even how long it had taken.

'This is so frustrating,' Nish said to Irisis that evening. They had made no progress at all.

'Give it a rest. You can't teach her in a day what takes most people years.' She turned to Ullii. 'Tomorrow, we must go after Tiaan. We have to go *outside*. We need you to find her. No one else can do it. Will you help us?'

Ullii tore off the goggles and put the mask back on. She was trembling. Putting her hands over her eyes, she shook her head from side to side.

Irisis stood up. 'What is it? Is she saying no?'

'I don't know,' said Nish.

Ullii also rose, looking up at them. Her fingers were curled into hooks. 'I will go with you,' she said in a despairing voice. 'Though I'm afraid. But if you leave me behind . . .'

'We're afraid too,' said Irisis.

'I'm very, very afraid,' shuddered Ullii. 'Clawers. Clawers everywhere.'

TWENTY-FOUR

The lyrinx's mouth opened wider. The front teeth were as long as her thumb and fearsomely sharp. Tiaan closed her eyes.

The creature dragged her closer, trying to say something. Only a choking noise came out, as if there was a bone caught in its throat.

'Chzurrrk!' it said. 'Zzhurripthk!'

She thought it was going to throw up all over her. Then, as its mouth yawned wider, she saw the crossbow bolt protruding into its gullet through the back of its neck. Blood ran down its throat. It tried to get its tongue at the obstruction but could not reach. It clawed at the back of its neck with its free hand, which had lost three fingers in the battle. The bolt was too deeply embedded to grip.

The creature gave a choking cough, which brought purple blood foaming up its throat. Another cough spattered Tiaan with the stuff. It was drowning in its own blood. Its eyes crossed; it gasped a breath which made a gurgling sound deep in its chest, like a plumber clearing a blocked sewer pipe, and its grip relaxed. Tiaan rolled out of the way as the lyrinx collapsed, still clawing at its neck. Its impact with the floor blew foam everywhere.

She stood up on shaky legs, watching the creature in the guttering flares. A whiff of pitch-smoke caught in her nose. It felt as if her air passages were on fire. Bent double with coughing, Tiaan circled behind the creature. The bolt had gone through the corded muscle to the right of its spine. The other beast lay nearby. It looked dead but she kept well clear. The live lyrinx tried to turn its head and gave another gasp.

Unlike other lyrinx she had seen, this one lacked wings, apart from a pair of vestigial nubs below its shoulders. Something seemed wrong about it – it did not quite seem to fit its body.

A spear lay on the ground. If she forced it into the lyrinx's neck beside the bolt, might it be enough to kill it? She raised the spear, staring at the bloody wound, imagining the gruesome thud of blade into flesh, the creature thrashing and screaming. Tiaan hesitated and with a pained grunt the lyrinx turned its head, looking her in the eye.

She willed herself to deliver the death blow. Her sheltered life had not prepared her for this. Tiaan had not killed a living creature before, but now she had to. She dare not risk leaving it alive to follow her.

The big eyes were mesmerising. Blue patterns ran up and down its neck. Tiaan felt an unexpected surge of compassion and wondered if the lyrinx was trying to control her. Some of them were mancers.

She plunged the spear into the wound. The lyrinx screamed and flung itself around, tearing the spear out of her hand. One thrashing leg caught her on the hip; it was like being struck by a battering ram. Before she could pick herself up, the lyrinx was standing over her, the spear still waggling in the back of its neck.

'Glarrh!' it rapped. 'Minchker!'

'I don't understand you,' she gasped. It was hard to make out what it was saying. A wonder it could speak at all with such an injury.

'Take . . . out,' it said in a bloody croak.

Tiaan hurt too much to move. Seizing her by the shoulder with its good hand, it squeezed so hard that her joints ground together. Claws pricked through her skin. 'Take out!'

There was no choice. 'I will. Let me go.'

It released the shoulder but immediately caught her leg. 'Go behind. Take out. Do not . . . try again.'

She edged behind, wondering if she dared defy it. It could tear her leg right off. Eyeing the mess her spear had made, Tiaan felt nauseated. Besides, it seemed to have done little harm, though a lesser creature, a human, would have been dead. Tiaan took hold of the spear. Dare she give it one hard thrust? The lyrinx crushed her ankle, a warning. Pulling the blade out, she tossed the spear on the floor.

'Take out . . . bolt!'

She put her fingers around the bloody bolt and pulled. She could not get a grip.

'It's buried too deep,' she said, repulsed by the gory wound.

'Use . . . spear.'

Her tentative efforts to lever out the bolt only made a bigger mess. The operation was horrible, not to mention the lyrinx's stifled groans. It must be in agony. She wished it would die, though maybe not even that would relax the manacle around her ankle.

'Keep trying!' It choked on blood. 'If I die – you too.'

She believed it. 'I have a tool in my pack that might help.'

'Show me.' It did not let go of her ankle.

She had to take everything out to get at her toolkit. Inside the folded canvas was a pair of pincers.

'Yes,' said the lyrinx. 'Use!'

Tiaan probed into the wound, gripped the base of the bolt and gave a mighty heave. It did not budge.

Taking a firmer grip, she put her boot on the back of the creature's massive neck and pulled with all her strength. The lyrinx screamed. Waves of colour pulsed from one end of its body to the other. It tossed its head, Tiaan kept pulling, and slowly the length of steel slid free. Purple blood pulsed from the hole, replaced by a clear fluid that congealed like the skin on boiled milk. The bleeding stopped.

She dropped the bolt and bloody pincers on the floor. The lyrinx convulsed from crest to claw, gave a retching heave that deposited a bucketful of bloody, foaming mucus on the floor, then rolled over to face Tiaan. What had she done? She had helped the enemy and now it would eat her anyway.

It opened its eyes. They stared at each other. It would be six, eight, maybe ten times her weight, and all muscle, bone and armour. Even with one injured hand it could tear her in half.

'Well, are you going to eat me, or what?' Her voice squeaked.

'What is your name?' The sound, formed deep in its throat, had a raspy, reverberating echo that was clearer than before, though it seemed to have difficulty shaping the words. Was it the injury, or the strange sounds in her language?

'I am called Tiaan Liise-Mar.'

'My name is . . . Ryll. What is your work?'

'I have none.'

'Everyone works, small human. You carry mechanic's tools.'

'I was an artisan.'

'Artisan? *Of controllers?*' It made a purring sound in its throat.

Why had she mentioned that? Alarmed, she tried to distract the creature. 'To my people I am good for nothing but *breeding!*'

Ryll looked uncomprehending. He gagged, swallowed and spoke more clearly. 'My mother has bred four little ones. She still takes her place in the battle line.'

'Some of our people say females should breed, and only men work and fight.' It felt wrong to be admitting it to this monster.

'No wonder we defeat you so easily,' said the lyrinx. 'You waste the talents of half your people. Your species is flawed.' His voice grew stronger, more confident, and Tiaan realised that he spoke her language rather well. Moreover, his accent was similar to her own. She wondered who had taught him.

'Females are too precious to risk. If we lose too many, our entire species is at risk. We must breed to survive.' Tiaan found herself mouthing arguments used to justify the breeding factory, arguments that even at the time had outraged her.

'As must we, human. What if we struck at your homes, where your defenceless women live with their offspring? Better they be armed and trained to defend their children. Better still, we will feed on you all. We are fittest.'

'You're nothing but barbarians!'

'How so?' Ryll said mildly.

'You *eat* us!'

'And you *don't* eat other animals?' said the lyrinx. Surely it was just pretending astonishment.

'They're just animals. We're intelligent. *We're human!*'

He gave a sniff. 'You smell like an animal to me, little Tiaan. That you are sentient does not make you better than other animals, or more worthy. Why should I not eat you, if I be hungry? Why should you not eat me?'

She shuddered at the thought. 'I couldn't! It would not be right. Besides . . .'

'Yes?'

'You would probably taste disgusting.'

'How did your unworthy kind come to dominate this world?' said the lyrinx. 'There are a hundred sentient creatures in the void, little Tiaan. We all ate each other as the need arose.'

'Are you going to eat me?' Her voice rose to the very edge of a shriek.

'No!'

'Why not?'

'I'm not hungry. Besides . . .'

The unfinished sentence hung in the air between them. Was it a threat of worse? Torture, to extract secrets vital to the war? Or . . . She'd heard horrible stories of what the other side did to prisoners. 'What?' she snapped. 'How will you use me?'

The lyrinx drew itself up and its rubber lip curled into what she interpreted as a sneer. Tiaan had to remind herself that this creature's facial gestures would probably have entirely different meanings.

'I cannot understand your kind. Why do you insult me?'

'Why do you make war on us?' said Tiaan.

'Because you have attacked us from the moment we came out of the void.'

'You started it!'

'We would say that *you* began it.'

'But it's *our* world. You're trying to take it from us.'

'You've turned Santhenar into a sewer. A ruined world. And it's not yours anyway.'

'It's our right . . .'

'How so?' said the lyrinx. 'Who gave such a right to human-kind?'

'We are the top – '

'In our philosophy no species can confer rights on themselves. The very concept is derisory. How dare you put yourselves above other creatures! Humanity destroys for the sake of destruction. Your kind deserves to be eaten.'

'Why must we fight and die?' said Tiaan. 'Why can't we live together?'

'That is not nature's way.'

Ryll licked his lips. Was he licking his chops? Had the conversation made him hungry? Tiaan moved back a pace.

He gave a gurgling chuckle. 'If I *was* going to eat you, *nothing* could save you.'

'Why aren't you?'

'You saved my life. A debt of honour.'

Tiaan almost made a sneering reference to lyrinx honour but thought better of it. What did she know about them, apart from the propaganda that came up the mountain?

'You forced me,' she said weakly. 'I was going to kill you.'

'But you did not, and thus I owe you.'

It was all too much. She could hardly stand up for hunger. She tried, her head spun, and Tiaan collapsed.

When she roused, the creature was looming over her. 'Are you injured?'

'I'm starving. I haven't eaten for days.'

'I often go a week without eating,' said Ryll. His knee wobbled and he sat down hurriedly. 'But then, I might consume a whole antelope, or a small . . .' He broke off. 'Your tiny belly would only hold one mouthful.' He gripped her thigh, the fingers curling all the way round. 'There's nothing of you. Eat! I won't harm you.'

'What are you going to do?' she asked, taking out one of the ration packets with many an uncomfortable glance at the creature that, even sitting, was taller than she. He was holding out his injured hand, staring at it. Previously, pieces of ragged bone had protruded from the severed ends of his fingers. No bone was visible now. The stumps were covered with smooth skin, pinkish grey.

'What are you doing?' she said.

'Regenerating my hand.'

'How?'

'It's just something we can do – there are animals of your world with the same ability.'

Ryll was concentrating so hard that droplets of perspiration appeared on his brow.

'Is that a form of mancing?' she wondered.

'I dare say. Without it, we would never have survived in the void.'

No further changes were evident. Regeneration must be a slow process, and an exhausting one, for Ryll went limp, his colours fading to pastel greens and blues. He could barely hold himself up now. She might escape after all, if she was quick. She'd better be, before the other lyrinx came back.

'You are different to the humans we meet – soldiers and armed men,' said Ryll. 'We can learn a lot about humankind from people like you.'

Tiaan methodically chewed her way through the ration packet, rice pasta layered with vegetables cooked to a thick paste. Was talking to this lyrinx treason? Saving its life, even under duress, must be.

She rose, watching Ryll from the corner of her eye. He put out an arm as if to restrain her, but had to let it fall. Her chance had come. Careful now; don't alarm him in case he's saving his strength. She went across to check on Pelf and the other man. Both were dead. Tiaan closed their eyes. The dead flesh made her shudder. Ryll's eyes followed her though he lay still, panting softly. Gathering her pack, she kept well out of reach.

'Where are you going, little outcast?'

She glanced at the entrance to the long tunnel. 'The other lyrinx went up there. I have to find another way.'

'You are brave,' said the lyrinx, 'but I fear you will die just the same. There is a blizzard blowing outside. Or . . .' Ryll tilted his head, giving her a cunning look.

'What?'

'You could come with me.'

'No!' She backed away. 'I know what you want. I'm not going to be a little grub to feed your hatchlings.' The thought nearly made her scream. She imagined herself lying helpless in a food chamber while its vicious young tore out her soft parts.

'We give birth, just like you,' said Ryll. 'Do you know so little about us?'

She knew nothing but dreadful rumour and what she had seen with her eyes.

'Besides, I owe you,' he went on.

'I do not wish to insult you again,' she said carefully, 'but how do I know you have honour?'

'I could have killed and eaten you a dozen times.' Ryll slammed his mighty fist down and his skin changed to the uniform grey it had worn into battle.

Tiaan backed away hurriedly. 'Now you reveal your true colours.' The pun was unintended, though it pleased her nonetheless.

Taking a crossbow and satchel of bolts from one of the dead archers, she fitted a bolt into the weapon. 'I could kill you.'

His skin faded to a sludgy green. Ryll slid sideways, his cheek striking the floor. 'I do not doubt it, in my present state,' he said hoarsely. 'Are you going to?'

Had he attacked she would have shot him, but while he lay helpless, watching her, she could not. At the mouth of the middle tunnel she took out her crystal, which was glowing as before. Ryll's eyes widened and Tiaan regretted her action. However, he did not move. He resembled a collapsed balloon, nothing like the flesh machines the lyrinx had been before the battle.

She hurried down the passage. After a few minutes' walking she was brought up by a body lying on the rocky floor. The head lay some distance away, only recognisable by its white hair – the unfortunate Hants. The eye with the cast was staring at her.

Stepping around the corpse, she continued, shortly coming to a dead end. The tunnel stopped at a smooth rock surface. The light revealed a lever down low. As she pulled it, the door rotated, letting in a blast of freezing air. The sky was gloomy grey, the same colour as the landscape. It looked ominous.

The wind went right through her. The cold was the worst she had ever felt. An icicle began to form on her upper lip. Tiaan ducked inside to put on the mountain gear that had belonged to Joeyn's wife. The gift warmed her and she spent a minute, head bowed, thinking of her dead friend. Opening the door again, she peered out. It *was* a blizzard and only the lyrinx could have made her go out into it.

The door opened onto a narrow ledge on a steep mountain-side. To her left a spindly tree was just visible through whirling snow, maybe a hundred paces away. To her right the ledge disappeared into white. The manufactory should be on the other side of the mountain, though in this weather she could not be sure of anything. On the other hand, she dared not go back inside. She mentally tossed a coin. Left looked marginally more attractive than right. She went left and began to trudge up the ledge.

Beyond the tree she came onto an exposed slope where the wind was like needles of black ice. Tiaan looked down and could see nothing. Up was the same. Gritty snow blew horizontally. Forward and back, she now lost the path within a dozen paces. It could have been any hour of the day. Which way should she go? She had no idea. Her steps grew reluctant.

A wild gust thumped her against the cliff. It might just as easily have carried her over the edge. The weather was deteriorating rapidly. She moved on and knew that she was failing. If I keep going, Tiaan thought, I'm going to die.

She headed back. Better the risk of the lyrinx than certain death by freezing. It *might* hold to its word. *Might* be a creature of honour. The cold and wind was indifferent. It would kill her and scream defiance over her body.

Head down, Tiaan plodded into the wind. Snow clotted in

her eyes, making it impossible to see. It seemed much further, going back. Surely she'd walked a thousand paces and still there was no sign of the place. Plod, plod, one foot after another. Trudge, trudge, ice crystals growing on her eyebrows, her ears going numb. Every step took an effort of will.

At last she saw the tree. The door could be no more than a hundred steps away. She counted each step to make sure. The weather had closed in, but even so, by the time she had reached ninety Tiaan expected to see the door. It should be a black hole in the grey mountainside. She went down a slope. One hundred, one hundred and one . . . Had she left the door open, or closed? If it was closed she would never find it. Ajar, Tiaan thought, but it was difficult to remember. Her brain felt like a frozen sponge.

One hundred and twenty-one, one hundred and twenty-two. She must have gone past it. She scanned the rock face but everything was crusted with ice. Could it have been two hundred paces? Tiaan could no longer remember. Maybe it had been. She kept going, but when she reached three hundred, she knew she had gone way too far.

Turning back, she soon found herself descending a precipitous slope she definitely had not climbed before. Again she turned but the path was icy and she'd only gone a few steps before her feet went from under her. She went flying through the air and buried herself in a drift.

Struggling out, Tiaan plunged neck-deep into another snow-filled hollow. She feebly scratched her way onto a ledge and foundered. An overhang blocked the way up. The snow was now falling as heavily as she had ever known it. It was a mighty blizzard and she would be lucky to survive.

Exhausted, Tiaan put her head down on the pack for a minute. The hedron dug into her cheek. She picked it out. It had a faint warmth. Holding it in her hands, she laid her head on the pack and closed her eyes.

TWENTY-FIVE

In the days Tiaan had spent in the mine, a deep, subpolar low had formed four hundred leagues south in the Kara Agel (the Frozen Sea) which lay between the boomerang-shaped Island of Noom and the steppes of N'roxi. It roared north across the Kara Ghâshâd (the Burning Sea), funnelled through the gap between the Smennbone Range and the Inchit Hills, passed directly across Ha-Drow on the Kaer Slass or Black Sea, burying the city of Drow under two spans of snow, then, still gathering strength, screamed across the inland sea of Tallallamel heading north. After dumping more snow on Lake Kalissi, a meteor crater with a curious spire island in the middle, it hurled itself against the ramparts of the Great Mountains in Tarralladell.

The mountains pushed the storm east where it found a gap in the chain, climbed the pass and began to empty its load on the branching ranges. Somewhere south of Tiksi the storm collided with a warm front moving up the coast from distant Crandor. The wildest blizzard of the century was about to strike the eastern mountains.

The wind had risen steadily all day. Now it screamed around the side of the mountain, scouring loose snow up into clouds. Tiaan began to feel really frightened. Unless a miracle happened she was going to die here.

Tiaan was trained to survive in the mountains, but this place was going to get colder and colder until it froze her solid. A snow cave was her only chance but it was too late to look for a suitable place. The best she could do was try to close off the space under the overhang.

She dug her knife into the snow plastered on the rock face. The blade went all the way in. Carving the compacted snow into blocks, she stacked them to make a curving wall on the outer part of the ledge. It was hard work, but useful, for the face turned out to be concave. Though not quite a cave, it offered shelter above and on either side.

By the time Tiaan's knife-point skated across rock, she had closed in two-thirds of her ledge. The visibility was falling; two steps from her shelter she could no longer see it. She stamped down the drift next to her wall, hacked it into blocks and continued raising the wall. Finally it met the ledge above, sealing her in. The space, about four strides long but only two across, looked like a white sepulchre.

It was getting dark. She warmed her hands in her armpits, for the crystal had gone as cold as the rest of her world and was hardly glowing at all. If only there was a way to draw power into it to warm herself. She tried to sense out the field but found nothing. Perhaps she was too far from the node, though that seemed unlikely.

Tiaan ate another ration pack, this one an unidentifiable melange of dried fruit, nuts and suet. It lay in her stomach like a brick. After rubbing her feet in a useless attempt to warm them, she wrapped the fur-lined coat around her and leaned back against the wall, trying to rest without going to sleep. She found herself dozing a couple of times, jerked awake then slipped into a restless sleep.

Outside, the storm was approaching its climax. Snow fell as it could not have fallen since the last Ice Age, at half a span an hour. Across the range it reached halfway up the great gate of the manufactory, but here, piled against the flank of the mountain, it was much deeper. By midnight it was four spans deep and falling as fast as ever.

In her snow cave Tiaan dreamed only of cold. She could feel

it sceping into the core of her. There was nothing but cold anywhere in the world. Nothing . . .

Help!

At first she did not know where it came from. It might even have been her own subconscious. The cry slid like an icicle along her congealing synapses.

Help!

A long dreaming, a slow cooling, a slowing down of every process in her body. Imperceptibly it crept towards the point from which there was no recovery.

HELP!

Tiaan shuddered in her sleep, slipping into a dream in which a single point of light moved slowly across a field of darkness. It left behind a few glowing specks. The point started another line, making a few more specks. Another line.

It was not until the hundredth line that her dazed dream-consciousness began to see an image in the specks. A series of horizontal lines, some verticals and two diagonals radiating up from one of the verticals. They made the sparest image that could possibly be made, though Tiaan's sluggish mind could see nothing in it but geometry.

Suddenly he was there. It was the young man on the balcony, his arms thrown up in entreaty.

'I'm here,' Tiaan croaked. Her mouth felt frozen shut.

He could not have heard, for there was no change in the image.

Help!

She groped for the globe, hedron and helm, checked that the crystal was in its setting and put the helm on her head, glacier slow. The frigid wire burned her skin but that did not register.

Tiaan played with the beads and the orbiting wires, rotating them into position after position, tuning the globe to the hedron. Suddenly, with the smoothness of two streams of oil merging, they were as one. The image of glowing lines vanished and the young man was there.

Who are you? he said directly into her mind, articulating every letter in that archaic mode of speech, W-h-o a-r-e y-o-u?

She spoke aloud. 'I am Tiaan. We spoke once before. I am an artisan from Santhenar.'

Show yourself to me, Tiaan.

Shyly, for he was obviously wealthy and of good family, while she was neither, Tiaan put together an image of herself. It was the one she had seen in the mirror at the breeding factory, after the attendants had done her hair and made up her face. That *was* her, after all. Not the ordinary her, but Tiaan nevertheless. She felt guilty about the little deception.

Tiaan! he sighed. *You're beautiful.*

She felt warm all over. 'What is your name?' she asked tentatively.

I am Minis, foster-son of Vithis, of Clan Inthis. First Clan!

She feasted on the image of him, so like the hero of her grandmother's tales. But he was in mortal danger, and so was she. 'I wish I could help you, Minis, but I am trapped.'

How? he said abruptly. *I cannot read your future.*

Tiaan wondered about the emphasis. Did he mean that he *could* read others'? She explained her situation.

Minis vanished and with a terrible pang of loss she slipped from her dream into half-wakefulness. Her whole body was shuddering with the cold. Her little cave must be buried deep. Tiaan did as many squats as her legs would allow, but at the end still felt cold, and a little drowsy. Was the air being used up? She attempted to enlarge her cave by tunnelling along the rock. She dared not remove any blocks from her wall. If the snow collapsed, it would pour in until it filled her shelter.

Ti . . .

Just the faintest whisper inside her head. Minis was calling her! Tiaan found the helm under a pile of snow, put it on and winced as the freezing metal seared her forehead.

Her fingers danced along the wires but she could not tune him in; her conscious mind knew not how to do what dream intuition had done previously. Tiaan panicked.

In her terror the loss of Minis seemed worse than the prospect of dying. She flung the wires and beads back and forth. It did not help. They were clustered together now and she knew that was wrong, but had no idea what arrangement had worked previously.

Tiaan lifted the globe and hedron above her head, shaking it furiously. She wanted to jump up and down on it until it was smashed into a tangle of wire.

Tiaan!

Startled, she dropped the globe. Her helm fell off and the little crystal rolled into the snow. She searched frantically for it. Everything was the same colour – the rock, the snow, the grey ice between her boots, the crystal. Ah, there it was!

She popped it into the bracket. Now, if only she could get . . .

Tiaan, stop it!

She froze at the peremptory tone, so reminiscent of Matron, Gi-Had and all the other authority figures in her life.

You're panicking, child. I can't find you.

Even worse was the word *child*. She had been cursed by that title since the day she began as a miserable floor scrubber, six years old. For Minis to use it felt like a betrayal.

She tried to concentrate. She must.

'I'm here, Minis.'

That's better. Show me where you are.

Tiaan concentrated on a mental image of her cave, and then of the mountain slope outside. She knew it was fuzzy but could do no better.

I don't like it, came another voice, a woman's.

You're wasting your time, said a third, a flat, despairing male voice. *She's going to die and so are we. It is written.*

Hush! whispered Minis. *Tirior, Luxor, not so loud. I read our time lines, so there must be a way. Tiaan, show us the devices you used to contact me.*

She mentally imaged the helm and globe.

Incredible, said the woman. *Where has she come by such artefacts?*

I don't know, Tirior. There was a mutter of talk in the background. Tiaan did not catch any of it.

Quickly, child! said the woman, Tirior. *Where did you find these devices?*

271

'I'm not a child!' Tiaan tried to sound mature, dignified. 'I made them.'

You made them? came the third voice, Luxor. How? Who are you?

She said nothing. Tiaan was not going to be treated like a juvenile.

You're intimidating her, Luxor. It was Minis's voice. *Please, let me talk to her. Tiaan, how came you to make such astonishing devices?*

The praise set her heart soaring. 'I am an artisan at the clanker manufactory in the mountains above Tiksi. Minis . . .?'

What is a clanker? asked Tirior.

She described their construction, operation and purpose. 'I make the controllers that draw power from the field, to make them go.'

What are these clankers for?

'We are at war with the lyrinx.'

Lyrinx? cried Luxor. *How did this come about?*

'When the Forbidding was broken, and Maigraith crossed the Way between the Worlds . . .' She hesitated, afraid they would not know what she was talking about.

That is also part of our Histories. Go on.

'That was two hundred and six years ago . . .'

Three hundred and ninety of ours, said Tirior, *but we have not forgotten.*

'The lyrinx came to Santhenar at that time, as did other fierce creatures that lived in the void between the worlds.'

Some also came to Aachan,' said Tirior. Her voice sounded kindly. *They did not last long. Tell us about yourself, Tiaan.*

'I am skilled in the working of fine metals, in forming ceramics and shaping and polishing crystals. That is how I make clanker controllers.'

What are controllers? said Minis.

'Mind-linked mechanical systems which enable an ordinary person to power and control a clanker.' She sent an image of an eight-limbed clanker.

Amazing! The flat voice of Luxor showed a flicker of interest.

His face appeared, so washed out that it was little more than outline. *Ingenious. How do you make it go?*

She explained how certain crystals could be tuned to tap into natural fields that existed around nodes, to draw a trickle of that power into the controller, and thence into the clanker itself.

You build such controllers? Where did the pattern come from?

Tiaan was becoming impatient. What did it matter how she made controllers? But, after all, she was not going anywhere. 'It's an old pattern I was taught in my prenticeship. I have made a number of improvements to it.'

Show us this pattern, said Luxor eagerly.

'You are not our kind. That would be treason.'

Then we cannot help you, he snapped.

Please, Luxor, said Minis. *Tiaan, I don't understand. You say you built these devices. How did you know how?*

'I needed something to amplify the signals from a faulty controller, so I simply made this globe and helm.'

That must have taken a long time. Months, surely?

'It took me a few days,' said Tiaan. 'That's what I do.'

Are there other artisans with your talent? She sensed awe.

'There are many artisans. I don't know how many have my talent. I have not travelled to other manufactories.' Then, with a trace of pride, 'But ours is said to be the best.'

What powers this device, Tiaan? Is there a crystal at the heart of it too?

Tiaan remembered that she had not shown Minis the hedron. 'A special hedron. I did not even have to shape it.' She held up the globe, visualising the perfect bipyramid of rutilated quartz at the heart of it, the twin balls of radiating needle crystals inside, the spark drifting across that cavity, the faint glow.

There was a long silence. A stunned silence, she realised.

What is it? said Minis. *What's the matter?*

The other two spoke among themselves. *Tell me!* cried Minis.

It's an amplimet! said Tirior in an awed whisper that clearly was not meant to carry to Tiaan. *There has not been one found in four thousand years. Just look at it!*

Does she even know what she has? Luxor's voice glowed with excitement. *Could she be a budding geomancer?*

Hush! Minis was back. *Tiaan . . .*

'Minis!' Tiaan interrupted. 'Why were you calling for help?'

Aachan is dying! he said harshly. *Our beautiful world is finished.*

'You are from Aachan?' she said incredulously. Tiaan knew of Aachan, the second of the Three Worlds. It was at the very core of the Histories and every child of Santhenar learned about it. It had been the world of the Aachim, until the Charon fled out of the void, took Aachan and enslaved its people. But at the time the Forbidding was broken, the Charon had gone to extinction and the Aachim became masters of their world again.

To think she was actually speaking to someone across the void – it seemed impossible. Subconsciously she must have known that Minis was from another world, but had not taken it in. Her dreams evaporated like a flake of snow in a frying pan. She could not help him. They could never meet. 'What is happening to Aachan?' she asked miserably.

The whole world is erupting. The very crust has cracked open in rifts five hundreds of leagues long. Aachan will survive it, but we won't! Our world may not be habitable for ten thousand years. Or ten million.

'How has this come about?'

An after-effect of the Forbidding being broken, we think. It began at that time.

'How long do you have?'

We think a few months. At the very outside, a year. Lava advances on us from all directions. The seas grow too hot to sustain life. Soon we will have no place to stand.

Tiaan went limp. Something caught in her throat, as if she had taken in a whiff of burning air. Minis was going to die.

Tiaan?

Tears flooded down her cheeks, forming icicles.

'Yes?' She choked. 'You're going to die and so am I. We're all doomed.' She was shaking. Tiaan could not help herself. Despair was a black Hürn bear, eating her from the belly out.

There may be a way! Minis's voice was a seductive whisper inside her head.

'How?'

We may be able to save you, through your amplimet. In return, you can do something for us.

'I will do anything!' she said eagerly. 'What would you ask of me?'

First we must save you. Listen carefully. Somehow you have stumbled on the ancient art of geomancy.

'Geomancy? Reading patterns in sand?' She could not conceal her scorn. It was the lowest fairground fakery of all.

Not that sad corruption, said Tirior. *True geomancy is the most powerful of all the Secret Arts, for it draws upon the very power of the earth. Mancing is always limited by power. Most mages keep it within themselves, or store it in small devices, or channel tiny amounts of power from places they don't understand. But geomancy offers unlimited power for those who have an amplimet and are able to use it. Imagine the power of an earthquake, the force that keeps your world in its orbit about the sun, the strength of the winds, the motion of the continents on their plates, the hot spots ascending from the very core of the planet. Those are the kinds of power a geomancer has at her disposal.*

But it is a dangerous power, said Luxor. *Geomancy is the most difficult of all the Secret Arts, and the most deadly. Your amplimet is the key, and all that has saved you is the clumsy nature of your tuning. You tapped the merest trickle of power, fortunately, or you would not have survived it. Nonetheless, you must have a strong talent for it.*

'Many artisans have died at their work,' said Tiaan. 'Burnt black inside. My headaches have been much worse since I made these devices. My arms feel hot and twitchy, and I have begun to see strange, impossible things.'

Oh? said Tirior sharply. *What kinds of things?* She glanced at Luxor.

'It's . . . hard to explain,' Tiaan said. 'Coloured shapes in the air that swell and contract, disappear and reappear somewhere else, different shapes and sizes and patterns. They remind me of . . .'

She broke off with a strangled cry. 'I'm going mad, aren't I? I've got crystal fever.'

What do they remind you of? Tirior asked with another glance at Luxor.

'Pieces of things!' Tiaan said through her hands. She let out a crazed laugh.

You're not mad, Tiaan. You're seeing beyond.

'Beyond what? You mean into the void?'

Not exactly. You're looking into the hyperplane.

'I don't understand.'

You and I live in a three-dimensional world, Tiaan, said Tirior. *Every object has length, breadth and depth. But the universe has more dimensions than that – as many as ten, some philosophers say, though we are incapable of imagining the others.*

'I still don't understand.'

You must have a most remarkable mind.

'I think in pictures,' said Tiaan. 'I used to think everyone did, until people began to tell me how unusual that was.'

Indeed. The amplimet must have lifted your inner seeing onto the hyperplane. You're beginning to see the fourth dimension.

It made no sense to Tiaan. 'But what am I seeing?'

Fragments of the strong field permeating ethyric space.

'It looks stronger than the field I'm used to.'

It is. That's why it's so useful. Since you can see it, you may be able to use it.

'There's power enough in the weak field for me, when it's there.' As she said that, Tiaan recalled the failure of the field at Minnien, which had caused the loss of fifty clankers. Had the lyrinx drained it like a well?

Again that exchange of glances. What weren't they telling her?

It's a . . . safer way, said Luxor.

Much safer, Tirior said smoothly. *Power takes a more direct path into the amplimet. And you can use geomancy where you can't see the weak field at all.*

'I don't understand,' Tiaan said. She felt utterly confused. 'I'm sorry. I can't help you. I don't know what you're talking about.'

There was a long silence. Tirior spoke low and urgently to Luxor, who grimaced. She put her lips to Minis's ear. He shook his head. She took his arm, hissed something he did not catch. Minis shook her off, disappearing from Tiaan's image. Shortly Minis reappeared, so close that he blocked her view of the others.

He looked into her eyes, smiled and her heart melted. *Tiaan, dearest.* Minis reached out as if to take her hand. *Please help me. I don't want to die. I* – he caught his breath. *Oh, Tiaan!* he sighed, gazing lovingly at her.

Tiaan was smitten. Suddenly, no promise was too rash if it would bring them together. 'Of course I will help you, Minis. If I can.'

Tirior edged into the image. *No one can understand the hyperplane, Tiaan. It's beyond our imagining. But we can still use it, just as you use the field without understanding it.*

'But what if I take too much power?' That had happened occasionally, if a squadron of clankers drew heavily on a small node, inducing reverberating *strangenesses* in the field. Whole clankers had vanished into nowhere, so these days they travelled well apart and followed strict rules about how much power they could draw. 'What if I tear open the wall between Santhenar and the hyperplane?'

Tirior staggered. Luxor's mouth hung open.

'What is it?' Tiaan cried.

Tirior drew the others away, speaking urgently. After some minutes they returned.

Never you worry about that. Just do exactly as we say and you will come to no harm.

'My head is burning,' said Tiaan.

The channelled power is leaking through you, said Tirior. *We must work fast. When you first saw Minis, am I not right, you just had a clumsy, shaped crystal? You only found the amplimet recently?*

'Less than a week ago. I've not used it yet, save speaking to you.' She began to feel faint.

Do not use it! This amplimet can channel so much power that it would burn you to a cinder. But if you employ it carefully, exactly as we say, it can save you.

'How?'

You are in deadly peril, Tiaan, and not just from freezing to death. From the attenuation of your signal we believe there may be as much as ten spans of snow above you.

Tiaan shuddered. That was the height of a good-sized tree. She could feel the cold weight of it hanging over her.

You cannot move until the storm stops and the snow crusts over. Even then you will be in peril of collapse, or avalanche. So you must wait for days. Have you food?

'Enough for a week. But I'll freeze before that.'

Listen carefully. You may be able to channel power through the crystal to keep you warm.

Tiaan tried to concentrate as Tirior gave instructions. They were long, complicated and difficult to understand, dealing as they did with unknowable concepts like 'topological morphometrics' and 'hyperdimensional wormholes'. Her arm began to twitch uncontrollably. She felt very cold.

'I can't hold the link,' she gasped.

Just one more . . .

Tirior faded away and Tiaan lacked the strength to get her back. Her toes were numb. Taking off boots and socks, she rubbed her feet. They were icy and her fingers had no warmth in them either. Frostbite could not be far off.

She could not think straight. How was she supposed to use the amplimet? She tried to work through Tirior's procedure but knew she was missing a couple of steps.

First, identify a nearby source of power. That was not hard; there was energy all around. The mass of snow on the slope contained enough potential to boil rock, though it would be the height of folly to tap such an unstable source, even had she been an adept.

Putting on the helm, Tiaan swept out in all directions, searching the way she used to map the field. She was looking for power she could use, such as from a hot spring. She found none. All possible sources were too small, too great, too hazardous or too incomprehensible.

Pain shrieked through her chest. Tiaan screamed aloud, fell

sideways and struck her ear on rock. The globe rolled across the floor, hit the snow wall and spun like a top. She could not reach it. Tiaan laid her head on the ground. It felt no colder than she did. It was too late.

TWENTY-SIX

*W*ake up!
   Cold! Galaxies of sluggish ice like frozen milk-mush,
slowly solidifying again.

Wake, Tiaan!

Grinding glacier; gelid blood separating into red, yellow and
clear. Eyeballs freezing from the outside in.

TIAAN, WAKE, MY LOVE!

That cracked the frozen crust. She groaned; she stirred.
Scales of rime fell from her eyelids. Everything hurt, as if
needles of ice were forming inside her.

You're dying, Tiaan!

'Want to. Better than this.'

No! he cried as if in pain. *I care about you. Save yourself,
Tiaan, and then save me.*

'How can –?' she whispered.

Use the amplimet. NOW!

'Afraid.'

You'll die if you don't. It's the only chance. For any of us.

She crawled towards the crystal, weeping icy tears. It hurt so
much. Tiaan reached out but it was still beyond her fingertips.
She could not go any further, until his shocking words gal-
vanised her. *Tiaan, my love!*

Tears of a different kind flowed out, sheer joy! Minis, her

280

tormented prince, *loved* her. He'd said so. And of course she loved him, though she had not realised it before. She would do anything for him.

Tiaan clawed her way across the ice, breaking fingernails, scraping breasts and chin and knees. The wires burned as she cradled the globe to her chest and sought out for a source of power. The field of the manufactory node was weak here, as if some other force repelled it. There was not enough in it to light a candle.

She saw not the least trace of a field. It took a long time to work out why. She was trying to force the crystal and it was resisting her. It could not be forced. It wanted to be cajoled. As she let go, something faint and foggy appeared, only to fade away.

She sat back, allowing her mind to empty of everything but the aura of the crystal. The faintest tracery appeared, spidery filaments in the fog. She was seeing further with the amplimet, and deeper, but not the normal, weak field at all. It was as if she was peering through the solid earth.

Lines and planes, spheres and clusters began to resolve. Were they different *kinds* of fields? They seemed more concentrated than anything she had encountered before.

Tiaan had no idea what they were, or what forces they might contain. The Art required understanding but she knew nothing about how the earth was formed or structured. If she tried to draw on these sources, she would surely kill herself.

Then, as she scanned across those varied shapes, one reminded her of something she'd seen before. It was a long dull plane cutting through the rocks, with occasional bright lenses here and there. It resembled the shear zone bisecting the long tunnel through the mountain. This shape must be a field associated with it. Tension, built up along the shear over hundreds of years, was overdue for release.

Clearly it represented a source of power, enough to save her if she could tap it. She focussed on the planar field. The amplimet made that easy. Mindful of Tirior's warning, she attempted to draw on the potential as gently as she could.

Nothing happened. Tiaan went over the visualisation, the tuning. All seemed correct. She imagined the sub-ethyric path and tried again. Still nothing.

What was she doing wrong? The Aachim had talked about this aspect of geomancy but she had not understood what they were saying. Perhaps she was not meant to draw power by the sub-ethyric path, but via the hyperplane. In that case, how?

Tiaan tried to return to the state where her inner vision caught glimpses of the hyperplane but of course it did not come. She leaned back, more drained than usual. Foolish to think that she could learn a new Art with so little instruction.

Lacking the energy to take off the helm, Tiaan nibbled the corner off a food cake and tried to take a sip from her flask. The drink was frozen solid; the metal stuck to her lips. She let the flask fall. Her head sank. As Tiaan drifted towards sleep, circles and segments began to float through her inner eye.

It was the hyperplane! Bringing up the field of the shear zone, she searched for a path through the hyperplane. It was like trying to trace the way through a shifting maze. Things were there one second and gone the next. Then, for the barest instant, she saw a tiny, thread-like path and snatched at it. The amplimet lit up and the globe grew warm under her fingers, blessed warmth such as she'd never thought to feel again. But it was not enough.

She lost the path but found another and took a trickle more power. Deep in the mountain the veins began to shear, one by one. The ledge gave the faintest little tremor. The wires were hot now. Not painfully hot; deliciously so. Tiaan rubbed the globe over her face and ears, but it soon began to cool. More power was needed. She drew harder and again felt that little tremor, that *heat*. Taking off her boots, she put her toes in through the wires.

After each attempt she warmed herself and rested before trying again. But that kind of warmth could not last here – the cold overwhelmed it. What she needed was the warmth of a bonfire, not a teacup, though it was impossible to pull such power through tiny paths. She went hunting for a bigger one. Tiaan knew what she was looking for this time.

There it was, a broad pathway. She drew power as hard as she possibly could and suddenly the globe was too hot to hold. Smoke curled up from the collar of her coat. Tiaan beat out a little smouldering patch.

Under the mountain, the webbing of veins across the fault snapped and the entire shear zone, three leagues long, unzipped. The marble side moved down, the granite up by the width of a hand. Not much, but the energy released was colossal. The whole mountain shook, radiating shockwaves in all directions.

The world seemed to turn inside out. Heat blasted from the globe. It was as if she had walked past the open door of one of the manufactory's furnaces. Orange streamers radiated out in all directions, ablating the snow away in a perfect sphere, as though washed out by boiling water. At a distance of several spans the surface froze as clear as glass. Tiaan opened her eyes, astounded at what she had done. Multi-coloured reflections sparkled off the ice. It was beautiful.

The mountain settled back in place and above her the snow began to flow like a white mudslide. It was little more than a bulge at first, but in a minute the whole side of the mountain was in motion. Inside her bubble the avalanche began as a whisper that swelled to a roar, louder than anything she had heard in her life. The snow layers sloughed away, one by one, and in places the weathered rock as well.

The stone at her back vibrated wildly. Tiaan held the hot globe and helm to her chest. The layers of the avalanche thundered over the ledge above her, plucking at her ice bubble and making a sound like an organ pipe. The surrounding snow was torn away, until with a shudder the slide had gone by, carrying its incomprehensibly huge load of snow, ice, rock, and an occasional tree, down until it half filled the valley bottom.

Silence. Tiaan opened her eyes, scarcely able to believe that she had survived. It was daytime, for she could see though the thick sphere of ice as if it were window glass. A wintry sun hung low in a clear sky. The storm had gone. Her sphere clung to the underside of the ledge like a soap bubble. Below and above were bare rock, a steep slope.

Minis, wonderful Minis, had saved her after all. Her heart swelled with love for him.

'Minis?'

The response seemed more distant than before. *Tiaan, you're alive! We thought* . . .

'There was an avalanche, but I survived it. What must I do? Tell me how to help you.'

It may be too late. He held a rag over his nose. *The eruptions grow ever worse.*

'Anything!' She was terrified that Minis would vanish before she ever met him.

Ah, Tiaan, you love too deeply and you trust too much. But if you would repay your debt, there is one way . . .

She was conscious of the debt and wanted to repay it. It was a sacred obligation. Even so, his use of the word shook her.

'Whatever it takes!'

Have you heard of a place called Tirthrax?

'Of course!' Tirthrax was the tallest and most famous peak in the Great Mountains, and therefore in the entire world. Some said in all the Three Worlds, though Tiaan knew not if that was true. Being interested in numbers, especially large ones, she knew that the monster peak was more than eight thousand spans high, or sixteen thousand paces, not that height was ever measured in paces.

And do you know that some of my people, the Aachim, once built a great city inside the mountain?

'I know a little of the Histories,' she said cautiously. 'I know that Aachim slaves were brought to Santhenar by Rulke the Charon, thousands of years ago, in the hunt for the Golden Flute. They gained their freedom long ago and built cities in the mountains. I did not know they dwelt at Tirthrax.'

Then I beg you – he seemed to be consulting a map – *make your way south across the mountains and thence west to Tirthrax. If* . . . *when you reach that peak, contact us and I will tell you how to get inside. Take the amplimet to the leader of the Aachim and beg him, or her, to use it. Only then will there be any chance for me.*

'What chance?' she whispered. Strange emotions stirred in her.

To come to your world. He seemed surprised that she had not realised. *It was foretold long ago, and again by me when I was a child.*

'Are you a seer?'

Of sorts, though seldom taken seriously by my own people. Ah, how I long to see beautiful Santhenar. And you, Tiaan, most beautiful of all.

Her heart leapt. These Aachim were a clever, strong species. They had beaten the lyrinx on Aachan. With their help, surely humanity could win the war. And, Tiaan realised, not only would she be with her love, as she was beginning to think of him, but she would be a hero. She would have helped to save Santhenar. No one would look down on her then. Her unfortunate birth would be irrelevant.

Can you do it? said Minis.

'Can you not see?' she asked softly.

It is given to no seer to see his own future. Nor can I see yours. I know I am asking a lot. Are you a traveller, Tiaan?

He was asking the world. In her lifetime Tiaan had gone no further than Tiksi, just a few leagues away. To Tirthrax would be a colossal journey. 'I am not, but for you,' she gazed at his face longingly, 'I will walk from one side of the world to the other.'

His eyes grew soft. *My little love. How I long to be in your arms. We have much to do, to be ready in time, and you have a great journey in front of you. You are our only hope, Tiaan. Whether you succeed, or fail, do so gloriously! In Tirthrax you will be honoured.*

And, remember, tell no one; they would not understand and would only try to stop you. Do not speak about your amplimet, either. To those who understand the Secret Art it is a crystal beyond price.

'Only one man ever knew, the old miner who found the crystal for me. Alas, my friend Joeyn lies dead in the mine.'

Minis stared into her eyes, then his face vanished. Tiaan stood looking at the space where his image had been, daydreaming of the first meeting with her lover, anticipating his caresses and their first night together. The thought was scary, but she was eager too. Tiaan was glad she'd had no other. She wanted Minis to be her first and only lover.

Another thought crept into her mind. Only one man ever knew about the amplimet, *and one lyrinx*! Foolishly, she had let Ryll see it. How was she going to keep it from him?

In a few minutes she was incapable of worrying, as the after-effects of geomancy smashed into her – extreme lassitude, hot and cold chills, and pain like a thousand needles pricking her all over. She lay back and endured.

First she must find a way out of this ice bubble, one that did not involve her falling down the side of the mountain. She was still hot and the amplimet radiated heat, though not enough to melt the walls of her prison. The clear ice looked to be quite thick; perhaps the length of her arm.

Tiaan roused, from a daydream about her lover, to reality. She was afraid of those disabling emotions that she had never understood; afraid of embarking on a relationship in which she might lose control. Afraid of the journey, too. It was a long way to Tirthrax. Tiaan did not know how far, but hundreds of leagues, certainly. It would be many months' journey, and she could not set out until spring.

The air felt stale. There had been plenty in the soft snow but none could penetrate the solid globe of ice. Before too long there would not be enough to keep her alive. The crossbow, she knew without trying it, would never break through.

Dare she try the amplimet again? There was nothing to lose. She sensed her way through earth and rock but the field of the shear zone was gone. She could not tell where it had been.

She sensed other auras though, near and far. The world was bursting with energies: the weight of rock on rock, heat seeping from deep in the earth, gas pockets below the limestone . . . But just because there was power, it did not mean she could tap it. Her skills were primitive, her control infinitesimal.

Seeking deeper, down in the wellsprings of the earth where the granite was cut by enormous veins, Tiaan came on a shifting aura about a crystal as large as an elephant, whose field was of a kind she had never sensed before. Created by pressure from the overlying rock, the force of the wind on the mountain and occasional little tremblers and avalanches, the field fluctuated wildly.

Tiaan sensed it out and in her mind's eye drew a blueprint of the path she wanted the energy to take, through the hyperplane back to the amplimet and then out at the shell of ice. Taking a deep breath, she adjusted the position slightly, then, as the field waxed, drew hard.

A sizzling yellow ray burst from the amplimet and struck above her head, shattering rock into fragments. Pieces of hot stone rained down, setting her hair smouldering. She smacked it away.

Agony, as if all that energy had speared though her. Tiaan screamed; she could not stop herself. Her foot kicked the globe, which spun around. She jumped just in time as the yellow beam flashed by, spattering gravel out of the wall. Another second and it would have taken both feet off at the ankles. A blister the size of an orange began to grow on one shin.

The beam brightened and a slab of rock exploded, sending cinders in all directions. One burned right through her clothes before sticking to her side. She ripped it off and the skin came too. Tiaan beat at the smouldering fabric. Her coat, lying on the floor where she had discarded it earlier, was also smoking. More rock exploded from the wall, and more.

She tried to shut off the flow of power but did not know how. The beam was roaring out of the amplimet and if she could just point it the right way it must burn through the ice in a second.

But Tiaan could not get near; it was too hot to touch. Now the rock was melting, flowing down the shelf to hiss on the floor. Her sphere began to fill with steam. Tiaan felt like the sorcerer's apprentice, having started something that she had no idea how to stop.

Snatching the helm off – it was hot too – she wrenched out its crystal. The yellow beam was unaffected. Molten rock poured down the ledge, melting into the ice.

Abruptly the beam went out. Tiaan squatted down, breathing through her sleeve. Minis had been right; geomancy was a deadly Art – far too dangerous for a novice like her.

The ice was pitted with hollows from fragments of red-hot rock. Molten rock had flowed halfway through the floor before its fire had been quenched.

The air was worse than ever. Tiaan brushed away the cooling cinders, packed up the geomantic globe, crystal and helm, and lay down on the shelf. It was growing dark outside. She closed her eyes, listening to the cooling rock slag cracking like toffee. There was no one to come to her rescue this time.

TWENTY-SEVEN

Ullii spent the night before their departure rocking. The shrieking of the blizzard even penetrated her earplugs, depriving her of the only perfect calm she ever got – sleep. She really needed it. The last few weeks had torn her from her self-contained existence and she was struggling to cope. For years she had lived in the little world of her mind. It was safe there, as long as she did not try to see too far, and was careful not to probe too deep. Some of those glowing knots in her lattice were not meant to be untangled. If she tried they would inflict terrible pain. She had been hurt in the early days, before she'd learned which were kind, or at least indifferent, and which cruel. Which were unknowing and which alert, constantly watching for spies, snoopers or those who, like her, were taking their first groping steps into the life of the mind. The powerful guarded their privacy jealously.

Now that refuge was lost. She was going to be thrust into the world outside, with its pitiless sun, constant racket and everything designed to torment her overloaded senses. Far worse, they would make her pick away at one of those cruel tangles in her lattice until she exposed what lay at its core. And then? The strong always attacked the weak. All she had to protect her was one young man, not an adept of any kind.

Nish had treated her kindly, but Ullii sensed something

289

burning in him. What did he really want? She did not count Irisis at all. Ullii had met dozens like her, people who were kind when it suited them, or harsh when that was more to their advantage. Irisis might be brave and bold, but she was quite selfish.

What would happen once she gave them what they wanted? Would they abandon her *outside*? Exposed to the nightmare of the senses, she would go insane.

So why was she going? Because Nish had been kind to her and that inspired her loyalty. It was no more than that. Ullii had never hoped for love, though she knew what it was. Love was another nightmare, inconceivable and terrifying.

She did so long for kindness, though. The memory of Nish's gentleness was a beautiful musty aroma tinged with spice and machinery oil. It was having her body caressed with spider-silk. Kindness was protection from splinters of light. Kindness was wax plugs in her ears. Kindness was absolute silence.

Nish's kindness kept her warm in the cold night. She wanted more of it. Whatever he wanted, she would give him.

Shouting woke Nish in the night. Jal-Nish was roaring at someone along the corridor. Time to go. Nish rolled out of his blankets. It was so cold! Having spent his youth in a centrally heated mansion, he could not get used to this place.

Dressed in five layers of clothing, he trotted to the refectory, where Irisis waited. They ate a hasty breakfast, by the end of which dawn-grey was highlighting the unwashed slit windows high above. Nish led Ullii down, only to hear Jal-Nish ranting again. The blizzard had left snow so deep that the gates could not be opened. It had to be shovelled away before the clankers, fitted with wide footpads, could be brought out to tramp down the area outside. They had just begun when the emergency bell rang from the gatehouse watch-tower.

'What is it?' Gi-Had shouted.

'Movement in the forest, surr. The enemy.'

'To your stations!' Gi-Had roared. People went in all directions. 'How many enemy, soldier?'

'At least six, surr.'

'Six,' the overseer muttered as he raced through the gates. 'And they're everywhere. It was no isolated band that attacked before. There's a careful strategy behind this and we're helpless to stop it. What are they really after? Our controllers or our artisans? Ah, poor Tiaan, I wouldn't be in your boots for anything.'

They spent the afternoon and the whole night on edge. The lyrinx were sighted several times, and once their catapults sent boulders slamming into the walls, but they did not attack. In the morning there was no sign of them.

Gi-Had liked this no better. 'Are they planning to attack, or trying to prevent us from getting Tiaan back?'

More hours were wasted while the clankers compacted a path to the mine and the village, so it was after noon by the time everyone assembled outside the gate, which was still being repaired.

There were sixteen in Irisis's party, which was to be led by Sergeant Arple, a professional soldier who had come up from the barracks at Tiksi, along with a troop of ten infantry, all that could be spared from the city's already undermanned garrison. They stood beside a scarred clanker. Its operator was handsome young Ky-Ara, whom Tiaan had once cast her eye over. His shooter was Pur-Did, a stocky man of nearly sixty years with warty hands and nostrils. His salt-and-pepper hair was shaved but for a ponytail at the back of his neck.

Two other groups stood by, each with a brand-new clanker, its operator, shooter and troop of ten soldiers. The party also comprised Perquisitor Jal-Nish, in overall command, Gi-Had his deputy, still under a cloud, Querist Fyn-Mah and a senior artificer. The civilians would travel with, or in, the clankers. Nish prayed that the machines were well made, for if anything went wrong he and the other artificer would have to fix it, brutal work in the weather they were expecting.

Light snow was falling as they formed up outside in their furs and fur-lined boots. The fall from the great blizzard had been tramped down as far as the mine, but beyond that they would have to ski.

The soldiers stood in their ranks, Arple in front. Beside them

291

were Nish and the senior artificer, a tall, dark-skinned woman called Tuniz, a native of distant Crandor. She was long and lean, short-bodied and as slim-hipped as a youth. Her wiry brown hair, cut to the width of a fingernail all over, stood up straight on her head. An elongated neck bore dozens of enamelled bracelets and her teeth were filed to points, which gave her an unwarranted fearsome look when she smiled, which was often.

Next, almost as tall, stood Irisis, then slender Fyn-Mah and wiry Gi-Had. Irisis had placed herself as far as possible from the querist, making no effort to conceal her dislike. Fyn-Mah acted as though she had not noticed. By herself at the end was Ullii, quite the smallest person there. Dressed in her layers of winter gear she looked like a little barrel. A broad-brimmed hat covered her earmuffs, goggles and mask. Her face was enveloped in a balaclava of spider-silk. She was fidgeting, shifting from foot to foot.

Nish felt a painful knot in his belly. A dozen lyrinx could be the match of this force, in rough country. He could see his fear mirrored in the faces around him.

Gi-Had looked distracted, staring back at the gate and tapping one foot.

'Our mission is a simple one,' said Jal-Nish. 'Artisan Tiaan has been captured by a lyrinx and we must get her back, whatever the cost. Whoever does so will be most handsomely rewarded. She has a talent this manufactory cannot do without.'

Irisis stamped one foot, making a loud clap. Jal-Nish gave her a warning glare.

'How did this come about, surr?' asked Arple, the sergeant. His upper lip was so deeply scarred and puckered that he looked like a man with two mouths, one above the other.

Gi-Had explained about the fight in the cavern and its grisly ending. The younger soldiers looked uneasy. 'I sent Gull and Hurny on to warn the manufactory and returned a different way for Tiaan.'

'A brave deed, surr,' said Arple. 'Not many have that kind of courage.'

'I was terrified,' Gi-Had admitted, 'but I am her overseer. It was my duty.'

292

'Get on with it,' grated the perquisitor, who despised heroes. 'Every minute the beast is carrying her further away.'

'Tiaan was gone from the battle cavern,' concluded Gi-Had. 'And so was a lyrinx I'd thought dead. Her gear was gone too. It must have taken her.'

'Why would it do that, surr?' Arple plucked at that upper lip.

'Perhaps they want her to teach them the craft of controller-making,' said Jal-Nish. 'We will take a shortcut through the mine. Once at the cavern, our seeker here,' he nodded at Ullii, 'will tell us where she's gone. To your places, *go!*'

Before they had moved a dozen steps, someone came flying out the gate, crying, 'Daddy, Daddy!' It was a little, dark-haired girl of five or six, with red ribbons in her hair. Racing up to the overseer, she threw her arms about him.

As Gi-Had lifted her up, five older girls appeared, walking demurely in a graduated line. Each embraced their father, then went back into the line. A plump, pale woman stood in the gateway, looking distressed.

When she stepped forward the perquisitor snapped, 'It's not a party, *probationary* overseer. Get moving!'

Gi-Had took a step toward his wife, stopped, gave her a jerky wave then turned away. Her face crumbled. The littlest girl began to cry. Gi-Had, frozen-faced, did not look back.

Ullii was to go in the last clanker, along with Irisis, Nish, Ky-Ara and Pur-Did, his shooter, who except in the most severe weather rode on top, at his weapons.

She had not seen a clanker before and, wearing both mask and goggles, Ullii could not see it now. She did not need to – her other senses were on fire with its strangeness. It stank: the tang of pitch distillate, the odours of sludgy grease and rancid fish oil. It also smelled of metal, spicy rations and the acrid odour that always accompanied the working parts of clankers. However, the stench of the clanker was overwhelmed by that of the soldiers, now breaking from their ranks.

The clanker, though stationary, was surprisingly noisy. Its workings made a low, thudding tick just on the edge of hearing through her muffs, the sound as irritating as an itch between the shoulder blades. The flywheels whined, pipes hissed, and every so often came a rattle as of a knuckle across a washboard.

That was nothing to the way she *sensed* it. This close, the clanker made a glowing knot in her lattice too bright to imagine, and the knots of the other machines blurred into it. The knot arose from the hedron at the heart of the machine, which drew power from the field, channelling it into the controller that powered the huge flywheels and worked the levers, gears and shafts to drive the iron feet so tirelessly on.

Controller and hedron both drew on aspects of the Secret Art, though not those kinds that mancers employed, and both glowed in her lattice. Even after she turned the forward fan of her lattice away, Ullii could sense the hedron and feel the power, as she had felt the heat and light and blast from the furnaces when Nish led her past them this morning.

A scream rose in her throat. Ullii had an overwhelming urge to tear off muffs, mask and clothes, and curl up in the snow. That would make things worse, but the panic was rising so fast she could not hold it back. She took a shuddering breath.

A hand came up over the nose holes in her balaclava. It was Nish. Catching at his hand with her gloves, she pressed it over her nose. Her head steadied. She took another sniff, tipping up her face to him. 'I'm better now,' she said softly. She did feel better, though strange – hot and liquid inside. A nerve twitched in her lip.

'We have to go,' Nish said. 'The soldiers are already out of sight.'

She could feel the clankers now. The other two flared in her lattice as they moved off with a *thud-thud* that shook the ground beneath her. The hatch was up in the plated back of the third clanker, Irisis gesturing furiously.

'I have to *know* it,' said Ullii.

Nish walked her around the clanker and Ullii touched the overlapping plates along each side, the thick metal legs, the firing platform on top. It felt like an armadillo, her favourite animal. Mancer Flammas had kept one in his workshop. She'd touched the creature, seen how it curled up, and modelled herself on it ever after. The memory made her smile and Ullii climbed willingly into the back of the machine.

Ky-Ara reached out with one long-fingered hand, making sure the controller was seated in its socket and that each of its twenty-four arms was correctly in place. He pulled down his 'crown-of-thorns', a metal headband set with eight pieces of crystal, equally spaced. Placing each hand into a wired glove, he reached forward and gripped two knobs. As he moved the right-hand knob, rainbows swirled in Ullii's lattice. The whine of the flywheels went up a notch as he fixed the field in his mind and drew power smoothly from it.

Ky-Ara's face went slack with bliss as the bond with the machine was established. His mouth fell open in a vacant grin – the flycatcher phase, Nish sneeringly called it. Ky-Ara would be as much machine as man until they stopped, and if parted too long afterwards would suffer the anguish of withdrawal.

Ullii was fascinated, though that changed as soon as the operator worked the starting lever and, with a squeal of plates and a rattling groan, the clanker moved. The sound went right through her earmuffs. The knot swelled until it filled her head. She tried to change the lattice but the racket ringing through her brain did not permit rational thought. She pressed her hands tightly over her earmuffs. It did not help. Ullii screamed, right in the operator's ear.

Ky-Ara, wrenched out of his bond, stopped the machine instantly. His head whipped around, mouth agape, eyes staring. 'What?' he slurred, in as much pain as she was.

'I've got her earplugs here somewhere,' Nish said to Irisis, rummaging in his pack.

'Take your hands away,' Nish whispered to Ullii. 'No one speak.'

Ullii slowly withdrew her hands. He handed her the plugs, which she pressed into her ears, then quickly put the muffs on. Nish signed to Ky-Ara.

With jerky movements he re-established the bond. The clanker lurched, stopped, lurched again. Ullii's hands flew up to her ears but stopped halfway. She could hear nothing. She smiled fleetingly, then worked on remaking her lattice so as to keep the fierce glow of the controller manageable.

Irisis put her boots up on the heatbank, a long metal box filled with hot stones. 'It's lovely and warm in here.'

'Enjoy it while it lasts,' said Nish, who had spent more than enough time in freezing clankers.

They were only halfway to the mine when there came a low rumble and the clanker stalled as if it had struck a barrier. A distortion wave passed through the machine, warping everything like a reflection in a fairground mirror.

'What's going on?' screamed Ky-Ara, waggling his knobs uselessly. He seemed on the verge of collapse. 'I've *lost* the field.'

They had all heard the tale of the failed Minnien field, clankers lost, an army slain. Nish leapt through the back hatch, drawing his borrowed sword, as did Irisis. Streaks of light plated across her vision. The ground shook underfoot, the forest trees lashed back and forth. The soldiers were crouched down with their shields over their heads.

'To your positions!' roared Arple.

The troops formed a ragged oval around the clankers, shields up, spears out. Irisis scanned the forest. If this was an ambush, they were too spread out to defend themselves.

Nothing further happened. Arple called the soldiers into a tight circle around the first clanker. The world stopped shaking. Irisis clutched at her pliance, which felt uncomfortably warm. That had not happened before.

'What was *that*?' shouted Jal-Nish.

'The enemy . . .' Gi-Had trailed off, worrying about his family.

'The artisan did it with her crystal,' Ullii said. 'It's burning her up.' She swooned, half out of the hatch.

'I can see the field again,' called the second operator, Simmo, through the top hatch of his machine.

Fyn-Mah looked to the perquisitor, who drew her aside. 'You also have some mancing talents,' he said quietly. 'What do you say that was?'

Irisis, whose hearing was keen, slipped into the forest and edged closer.

'Power,' said Fyn-Mah, 'as I have *never* felt it used before. And not far away.'

'I thought so too. But Tiaan is just an artisan. She has no mancer training.'

'Look to her heritage . . .' began the querist.

'Hush! Don't talk about that.' He glanced over his shoulder but did not see Irisis, who had slid behind a tree. 'She's stumbled onto something new.'

'How do you mean?'

'That kind of power, enough to shake the mountain, could not have come from the weak field.'

'Well, other people have made such discoveries. I don't know that any survived to use them.'

'The ancients did!' he said vehemently. 'The Histories are full of Rulke's marvels, and what Yalkara did. Can't you see? This could be the answer to that failure of the field at Minnien. A new, stronger force?'

'Nunar did write about such things,' she said slowly.

'With such power at our disposal, impossible things become possible. We won't just win the war, we can wipe the enemy off the face of the globe. There *is* a way, Fyn-Mah, and if we bring it to the scrutators *we're made for life*. We've got to bring her back alive, whatever it takes. We must find out what she's discovered.'

'Indeed,' said Fyn-Mah. 'To say nothing of this "crystal". It would be tragic if she died using it and the secret was lost.'

Jal-Nish gave her a curious look, as if there was sarcasm in her words, then signed for the column to move off. The other two operators helped an ashen Ky-Ara into his seat. 'I thought the field was gone,' he said over and over to his clanker. He rubbed the controller with his cheek. 'I thought I'd lost you.'

Irisis got in beside Nish and Ullii and sat quietly, trying to digest what she had heard. Had Tiaan made a brilliant breakthrough, or was it just this new crystal she'd found? Whatever it was, it could be as much to her advantage as Jal-Nish's. For the first time in years Irisis allowed herself to hope.

TWENTY-EIGHT

The fumes were worse than ever. Tiaan rolled over and broke into a fit of coughing that sprayed the stone red. It felt as if she was bringing up specks of lung. She rested her forehead against the rock. Why did it take so long to die?

Thump! Something landed on top of the ice globe, knocking a cold cinder down on her head. She rolled onto her back. A shadow clung to the outside like a kitten to a ball. Vaguely outlined against the stars, it looked like a Hürn bear; a big one.

The creature scratched at the ice, the sound reverberating in her ears. Moving under the shelf, she pressed her nose to a crack in the stone and breathed deep, trying to suck fresh air out of it. The grinding grew louder. Wiping her streaming eyes, Tiaan sat with her crossbow loaded. It made her feel better.

The beast sprang in the air and came down reversed, clinging with its back feet, scraping with one forefoot. She closed her eyes. Though everything hurt, Tiaan could feel herself drifting off.

Another thump; the scratching resumed. She did not look up. Breathing was taking all her strength. The crossbow slipped from her hand. A louder thump. Again the bear had reversed position. Its legs drew back and kicked at the circular gouge.

The outer half of the sphere split off in a ragged circle and freezing air rushed in. Tiaan gulped it down. It tasted better than the fine wine her mother had occasionally offered on her visits to the breeding factory.

The creature's head came over the edge of the ice. It was not a Hürn bear at all, but a lyrinx. There was frozen blood down its front – one of its victims, no doubt. She felt for the crossbow. Her eyes were all blurry. Ryll slowly came into focus.

'Can you cling to my back?'

'No!' she gasped, backing against the rock. 'No!'

He took the crossbow away, pulled her out and tucked her under one muscular arm. She caught a whiff of his odour – strong, gamey, though not unpleasant. Tiaan did not struggle. There was no point.

'Where are you taking me?' she said hoarsely.

'Don't be afraid.' He began to climb up over the ice, seemingly unburdened by her weight. 'I am paying my debt.'

'Pack!' she croaked.

Ryll stopped. 'What is the matter?'

'I must have my pack!'

He resumed the climb. 'I will come back for it.'

Tiaan sagged. Whatever he planned to do with her, or to her, she was too weak to resist.

The darkness was complete, not the least pinpoint of light anywhere as Tiaan came to. Rock pressed against her shoulder blades. She felt around. More rock. It felt strange, having no idea what space she was in. Tiaan wished she had the senses of a bat, to move carefree through the dark. She was not cold, but so weary that merely moving her arms exhausted her. She felt acutely aware of her body. Every part was tingling; she could feel every nerve strand. What damage had the amplimet done to her?

The air was still. Silence surrounded her, and smells – the odour of blood and meat, the bodies of the soldiers, and a different kind of odour that must be the dead lyrinx. She was in the cavern.

'Hello!' she said. The sound came back in dull-edged echoes. 'Hello?' she shouted. 'Ryll!'

Echoes but no reply. This was her chance to escape, and

Tiaan felt a sudden pang of homesickness for the smell and the racket of the manufactory, and even her cold little sleeping cubicle. If only she could go home.

She was imagining that she could when she had a vision of Minis's reproachful face. *But you gave your word, Tiaan.*

She groaned aloud. She would not go home, but how could she go after Minis? Tirthrax was hundreds of leagues away, through some of the most inhospitable country in the world. It would take years, even if she had plenty of money and supplies. And everywhere she went, guards would question her, officials demand her papers, and throw her into the cells because she had no right to be there.

It was absurd to think that she could walk to Tirthrax. Quite impossible. Give him up, she told herself. You *just* can't do it, and no one could expect you to. But *where* could she go?

Minis, she thought. *My poor, lost love.* You picked the wrong person. I would save you if I could, but I can't. I'm just not strong enough. She lay on the floor and wept.

Tiaan felt washed out. Why had Ryll saved her life then left her here? Had he fled with her amplimet? Was it what Ryll really wanted? Her outstretched hand touched the webbing of her pack and she felt inside. The helm was there, and the small crystal.

Emptying her pack, she scratched frantically through the contents. Her tools fell out of the toolkit, to tinkle on the rock floor. Clothes, food rations, sleeping pouch, soap, all were there. The amplimet was not.

Ryll had left her halfway up the sloping floor, well away from the bodies. She went down, looking for one of the torches. The bloody smell grew stronger. Her hand struck something rigid – a dead soldier.

Tiaan ran into three more bodies, then a tunnel. She must be near the second, third or fourth tunnels, for that was where the battle had been. After working that information into a mental picture of the chamber, she knew where to look. The bundle of tarred sticks must be to her left.

It was a surprisingly long time before she found them. She

came up against the back of the dead lyrinx, slipped in a puddle of jellied blood and lost her mental map. Trying to get it back, arms out, she walked slap-bang into the torches.

One had a sticky patch of tar on it that had not burned. Striking sparks into a pinch of tinder, Tiaan used the small flare to light the torch. The flame dazzled her. Seeking out the tar pot she replenished the torch and in its smoky light searched the cavern from one side to the other, and the tunnel that led back to the outside. She did not find the amplimet.

Nor did she find her pincers, used to draw the bolt from Ryll's neck. The empty space in her toolkit was like a freshly pulled tooth. She found bloody evidence of the place Ryll had fallen, the muck he'd heaved up afterwards, and even a mark on the floor, in purple blood, that had the outline of the pincers. Both pincers and bolt were gone.

Ryll appeared behind her. She let out a strangled cry. The light in his hands came from the amplimet, reflecting eerily off skin now coloured in washes of yellow.

'What are you doing with my crystal?' she said wildly. Withdrawal had made her reckless.

He gave a mild, toothy smile. Did that mean he was amused, or hungry? 'I can't see in pitch dark,' he rumbled.

Tiaan, regretting the tone of her voice, edged backwards.

The smile broadened. 'I'm not going to eat you, little human.'

Not very reassuring. 'Wh-where have you been?'

'Checking the tunnels to make sure no one came after me.'

'Was anyone coming?'

'Not *that* way!' With his injured hand, he indicated the passage back to the crystal mine. The regenerating fingers were now the size of a child's. 'The rocks have moved. The tunnel is blocked.'

'What did you do with my pincers?'

'What?'

'The tool I pulled the bolt from your neck with. It was lying just there.' She showed him the bloody outline.

'I did not touch it,' he said.

'It was with the bolt. You must have taken them.'

301

'I did not. Why would I?'

'Then someone has been here!'

'One man came back – the leader. I can smell him. But he went again.'

Fear pricked her. Gi-Had must have come looking for her and found the artisan's pincers. Helping the enemy was a capital offence and now he had evidence of it. Tiaan put her hands over her eyes, trying to think. She could not. She was too afraid. When she opened them, Ryll was staring at her.

'What do you want me for?'

'My debt of honour,' he replied.

'You saved my life. The debt is paid!'

'Not if you're going to die as soon as I go.'

'You have a stern moral code,' she said sarcastically.

'Indeed! Otherwise, why have a code at all? I will escort you home.'

If she went back, Gi-Had would probably have her executed for treason. 'I no longer have a home.'

He looked thoughtful. 'Where do you wish to go?'

Tiaan felt panicky. Where *could* she go? All destinations were equally hopeless. In that case she might as well attempt the impossible and head for Tirthrax. No doubt she would die on the way but at least she'd be keeping her promise to Minis. It made her feel better. 'I want to go south! Over the range to Tarralladell.'

'Have you family there?'

'No, but further west, in the mountains of Mirrilladell, I am going to find a man I have never met.'

'Ah! An arranged mating?'

Tiaan blushed. 'In a way; not yet, but I hope . . .' She did not go on. It was too unreal.

'To cross the mountains in this season . . .' he mused. 'Well, south of here they are smaller, and there are passes, but even so,' he gave her a sideways glance. 'It will not be easy.'

'I can't wait till spring. I might be too late.'

'To my mind, if he cannot wait that long to mate with you,' said Ryll, 'he is not a good choice.'

Again that disturbing use of the word 'mate'. She had to

remind herself that lyrinx were alien, with an entirely different culture and way of life. Perhaps love was meaningless to them. 'I didn't ask your opinion,' she snapped.

'You could take ship around the Horns, then sail across the inland sea.'

Tiaan consulted her mental map of Lauralin. 'At this time of year? That would be as dangerous as going over the mountains, and the entrance to Tallallamel may be frozen over. Anyway, no ship would take me. I have no papers.' However she went, travel was expensive. Would she have enough to go so far? She had no idea. She had not opened Joeyn's money belt but surely there could not be much in it.

'You speak our language well, Ryll,' she said tentatively, using his name for the first time. Naming him seemed to change their relationship.

'I was brought up with captive humans, so as to learn. I am one of the most fluent.'

He regarded her steadily. She could not meet his gaze. Her world kept turning upside down.

'May I have back my crystal?' She had to work hard to keep the quaver out of her voice. He tossed it to her and as soon as she caught it Tiaan felt better.

'What do you know about the tetrarch?' He was looking at her intently.

'What is a tetrarch?'

'You don't know?'

'I've never heard the word before.'

Ryll held her gaze for a moment, said 'No matter,' and stalked across the cavern in that strange, sway-backed stride. She watched him all the way. What did he want from her? The secrets of power – hedrons and controllers? Was the tetrarch a similar kind of device?

Ryll bent down, put his foot against something on the floor, and wrenched. There came a gruesome butchering noise. He stripped the trouser leg off a haunch of soldier and began to feed noisily. Tiaan wanted to vomit. The creature really was a beast, for all that it could talk.

The lyrinx tore off a piece of meat that would have fed her for days, chewing and swallowing with a few head-back gulps.

Tiaan gagged. Once he had what he wanted he would eat her too.

Ryll strolled back, gnawing on a thigh bone.

Putting her arms across her face, she turned away.

'Are you sick?' he asked.

'You're eating my people!' she screeched.

'They were not your friends, surely?' Ryll seemed surprised.

'Eating human flesh is disgusting!'

'It tastes good to me.'

'There's nothing wrong *with* it! It's just wrong to *eat* it. It makes me want to vomit, seeing you . . .'

'Only human flesh?' he enquired, cracking the bone over his knee and hooking out a quivering length of marrow with one claw. It went down with a slurp.

'And scavengers and carrion eaters,' she conceded, unable to look.

'Do humans see themselves as carrion eaters?' said Ryll with a puzzled frown. Waves of colour washed over his skin, like watercolours being mixed on wet paper.

'Certainly not! It's just that . . . human flesh is sacred to us.'

'Would it help if I ate where you could not see?'

'I'd prefer you didn't eat us at all.'

Shrugging, Ryll tossed the bones to one side. 'I will take you into the mountains.'

She did not believe him. The creature was toying with her. She had to escape. 'Now?'

'Later tonight. There was a thaw today. As soon as it sets hard we will go.'

Tiaan slept badly, with unpleasant, fractured, crystal dreams. She woke to find Ryll standing over her. With the torch fluttering, he looked particularly menacing. She jumped up. 'What do you want?'

Ryll stepped back a pace. 'Time to go. You have food?'

'Enough for a few days. How long will the journey be?' It felt unreal. They might have been discussing a picnic, except that the feast would probably be her. She wished she was a quick-thinking hero who would instinctively know to escape.

'We are here.' With a long yellow claw he drew on the floor, a shape like the head of a fork with two tines, one rather longer than the other. It made an unpleasant scratching sound on the marble. 'Here is your city of Tiksi.' He marked a point just north of where the longer tine met the head of the fork, which repre-sented the main mass of the Great Mountains. 'To cross the first range to the land you call Buh-rr . . . Bhur . . .'

'Burlahp!' she corrected.

'Buhrr-larp! That is about ninety slgurrk.' Ryll thought for a moment. 'Which would be about ten of your leagues, were we able to fly.' He grimaced.

A strange expression crossed his face, almost a shudder, and the vestigial wings stirred involuntarily. He snapped them down. 'Across Buhrr-larp is fifteen of your leagues, and ten more across the second range.' He indicated the second tine with his claw. 'This is the land you call Tarralladell. It is a long way from Mirrilladell, your destination.' His yellow eyes searched her.

'To walk to Buhrr-larp might take as little as six days, or as much as twelve, depending on the weather. That is, if I carried you. I will get food on the way.' Noting her horrified look he said, 'Mountain goat, fish, or maybe a small Hürn bear. Fill your pack, in case.'

Tarring up a torch, she rifled the dead soldiers' packs. There was more food than she could carry – dried meat and fruit, tiny onions, cheese and rice balls, some starting to go mouldy. Ryll was busy across the other side of the cavern, feeding again, judging by the nauseating rending and gulping noises. He did it in the darkness, thankfully.

By the time she had packed, he was on his way back, wiping his enormous mouth on a rag torn from the seat of a soldier's pants. Tiaan turned away, busying herself with her gear. She did not want to know.

'Ready?' he asked.

'Yes.'

'Bring one of those spears, in case of a bear.'

How little he feared her. 'I already have a crossbow.'

She took a few more bolts, just in case, and was surprised that he allowed her. A spear would not help her against a Hürn bear, for she felt so weak that a breeze might blow her away. However, Tiaan had a good eye and the crossbow had been her weapon of choice in defence training. She might, just possibly, bring down a lyrinx with it. That made her feel better, though the crossbow was an awkward weapon and took a long time to reload.

Now heavily laden, she followed Ryll down the passage. Outside he turned left, the direction she had taken after first leaving the tunnel. It was cold, but there was no wind and the moon was shining. They went along the ledge past the old tree, which somehow had survived the landslide. The stars were out.

A beautiful night for walking, were it not for the company.

They continued until dawn, getting in a good five or six hours. It was hard going, up and down all the time, though at least the snow had a solid crust. Ryll seemed to know exactly where he was going. After half an hour he left the ledge and headed up through unmarked snow, sometimes across alpine meadows, sometimes along ledges which fell into chasms hundreds of spans deep. As it grew light his skin plates changed colour. In a few minutes he was as white as a Hürn bear, disappearing into the landscape.

Tiaan felt a mixture of emotions. Did he really have a code of honour, or had he some ghastly use for her? What twisted purposes, what warped desires, what strange lusts might he be planning to slake upon her?

Tiaan stopped abruptly, staring at the monster's back. One hand slipped down to the butt of the crossbow, though she did not draw it. She could not shoot Ryll from behind. Even had she been able to, the armour was thick there. To kill him she would have to hit him in the eye, the throat, or send a bolt between chest plates and ribs, into the heart. Assuming it was in the same place as hers, of course.

Ryll spun around, going into a crouch. The retractile claws extended. 'I have a sense for danger, small human.'

She hastily moved her hand from the weapon. What was she thinking? Even with a loaded crossbow she could not expect to beat an alert lyrinx.

He came back, took the bolts and packed them in a pouch at his waist. It was the first time he had used his regenerating hand.

'I need a rest!' she said in a croaky voice. 'And breakfast.'

'Strange creatures, you humans,' said Ryll. 'What a handicap, needing to eat three times a day.'

'I don't *have* to eat three times a day!' she snapped. 'But I do need to rest. I'm an artisan, not a mountain climber. At least, I was an artisan . . .'

TWENTY-NINE

The clankers had taken a mine tunnel that ran through the mountain. Late that night they stopped, everyone ate and those not on watch dozed on the uneven floor. Though exhausted, Irisis could not sleep. Ullii was walking about in the dimness further up the tunnel, without goggles or earmuffs, eating little balls of sticky rice. She took little else, for anything flavoured or spiced tasted unbearably strong to her. Finally, bored senseless, Irisis strolled up to see what the seeker was doing. She seemed to find the rock an endless source of fascination, sometimes staring at one vein or crystal for ten minutes or more.

'There is magic in these rocks,' said Ullii.

'Oh?' Irisis was careful to speak softly.

'It's in the lattice – there and there. And there!' She pointed in various directions, through the rock.

'We find the controller crystals in this mine,' said Irisis, wondering if they might use Ullii's talent to locate better ones than the miners could, in their blind delving. Especially blind now that the best, Joeyn, was dead.

'I know. I can *see* them. The mountain is like a pudding full of crystals.'

That was something to explore, if they came back. It would be another mark in her favour.

*

Gi-Had pushed the lever. The door swung back against the wall and the column passed into the other mine, torches held high, weapons at the ready. Following a zig-zagging path through tunnels that were barely wider than the machines, they eventually emerged in the cavern where the battle had occurred. Everyone except Ullii got out, examining the remains of human and lyrinx in silence. Someone retched noisily by the far wall. Ullii put her head out the back, took one whiff and retreated, slamming the hatch down.

'I can't blame her,' Nish said to Irisis. 'What a gruesome place.'

Gi-Had described the battle in clipped sentences, then walked away with Jal-Nish. They squatted down, staring at the floor. Nish crept closer, wondering what they were doing.

'I found the pincers just here,' said the overseer, pointing to the floor. Taking a small package from his pocket, he handed it to the perquisitor

Jal-Nish held something up. 'Her finger marks are on the pincers and the bolt.'

'Doesn't prove she helped him,' Gi-Had said unhappily.

'I'll keep them, *just in case*.'

They came back towards the bodies. 'We'll collect the remains for burial on the way back,' said Jal-Nish. 'Move on.'

When Irisis climbed in, Ullii was shivering and had stuffed a spare pair of earplugs up her nose. Breaking through to the outside, they found the sun rising on a cold, breezy but clear day. Breakfast was handed around while snowpads were fitted to the feet of the clankers. Jal-Nish came up to where Nish stood with Irisis and Ullii.

'Well, Cryl-Nish, let's see if your monkey can do her tricks.' His voice expressed all the doubt in the world.

Irisis felt just as doubtful. Ullii had as good as said that Tiaan was dead.

'Can you find Tiaan for us, Ullii?' If Nish doubted, he did not show it. 'Remember the controller I showed you. Tiaan made it, and maybe you can get a trace . . .'

Ullii turned her masked face diagonally up the slope. 'I can *see* her crystal!'

'Where? Are you sure?' cried Jal-Nish, reaching forward as if to shake her. Nish threw his arm out and the perquisitor drew back.

She pointed to the south-west. 'That way.'

'How far?'

'I don't know.'

'Can you see Tiaan?'

'Crystal is too bright.'

'Well, when was it here?' Jal-Nish snapped.

She went blank for some time. 'It was here for days.'

'She could not have moved in the great storm,' said Gi-Had. 'Or immediately after. Not until last night at the earliest.'

'She must be close by,' cried Jal-Nish. 'Spread out. Look for her.'

'She did a great magic here,' said Ullii.

'Did she now?' Jal-Nish breathed. He exchanged glances with Fyn-Mah, and Irisis knew it had to do with the event of yesterday. 'I did not know she had any. What kind of magic, I wonder?'

Ullii had no idea. 'The crystal glows by itself.'

'What do you mean?' Fyn-Mah drew close to the seeker.

'It shines all the time now. It is the brightest thing in my lattice.'

Again that exchange of glances. 'Tell us everything about this crystal,' said the perquisitor.

Ullii shaped it with her hands. 'There is a black star in either end, and black needles down the centre. A little spark runs along them.'

Jal-Nish drew Fyn-Mah away and Irisis did not hear what was said next, though they seemed to be excited and disturbed. To Irisis, born with a hedron in her hand, it was fascinating. It offered hope. Irisis knew her talent was not gone, just buried where she could not find it. She had lost confidence in herself, that fourth birthday, and unless she recovered it she would always be a fraud.

This crystal was more powerful than any Irisis had ever heard of. If she had it, she *would* believe in herself. To be a true artisan mattered more than anything in the world. What she would not give, or do, for that!

310

A soldier came running down the slope. 'Fresh tracks, surr! One lyrinx, one human with a light tread.'

'Whatever magic Tiaan used,' said Irisis, 'it didn't get her away from the enemy.'

'Maybe the seeker will prove useful after all,' said Jal-Nish. 'Move!'

They scrambled into the machines. The mechanical feet pounded away, the soldiers following on the trodden snow.

'Why are we going so slowly?' Nish said to himself after they had been crawling for a good while.

Irisis touched her pliance and said, 'The field is weak here.'

'Why?'

'Perhaps something interferes with it.'

He turned the other way. Ullii, who wriggled and squirmed as much as any two-year-old, had taken off everything except the spider-silk underwear, which fitted her like another skin. Resting her head on Irisis's shoulder, she fell asleep.

Nish's eyes never left the seeker. They ran up and down her curves, the small, pointed breasts, the curvy hips, the shadowed area between.

'Haven't you anything better to do?' Irisis said coldly. 'You're such a pervert, Nish.'

He flushed, looked away, then sat up at shouts outside. The clanker ground to a halt, shuddering on its eight legs. Nish got out, walking awkwardly. Irisis followed, pulling the hatch down behind her.

They had come up a steep slope winding around the side of a mountain. All around towered higher peaks, with sheer faces of dark rock mostly bare of snow. They were much more forbidding than the range in which the manufactory was set.

'What's the matter?' She went to the front of the line.

Ahead, an outcropping layer of flinty rock formed a small cliff, impassible to the clankers. Nish's eye traced the outcrop around the mountain. It ran for at least a league.

'What about there?' Jal-Nish pointed.

The three operators went into a huddle, muttering to one another, then broke up, avoiding Jal-Nish's eye.

'Well, come on, damn it!' he roared.

'It's not possible, perquisitor,' Gi-Had said quietly.

'Then why don't they say so?'

'It's a . . . it's the way of their culture; if you force them to an answer they'll say yes because they don't like to be the bearer of bad news. But it still won't get us up there.'

'Damn fool culture! If they'd told me that in the first place . . .'

'They are telling you, but you're not listening.'

'You tell me, then! *Where?*'

Gi-Had rubbed his jaw. 'Perhaps over there.' He indicated behind them, where the outcrop was notched. 'Try there!' he called.

The operators moved their machines backwards, which looked even more ridiculous than the clankers' forward motion. With their overlapping, curving plates of armour they were like eight-legged armadillos. Down the beaten track of their passage they thudded, then turned diagonally up the slope.

Nish slogged through the snow up to the notch. He was sweating by the time he reached it.

'I don't know,' Gi-Had frowned. 'It'll be a pinch, even if we can get up to the gap. The first bit's too steep, and with the weak field here . . .'

'What if we built a ramp of snow along here?' said Irisis.

'Good idea!'

It took hours, even with thirty soldiers labouring with their camp shovels, but finally a ramp of compacted snow was constructed up to the outcrop.

'It's still pretty steep,' said Gi-Had. 'What do you think?' he asked the huddled operators.

Again they muttered among themselves. 'What now?' Jal-Nish exclaimed, practically tearing his hair out. 'We'll lose Tiaan!' He pounded the side of the clanker. The operators turned as one, glaring. Ky-Ara clenched his fist. Jal-Nish snatched his hand away.

'What's it matter?' Nish interjected. 'The seeker can always find her again.'

'That's the attitude that got you in your present trouble, boy!' Jal-Nish grated. 'It matters, idiot son of mine, because the country beyond those peaks is a great plateau. You would have known that, had you bothered to consult a map before we left. Up there we can run them down. Not even a lyrinx has the endurance of a clanker, and it must stop to rest. But beyond the plateau lies Nyst, a land of crags, canyons and crevasses. A lyrinx can go places where no clanker, indeed no soldier, can follow. That's why we've got to catch them. If we don't do it in the next few days we never will. And if the beast finds his friends . . .' The perquisitor broke off, staring at the snow bank. His round chest, which merged indistinguishably into the swell of his belly, was heaving. 'Just get up there!' he spat at the operators.

They scurried back to their machines, the metal feet began to compress the snow and Simmo's clanker crept up the steep slope. Two-thirds of the way along, the front feet began to slip. They pounded on the spot, digging potholes beneath each foot, then stopped. Gi-Had gestured to Arple. The sergeant roared orders. Six soldiers trotted up behind, put their shoulders to the clanker, and Gi-Had shouted 'Go!'

Again the feet skidded. 'Heave!' cried Arple and the soldiers heaved. The clanker inched upwards. 'Heave! Heave!'

With each heave it went a little further but it did not take long to exhaust the soldiers. They held it while another gang took their place, and shortly they had it up and over, onto the gentler slope above.

'Next one won't be so easy,' Gi-Had observed laconically. 'It's pounded the track to ice.'

'Run a cable from the first,' said Tuniz the artificer, scratching her spiky head. 'It can pull the others up.'

'Don't know about that,' said Gi-Had, but gave the orders.

The two clankers started. The first was going slowly, buried to the belly in soft snow. Ky-Ara's machine began to catch up to the first as it approached the icy section. The rope sagged down to the ground.

'Shit!' cried Gi-Had, waving his arms at the operator. 'Slow down! You've got to keep the rope taut.'

Ky-Ara's clanker hit the icy patch, travelling fast. The legs thrashed, sending stinging chips of ice everywhere, but could not get a purchase. The machine began to slide backwards.

'Hold it!' roared Jal-Nish.

Two soldiers ran and put their shoulders to the rear of the machine. Arple screamed, 'Get back! No! No! Get out of the way!'

The soldiers looked from one to the other, not knowing which order to obey.

'Jump clear!' roared Arple, but it was too late. The tow rope twanged tight and as smoothly as a pendulum the clanker slid sideways across the ramp, sweeping one soldier off the edge. The other tripped and the pounding metal feet went over him. He gave a single horrible scream. The clanker toppled off the edge of the ramp, hanging from the cable, to thump into the steep slope. Ky-Ara shrieked in anguish, the sound like a saw blade on glass.

Simmo cried out as the weight pulled his machine backwards to the brink. Nish could not bear to think what the strain must be doing to the mechanisms. For a long minute it seemed the first clanker would come down on the second, but Arple sent another troop running and they heaved a rock behind the legs just in time.

When the clanker had been stabilised the sergeant came storming across, smoking with rage. He lifted Jal-Nish by the front of the coat, a considerable feat. 'If you ever, *ever* give an order to my troops again,' he said savagely, 'I'll make you wish you'd been smothered at birth, perquisitor or not. You give your orders to me. No one else! Is that understood?'

'Yes,' squeaked Jal-Nish.

'Let it be so!' Arple dropped him in the snow and ran to his fallen. The soldier who had been swept off the ramp had suffered only bruises and a sprained wrist, but the other had broken every bone between his thighs and the lower ribs. The sergeant hacked his pants open. Blood trickled from the soldier's bowel.

Arple, who looked the toughest and most unfeeling sergeant Nish had ever met, squatted down beside the soldier and took his hand. 'I'm sorry, Dhirr,' he said. 'I can't do anything for you. You're going to die.'

Dhirr gave a gasp that wracked his long face to the roots of his receding hair. 'My wife is pregnant. Our third! What is she going to do?'

'She is doing great service for our country,' said Arple. 'And so have you done. She will be well taken care of.'

'But my children . . .' he jerked, groaned and fell sideways.

Arple listened at Dhirr's chest. 'He breathes, for the moment. Put him on a stretcher. He can go in the clanker once we get it up.'

Ky-Ara was hysterical and had to be consoled by Simmo. The two men stood with their arms around each other, Ky-Ara weeping enough to frost his coat.

'There'll be trouble with that fellow before we get back,' said Gi-Had to Irisis, who was standing next to him.

'He's an emotional man, even by the standards of operators,' she agreed. 'After his controller failed last month he bawled for a week.'

They spent all morning recovering the second clanker and lifting it onto the ramp with pulleys and ropes carefully anchored. Everything was done in consultation with Gi-Had, Arple and Artificer Tuniz, who was years ahead of Nish in her trade and proved unexpectedly useful in this task. Nish was glad they did not consult him, for he had no idea what to do.

While that was going on, the soldiers cut a path through the soft snow for the first clanker, pounding the surface down hard. Other soldiers dug corrugations across the icy patch for the iron feet to grip on.

The clanker was not much damaged, fortunately, just a connecting rod bent and one of the armoured panels dented and scraping with every movement. Tuniz and Nish had the repairs done by the time the third clanker was heaved up. The accident had cost them five hours.

The perquisitor had not spoken since his encounter with Arple, but there was a thunderous look on his round face that boded ill for the sergeant if ever Jal-Nish had the advantage of him. He was not a man who could easily come to terms with humiliation, to say nothing of the challenge to his authority. But for now it would be put aside. The pursuit must go on.

THIRTY

Jal-Nish drove them hard for what remained of the day and most of the night. The field was strong here but the country unknown, so they crept along under the light of a single flare. That was risky but Jal-Nish dared not stop. The clanker operators were issued with spicy nigah leaf, to keep them awake. The army sometimes used the drug to combat cold and fatigue. Everyone was on edge, knowing how vulnerable they were. Half a dozen lyrinx, attacking from the darkness, could slaughter them all.

Just after dawn, most of the way across a domed plateau, the hunt again came upon tracks in the snow.

'It's them!' shouted one of the soldiers.

'I can't see anything.' Gi-Had was up on the shooter's platform, staring through a spyglass, when Nish and Irisis scrambled out.

Jal-Nish squatted to examine the smaller prints. 'It's Tiaan's boot all right. I don't understand it. It's as if she's going willingly.'

Arple inspected the evidence, stroking his scarred lip. 'If you can tell that from a bootprint you're a damn sight better tracker than I'll ever be.'

'She hasn't run away!' Jal-Nish said.

'Would you run from a creature three times as big and twice as fast? If I were her, I'd do exactly as it told me.'

'That's why you're a sergeant in the Tiksi garrison rather than a general at the front,' Jal-Nish sneered.

Arple reared up before him. 'Have you ever fought a lyrinx, perquisitor?'

'No.' Jal-Nish drew back.

'Then shut up before you make a fool of yourself. You don't know what you're talking about, and if there's one thing I despise it's the ass that flaps his mouth from the safety of an armchair. I've seen hundreds of my boys dead at the hands of lyrinx, *perquisitor*. Dead and eaten! Better men than you'll ever be, just fighting for their families and their country. Don't talk to me about lyrinx. Don't tell me my job. And don't sneer at my courage until you've proven your own.' He stalked away, head held high.

Gi-Had said quietly, 'He may be only a sergeant, surr, but Arple's been up north fighting lyrinx for fifteen years. He's killed five of the beasts, two all by himself, and that makes him as tough a man as you'll ever meet.'

The column moved off at a faster pace, following the marks in the snow. The soldiers had skis on now, since the way ahead was flat. Irisis chuckled.

'What's so funny?' Nish asked.

'It's good to see someone get the better of your father. He's such a hypocrite.'

Nish had enjoyed the sight too, though family loyalty would not allow him to show it. 'It remains to be seen if Arple *has* got the better of him. My father is a ferocious enemy.'

Up the front, metal screamed and the machine shuddered to a stop. 'That doesn't sound good,' said Irisis.

Nish got out. 'What's wrong?' he asked Pur-Did, who was squatting by the front leg.

'Rod's jammed, I'd say. You'll have to pull it down.'

Nish cursed. It would be a hideous job in the freezing conditions and he would not be able to wear gloves.

Tuniz and Nish spent an hour and a half taking the leg apart. It proved the very devil of a job and when it was stripped down they could find nothing the matter with it. Tuniz sat back on her haunches, sucking a skinned knuckle. 'Well, this is a puzzle,' she grinned.

Nish repaid it with a scowl. 'You're awfully cheerful about it, senior artificer.'

'Tuniz, please. I hate titles. Things generally go easier if you can have a laugh.'

Nish found that he liked working with her. 'You're from Crandor, aren't you? How did you end up so far from home?' She had been at the manufactory for nearly a year but he knew nothing about her.

'Let's put the leg back together, eh?' She talked as she worked. 'Yes, I'm from Roros, one of the biggest cities of Crandor. My man was an artificer with the navy. I hadn't seen him in three years, and the children . . .' She broke off, wrestling with a rod that did not want to go into its socket.

Nish steadied the mechanism. 'How many children do you have?'

She bit her lip. 'Two boys and a girl: seven, five and four years old. News came that my man was lost. His ship ran aground, down the coast from Tiksi. Then I heard he wasn't lost, but captured by the enemy. The army wasn't going to do anything, so I came after him.'

'How did you get permission?' Nish asked.

'I . . . didn't. I left the children with their grandparents and stowed away.' Her brown eyes met his. 'I was too late. My man had been eaten. I tried to get home, but with the war, and no papers . . .' She paused. 'I had to turn myself in, and this manufactory needed a senior artificer, so I was sent here.'

'You must miss your children.'

'I never stop thinking about them. Or my man.' All the cheer was gone. 'Let's get this finished.'

The reassembled leg worked and they continued. Nish's frozen hands had lost skin in a dozen places.

'I hate being an artificer at times like this,' he said to Irisis, just as his father walked by.

'It might be different if you put a bit of effort into it,' Jal-Nish said frigidly.

They kept on going, faster than before. As the clanker hit a bump, a gasp escaped from the injured Dhirr. His eyes fluttered open then closed. Irisis nudged Nish in the ribs. He looked around. 'What?'

Ullii was staring at Dhirr, her back arched like a cat confronting a snake.

'What is it, Ullii?' said Nish.

She backed away from the injured man until her elbow struck the metal side of the clanker. Looking around wildly, she lifted the earmuffs and forced in her wax plugs. Taking the goggles off, she stared at Dhirr. With undue haste she put the mask on over the goggles and reached blindly for Nish's hand. He put it in hers. She pressed it hard against her nose, which appeared to calm her.

The clanker pounded on, going fast down a gentle slope. The view out the front porthole was solid grey.

'What's the matter?' Nish asked, lifting Ullii's mask so she could read his lips.

She withdrew his hand but did not let go of it. 'I can see his pain.'

'See his pain?' Irisis echoed.

'A blood-red clot in my lattice, with hooks all over it. Digging, tearing hooks. I tried to help him but underneath the red was blinding yellow. It burned. *He hates me!*' Her back began to arch again. 'I just wanted to be kind to him,' she said in the voice of Irisis.

'Dhirr doesn't know what he's doing. He's in too much pain,' Irisis said with rare insight. Then, softly to Nish, 'Maybe he's got a latent talent for the Secret Art. Many people do and never know it. Perhaps she probed too deep and his unconscious mind hit back in self-defence.'

The clanker stopped suddenly, throwing them forward. The soldier groaned. They got out to see what the matter was. This time Ullii leapt through the hatch as Nish was about to close it.

'It's the front leg,' said Ky-Ara. 'You'll have to pull it down again.'

'And this time do it properly,' scowled Jal-Nish. 'If the beast gets away because of your incompetence . . .'

'Are you suggesting that *I'm* incompetent?' said Tuniz, standing up tall and straight and showing her filed teeth. She towered over the perquisitor.

'No,' he said faintly.

They went through the whole tiresome business again, but could find no fault. 'Would you check the controller, please, Irisis?' said Tuniz.

'It's one of yours, isn't it, Irisis?' Nish said furiously, sucking his battered fingers.

The controller proved to be the problem and Irisis had it fixed within minutes. The constant shaking had disconnected one of the controller arms from its stub.

On they went, but had only been going a few minutes when the clanker drifted to a stop.

'What now?' screamed Jal-Nish from the next machine. The afternoon was waning.

'Lost the field,' said Ky-Ara, taking off his crown-of-thorns. Getting out, he went into conference with the other operators. Everyone assembled outside.

'Where is she now, seeker?' said Jal-Nish.

Ullii did not hear. Nish tapped her on the shoulder. She lifted the mask and he signed for her to take the plugs out.

'Where is Tiaan, seeker?' Jal-Nish repeated, more loudly. The frustrations were telling on him and he was not a man to take failure well.

'I can't see her,' Ullii said in a small voice.

'Why not, damn you?' He raised a pudgy club of a fist.

She backed away behind Nish.

'It's Dhirr,' Nish interjected before Ullii could go into one of her states. 'We think he has an undiscovered talent for the Art. He's broadcasting his agony and it's clouding up her seeking.'

'Bah!' Jal-Nish stormed up to the front of the column.

The others followed. Everyone gathered around in a straggling circle, stamping their feet to keep warm. The sky was clear now but a keen wind was blowing.

'We've lost them!' The perquisitor tore viciously at a length of sausage with his teeth.

'They can't be far ahead,' said Arple. 'There's no snow in these tracks. We'll catch them down below. There's a big river there. Take care, operators; it should be frozen, but you must not go onto the ice until I've tested it. There may be places where a man can pass safely but a clanker would fall through.'

'What's the matter with the field?' Nish asked Irisis.

'Can't be too serious. Ky-Ara's on his way back, and he's smiling.'

The operator resumed his seat. 'I have the field,' he called.

Jal-Nish had perked up. 'The river is very good news. I've a trump set aside for just this contingency and it should be in place now.'

'What is it?' Arple asked.

'You'll see!' Jal-Nish looked unnaturally smug. Clearly he was not going to say.

Arple called to his troops. 'There's no more than an hour of light left. If we're to catch them . . !'

'I've seen them!' cried one of the scouts, skiing across from a lookout. 'They're not far. This side of the river.'

Arple issued directions in a low voice, ending, 'Go at them, hard as you can. The perquisitor promises a *quile* of silver to anyone who takes the woman alive, and another for her crystal.'

'And death by quartering should anyone harm her!' Jal-Nish added. 'So shoot over their heads, if she's close to the beast.'

'Advance guard, take the heavy crossbows and ski out to either side,' Arple ordered. 'Be ready to cut off any breakout.'

They hurled themselves in and the machines pounded down the slope. The clankers, going full speed for the first time, drew ahead of the soldiers. The slope steepened. To either side the snow had been stripped away by avalanches that terminated in untidy mounds near the river. Ullii began to make that keening sound behind them. Nish tried to see out through the front porthole but Irisis's head was in the way.

'What's happening?' he said irritably. 'Give me a look.'

She pushed him away. 'We're gaining. The lyrinx is carrying her now. It's running. I never thought any creature could go so fast. The skiers are faster though. They're coming round on either side. They're bold! It could tear them apart.'

Irisis fell silent. Nish tried to shove her out of the way so he could see, but she pushed back.

'Stop that!' snapped Ky-Ara. 'I can't concentrate.'

Nish withdrew sullenly. 'Irisis?' he whispered.

'The lyrinx has gone in between the rocks. If it's going to stand and fight there, it'll be bloody. Ah, there it is again.'

There came a sharp snap above them. The clanker jerked, flinging them forward. 'We're firing!' said Nish. 'Can you see?'

'I've lost sight of it. That was close! The ball smashed the top of a boulder to splinters. I wouldn't like to be standing next to that!'

The threaded rods of the catapult whirred as the shooter wound it back to reload. Another clanker fired. 'Just to the left of the beast!' cried Irisis. 'They're taking a risk.'

'Better she's dead than helping the enemy.'

Tiaan and Ryll had spent all day, and a good part of the next, crossing a vast plateau dotted with boulders that protruded through the drifts from the great blizzard. There had been no landslides up here. Tiaan was alert for a chance to escape but it never came. Ryll watched her ceaselessly and he could walk as fast as she could run.

Around the middle of their second day, he stopped so Tiaan could eat. Having no need for food, he climbed onto a boulder to keep watch. He spent a lot of time doing that. The sun came out brightly. His eyes began to water, even after he closed them to slits. For a moment he seemed confused. Did the lyrinx have a weakness?

Tiaan unwrapped a packet of rice balls. Threads of grey mould webbed the surface and the interior too. She bit into the ball. There was no food to waste. Tiaan was used to indifferent food – the only times she'd eaten well had been when she'd visited her mother.

The rice ball smelled bad inside and made her stomach heave. Tiaan began on a piece of jerked meat. It reminded her of the conversation about eating human flesh. Her jaws ached; the soggy texture repulsed her. Suddenly the whole idea of eating meat was nauseating. She spat it on the ground. No doubt Ryll would find that equally incomprehensible. Tiaan pushed it under the snow with her boot.

They set off but Tiaan began to fall behind. The lyrinx kept up a pace that would have been difficult to meet when fit, and she now felt decidedly uncomfortable. Her stomach began to bubble like a witch's cooking pot; the revolting taste kept rising up her throat. Plodding on, head down and in misery, her lunch came rushing up without warning.

Afterwards she felt no better. A sharp pain crept down her bowel; she had to concentrate hard not to soil herself. The lyrinx was staring at her as if committing everything she did to memory. Maybe he was; Ryll was a keen student of humanity.

Another spasm doubled Tiaan over. As she was washing her mouth out, the lyrinx squatted beside her.

'Is this a common difficulty with humans?'

'The food is bad,' she gasped, wiping tears from her eyes.

He opened her rations, sniffed everything and tasted a mouldy rice ball. 'It would not harm me.'

'Well, you're tougher than I am!' she snapped. Tiaan pretended that it was just a passing illness. If he knew how bad she felt, he might eat her.

They set off again but within half a league Tiaan was forced to stop. She went behind a rock, which eased the pain in her intestines somewhat. She'd just come out and was miserably contemplating her pack when Ryll sprang from his watch boulder and bound her wrists with a strip of leather before she realised what was going on. Swinging her onto his shoulders, he put the pack under his arm and ran.

His strength was phenomenal – he ran in great, thudding strides, much faster than Tiaan could ever have sprinted.

'What are you doing?' she cried, struggling helplessly.

He made no reply but as they went over a rise she saw the dark shapes of soldiers against the snow, well back.

Ryll increased his pace. The soldiers began to fall behind. He ran for half an hour, as near as she could judge, before stopping on a gentle hill dotted with boulders and springing up on one.

Thud-thud, thud-thud, a sound Tiaan knew very well. Over the rise behind them came the blunt snout of a clanker, its mechanical feet pounding rhythmically. Another appeared to one side of it, and a third. Then the soldiers, at least thirty.

Such a force would easily kill a single lyrinx, especially a flightless one such as Ryll. A clanker was better armed and armoured, and could go full speed for as long as the field allowed it to. Its weapons included the catapult and also a javelard that could send a heavy spear in one side of a lyrinx and out the other.

Snatching her from the rock, Ryll bounded off, but before they'd gone far he let out a roar and threw himself to one side. Tiaan fell, breaking through the crust into grainy snow. The impact winded her. A long spear stuck, quivering, in the ground some way ahead. It had gone straight over their heads.

Tiaan scrambled to her feet. Her belly felt no better. Was this her chance to get away? She tried to run for it but the lyrinx struck her behind the knees with one leg. She went face first into the snow. Another spear shattered against the rock to her right.

Ryll ran with her, taking advantage of what cover there was. An occasional glimpse showed the racing clankers, the shooters on top frantically cranking their javelards. The spears were no longer than an infantryman's javelin but thicker, with a head of hardened steel. Propelled by a mechanism like a giant crossbow they would destroy any living thing they hit.

The lyrinx was moving as fast as a trotting horse, the breath whistling in and out of his lungs. His grip threatened to force what remained in Tiaan's belly out either end. She could hardly breathe. Her eyes were watering and freezing on her cheeks.

Ryll began to outpace the clankers, which were slower in this rocky country. Another spear was fired but it fell well behind. However, after a further half-hour of full-speed running, Ryll stopped and bent over, gasping. For an instant she saw panic in his eyes.

He continued, plunging down the edge of the great dome they'd been crossing for the past two days. The slope steepened below them and was scored with the paths of avalanches. The clankers had spread out, while soldiers on skis were curving round on either flank. Ryll could only go directly forward. If he turned, he must be killed. Already the clankers were drawing closer and would soon be within firing distance. There was no escape.

Tiaan considered what would happen when they killed him, as they must. If they judged her a collaborator they might execute her on the spot, or take her back to the breeding factory. She'd rather die.

They headed down the steepening slope. Ryll sprang onto one of the slides, here stripped of its snow cover, taking reckless leaps that had the snow slipping underneath his feet. A misstep at this speed and they were both dead.

Crack! A ball of rock exploded against a boulder to Tiaan's right, peppering them with shrapnel. The lyrinx yelped, rubbing one eye with his free hand. His feet slipped on ice and he nearly went down. Tiaan shrieked.

Ryll recovered and ran harder. Another ball went over their heads, neatly taking the cap of snow off a tall boulder ahead. The lyrinx darted left, weaving among the rocks. In their cover he set her down to catch his breath. Their eyes met. She could not read his expression.

The clankers were coming down the slope in three prongs, the advance guard now speeding ahead on their skis. Only minutes left. Why did Ryll not abandon her?

Below, the slope was an obstacle course of boulders, torn-up trees and avalanche mounds, treacherous conditions that would be impossible to run through, though a few strands of undisturbed snow wound between the avalanches. There the crust would be hard enough to move on. Beyond, a gentle rise concealed what lay ahead. Down to their left it looked like a frozen river.

Another ball splintered a solitary tree ahead of them. Ryll took off with Tiaan under his left arm. This was difficult terrain for a clanker. He scooted along a ribbon of snow between the debris. They crested the rise and ahead lay a broad, winding river, iced over except for necklace beads of dark water along the centre. Beyond, Tiaan could see another snow-covered dome. There was nowhere to hide and the clankers must catch Ryll as he laboured up the slope. Wherever he went, the machines would run him down. She kept hearing Minis's cry, *Tiaan, Tiaan, why have you forsaken me?*

The day was fading. Darkness could not come too soon. The lyrinx kept going. She had to admire Ryll's courage. They went over a second rise and the expanse of the river stretched before them. With a guttural cry Ryll skidded to a stop.

Below, on the ice at the other side of the river, stood a fourth clanker and ten more soldiers, five in a curving line on either side. The loaded catapult was aimed directly at them. Suddenly the ball was not there. Something whined over their heads to embed itself behind them. A cloud of snow drifted on the breeze.

Ryll sprang onto the terminus of an avalanche. Bounding recklessly from one ice-covered boulder to the next, he let out wild roars of defiance. One false step meant the end. She could sense the thrill of peril, of him pitting his strength against them all.

He took four great leaps, one after another, skidding, claws scrabbling for a grip, teetering, steadying, the great thigh muscles driving him on. Three times Tiaan thought he was going to fall and crush her. Three times he just made it. Across the river the soldiers were frantically regrouping. With a last bound he made it down off the toe of the avalanche and raced toward the river.

Ryll almost got across. He would have, had not one of the following clankers hurtled down the slope just as recklessly, and found a clear passage to the river well downstream. Ignoring Arple's instruction, it was already ploughing across the snow-covered ice.

Emitting a deafening war cry, Ryll ran onto the ice. The surface was slippery; wind had blown the loose snow away. The clankers were not so encumbered. They converged from four directions, blocking any escape. Making a superhuman effort, Ryll gained the middle of the ice. It was not enough. They were surrounded.

The clanker bounced and jerked on uneven ground. Their headlong passage slowed. 'Can you still see them?' cried Nish.

'Just now and then,' Irisis replied. 'The lyrinx is weaving through the boulders. We'll have to go round. Ah, it's a bad place for an ambush. I can't see the beast. There it is – it's out the other side – it's got her under its arm. The lyrinx is really flying now. It's going down a track between the avalanches – too narrow for us.'

Nish was practically jumping up and down. 'Let me see, you selfish tart!'

Irisis held him away. 'Stop it! You're upsetting the operator.' She turned back to the porthole. Her voice had gone flat. 'It's getting away. It's up on the avalanche, bounding from rock to rock. It's like a mountain goat,' she said with a trace of admiration. 'The only chance is to get it with a spear.'

'Our shooter is loading one now,' said Nish. 'I can hear the ratchet going.' He knew the sound intimately; one of his principal jobs as artificer was to adjust and repair the javelard, which could shoot a heavy spear a third of a league. It was deadly accurate in the hands of a skilled operator, though not from a moving clanker. Especially not on uneven ground.

A bell rang in front of the operator. The clanker stopped. The sighting mechanism creaked above them. *Crack!* Again the clanker jerked, though not as hard as when the catapult had fired. They moved off again. It was snowing. The wind intensified, whirling the flakes about. The weather was turning bad.

'Any luck?' cried Nish.

'No. We're too late; it's nearly to the ice . . .'

Her voice trailed away. Perhaps she was thinking through the consequences of failure, for them. Nish certainly was.

'It's on the river. The ice must be thin; I can see patches of water. Arple will never risk the clankers out there.'

'We've lost,' Nish said dully.

'Oh!' Irisis exclaimed. 'Brilliant. Your father did have a trump after all. Oh, yes!'

'What?' he said frantically.

'There's another clanker coming down the far side of the

river, with a squad of soldiers. He must have sent them out secretly, before the blizzard, just in case.'

'A lucky guess!' Nish felt miffed that, after all, the success would be his father's.

'Maybe. The lyrinx would have had to cross this river some-where. From a high place they could have seen our flares in the night. Plenty of time to get into position.'

'The beast has stopped,' Irisis continued in a low voice. 'It knows it can't get away.'

The clanker stopped too. 'Are we close?' Nish was practically screaming with frustration.

'Just at the edge of the river.'

Pulling the hatch up, he leapt out. Ullii, who had been silent during the long chase, let out a wailing cry and snatched at his hand, but too late. Irisis went after him. Ullii crept out too. The light was fading; snow began to fall more heavily. Jal-Nish was making hand-signals to the fourth clanker.

'I'm not sure this is a good idea,' said Irisis, stumbling on blocky ice.

'It's a lousy one.' Nish kept going. 'But I'm not going to cower inside after all we've been through. I want to see it taken.'

'Tiaan isn't even running,' said Irisis. 'Maybe she *was* the spy after all.'

'I'll have none of that talk,' grated Gi-Had, peering through his spyglass. 'Her hands are tied!'

'She's more afraid of us than of it.' A rare interjection from Ullii, beside Nish.

Only Nish heard, but he was too distracted to notice. The wind drifted clouds of snow across the ice. Nish could hear it howling through the rods and wires of the javelard. He shivered. It was going to be a miserable night, whatever happened.

In a movement too fast to see, the lyrinx pulled Tiaan up before its chest. Gi-Had called out to it to surrender. It did not move.

'What are we going to do?' said Nish. 'If we fire, Tiaan will surely die.'

'I want her alive,' grated Jal-Nish. He called Fyn-Mah over. 'Is there anything we can do?'

'Not at this distance,' the querist said. 'Besides, there's people watching. The Secret . . .'

'Damn the rules! Try!'

The querist shrugged then made a circle of her fingers and sighted through it. She whistled between her teeth, her black hair stood up and a globe of mist condensed in the air several paces in front of her.

Ullii screamed as there came a clap like two shields being struck together. A cloud of loose snow was kicked up to the right of the lyrinx. A roar echoed back and, as if hit by a fist of compressed air, Fyn-Mah was tossed off her feet.

Nish helped her up. The querist's lip was bleeding. 'It's too strong,' she mumbled, cross-eyed. 'Reflected it back.'

Irisis was staring at her pliance, which momentarily glowed a baleful green before fading.

'What is it?' Nish said.

'I have no idea, but something just activated my pliance and I saw the field as clear as day, streaming out in all directions.'

'Was it the beast or Tiaan's crystal?' Jal-Nish demanded.

'I don't know,' said Fyn-Mah, 'but the lyrinx is strong in the Art. Too strong for me.'

Irisis was pleased at the admission. The snooty querist was not as capable as she made out. 'We want the crystal too,' Irisis reminded them.

Jal-Nish gave her a considered glance. 'Indeed we do, but we want Tiaan more. I'll have the head of anyone that harms her. If the beast doesn't surrender, Arple, fire when I say the word. *For its legs.*'

'What if you hit Tiaan?' said Gi-Had.

'She doesn't need legs to be an artisan.'

Ryll stopped midway between two beads of clear water. The ice was thinner here. Tiaan felt it bow beneath their weight.

'Release the prisoner, lyrinx!' screamed Gi-Had. 'Hold your arms high.'

Ryll clutched Tiaan to his chest. She could feel his muscles quivering. 'Shoot me and she dies,' he roared back.

Tiaan looked from one clanker to another. Their javelards seemed to be pointing directly at her. But surely . . . surely they were not shooting at her.

'Fire!' snapped Jal-Nish.

The revelation struck her. If they could not get her back, they would kill her rather than allow her talents to be used by the enemy.

The clankers fired. They *were* trying to kill her. Ryll moved so fast that she had no idea what had happened. They went head first into the water. The shock was so great that Tiaan felt her heart stop beating. Her lungs went into spasm. It was as if she had been buried in ice.

THIRTY-ONE

As the lyrinx dived through the hole in the ice, Irisis let out an involuntary cry of anguish. The clankers fired, one first, followed by the other three together. Two javelards went through the hole. A third whistled over the heads of Jal-Nish and Gi-Had, to plough into the toe of an avalanche mound. The fourth hit to one side of the hole and went skidding across the river. Its bladed tip carved the ice with an ear-piercing shriek, it curved around in an arc, sending up a spray of ice like a turning skier, and slammed into the front foot of the fourth clanker.

'Stop!' roared Arple, waving his arms. 'You'll kill somebody!' He ran to the ragged hole, which was about the size of a clanker. The other troops followed. 'Careful. It's thin here!'

It was getting dark. The snow fell thickly now. Jal-Nish was beside himself. His face had gone purple. 'If it's got away with her,' he choked, 'if the crystal is lost, I'll have every man whipped to within an ell of his life.'

The soldiers went still in their ranks. Arple stalked to the nearest troop and ordered them to be silent. He turned back to the perquisitor. 'I'd be careful of making threats out here, all alone,' he said quietly.

'Are you threatening *me*?' cried Jal-Nish.

'I'm a loyal soldier, surr.' Arple touched his helm. 'I'm trying to protect you. My troops have done their best ever since we left.

331

We followed your orders, surr. Had we been able to fire at will we would have had the beast.'

Jal-Nish spun the other way, his round belly quivering. He looked as if he was going to burst.

Nish went to him, stepping carefully on the ice. 'Are you all right, father?'

'If she's lost . . .' Jal-Nish began. His purple face went soggy. For one horrified moment Nish thought his father was going to burst into tears. 'Aah, Cryl-Nish! She could have made me.'

'She could still be alive, father. There's still a chance.'

Jal-Nish waved him away. Nish hurried towards the hole. 'Did you see blood in the water?' he asked Arple.

'No, but doesn't mean we didn't hit the beast. The water is really racing under the ice.'

Jal-Nish stalked toward them, holding his face rigid. 'The artisan must be found, sergeant, and her crystal. I . . .' He hesitated. 'She has secrets. She is vital to the war.'

Arple snapped to attention. 'The war!' He began shouting orders. One clanker headed downstream. 'Troops, fall into pairs. Tar up stakes, light them and go down the river as far as the bend. Check every patch of water; be very careful. Nix and Thurne, head upstream. I doubt that a lyrinx could swim that way – they're hopeless in the water – but we'll take no chances. Stay in pairs. Move carefully. Beware of the ice. And if the weather closes in, follow the edge of the river until you see our flares. We'll camp here.' He indicated the jumbled rocks by the river bank.

'Lyrinx are much tougher than we are,' Arple continued. 'Never think that one is dead until you see its corpse, preferably with the head well severed from the body. And even then, give it another ten minutes. Many a soldier has seen his guts spilled on the ground from a dead lyrinx's last reflex.' The soldiers hurried off, their flares disappearing in the whirling snow.

He turned away. 'We must set the camp up while there's light, perquisitor.'

'Damn the camp, I want every man . . .' Jal-Nish broke off, as if realising how foolish he sounded.

'It's got to be done now, surr,' Arple insisted. 'For our own

332

survival. And if the artisan *is* found we'll need fire and hot food to save her.'

He gave orders to search the avalanche mounds for firewood. The remaining soldiers went about the set-up efficiently, slinging tents in the shelter of the boulders, making a latrine around the back, fetching water and erecting the pitch-burning cooking stoves. The clankers were drawn up side by side. The fourth was a different design from the others, shorter but more bulbous and with lengths of rod bound to the top. Nish wondered what they were for. Its troops, in white uniforms, were led by a tall, stern-looking sergeant, Rustina, a young woman with long red hair. That was unusual – only rarely were women of child-bearing age permitted to become soldiers. No one knew anything about her and Rustina's troops were close-mouthed.

'What are your orders, perquisitor?' Arple asked when everything was organised.

'Search all night!' Jal-Nish said curtly. 'Tiaan must be found. And if we can take the beast alive, so much the better. If it *has* survived, it will be weak.'

'No one could survive in *that* water, surr.'

'I still have to see the bodies. The scrutator will expect no less.'

'They would be a league downstream by now, under the ice.'

'Would you like to explain that to the scrutator?' Jal-Nish hissed.

'No,' said Arple calmly. 'I would not.'

'And neither would I. We'll search every hole, and the banks around.'

Irisis joined a search detail. Nish went with one of the clankers up the slope to a gully where earlier they'd seen a stand of straggly pines. An axeman soon brought down a dead tree and the clanker dragged it back to the camp, where it was cut into fuel for the night. The soldiers gathered cones and kindling, not wanting to use the precious pitch stores unless they had nothing else. They could be trapped in a blizzard for days up here, even in autumn.

Irisis returned alone from the search as the fire blazed up.

She looked depressed. 'No sign of either of them,' she said to Jal-Nish, who grunted and walked off.

'Where's Ullii?' Nish asked.

'How should I know?' Irisis snapped.

They found her among the boulders, close to exposure, wearing only her spider-silk undergarments. 'What are you doing out here dressed like that?' Irisis scolded. 'Have you no sense at all?' Taking off her coat, she wrapped it around the small woman and carried her back to the fire. Ullii was too listless to protest.

'He was coming after me,' she whispered. 'He wanted to hurt me.'

'Who?' said Irisis, head snapping up. 'The lyrinx?'

'The man inside. He was picking at the lattice, trying to get into my hidey-hole.'

'What is he doing now?'

'I can't see him,' she whimpered.

Nish and Irisis went to the clanker, wondering. They found only the body of Dhirr, tormented mouth open, fingers hooked as if he *had* been trying to get at the seeker, though no doubt it was only a death spasm.

'He's dead!' Irisis said soothingly. 'He can't hurt you now, Ullii. Hop in; it's warmer than outside.'

Ullii would not go into the machine, even after they'd carried the body out and left it with Arple for burying. They dressed Ullii, who squatted between the boulders on the far side of the fire, mask well down over her eyes.

Nish stood by the blaze, warming his hands on a mug of soup. He could hear his father's voice through the wall of one of the tents.

'That was a good bit of work you did today, sergeant.'

Rustina's nasal accent replied. 'It was close, surr, but I wish it had been closer. A lucky stroke that we were in position in time. We were near to perishing in the great blizzard.'

'I was worried,' said Jal-Nish.

I'll bet you were, Nish thought. Worried that you'd be blamed if they were lost. The only thing you care about is becoming scrutator.

334

'We could see foul weather coming from up top,' came Rustina's voice. 'We'd planned for it and took shelter in an old mine tunnel. Lucky we got there in time. The blizzard came on faster than we expected. Without shelter we'd have been frozen solid.'

'I knew you wouldn't let me down,' said Jal-Nish.

Nish was disgusted. For the first time in his life he saw that ambition wasn't everything.

In a bitter voice she replied, '*No one* wants to destroy lyrinx more than I do, surr.'

It was not until they had finished their dinner, and those not on watch or out searching were preparing for sleep, that anyone thought to ask Ullii if she could *see* Tiaan.

'I could not see her when I was in the clanker,' she said. 'The evil man cried out and tried to claw me. I ran away and then I saw her crystal.'

'That was just after Dhirr died,' Irisis said to Jal-Nish. 'He'd blocked her inner sight.'

'And then what happened?' asked Jal-Nish.

'I saw her!'

'You already said that.'

'No, I saw *her*, through my goggles.'

'As well as in your mind?' Irisis asked.

'Yes! But the clawer jumped into the water with her. I could not see her after that. Or her crystal.'

'You could not see her with your mind?' Nish guessed.

'She went out like a lamp.'

'She's dead!' said Irisis. 'She either drowned or froze, and the hedron fell to the bottom. The cold put it out too.' She turned away, looking bleak.

'We should keep looking,' said Fyn-Mah, who had scarcely uttered a word since her failed mancing.

'Of course we will,' Jal-Nish snapped. 'We're not here to guess but to *make certain*.'

It blew a gale in the night. Arple called his troops in and even Jal-Nish knew better than to argue. The sentries had one of the most miserable nights of their lives and it was still blowing hard when dawn came.

Nish's fingers were so cold that it hurt to bend them. He said nothing – as a child his father's belt had taught him not to complain. As soon as it was light he joined in the hunt, walking as fast as he could in the conditions, up and down river, across and back, with Irisis. He found nothing. No one did.

Jal-Nish refused to give up. The day passed and the following night, which was, if possible, even more bitter. The day after that dawned bleak and blizzardy. The soldiers began to mutter among themselves and not even Arple could stop them. The querist spoke to Jal-Nish several times during the day but he would not relent.

Finally Artificer Tuniz, after a long consultation with the clanker operators, spoke to Fyn-Mah, who accompanied her to Jal-Nish. Nish, waiting to go on watch, overheard their conversation.

'We must go back, surr,' said Tuniz, 'else we are liable to lose the clankers.'

He turned sharply. His round face was pinched and hollow, the full lips a bloodless grey. The perquisitor looked like a man who had failed and could never accept it. 'How so, artificer?'

'It's just *too* cold. The oil goes hard and does not do its job. If it gets any colder, and the oil freezes, we won't be able to move the clankers at all.'

'Then warm it up! You can do that, surely?'

Tuniz smiled with those filed teeth. 'Aye, but it will just go hard again. And there's another problem. A worse one.'

'What now?' Jal-Nish hated it when someone tried to convince him against his own conviction.

'The metal of the linkages gets brittle in this kind of cold. If we break just one, we'll have to abandon the clanker, and by the time we come back it will be buried for the winter. In the thaw it will rust solid.'

'Very well,' Jal-Nish said, bitter in his failure. 'We leave at dawn.'

THIRTY-TWO

Tiaan dreamed that a lyrinx's huge mouth had closed right over her head, to bite her off at the neck. She dreamed that she was whirled in visible currents of water, blue and green and purple. She dreamed that she had swallowed a fish, which was flapping around inside her left lung, its spines prickling.

Piercing, brittle cold; the worst she'd ever felt. A blow in her chest; another. Something with an overpowering gamey smell went over her face.

Thump, thump, thump, fading to nothing again.

Her fingers and toes hurt so much that she woke weeping. She was wrapped in something that itched and her feet felt as if they had been rubbed with broken glass.

Tiaan opened her eyes. She seemed to be in a cave, the entrance closed off by a hanging. A fire blazed behind her, another not far from her feet. Ryll squatted there, rubbing her feet and calves. The claws were retracted. His hand looked fully regenerated. He had a massive bruise above his right eye.

'My feet feel like icicles that you could snap off,' she whispered, too listless to question or even wonder.

'There is broth.' He busied himself at the fire, returning with one hand cupped. 'Open your mouth.'

She opened up but, thinking what he might have made soup from, snapped it closed again.

'What is wrong?' the lyrinx asked.

'It's not . . .'

Ryll smiled, the first true smile she had seen on him. It was frightening – so many teeth – but disarming too. 'It's bear soup. A big old Hürn male, past his best. You're wearing his skin.'

Tiaan, becoming aware that she was clad in nothing else, flushed.

'Open!' said Ryll.

She shook her head, able to think of nothing but that she lay naked in a bearskin at the mercy of this . . . predator.

Ryll pinched her nose until Tiaan was forced to open her mouth. The soup dribbled in. It was hot. She gagged, swallowed, found it good and swallowed again. A delicious warmth spread through her belly.

All dignity gone, she nuzzled at his hand like a starving calf, desperate for more. He filled his hand over and again from the hollow stone in the fire. Shortly, her stomach aching, Tiaan lay back. The cold was fleeing from her middle, though her feet and hands still felt dead. Ryll's eyes did not leave her.

'How did we escape?' she asked. She could not remember those last seconds.

'I wrapped myself around you, trying to keep you warm, but you died.'

She sat up, staring at him. She felt a tremendous pain in her chest. 'What?'

'The shock stopped your heart. I could not keep you warm enough. I went downriver a long away. Maybe half a . . . league, before I could get out.'

'How did *you* survive?'

'I nearly drowned. It was the greatest terror of my life. We do not like water.'

'Why not?' she croaked.

'Swimming is hard for us. We do not float, and our wings tangle in the water. Fortunately,' and she could sense his bitterness, 'I have no wings. I found a hole but the ice kept breaking

338

off. *I couldn't get out!* I nearly went mad with panic.' Black jags shivered across his chest plates. 'The current pushed me under but, luckily, jammed me between a rock and the ice. I burst through and ran with you. Then came the piece of luck that saved your life. I found a cave in a gully, and in it was an old bear.'

'A bear?' she echoed.

'I killed it, that you might live. There was no time for anything else. You had not breathed for half an hour but I knew the cold could have saved you. I've seen that before, with humans. I dared not make a fire. I took out the guts of the bear, put you inside and packed them in again. When you began to warm up, I struck you in the chest until your heart started beating.'

'That's why it hurts so much.' Her chest felt battered black and blue, and the bloody offal stench came from her.

'You breathed, but did not wake. I thought you never would. Three days have gone by since we went into the river. In the middle of that night I carried you away. I knew there were caves here.'

'How did you manage?'

'We are tough. How has humanity given us such trouble when you are so little and puny and weak?' Going to the entrance, he pulled the skin to one side and stared out.

'Where are my clothes?' she asked.

'Everything is wet.' He pointed to her pack, which lay behind her.

She emptied it. The contents were sodden, ice-crusted.

'Could you make a line for me?' She held out the rope. Every movement hurt her chest.

'I have much to think about.' He returned to the door.

Turning away, she opened the bearskin. The area between her breasts was bruised yellow and purple. He must have struck her many times with those hard hands, but he'd saved her life. The question she kept coming back to was – why?

Tiaan tried to make a drying line while holding the skin around her. It proved impossible. She was too weak; the uncured skin was heavy.

Ryll snorted. His face was distorted in what she assumed was amusement. Yellow streaks around his mouth made a smile as wide as a shovel.

'What?' she said furiously.

He let out a great bellow, unmistakably laughter. His chest pumped, his leathery cheeks inflated like a trumpeter.

'What are you hiding, little one? Had I not stripped off your wet clothes and put you in the bear you would have frozen to death. I massaged every part of you to keep the blood flowing.'

She ducked her head in mortification. When she finally looked up again, he was still staring at her middle. She managed to pull the skin up that far.

'You are a mature woman,' he said. 'Have you been mated?'

'No,' she said uncomfortably.

'You have only just matured?'

'I am twenty. I have been a woman for six years.'

Ryll looked sympathetic. 'You are not permitted to mate *either*?'

For some reason she found his sympathy irritating. 'I *choose* not to mate!' she said sharply. 'I have had many offers.' That was not true. Her cool manner and total absorption in her work had been off-putting to suitors and, after all, in the manufactory there were many more women than men.

'You choose not to mate?' he said incredulously. 'But when you are ripe you *must* mate, if you have been matched.'

'Human females do not go on heat. We can mate anytime we choose. *Or not!* I have waited six years for my lover, and now I am going to him.' Poor Minis. There had been no time to think of him with all her own troubles.

'Your customs bewilder me.'

Ryll was staring at her, as he must have while she was unconscious. This alien creature had been examining her, while she lay all unknowing. 'I feel so . . .' To her horror, Tiaan began to cry, great choking sobs. Once begun, she could not stop.

The lyrinx regarded her impassively. Eventually the tears reduced to sniffles. She wiped her face and sank down in the skin, next to the fire.

'What was that called?' asked Ryll.

She found herself smiling at his curiosity. 'I was crying. Also called weeping or sobbing.'

'I know those words. Why do you cry? What does it do?'

'I felt sad, and embarrassed and ashamed; and afraid.' She had to explain those emotions as well.

'Why did you feel that way?'

'Because you're a male and you had the advantage of me while I knew nothing about it. You might . . .' As the thought occurred to her, Tiaan's mouth opened wide and she tried to get away. Her bearskin, dragged into the fire, began to smoulder.

He sprang to beat it out. She limped the other way, putting the fire between them and making an incoherent sound in her throat. She felt a churning, vomitous horror.

He went still, baffled. 'I don't understand. What emotion are you feeling now? Why were you afraid? I was not going to eat you.'

'You're a male!' she choked. 'And . . . And . .' She could not say it.

The bony crest on Ryll's head flashed from lizard-grey to brilliant reds and yellows. Without a word he stalked to the mouth of the cave, tossed back the skin and hurled himself through.

Tiaan watched him crash down the steep slope. She could not even think of escape. Her muscles felt so wasted she could not have walked a hundred steps. Shrugging off the bearskin, she examined herself. There were scratches and bruises all over her body. Making a drying line with the rope, she cracked ice off her clothes and hung them near the fire, stood her boots upside down beside it and unpacked the rest of her gear. Hacking strips off a chunk of bear meat, she put them on a hot stone to sizzle.

In a scrap of bearskin Tiaan found yellow fat – rendered bear tallow. Scooping some up in her fingers, she began to work it into her boots. Her precious tools had specks of rust. She rubbed them clean and coated them all with fat. The missing pair of pincers cried out to her.

The meat was giving off such appetising aromas that Tiaan's mouth watered. Cleaning her hands with snow, she sat down to dinner. It was as delicious a meal as she had ever eaten – chewy and with a strong flavour. She ate the lot, put more on and packed snow into her pot to melt.

Her belly was full and Tiaan was sitting by the fire, combing the knots from her hair when Ryll reappeared. Nodding curtly, he squatted by the fire and began rubbing bear fat into a patch of torn skin on his arm.

She watched him in silence. His every movement simmered with barely controlled energy, whereas she felt as if she had been living off her own body.

'If I have offended you, I'm sorry.' It sounded the right thing to say. Did he have any concept of what 'sorry' meant? She hoped so. Her life depended on his whim.

Ryll glared at her from under those massive brow ridges. His eyes caught a ray of light coming in through the entrance.

'I am not a man, little one. I am lyrinx, *unmated male*! You have insulted me deeply.'

She did not know what to say. 'I can only judge you by my own kind.'

'We do not, we *cannot* mate without invitation. It is unthinkable!' he glared at her. 'Can it be that human males would dare such a crime?'

'Time was when it was almost unheard of,' she said, remembering things her grandmother had told her. 'Men and women were equal once, but our kind have changed since the war began. Men have to sacrifice their lives in battle, and women must breed new men. Their sacrifice is deemed greater than ours.'

Ryll's enormous mouth flew open, showing the purple scar at the back of his throat. 'Decadent species! We will overcome you sooner than I thought. Besides,' he went on, 'what would be the point of mating with another species?'

A number of points occurred to Tiaan though she did not raise them. 'You do not mate for pleasure?'

'Of course we do. *Once we are matched.*'

The conversation made her uncomfortable. She finished her hair, put the brush away and sat forward, soaking up the warmth of the fire. Something occurred to her.

'What did you mean when you said you were an *unmated male*?'

Again his crest flushed, this time bright yellow. 'I have not yet been chosen by a female as her mate.'

'Are you not old enough?'

'I am old enough!' The words came out in a snarl.

'Then why?'

'I am incomplete!'

She looked him over, comparing him to the other lyrinx she'd seen. He might be smaller, though certainly no less fierce. What was different?

'Have your wings not developed yet? Is that the reason?'

'They will *never* develop! I am a wingless monstrosity, a degenerate creature. For the good of our kind there must be no more of me. Ah, but still I want to mate. It is the very purpose for which we exist.'

'Do lyrinx use their wings much?'

'Our ancestors flew everywhere in the void. We mated in the air. On this world we are too heavy. We can fly, those of us with wings,' he said bitterly, 'only by a monumental expenditure of what you call the Secret Art. Of course, many lyrinx are not adepts of the Art and cannot fly on Santhenar at all. Apart from the first mating flight, which requires at least one flier, lyrinx do not fly unless we have no choice. The after-effects of the Art are quite . . . Well, we suffer.'

'Then surely wings are a handicap and you are better off without them.'

'We are winged beings!' His crest engorged until it was almost black. 'Wings distinguish us from other intelligent creatures. It is as if . . .' He stared at her, '. . . as if you were the only female on your world without breasts. How would you feel?'

'I would feel incomplete,' she murmured, rather shocked.

'Without wings I am scarcely lyrinx at all, and no female will choose me for her mate. So what am I for?'

THIRTY-THREE

Morning came, and Ullii lay in her tent, waiting for everything to be ready so she could slip into the clanker without meeting anyone. Now that her senses were mostly under control, people were her greatest problem. Life had taught her to be afraid of everyone.

Through the earmuffs she could hear shouted orders, the noise of tents being taken down, the hiss of heated oil being poured into the machines. Jal-Nish was stamping about in a foul mood, roaring at everyone. It must be time to go. Ullii tried to find courage for the dash from tent to clanker. It was an ordeal she had to force herself to face, every day.

Irisis's head appeared inside the tent, startling her. 'Ready?' she said so loudly that it hurt.

Ullii could sense bitterness in her too. It had been there ever since Tiaan and the crystal went through the ice. Grabbing her little pack, Ullii scuttled out. Irisis scanned the tent, gathering the earplugs and coat the seeker had left behind. Ullii was halfway to the clanker when her path intersected Jal-Nish's. She stopped dead, feeling panicky. He grimaced, went to go round, then recognised who it was.

'If it isn't the little seeker. How are you today, *girl?*'

She stared down at her boots, unable to think of an answer. Jal-Nish inspected her like a grub in his breakfast. 'Idiot child!

How I ever thought you'd be any use, I can't imagine.' He brushed past.

She was about to scuttle away when he spun around, staring at her. 'What about Tiaan and her magical hedron? Do you see her now?'

'I . . . haven't looked,' she said, almost inaudibly. She could not face him alone. His voice hurt her ears. His face was cruel.

'Why not?' he roared, giving her a buffet across the cheek with the back of his hand that knocked her off her feet.

Ullii screamed and tried to curl up into a ball. He lifted her, straightening her body with his strong hands. 'Don't!' he said coldly. 'Or I'll tear off your goggles and earmuffs. So help me, I'll strip you naked and cast you into the snow. Now answer . . .'

Nish and Irisis came running. 'Father, stop!' Nish yelled. 'You'll . . .'

'Don't tell me what to do, boy!' growled Jal-Nish, 'or you'll find out what happens to people who fail. The scrutator is not a forgiving man. I've not let him down before and I'm not going to now. I don't care who I have to break; I won't give up. What do *you* want?' he roared at Arple, who was running up from the other direction.

'I would suggest, surr . . .'

'This is perquisitor business. Interfere and I'll see you quartered for treason!' He spun back to Ullii, whom he'd let fall. She crouched on the ground with her arms up over her face. 'Stand up, girl. Look at me.'

Ullii stood up, blank terror etched into her.

'*Why* have you not looked, seeker? *Why* did you not try to see Tiaan and her hedron?'

'No one asked me to,' she whispered, reflecting his voice back at him.

The blow came out of nowhere, knocking her down. Ullii tasted blood, boiling-hot and metallic. The goggles and earmuffs came off; in broad daylight it was like being stabbed through the eyes with shards of glass. She overloaded, convulsed and screamed until she went into a fit.

Irisis walked calmly up to Jal-Nish and, as Nish gaped, struck

345

the perquisitor in the face so hard that he crashed backwards into the snow. His proud nose was flattened against his face and blood poured out of it.

'You're a fool and a fraud, Jal-Nish! No true perquisitor would ever act in such a brutal way. How much did you pay for your position?' Spitting in his face, she walked to the sergeant, held her arms out for the manacles, and said, 'Do your worst. I care not!'

Arple waved her away. 'I have no orders concerning you, artisan.'

'You have now!' raged Jal-Nish, staggering across the packed snow. Blood formed lurid icicles in his beard. 'Take her head off at the shoulder blades and hurl it into the fire.'

'No valid orders,' said Arple, folding scarred arms across his tree-trunk chest.

'So that's the way it is, is it?' Jal-Nish's voice grew soft with menace. 'I'll reserve *my* orders for you both. There are worse things in life than death. Before I'm finished you'll be begging for it. *Cryl-Nish!*'

Nish was bent over Ullii, trying to calm her. 'Yes, Perquisitor Hlar?' He made a point of the formality. It was as far as he dared go.

'I'll be dealing with you as well. For incompetence! Get the seeker fixed up at once.'

Nodding curtly, Nish carried Ullii to the clanker. Irisis came behind with goggles and muffs. Nish put them on the seeker. As he was bathing her bruised face with a cloth steeped in warm water, Ky-Ara and Pur-Did staggered up, carrying the heatbank between them on its long handles, and slid it into the middle of the clanker. Having been standing in the fire, it was practically red-hot.

'Why did you do that?' Nish said to Irisis, who was staring blankly out the front porthole.

'I've had enough of your father!' she said fiercely.

'But Irisis, when we get back, he'll destroy you.'

'I'm ruined anyway. The crystal was my last hope. I've disgraced the family and my shame will be in the Histories forever, so how can I make it worse?' She gave a bitter chuckle. 'I've

346

never enjoyed anything so much as popping his proud nose. How he squealed! Just like a rat in a trap.'

Nish did not share her pleasure. He could not bear to think what Jal-Nish would do in revenge.

Irisis warmed her hands at the heatbox. Nish sat patiently, holding Ullii's hand. She did not stir for an hour, and it was another hour before she would sit up. She was staring through the rear porthole when she stiffened and shrank away. Nish peered out. Jal-Nish was pacing back and forth, his face swollen beyond recognition. After he had gone by she sat up again.

'What happened to the perquisitor?'

'He hit you,' Irisis said. 'So I hit him harder, to teach him not to hurt people.'

Ullii then did the strangest thing. She pulled up the goggles and for the first time they saw her strange, almost colourless eyes clearly. They shone as if coated in glycerine.

'You did that for me?' she said. Seizing Irisis's hand, she brought it up and buried her nose in it. 'You are kind too.'

Irisis looked uncomfortable, which she tried to cover up by rolling her eyes at Nish. 'I'm a mean bitch,' she said under her breath. 'Don't read too much into a single rash act.'

'Are you ready to look for Tiaan?' Nish said shortly. 'Can you . . .'

'Of course!' Ullii was transported, positively bubbling now as she put on the mask.

Jal-Nish rapped on the back hatch. 'Well?' he snapped.

Nish flipped the hatch open, forcing the perquisitor to leap out of the way. 'She is looking.'

'And?' cried Jal-Nish. 'Come out, seeker.'

Ullii climbed out, keeping well clear of him.

'What can you see, seeker?' said Jal-Nish.

She said nothing. 'Tell us what you see, Ullii,' Nish said, taking her right hand.

She flung out her left. 'I can see her!' She pointed to the south-west.

Clearly the perquisitor had expected nothing. 'Are you sure?' he said incredulously. 'How far?'

'Not far. Her crystal is shining like the morning star.'

Irisis let out a strangled cry. The sun broke through the overcast for a moment. Jal-Nish smiled. It was not a pretty sight. He gave a jerk of the head. 'After her!'

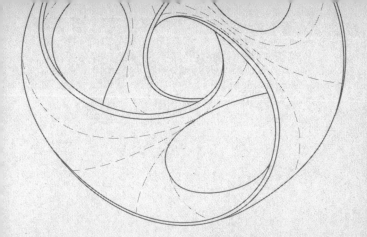

PART FOUR

FLESH-FORMER

THIRTY-FOUR

'Get up! We're going.'

Tiaan snapped awake. Ryll was at the entrance, staring down. She rolled out of the bearskin, too panicky to feel self-conscious. The lyrinx must have turned her clothes during the night for, apart from the heavy coat, they were dry. She dressed quickly in four layers of clothing, all smelling of smoke. The boots were still damp but at least they were warm.

In five minutes she was ready. 'What's the matter?' She stood by his side at the entrance.

He simply pointed down the mountain. Far below, two columns of marching soldiers, and the four clankers, crawled like grey caterpillars across the snowfield. Their tracks ran across the landscape, perfectly straight, all the way from the river. The awful memory came back – the four clankers surrounding them on the ice, firing their javelards. Trying to kill her. Her own people would sooner do that than allow Ryll to get away with her! Her loyalty to the manufactory vanished. She would have to make her own way in the world now. For the moment that must be with Ryll, since there was no possibility of escaping him.

'How did they find me?' Ryll murmured. 'I covered my path well.'

'The fire?' said Tiaan, though it gave off little smoke and the entrance faced away from the river. 'Or carrion birds?'

'See how straight their tracks are? They must have a way of finding you; *or your crystal.*'

'I was not aware that could be done at any distance.' She knew so little about the Secret Art, even as used in such systems as she had been making for years. But then, the lyrinx had been able to detect the aura from controllers . . .

'Must I tie your wrists again?' Ryll asked.

The feeling of helplessness when she had gone into the river with bound hands had been terrifying. 'I won't try to escape.'

'There would not be much point to it.'

Ryll slid along the edge into the shadows, then headed up. The face of the mountain was steep. In her state the climb proved impossible and after the first stumble he tucked her under his arm. Ryll seemed untroubled by the extra weight, but he could cling with the claws on his hands and feet.

Toward the top he tied her to his chest. 'In case you fall,' he said.

She tried not to think what would happen if *he* fell.

They followed a path of his choosing for three days. Tiaan had no choice in the matter; she had no idea where they were going, though they were heading south-west, roughly the way she wanted to go.

She saw the clankers several times on the first day, but they fell further behind and by the afternoon there was no more sign of them.

Each day was much the same. They began at dawn with a feed of bear meat – roasted for her, raw for him – then walked for as long as Tiaan could keep up. When she flagged they stopped, Tiaan ate, he put her on his back and kept going until dark, or after dark if the country permitted it. Finally they would stop for dinner and sleep in a snow cave, or under an overhang.

'I believe we've lost them,' Ryll said on the afternoon of the third day.

Tiaan rested behind a windswept boulder. The weather had been good these last days but an ominous bank of clouds was building in front of them. 'We'd better find shelter for the night, and tomorrow too.'

'I know a place.' The lyrinx indicated a steep-sided plateau in the distance.

She gauged the progress of the cloudbank. 'We won't make it.'

'There's nowhere else.'

Swinging her up on his shoulders, he began to run. Used to it by now, she merely clenched her thighs about his neck as if astride a horse and hung on, enduring the thumping ride. It was a race, and one they were going to lose. The overcast came in quickly, with chilly gusts and scattered snowflakes. Before they reached the base of the plateau, it was snowing hard.

He stopped at an outcrop of yellow rock, a broken cliff that went up further than she could see. 'Better find a cave,' Tiaan said.

Ryll swung her down and ranged along the base of the plateau, which rose abruptly from the plain. The incessant wind had blasted the rubble to dust and blown it away.

'What about this?' she shouted, for they were passing a series of small caves like a giant honeycomb in the rock.

'I know where I'm going.'

She felt a twinge of unease but the storm was on them and there was no choice but to follow him. After some minutes, when visibility was down to the distance she could have spat a plum seed, Ryll went sideways into a slot no wider than her shoulders. A pattern of clefts cut the rock into stacks. She tried to map the way but soon lost the sequence, for every turn looked the same. Finally the lyrinx slipped into an even narrower gap, squeezed though a tight space and stopped.

It was calm here, the snow falling vertically. Grasping a rope that she had not noticed, he gave a series of tugs.

'Get on my shoulders!'

She complied, now thoroughly alarmed. The rope jerked twice, Ryll took a firm grip and was drawn steadily up. The ground disappeared in the whirling snow, which was worse than looking down on the drop.

The rope stopped suddenly. The strain was showing on Ryll's

face and the knotted arms began to tremble. He looked up anxiously. Without warning the rope jerked again, so hard that his hands slipped on the fibres. Ryll let out a truncated cry. Tiaan almost wet herself, but his grip held.

Near the top they stopped again. He was really straining now. Another jerk and she saw flat ground, the edge of the plateau. A gust blew them sideways. Tiaan was sure they were going to fall.

She screamed, and again as a lyrinx much bigger than Ryll snatched him off the rope. She went backwards off his shoulders but Ryll's hand found her ankle. As they were hauled in, she went close to dashing her brains out on the cliff edge.

Ryll stood her on her feet but had to hold her up, for Tiaan's knees had turned plastic. Three lyrinx stood in an arc in front of them. Two were much bigger than Ryll, the third about his size. All stood in a crouch, arms curved, fingers flexed. Their skin colours rippled in unison, in waves of brilliant yellow and red. Warning colours.

'Thlrrpith myrzhip?' said the middle one in an aggressive voice.

'Myrllishimirr, ptath vozzr!' Ryll sounded defensive.

'Sklizzipth moxor! *Tcharr!*'

The lyrinx to Tiaan's left sprang and caught her by the arms. Its other hand grabbed her legs and raised her in front of its face. It was either going to tear her limbs off or bite her head from her neck.

'Thlampetter rysh!' roared Ryll. 'Thlampetter rysh *narrl.*'

The lyrinx froze, looking from one of its fellows to the other, and then to Ryll.

'Rysh *narrl?*'

The pressure eased slightly.

Ryll pointed over the cliff into the snow, blasted about by wild gusts of wind. The creatures spoke among themselves, after which one remained behind while the others escorted Ryll away from the cliff, the lyrinx still carrying Tiaan like a forgotten parcel.

After a bitterly cold trek that lasted an hour and more, a curved ice wall loomed up in front of them. The leading lyrinx pulled aside a set of skin doors, hanging one after another, went on hands and knees through a tunnel, another skin door, and into a large room. It was domed, like a big igloo, and made of sawn ice or pressed blocks of snow. The room was empty apart from some skins on the floor. Several crawl passages ran off it. The first lyrinx went down the one to her left.

Her captor put Tiaan on her feet. A long conversation followed in their language. Tiaan had no idea what was going on, though clearly Ryll had been heading here all the time. He'd had no intention of taking her across the mountains. His code of honour was no more than a lie. She felt bitterly disappointed, though she was aware how foolish that was. The lyrinx were enemies.

'What do you want me for?' she said to Ryll.

'To help us with the war, of course.'

'But . . . you said you owed me a debt.'

'I repaid it when I saved you after the avalanche. I saved your life again on the ice when your own people would have killed you.'

She looked up at his fierce face. 'You never said that the debt had been repaid.'

'Can you not reckon up the weight of your obligations? We *are* at war, human!'

Tiaan felt like a fool. How could she have trusted him? 'You did not tell me!' she hissed, as if that was an excuse.

'I left you unwatched after I saved you the first time. You had the chance to escape and did not. After all I have done for you since, I count you deep in *my* obligation.'

'I will not betray my people,' she said uselessly, but he had gone.

Tiaan considered her position. His kind would always be enemies of humanity. What was he going to do to her now? He had not brought her all this way for nothing.

A large lyrinx came through the passage directly in front of her. It had a green crest and breast-shaped chest plates, by which Tiaan assumed it to be female. The crest was badly scarred, the first three peaks missing and the scars lacking pigment. Female lyrinx were the same size as males, or sometimes bigger, she noted. Others followed, including Ryll. Soon eight stood in front of her. Ryll spoke to the first in his own tongue. Two others, both with green crests, bore young. All had folded leathery wings, unlike Ryll's useless stumps.

'Bring out your devices, Tiaan,' said Ryll.

She shook her head. With one bound the lyrinx that had attacked her at the clifftop took her by the throat and shook her hard.

'Glynnch!' the large female said peremptorily.

The lyrinx dropped her on the floor. Ryll shook out the contents of her pack, handing Tiaan the globe, crystal and cap. As she met his eyes, resistance drained out of her.

She made sure that the wires had not been bent by the journey, and that the small crystal was secure in its setting. The globe was squashed on one side. Her fingers worked it back into shape, checking that the beads would slide freely in their orbits. The lyrinx did not take their eyes off her.

Tiaan lifted out the hedron, or amplimet as she now thought of it. It was warm to the touch; unusually so. Did that mean this place lay over a node? The crystal felt heavier than usual. Ryll caught her elbow, holding it up so they could all see it.

A spark leapt the gap between the central needles, flaring into a yellow light that made her flinch. It was much brighter than before. The lyrinx cried out as one.

'Thlampetter rysh!' said Ryll. 'The crystal key. And she is the keykeeper.'

He went into a huddle with the other lyrinx. There was a heated conversation with much arm-waving, thumping of each other's chests and lurid changes of skin colour and pattern. Ryll seemed unusually submissive – they struck his chest so hard that he rocked backwards, while his blows were mere taps, done with lowered head.

From the way they spoke to Ryll, and their body language, Tiaan could see that he was held in low esteem. Was that because he was an unmated male, or was it because of his deformity, his lack of wings? Whatever the reason, the all-competent, all-powerful protector of recent days was revealed to be power-less here.

A long debate followed, of which Tiaan understood not a word. After some time she was escorted to a smaller room whose entrance was then blocked with a slab of shaped ice. The room was like an igloo made of compressed snow. She might have cut her way out but Ryll had taken her knife. Nor could she budge the block that plugged the tunnel.

Tiaan paced across and back. The room contained nothing but a skin with long, silky white fur. Too big to be any kind of wildcat, and too coarse for mountain ox, it was probably from a snow bear. She sat on it, considering the possibilities.

Either Ryll would lose his argument, whatever it was, and the lyrinx would eat her, or they would force her to teach them about the amplimet, and the making of controllers, and how best they could be disabled or adapted to their own purposes. And then they would eat her. What would happen to Minis then? Tears welled in her eyes.

Already she felt the first pangs of withdrawal. If they kept the amplimet for long enough Tiaan knew she would do anything, just to hold it again. But how could she? Wrapping the skin tightly about her, she lay down on ice and tried to sleep.

The slab ground out of the way and a lyrinx shimmering with purple colours dragged her into the main room. Tiaan's eyes darted around but the grip was unbreakable.

'You will show us the use of your devices,' said Ryll.

Where did the boundaries of treachery lie? Was it betrayal if she revealed what she knew under torture? A true hero would provoke them into killing her, to avoid being forced to betray humanity's secrets. That required more bravery, or gratitude, than Tiaan had in her. Besides, she had given her promise to Minis; and her love.

'At once!' barked the largest lyrinx.

Tiaan was no hero, just very frightened. The helm felt burning cold. She warmed it in her fingers, then placed the amplimet inside the globe. She concentrated hard; her fingers moved the beads, seeking some elusive pattern that might enable her to tune in to the field about the node here. The glimmering of a plan came to her.

Could she tap into the field and direct it against her captors, to disable or kill them all at the same time? Probably not. It was hard to take that kind of power from the weak field. For what she required, only geomancy would do, but Tiaan was afraid of that Art. Her failure in the ice sphere had taught her how little she knew about it, and how deadly it was.

While she was thus preoccupied, her fingers had been working of their own volition, testing patterns and permutations randomly. She began to pick up a field. At least, she thought it was a field, though like none she'd ever seen before. It looked like two red suns whirling around each other in a halo of orange mist, beautiful but alien. Tiaan assessed the mind-image. Was there anything she could do with it? The red orbs looked dangerous; she dared not go near them. What about the mist? There seemed a little power in it.

The mist drifted, spread and closed around her, dark and menacing. Tiaan was trapped in orange fog. A hot surge went through her and the amplimet let out a brilliant violet flare. One of the lyrinx yelped. The others shielded their eyes. Her head was reverberating. She slid sideways to the floor, hands over her ears, trying to block out the sound. Her head hit the ice, the helm flew off and the flare went out.

Ryll picked her up. Water was dripping from the roof. As Tiaan took her hands away from her ears, her sight came back. The lyrinx, eyes watering, looked around in confusion. Tiaan made a mental note of that weakness. The amplimet was gently glowing as before. Tiaan had no idea what force she had tapped.

'Well, Besant,' said Ryll. 'Do you believe me now?'

Besant, the large female with the scarred crest, twitched her face muscles. Was she reluctant to make the concession to a deformed, unmated male?

'You have done well, Ryll,' she said in a deep voice. It took some time for Tiaan to recognise it as the common speech, so thick was her accent. 'The device has tapped an unknown source of power. The human may teach us much. I will send her to Kalissin.'

'And me?' Ryll said, too eagerly. 'Is this my chance? Shall I be mated now?'

'This could improve your desirability. I give you leave to seek a mate, though I doubt very much if a mate would choose *you*.'

They allowed Tiaan back her possessions, except for the amplimet, knife and crossbow. She was returned to her room, fed several times on charred strips of bear meat and water, and taken outside occasionally by Ryll to use a pit dug in the snow. Once she went by a pair of lyrinx squatting over a small, mushroom-shaped object, their hands shaping the air around it.

'What are they doing?' she asked.

'Watching,' said Ryll, and would say no more.

Tiaan expected crystal dreams that first night, and hoped they might be of her lost lover. Her dreams turned out to be horrors unlike anything she had ever imagined. She dreamed that her room was full of cages, each containing a warped travesty of the wild creatures she knew.

A misty orange field swirled around the cages, squeezing the creatures in whirlpool coils. They shrieked in agony, blood dripped from mouths and other orifices, and one by one they began to change. Flesh and bones deformed, skin and sinews stretched and crackled. Teeth shattered and fell from gaping mouths, to be replaced by new ones as sharp as the teeth of sharks.

Soon those creatures that survived were transformed into staring monsters. Their eyes were fixed on her. Tiaan paced back and forth all night to keep the dreams away.

The following night she also dreamed, but these were withdrawal dreams, a desperate craving that grew worse with every hour she was parted from the amplimet. Her body was wracked with aches and longings. She thought of nothing all day but how she might recover the crystal, and dreamed of nothing all night. That was the worst thing about withdrawal – it took so long to get over. Some people never did.

'What is the matter?' Ryll asked her on the second afternoon, when she lay shaking on her skin, tormented by her longing. 'Are you ill?'

Tiaan was in no state to think up a cover story. 'I must have the crystal,' she whispered. 'Please. I cannot bear to be without it.'

'Ah!' he said, and went out.

Only later did Tiaan realise that she had given him the perfect hold over her.

THIRTY-FIVE

Following Ullii's directions the searchers went straight to the last of the caves. Irisis was at their head. A pair of soldiers approached the bearskin door, spears at the ready. Irisis, with recklessness born of despair, thrust past, tore down the skin and leapt inside. The cave was empty.

'She's gone!' Irisis said bitterly.

'And within hours.' Arple had uncovered red coals from the ashes.

'Now do you see the worth of your seeker,' said Nish from the entrance, 'and give her credit for what she's done?'

'Indeed,' replied the perquisitor. 'She's proven her worth. We'll find many uses for her in the war, I'll be bound.'

As Irisis came out, Ullii shivered and drew closer to her friends. With a harsh laugh Jal-Nish turned away, ordering a search of all the caves and signalling down to the clankers to recall the other squads.

Fresh prints led up the mountain. The climbers followed them, while far below the clankers headed up the valley. The forces rejoined late in the afternoon.

It began to snow that evening. They tried to follow the tracks with flares, but after dark lost them in the deepening snow. Making camp in the shelter of a bluff, they had a full night's sleep for the first time in many days. In the morning Ullii was again called upon. She pointed more south now, and was required to show the way many times in the next days, for they saw not a single track in that time.

The snow was heavy going and the clankers, with their broad footplates installed, could make no better time than a slow march. They were plagued with freezing oil and breakdowns, which Nish and Tuniz were called upon to fix. Nish discovered just how much he loathed his trade. He always ended up with bloody, frozen fingers and his father's curses ringing in his ears. Every operation was ten times as difficult as it had been in the workshop. Even unflappable Tuniz was heard to swear on occasion.

It was not windy, but intensely cold, especially in the clear nights. On the third afternoon a blizzard blasted down on them. They could not move at all the following day, and the fifth brought wind to whirl the fresh snow up into clouds. They struggled on, slower and slower, and finally the clankers shuddered to a stop.

'What is it?' screamed Jal-Nish. He had to scream to be heard over the wind. Everyone gathered behind the clankers.

'Field's too weak,' said Simmo from the second machine. 'We've been running on the flywheels for the last quarter-hour but they've run down.'

'Does that mean we're stuck here? Incompetent fools!'

'There's another node ahead, surr, and it's a strong one, but we're having trouble drawing from its field. It's strange, perquisitor, surr. I've never seen anything like it.'

'What do you mean?'

Simmo conferred with the other operators before answering. 'Seems to be a double node. We've never come across such a thing before. We can't work it out.'

'Then get the artisan to show you. That's what's she's here for. Artisan Irisis, get over here.'

Irisis froze, her guts churning. This was it. She was going to be exposed. She would never fool Jal-Nish. Looking despairingly around the circle of pinched faces, she caught Nish's eyes on her. He was stricken.

She assumed her famous arrogant expression. At least she

would go down fighting, and when the worst did happen she would take the perquisitor with her. Clutching her pliance, Irisis strode forward.

'I expect I'll have to modify the controllers,' she said.

'How long will that take?'

'As long as it takes, surr. We can't take risks up here.'

'Get on with it.'

Climbing into the clanker, Irisis began to pull the controller apart. Ky-Ara crouched beside her, watching her every move as if she was operating on his own child. He whimpered as she removed each controller arm. It was hard to concentrate.

'Ky-Ara,' she said pleasantly, 'would you be so kind as to bring the other controllers here?'

He went reluctantly, with many a backward glance from those liquid eyes.

'Nish!' Irisis called. Nish came out of the huddle. 'Stand guard on the hatch and don't let anyone through.'

'What about Ky-Ara?'

'Especially not that whimpering fool. Or your father.'

Ullii came trailing up behind Nish, thrust her head under his arm and peered in through her goggles. Nish indicated her with an inclination of the head.

'Come in, Ullii!' snapped Irisis. 'But don't say anything, all right?'

Creeping in, Ullii sat down in her seat.

Irisis worked steadily for an hour or so, visualising the strange double node with her pliance and trying to tune Ky-Ara's controller to the field. In spite of the cold she began to sweat. The double node was the strangest she'd ever encountered, a large glowing globe and a smaller one, orbiting each other. Orange mist whirled around and between the two, flowing from one to the other and emitting occasional bright pulses. It disturbed her, and when she tried to visualise the associated field her brain hurt, the way her nose did when she caught a breath of pitch smoke. There was something noxious about this field. It fluctuated from weak to strong more quickly than her defences could cope.

Irisis pulled away, her heart pounding. Something was very

wrong. Even if she could tune the controllers to the node, she was afraid what would happen when she did.

Someone rapped on the back hatch. 'What's going on?' came Jal-Nish's cry.

'Don't let him in, Nish.'

The hatch was jerked open. 'Well, artisan?'

'It's proving unexpectedly difficult.'

'Why?' There was a dangerous glint in Jal-Nish's eye.

'I've never worked with a double node before and I don't think anyone else has either. If I get it wrong it may burn out the hedron and the clanker will be stuck here for the winter.'

'Bah! Fyn-Mah always said you were a fraud.'

After some hours Irisis had worked out how to tune the controller to the field, though she had no idea if it would be able to cope with the dangerous fluctuations in intensity. She could not do the test herself, since she lacked the ability to draw power from the field. Irisis planned to have Ky-Ara do it. It was the only way she could think of to escape her fate. But if he refused . . .

Ky-Ara was eager to help. He would have agreed to anything to get her out of his seat. Irisis had been counting on that. It was the reason she had done his controller first. The other operators were tougher.

She was sitting beside Ky-Ara, explaining what to do, when Jal-Nish heaved Nish out of the way and pushed through to the front of the clanker.

'What do you think you're doing?' he snapped.

'I . . .' A shiver went up her spine. 'I'm showing Ky-Ara how to carry out the test.'

'Be damned! That's artisan's work. I wouldn't risk an operator on it if I had a dozen to spare.'

'But he's the one . . .' she began desperately.

'Never! I can lose you, if it goes wrong. I can't lose him.'

Irisis swallowed. 'Then I'll need him to help.'

'You'll do it on your own, artisan. What's the problem? You were acting crafter a few weeks ago. You must have done this a thousand times.'

'It's just . . . not this kind of node,' she said, almost inaudibly. Irisis glanced at Nish as if for help, but he was looking down, picking ice off his boots. Well, this is it, she thought. My nightmare has come at last. If I *could* do it, I'd pull so much power from the field that it would blow the clanker apart and anthracise everyone in it. The apocalypse had a violent appeal, but it was just a dream.

'Very well,' she went on. 'Everyone must stand well back, in case something goes wrong. I don't think this kind of node has ever been used before.'

'Just get it done,' said Jal-Nish. *'If you can.'*

Was this a malicious game, she thought, to humiliate her in front of everyone? It was just the kind of revenge the perquisitor would go for.

Jal-Nish took her advice and moved a long way from the clanker. The querist remained where she was. Did she do that to mock Irisis?

'You'd better go too,' Irisis said to Ullii and Nish. Nish did not meet her eyes, as if trying to distance himself from the humiliation to come. She could not blame him.

He stayed, though, and Ullii did too, which was surprising. Or perhaps Ullii knew there was no danger at all. Irisis began, using the controller to sense out the fluctuating field. It was so much stronger than using her pliance. It had to be, to drive the massive weight of a clanker.

Allowing those baleful globes to orbit freely in her mind, but keeping well away, Irisis concentrated on the spirals of mist that whirled between them. She was searching for one that was strong but not too strong. Her missing talent *might* come back.

She passed by one, then a second, a third. The eyes of Nish and Ullii never left her face. Irisis imagined what was to come. Utter humiliation. Jal-Nish would not dispose of her here – her abilities could be needed on the way home – but once back at the manufactory he would make a public spectacle of her. Chroniclers and tellers would be imported from a hundred leagues to spread the tale of her downfall and to describe, in loving detail, her fitting punishment.

'Hurry up, artisan.' The perquisitor had his head in through the back hatch.

It was now or not at all. Irisis seized on one of those whorls and tried with all her strength to draw power. Nothing happened. Gritting her teeth, she wiped icy perspiration from her brow and tried again. Again nothing.

The perquisitor laughed. How Jal-Nish was enjoying this. 'You can't do it. You're a fraud, Irisis. You've always been a fraud. What a cautionary tale this is going to make. I can't wait to see the faces of the House of Stirm as the story is told.'

'I *can* do it!' she ground out. How dare he attack her family! Everyone knew his ancestors were upstarts who had whored and bribed and battered their way to the top. If she could have anthracised him she would have done it on the spot.

She tried again and again, until the sinews in her neck stood out like knotted cords. Irisis bared her teeth; a groan escaped, but not the least trickle of power came though into the controller.

Jal-Nish laughed aloud. Irisis wanted to smash his face in, but that had got her into trouble in the first place. She looked around wildly. The seeker had taken off her goggles and was staring at Irisis with frightening intensity. Strangely, it made the artisan think of scribbled marks on fans.

Closing her eyes, she prepared for one last try. Irisis plunged into a knot of that red mist, but now it was like a knot on a fan. As she hurled herself at it, the knot began to unravel, and then to open up like a rosebud, and a path unfolded inside that was unlike any path she had ever seen before.

Suddenly Irisis saw the way that had been closed to her and pulled so hard that she blacked out for an instant, cracking her head on the side of the clanker.

The clanker did not budge; the controller arms failed to flex in the slightest degree. She had failed. Irisis looked up for the cruel vindication on Jal-Nish's face.

The perquisitor had his head to one side. 'What's that?'

Her head was ringing; she could not tell.

'I don't know,' she heard the querist say.

'Flywheel spinning,' said Ullii.

The faintest ticking sound became a whirr, a hum, then a whine as the paired flywheels spun up to full speed. Somehow, incredibly, miraculously, the controller was drawing from the field.

'You did it!' cried Nish, hugging and kissing her on the brow. 'I knew you would.'

'It *is* her job,' Jal-Nish said sourly. 'I don't see why you're making such a fuss about it. Get the others fixed and let's get after the lyrinx.'

Irisis tuned the other three controllers to the field and instructed their operators on how to get them going. When that was done she went back to her clanker and touched Ullii on the cheek with her fingertips, silent thanks. She had no idea what Ullii had done, or how she had shown her the way, but that did not matter. It was done and she had a temporary reprieve. Nothing else had changed. Irisis knew she could no more do it by herself than before. Her need for the crystal was as urgent as ever.

On the afternoon of the fifth day they caught a glimpse, when the weather cleared briefly, of a cliff-bound plateau not far away. From Ullii's latest directions, the lyrinx had gone straight toward it. They went carefully thereafter, not moving until dark and travelling though the night. Jal-Nish was working on a plan to take the enemy by surprise. He spent a lot of time with Rustina, the red-haired sergeant of the troop which had joined them at the river. The two squatted by themselves, he talking, she drawing with her knife on the snow. Whatever was decided Jal-Nish kept to himself.

'No doubt father is planning to spring another triumph on us,' Nish said sourly to Irisis.

'He has to keep proving his cleverness . . .' She broke off as Jal-Nish approached.

'What if they have a town there?' Nish said to his father.

'Up there? At most it will be a small clan grouping.'

They reached the cliffs some hours before dawn, having veered away from the lyrinx's path in case a lookout was kept.

There was no danger at the moment, for the air was full of blown snow and the top of the plateau could not be seen. They camped in a fold behind a hill, a hiding place if the weather cleared suddenly. Conference was held at the base of the cliff. Everyone was called to it, even Ullii, though she was allowed to watch from the open hatch of the clanker.

'What do you know of this place?' the querist asked Arple.

'I've heard of it,' the sergeant replied, his hand upon the yellow riven rock. Wind had fretted it into little clusters of box shapes, outlined a deeper yellow-brown. 'People dwelt up there once, shepherds of mountain sheep and goats, but the weather turned cold forty years back and one year there was no summer at all. The flocks starved; the people died or left. Nothing can survive there now.'

'Except lyrinx!' Jal-Nish said sourly. 'And surely they do not eat the rocks. Who among you has been atop? Speak up and you will be rewarded.'

'I believe Wulley is acquainted with the place, surr,' said Arple after a long hesitation. 'Wulley . . .'

A hard-bitten veteran spoke from the shadows. His voice was as soft as butter and never rose above a whisper. Irisis's eyes sought him out in the darkness. A heavily muscled man, though with the legs of a dwarf, his face was scored with scars, clan marks. Another went across his throat, which explained the voice. She wondered how he had survived such a wound.

'I know it from when I were a kiddie, surr. Were a robber band there for a while. Brought terror and ruin to Yellow Nodey, Consummine, Tungstate and a dozen other villages nearby.'

'I did not know there were any villages up here,' said Jal-Nish.

'Aren't any more. Famine and plague got what the robbers did not, more'n thirty year ago.'

'What do you know of this plateau, soldier?'

'Garrihan it's called, surr, which means tabletop mountain in our dialect. Least, it used to. I'm the only one to speak it now, and when I'm gone . . .' He trailed off.

'What's on top of Garrihan, Wulley?' asked Arple.

'Top is shaped like an egg, surr. The pointy end faces us. It'd be a solid day's march across, in the snow.'

'It's about three leagues long,' said the querist, who was holding a map up to the light. 'And two wide. It would take a good force to watch all that edge. It's flat you say, Wulley?'

'Pretty much. There's gentle hills and gullies down the other end. No high places where they could keep watch, though.'

'Where would they camp if they were up there?' Jal-Nish asked.

'Down the round end. In the gullies you can get away from the wind, and there's water, when it's not frozen.'

'Sounds like this end is the best place to go up,' said Jal-Nish, 'if the weather stays bad. Show us on the map, soldier.'

Wulley came out, walking like a bear on its hind legs. Irisis pressed closer. Pointing to the eastern side of the round end with a battered, nailless finger, the soldier said, 'Was a stair here, when the robbers held it. That'll be guarded, if the beasts haven't destroyed it. Lyrinx don't need stairs. Village was here. Winds are perishing anywhere else.'

'Where would you go up in secret?' Arple asked.

Without hesitation, Wulley replied, 'Just here, across the tabletop from the stair, surr. The edge is all broken and there are rocks and boulders. Easy to hide but hard to guard. You can't see far. Bugger of a climb, though.'

'We're ready for that,' Jal-Nish said smugly. 'The troop that came with the fourth clanker are all climbers. I'm prepared for every contingency.'

Except my fist in your face, Irisis thought, taking some satisfaction from the damage she'd done. His handsome nose was ruined and every breath wheezed in his sinuses.

Jal-Nish's news was a surprise, even to Arple, for the new squad had kept to themselves.

'We'll move the camp down there, out of sight,' Jal-Nish continued, 'and my climbers will come to the base of the cliffs while it's still dark. Unless the weather clears they'll go up at first light, make reconnaissance and prepare the way for the rest of the force. By this time tomorrow the lyrinx will be history.'

THIRTY-SIX

They arrived in position just as a slate-grey dawn broke. The wind was shrieking but they found a relatively protected north face. Rustina paced back and forth, scanning the cliffs for a suitable place to climb.

'Here, I think!' She placed her gloved hand on the layered rock.

A flurry of snow whirled up the gully like a miniature tornado. Irisis watched the white flakes spin. Obsessed with the crystal now, she dreamed about it every night, and in her waking moments fantasised that it would give her back her talent.

The rest of the squad were carrying enormous packs, which they placed at the base of the cliff. Rustina motioned them away. 'No, over there! Move it well back! If we're discovered they could wipe us out with a few boulders.'

Soon they were ready. Irisis turned her back to the wind and watched. The first two climbers received their final instructions. Both were like Rustina: tall, lean and long-limbed. They wore clawed, retractable spikes strapped to wrists and boot toes. Each carried an ice axe spiked on one end, and a small pack. A length of rope connected them.

Rustina clapped each on the shoulder and up they went, climbing with surprising swiftness, using crevices Irisis could not see. They looked like four-armed spiders creeping across the stone. Soon they disappeared into the blasting snow.

Jal-Nish stood with his arms folded. Arple was some distance away, as rigid as if on parade. Blown snow had caked in his furrowed upper lip. More than ever it seemed like a second mouth. Rustina strode back and forth, red hair flying, thin lips tight. The minutes ticked into an hour. They heard no sound, not that anything *could* be heard over the wind. The sergeant muttered to herself. Jal-Nish began pacing nervously, casting anxious glances up. Arple still had not moved.

With a squeal of metal on stone something bounced off the rock above him. Landing with another scrape, it pushed off and came down another couple of spans. It was one of the climbers, bounding on a rope. His feet struck the ground.

'All's well so far,' he said, beaming. 'No sign of them. We've set up, up top.'

Jal-Nish came running across. 'And the weather?'

'Wonderful!' The climber gave a fierce grin. His gums were stained bright yellow from chewing nigah leaf, which dulled the senses to cold. Rustina had issued rations of it to her troop, though she did not take any for herself. 'It's blowing a gale, surr. Visibility no more than twenty steps.'

'You saw no tracks, no path?'

'No, surr!' By way of emphasis he spat a yellow gob on the snow.

'And the clankers?'

The climber scratched his head and spoke briefly to Rustina. She nodded.

'I believe it's possible, surr.' They went into a huddle. Irisis did not hear the rest. Soon after they broke up.

'Get your troops up, sergeant,' Jal-Nish said. 'Quick as you can! Put the defences in place and set up the lifts. Arple, send for the camp and the clankers. We're going to take them up.'

Arple looked dubious but rapped out his orders and a soldier skied off to the camp. Rustina's troops brought the strapped bundles of rods out from under an overhang. They had been bound to the top of the fourth clanker. Irisis had often wondered what they were for. They also carried bags with pulleys, clamps, coils of rope and other equipment. Rustina went back and forth, carrying loads the equal of the strongest soldiers. She drove herself the hardest of all. Finally, the rest of her squad donned their packs and went up the cliff, using the rope.

Irisis sat on a rock. The troops were well drilled and there was nothing she could do to help. How were they going to get the clankers up there? It seemed like madness, in this gale, especially after the fiasco that had killed Dhirr.

Soon the rope jerked. Rustina signalled back and the troops tied on the bags and bundles of equipment, which were lifted with no more than an occasional clink of metal against the yellow cliff. The rope came back down. The remaining soldiers were hauled up, Rustina last of all.

Jal-Nish stood back, looking anxiously around. They were particularly vulnerable now, if the weather cleared or a scouting party ran into them down here, with Arple the only trained soldier to protect them. Even the eleven above would have trouble with a pair of lyrinx. If there were more, they would be annihilated.

A couple of hours went by before the soldier returned, skis whispering on the snow. The others followed. They gathered around in their ranks, were briefed and hauled up in a rope chair.

Arple went with them to inspect the defences. Shortly the first of the clankers came clunking along, followed by the others. Heavier ropes were taken up, then Artificer Tuniz, anxiously showing her pointed teeth.

Nish wandered across. 'What's going on?'

'Most of the troops are atop,' Irisis said. 'They're setting up a structure to lift the clankers.'

'They're mad!'

'Well, you'd know, being an artificer.'

'Tuniz is a better one, fortunately.'

Tuniz reappeared, lowered in the chair, and began issuing orders. The first clanker was moved into position and tied fore and aft. She signalled with the original rope.

The haul ropes went taut and without any apparent effort the clanker lifted off the snow and began to rise upwards, to disappear in the thickening snow.

'How?' began Nish.

'I've no idea.'

It turned out to be brilliantly simple. The rope at the top passed over a series of pulleys held up by a frame made from the rods, and down over another frame and pulley. The other end of the rope was tied to a boulder which acted as a counterweight. Another structure of ropes and pulleys enabled soldiers to brake the boulder's descent.

The boulder struck the ground. Tuniz waited for the signal that the clanker was on solid earth, checked and had it confirmed, then untied the rope. The end went up, the other ropes came down and were tied around the second clanker, which was lifted with another boulder. And so it went on.

'There you are,' crowed Jal-Nish as the last clanker, with Ullii still inside, rose smoothly into the air. 'It's all gone perfectly. That's what happens when you do things yourself.'

Irisis held her breath and stepped well back. If anything would call the wrath of fortune down on them it was statements like that. However, the signal soon came that everything was all right.

'Perfect,' said Jal-Nish. It was only mid-afternoon. 'We'll camp up top, send out our scouts and prepare to move in the night. As soon as we find them, we'll strike with everything we've got. I want to see waterfalls of lyrinx blood. No one will get away this time.'

'What about Tiaan?' said Irisis.

'I'm working on a plan,' he said smugly, wanting them to ask so he could have the pleasure of refusing to answer.

Irisis said nothing, nor did Nish. They went up in the chair. The wind was blowing off the plateau, reducing visibility to a few paces. They ate their fill of cold food and tried to sleep.

Irisis was woken in the night by a hard hand on her shoulder, a soldier she did not recognise. 'We've found them. We're going in twenty minutes, artisan.'

Irisis had slept in her clothes, so it only took a minute to pull on her icy boots and she was ready. She chewed on a strip of smoked fish. The others were gathered in a space between large boulders, where they dared a little light.

'They're here,' said Arple, drawing a chart in the snow with the tip of his knife. 'A collection of linked snilau.'

'What's a snilau?' Irisis asked.

'An ice house – igloo! There aren't many; the scouts guess at around ten lyrinx.'

'Still a formidable force, even with our clankers,' said Rustina, gnawing on a raw potato.

'But some may be children. We'll attack at dawn, bombarding the snilau with rocks from our catapults. With luck we may kill half of them in their sleep.'

'And maybe Tiaan too,' said Nish.

'I've a plan for her,' Jal-Nish said. 'Move out!'

The soldiers went ahead on skis. The passengers withdrew into the clankers, which moved off slowly, to make as little noise as possible. That was not such a risk, with the wind positively howling in their faces, but a lyrinx patrol could be anywhere.

They sat in silence for most of the journey. The clanker was frigid, since they'd had no fire to warm the heatboxes. Sometimes a furious gust would rock it on its sturdy legs. Ullii had been consulted several times, to ensure Tiaan was at the snilau. Her directions always confirmed the scouts' advice.

Ullii became increasingly edgy as they approached. Unable to sit still for a minute, she moved forward, then back, swayed from side to side, twitched her legs, rapped her knees with her knuckles, flexed her fingers and toes. The closer they got the more anxious she appeared. Peering through the porthole into the darkness, she turned to Nish and her eyes were wide.

'It's horrible!' she whispered.

'What?' Nish stroked her hand. Irisis shot him a dirty look.

'It's horrible!' Ullii shuddered.

It was dark in the clanker and the seeker was not wearing her mask. Occasionally Irisis caught a gleam from her owl eyes.

'After tonight, nothing will ever be the same again,' Nish said soberly.

Irisis wished he had not spoken. What would happen when they got Tiaan back? Whatever it was, Irisis knew *she* would not be returning to her safe artisan's position at the manufactory. Her stupid assault on Jal-Nish had ended those hopes forever. Why had she done it? Could it be that she cared for the little seeker? Or had it just been black despair, a kind of death wish?

The clanker stopped and someone opened the hatch from outside. 'We're in position,' Arple's voice issued from the darkness. 'It's just coming dawn. Ready?'

Irisis jumped out, easing her sword in its scabbard. At the telltale scrape Arple said, 'I'd advise you to keep well back, artisan. Leave the fighting to them as knows how.'

'I've done my training,' she said. 'I'll not stand by when there's work to be done. Besides . . .'

'Yes?' He turned back.

'I have no future, sergeant, after the other day. Unless we get back the crystal. And maybe not even then . . .'

'Aye,' he said. 'Nor I. Still, we do what we must.'

Dawn broke. It was still blowing but the snow had stopped during the night. 'There!' said Arple, standing at Irisis's shoulder.

By straining her eyes where he pointed she could just make out the curving shapes of the ice houses, white against white. One of the scouts came running. 'We ran into one of their sentries, over east. It must have been coming back from watch. We hurt it bad, but it killed Marti.'

'Where is the beast now?'

'Back there about a league. We toppled it down into a gully, but lost it in the snow. It's got a great gash in the leg.'

'Can it walk?'

'Only stagger, surr.'

'Keep watch. We'll leave it for the moment. I want everyone for the assault on the ice houses. We'd better attack right away, in case it has some way of sending a signal.'

'First we find the artisan, alive,' Jal-Nish said nasally. He was having trouble breathing through his crushed nose.

'No one could guarantee that, surr,' said Arple. 'We don't know where she is.'

'We soon will. Seeker, get out here!'

Ullii emerged warily from the clanker.

'Where is the artisan and her crystal?'

Ullii pointed towards the snilau.

'Which one, seeker?' Jal-Nish said patiently. Now that things were going to plan he had gained control of his temper.

Ullii looked panicky. Nish gave her his hand to sniff. She gulped, then steadied on her feet. 'I . . . I can't tell.' She braced herself as if expecting a blow.

Nish ran across to Fyn-Mah and whispered in her ear. They came back together.

'Ullii,' Fyn-Mah said in her pleasant voice, 'I have here a map of the snilau.'

Ullii looked down at the slate, which showed the ice houses in a spiral pattern. She smiled. 'It's like a snail. I like snails; they know how to hide.'

'Can you see any of the lyrinx?' Nish asked softly.

'Of course,' Ullii said brightly. 'I can see all of them.'

'What?' cried Jal-Nish. 'Why didn't you say so?'

'Because no one . . .' She broke off. That had been the wrong answer last time.

Arple pushed through the throng gathered around her. The tough sergeant went to one knee before her. 'Seeker, it will save many lives if you can tell us where the enemy are. Please try.'

She closed her eyes behind the goggles, then walked along the ridge, turned, looked down to the ice houses and came back.

'There are fourteen lyrinx.' Her voice was barely audible. 'Five here; three here; two here; three here; one here.' In turn she pointed to five of the outside snilau.

'More than we thought,' said Arple. 'I don't like the odds, surr.'

'Then you'd better make sure of them with the catapults.'

'And Tiaan?' asked Arple of Ullii.

'She is in the big one in the middle.'

'That's wonderful!' Arple ran to the clankers to give orders.

'See that she is not harmed or I'll be taking heads,' Jal-Nish growled.

'Ready?' Arple called to the shooters. Each had his catapult loaded with a round ball of stone and two more beside it. They signed that they were. 'Rustina, take your troops out and around the left side to cut off any escape. We'll fire in three minutes. After the third firing, attack the ice house in the centre. You are to take Tiaan alive, and her crystal, before anything else. Go!'

Rustina saluted and her squad skied down the slope. The other troops were given their orders, and they too moved out. Irisis could hear Arple counting under his breath. 'Ready?' he called to the shooters. 'Fire on four!'

He lifted his arm, beat it up and down three times, then slashed it down. 'Fire!'

The catapults went off as one. The clankers jerked. The shooters wound their handles frantically. 'Fire at will,' yelled Arple.

Irisis saw splashes of snow where the balls had landed. Two had missed, though not by much. One had definitely hit the nearest snilau and the other may have. It was hard to tell, everything being white.

The catapults fired again, one, then two together, then a long pause to the last. 'Hurry it up, damn it,' cried Jal-Nish.

Three hits this time, including the last, which appeared to have demolished most of the end ice house.

'Good work!' said Arple. 'Now the third! Remember, keep clear of the ice house in the middle!'

They fired their third missiles but this time Irisis could see nothing though the clouds of snow.

'Two more hits!' said Arple, peering through a spyglass. 'I can see something staggering about. A lyrinx. Looks like it's lost a leg. Ready your javelards!' yelled Arple. 'Move! Find the artisan.'

Irisis jumped in. The four clankers raced down the slope. The terrain was bumpy; they bounced and thudded all the way.

'What's happening?' she said, for Nish was hogging the line of the view hole.

'Rustina's troops are just reaching the ice houses,' Nish said. 'I can see three lyrinx now . . .'

'What?' cried Irisis, for he had fallen silent.

He took a long while to answer, and she heard his amusement, getting his own back on her. Irisis, in no mood for it, jabbed him in the ribs. 'A flurry of snow,' Nish said. 'I can't see anything.'

The clanker roared around in a wide circle before stopping abruptly. They could hear fighting over the wind – the bellowing of lyrinx, the clash of sword on armoured skin, screams of agony – some human, others not. Irisis leapt out.

'Where are you going?' yelled Nish.

'After the crystal. Stay here. Look after Ullii.'

'But . . .' Nish began.

'Someone's got to guard her, and the clanker. And who's to say you won't be in more danger than I am?'

That was true enough. Anything might happen. Somebody had given Nish a short sword, which he drew. He was competent in the weapon, for a civilian. Few people were not, in these times, though he had not handled one in ages. He'd neglected his practice, working so hard at being an artificer. Nish regretted that now.

It was hard to see. The wind had come up with the dawn and the air was full of drifting snow. Nish climbed onto the clanker, next to the shooter, Pur-Did, whose javelard was aimed at the ice houses some thirty or forty paces away. Too close, Nish thought. A lyrinx could cross that distance in a few seconds.

He caught sight of a squad of soldiers hacking at the blocked entrance of the central snilau. Good, Nish thought. This will soon be over and we can go home.

A wild melee began outside the right-hand snilau, whose roof had collapsed. Two lyrinx were fighting five or six soldiers who had discarded their skis and were attempting to trap the enemy against the wall. They were handicapped by the deep snow.

The lyrinx went backwards, not seeming to defend themselves. 'They don't appear as tough as I've been told,' said Nish. 'They . . .'

One lyrinx did a backward somersault, landed on the rubble of ice blocks and, in a series of movements too quick to follow, hurled blocks the size of sheep at three of his opponents. One ducked, receiving only a blow on the shoulder. The other two, struck in the middle, went down.

The second lyrinx leapt among the other three and with quick swipes sent two of them flying. Blood sprayed through the air. The last man on his feet back-pedalled and began to run. The lyrinx hurled one of the bodies at him, bringing him down. The soldier stuck the lyrinx with his sword as it came for him, but it did not stop the creature.

The other had already finished off his three opponents. Nish felt sick. Six soldiers dead and it had taken only a minute. As the second lyrinx straightened up, the javelard snapped. The missile went through the lyrinx's chest and out the other side. It fell among the bodies.

The other lyrinx looked up. Pur-Did furiously cranked his winder but the beast, after a swift look at them, ran towards the central ice house.

'After him!' Nish called down through the hatch.

'My orders are to remain here unless one gets away with the artisan,' said Ky-Ara.

A wild gust raced across the plateau, carrying a cloud of snow. Within seconds Nish could not even see the ground. Wiping snow grit out of his face, he caught the eye of the shooter, who was doing the same.

'Nice day for it,' the man said cheerfully, sucking air through his warty nostrils.

'Yeah! And in a minute we might all be dead, with our guts trailing over the snow.'

'Could do.' Pur-Did brushed snow out of his javelard, making sure that nothing could foul the mechanism.

The cloud thinned. Nish scanned the area for enemies. A wild struggle was going on between the ice houses. He looked the other way, in case a lyrinx had sneaked around behind them. Half a dozen soldiers had what appeared to be a very pregnant lyrinx down on her knees, and as he watched they ran her through. Two infants were despatched just as ruthlessly, their heads completely severed from their bodies. The mother gave an agonised scream, then she too was beheaded. Nish could not watch.

THIRTY-SEVEN

Tiaan was woken by thuds and crashes that shook the building. A gloomy light came through the ice. She ran to the entrance but the plug remained in place. 'Ryll?' she yelled through the space around the block. 'What's happening?'

There was no answer. She heard more thuds, a roar of pain from a lyrinx, higher screams. With a *hiss-thump*, something came through the wall, pinning the bearskin to the floor. It was a spear from a clanker javelard.

Tiaan did not waste time wondering how she had been tracked, or how they had got clankers up here. Somehow they had, which showed an absolute determination to take her back or destroy her. Why? It could not be because she'd run away from the breeding factory. No runaway was worth such a hunt. Was it because she'd saved the life of the enemy? It could be. The Histories of the lyrinx wars contained many tales of treachery and, whatever it took, the traitors were always hunted down. The Council of Scrutators believed in making examples.

They must also be hunting her because she was an artisan. The secret of controllers would be invaluable to the enemy and Gi-Had was making sure they did not get it.

Either way she could never go home. And to make matters worse, withdrawal still ebbed and flowed within her. When a pang struck she was incapable of thinking about anything else.

381

Throwing on her coat, she took up the spear and waited. Faint cries came from outside, and the roars of lyrinx. The building shook as if a catapult ball had struck it. Ice fell from the roof.

The trapped feeling grew. Tiaan hacked at the wall with the spear, but had not made more than a fist-sized indentation when there came a ghastly echoing scream from outside, a lyrinx death-cry, surely.

The sounds of battle continued. Tiaan had just resumed her futile work when the ice plug was thrust in and Ryll's head appeared. He scrabbled through the gap, kicked the plug back and gasped, 'Get ready!'

'My people have come!' She did not say it with any joy.

'And they tried to kill you before.'

Ryll began to claw at the wall: across, down, across, up, with the same furious energy as he had shown in scouring his way into her ice sphere after the avalanche. The raking strokes flung ice halfway across the room. There was an intense look on his face that she had not seen before. Fear? Or fury at what was happening outside?

The plug ground forward. Ryll leapt across the room and slammed it back. Anguished cries came from the other side. He jammed the spear into the ice in front of the plug, bound her wrists with a strip of leather and resumed his frantic work.

The plug moved, hit the spear and stopped. His gouges in the wall had now outlined a block almost her size. Putting his shoulder to it, he heaved. The block did not budge. Shaking his head, Ryll gouged faster.

Another blow shook the plug, snapping off the point of the spear. The plug crept forward. Was it better to be captured, or taken by Ryll? Could she escape both? Indecision paralysed her.

The plug was heaved through and a soldier's head appeared, a savage, bloody, human face. Tiaan shrank away.

The soldier cried, 'Run, artisan!'

Ryll jerked her against his side. 'If you want to see your crystal again,' he said in her ear, 'you'll come with me.'

Tiaan tried to swallow. Her dry tongue rasped against the roof of her mouth.

The soldier's face hardened and he levelled the crossbow. From this distance he could not miss. His finger tightened on the release. Ryll twisted violently but the impact slammed him into the wall and her hand slipped free. A gasp escaped him. The soldier dropped the crossbow and lunged at Ryll with the spear. Ryll slashed and then weaved away, holding his shoulder. The soldier went after him.

Tiaan took two steps but a pang of withdrawal drove her to her knees. She cried out with the agony of longing, so strong that she lost track of the struggle on the other side of the room.

A blurry face appeared in the tunnel. Irisis crawled through, carrying a bloody sword, and fell on the pack. Not finding what she was looking for, she put the sword tip to Tiaan's throat. The withdrawal eased.

'Where is it?' Irisis ground out. 'Where is the crystal?'

'They took it from me,' Tiaan whispered. 'Can't you tell?' She held out a shaking hand.

Irisis glared into her bloodshot eyes. Tiaan caught her breath, expecting to be skewered through the throat, but Irisis turned away.

'What are you doing?' cried the struggling soldier. 'Take her!'

'She doesn't matter,' snarled Irisis over her shoulder as she scrambled down the tunnel. 'The crystal does.'

Ryll drove the soldier back to the tunnel with sweeps of his good arm. The man took refuge there, roaring, 'Help! I've found the artisan.'

Tiaan watched, numb inside, her arms around her pack. Nothing mattered now but the crystal – she had to get it back.

Ryll kicked ice in the man's face, grabbed her, hit the block with his good shoulder and it fell through. Freezing air roared in. Wrapping his arms around her, he forced through the wall with his back. As the soldier darted forward, stabbing with the spear, Ryll leapt onto the domed roof and kicked with both feet. The block fell in, then the ones on either side. He almost went with it as the rest of the roof collapsed.

The soldier disappeared under the ice blocks. Ryll gave a convulsive twist in mid-air, his vestigial wings flapping uselessly, and tumbled off the side. Tiaan saw her chance to escape them all. She ran around the corner but her legs stalled, as if she was hobbled. She tried to go on but the withdrawal would not allow her. She must be going the wrong way – away from the crystal.

Ryll hobbled into view, his muzzle darting from side to side. Not seeing her against the wall, he went the other way, disappearing into the driving snow.

Where could the crystal be? Probably in the main ice house. Creeping along the wall, she came face to face with Gi-Had. Each stopped, staring at the other. Gi-Had was terribly wounded. Claw marks across his chest had exposed ribs and breast bone. His coat was crusted with frozen blood.

Even so, his face lit up. 'Tiaan!' He threw out his arms. One bloodstained hand had two fingers missing.

Tiaan stalled, her mouth open. His reaction made no sense.

He took a staggering step toward her. 'What is the matter, artisan?'

She choked. 'I . . . can't,' she gasped. 'Must find the crystal . . .' She backed away.

'Why, artisan? *Why*?' Gi-Had fell to his knees.

She turned, desperate to escape the look in his eyes, but crashed into Ryll, who grabbed her. She struggled weakly. As the lyrinx carried her away, she caught a last glimpse of the overseer, supporting himself on the tumbled blocks of the ice house. He was staring after her. She knew she would never see him again. Despair and self-loathing boiled up inside her.

Ryll ran through the fog and ducked behind another ice house.

'Where are you taking me?' she gasped.

'Far away,' the lyrinx said.

'What about the other lyrinx?' Her mouth was dry.

'They will die defending us,' Ryll said gravely.

'Even the children?'

She could see the pain on his face now, more poignant because he was unlikely ever to have children of his own. 'Alas! There are many soldiers and four clankers. You humans are deadly ingenious. We had no chance. The catapults killed three of us in our sleep.' His head darted around, then he jerked her back.

Two soldiers ran across the gap between the ice houses, calling out to a third Tiaan could not see. 'The roof's collapsed. She must be under it.'

'Irisis was in there too,' said the other.

Ryll's hand went across Tiaan's mouth. He dragged her the other way.

'Where is my crystal?' she mumbled. Without it, her dreams were nothing.

'Gone with Besant. It is safe with her. You'll see it again, soon.'

The withdrawal eased at once. Tiaan looked around. Purple blood ran in a thin stream from his shoulder. Behind them the wind blew a clear passage through the snow clouds.

'There they go!' someone roared.

Something flashed between the two furthest snilau. Nish squinted against the snow.

'Hey! It's Tiaan. The beast is getting away with her. Get moving, Ky-Ara.'

Pur-Did thumped on the roof and the clanker began to move, sluggishly and with much groaning of the drive trains. He tried to aim the javelard but the pair had disappeared. Nish opened the top hatch.

'What's the matter?' he yelled down.

'Oil has gone cold. I can't go any faster until it warms up.'

'Anything I can do to help?'

'Not a thing!' Ky-Ara was manipulating the knobs in jerky motions that betrayed his anxiety. 'Not a damn thing!'

Ullii huddled up against the back corner, shaking. Any kind of violence was unbearable to her. Nish wondered what had happened to Irisis. He'd not seen her since the skirmish started. She could well be dead.

The clanker ground around in a great circle before Pur-Did picked up tracks heading toward the edge of the plateau, which was not far away.

'Follow them!' Nish shouted, unnecessarily. The shooter smiled at his naive enthusiasm.

Ky-Ara called up through the hatch. He sounded uneasy. 'I must let the sergeant – '

'No time!' Nish yelled. 'If the wind comes up we'll lose them. They'll be over the edge, and by the time we get the clankers down they'll have gone into the mountains where we can't follow.'

If there's anyone left to follow, he thought. The carnage had been terrible. They might run their quarry down only to find themselves alone. And then, barring a lucky shot from the javelard, they would also die. How quickly the advantage had been lost.

The clanker turned onto the tracks, bumping lethargically along. Nish cursed their slow pace. The lyrinx had seemed to be limping but must be going faster than this.

Up ahead, the footprints descended into a gully, ploughed through deep snow, and up onto the side where the cover was thin. The operator kept going straight.

Nish swung inside, ignoring Ullii cowering in the corner. 'Down there!' he cried, pointing. 'Can't you see?'

'Deep drifts that way,' said Ky-Ara. 'We'll never get through them. It's quicker along the rim.'

The clanker did seem to be speeding up. They tracked along the edge, a shorter distance than the winding gully bottom.

'I can see them!' Nish roared. He stuck his head out the back. 'Fire! Fire, damn you!'

The man did not fire. 'Bloody fool!' said Nish, climbing onto the top. 'What's the matter?'

Pur-Did said patiently, 'I can't train the javelard that low.'

Nish threw himself back in, issuing instructions. 'Down there! He's got to have the front pointed down or the spear will go over their heads.'

'We know our jobs, artificer,' Ky-Ara said coldly. 'Keep out of our way and let us do them.'

He slowed, turned and tipped the front over the edge. The mechanical legs pounded. The lyrinx came into view, running down the valley, hauling Tiaan by one arm. The beast was limping badly. Oh, for a crossbow!

Fire! Nish said to himself. Now; *now*!

The shooter did not fire. The angle was still not right. Nish felt like kicking him off his seat and using the javelard himself.

'Just not low enough,' Pur-Did called through the hole, picking icicles from his warty nostrils. 'Try a bit further down, Ky-Ara.'

Ky-Ara reversed the machine, its iron footpads squealing as they cut through snow to stone beneath. Gravel showered down the side of the gully, the clanker turned and, moving much faster now, clattered along the rim. A few hundred paces on they tried again. Here the rim was benched, allowing the clanker to get further down. Ky-Ara moved it into position. They waited.

Tiaan and the lyrinx appeared. Her hands were bound, though surely she could have outdistanced the hobbling creature had she chosen to. Was she a traitor after all?

Agonising seconds passed but still the shooter did not fire. 'Go!' Nish roared, pounding on the roof.

'Damn thing's jammed.'

Soon it would be too late. The lyrinx had only checked for an instant. As it continued, Nish noticed something strange about this one. It had no wings.

'Free!' yelled the shooter. 'Turn around, Ky-Ara. If we can't get it coming, we'll get it going.'

'Blasted shooters!' cursed Ky-Ara. 'Useless clowns.' He turned, backed, turned again. Nish kept his eye to the porthole. The fleeing pair ran right below them. A pang struck Nish's heart. He did not want her to die.

'A bit further down at the front,' Pur-Did yelled.

Ky-Ara hesitated. 'We're too close to the edge.'

Nish's fury boiled over. Was he the only one who wanted to catch them? 'If you don't want to be a clanker operator, *just say so!*' he said in a deadly voice. 'I'm sure my father the perquisitor can replace you.'

Ky-Ara choked, looked around wildly, and then edged the machine forward, sideways and forward again. His teeth began to chatter as he waited for the call, 'Enough!'

It did not come, because rock beneath the right-hand side crumbled and they slipped sideways. A whole slab gave; the clanker tilted over. Ky-Ara moaned, frantically working to right the machine, but it was too late. The clanker rolled, crashed onto its roof and kept rolling.

Ullii screamed. Ky-Ara did too. Nish put his arms over his head and went with it. They rolled three times before landing upside down with a bone-shaking crash that pushed the front half of the roof in. The clanker rocked back and forth, metal plates squealing, then came to rest. Loose objects rained down, including Ullii's goggles, which smashed.

Ky-Ara hung from his straps, making the most ghastly keening sound Nish had ever heard, like a rabbit being dismembered by an owl. Blood trickled from his left nostril. The clanker was wrecked and the operator would never get another one. 'Incompetent fool!' Nish said, trying to ignore his own contribution to the disaster.

Up the back, Ullii lay curled up in the corner, still screaming. She had lost her mask and earmuffs. Crawling across, Nish put his hand over her mouth and nose. After several deep breaths she stopped screaming. Placing the earmuffs and mask on her, he pushed at the hatch. It was jammed; he had to kick it. He and Ullii scrambled out.

The machine had crashed onto a boulder, crushing javelard and catapult. Pur-Did lay further up the slope, a bloody smear against the rocks. The machine had come down on top of him.

Tiaan and the lyrinx had disappeared around the bend. Nish was furious with Ky-Ara, and with himself for pressuring him. The whole manufactory had slaved for a month just to produce this clanker. His feelings for Tiaan seemed to have vanished.

Screams came from inside the crashed clanker, unnervingly high-pitched and shrill. It did not sound like a soldier.

Tiaan ran past, turned the next bend and there in front of them, extending well out over the abyss, was a wooden platform decked with round timbers that rattled in the wind. A curving walkway ran to it. Besant stood on the edge, beside a strange structure shaped like a bird's wing. The pack strapped to her chest surely contained the precious crystal.

Tiaan ran forward with a glad cry but had just set foot on the walkway when a catapult ball shattered the timbers to splinters. Ryll dragged her to safety. Whatever Besant had planned, they could no longer reach her.

A second clanker had come over the slope to their right, firing across the outcrops and boulder fields along the edge of the plateau. The shooter trained his javelard on the lyrinx while the operator worked furiously to place another ball in the catapult. She knew them both, Rahnd and Simmo.

'Go!' Ryll roared. 'Fly, Besant!' He pointed further along the cliff.

She made an arm gesture Tiaan could not interpret, held the wing out and, as a spear shivered through the platform, dived off.

Tiaan held her breath as the wing curved around, caught an updraft and lifted. Besant's great wings unfurled and she rose above it. Tiaan felt a fizzing sensation behind her temples, like sherbet dissolving on the tongue. Though she had never experienced it before she knew what it had to be. Besant was using her own strange version of the Secret Art to keep her massive weight aloft.

She spiralled around, the wing flier trailing below on ropes. The clanker struggled to train its catapult on her. Besant pointed with one arm to a flat place further along the escarpment.

Ryll set off at the fastest limp he could manage, with Tiaan dragging behind. He kept to the shelter of the boulders and she lost sight of the clanker. She saw Gi-Had's tormented face again. He was a decent man. Had he really ordered this force to kill her, or had she just imagined it? Tiaan felt guilty, ashamed. She wanted to run to the machine, give herself up and take the consequences. She tried to pull free.

The lyrinx held her effortlessly. 'Besant has your crystal. If you don't come you'll never see it again.'

As they reached the flat spot the clanker fired. The spear carved an arc across the sky, passing between Besant and the wing. Tiaan breathed again. Besant turned, heading toward them on a long, sweeping trajectory.

'As she comes by,' said Ryll, 'jump for the harness hanging below the wing. Fasten the straps around you.' He gripped the bolt buried in his shoulder and with a groan and a furious flickering of skin colours, wrenched it out.

'Yes,' she said. Wherever the amplimet went she had to follow. Without it she would go insane. She stared at Ryll's haggard face. 'What about you?'

He studied the bloody bolt. 'I stay behind to defend you.'

'To die!'

'To do my duty, that others more worthy may live.'

Besant came streaming in. Tiaan tensed but as the flier approached an updraft hurled the wing upwards, away from the cliff.

'Ready?' Ryll said.

'My hands are numb.' She felt numb all over. Only an acrobat could make such a leap.

He slashed the bonds at her wrists. Tiaan flexed her fingers but could not feel anything.

'Jump!' cried Ryll as the wing rushed past.

'I can't. I'll miss!' That was certain – it was too far out. And was the fate that awaited her in the lyrinx lair any better than at the hands of her own people?

THIRTY-EIGHT

Nish wrested his sword free. If the beast got away with Tiaan, he was dead, and it would be his own stupid fault. He raced after them, the masked seeker stumbling and wailing behind. He should have left her in the clanker but could not abandon her to the dead man and the mad one. Her screams had gone right through him.

He ploughed around another bend and ahead was nothing but open sky – the precipice. Tiaan and the lyrinx were just ahead. Further off, on a cantilevered platform built out over nothing, stood a larger lyrinx.

'Stay here, Ullii,' he said, letting go of her hand. 'The edge of the precipice is just over there.'

'I can *see* it.'

Nish ran and knew he would be too late. The large lyrinx, a green-crested female, opened her mighty wings to carry Tiaan away. He shouted and waved his sword uselessly.

Tiaan had just put her foot on the walkway when it exploded into splinters. Simmo's clanker was rattling down the slope with several people hanging onto the outside. Nish could have wept with relief.

The big lyrinx dived off the platform and Ullii screamed so loudly that he ran back. 'What's the matter?'

She rolled into a protective ball, hugging her head with her arms. As she seemed safe enough, and well away from the cliff, Nish left her there.

Rahnd, Simmo's shooter, fired the javelard and missed. Tiaan and the wingless lyrinx ran along the cliff. Rahnd fired the catapult. The ball went so close that it rippled one wing of the flying lyrinx.

'Fire at the wingless one!' Nish screamed.

Rahnd, a dark, burly man with no front teeth and one leg noticeably shorter than the other, held up empty hands. He'd spent all his missiles. The clanker groaned to a stop some hundred paces up the slope, where boulders and outcrops prevented further movement.

The passengers jumped off. Jal-Nish was among them, along with Fyn-Mah, Tuniz and red-headed Rustina, whose shoulder and side were covered in blood. Seeing no sign of Irisis, Nish caught his breath. Rahnd sprang off, attacking a rock with hammer and chisel.

'Ky-Ara's clanker is wrecked back in the gully,' Nish shouted, pointing. 'It still has spears.'

Rahnd set off with a lopsided, lurching stride. Nish went to meet the others. 'Where's Irisis?' he gasped. 'Is she . . .?'

Rustina pointed over her shoulder. Irisis, just levering herself through the back hatch, had a bandage wrapped around her thigh. Her garments were rent down the side, the left sleeve of her coat hanging by a few threads. Jal-Nish was grim of face but unharmed.

'We've got them!' Nish exulted, pointing to the lyrinx hobbling along the cliff, still holding Tiaan.

'We'll crow when we have them in our hands,' said Jal-Nish wearily. 'And considering there's two lyrinx, and we . . . Ah, I'm mortally weary. Let's get it over.'

Irisis limped down. 'Where's the crystal?'

'I presume Tiaan has it,' said Nish.

'She hasn't! I searched her pack at the ice house.' Irisis was very pale.

Jal-Nish's head whipped around. He gave Irisis a smouldering stare.

Nish asked no questions, though he wanted to. 'Then the flying one must have it. Look! She's got a little pack on her chest.'

The flying lyrinx swooped down toward the pair on the cliff, trailing the wing. 'What's she up to?' Jal-Nish muttered.

'I've no idea,' Fyn-Mah replied. Her lips were blue; her eyes had gone a murky yellow.

'Aim for the flying one!' Irisis roared at the clanker. 'It's got the crystal!'

'How do you know?' snapped Jal-Nish, his mood deteriorating by the second.

'I'm an artisan, *remember*?'

The shooter had not returned but Simmo was staggering up the slope carrying a lump of rock. Turning the catapult around, he aimed at the flying lyrinx and fired. The missile sang through the sky but did no damage.

'I'm surrounded by incompetents!' Jal-Nish spat.

'Even Rahnd would be lucky to do better,' the querist said quietly. 'Precise shooting requires round shot.'

'Get up there, Tuniz,' Jal-Nish ordered. 'Round rocks for the shooter! The rest of you, after the wingless beast. Kill it or put it over the cliff. Keep Tiaan alive at all costs. We'll attack together.'

'Do you think we should try to use power against it?' Fyn-Mah said quietly to the perquisitor.

'After what happened last time?'

'It might make the difference.'

'All right. We'll take the wingless one. See if you can bring the flier down.'

The wingless lyrinx was limping along the edge of the cliff, holding Tiaan by the wrist. It was a difficult position to attack. They could not run at it without risking going over themselves. Nish fell in beside Irisis as they moved to cut it off.

'How's your leg?'

'Very painful.'

The flying lyrinx, now soaring high, came swooping down with the delta-shape gliding along below. Irisis was the first to realise what it was for. 'Shoot!' she screamed at Simmo. 'They'll get away on the wing.'

393

Jal-Nish and Rustina converged on the wingless lyrinx. The perquisitor, out in front, moved with deliberation. Rustina was all over the place, hacking wildly. The sight of the creature, holding Tiaan as hostage, had driven her into a frenzy.

'Calm down, sergeant. Try to hamstring it!' roared Jal-Nish. 'I'll go for the throat.'

The lyrinx, now holding Tiaan against its chest, slashed at Jal-Nish but missed. Rustina got through the creature's guard to prick it on the hip, though not to any noticeable effect. It clouted her in the belly with a backhand, slamming her head-first into a boulder. Jal-Nish, finding himself without support, scrambled backwards but could not get out of reach of the mighty arm. The creature's claws raked him across the face, the shoulder, then the chest. Jal-Nish screamed. The lyrinx backhanded him across the head, like swatting a fly, and the perquisitor went down, blood pouring out of him.

Only Nish and Irisis were still armed and able. Their eyes met. 'It's over,' Irisis said calmly.

'We tried our best.'

'What say you, Nish, old lover? To the death?'

Her words warmed him. 'To the death!' he echoed, sure that his father was dying and he was going to.

Nish and Irisis flung themselves at the lyrinx, their swords weaving a net of steel in front of them. It was retreating slowly, more intent on what was happening in the sky than overcoming them. Kicking a clot of icy gravel in their faces, the lyrinx ran a few steps then stopped.

The flier came sweeping in. The wingless lyrinx let out a howl of frustration as again the wing bucked in the updraft. Nish and Irisis attacked from behind. Nish landed a blow on the thigh that went between the plates and drew dark blood. Irisis followed it up with a stab to the back, directly into a plate.

Tossing Tiaan to one side, the lyrinx whirled and kicked Irisis's legs from under her. Nish heard something break and she fell near the edge of the cliff. He launched a furious attack, which the lyrinx fended off absently, one eye on the scene in the air.

Fyn-Mah was standing on top of an outcrop, holding her arms out as if carrying a basin of water. Whipping them apart, up and down and up, across and back, she carved an extended infinity sign in the air. Powdery crystals followed her fingers. With a flick of her hands, the shape tumbled through the air, to vanish in an explosion of ice just below the flying lyrinx's left wing.

The wing dipped sharply as if the air had collapsed below it. The lyrinx tumbled, recovered, there came a whistle-crack and the rock erupted upwards beneath Fyn-Mah's feet, sending her head-over-heels. Fragments of stone sang through the air, trailing mist. The shattered top of the rock steamed. A trickle of water ran down the side, froze and all was still again. Fyn-Mah could not be seen.

The wing swept down. Nish roared 'Fire!'

A ragged ball of rock tore between him and the wingless lyrinx, so near that the wind ruffled his hair. 'Not at me, you cretin!'

Nish attacked again. The lyrinx lunged, swinging wildly. Nish tripped, landed flat on his back, and the sword jarred out of his hand. He stared up at the beast, knowing it was going to tear him apart.

Tiaan lay on the ground, watching the struggle. Whether Ryll won or lost made little difference now. Besant would get away with the amplimet and her dreams would end.

But Ryll's attackers fell, one by one. The violence made her feel sick. Irisis screamed and crashed down by the cliff. Tiaan caught her breath in case she went over. She was beyond any ill-feelings for Irisis now.

Nish attacked boldly, looking ten times the man who had pestered her a few weeks ago. He looked as if he had suffered. He too went down.

Her eyes met his. 'I'm sorry,' Tiaan said.

'So am I!' he said stiffly.

Ryll raised one foot. 'No, Ryll!' she cried. He was about to bring it down when there came a wild, shuddering shriek and Ryll turned aside. She was glad Nish would survive.

As Ryll dragged her away, Jal-Nish, a blood-drenched caricature of a man, staggered to his feet. 'Don't let it have her!' he gasped. 'If she can't be taken, *kill her!*'

Tiaan's uncertainty vanished. She screwed up her courage for the leap. Again, wind caught the wing before it got to her, kicking it up and out, though not so far out this time. She could *almost* get there. She tensed, knowing that it was just too far away.

A blow in the back, a crushing grip around her waist, then she was flying through the air under Ryll's injured arm. Their trajectories converged. The wind lifted the harness dangling below the gliding wing. She could never have reached it but Ryll's upstretched fingers closed around a loop of leather. Tiaan caught a trailing rope and wrapped it around her wrist.

The wing stalled under their weight and began spiralling like a leaf on the tow ropes. Tiaan was torn from Ryll's grip. She fell, was brought up by the rope and felt a gruesome pain in her shoulder, as if it had been pulled from its socket.

The shock almost folded Besant's wings up. She flapped harder and the fizzing boiled over in Tiaan's head as the lyrinx expended more and more of the Art in her effort to stay in the air. Below, Tiaan heard those terrible screams again.

Ryll hauled her up. 'What's the matter?' He held her tightly as they carved a figure-eight through the air.

'My arm. . .' She fought tears which the wind froze on her cheeks.

He muttered something in his own tongue, pulled himself into the crutch loops of the harness and let go of his rope. Buckling himself in one-handed, he lashed her to his chest then made frantic hand-signals to Besant, who was barely in control. The wing was still whirling, dragging her down. They swung around in an arc on the end of the ropes, drifting directly towards the clanker. Rahnd was back in his seat, tracking them with the javelard. From this distance he could not miss.

Suddenly another lyrinx stood up on the rocks, one leg drenched in blood. It was the sentry that had been wounded before the attack began. It sprang but fell short. Simmo lurched the machine forward, trying to run the beast down. The lyrinx caught the side plates and flipped itself up on top. The machine bucked and hopped as Simmo tried to shake the attacker off. The lyrinx slipped in its own blood but managed to catch hold of the spear in the javelard. As it dangled there, Rahnd fired. The spear carried the lyrinx down among the boulders.

The clanker clumped around and Tiaan saw Rahnd wrench the loaded catapult onto their path as they swept inland. She held her breath. Ryll, holding her against his chest, made a helpless choking sound.

The injured lyrinx came out of the rocks, hurling the bent javelin. Rahnd ducked. Springing up on the front of the clanker, the lyrinx threw itself directly at the catapult. The ball went straight through the creature and its remains spun into the snow.

Ryll gave a muffled cry of grief. Tiaan let out her breath and gasped another. They shot straight over the clanker as Rahnd frantically tried to reload the javelard. It was too late. They were away.

Ryll took the control ropes and brought the front of the wing down slightly. The wing lifted – it was flying! It seemed miraculous to Tiaan. The strain went off the tow ropes; the fizzing in Tiaan's brain died away. Besant did two great circles and turned towards the south-west, to Kalissin, wherever or whatever that was.

THIRTY-NINE

Rahnd kept firing until Tiaan was well beyond range.

'Enough!' Nish collapsed on the rocky ground beside Irisis, feeling incredibly cold, weak and helpless. Despite everything, Tiaan was lost, and the crystal too. If only he had not pressured Ky-Ara. With two clankers, the lyrinx could not have escaped. You fool! Nish thought. You absolute, bloody fool.

The expedition had been a catastrophic failure and someone would have to pay for it. Most had already, including his father. Back a little way, he lay among the rocks like a bloody pile of rags. Nish could not bear to look.

'Well, that's that!' said Irisis. 'I've a mind to roll off the cliff.'

Nish clutched her hand.

'Don't worry,' she said. 'I've already failed at that. We'll face our fate together, Cryl-Nish.'

He followed the specks, dwindling into the infinite sky. 'By this time tomorrow Tiaan will be a hundred leagues away and not even Ullii will be able to find her. What a disaster!'

Irisis eased her leg, letting out a pained grunt.

'How is it?' he said.

'Kind of you to ask. The broken bone hurts so much I can't even feel the other wound.' She gave a short laugh. 'Break the other leg, why don't you? It might take away the pain of the first.'

'Sometimes I just don't understand you,' Nish said.

'Good!'

'Let's get you away from the edge of the cliff. It makes me nervous.'

'I'm happy where I am,' Irisis protested, but he took her under the arms and hauled her up the slope, her feet dragging over the bumpy ground. There were tears in her eyes by the time he got her there. 'I don't much care for your bedside manner, Nish.'

Nish hardly noticed. Guilt was eating him up. Staring distractedly around him, he began to shiver. It was bitterly cold now that the action had finished.

'Better see to your father. He's a lot worse than I am.'

Nish looked across and away, terrified of what he would find there. 'I'll send back to the ice houses for help.' He waved at the clanker.

'I wouldn't bother,' Irisis replied. 'There won't be anyone coming.'

He spun around, mouth hanging open.

'That's right, Nish. The rest were wiped out at the ice houses. Every man!'

'And the lyrinx?'

'All dead.'

More than forty people brutally slain! Nish could not take it in. He'd known them all; had shared a joke with most of them over the past week or two. How could so much life have been lost, so quickly?

His father began to wail shrilly. He was still alive, at least. Nish ran to him, bent over and froze. Jal-Nish, his handsome father, was a ruined man. His face had been torn open. One pulped eyeball dangled from its socket and most of his nose had gone. The left cheek had been peeled back from ear to mouth in three separate rents. Nish could not bear to look at him.

Jal-Nish fell back into unconsciousness. There were deep gouges across his chest and his arm was terribly shattered and torn. Nish looked around for help. The only survivors were Simmo, Rahnd, Rustina, Tuniz the artificer, and Irisis. No, the querist was alive as well, staggering out from the rocks where she'd fallen. Tuniz was unharmed. Rustina had broken bones in her arm, a swollen right wrist, a wobbly jaw and many bruises, but at least she could stand up. Irisis was being carried up the hill on a stretcher. And then there was Ullii, huddled up behind a rock, but she was no use at all. Her eyes had turned inward. She was incapable of speaking.

'What's the matter with her?' asked Fyn-Mah, sitting down abruptly.

'She began screaming when the lyrinx first took off,' Nish said. 'I suppose the Art was burning her. Is anyone a healer?'

'I know a little field medicine,' Rustina whispered. Tuniz had to help her to her knees beside the perquisitor, and then to hold her up.

'He's going to die, isn't he?'

'I'd say so,' the sergeant replied. 'Though I've seen men recover from worse.' She took Jal-Nish's wrist with her left hand. 'Well, the pulse is strong. Maybe he has a chance . . .'

'I'll do *anything*.' Nish was only now realising how much his arrogant, demanding father meant to him.

'The arm will have to go,' said Rustina. 'The upper bone is smashed to pieces and no one could fix it.' She looked up as if gauging his courage. 'You'll have to do it.'

Nish imagined hacking his father's arm off at the shoulder, like a butcher carving through a joint. 'I can't . . .'

'We all must do . . .' Rustina began.

'He can't do it, sergeant!' snapped Irisis.

'Then the perquisitor will die, and it's probably best. If he did survive, he'd be in torment for the rest of his life, and a horror to look at. Would he want to live?'

'My father can't die!' cried Nish. 'Give me the knife.'

'I'll do it,' said Irisis. They all stared at her. 'It's the leg that's broken, not my arm. I have a steady hand and a good eye.'

Those who had seen her coolly take the shard from Nish's neck knew that. And her metal work was the best anyone had ever seen. Half the women of the manufactory wore jewellery Irisis had made in her spare time.

She had to perform the operation sitting, with her splinted leg out straight before her. It was rather awkward. Nish knelt on the other side, holding his father still, for even in his unconscious state Jal-Nish jerked and twitched.

It took surprisingly little time to remove the arm at the shoulder. Rahnd cauterised the wound with a metal plate off the clanker, heated over a fire of scrub branches. The smell was horrible. Worse, the searing shocked Jal-Nish back to consciousness. His screams could have been heard across the plateau, especially when Irisis began to sew his face back together. Three people had to hold him down.

'Let me die!' he kept shouting, his one eye staring at them, unblinking.

Finally the ghastly operation was done, the wounds painted with warm tar and bound up. They put Jal-Nish in the clanker with Irisis and Rustina, who had collapsed, moaning and holding her belly.

'The beast struck her in the middle,' said Nish. 'Maybe it's burst her belly.' He pulled her clothes up and went still.

'What is it?' said Irisis.

Rustina was unmarked but for a set of old scars that carved all the way across her midriff. 'Lyrinx claws. How did she ever survive? She must have been torn right open.'

'She was only a child when it happened,' said Fyn-Mah. 'There was no possibility of her having children so she was allowed to join the army. All she's ever wanted since was to kill the enemy.'

Ullii was still crouched behind her rock. Nish could get no response out of her, no matter what he did. He carried her to the clanker, whereupon she came to life and sprang out again.

'He's screaming!' she moaned, though Jal-Nish, sedated with a heavy dose of nigah, was silent.

Nish let her go. He had no energy left for her.

On the way back they managed to right the crashed clanker, but the flywheels had torn from their mountings and the machine had to be abandoned. Ky-Ara sat beside it, weeping silently. The death of Pur-Did seemed a far lesser tragedy than the loss of his machine. Clanker operators rarely bonded with their shooters.

They buried Pur-Did in the gravel and put Ky-Ara in the good machine, but as soon as they clattered away he began to scream and wail, and had to be held to keep him from leaping out.

'I can still *see* the clanker,' said Ullii.

'Of course you . . .' Nish began, trudging beside her, before realising that she had her mask on. Besides, she was looking the other way. They had left the controller behind.

He ran back for it and, reaching in through the back hatch, passed the controller to Irisis. 'Give him this.'

Cradling the controller in his arms, Ky-Ara fell silent. The bond between operator and clanker went through the controller, which was specifically attuned to both. A clanker whose operator was dead was just scrap metal until another controller could be fitted, or a new operator trained to use the old one.

It was a major handicap in battle, though better than the alternative, which would have allowed the enemy to turn a captured clanker on its own troops.

Ullii began to scream as soon as they crested the hill, even before they set sight on the dreadful scene at the snilau. 'Waves through the body!' she kept saying. 'Waves of flesh.'

There they found carnage such as Nish had never seen before. More than forty human bodies lay strewn all around, clawed and rent worse than any Hürn bear would have done, as well as a dozen of the enemy. Fyn-Mah called Nish down to help check that all the lyrinx were dead, and to see if any of their troops remained alive.

'Wait!' cried a weak voice. Rustina climbed shakily out of the hatch.

'I don't think . . .' Nish began.

'They are my troops, artificer.'

There was no arguing with that. They checked the bodies one by one. Rustina called out the details of each, including the way they had died, Fyn-Mah wrote it down and they collected any valuables for the families. All the troops were dead and all their sergeants except for Rustina. The operators and shooters of the other clankers had also been slain. Gi-Had lay behind a low wall of ice blocks, where he had been defending a group of injured soldiers. As overseer, the man had been such a powerful presence. Now he lay lifeless on the red-stained snow and Nish was startled to realise what a small man Gi-Had had been, not much larger than Nish himself. Nish closed the half-frozen eyes and stood with head bowed, profoundly sorry. Despite the whipping, the overseer had been the best of men, in his way.

As he walked off, all Nish could think of was the parting scene at the manufactory: the pale wife, the five girls in a line, and the littlest one, with the red ribbons, crying. Daddy was not coming home.

Several soldiers had died recently, as much of the cold as their injuries. Arple, though suffering a dozen wounds, could not have been dead more than a few minutes. He had dragged himself to one of his troops, leaving a bloody trail, and his body was still warm. The most decorated soldier in Glynninar had met his match.

'What were the lyrinx doing here?' Nish said when the work was done and all the enemy bodies had been checked, warily.

Fyn-Mah looked around, lowered her voice and said, 'We don't know, but . . .'

'Yes?' Nish prompted.

'It's not the first time we've come across small groups inhabiting the most hostile places. Locations with no strategic value whatsoever, though usually at a powerful node.'

'And it's a most strange node here.'

'Indeed. A double. We think . . .' She broke off and walked rapidly toward the largest snilau, a multi-chambered one around which the others spiralled like the whorl of a snail shell. The side and roof of the main chamber had fallen in. They went through the hole, Nish with his sword at the ready as Fyn-Mah searched through the debris of ice blocks.

They found nothing in the larger chambers except rugs and furs, some laid over blocks of ice to form rude benches, chunks of frozen meat (not human), several leather buckets and a few other tools. However, in side rooms the querist discovered a series of cages. Some were empty; others contained small, unearthly-looking creatures. All appeared to be dead, yet Fyn-Mah inspected and described every one with meticulous care.

In a cage at the back they found a live creature the size of a mouse, though shaped like no animal Nish had ever seen. It had a long slanted head with protruding sabre teeth, a spined backbone and a clubbed tail. As they approached, it pushed itself up on spindly legs, let out a mewling cry then fell down again.

'What *are* these beasts?' Nish asked.

Fyn-Mah kept writing. 'Finish that, would you.'

Putting his sword in through the bars, Nish crushed the creature.

'They've been *flesh-formed*,' Fyn-Mah said. 'Certain lyrinx have the talent to force small creatures to grow differently, to a pattern they make in their minds. But it can only be done in certain places; at nodes. That's all we know. *Why* do they do it? Is it for food, or culture, or worship? Are they toys, or art? We know so little about the lyrinx. But it may also be – '

Flesh-formers! Nish shuddered. 'That's what Ullii was trying to tell us. "Waves through the body," she said.' He felt his own flesh crawling. 'Or maybe,' he mused, teasing the logic together, 'they're trying to create a weapon. One we'll have no defence against.'

'Maybe they are, artificer. We would very much like to know.'

He came to an instantaneous decision. 'I'd like to find out.'

She looked surprised, the first time he'd seen such a reaction from her. 'Are you man enough for it?'

'Probably not.' A rare admission, for him. 'Though I know languages, and people, and machines. Flesh-forming may have similarities to metal-working.'

'And many differences too.'

'I've grown up with examiners and perquisitors. I'm as qualified as most people.'

'You lack what may be the most important qualification of all,' she said. 'You have no talent for the Secret Art.'

'But I have been working with the seeker, and she can sense out the Art.'

'Not the same thing at all.'

'And there is Irisis.'

'A fraud,' said Fyn-Mah, 'without the talent of the artisan she pretends to be.'

Nish turned away so she would not see his shock. Was there no secret the querist did not know?

'She is brilliant at getting her people to work together and bringing out of them more than they know. She is already a master crafter. She had to become one, to survive.'

'Whatever!' Fyn-Mah said disinterestedly. 'Your own capacity for hard work is undoubted, artificer. And your intelligence. Your judgment can be faulty, however, and there is a question-mark over your integrity. Do you have the guts to keep going, whatever it takes?'

'Did you see what they did to my father?' he said in an almost inaudible voice. 'If Jal-Nish does not die, he will never be a whole man again. For all our differences, he is still my father. He has many faults, as do I, but lack of loyalty is not one of them. I will make up for this affront to him, whatever it takes.'

The querist looked him in the eye. 'I believe you will, Cryl-Nish. Very well, as leader of this force, you have my warrant to follow this question through. You have three months. After that, it will be at the discretion of Jal-Nish's replacement as perquisi-tor – or of your father, if he recovers.'

With a last look around at the devastation she headed back to the clanker. Nish studied the small corpses, and the cages, won-dering what he had let himself in for. Then, thinking about what lay ahead, he doubted if it would matter. Such a small, battered force as they now were might not get the clanker down the cliff. And if they did not, they would all die.

FORTY

Tiaan and Ryll soon left the plateau far behind. With Besant's great wings thudding rhythmically above, in less than an hour they had cleared the mountains and were gliding over a hummocky land, largely treeless, which contained one enormous lake after another. Burlahp, she knew the place to be, though only as a name. Beyond the southern end of the lake was a city. Comparing its location with a map in her head, she deduced it to be Nox.

Ahead loomed another range, the second and shorter tine of the fork, though equally wide and high. The sun was heading down and Tiaan could feel the cold seeping into her core.

'Ryll?' she said weakly.

'Yes?'

'I'm freezing. Is there far to go?'

'Many hours.'

'I'll be dead by then.'

He hauled her up and bound her to his chest, face out, with her coat double-thickness at the front. He must have opened his skin plates a little, for she could feel the warmth seeping from his chest and belly, like a hotplate running down her back. It felt wonderful. Disturbing too, though she did not want to think about that.

Before the sun had set she was able to catch some of the thrill of flying, or gliding – the silent movement through the air, their almost imperceptible progress against the mottled lands below, the strange viewpoint that flattened the world into an embroidered bedcover.

It was dark before they reached the second range. The cold intensified and the night became a struggle to keep warm, even with Ryll against her. She worked her fingers and toes constantly, warmed her nose and cheeks with the palms of her hands, but it was never enough. Neither was Ryll as warm as he had been.

The night, nearly fifteen hours long, was an eternity. Her shoulder hurt at the least movement. Tiaan desperately wanted to sleep but knew she risked frostbite if she so much as dozed. That desperate craving for sleep and warmth dragged every minute into an hour. Another craving was even worse – her longing for the amplimet. She could see it in her mind's eye, bound to Besant's chest, too far away to give her any comfort. She wanted it badly and could not have it.

Sometime during the night her frigid daze was disturbed by Ryll tugging on the lines. They jerked back and he went forward in his harness, tilting the front of the flier down. Again Tiaan felt the fizzing behind her temples that indicated Besant's Art. Down they went, so steeply that the wind tried to pluck her from Ryll's chilly embrace.

Eventually he levelled out. It was warmer here. Another eternity passed. Ryll felt cold against her back now and scarcely moved. How must he be suffering from that bolt in the shoulder? Perhaps he was dying. Had he given the warmth of his body to save her, at the cost of his own life?

The fizzing had faded long ago. Had Besant's mancing burnt *her* out too, on this monumental journey?

A low red sun tipped the horizon. A thin ray touched Tiaan's face, warming her out of all proportion to its power. She shook herself. Ryll gave a frosty groan and ice fell from his nostrils.

Light touched the clouds below them. They were flying above a dense overcast, an infinite layer of grey. Shortly a circular gap appeared to their right. Ryll headed toward an opening like the eye of a hurricane.

As they came over the hole, Tiaan saw far below a circular lake with rivers flowing into it like spokes of a wheel. In the centre stood a rocky peak, strangely bare, though the landscape around the lake was covered in snow and forest. They headed in plunging spirals toward the peak. Below the clouds they entered a rising column of warm air that buffeted the wing violently. Without warning it tilted up, a long fluttering strip of fabric tore free and the wing stalled.

Besant screamed something, her Art fizzed momentarily, then went out. Tiaan looked up to see the lyrinx's wings collapse under her weight. She fell out of the air, plummeting towards them.

'Cut free!' she cried, a harsh croak as she shot past so close that the flier rippled.

Ryll was reaching out with a blade to cut the traces when Tiaan gasped, 'No! She's got the crystal!'

Making a violent manoeuvre that dragged the front of the wing down, Ryll plunged after her. As Besant's weight came on the lines, the wing structure groaned. Ryll gripped the struts under the greatest strain, holding them together. The loose fabric cracked like a whip as they went into a vertical dive toward the peak.

Ryll shifted backwards, trying to compensate for Besant's dead weight. The dive became shallower. He aimed the wing toward the top of the peak but it kept crabbing sideways. Besant was not moving, though the leathery material of her wings was extended.

They drifted over the peak, again passing through hot air that rocked the wing, though this time Ryll did not lose control. Not far to go now. They swept across the water, still going incredibly fast. He wrenched them back on course. The peak was a jumbled mass that looked like welded rock and metal, oily green-black and rusty-red, quite devoid of vegetation. Ryll seemed to be aiming for a smooth area pitted with holes and clotted rock mounds, surrounded by spires.

Besant, hanging five or six spans below them, would hit and pull them head-first into the ground. Ryll tried to haul her up but the wing creaked and cracked. Below, figures issued from a hole in the rock, small from this distance but recognisable as lyrinx.

'Besant!' he roared. 'Besant, wake! *Thylymyyx fushrr!*'

She did not respond. He shouted the same words again, jerking on the lines as hard as he dared. No answer. The top of the peak came up, too quickly. They were drifting right at the spires.

'Besant!' he screamed, so loudly that it hurt Tiaan's ears. 'Wake or we are ended and the war is lost.'

Besant gave a faint convulsion. One leg kicked. She raised her head and her left wing extended, clawing them round the main peak straight toward a smaller spire of iron.

Ryll flung his weight sideways. The wing flier banked, shot past the spire, just skimmed another; and then Besant's wings flapped twice, lifting her weight. They soared up and over, slowing rapidly. They were going to make it.

But Besant was finished. One wing tore, she struck the edge of a third spire and fell thumping all the way down. The wing flier turned upside down and broke in two. They plummeted a couple of spans to the ground, Ryll landing on his back with Tiaan on top of him.

She lay there, stunned and aching all over. Three lyrinx came bounding up. Slashing her free, they hauled her off Ryll, who was unconscious. The largest lyrinx spoke to Tiaan in a language she did not know. Another ran to the crumpled figure of Besant.

'I do not understand you,' Tiaan said carefully, using the common speech of the south-east.

Ryll sat up, shaking his head. A horrible groan rent the air. It was Besant. The lyrinx turned to her. She tried to roll over but purple blood ran out of her mouth. As they attempted to lift her she gave a wracking cry.

One lyrinx began stripping the broken flier down to its wooden members. Another carried several struts and a piece of fabric across and lashed them into the shape of a stretcher.

A third wiped blood from Besant's mouth, gibbering at her in that strange tongue. Her hand pointed to a small pack bound between her breast plates. Someone unfastened it, drawing out a leather case. The lashings were untied. A female gasped, her crest went a luminous green and she held the amplimet high. It glowed much more brightly than usual. Light was positively flooding from it.

Besant choked out a few sentences, in one of which Tiaan heard her name, somewhat mangled, 'Tee-yarrrn.' The lyrinx swung around, all staring at her. Besant continued, her voice rising.

'Myllixyn thrruppa harrh, *ghos tirri Ryll!*' She screamed out the last three words, flung an accusing arm at him and slumped sideways, coughing purple bubbles.

The lyrinx who had cut Tiaan's ropes covered the ground to Ryll in three great bounds, hauled him to his feet and struck him hard on the forehead, three times. Ryll bowed his head and held out his hands. The lyrinx bound him swiftly, Ryll showing no emotion, nor any reaction to the pain as his injured arm was jerked about. He was led away.

Another collected his pack, and Tiaan's, and pointed toward the sinkhole. She moved that way. The remaining lyrinx had eased Besant onto the stretcher and were rigging ropes on a tripod above the hole. Tiaan was led down a narrow iron ladder whose rungs were uncomfortably far apart.

The first thing she noticed was the noise, or rather, music, a low droning that went up and down like someone blowing through long tubes. It was in the background all the time. Sometimes the sound went *so* low that she could feel it in her bones.

As she stumbled into the dark, Tiaan wondered if she would ever see the outside again. It was the strangest place she had ever been. The inside was like a frozen foam of grey, rust-streaked iron, every surface being curved like the interior of a bubble. A long way below, past various guard chambers and working spaces whose purpose she could not discern, she entered a large circular chamber shaped like two saucers, one right way up with another upside down on top of it.

She was taken down a sloping floor to the depressed central section. To one side stood a round table, a pitcher and a set of mugs the size of small buckets, all made of iron. Ryll was led in, followed by Besant on her stretcher, her breast plates streaked with coughed–up blood. The stretcher-bearers set Besant down on the rim. Some dozens of lyrinx took up positions around her.

A young female, whose skin plates were so soft and unpigmented that Tiaan could see her breasts through them, gently held up Besant's head. A huge female bent over her, in the attitude Ryll had adopted when regenerating his hand. She stood up, shaking her head.

'Would you speak, Wise Mother?' she said.

Besant mumbled in her incomprehensible language. Every word brought bubbles foaming out of her mouth and nose. Again she spoke Tiaan's name and everyone stared at her. A massively built male, with green eyes shaded by brow ridges like shelves, produced the amplimet. It lit up the room with streamers of radiant light.

He gestured to Tiaan. The big female, who had yellow skin plates and sagging wattles at neck and chin, spoke Tiaan's language in a crackling voice. 'I am Coeland, Wise Mother of Kalissin. Show us the devices, human.'

Not daring to disobey, Tiaan donned the helm, held the wire globe in her hands and waited. Everyone was watching her.

'The amplimet goes inside,' Tiaan said.

Coeland gestured; the male with the brow ridges brought the crystal across. Before he reached her Tiaan felt the potential of it, stronger than before. There had to be a powerful node here.

Her craving for the amplimet was unbearable. Tiaan's eyes watered. She opened the globe so he could place the crystal inside. The light flared. He cried out and dropped the crystal. She caught it in her hands, a moment of painful bliss, then slipped it into the globe, closed it and fastened the catch. The lyrinx sprang out of the way as if it had bitten him.

Tiaan put down the globe. The field was so bright here that she could visualise it with her eyes open. The node must be a monster. She moved the helm on her head, afraid of the amplimet now. It was definitely channelling power by itself, much more than before. It had nearly killed her in the ice sphere, and there it had been much dimmer.

'Show!' Coeland said imperatively.

Tiaan adjusted her helm, reached for the globe, shrieked and snatched her fingers away. The wires were too hot to touch. Suddenly the metal table, pitcher and mugs were pulled up to the ceiling, where they stuck as if magnetised. Water rained down, sizzling on the wires. Her hair began to smoke. Ryll lurched forward and knocked the helm off with his bound hands. The light died down. He caught the falling table and pitcher, though the mugs clanged on the floor.

'You see,' he said to the Wise Mother. 'It taps great power but it is a dangerous device to control. She does not know what she is doing.'

'The field is strong here,' Tiaan said shakily, inspecting her fingers, which had lines burned across them. What if they thought it too dangerous and disposed of her? 'It takes time for me to learn a new field before I can control the flux of power.'

'We'll see about that,' said the elderly lyrinx. 'Tell us about the tetrarch, human.'

Again that question. 'I don't know what a tetrarch is,' Tiaan said.

Again that interrogative stare, as if the lyrinx was trying to read her for the truth.

'It is a person we would very much like to find.' She turned to Ryll. 'Besant accuses you of cowardice, wingless one! You were to remain behind. How do you defend yourself?'

Ryll shook his head. He sat holding his shoulder, which was inflamed around the crossbow wound. 'No defence.'

'Then Wyrkoe will be your defender.' At her gesture a tall, slender female stood up.

'No!' said Ryll. 'No defence.'

Wyrkoe sat again.

'In that case you must take the consequences. You will be neutered at first light.'

Tiaan was shocked. What was the matter with Ryll? Was he

412

too proud to defend himself, or had he given up? She looked around at the hard faces. After all he had done for her on the journey she could not see him treated so unjustly. Dare she?

'I will defend Ryll!'

Her words exploded into the silence. Every head jerked up, except one. Ryll's sank to his ankles. 'No!' he groaned.

Had she shamed him? It seemed so, from the malicious stares of the other lyrinx. One even laughed, or so she interpreted the braying sound. But to be *neutered* – how could he suffer that? It did not occur to Tiaan that it might be a blessed relief, an honourable way out.

'Very well,' said Coeland, 'defend your *hero*, human.'

Tiaan took a deep breath. Ryll let out another groan but it was too late. The order had been given.

'Had Ryll stayed behind I would have died and my crystal would have been lost, for I could not have caught Besant's flier.' She explained the details of the escape. 'Had Ryll not jumped, carrying me, I would have been captured.'

'He should have harnessed you in and cut himself free!' thundered the Wise Mother. 'Besant, the greatest of our clan, lies dying, sacrificed for a wingless travesty.'

'I could not have flown the wing,' said Tiaan. 'My shoulder is dislocated.' She had to explain the term.

The young female with the transparent skin took off Tiaan's upper garments and worked the arm. Tiaan gritted her teeth. The lyrinx, with a quick movement that made Tiaan shriek, popped the shoulder back in place. She then put the arm in a leather sling and pulled Tiaan's shirt over it.

'Ryll might have done the same,' Coeland observed.

'I still would not have been able to use my arm,' said Tiaan.

'Pfft!' Coeland made a dismissive gesture. 'Such weak creatures.'

'I could not have flown the wing!' Tiaan said furiously. 'And without Ryll giving me the warmth of his body I would have frozen to death. Anyway, had it not been for his foresight and courage you would never have had the amplimet at all.'

Coeland sat up at that and Tiaan was made to tell her the

whole tale. When it was finished the Wise Mother said, 'Ryll is cleared of the charge of cowardice, though you should be aware, *human*, that he would have preferred life as a neuter than to be defended by you! Take him away and attend his injuries.'

FORTY-ONE

Kalissin was a most special node, a place where the latent energies of the earth might conceivably be tapped – if someone was strong enough, and foolhardy enough, to try. Fifty thousand years ago a rock and iron comet from the depths of the void had plunged to ground here, making the planet ring like a gong and blasting up such a cloud of shattered rock that the entire globe had been plunged into darkness. An age of ice followed that had lasted for thirty thousand years.

The remains of the comet had buried itself deep in the crust of Tarralladell. The rocky parts were fused to glass but the iron core formed a deep molten pool that stayed liquid for twenty thousand years until, buoyed by up-seeping gases, it began to rise again. Expanding gas blew the iron into foamy cells that swelled until the mass forced its way to the surface, melted up though the receding ice sheet and set into a solid spire.

Now it made a pinnacle two hundred and sixty spans high, rising out of the island in the centre of the lake that filled the comet's impact crater. Inside, the pinnacle was like a honey-comb built for giants, a frozen froth of iron. Outside, its upper parts, pointed like a collection of witches' hats, were streaked red and rusty-brown. Clots of greasy green shattered rock and glass were welded to it here and there. The lower part was enveloped in country rock dragged up with the pinnacle and layers of windblown dust accumulated after the ice disappeared.

The skirts of the pinnacle were clothed in tall trees, quite unlike the spindly pines elsewhere in Tarralladell. Here and there lay steamy pools, ponds of bubbling mud and cracks from which warm water ebbed, coating the rocks in multi-coloured salts. The upper parts of the pinnacle were bare of all but lichen, though being warm in that frigid land they were a favoured nesting site of eagles and many other kinds of bird.

No one came to collect the eggs. Kalissin Spire had been known as a place of evil spirits long before the lyrinx secretly entered it. No humans crossed the uncannily warm waters of the lake. Just to look up told them what a forbidden place it was. The skies of Tarralladell were overcast for half the year but over Kalissin a circle of clear air was often ringed by great storms, and the iron fangs of the spire were struck by lightning more frequently than any other place in that land. The evil ones were recharging their death spears, folktales told, preparing to wreak havoc on the world in their night ridings. And just occasionally, a fisher on the furthest shore of the lake would look up to see winged creatures wheeling and soaring high above, and know it was all true.

Being a creature of the void from which the lyrinx had come, the remains of the comet drew the invaders to it. The crater, and particularly the honeycombed iron peak, were things they knew and understood – part of their own environment, in a way. But it was more than that. Comets are bodies of unimaginably vast energy, and this one had not expended all its potential in its fiery plunge into the ground. The fall, the impact, the melting and the rising of that iron froth had created an instability. The metal shaft which ran deep into the earth was out of equilibrium with its surroundings. That instability, that node, represented a mighty pool of energy waiting to be tapped.

Comets are strange things. Wandering the heavens for billions of years as they do, their matter attains inexplicable properties of great value to practitioners of the Secret Art. Lyrinx who had this ability coveted cometary iron above all things, and Kalissin Spire represented the very acme of their desires. They brought their best and most creative intelligences here, to envelop themselves in the energy fields; to eat, breathe and sleep surrounded by this, to them, most magical of all substances.

Kalissin was their greatest workshop and laboratory. Here the lyrinx in their individual cells went about their urgent project. Clankers had inflicted enormous casualties on them and they were not numerous enough to support such losses. They had to find a defence.

Unfortunately they had not discovered how to tap the power of Kalissin. Just being within the fields helped, but it was not enough. It was frustrating to be surrounded by more power than they could ever use, and not be able to draw on it. They wanted the amplimet; more importantly, to find out how Tiaan used it to take power from the field. All this Tiaan learned, directly or indirectly, in her first days in Kalissin.

A week went by. Tiaan was fully recovered, apart from a tenderness in her shoulder. The lyrinx had not treated her unkindly, and fed her better than she had ever eaten at the manufactory. At first she insisted on being shown the source of her meals, but soon realised that they respected her beliefs and taboos. The lyrinx would no sooner have fed her human flesh than they would have eaten their own dead. Besides, they mostly ate fish from the lake. Tiaan was soon sick of their diet: grilled fish, a kind of soupy algae, and a root vegetable like a pungent turnip. She had the same every day.

She was housed in a cluster of rooms near the top of the pinnacle. Their shape, like iron bubbles, was hard to get used to. The walls were curved, dark metal with streaks of rust. Her bedroom had a circular hole cut through to the exterior for fresh air, and a cap of green volcanic glass to close it when it was frigid outside. She seldom did. The iron conducted heat up from the depths, keeping the whole of Kalissin warm. The hole was too small to squeeze through.

The droning music was less audible here, and higher-pitched, more like a raspy oboe. The lyrinx had bored holes through the

417

outer bubbles to make wind horns. The wind blew constantly around the heights and the horns never stilled their mournful voices.

None of these things gave Tiaan any comfort. Desire for the amplimet was a constant ache and the pangs grew worse every day, though she was helpless to do anything about her craving. She had learned to undo her door lock the first night but was caught within minutes. They did not harm her, but simply returned her to her room and fixed a bolt on the outside.

Every day they questioned her about the amplimet and the nature of her art and craft. She refused to answer, though with each day's separation from the crystal that grew harder. Soon, Tiaan knew, she would tell them everything, just to have it in her hands for an instant. And she had to have it. It was her only hope of getting free. Most important of all, it was the key to Minis's survival. In all her troubles she never lost sight of that ultimate goal – to get the amplimet to Tirthrax in time.

How she regretted telling Ryll about withdrawal, but it was too late for that.

'What are your people doing here?' she asked Ryll on the eighth day. 'Are you trying to make your own clankers? Is that why you're so interested in my craft?'

'We would hardly duplicate the weapons of our enemies,' he said coolly. Relations had been strained since she'd defended him.

'Why not?'

'That way lies degeneration. It would be going against our own nature. Any device we use must come from the wellspring of our lives and traditions.'

'But surely it would be easier . . .'

'What do we care about *easier*?' he said savagely. 'We are not *human*! We do not exist to make things easier for ourselves! *Better*, yes! It is the struggle that matters, else we will soon be as depraved as . . .'

He had been going to say 'as you'. She forbore to state that it would be worth it to win the war. It was already clear that, to them, the end did not justify the means. Only means that were part of their culture would ever be employed. 'What *are* you trying to do?'

'I can't tell you that.'

Another difference between lyrinx and humans. They did not lie, as a rule. They just refused to answer.

'Then what do you want me for? Since I've been here I've done nothing but eat and sleep. I begin to worry that I am being fattened for your dinner table.' She tried to make a joke of it, but was not convincing.

Undoing the cap on her window, he thrust his muzzle into the opening. When he finally pulled away there was a ring of ice around each eye. 'We're watching you and learning about your kind. We think you will be able to help us.'

Tiaan shivered. An icy wind was blowing straight in today. 'Your own efforts with my amplimet have not been successful?'

'What makes you think that?' he said, interested.

'Your manner with each other, and the tones of your voices. I am learning about lyrinx, too.'

'What else have you learned?'

'You never talk about your Histories, Ryll.'

He closed off at once. 'We are the lost people. We *have* no Histories.'

'What do you mean?'

She did not expect an answer, but after striding about the room in some agitation, and closing the door, Ryll came back to her.

'We *patterned* our unborn children in the void, that our kind might survive. And we did. We thrived. Thereafter we did it again and again, patterning our babies in the womb to meet each new threat. We survived; we increased; but we do not *fit*. We no longer know who we are.'

There were hundreds of lyrinx in Kalissin and a good proportion had one deformity or another – lack of wings or claws, inadequate armour or pigmentation, inability to change the colour of their skin. Tiaan wondered about that. Were they reverting to what they'd been before they re-formed their bodies in the void? None of them, even the normal ones, quite seemed to belong.

The following day she was taken down a series of iron ladders, some straight, others corkscrewed, to a series of rooms halfway down the spire. The temperature increased with every step and in these middle chambers it was unpleasantly warm.

Ryll led her into a chamber where the central walls of a cluster of bubbles had been cut away to make a room shaped like a strawberry. In one corner of that uncomfortable space a small female lyrinx stood at a bench made of honeycombed iron, surfaced with rock glass the palest tinge of green. She was the one who had fixed Tiaan's shoulder at the trial, the one who lacked pigment in her skin. At the back of the bench sat a box made of iron wires and green glass, like a tank for fish.

The lyrinx wore Tiaan's helm. The globe sat on the bench. The creature was manipulating the beads. Her claws were retracted and the thick fingers surprisingly dexterous, though the glow emitted by the amplimet was unchanged no matter what she did.

Tiaan was drawn to the crystal. She could not help herself.

'This is Liett,' said Ryll to Tiaan.

Tiaan did not hear. Stumbling toward the bench with a dazed look on her face, she reached out for the amplimet. Ryll dragged her back.

Desperate for it, Tiaan tore free, darted around the startled lyrinx and sprang. Ryll caught her in mid-air, carried her to her room and locked her in.

'You will not touch the crystal again until you agree to help us. Do you hear me?' Banging the door, he slammed the bolt home.

Tiaan paced the room all day, growing more despairing each minute. The craving was unbearable. She paced out the night too, finally collapsing on her bed at dawn.

Ryll woke her soon after. He had the crystal in one hand, no doubt to torment her further. Tiaan threw herself on him like a savage, clawing and biting. He seemed surprised by her fury but simply held her in one hand until she was spent.

'Do you agree?' he asked calmly.

'No!' she snarled. Tiaan felt dazed, unreal. This close to the amplimet she could pick up traces of the field spiralling about Kalissin node. Tears of longing poured down her cheeks.

He walked out and bolted the door. By the time he returned the following day Tiaan felt sure that she was going mad. She had not slept, her hair was a riot, her eyes yellow and brown pits. She had broken her fingernails clawing at the door. Her forehead was bruised from banging it on the wall.

She lay on her back, looking up at the amplimet. She no longer had the strength to fight.

'Well?' he said. One facet of the crystal flashed at her.

She laid her head on the floor. 'I will help you,' she croaked, holding out her hand.

'Come down.' He walked out.

Tiaan followed him back to that strawberry-shaped room. 'This is Liett,' Ryll said.

Tiaan repeated the name, '*Li*-ett,' pronouncing it the way names were sounded in her part of the world.

'No, Li*et-t*.' She emphasised the second syllable and ending with a distinct *t-t* sound, like tapping the bench with a fingernail.

Tiaan tried again. 'Lee-*et*!'

The lyrinx parted her lips in a gesture that might have been a smile or a grimace. 'Just call me Leet!'

Tiaan moved closer to the bench, distracted by a scuttling movement in the box. Inside crouched a creature like nothing she had ever seen before. It was about the size of a mouse, with the general form of a lyrinx-like biped, though a savagely distorted one. Fur took the place of chameleon skin and it had enormous pink eyes.

It scuttled about on all fours. Its feet were padded hoofs, while the muscularity of its back looked more suited to the carrying of heavy loads than to walking upright.

'What is it?' Tiaan asked.

'A thramp!' Liett replied. 'Just observe, small human.'

Liett placed her hands around the walls of the cage, gently but firmly, and strained. Tiaan felt a fizzing sensation, though subtly different in pitch and *colour* from the one Besant had caused in the night flight. The sensation stopped and Liett jerked her hands away, panting with the effort.

She stood up, shaking her head as though trying to dislodge something caught in her colourless crest. Her fingers pressed the spot, over and over. Finally she sat down and closed her eyes.

Tiaan watched the little creature, which had fallen over and was kicking its back legs in uncoordinated spasms. Then, before her eyes, the pads of its feet began to thin and elongate. It happened so imperceptibly that at first Tiaan thought she'd imagined it. She had to compare what she was seeing now with its original self, like a blueprint in her mind, before she was sure.

'Are *you* a flesh-shaper?' she said to Ryll, recalling her dreams in the ice house.

'Some of us are.'

Had they done this to *her* while she slept? Was she subtly altered from before? She inspected her hands and the horror must have been evident on her face.

'Not you, Tiaan!' Ryll seemed amused.

'Why not?' she cried, backing away.

'Many reasons,' said Liett. 'But most important, you are too big.'

'Oh?'

'Even our greatest adepts can't flesh-form a creature larger than a rat. It takes too much out of us. The work is painful and quite draining. We can't channel power from outside us, as you do. Even if a dozen of us worked together, to flesh-form a creature the size of a cat would drive us to insanity. *Even here.*'

'I saw you shape new fingers,' she accused Ryll.

'That was regeneration, which is quite different. I was replacing what was lost, not creating a new organism. Our bodies can regenerate even if we are unconscious.'

'But in the void . . .'

'Also different.' He glanced at Liett. 'We were subtly shaping our unborn selves. Gently.'

Tiaan went back to the thramp. 'If you had a hundred working together, or a thou – '

'That many wills can't be focussed,' said Ryll. 'A hundred is worse than ten.'

'Moreover,' Liett went on, 'you would know it if we tried to work on you. Flesh-forming is torture. This creature has been sedated. Even so, the trauma will probably kill it.'

The thramp was now lying on its side, panting. Its eyes were staring.

'It does not look so bad.'

'The worst is to come,' said Ryll. 'Liett has just transformed the skin and muscle beneath it. To mould the bones and organs will take days. Flesh-shaping is a very slow process, with many failures, despite what your tellers may have told you.'

'Then why do it?'

'Small creatures can be . . .' She trailed off at a warning glance from Ryll, then continued. 'We have a hundred shapers here, and more at other nodes, as you call them. Once one shaper finds the way, others can follow. But one day we will learn to use the power this place bathes in. We will not fear your clankers then, *human*.'

'That's why you wanted our controllers!' Tiaan exclaimed. 'And me. You can't use the field and you want me to show you how. I won't. *Never!*' Why, *why* hadn't she taken that chance to escape, back at the ice houses?

'Oh yes, you will,' said Liett, with a glance at the amplimet. 'You will beg to help us.'

FORTY-TWO

That night Tiaan dreamed the earthly structure of Kalissin Spire and woke afraid. The very crust of the world seemed out of balance here. The land was imperceptibly rising, returning to its elevation before the ice sheets had weighed it down. Below, the fluid mantle drifted, immeasurably slow, to compensate.

Her dreams spoke to Tiaan after she was allowed to touch the amplimet. The fields churned all around her, and she sensed another potential. Beneath the iron spire the magma had subsided, leaving an empty chamber. Cooling, shrinking rock had cracked in concentric circles around the base of the spire, which was sinking, unleashing geomantic forces of many kinds.

Tiaan was woken by the wailing of pipes, not far away. They had been going for days now, playing the sorrowful songs that had been the life and death of Besant, Wise Mother of a lyrinx clan for more than eighty years.

Myrriptth	*tzzrk*	*yllishyn*
N'harrth	*girrymirr*	*N'voxur*
Ynnirysh	*thylrjizz*	*myrzhip*

The alien syllables rasped on, hour after hour. Another dream flooded back and Tiaan threw herself out of bed, kicking the sheet of woven rush fibres away. Her skin crawled.

Running to the window and tearing the cap open, she thrust her face through. Freezing air belted her in the face. She gulped down mouthfuls of it, so cold that Tiaan felt clots sinking into her lungs. She welcomed the frigid metal against her skin as she went through her second dream, over and again.

Flesh-forming was a talent unique to lyrinx, honed over the aeons they had spent in the void, when being able to physically adapt their young to new environments had been the ultimate way of surviving. In her dream they had been flesh-forming her, turning her into a monster, an eight-legged beast alarmingly similar to a clanker. When they were finished they would send her out to destroy clankers and kill soldiers, the ultimate betrayal of her own kind. As if she had not done enough harm already. By withholding the crystal, they could force her to do anything, no matter how degraded.

The room trembled, just a shiver. It might have been the spire contracting in the night cold, or an earth trembler far away. Or the stone at the base of the spire preparing to give way. That dream came back too, lifting the hairs on the back of her neck. This place had such potential, but the spire was hanging over an abyss.

What did they really want her for? To draw power through the amplimet? To make a controller that would enhance their hideous flesh-forming? Or, most horrible of all, to flesh-form *her*? Despite what had been said about size, that dominated her dreams. It made her shudder to think what they were doing. It was indecent.

The bolt cracked and the door came open. It was Liett. With her thin skin she sometimes looked almost human, apart from the wings.

'Come!' Liett took Tiaan's wrist. Small she may have been, and soft-skinned, but she was many times stronger than Tiaan.

'I'm not dressed,' said Tiaan.

'It's hot below,' said the creature, as if that was all that mattered.

No doubt it was to them; they had no need of clothes. Tiaan grabbed a sheet and wrapped it around her as she was hauled away. Liett did not like Tiaan. Tiaan did not care for her either.

She went down the ladder ahead of the lyrinx, the rough edges digging into her feet. She was not used to going barefoot. A long way down Liett said, 'Stop here.' Ahead, an iron–grey bubble had a ragged hole knocked through into the chamber next door.

'Where are we going?'

'To work. Go through.'

She ducked through the hole and Tiaan followed. Though wide, it was not even shoulder-high. Liett pulled a hidden door closed. Tiaan found herself in a larger, triple bubble, the common walls of which had been cut away above waist height to form a stalk on which was mounted a cloverleaf tabletop of polished iron, some two spans across. On one of its lobes sat her amplimet, globe and helm. Other benches set in the walls at the height of her throat contained glass and metal cages like the ones she had seen previously. The room was lit by a round hole in the wall, filled in with glass a handspan thick. The sun was coming up.

Liett pulled out a high stool, the seat also clover leaf-shaped, and pointed to it. Tiaan climbed up. The seat was uncomfortable and she did not like being clad in a sheet. It reminded her of the breeding factory.

The lyrinx busied herself at another bench. She was only the size of a tall man. A soft, translucent green crest ran from her forehead to the nape of her neck, indicating that she was a mature female. Children had colourless crests.

Liett was heavily built compared to a human male, though slight relative to other lyrinx, male or female. Her shoulders were wide, the torso long with a small indentation at the waist. Her hips were broad, her short legs muscular, her feet wide. The wings were folded flat against her back.

It was her skin that most distinguished her from every other lyrinx. On them it was leathery, with hard plates that protected the genitalia and vital organs of the belly and chest, and more flexible plates elsewhere, while its chameleon pigments completely concealed the soft second skin beneath.

On Liett the outer skin was thin and completely transparent, like a layer of jelly spread over pale-grey inner skin. Even the parts covered by her undeveloped skin plates were visible. She looked almost human, if the wings were discounted.

'How is it . . .?' Tiaan thought better of it.

'I am incomplete,' Liett said with a sideways twist of her mobile mouth. 'I have to wear *clothes* outside.' She used the word as if it were a depravity, or a fatal weakness. Perhaps it was, to them. 'And I cannot *skin-change*!'

'Why does that matter?'

Liett cracked a wing at Tiaan's face. 'It matters!'

Tiaan jumped backwards, knocking over the stool and landing hard on it, legs asprawl. 'Ow!' she yelped.

Liett effortlessly lifted her onto the stool. Tiaan rubbed her back.

'Skin-change is speech and reply, fear and curiosity, and an embrace with a lover. It is half our lives. I am blind without it.'

Tiaan had often noted Ryll's colour-changes without realising that they were a form of communication. 'Tell me . . .'

'To work!' Liett said abruptly. 'Take up your devices. Try to follow what I am doing.'

She placed her hands on a cage which had wire bars instead of glass. The creature inside snapped at her fingers. Liett put a larger cage over the first and closed her eyes.

Tiaan felt that familiar fizzing. She gladly took hold of the amplimet, closed her eyes and allowed her mind to drift into the one pleasure of her life, her romantic daydream about Minis. It was an escape she used more and more, though worrying that he was becoming an obsession.

'Well?' Liett said sharply.

Tiaan opened her eyes to find the lyrinx looming over her, one ebony nipple staring at her like an accusing eye. She started and nearly fell off her stool.

'Can you see what I am trying to do?'

'Not yet,' Tiaan said guiltily. 'It's hard . . .'

'Hmpf!' Liett went out.

Shortly Ryll appeared, carrying three cages suspended by cords. Sliding them onto the bench he came around the side, stopping abruptly when he caught sight of Tiaan in her sheet.

'Where are your clothes?'

'Liett was in a hurry,' she said tersely.

He spun on one leathery foot and went out, soon returning with her garments. Tiaan dressed in haste. She had just finished when Liett reappeared. She stood in the doorway, tension evident in every muscle. Her claws were extended. She growled at Ryll in their language.

'How can she work if she's . . . *thyllxish?*' he hissed back.

With a toss of her head Liett stalked to the bench, her toe claws clacking on the floor. The sound was irritating.

Tiaan bent over the amplimet but could not concentrate. She could feel something in the air, a tension she had not felt with Ryll before. Looking sideways, she saw him staring at Liett's buttocks. She had not noticed previously, but it was an obvious difference between the sexes. Ryll's were muscular but flat whereas Liett's were extremely fleshy and prominent.

Tiaan could see the smouldering sensuality in her, and the desperate ache in Ryll to mate. It made her uncomfortable.

Liett put down the caged creature she was working with and bent over to pick up something from the floor. It was a display; a tease or a taunt. Ryll let out an involuntary groan.

Liett spun around. 'What are you . . .?' She broke off, as Ryll turned his back.

'Never!' Liett raged in Tiaan's language. 'Not in a hundred eternities would I allow you, *wingless one!*'

Ryll's crest coloured red, then purple. Bright spirals shimmered across his chest plates, gorgeous patterns that could only have been a reply to her taunt. He stood in a loose-limbed crouch, the colours so intense that they lit up the dim room. Tiaan had never seen anything so beautiful, futile or sad.

'Think you that I would mate with *you?*' he spat. 'Better no mate at all than one as naked as a human. One with no colour at all. *One who cannot skin-speak.*'

Liett's wings flashed out to full size, spanning half the bubble-room. They were beautiful, like pearly, translucent milk. She looked majestic. It made Ryll's lack all the more evident. Extending one hand, waist-high, she slid her claws out like oiled machinery. 'Open your groin plates again! I will neuter you this minute,' she hissed.

Tiaan ducked under the bench and pulled the stool in front of her. She could imagine the ruin if they fought. Fortunately, before it could begin another lyrinx entered the room, head and shoulders bowed to pass through the opening. It was the old female, Coeland, matriarch of the spire clan.

'How are . . .?' As she took in the attitudes of Ryll and Liett, her cheek plates hardened. 'What is it?' Her voice was a file rasping against steel.

Ryll hung his head, his crest dulling to the colour of his skin. Liett glared at him but would not meet Coeland's eyes. Neither answered.

'Well?' Coeland roared. 'We *are* at war, remember?'

As the silence lengthened, it became clear that neither could reveal the source of their disagreement without losing face.

'Very well,' said Coeland, 'when this is over you are both sentenced . . .'

She broke off, noticing Tiaan cowering under the bench. 'Ah, human. Come out. Explain the problem.'

Tiaan remained where she was, holding the stool in front of her like a shield. Out of the corner of her eye she could see Ryll staring at her. She knew what he was thinking. Don't reveal my shame!

Crossing the distance between them in two quick strides, Coeland caught Tiaan by the wrists. The claws dug in as she dragged Tiaan from her hide and tossed her on the bench. The huge eyes seemed to see right into her head.

'How do I know what lyrinx fight about?' Tiaan said, trying to evade the eyes.

'You weren't so coy the day you arrived.' Coeland's hand squeezed until Tiaan thought her wrist bones were going to splinter. Blood ebbed from the claw punctures. She cried out.

'You may speak,' said Ryll. 'I would not have you harmed on my behalf.'

'Ryll is desperate to mate,' Tiaan gasped. 'Liett too. But neither wishes to mate with another who is flawed. Liett flaunts herself, taunts him, and then threatens to neuter him if he approaches her.'

'Is this true?' Coeland asked.

'Yes!' Ryll said in a choked voice.

'Yes, Wise Mother!' said Liett. Her eyes flashed fire at Tiaan and Ryll.

Coeland sprang at Liett, striking her so hard across the flat of her forehead that the small lyrinx went tumbling across the room to land with her backside in the air. Picking Liett up, the Wise Mother held her out at arm's length.

'You will work with him without complaint,' she said through bared teeth, 'or I will have Ryll neuter *you*!'

'But I am your daughter!'

'All the more reason to do your duty,' Coeland said coldly.

'He is nothing but a beast.' She tried to spit in Ryll's direction but it merely dribbled down her chin. '*He has no wings!*'

'And you, my unfortunate child, have skin like a human, a far worse handicap. You cannot skin-speak, and you cannot go outside without skin paste, or *clothes*. You have never proven your worth. Ryll, wingless though he may be, is a hero who has given everything to bring this treasure to us. You will work with him or he will neuter you at my command. Will you?' She lowered Liett until her feet touched the floor.

'I will,' Liett said softly, laying her cheek submissively on her mother's arm. But as she did so her eyes flashed at Tiaan, such a baleful glare that Tiaan had to turn away.

'And you, Ryll?' said Coeland.

Ryll bent until his forehead touched the Wise Mother's feet. His crest went purple, then red, before fading to grey. 'I will do my duty,' he said, equally softly.

FORTY-THREE

The following day Tiaan learned what they wanted her for. The cages were constructed of finely drawn cometary iron, with floor and sometimes walls of rock glass formed by the impact. Each had particular properties that enhanced the flesh-forming Art. She was required to channel power from the Kalissin fields into the iron filaments so as to induce a smaller, more concentrated aura inside the cage. The lyrinx hoped, by this, to grow their flesh-formed creatures larger.

'I will not do it,' Tiaan said with a shudder.

Liett whirled, caught Tiaan's head in the claws of one hand, and squeezed until they broke the skin in five places. Tiaan dared not move. The lyrinx was strong enough to tear her face off. Liett held her for a minute, then Ryll cried 'Enough!' and Tiaan was released.

'Will you do it now?' Ryll asked, soft-voiced.

'No.'

Liett bared her teeth but Ryll simply plucked the amplimet from Tiaan's fingers and placed it on a high shelf. Taking her by the arm, he led her up to her room and locked her in.

Tiaan knew what to expect now, and perhaps because of that, withdrawal seemed to come on more strongly than ever. Or perhaps it was knowing that Ryll would never relent. Within twenty-four hours she was climbing the walls. By the following dawn she began screaming, which aroused the worst memory of all, the horrible night that had seen her banished to the breeding factory. When Ryll appeared she just gave in.

One touch of the amplimet and the withdrawal was gone. Within an hour she was at the bench, ready to do whatever he required. Tiaan blocked out the betrayal – she had to.

However, after hours of trying she laid the amplimet aside, unable to visualise the strange field here. Her normal way of seeing it did not work. 'I can't do it.'

Ryll scowled. 'Another attempt to delay us, artisan?'

'It's not like the field I'm used to,' she stammered, afraid of their fury.

'Try harder!'

She did, no more successfully, but that evening, fiddling with a piece of iron on the bench, Tiaan noticed that it had smaller particles clinging to it. She tried to pick it up and had to wrench it off the surface. It was a little magnet, and maybe the bench was a bigger one. *Perhaps the whole spire was!*

The room vanished and suddenly she saw it. She was standing inside an iron spire jutting up from the earth, its feet in fire, tip crusted with ice. She could image the heat flowing from one end to the other, radiating out in all directions before being swallowed by an ocean of frigid air.

Now Tiaan sensed a different, subtler force. The iron spire seemed to be made up of horizontal bands, oriented one way or another, out of which swept fields of force in elongated, intersecting loops. It was like ... Tiaan struggled to think of any comparison. Then she had it – an exercise Crafter Barkus had given her before she even began her prenticeship.

He'd had her stroke a piece of iron with a lodestone until it was magnetised and she could pick a nail with it. Later he had sprinkled iron filings on a piece of paper and moved the nail around underneath. The filings had formed curving patterns sweeping from one end of the magnet to the other.

The shape of the fields (for there were at least two here, unlike other nodes she had experience with) told her that the spire was an enormous magnet or collection of magnets. Tiaan had done other experiments with magnets, making other patterns. By moving a magnet inside a coil of wire she had made circular patterns around the wire. They had fascinated her so much that she fell behind in her work and had been reprimanded by Crafter Barkus. Tiaan had never gone back to magnets. There had been no time for toys at the manufactory.

What might a magnet as large as a mountain be able to do? What power it must have!

'I can see the fields,' she said.

Weeks went by, a time of the most exhausting mental labour. Day after day Tiaan spent on her stool, exploring the unusual paired fields, working out how to channel them safely, and then creating the aura in the cages. The work left her head throbbing at night, and sometimes it still ached when a hostile Liett hauled her from her bed in the morning. And every time, after using the amplimet, Tiaan dreamed the wildest crystal dreams about flesh-formed monsters.

They worked every day for all the waking hours. The lyrinx kept no holidays or feast days. Nor had they any concept of recreation, so far as she could tell. If they had a culture she saw no signs of it, apart from the wind music. The place was undecorated: no artworks or pottery, no furniture except of the most rudimentary kind. She knew the lyrinx could read and write, though she saw no books, scrolls or any other kind of document. But of course this place was a workshop and laboratory, dedicated to the war. Their homes, or nests, could be completely different. Moreover their language was incomprehensible, to say nothing of skin-speech. Their greatest poets and orators might have been reciting beside her and she would have known nothing about it. Alternatively, Ryll might have been telling the truth. Perhaps the lyrinx were a lost people, without even their own Histories.

Despite her efforts, the lyrinx did not seem to be making progress. Tiaan was glad of it. They were careful to hide the real purpose of their experiments from her, but the procession of bizarre, flesh-formed creatures that writhed and squealed and

433

expired on the bench was terrifying. She could not bear to think how the lyrinx would use them, if they succeeded.

Tiaan despised herself for collaborating with the enemy. As the work progressed she became filled with self-loathing. She rebelled many times, and each time they simply took away the amplimet. Each time the agony was greater.

The lyrinx became increasingly frustrated with their inability to understand the amplimet and the fields Tiaan could tap with it. For years their most talented mancers had been working with captured controllers, but to no effect. They simply could not use such devices.

Each day, after her other work was done, they interrogated her, trying to wrest the secret from her. They made Tiaan demonstrate her art from first principles, as if teaching the lowest prentice. They had spent weeks watching and studying her while she explored the fields below and around the spire. They monitored her with strange instruments, some half-mechanical and half-alive, like living versions of her controllers. Coeland suggested that she was deliberately thwarting them. Liett made veiled threats.

It made no difference. They understood how her devices worked, and the nature of the fields here. They could sense the raw power the spire was bathed in – that was why they had come here in the first place. They could visualise the fields with the captured controllers and with her amplimet. But they could not draw that power, no matter how hard they tried, or how cleverly. The ability simply was not in them.

I must be the rankest coward on Santhenar, Tiaan thought one night as she lay in bed, hands pressed to her throbbing temples. The day's work had been particularly gruelling. I deserve to be killed and eaten.

She felt strangely detached from her body, as if a crystal dream was coming. Or was it crystal fever? They had driven her so terribly hard lately. She drifted into a daze where the ache persisted and she was still aware of the room, but everything was subtly shifted.

Crack! Lines of fire lashed across her back and curled around her side, ending in blinding stings on her belly. *Crack!* More lashes, crossing the first.

An image, distant and out of focus: a man hanging suspended from an engraved dome. Another, across the room, hurling punishment stars at his unprotected body. Each star had a soft central core trailing many thread-like tentacles, like those of a jellyfish. And like a jellyfish they wrapped around, stinging and burning.

There was something about the prisoner – the tall, well-proportioned frame, the dark hair hanging like a mop over his face. Slowly she brought him into focus and her own pain faded, becoming no more than a silken cord across her back, a caress.

The man threw up his head in agony. His lips were drawn back from his teeth. He seemed to be staring right into her eyes, reproaching her for her oath-breaking. 'Faithless friend,' he sang out between the strikes. 'Why have you forsaken me?'

It was Minis, her love. He had raised his people's hopes and she had let him down. Tiaan came fully awake and the daydream disappeared. He was the reason she was still alive; only she could save him. It was her destiny, and once she did, the Aachim would change the balance. With their aid, humanity would be able to stand up to the lyrinx. She would no longer be a traitor. Tiaan would be the woman who had saved the world.

But first she must escape from Kalissin and make her way a hundred leagues across country to Tirthrax. That would not be easy. Tarralladell and Mirrilladell, scoured bare by ice sheets over thirty thousand years, were a mass of rivers, swamps and elongated lakes that ran south from the Great Mountains to the inland seas of Tallallamel and Milmillamel. There was no crossing this country from east to west, after the thaw. No roads or bridges went that way. All but local traffic moved north–south, by boat in the summer and by keel on the ice in winter, though winter was so cold that few people travelled at all. They huddled in their huts and prayed that the food would last until spring. How was she to cross such country alone?

The latch rattled. Leaping out of bed, Tiaan flung on her clothes. If she did not, Liett would haul her down to work naked.

Liett seemed particularly irritable today. Tiaan had her pants on but only one arm through her sleeve when she was dragged out the door. She felt foolish, stumbling behind the hurrying lyrinx, trying to dress one-handed.

In the work chamber, Liett thrust her across the room. 'Get to work! And see that you do better than yesterday, or today may be your last.'

That only made things worse and the day turned out as unproductive as all the previous ones. By nightfall Liett was trembling with frustration. Several times, looking up from her work, Tiaan noticed the lyrinx staring at her. The expression in her eyes was disturbing. Suddenly Liett sprang up, strode to the door and flicked the fingerlock. Tiaan wondered why.

Returning to her bench, the lyrinx began arranging her incubation jars. Tiaan put it out of mind and was concentrating on the field when Liett took her from behind and held her arm down flat. Using an implement like a leather worker's punch, Liett cut out a disc of skin and flesh, the size of her little fingernail, from the inside of Tiaan's left arm.

Such a small wound, but Tiaan slumped on her stool, feeling faint. Liett macerated the sample into particles too tiny to see and stirred it into a jar of yellow-tinged fluid, like broth. Air bubbled through the fluid. She spent the rest of the day there, concentrating hard while Tiaan trickled power to maintain the aura inside the metal bars. Liett changed the fluid several times.

A day later a glob of matter began to grow at the bottom of the jar. On the third day buds formed into two limbs, then four, then many, then back to four again. Its shape seemed not fixed; or was Liett's flesh-forming constantly changing it? Tiaan suspected that Liett had added other tissue to the jar when no one else was there. Once she noticed a fresh circular scab up in the lyrinx's armpit. Had she used her own tissue? If so, she had taken pains to conceal it. Perhaps that was forbidden.

After a week the creature began to grow rapidly, the limbs branching over and over again until it resembled a four-armed starfish, each arm terminating in a dozen smaller ones, like fingered, coiling tentacles.

In a fortnight, when the creature's body was the size of an egg and the limbs spread to six times that size, it began to show signs of coordination, if not intelligence. All the lyrinx in the spire came to see it, crowding into the room in small groups. There were hundreds of them. Gloom settled over her. She would never escape.

Tiaan rubbed her arm. The injury had been slow to heal and the neat circular scar still ached. Repelled, horrified and fascinated in turn, she could not keep away from the jar. The creature was unique, bizarre. Each of its extremities was different: some like fingers, others resembling claws or probes, bundles of feathers or threads as fine as silk. Some she could imagine a purpose for, others she could not. What did Liett have in mind for it?

The creature began to grow scaly plates all over its body. The plates thickened until the arms could no longer move. It lay on the floor of its jar for a day, whereupon Liett took it out and killed it with a single thrust from a carefully cleaned knife. As she did, pain sheared through Tiaan's head. It passed without after-effects, apart from uncomfortable feelings of empathy for the dead animal.

Liett dissected the corpse, made notes and reduced it to pulp for her next experiment. However, the next three attempts were failures; the creatures terminated within a few days.

Ryll was as busy with his own flesh-forming. His creations were all of a type – an elongated body, heavily armoured and spiked on the underside, long, armoured legs, a spiked club for a tail and a spiked, fanged, plate-armoured head. His experiments likewise were not going well. Tiaan often saw what she now recognised as stress-patterns on his skin: chevron shapes in blacks and reds.

Tiaan could not fathom why that particular form was so important to him, and Ryll would not say. He made his creatures over and again, using tissue samples of unknown source. Each time, when they reached the size of a fat mouse, Ryll collapsed from the strain. His creatures would keep growing for a day or two before falling down in a twitching, uncoordinated mass. Ryll would groan and bang his sensitive crest on the wall. There would be yet another conference with Coeland and other senior lyrinx, much shouting, yelling and violent skin-talk, then they would all go away and Ryll, as soon as he was able, returned to his work.

'I wonder . . .' Ryll said late one night, about a month after Liett had taken the sample from Tiaan's arm.

Tiaan looked up from the crystal. The work made her nauseous and all she wanted was to go to bed and shut out the world. It was hotter than ever down here; she could not adjust. For most of her life she had been cold. Now she yearned for it. She slept with her window open, whatever the weather. When not sleeping she stood at the window, staring across the lake to the smudges of snow-blanketed forest in the distance, and wondering if she would ever reach it. In the two and a half months she had been held here, there had been no chance to escape. She was not permitted to go anywhere unescorted and was always locked in at night.

'What?' Tiaan said, indifferent.

Ryll was staring at the many-armed creature growing in Liett's jar. It was still tiny – no bigger than a thumbnail.

He looked over his shoulder. The gesture seemed furtive. His colour changed to iron-greys and browns, a camouflage so brilliant that Tiaan could only see him when he moved. She did not think Ryll had any idea he'd done it. What was he up to?

Liett had gone to her chamber some time ago and would not be back until the morning. She began early; Ryll worked late, perhaps so that they needed to spend the least time in each other's presence.

Striding to the door, Ryll thrust a finger in the lock. It gave a gentle snick. Furtively he picked up Liett's jar and carried it to his bench. He fed his own creature, the size of Tiaan's thumb, a knockout pellet. It went still. In seconds Ryll had it out of the cage, made a careful incision from neck to tail, clamped the major blood vessels, scooped Liett's tiny creature from the jar, blew it dry then put it into the incision, with the body at the base of the skull and the tentacles trailing down the back.

With deft stitches he fixed the creature inside, rejoined the blood vessels, sutured the wound and spread a clear jelly over it. Tossing the needle on the bench, Ryll held his armoured creature in one hand and began flesh-forming. Tiaan's brain fizzed.

After an hour or so, the creature gave a single, feeble kick. A thread of purple ebbed out under the jelly, which had formed a clear skin. The creature kicked again and lay still.

Tiaan crept across to stand beside Ryll, who looked saggy today. 'Are you all right?' she said.

'The heat down here does not suit us. We are beings of the cold void.'

She had noticed how sluggishly he moved in the lower levels. 'It does not seem to bother Liett.'

'Liett doesn't have skin armour.' He turned back to the cage.

'Is the creature dead?' she whispered.

'Not yet!' A muscle twitched in his neck. 'But it's in shock. I should not have tried. It's too small.'

'Could you not start at an earlier stage, as with your own children in the void?'

'We don't know enough about other animals.'

They watched the creature for hours. It did not move, or even look to be breathing, though Ryll said it was still alive. Finally, when it was nearly dawn and the creature lay as limp as ever, Ryll rose.

'I must sleep, at least for an hour.'

'And I. Liett will be coming to drag me out in two.'

She dozed with her mind full of flesh-formed images and woke feeling hot, claustrophobic and not a little horrified that a part of her had gone into the creature. She was at the window, gulping down lungs of frigid air, when the bolt clicked.

Liett flung the door open. 'Come. I have had an idea. We must work swiftly. You will channel power for me and there can be no mistakes.'

Tiaan dragged herself down the ladders, wondering what would happen when Liett discovered what Ryll had done.

'What is the matter with you today?' Liett snapped. Tiaan had stalled halfway down, hanging from the ladder like a dead spider.

'I worked most of the night with Ryll.'

'Waste of time!' Liett gave her a playful buffet that crashed Tiaan into the wall.

Liett squeezed through the entrance, scowled at Ryll, who was frowning down at his creature, and headed for her bench. Tiaan's brain began to fizz. There was barely any colour in Ryll's skin, and no pattern, just a uniform dull grey. It must be taking all his Art to keep the creature alive.

'Where's my snizlet?' Liett held her jar up to the light. Ryll was too preoccupied to answer. 'What have you done with it?' she screamed.

He did not look up. She bounded across the room, lifted Tiaan by the shoulders and shook her. 'What has he done with my snizlet?'

Tiaan's head was nodding so hard she could not speak. She simply pointed to Ryll's armoured creature.

Liett dropped Tiaan and flung herself at Ryll. Her claws scored down his side, carving a gash between his skin plates. Setting down the cage, he whirled and lashed out.

Liett ducked out of the way. She was brave, but her soft skin made her almost as vulnerable as a human. She struck at him, drawing blood on his brow ridge. He crouched, preparing to spring. Tiaan covered her eyes.

'Stop!' roared a deep voice from the door.

The two froze in place. Coeland levered herself through the opening and stood up. Several more lyrinx followed.

'Well?' she said in a dangerous voice.

'He stole my snizlet!' said Liett. 'He took it without asking and put it in his rrhyzzik, there. And now it's dead!'

'Is this true?' Coeland asked coldly.

'It is true that I took it,' said Ryll, 'but it's not dead yet.'

'I demand satisfaction on his body!' shouted Liett. 'Just last

440

night I understood what I was doing wrong. Now I'll have to start again.'

'Do you make a pleading, Ryll?' Coeland asked.

'The answer is in both our work,' he answered. 'Rrhyzzik is well designed for the . . .' he glanced at Tiaan, 'the job, but it's a dumb creature; unbiddable. Her snizlet is a brilliant sensor and adaptor, though too weak to survive outside. Yet mate the two together, hers inside mine . . .'

'Never!' cried Liett. 'His rrhyzzik is as much a monstrosity as he is. It will never do . . .'

Something clacked in the cage. The creature pushed to its feet, swaying like a newborn calf. Its spined snout quested the air. It took a step forward, fell down, got up again, then took another wobbling step, and another. With each step it grew stronger.

The lyrinx gathered around, even Liett. In a minute it was practically gambolling. It did a running jump, flung four legs in the air at once, somersaulted and landed facing the other way. It pressed against the bars, staring at them, and there was undoubted intelligence in its eyes.

Ryll let out an ear-splitting whoop. 'We've done it!' he roared, lifting Liett high and twirling her around while she batted at him half-heartedly. She was laughing, though. He put her down again, giving her a great kiss on the bridge of her nose. 'Liett, your snizlet is the most *brilliant* work I've ever seen. Together we've done it!'

She rubbed furiously at her nose. He extended his arm to her. After a considerable hesitation, she clasped it, her hand about his biceps, his about hers.

Coeland grinned wide enough to have swallowed Tiaan's head, clasped arms with both of them, and turned to the entrance. 'Back to work! Grow it to size, Ryll, and you shall have your heart's desire.' She nodded to Liett. 'Perhaps you too, daughter, if you have worked out what it is. This is only the beginning.'

FORTY-FOUR

Ryll and Liett had solved one problem, but not the other. It was a killing strain to get their creatures to the size of a rat, but there the growth always stopped.

Tiaan was pleased about that. She did not like the look of the new creature, and the way it fed was absolutely terrifying. Once Ryll tossed in a live rat and after a few seconds of paralysed staring it tried to dart away. The flesh-formed creature was on it with a single bound and literally tore its head off. What would the creature be like if Ryll could grow it to full size? What *was* its full size?

There were several more crises in the following week. One day the creature began to race around in circles, snapping at its tail and convulsing as if it was trying to tie itself into a knot.

'Snizlet and rrhyzzik are trying to reject each other,' said Ryll.

'It's driving it insane,' said Liett, standing so close that her shoulder touched his. His broad hand lay on the shelf of her buttock. Their relationship had been transformed.

In the morning the animal lay on its side, panting. A line of sores had formed along the suture scar; red streaks radiated away from them. Tiaan could feel its pain as if it were her own. 'Put it out of its agony,' she begged. 'No thing should suffer so.'

'It's not going well, Ryll.' Liett slid her hand around his hip. 'What if we were to kill it, and build it anew?'

'The two haven't integrated yet.' Ryll slipped his own hand lower. Tiaan could not decide if she was fascinated or repelled by this public display. 'I think it would just make one, or the other.' He went to the cage. 'Tiaan, give me all the power you can. I'll try to force integration.'

'I don't like it.' Liett lay a soft-skinned hand on his arm. 'This risks burning insanity into its very makeup. Better to start again than create a creature we can't control.'

He looked deep into her eyes. 'Let's try first, shall we? If we fail we'll kill it and start afresh.' He pressed his hands around the cage but the field did not appear. 'Tiaan?'

She was still staring at the miserable creature. 'This is wrong. Let the poor thing die!'

'Make the aura!' he snarled.

'I won't help you any more.'

Ryll sprang across the room, furious in his wrath, and snatched the amplimet from her hand. One claw tore the skin of her palm and Tiaan felt an audible snap as her bond with the crystal was wrenched apart. It rocked her on her stool.

'No. This has gone far enough,' she whispered, staring at the bright beads welling up on her palm.

This time Tiaan was held in a large spherical chamber at the bottom of the spire. It had no window and was stiflingly hot. The room was empty but for a bracket at the ceiling. Ryll hung the amplimet there and locked the door.

She sat on the floor, which proved so unpleasantly warm that she had to get up at once. Her eyes were drawn to the amplimet, hanging four spans out of reach and utterly unattainable. Withdrawal struck her in the face. Tiaan let out a wail of despair and longing.

Twenty-six hours she spent in that room, pacing back and forth. There was nothing to sit on, nothing to lie on. If she stayed in the same place too long her feet hurt. She did not sleep; could not; it was sweltering, and down here the amplimet emitted a harsh glare that she could feel through the back of her head.

Several times Tiaan dozed on her feet but the agony never stopped. It would just get worse and worse and in the end she would break as she always had.

On the morning of the second day she gave in. Rapping on the door with her boot, she said to the lyrinx who opened it, 'I will do it. Take me to Ryll.'

The creature still panted on the floor of the cage. It looked thinner than before and so did Ryll, who had been working non-stop to keep it alive. Liett was not there; she had been called away to another project. Ryll often looked around as if to ask her something.

Tiaan climbed onto her stool and reached down for that source of power she had tapped before, the lines of force that surrounded and passed through the great magnets of the iron spire of Kalissin.

Over the past weeks she had gained some facility at drawing on that power, taking the barest trickle from it, though she was always aware that it was like filling a thimble from a waterfall. All around was power a billion times vaster than she could handle. One mistake and it would anthracise her.

'Hurry!' Ryll choked. 'It's failing.' He looked as if he was drying out inside. His skin had gone baggy.

She channelled power into the cometary iron strands, drip by drip. An aura sprang to life about the cage. Immediately Ryll looked less haggard.

They worked all evening, though Tiaan had no insight into what Ryll was doing. By midnight the red lines of inflammation were fading, the sores less swollen and scabbing over. They continued through dawn and the following day. Only when the sun was setting through a porthole did Ryll call a stop. The creature kicked once or twice then settled into sleep. The crisis appeared to be over.

Tiaan, after two nights without sleep, was so exhausted that she could not even take the helm off. She lay on the metal floor. It felt as if the channelling had worn parts of her away.

'Shall I carry you to your room?' Ryll said, bending down.

Pillowing her head on her arms, she snuggled down and closed her eyes. 'Perfectly comf . . .' Tiaan fell into sleep.

Moonrise over a boggy plain. The luminous light reflected brassily off a hundred thousand little ponds, some no bigger than a table-cloth. Rushes threaded their way between them.

Tiaan was sitting on a reedy mound, the sole vantage point in that dismal scape. It moved as she did, like a sodden, floating haystack. There was no track through the mire; no escape!

A movement caught her eye, some way off. The reflection of the moon on one pond had been eclipsed momentarily, as if something had disturbed the smooth plane of water. She stared at the spot for ages. The blink did not recur, but as Tiaan resumed her watch there came another flash to the left of the first, and a third to her right. She looked behind her but saw nothing. All was dark there.

Turning back, Tiaan saw that the ponds were winking every-where, the flashes of light and darkness getting closer. Whatever caused them was headed directly towards her.

The moon rose higher. A cool breeze made her shiver. Tiaan stood up, staring at the approaching streamlines. She caught the distant chuckling of agitated water, growing ever louder until it became a thrashing roar like the wind-driven paddle-wheels in the coastal fish ponds below Tiksi.

Then she saw it – an elongated shape diving into a pond not fifty paces from her mound. It thrashed across, thick legs moving like paddles and sending gouts of water high. The moonlight illuminated the translucent tips of spines. It resembled Ryll's creature, only grown monstrously large. An elongated head, an enormous mouth full of teeth, spiky sides and underneath, a spiked club for a tail. Worst of all was the glittering intelligence in its eyes.

Another creature left a trail across a nearby pond. They were everywhere, pounding toward the mound as if racing to get to her first.

She stood up on tiptoe. Now the dark behind her was cut by hundreds of phosphorescent trails. The moon reflected off bleached eyes and grey teeth. Tiaan whirled around and around. They were everywhere; thousands of them. She felt at her waist. No knife; no weapon at all.

The creature she had first seen was ahead of the others. It hurled itself into the pond next to her mound, sending up twin deluges. Mud and reeds were flung in the air. It was three times her size.

It reached the near side of the pond. The flat feet slipped on the wet stems of her mound. Claws snapped out, took hold, and it came out of the water in a rush. Its spiked snout gaped. It lunged.

Tiaan screamed and woke up. It was just a crystal-induced nightmare, to be expected after such overuse of the amplimet.

As Tiaan stood, she saw something fingered in a beam of moonlight from the window. It was Ryll's creature in its cage.

Come closer.

She spun around, thinking that someone had whispered behind her, though the sound had been unlike any lyrinx voice. The room was empty. Tiaan approached the cage. The creature pressed its snout through the bars. Its eyes were fixed on her.

Closer, closer!

Tiaan stared at the little beast, which was like the one in her dreams, only small. It looked . . . She did not know what, but deadly.

Hungry.

Recalling the fate of the rats it fed on, she reached for a strip of dried flesh in a basket and held it out, carefully. The creature watched her, unmoving. It was not looking at the meat. Its eyes were fixed on her fingers.

Hungry!

Tiaan moved closer, reaching out until the strip touched its snout. She felt mesmerised by the eyes; the call.

It sprang, hitting the bars so hard that the cage jerked forward. The jaws snapped just a breath away from her fingers. She leapt backwards with a squawk and the forgotten helm fell off. Instantly the whispering in her head stopped, the mesmerising power of its eyes faded. The creature, vicious though it was, was just a wild animal.

It had bent the bars. Tiaan put a heavier cage over the first, weighed it down with a block of metal and went out. A guard escorted her to her room, where she locked the door behind her.

Three times that night she woke in a lather and ran to the door, to check that it was still locked.

Tiaan told Ryll about the incident, though not about the impulses it had put into her head via the helm. She did not want him to know that – he might be even more pleased with his creation.

The following morning she woke with a streaming nose and a throat so sore that she was unable to eat. She was confined to bed; there was no possibility of working.

Three days later, when she returned to work, Ryll's creature had grown to twice its previous length. It had a body the size of a small house cat, longer and thinner legs, and segmented armour plating through which the spikes grew. A reinforced cage was required to contain it.

'It's going wonderfully well,' Ryll exulted as she took her place on the stool. 'Come see.'

She did not move.

'Come on, Tiaan.' He took her hand and pulled. Her reluctant feet dragged across the floor.

The creature fell into a crouch, its eyes fixed unblinkingly on her. It began to hiss. The flattened spines erected and the neck skin inflated into spiked rings.

She stopped dead. It was trying to get at her mind and it felt stronger now. Had she been wearing the helm, Tiaan was not sure she could have resisted it. *Hungry!* was a whisper inside her head.

Ryll urged her forward by the elbow. She allowed herself to be drawn closer. No harm could be done to her while he was here. As Tiaan took the last step the creature launched itself at the bars. The cage, which had no bottom, rocked and might have toppled had not Ryll slammed a fist on it. The creature twisted and flashed for the opening but the side came down, pinning it to the bench by the tip of one spine.

Pulling away, it flung itself from one side of the cage to the other, letting out ear-piercing squeals of rage and frustration. It attacked the bars with its teeth, breaking several, then just as suddenly sat on what passed for haunches, staring at Tiaan. The look in its eyes made her catch her breath.

'It's a wild thing!' Ryll scratched his cheek cheerfully.

She was backing away when the animal protruded a rolled blue tongue through warty lips and squirted something at her. The fluid struck her brow, eyebrow and left eyelid, and immediately began to sting and blister.

She cried out, vainly trying to wipe the clinging, noisome stuff away. Ryll bounded across the room and heaved half a bucket of water at her face. The next second she was hanging upside down, her ankle clutched in his hand, while he scooped water and washed the poison off.

In a few minutes it was gone, though where the venom had landed was covered in fluid-filled blisters and the hairs of her eyebrow were falling out. Ryll sent a guard to her room for Tiaan's pack. She changed her clothes, washed the contaminated ones and spread them on the warm floor to dry. They continued their work.

'I'm afraid of this creature,' she said to Ryll that evening. 'It *hates* living things.'

'The rrhyzzik and snizlet aren't completely integrated. They're fighting each other; that's why its behaviour is so odd.'

It's more than odd, she thought. It's an obscenity, and I helped to make it. 'What if . . . you can't fix it? What if it turns on you?'

'Me?' He laughed. 'That little thing! I'd kill it and start again. It will be easier next time.'

She said nothing. If only she had pretended to be stupid from the beginning, this could never have happened.

An hour later the creature collapsed and began to twitch. The twitching became an epileptic thrashing that grew more violent every second.

'What is it?' Tiaan whispered. The sight was unnerving.

'Something has gone wrong with its brain,' Ryll replied. 'I'm not sure I can fix it.' He seemed more uncertain than usual, not a reassuring sign. 'I don't understand what the problem is.'

'Then let it die!' She prayed that it would, swiftly.

His face and throat went black, then green, then white. Was it anguish, resignation or resolve? Even after all this time she could seldom read his skin-speech.

'It's so close,' he whispered. 'Seventy years we've worked on this project. I know I can do it! Surely one more day will be enough.' His forehead blushed red and he seemed to make up his mind. 'Make the aura again. I have an idea.'

They went back to work, Ryll flesh-shaping the creature's brain, working in ways she could never understand, while she poured power into the aura around the cage.

He began to look haggard and baggy again. 'I need more, Tiaan,' he said in a cracked whisper.

'I can't safely give you more.'

'Then do it unsafely! I'm nearly there. I can't stop now.' There was a reckless gleam in his eyes.

Her head was burning, a bad sign. 'I'm afraid.'

'I'll protect you. Do it!'

How could anyone protect her from what she was afraid of? There *was* no protection. Setting the helm more tightly on her head, Tiaan tuned the amplimet to the looping fields surrounding the spire.

There was a barrier beyond which she dared not cross. Tiaan could feel the energy there, unlimited amounts of it, a great, worldwide field intersecting with smaller fields surrounding the spire. How to draw from it without taking too much?

As she considered what to do, Ryll let out a chicken-like squawk and crashed to the floor, where he began to twitch. This turned into a violent, uncoordinated thrashing. Had he driven himself over the edge, or had the creature taken over his mind? Should she stop, or keep going? What if she was just feeding power to the animal? Surely Ryll could stand more than it could. But could she?

Sensing out a minor loop of the field, she tapped it and a flood of power surged into her. Too much. Her head felt boiling hot; she grew faint and had to hold herself up with her arms.

Then, ever so slowly, a block began to dissolve, like a

rock-salt door in the path of a flood. It softened, pinholed in the middle, and the current tore through it.

'Yes!' Ryll roared, kicked both legs in the air and lay still.

The creature screamed, the sound reminding Tiaan of a woman who had gone insane in the breeding factory. The little beast convulsed and tried to tear the spikes off its tail. Colours chased themselves across it.

Tiaan pulled off the helm. The flow of power ceased. She wobbled across to Ryll, thinking him dead. Strangely, that bothered her. They had been together for over three months, and in spite of everything, she liked him.

His lips had coloured an oily green, the rest of his skin fading to grey. He was breathing. She sat by him, wondering if she should run for help. He did not look unconscious; more like asleep. The creature lay on its back, legs spread like a dead cat, though it was also breathing.

Was this her chance? She staggered to the door. It was locked and her fingers weren't strong enough to work the fingerlock. She pounded on the door but it made little sound on the solid metal.

Tiaan went back to the bench. Ryll and the creature lay as before. There was nothing she could do. Taking up the globe, she saw that it was bent out of shape. Tiaan got out her toolkit and began to reconstruct it. The time passed quickly. It was good to be working with her hands again. She had not realised how much she'd missed that. When the job was done she lay on the floor and dozed.

It was early morning when she woke and went to check on Ryll. He opened his eyes, giving her a warped smile. 'You saved my life!' His voice was a cracked rasp.

'A life for a life,' she replied more boldly than she felt. 'I hope you remember that.'

'I will.'

He looked across at the cage. Lyrinx smiles were always disturbing but this one showed more tooth than most. 'I believe we've done it, Tiaan.'

She did not respond.

'The snizlet and rrhyzzik have melded into one.'

The backs of her hands prickled. 'I only did it to save you; and myself,' she muttered.

'Look at the little beast. I don't know what you did, but it's worked. It may even grow to full size.'

She prayed that it would not. He trudged to the cage, but had to prop himself up on the bench. The creature was up on its back legs, gripping the bars. Its snout was cocked to one side as if listening. It was bigger than before, and leaner.

'I'm going to call it *nylatl*,' said Ryll. Reaching for the meat bowl he dug a hole in a piece of meat with one claw, pressed in a pellet the size of a grain of wheat and tossed the meat through the bars.

The nylatl stared at the food, turned it over and over on the floor and sniffed it carefully. Only then did it bolt the morsel in a single gulp.

'What are you doing?' asked Tiaan, keeping well back.

He held up his hand, watching the nylatl intently. After taking two steps the legs on its left side collapsed. It fell down; its eyes closed. Ryll prodded it with a piece of metal. It did not move.

He whipped off the cage, punched six tiny circles of flesh from the back of the creature and popped them in a jar of fluid. Ryll dug ointment from a jar with his fingers but, reaching over to put it on the wounds, he stopped, looking shaky. Resting both forearms on the bench, he said, 'Ah, I ache all over.'

A sharp pain cleaved through Tiaan's head. She lost vision for a second and in that darkness smelled the nylatl, a hot odour like slightly-off meat.

Hurt!

As her vision came back, the nylatl kicked one leg, flipped upside down and sank its claws into Ryll's arm.

Hate!

Before he could grab the creature it shot into the air and landed on his head. The back claws dug into his neck, seeking the joins between his skin plates. The claws of its front legs carved furrows across Ryll's long brow, going for the eye-sockets.

Ryll flung an arm across his eyes. The other hand flashed back, trying to rip the nylatl off his head. One of its poisoned spines penetrated his palm. Roaring in agony, Ryll snatched his hand away. Clear venom dripped from the spine. He tried again but the fearsome mouth took a piece out of his hand at the base of the thumb.

Hungry!

She watched, open-mouthed. Ryll tried to prise the creature off with an iron bar. It dug its front claws into his brow ridges and the rear ones into his neck, pulling its segmented body down over his skull like a cap. Venom began to seep from the down-pointing spines. Already Ryll looked disoriented. Soon those spines would plunge into his skull and inject their poison. Ryll would be dead and it would start on her.

Brains! Ahhhh!

Perhaps it was a paralysing venom and the creature would tear Ryll's head open and eat the contents while he was still alive. She watched helplessly as the nylatl tightened its grip.

FORTY-FIVE

Tiaan ran to the locked door, screaming 'Help!' so hard that it hurt her throat. She pounded on the metal. There came no response. No sound could penetrate the thickness of iron. What could she do? It was whispering in her mind, the same thing over and over.

Hungry! Hungry! Hungry!

Ryll had managed, by reaching behind his head, to catch hold of the back of the creature where he could avoid the spines, though his arm was at such an awkward angle that he could not tear the nylatl off. He dared not use his other arm lest the beast gouge his eyes out.

The nylatl arched its back, pressing another spine into Ryll's hand. He clung on grimly but Tiaan could see he was weakening as the venom took effect.

She ran around, looking for any kind of weapon. There was not much in the room – the lyrinx used few tools. Grabbing one of the glass and wire cages, she darted behind Ryll, planning to whack the nylatl off. It was the bravest thing she had ever done. If it went for her it would claw her face off.

Tiaan lunged, swinging the cage with all her strength. The nylatl's head twisted around, the blue tongue aiming a squirt of venom at her eyes. She ducked and the cage smashed against Ryll's head. He grunted; the nylatl squealed.

The venom splatted on the top of her head, burning straight through her hair. She ran for the water barrel, plunged her head in and scrubbed frantically. Strands of hair floated on the surface.

Brains!

She spun around, water pouring down her face. The nylatl was staring at her. Its claws lifted and dug in like a cat on an armchair.

There was only one thing left to do, and it might well be worse than doing nothing. She crammed the helm on, grabbed the globe, oriented the long side of the amplimet so that it faced Ryll's head and strove with all her might for power.

Instantly the whispering in her mind grew to a mad shriek.

HUNGRY! BRAINS!

The nylatl's thoughts crashed around inside her skull like a blind bat, full of incoherent rage. The forced integration must have broken its mind, but its was a deadly cunning insanity. The nylatl wanted to gouge its way into Ryll's head and take over his body as its own had been invaded. It wanted to make her suffer too, as it had suffered in the integration. And it wanted to destroy and consume, as its own nature had been destroyed and consumed. It was full of malice.

The spire's magnetic lines of force whirled about her, but even as Tiaan drew power from the field she knew it could not work. That power, the kind that had been used to create the nylatl and make it grow, only fed the creature. She had to have something different, *stronger*. So strong that the beast would be completely overwhelmed. No choice but to use her fledgling geomancy again. This nylatl could not be allowed to live. If it could overcome a lyrinx so easily, what would it be capable of when it was fully grown?

Down her senses went, to that hollow beneath the base of the iron spire of Kalissin, from whence the magma pool had retreated ten thousand years ago. The domed roof rock formed a series of concentric cracks under the weight of the spire, though the iron froth was still welded to the rock it had penetrated in its molten rise.

To make the roof fall was far beyond her powers, or anyone's. It might remain in place for another hundred thousand years before gravity finally pulled it down. But just the fall of a fragment into that pool in the distant depths would provide enough energy for her purposes. It might release more than she could handle, and then she would die. Tiaan hesitated, but only for a second. If she did nothing they would both die.

Ryll groaned, breaking her concentration. He was on his back, kicking feebly. His head was covered in purple blood. The bent arm still strained but he was failing.

'Help!' she roared, but no one could hear.

Bat's claws scored through her brain, the nylatl trying to stop her. The pain was excruciating. Tiaan could barely see though it, with her strange, three-dimensional artisan's vision, to that source below the spire.

Her sight began to break up. Pinholes appeared in everything she looked at. They grew larger and through each she saw a nylatl's staring eye. It was, despite her efforts, getting at her mind.

Her geomantic strange-sight passed through half a league of solid rock, scanning across the surface of the dome, seeking a piece so precariously held that the gentlest of nudges would release it. She tried one, then another, but the meagre skills the Aachim had taught her were not enough. Tiaan began to panic. She had no idea what she was doing. It could not work.

Ryll let out a ghastly, quivering shriek. She had to succeed. There – a small column of rock was jointed all around in a perfect hexagon, and it was almost cracked through at the top. She used what power she could gather from the fields but could not budge it. *More!* She drew more. Her head seemed to be boiling like a kettle. She felt the rock crack, but it did not fall.

Tiaan lost focus. With the mad shrieking in her head, and Ryll's cries and thrashing before her, she could not visualise the source.

Her eyes sprang open. Ryll's hand lost its grip on the nylatl and fell smack against the floor. The creature dug in its claws. One spine had pierced his scalp and was going up and down, trying to penetrate his skull. The nylatl's skin was striped in brilliant reds, yellows and blacks, like a poisonous caterpillar. Ryll flashed in delirious, psychedelic colours.

She could not waste a second. Tiaan found that hexagonal column again and suddenly she knew how to use it. The Principle of Similarity, one of the vital principles used by artisans, was the perfect choice here, for the rock column had the same shape as the amplimet. Power cascaded from the field into the crystal and she hurled it at the crack.

It parted. Friction held the column for a moment, and then it fell. She drew power from its motion, just a trickle at first but increasing as it accelerated into the magma chamber.

The bead of light in her amplimet swelled. A focussed beam burst forth. She directed it onto the nylatl. It was not bright enough to hurt it. Not yet. The nylatl arched its back. Ryll kicked weakly. The beam slipped off the creature.

'Don't move, Ryll!' She hoped his hearing had not closed down. Her head felt eaten away inside. The nylatl began to struggle desperately.

In her mind's eye Tiaan could see the column falling as if she was watching it in slow motion. It accelerated toward that glowing pool of magma.

Her head felt as hot as that magma; white heat licked down her backbone; every nerve fibre in her body was ablaze. Her senses were shutting down one by one. She could no longer feel her feet on the floor. The hot carrion smell of the nylatl vanished. Ryll's agonised wails cut off. The shrieking chuckle of the creature faded away.

Her sight began to break up at the edges; her eyes felt full of pinpricks. Tiaan clung grimly to sight; she must be able to see to aim. The last she saw, as her vision was going completely, was the nylatl arching up on Ryll's head, preparing to hurl itself at the real enemy – her!

The black column plunged into the pool, giving up its energy in a burst that blacked Tiaan out. She did not see the brilliant purple light that burst, fan-like, from the amplimet. She tracked the creature's leap through the field. Just the edge of the fan caught the nylatl, burning the ends off its spines and heating its skin to blister point. Its overheated muscles spasmed, hurling it against the wall so hard that it was knocked senseless.

She did not see the central pulse heat the wall to white-hot, until the metal ran down and puddled on the sloping floor. With an explosion of sparks the light burst through, carving a ragged hole to the outside. Tiaan saw and felt nothing. She lay senseless. The amplimet went out.

There were shouts outside, the lock was forced and Liett scrabbled through the entrance, bent low, followed by Coeland. They stared at the destruction. A red pool of iron, large enough to fill a number of wheelbarrows, was congealing on the floor. Ash and cinders lay everywhere. The room was as hot as a sauna. Ryll crouched in a groaning, lacerated heap.

'What happened?' Liett shouted.

One of Ryll's arms twitched. Liett lifted his battered head onto her knee, wiping blood out of his eyes. She stroked his dull crest. He rolled his head and his eyes lit on the nylatl, lying against the wall. It was covered in pus-coloured blisters. Smoke curled up from several of the spines. Its skin was a bilious yellow. It looked dead.

'It tried to kill me, Liett,' Ryll gasped. 'Tiaan twice saved me. Is she . . .?'

Coeland bent over her. 'She lives.'

Ryll's eyes widened in terror. 'The nylatl moved. *Kill it!*'

The creature shot past them, hurtled through the doorway and disappeared.

'Sound the alarm!' Ryll choked. 'Find it, and destroy it!'

Coeland and Liett went after the nylatl. Ryll forced himself to his feet, glancing at Tiaan, who lay as before. He eyed the hole in the wall, saluted Tiaan with a shaky hand and went out. The door slammed. The lock clicked.

Tiaan felt her senses coming back in the same order as they had disappeared. She tasted blood from a bitten tongue. Her scalp throbbed. She smelt lyrinx blood and carrion. And something else – fresh air on her face. Cold air!

The chance had come – the only one she'd get. She did not move as the lyrinx checked her, nor even as the nylatl got away and the two went after it. Only after Ryll had gone, locking the door behind him, did she climb to her feet.

The smell of freedom made her eyes water, or maybe it was the fumes. She opened her eyes and saw nothing. Tiaan almost panicked, then the room brightened as if a lantern had been turned up and her sight was back.

There was a gaping hole in the wall, large enough to get through. She put her head out. The metal was still hot but cooling rapidly. The spire, clotted here and there with rock, was steep, though not so steep that she could not climb down.

She had to take the chance even if she was caught within minutes. Tiaan stuffed her devices into her pack and threw it over her shoulder. A bare blade lay on the bench, the one Ryll had used as a scalpel. She took that too. The amplimet was on the floor. Tiaan pressed it to her lips, gave thanks for the miracle and packed it away. Finally she put a finger in a clot of Ryll's blood and wrote crudely on the wall, 'Two lives! My debt is paid!'

She doubted that it would stop the lyrinx from coming after her, but Tiaan wanted it to be on the record. If she was captured she would fight them to the death. Better that than be forced to collaborate again, even for Minis.

Laying a stool across the hot aperture, she crawled out and began to pick her way down. Tiaan felt hot and cold and shivery, an inevitable result of so abusing her talent. Still, she could walk, and climb, and defend herself if she had to.

It was further than it looked, and steeper. And much, much colder. After months inside the unnatural warmth of Kalissin, Tiaan was quite unused to the winter cold. Yet even the outside of Kalissin was considerably warmer than the rest of Faralladell. It would be perishing on the other side of the lake. Out of sight of the aperture, she put on her mountain clothing.

She hoped they had not yet caught the nylatl. With luck, not that she'd had much of that lately, it might be an hour or two before they discovered she was gone. Tiaan did not build up her hopes. The chance of getting away was remote.

She tried not to think of the nylatl escaping. Tiaan could still see the look in its eyes as it prepared to abandon Ryll and leap at her. She would have no chance against it, if it got out.

Not far to the bottom now. There was little likelihood of being seen from inside, for the windows were small and it was easy to keep away from them. Tiaan squinted across the lake but the mist-wreathed water blurred into the snowy shores beyond. There was no colour in this landscape. It might have been two leagues across, or five.

It was approaching noon by the time she made it to the bottom of the spire, which rose out of a collar of angular rubble clothed in dense broad-leaved trees. They looked quite out of place here.

The ground was warm – Tiaan could feel it through the soles of her boots. The air was too, though only near the ground. The wind blowing off the lake felt dank.

She negotiated her way through shoulder-high ferns. Cushiony mosses lay underfoot and the forest had a moist organic reek she had never smelt before, though she associated it with the warm forests of the north. It was not far down to the water. When she reached it Tiaan looked back.

The sun's slanting rays passed between the cloud layers to paint the dark spire in reds and browns. Halfway up she saw her ragged escape hole. There was no sign of pursuit. Perhaps Ryll, honourable creature that he was, considered the debt repaid. Had he given her this chance?

She turned away to cast along the shore for a boat. Tiaan felt sure there must be boats, for the diet in Kalissin normally consisted of fish, frequently fresh. She *had* to find a boat; the island was too small to hide on. She hurried along the edge of the forest, next to the strand. Even a log would do.

The sun emitted a gloomy, umbrous light that made the lake seem blood-brown. It was, Tiaan thought, the kind of light the afternoon sun would make setting through the reek and fume of a burnt city.

Her calves were aching. She'd lost fitness in Kalissin. Perhaps the lyrinx used lines, or nets, or even, unlikely as it seemed, scooped fish up from the air as a pelican did. She smiled. They would surely not waste the Secret Art that way.

Standing on the shore, she contemplated the sullen waters. Tiaan could swim, though she had not since childhood. She put one finger in the water. It was cold, but not freezing. She figured she could swim as far as she could see – about a hundred spans.

Walking on, she came to a path. Tiaan followed it up through the forest, peering into the dim undergrowth on either side. No boat. She crept along the upper edge of the forest and down the next path to the water again. No boat. What was she going to do?

As she continued along the shore, something small and dark emerged from an open porthole at the very top of the spire and crept into the shadow. The nylatl had been hurt badly by Tiaan's blast and the impact with the wall. Muscles had been torn, armour broken. Its skin was weeping, the spines burnt to dribbling stumps and one rear limb dragged. The nylatl had an overpowering urge to find a dark space and hibernate for a month, while its body repaired itself.

It could not hide here. Even if it burrowed into the warm earth its enemies would find it. Besides, it had to feed first. It had to find the creature that had so damaged it, and the terrible crystal. It sniffed the air and caught a scent. The nylatl began the painful climb down.

Hungry!

FORTY-SIX

Tiaan started on a piece of dried fish left over from the previous day, that being the only food she had. It softened in her mouth into flakes with a salty, heavily smoked flavour.

Something whooped in the trees on her right – she hoped it was a bird. Wavelets lapped on the shore; dull, oily surges. There was a smell of rotting vegetation. The overcast seemed to have grown more dense and banners of fog now drifted on the lake.

The strong flavour was not pleasant. Tiaan packed away the fish, drank a few mouthfuls of lake water and kept going. Not far along she saw a lyrinx print in damp sand. Whoever made it had been coming from the forest. Following the marks back, she found a faint path.

Tiaan traced it up through the forest, which was unnaturally luxuriant and hard to see in. After many false turns she crossed over a gully and found, at the top of a gentle slope, a beaten track that led toward the spire. From the track they had taken various ways down to the water.

She followed each way one by one, searching in the undergrowth on either side, but without success. About to head down another trail, Tiaan realised that she had been looking in the wrong place. They would keep the boat, or boats, up where the path first branched. Of course they would not leave it on the shore, where a gale might damage it.

The round shape to her right was not a boulder – there were no round boulders here. It turned out to be a circular boat made of leather, if boat it could be called at all. It was exactly like a high-sided bowl, the leather stretched drum-tight over a wooden frame. Something hung down inside, like a soft leather curtain with a drawstring. The craft had a floor of woven cane.

It turned out to be manageably light. A paddle stood against a tree, along with a rolled net. Tiaan tossed both into the boat and began to drag it down the path. It caught on a snag. Afraid of tearing it, she took everything out, lifted the boat above her head and staggered to the water.

By the time she got there Tiaan could not go another step. She put the boat at the edge, dropped her pack in and squatted down, panting. Somewhere above came a snap, like a door closing. Tiaan sprinted back for the paddle. The boat was useless without it.

'Snggrylkk!' The cry came from the forest.

A similar cry answered to her left. The lyrinx were out! Grabbing the paddle and the net, she ran. As she reached the beach Tiaan saw a lyrinx pounding around the shore. Another was thudding down the path.

No time to think, no chance of defending herself. Hurling in paddle and net, she ran into the water pushing the boat. It was so light that it skated across the surface. In thigh-deep water she tried to jump inside but bounced off, pushing the boat further out. Tiaan tried again, this time going in head first and striking her cheek on the circular blade of the paddle. The boat tilted right over. She yelped, thinking it was going to capsize, but it righted itself and rolled nearly as far the other way.

Tiaan had never been in a boat before and was not impressed by this one. As she stood up it tried to roll over. Throwing her weight the other way, she managed to keep it upright and, balancing precariously, looked back. Three lyrinx stood at the shore.

They seemed reluctant, then two pushed forward a third, a tall female. They were afraid of the water and poor swimmers, Ryll had said. She hoped they were not fliers. Tiaan reached down with the paddle. The water was about chest-deep on her; only waist-deep for them. Not deep enough.

Digging the paddle into the water, she gave a mighty heave. The boat simply revolved in place. She tried paddling the other way; it merely changed the direction of rotation. Wretched craft!

The lyrinx was getting closer. Probing for the lake bed, Tiaan thrust hard and the boat moved away. The lyrinx pushed forward gingerly, letting out a mewling cry as the water came over her hips. She looked back at her fellows, who urged her on with shouts and hand gestures. Tiaan recognised her now. It was Wyrkoe, who had been appointed to defend Ryll that first day in the spire.

Wyrkoe was only a few spans away, within springing distance had she been on land. She seemed to be finding courage. Her chest inflated, the crest stood up and her skin changed to an iridescent red. Tiaan watched, paddle upraised. The boat slowly drifted.

The lyrinx sprang but fell short and the water went over her head. She came up again, making an awful grating squeal. Her eyes were wide, her mouth agape.

The boat had stopped moving. Wyrkoe was little more than a paddle length away. Two steps and she could tear the boat open. She rubbed water out of her eyes and took a deep breath. Tiaan dropped the paddle and, as Wyrkoe leapt, threw the net over her.

The lyrinx slipped, thrashed her arms and became tangled in the net. Again she went under and took a long time to come up. She rose just above the water, striking helplessly at the meshes, only to slip below.

The look of terror on Wyrkoe's face was awful. If Tiaan could have taken back that cast of the net she would have. Knowing that she had just killed someone almost as human as herself, she poled away.

The other lyrinx splashed out. Tiaan managed to maintain a wavering line into deeper water, where a breeze caught the boat and drifted it south. Safe for the moment, she watched the pair retrieve Wyrkoe and drag her back to shore, where they disentangled her from the net. Wyrkoe did not move. She must have drowned. Tiaan could not come to terms with it.

Shivering in the breeze, she stared at the dark shapes on the shore, allowing the wind to drift her where it would.

An hour later she was squatting loosely with the drawstring fastened about her neck, not exactly warm but protected from the worst of the elements. The boat drifted in and out of banks of mist. The spire of Kalissin had long since disappeared. The snowy shores of the other side of the lake were equally invisible and unknown. For all she knew, Tiaan could have been drifting back toward the island.

She was gnawing on another piece of her dried fish when something cast a fleeting shadow and a lyrinx came plummeting out of the sun. All she could see was its outline against the blinding light. Tiaan scrabbled with the drawstring, which knotted up, trapping her inside. The lyrinx flattened out into a swooping glide, the claws of its hind legs extended to snatch her from the water. Unable to get the knot undone, all Tiaan could do was watch.

At the last instant she threw her weight to one side. The boat rolled, she felt the wind as the creature went by, then Tiaan's head hit the water and the boat kept rolling until it was upside down. Her weight pulled down the leather collar, hanging her head-down at the bottom of a cone. Water began to trickle in around the drawstring, which had drawn tight about her neck.

Tiaan gasped and a mouthful of water was forced up her throat. She heaved sideways. The boat rolled, though not enough – her weight, hanging low, gave the craft the centre of gravity it had previously lacked.

Though Tiaan jerked again and again, it was no use. No matter what she did she could not right the vessel. She simply was not heavy or strong enough. If she did not choke she was going to drown.

As her lungs began to heave and the water pushed up through her sinuses, Tiaan was lifted, boat and all, into the air. The lake rushed past; her head fizzed. The lyrinx was using the

Secret Art as it had never used it before, to lift the boat and her on its inadequate wings.

Tearing at the strings, Tiaan gave a last convulsive spasm, like a fish trying to hurl itself off the hook. The boat slipped free, revolved in the air and struck the water hard. She caught another breath as it rolled, but this time Tiaan used her weight to keep it rolling. It came upright, she managed to balance it the other way and her fingers, which had found the blade in her pack, hacked the cord from around her neck.

Tiaan clung to the side of the boat. The lyrinx was wobbling through the air not far away. Clearly it had nothing like the strength of Besant. Its wings hammered, slowly climbing as it came around for another attempt. She recognised this lyrinx too – a small, slight thing that had stood guard outside her door in the early days. It had treated her kindly enough. She did not recall its name.

Putting the knife in her belt, Tiaan took up the paddle and prepared to fend her opponent off. It took a long time for the lyrinx to beat its weight to altitude. It took no time at all to hurtle down, in a steep dive with its wings folded back. The lyrinx flattened out, screaming low across the water at her.

She lifted the paddle over her shoulder then swung it hard as the creature approached. It dipped its wings left and right, the blow missed and the claws went through her hair. Screeching something she did not understand, it turned and, without climbing, headed straight back.

This time Tiaan held the paddle in front, blade outstretched. The lyrinx thrashed its wings, struggling to maintain height. It was going slowly now and must be tiring. It came at her, mouth open, claws extended. At the last instant she thrust out the length of the paddle. She went right through its guard, striking it on the chin. The paddle was torn from her hand. The lyrinx tumbled, flapped furiously, and, as the boat tipped, wheeled through the air. One wing struck the water and it was going too slowly to recover.

It went head first into the lake, making a mighty splash. Tiaan struggled to stop the craft from capsizing. As she hung on the rim, the boat rocking wildly, the lyrinx's head broke the surface. It tried to get on top of the water but was too heavy. Its terrified eyes rolled, the limbs churned helplessly, then its weight pulled it under again. Bubbles marked its disappearance.

Tiaan looked around for the paddle, which was floating a few spans away. It might as well have been on the dark face of the moon, for there was no way of retrieving it. She dared not reach down as far as the water. If she went in, Tiaan knew she would no more come out than the lyrinx.

No wonder they were afraid of the water. The massive bones and muscles, the armoured skin that made them such a terror on land, the great wings, all were deadly encumbrances in the water. The creatures were simply too dense. If they could swim at all, it would only be feebly. A fatal weakness in this land, half lake and the rest river and bog. All the more marvel that Ryll had got her out from under the ice that day.

She pulled her hat down over her eyes, her eyes closed and Tiaan slept the sleep of exhaustion. The wind carried her south, rocking like a cradle on the water.

Near sunset another lyrinx, with practically transparent wings, began to circle high above. It stayed well up. The water meant certain death this far from land, even for such a lightly built, unarmoured lyrinx as Liett.

But Liett was strong in the Secret Art, one of the best fliers of all. She would watch, wait and report back. When Tiaan found land in a day or two, she would be easily followed. The snow blanketing Tarralladell would make it difficult for her to move, and impossible to travel without leaving tracks. The hunt had been called off. The lyrinx had learned what they could from her. They now wanted to find out where she was taking her marvellous crystal. They suspected a secret city in the mountains, a place it would be worth almost any sacrifice to learn about.

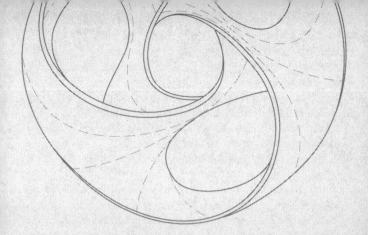

PART FIVE

GEOMANCER

FORTY-SEVEN

The journey back to the manufactory was a nightmare Nish thought was never going to end. There was no way to bury the bodies in the frozen ground, and no fuel to burn them. All they could do was lay them out side by side, pile ice blocks over the top, bow their heads and think that if they'd done this or that it might have turned out differently.

After loading the injured into the clanker, they took the controllers from the remaining two and set out for the far side of the plateau where the lifting frames were hidden. The other operators being dead, there was no way to bring their clankers back. At the cliff they unloaded the injured, preparing to send them down on stretchers to whatever shelter could be found below. There was none up here – the gale was unceasing.

Nish had never worked so hard, erecting the frames and arrays of pulleys, roping the clanker, tying on a boulder at the base of the cliff to serve as a counterbalance. The only able-bodied people were himself, Simmo and his shooter Rahnd, Tuniz and Fyn-Mah. Irisis, with her broken leg, could not help though she had remained up top. Rustina could use only one hand. Ky-Ara, though overcome by inconsolable grief at the loss of his clanker, could at least hold a rope. Nish's father was delirious and had to be sedated with nigah extract. Ullii was useless.

It was not enough. There were simply too few people to do

all the work, for a minimum of six were required to swing the clanker out over the cliff, and another four on the rope that would brake its descent. They had to make do with four and two, and add extra pulleys so they could lift the weight at all.

'Ready?' called Tuniz.

'Yes!' Nish held the braking rope taut. Ky-Ara stood behind him, hanging on listlessly.

'Lift!' Her team hauled on their rope.

Nish thought the heavily laden clanker was not going to move at all. The rope went taut and the four strained until their joints cracked. Finally it lifted, ever so slowly.

'Hold!' yelled Tuniz. Tying the end of the rope around a rock, she ran to swing the arm out. It did not budge. She threw her weight against it, the arm freed suddenly and the artificer almost went over. The clanker dropped, pulling the team off their feet. The rock tore out of the ground and the machine fell sharply, for Ky-Ara had let go of the braking rope. Nish could not hold the weight. The rope scorched through his hands and he had to let go.

The clanker hit the cliff, rotated and crashed on its other side, buckling the armour plates. Simmo gave a cry of anguish. Nish thought the machine was going to fall all the way, but after a few jerks the counterweight held it.

'Useless clown!' Nish roared at Ky-Ara. 'Why did you let go?'

Ky-Ara just stared vacantly at him.

Now they encountered another problem – the counterweight was heavier than the clanker. That had not mattered on the way up, but they would have to add weight to the machine for it to descend.

'Perhaps if one of us were to go on the shooter's seat,' said Fyn-Mah.

'No!' Tuniz said sharply. 'If it falls we've lost another person and we'll never get it down.'

They manoeuvred a small boulder onto the seat. Nish felt the tug immediately and began to pay the rope out. The clanker went down, swinging in the violent updraft and crashing repeatedly into the cliff. Every blow, every impact that tore free another leaf of its armour, caused Simmo to wail in torment.

'Slow it down!' he screamed, in tears.

Nish tried his best but the rope hissed through his fingers, burning welts across his palm. 'Ky-Ara!' he screamed. 'Hold the damn thing! Ky-Ara?'

Ky-Ara had dropped his end and wandered off. Again Nish was forced to let go. The wildly swinging clanker crashed into the ascending boulder. Both stopped, revolving around each other, and a section of armour fell off.

'I can't hold the brake rope by myself!' Nish said furiously. 'It needs at least three. What's the matter with you, Ky-Ara?'

The operator gave him a bland stare. Fyn-Mah and Tuniz came running and hauled on the clanker's rope. Nothing happened. The cables were twisted around the bent struts and protruding leaves of armour. No matter how hard they pulled they could not free them.

'Someone will have to go down,' said Rustina.

'Be a harder job than it looks!' Tuniz stared at the mess, rubbing a white spot on her nose. 'Especially in this wind. Any volunteers?'

'I'll go,' said Nish, 'if no one else can.' He did not want to, in fact doubted that he could do anything useful, but volunteering was better than being ordered. He had to redeem himself, if that was possible after the last disastrous week.

'Well, *you* can't go, Tuniz,' said Rustina. 'You're the senior artificer. But I suppose we can afford to lose *him*.'

'I'll go,' said Simmo, pushing past Nish. 'It's my clanker and my right.' His eyes were fever bright.

'I don't know,' said Rustina. 'What do you think, querist?'

'We can't afford to lose an operator either,' said Fyn-Mah, 'though Ky-Ara is getting better. But could he even operate this clanker?'

'He could, if he put his own controller in place of mine,' said Simmo, hopping from one foot to the other. He took hold of Fyn-Mah's arm. 'Please. This machine is my life. Besides, I may have to operate it to get free. No one else can.'

'Oh, very well,' said Rustina. 'You have no further objections, Fyn-Mah?'

'Get it done!'

Ky-Ara suddenly looked radiant and Nish wondered why. Simmo went down a rope, landing gently on the shooter's platform. The updraft kept tugging the machine away from the cliff and the weight of the boulder slamming it back.

'He'd better hurry,' said Tuniz, 'or the clanker will be a pile of scrap.'

Simmo wept as he inspected the damage. He tried to untangle the ropes but there was so much weight on them that it proved impossible. He tried to untwist them by rotating the clanker out past the boulder. The pressure of the wind would not allow it.

'What's he doing now?' Nish wondered aloud.

Simmo had gone inside and was sitting in his seat. The clanker's legs moved back and forth, the front pair scratching against the counterweight.

'Smart idea,' said Tuniz, walking backwards along the cliff edge with her rope. 'He's trying to spin the counterweight around the clanker. Take hold of the braking ropes, just in case.'

They did so and braced themselves. The clanker's metal feet screeched on the stone and it rotated the right way, a full turn. 'Oh, brilliant work!' exclaimed the querist. 'Twice more and he'll have it.'

Simmo tried again. This time it took quite a few attempts but finally the counterweight swung another turn. The legs thrashed, ground against the slowly rotating boulder and caught on something.

'No! Back off!' Tuniz yelled. 'Ky-Ara, you can free it. Pull hard, *that way*!'

'What's the matter?' called Fyn-Mah.

'The counterweight rope's caught around one leg. Stop or you'll break it!' she roared with all her might. 'Pull hard, Ky-Ara, that way!'

Simmo did not hear and Ky-Ara just let go of his rope. The legs jerked, the rope snapped and the counterweight dropped out of its rope cage. They watched in horror as the clanker fell, slowly at first, faster as it ripped the twisted ropes apart. The broken end whipped up, lashing about before it went through the pulley.

The clanker rolled over in the air and landed upside down on one of the boulders, splitting open down the middle. Armour and leg parts went flying in all directions. The pair of iron fly-wheels spun across the snow, out of sight. The smash came echoing up. Silence fell.

Irisis hopped to the edge on her crutches, then shook her head. Nish caught a faint smile on Ky-Ara's face, but when he checked again the operator had composed himself.

They looked at one another. 'Simmo's dead, of course,' said Fyn-Mah.

'The impact would have broken every bone in his body,' Tuniz replied. 'Now what do we do?'

'We ski back to the ice houses,' Fyn-Mah ground out. 'We put Ky-Ara's controller into one of the clankers and he brings it back. And this time we work out how to get the damn thing down without breaking it!' Her voice was as bleak as ice. No doubt she was wondering how to explain yet another disaster on this catastrophically failed hunt.

Nish and Irisis exchanged glances. 'I'd be keeping a close watch on our operator if I were you,' she said quietly. 'Ky-Ara did that deliberately.'

'Yes,' said Nish. 'He knew he'd never be given another clanker.' That reminded Nish of his own part in the affair. Had he not pressured Ky-Ara, the clanker would not have been lost, nor Tiaan, nor her crystal. And back at the manufactory, at the enquiry into the failed expedition, his, Nish's, folly would be revealed. What then? He was doomed.

It took two days to get the other clanker down and there were many times when Nish thought it was going to end up in the same condition as Simmo's. The weather stayed unchanged, bitterly cold with gale-force winds. Nish had frostbite on the tip of his nose, and the querist in her fingertips, by the time they untied the machine at the bottom of the cliff.

They climbed in but it refused to go, for the oil had set hard and in the blizzard that followed they could not even see who they were standing next to. Fortunately there was dry scrub in the ravines cutting into the plateau. They made a fire there, a roaring blaze under an overhang, or they would not have survived.

Irisis had not mentioned the lost crystal again. She was recovering well, hobbling about on her crutches, though she would not walk unaided for at least six weeks. However, she suffered her disability without complaint and was the most cheerful of the crew except for Ky-Ara, who was in ecstasies of bliss at having a clanker again. He had quite recovered, apart from occasional headaches and memory loss. There were times when he had to ask the names of the people around him. He often asked what had happened to Simmo.

Ullii had retreated into herself since the attack. The horrors of the battle at the ice house, or perhaps the flesh-forming, had rewoken some primal fear in her. She spent the days with mask on and earplugs in, and often a black silk bag over her head. Nish did not try to bring her out. He no longer had the strength. He asked her several times a day if she could see Tiaan. The answer was always no.

The greatest worry was Jal-Nish. The perquisitor's shoulder and chest were already healing but his face had not. The rents were hideous, weeping wounds, so ghastly that no one could bear to look at him, least of all his son. Worse, Jal-Nish had caught a brain fever that made him rant, curse and attack whoever came near. Twice, after taking food to his father, Nish had to have the iron fingers prised from his throat. The perquisitor was surprisingly strong, considering the butchery that had been done on his shoulder.

Irisis was his main target. Sometimes Jal-Nish cursed her for hours without stopping, in a gurgling, pus-sodden voice. He blamed her for seducing his idiot son, for what she had done to Tiaan, but most of all for saving his life instead of letting him die.

Irisis seemed unaffected by the abuse. She took her turn changing his dressings until the day the weather turned and they were about to head for home. She limped up, carrying a mug of hot broth for Jal-Nish. He threw it in her face, knocked her off her crutches, and was about to grind his boot into her throat when Nish and Ky-Ara dragged him off.

'Slutting bitch!' Jal-Nish screamed. 'You're a liar and a fraud, Irisis. I'll see you in the breeding factory when I get back. You'll never be an artisan again.

He ranted and cursed, and kept it up for an hour until Ky-Ara, the only one able to get on with him, took him tea doped with nigah syrup. After that they kept him sedated twenty-four hours a day and his good arm was bound to his side.

Three weeks had passed since the battle at the ice houses, before they came in sight of the manufactory, and such labouring days they were in the bitterness of the mountain winter that many times Nish thought they would not get back at all. No one travelled up here at this time of year. Had the clanker not been so well built they would all have perished.

Finally they found their way back over the mountain through which the mine tunnels were delved and looked down to see the grey bulk of the manufactory on the other side of the valley. They had been gone for more than a month.

Irisis levered herself out of the back of the clanker. As Nish handed her the crutches there were tears in his eyes. Everyone stared down at the manufactory. The only one not glad to see it was Ky-Ara. He looked agitated, and though it was as cold as ever he was sweating and casting anxious glances at the querist.

'Should not the furnace chimneys be smoking?' Fyn-Mah said, coming up between them.

'They must have gotten slack while the overseer's been away,' Nish replied lightly.

Fyn-Mah held a spyglass to her left eye. It moved slowly across the landscape, then the hand holding it fell to her side. 'There's not a chimney smoking anywhere. Not at the manufactory, the galleys, the laundries or dormitories, or even down at the mining village.' Her voice cracked. Nish caught her eye and her self-control failed. 'The lyrinx have come!' Fyn-Mah looked as if she was going to cry. 'All those children.'

'Damned hypocrite!' Irisis muttered.

'Dangerous ground, artisan,' said Fyn-Mah glacially.

Irisis yawned in her face. She did not seem to worry. 'What

do you care for the children? I don't see any evidence of you doing your duty.'

Fyn-Mah crushed one fist into another, then pulled the tall woman to one side.

'How dare you lecture me on duty, after the crimes you've committed?'

'There is no bigger crime than preventing conception.' Irisis quoted one of the many regulations that governed their lives.

Fyn-Mah went so cold that Nish, watching from some distance away, could scarcely bear to look.

'I'm barren!' she hissed. 'I've been to eleven healers and none can do anything.' She pressed her palms against her eyes. 'All I ever wanted was children, and to be mocked by you . . . you . . .' To Nish's horror, she burst into tears.

Irisis was struck dumb. It was all perfectly clear now: the iron self-control, the impression that she was keeping the whole world at bay. And yet, she recalled, when the manufactory was attacked that first time, the querist's first thought had been for the children.

'I'm sorry,' said Irisis.

Fyn-Mah did not react.

'I am truly sorry,' Irisis repeated. 'How you must despise a cheat and liar like me.'

'I don't despise you,' said Fyn-Mah. 'I pity you, for you have everything and yet it's worth nothing.'

Irisis might have done a lot of things, but in one of those rare impulses that turned everything upside down, she threw her arms around the querist and would not let go. After a while the smaller woman stopped struggling and buried her face in the artisan's coat.

'We'd better go carefully,' said Rustina, 'and be prepared for anything.'

They gathered stones for the catapult, storing them in the metal basket on top. Tuniz sat in the shooter's seat. Nish climbed up beside her, armed with a spear and his short sword. They went down at normal pace, since the clatter of the clanker could not be disguised, rattled across the frozen stream and up the hillside towards the manufactory, skirting around the forest to meet the road higher up. They would not have much chance in the open, but none at all in a forest ambush.

The clanker thudded up the hill, turning onto the Tiksi road. The gates of the manufactory dangled from their hinges. There was more damage inside, as well as head-high drifts of snow, but no tracks.

'Looks like it happened some time ago,' said Tuniz. 'That drift didn't get here in a day.'

They went down the central walkway, weapons at the ready. Irisis, hobbling past the cold furnaces, peered in and shook her head. 'They must have been out for at least a week.'

'And they'll be the very devil to get back into operation,' said Tuniz. 'This one has a load of iron set hard in the bottom. How are we going to get that out?'

They found no one, nor any great signs of violence inside. There were no bodies and the place had not been sacked or looted, though all the crystal was gone from the artisans' workshops. Sitting in a courtyard out the back, where a meagre sun just managed to top the wall, they ate a dismal lunch.

'It looks as if the place was attacked and everyone fled,' said Nish. 'Though all the lyrinx came for was the crystal.'

'Or to put the place out of action,' said Fyn-Mah, composed again.

'I suppose you're in charge here now,' said Irisis to the querist.

'I suppose I am. And I'm loath to abandon this place, since it's the best mine and the best manufactory in this area, but we can't stay here without a guard. We'll head down to Tiksi, where I dare say we'll find our workers and miners. I'll see what's happened and seek advice from the scrutator, if I can commandeer a skeet. And there,' she lowered her voice, 'we'll have to do something about our operator.'

'I don't know that there's any proof . . .' Nish began. He looked up to see Ky-Ara hurrying out.

'No proof is needed to put him where he can do no more harm!' Fyn-Mah said savagely.

They were getting up when they heard the clanker rattling down the track.

'What's he doing?' Fyn-Mah shouted.

Nish ran to the front gate. The machine was already out of sight. 'He's gone renegade,' Irisis said, clacking towards him on her crutches. She began to laugh.

'What's so funny?' said Nish. 'Now we've got to walk down to Tiksi.'

'How else could this bloody fiasco of an expedition end?' she snorted and, tucking the crutches under her arms, set off down the hill.

They went by the mine and the village. Both had been evacuated. The weather being good, they continued down the mountain and reached the gates of Tiksi at dusk. There they found scenes of confusion and chaos. Spikes were being installed on top of the city walls and a massive new gate constructed outside the old one.

'That won't keep lyrinx out for long,' said Tuniz after they had gone through. She turned to stare at the stonework with a professional's eye.

'I don't suppose it will.' Nish plodded apathetically beside her. After so long on the road, all he wanted was a hot bath. He planned to lie in it until his skin peeled off, then go to bed and not get up for a week.

Irisis was not laughing now. The crutches had taken the skin off under her arms and every step brought a gasp.

Nish saw his father settled into bed at an inn and called a healer to attend him. Jal-Nish was docile after the weeks of sedation, but Nish gave the appropriate warnings. He found a quiet room for Ullii, who remained closed off, advised the maid how to treat her, and attended to a dozen other urgent matters. Fyn-Mah had gone to see the master of the city.

Finally, around midnight, he had just taken his clothes off and was putting one grimy foot in the bathwater, which was barely lukewarm, when someone pounded on the door with a spear butt.

'Cryl-Nish Hlar! Cryl-Nish Hlar!'

'Yes!' he snapped.

'You are called to attend the master.'

'I'm in the bath. I'll be out directly.'

'He said you were to come *immediately*!'

Nish cursed the man under his breath. 'It will take a few minutes to get dressed.'

'Make it quick!'

Nish gave himself a quick scrub with a cloth, removing the surface grime. Whatever the urgency, appearances were important. He found clothes in his pack which, though not clean, were better than the ones he had on. Before he was ready the soldier began pounding on the door again. Nish was hurried through the streets and up the steps of the master's mansion. There he was ushered into a small room crowded with people. He recognised many faces from the manufactory, including Foreman Gryste and, surprisingly, Muss the halfwit. Irisis and Fyn-Mah were there too, as well as the master of the city and a small, thin man Nish had never seen before. He sat at the end of the table and even the master seemed in awe of him.

'Cryl-Nish Hlar!' announced the aide, and the small man turned a pair of mild black eyes on him. They were shaded in deep sockets by eyebrows that formed an unbroken black band across the bridge of the man's nose.

'About time!' he snapped. 'Where have you been, Artificer Cryl-Nish?'

'I had to settle my father, surr. He is Perquisitor Jal-Nish . . .'

'I know your damned father! Sit down! Querist Fyn-Mah has given me an outline of this disaster. Four clankers lost, and forty soldiers, for absolutely no gain. Such incompetence I cannot comprehend. I've a good mind to send the whole blasted lot of you to the front-line.'

An audible shiver passed through the room. He let the sentence hang in the air while he glared at each of them in turn. Nish tried to meet his gaze but had to look away. This was a man very much used to dominating others. He had an exceptionally thin and angular face that looked to have had all the meat pared from it, leaving mere bone, skin and sinew. His cheeks were sucked in so far that Nish could see the outline of his teeth. A straggle of beard on the chin emphasised its spade-like quality.

'Humpf! Useless lot.' His eye fell on Nish again, who was seated next to Irisis. 'Especially you pair! What was that fuss all about?'

Neither said anything, since they had no idea what the question meant.

'Fornication! That's what! I blame you two for the whole sorry mess.' The man sighed. 'In the meantime, there's work to be done. It's a tragedy Tiaan is lost to us. A double tragedy that the curious crystal is gone as well. And to cap it all, your clanker operator's run off with his machine. Who the hell was running the show?'

No one spoke. Fyn-Mah looked stricken. 'I was, surr, after the perquisitor was injured. I take full resp . . .'

'Humpfh! I sent Jal-Nish. The responsibility is mine. Don't suppose the fellow will get far, anyway. Now, how do we get out of this mess?'

Again no one spoke.

'You lot don't have a quile of initiative between you!' He twirled his whiskers around a finger and pressed the coil in through his lips, sucking on the strands. 'We can't give up the manufactory. We *won't* be intimidated. It goes back into operation as soon as possible. And the mine. But I need an overseer.' He considered, sucking furiously.

A chair scraped halfway down Nish's row. A big, barrel-chested man stood up. 'I would like to put . . .'

'Sit down, *Foreman* Gryste,' said the thin man. 'Artificer Tuniz, you have come out of the excursion with some credit. You will be overseer. I shall give you two weeks to get the manufactory operating again, and then I want a clanker from it every fortnight.'

Gryste rocked back on his chair, dismayed, then angry.

'It can't be done!' said Tuniz flatly.

'I can do it, surr,' said Gryste.

'Good! See you are the best foreman the manufactory has

ever had or I'll have your head. Overseer Tuniz, find a way! You will have the support you need.'

'I have children in Crandor, surr,' she said softly.

'You should never have left them.' He bit his knuckles. 'After one year, if the manufactory meets its goals – all of them – I will send you home.'

'Thank you, surr.' Tuniz was beaming from one side of her face to the other.

He rotated in his chair. 'Artisan Irisis. I know everything about you!' He glared at her so fiercely that Nish thought she was going to be sent to the execution block. 'Including that you manage your artisans better than anyone. You will be acting crafter, your job to produce controllers as fast as you possibly can.'

'I'll need more artisans and prentices,' she said calmly. Nish admired her self-possession, for she must have been expecting the breeding factory, or worse.

'You'll have them as soon as I can march them here.'

'And better defences for the manufactory and the mine.'

'Masons are being collected right now, and a detail of two hundred soldiers is on its way. I've had a warrant made up for you. Collect it before you leave. Buy whatever you require and be prepared to go back by the end of the week.'

'What I need is crystal,' said Irisis. 'The lyrinx cleaned out our stores. I must have miners who can find the kind we need.'

'Wasn't there an old fellow . . . Joeyn?' said the thin man.

'He's dead, and the others are mere metal miners. They can't tell crystal from muck.'

'I'll have miners sent here, though it may be a month before you get them. Too long . . .'

'I have an idea, surr,' said Irisis. 'If you're prepared to listen.'

He raised half of his continuous eyebrow.

'When we were in the mine,' Irisis said, 'the seeker said she could see crystal in the mountain like raisins in a pudding. What if . . .?'

'Already you prove your worth, Crafter Irisis. Get to it! She will guide the miners.'

He swung around again. 'And now for you, Cryl-Nish Hlar. What am I to do with you?'

Nish caught his breath, but this time he held the man's gaze. It was like looking into an empty shaft – his eyes gave nothing away.

'Humpf!' said the man. 'The reports I've had of you are not *entirely* unfavourable. You have a little project for Fyn-Mah, I understand. Concerning what was found up in the ice houses? And there's your work with the seeker. Where is she?'

'In her room at the inn,' said Nish.

'Not much damn good there! Send her down for examination. Go back to your bath, boy, while I consider how I can use you. *If at all!*'

Nish felt piqued that Irisis had been rewarded handsomely while his life still hung by a thread. 'Ullii requires special handling if you are to get anything out of her, surr. It might be better . . !'

'Damn you, boy!' the man growled. 'Don't tell me my job. I'll fetch her myself. Now clear out, the lot of you!'

They hastily vacated the room, even the master of Tiksi, whose chamber it was.

'Give me a hand, Nish!' said Irisis as they went down the front steps. She looked faint.

'What's the matter?'

'These wretched crutches have chafed the skin off,' she muttered.

Nish gave her a curious glance. 'No, what's really the matter?'

'I'm going to be exposed, that's what! I can't do it, Nish.'

'Of course you can. You're a brilliant team leader. Who was that, anyway?'

'You, with all your contacts, don't know?'

'No!' he said. 'I have no idea.'

'That,' she paused dramatically, 'was the scrutator himself. Xervish Flydd!'

FORTY-EIGHT

As the boat drifted away from the seeping warmth of Kalissin, the water became progressively colder. Tiaan woke, feeling the chill coming through the leather.

It was dark; just a trace of moon. The craft was rocking wildly and driven sleet stung her cheeks. In this wind the boat must soon fetch up on the shore. Then she had to discover how to get to her destination, preferably without telling anyone where she was headed.

Better stay with the boat, at least until she found a village. It would be easy enough to fashion a paddle. She could even make a scrap of sail, perhaps sailing down a river to the inland sea. The wind was blowing towards the south, roughly the way she wanted to go. She'd head along the shore until she found an outlet flowing in that direction, to Tallallamel, and keep going until she got there.

Wrapping her coat around her, Tiaan drifted, somewhere between waking and sleep. She ached all over and the top of her head throbbed. She probed it with her fingertips. A clump of hair was gone, the skin beneath blistered.

The boat was being banged against something hard, a crust of ice stretching between round rocks. It was still dark and she was freezing.

Easing the craft along the rocks into a cove, she climbed out. The ground was crusted snow. Ahead lay sparse forest, old pines with straggly limbs. Pulling the boat from the water, she marked its position and went towards the trees.

She'd need a fire to survive the night. A little way inside the forest Tiaan began to gather twigs from above her head. It took a lot of effort with flint and tinder to get a fire going, for the wood was damp. Fortunately she had plenty of experience – damp wood was the only kind they had at the manufactory. Soon she was warming her hands at the blaze and making soup from dried fish and lake water.

She did not care what it tasted like; the warmth was all that mattered. Later Tiaan made a second fire, put boughs between the two for a bed and lay down in her sleeping pouch. It was one of the most uncomfortable nights of her life.

The following day she poled along the edge of the lake, searching for an outlet. Tiaan did not find one, though on the morning after she encountered a good-sized river which flowed south. Paddling into it, she let the current carry her along, and shortly passed a hut on the edge of a patch of forest. She kept going, hoping for a village, but before long came around a bend to find ice from bank to bank. The river was probably frozen all the way to the inland sea, and clear upstream only because the lake was warm. What now? She could not walk to Tallallamel. Tiaan poled back towards the hut, taking a small piece of silver from Joeyn's money belt and putting it in her pocket.

The hut was built on a gentle rise and constructed of wattle and daub, shaped like a squat vase. The walls were thick, the roof rising to a peak. A slanted, pointed cowl kept snow out of the smoke hole.

A miserable dwelling, but the walls were in good condition and a child playing in a tree outside had rosy cheeks and a well-fed face. No doubt the family made a good living from fish. Poling her boat to the shore, Tiaan stepped onto the snow, which crunched underfoot.

The child looked down.

'Hola!' said Tiaan.

'Myrz!' said the child, jumping off the branch. Dressed in furs, it was a round ball of a creature of indeterminate sex. Its hood fell back, revealing pale skin and long hair a quite remarkable colour, blond with the faintest hint of lime. The child was seven or eight, she supposed. She had heard tales of pale-skinned, green-haired people who lived beyond the mountains, but had never seen one before. There were not a lot of visitors to the manufactory and most were like her – black of hair and olive of skin.

Tiaan had no idea of the language. She knew only the dialects of the south-east peninsula and the common speech of eastern Lauralin, which was not as well known as it might have been. In many places only scholars, tellers and traders knew it. She spoke to the child in the common speech.

'I would like to buy some food, please.'

'Myrz?'

Tiaan mimed putting food in her mouth.

The child laughed. 'Mitsy-pitsy. Flar hyar!' It trotted off to the hut, looking back at intervals to see that Tiaan was following. At the entrance the child pushed aside a hanging door and slipped inside, calling out.

Tiaan waited. She'd left her pack in the boat and was afraid it would disappear if she let it out of her sight. The child's head appeared beneath the hanging. 'Blazy mirr!' It made hand-signals that seemed to be saying, 'Come in.'

Casting an anxious glance at the boat, Tiaan crawled inside. It was surprisingly warm. The air had a thick tang of smoke, fish stew and the ripe smell, not unpleasant, of humanity. Three women squatted on the floor, which was considerably lower than the ground outside. A small fire of pine logs glowed in a stone-lined pit. An iron cauldron hung above it on a pole supported on two forked sticks embedded in the floor. A heap of firs against the far wall made a communal bed.

The women might have been triplets, at least to her eyes, for they all had long faces, the same pale lime hair and thin, prominent noses. They got up, fleshy women all, and rather taller than she was. Now Tiaan saw the differences. They must be sisters, the one nearest her older than the others. The second was the youngest and had a round scar on her chin.

'Hello,' said Tiaan in common. 'My name is Tiaan Liise-Mar.' She pointed to her chest. 'I would like to buy some food.' She pantomimed that as well.

The oldest woman, the most plump and buxom of the three, tilted her head to one side, puzzled. She debated with the others then turned back to Tiaan. 'Vart iss "buyy"?' Her accent was extremely heavy.

'It means "pay for with money".'

They looked uncomprehending. Tiaan fingered the piece of silver out of her pocket, showing it on the palm of her hand. She hoped that was not a mistake.

The oldest woman looked even more puzzled, then took up the piece of silver, examining it in the firelight. She passed it to the others. The middle one tasted it, the other tested it with her teeth.

'It's silver,' said Tiaan. 'Money for food!' The smell of the stew was making her salivate.

'Mun-ney!' said the older woman, and burst out in a great roar of laughter, displaying a dozen yellow, angled teeth. The other women laughed just as heartily, whereupon the first clapped Tiaan on the back with a meaty hand and tossed the silver back to her.

'I Fluuni,' she said. 'Middle sister iss Jiini; little sister iss Lyssa. Daughter iss Haani.'

Tiaan repeated the names, sounding them in the Tiksi way with extended vowels. From the hysterical laughter, she had got them completely wrong. 'I am Tiaan,' she repeated.

They repeated her name, mispronouncing it as badly. Lyssa dipped a wooden ladle in the cauldron, spilled the contents onto a square wood platter and handed Tiaan an implement like a spoon with teeth on the end, also made of wood.

She took it, not knowing what to say. What payment would they require? The plate contained a thick, bright-yellow mess. She could smell fish, though it had long since fallen to pieces. There were long fibrous sections of vegetables that might have been parsnip, dark unidentifiable grains, a hint of onion.

'Eat,' Fluuni said.

Tiaan took a mouthful. It was a peculiar combination of flavours, but delicious. She heaped up her implement. The women and the child were staring at her expectantly. 'Good!' she said. They did not understand. 'Very good!' She smacked her lips, patted her stomach. Still the stares. Had she committed some terrible blunder?

She shovelled in some more, swallowed, and to her embarrassment her stomach gave a great rollicking gurgle. Beaming smiles appeared. Haani clapped her hands.

Tiaan finished the stew. Immediately another ladle was emptied onto her platter. Her stomach was groaning from the first but they were looking at her so expectantly that it seemed ill-mannered to refuse. By the time the second was gone she was bursting, heavy-bellied and drowsy. Fluuni immediately dipped the ladle again. Tiaan leapt up, cried her thanks and bowed from the waist. They did not know what to make of this either.

They offered her tea made from mustard seeds. Its pungency went up her nose. Tiaan sneezed and tears ran from her eyes.

Afterwards she felt really sleepy. It was ages since she'd had a decent night's rest. Leaning against the wall she closed her eyes, snatched them open again and fell fast asleep.

When she woke it was just as smoky and gloomy and Tiaan thought she'd slept only for a few minutes, though she felt unusually refreshed. The room was empty. She crawled through the door and to her horror discovered that it was near dusk. She'd slept the day away.

Her eye wandered along the river bank. The boat was not there! She hurtled down to the water. No sign of it anywhere, nor of her pack and its infinitely precious contents. Tiaan sprinted back to the hut, crashing into Lyssa, who was carrying a load of wood from the forest. Sticks went everywhere.

Tiaan helped her pick them up. 'Where is my boat?'

'Bote?' Lyssa replied.

Tiaan made paddling motions with her hands. 'Trall!' said Lyssa, going around the back of the hut. The boat was leaning against the wall, upside down. Water draining from it had frozen on the ground.

'What did you do with my pack?' She tried to say it in sign language. Lyssa led her inside and Tiaan saw the pack not far from where she'd gone to sleep. She went though it while Lyssa looked on with a faint smile. Everything was as it had been before.

Tiaan felt embarrassed at her suspicions. Getting up, she cried 'Thank you; thank you!' and threw out her arms.

Lyssa beamed, folded Tiaan in her own arms and gave her a long warm hug. Her doughy flesh reminded Tiaan of her mother, back when Tiaan had been a little girl and Marnie had time for her. Before she'd been rejected for the next child, and the one after.

By this time it was dark. Shortly the two sisters appeared with Haani. They began preparing vegetables, peeling onions and garlic from bunches hung at the ceiling, and a variety of roots which they brought from a cellar whose trapdoor was in one corner.

Tiaan offered to help but they sat her by the fire, the place of honour. Dinner was a slab of husky black bread placed in the bottom of a platter and the liquid from the fish stew poured over it. She ate every scrap and mopped her plate with the crusts.

Following that, Lyssa sang to Haani. It seemed to be a long tale, perhaps part of the Histories, or the Histories of the family. Tiaan did not know the language. It went on for at least an hour, a story full of drama and tragedy, fire and passion, and tender lovemaking too, judging by the wistful look that crept across Lyssa's face. The older women sat mending their clothing as they listened.

Finally the Histories had been sung. The child sat droopy-eyed while they undressed her, gave her a perfunctory clean with a wet rag and put her to bed in the middle of the furs. Then they laid down their work and looked expectantly at Tiaan. Evidently she had to sing for her supper.

Had she been asked to sing at the manufactory, Tiaan would have been so mortified that she could not have made a single note. But these people did not know her, they would never see her again, and besides, she owed them for the food, shelter and kindness.

She had not sung since she was a child in the breeding factory. A nursery rhyme popped into her head, a cautionary tale about a frog and a butterfly. She sang it in a hoarse, scratchy voice, not well at all, though Haani seemed to like it.

When she finished, Lyssa put her finger across Tiaan's lips, went to the fire and began stirring some kind of aromatic balm into a mug. It had a lemony, minty aroma. She squeezed in honey from a red-black comb and passed it to Tiaan with a smile.

Tiaan sipped from the mug, which eased her dry throat, and began to hum another tune. She made up the words as she sang. It was to the father she had never known and could not know. He must have died in the war, else he would have come back for her.

The sad song ended. Her eyes were moist. Again they clapped, and the child settled in bed. Only then did Tiaan raise the topic that was preoccupying her.

'The river is frozen. How can I get to the sea?'

'Fro-sshen?' said Jiini, the quietest of the three.

It took a lot of sign language to convey Tiaan's meaning, and then not very well. She had to take them outside, point to the river and try to sign that it was blocked by the ice. 'Sea' she could not convey at all.

The great southern inland sea was nearly three hundred leagues long. The smaller, western end was called Milmillamel. What was the larger? It took ages to call a map of Lauralin, like a blueprint seen long ago, into her mind.

'Tallallamel,' she said. 'I go to Tallallamel.'

'Ah!' said Lyssa. 'Tiaan go Tallallamel Myr.'

They grinned and chattered among themselves, then Fluuni said, speaking slowly and distinctly, 'Tiaan must leave boat. Tiaan shee.' She corrected herself, 'Tiaan skee river, ya?'

'Ski down the river to Tallallamel?'

'Ya, ya!' said the three women, nodding vigorously. 'Skee to Ghysmel, ya.'

Tiaan presumed Ghysmel was a city on the coast. 'How far is that?' Blank looks. 'How many sleeps to Ghysmel?'

Jiini held up six fingers. 'Nya!' said Lyssa, pushing her sister's hand down and holding up eight fingers. Fluuni nodded vigorously.

Eight days of skiing. That wasn't so bad; Tiaan was an accomplished skier. That was how they got around in winter, at the manufactory. Skiing all day might test her out though.

Having established that money was foreign to them, Tiaan was at a loss how to proceed. However, after some hard work she bartered her leather boat for a pair of skis and food. No doubt they already had a boat, though Fluuni's eyes lit up as soon as Tiaan made the offer. The leather was soft but strong, much more valuable than a pair of skis, which were easily carved in a few evenings.

They insisted on filling her pack with food – bundles of stiff dried fish, dried meat, a comb of honey, a round of cheese probably made from deer milk, a string of onions and much more. She had to stop them – there was more than she could carry.

It was late. The women crawled into the nest of furs, with the child in the middle. Fluuni indicated the space nearest the fire. Tiaan was soon asleep.

Her dreams were pleasant ones, for once. These strangers, whom Tiaan had known for only a day, felt closer and more caring than anyone she knew. It was like lying in her mother's bed as a child.

Tiaan woke in the night and thought she was back with Marnie. Turning over, disoriented, her outflung arm struck the pack. The fire had died down and the hut was absolutely dark. It made her feel claustrophobic.

Tiaan felt inside the pack, wanting a glimmer of light to break the confined feeling. As she touched the amplimet it lit up and a shock raced along her arm. The pack glowed garnet-red for an instant. What had happened? It had not done that before. Recalling how the soldiers had seemed to be able to track her, she felt a moment of unease.

But that had been a long time ago, and at least a hundred leagues away. Could they have tracked her to Kalissin? It did not seem possible, but the lyrinx were within easy flying distance.

Her heart was racing. Tiaan crawled to the entrance. It was still dark outside. She settled down again. She'd go at dawn and hope it snowed to cover her tracks.

Tiaan groaned aloud. Fluuni rolled over and put an arm about her waist. It would have been comforting, had not her problems been so insoluble. Tiaan lay awake the rest of the night, twice slipping out of bed and lifting the flap. The second time the sky was pale in the east.

She was tying her boots into the ski bindings when Jiini came out. She went into the forest to relieve herself, then helped Tiaan with the adjustments. Shortly Fluuni, Lyssa and Haani emerged. No doubt they always rose with the light.

When Tiaan went in for her pack the cauldron was over the fire. She took a large bowl of fish stew, then gave thanks to the women, who each embraced her. She shook hands with Haani, who smiled shyly. Tiaan donned her pack and skied towards the river, the four watching how she went and laughing – no doubt commenting on her strange style. She turned to ski along the bank, waved and pushed off, settling into the striding rhythm.

It was hard work for muscles that had not skied in months and she stopped as the ice came in sight. She must not pull a muscle and cripple herself.

Sitting on her coat on a tree trunk just above the ice and, watching a pair of deer grazing on lichen, she was startled by a high-pitched, keening cry coming faint down the river. Some chance reflection off the water must have carried it to her. Tiaan recognised it instantly. *The nylatl!*

FORTY-NINE

Tiaan's first impulse was to flee. She could easily outrun it on skis. But the women and child would have no chance if it attacked.

Was it hunting her, or the amplimet? Tiaan had noted the look in its eyes when it had seen the crystal. Taking out the blade, hopeless weapon though it was, she headed back. It took all the courage she had.

Tiaan refused to think about that. If she had, she would never have been able to continue. The nylatl could be on the other side of the river, hunting a deer or a rabbit. If it was hunting *her*, going to the hut might lead it to them. She stopped halfway, not knowing what to do. Then she heard the scream.

It was a woman's scream, shrill and cracked at the end. A cry of agony, for herself or for someone she loved. The nylatl must be there, *at the hut*.

She skied back as fast as she had ever gone. As she went, Tiaan tested the blade with her thumb. It was viciously sharp. A violent, bloody rage grew in her. If the nylatl had hurt them she would rejoice as she carved it open.

No further cry came. She heard nothing but the pounding of her heart and a roaring in her ears. This time she saw no living thing along the river. It was as if the entire world had gone into hiding.

Her knees felt soft by the time she curved around the river bank, shot through a straggly patch of pines and came out in a clearing. The hut was visible beyond the next patch of trees. All looked just as it had been before. She pressed on but saw no one.

'Fluuni?' she said softly. 'Jiini? Lyssa?'

No reply. 'Haani?' she whispered. The child did not answer either. Perhaps they'd gone up to the lake to fish or try out the boat.

She slid forward a few more ski lengths. The back of the hut came into view, the boat leaning just as she had left it. Something stabbed Tiaan in the heart. She scanned the surroundings: up in the trees, down to the river. She saw nothing, but the nylatl could camouflage itself as well as a lyrinx. Going a bit further, she saw a large, crumpled shape in the shadow behind the hut. It looked like one of the women.

Tiaan tore at the ski bindings, which did not want to come off. Her foot caught, she tripped and landed on her palms. The blade went skidding across the snow, to stop just before the woman's face. Her lime-blond hair lay on the ground. Tiaan recognised the coat.

'Jiini?' she whispered, reaching forward to brush the hair away. It was red at the ends, as were her furs and the ground beneath her. There was not enough left of her face to be recognisable. She was unquestionably dead.

As Tiaan crouched there, blade in hand, she became aware of a strange sound coming from inside the hut. A sort of *rending* noise. There was only one way to go in. Tiaan took a run-up, hurled herself at the low hanging and landed inside.

The sight that met her eyes was worse. Lyssa lay on the floor, even more horribly eaten than her sister. There was blood halfway up the walls and the scanty contents of the hut were scattered everywhere. Fluuni lay against the far wall, eyes staring, furs soaked in blood. A stone mallet, the kind used for pounding meat, hung from one hand.

The gruesome noise was coming from Lyssa's body, which was moving though she could not possibly be alive. Tiaan's hair stood on end. The nylatl must be inside her, feeding. And where was little Haani?

She circled around the fire pit, watching the body warily. Her foot grated against something – a carving knife. Taking it in her free hand, she held it out in front of her.

Something moved in Lyssa's middle. It looked gruesomely like an eye staring at her out of wet flesh. Tiaan wanted to scream; wanted to be sick. She had to remind herself that Lyssa was dead and could feel nothing.

The nylatl came flying out, covered in blood and glistening strands. It skittered across the floor, directly at Tiaan. It was fast, though not as fast as before. Hopefully its injuries still troubled it. It seemed bigger too: the size of a small dog now.

She ran to her left, keeping cauldron and fire between her and it. It shot right over, at her face. She got the carving knife up in time, batting the beast away, though without wounding it. Her head began to throb and again her eyes were full of pin-pricks. The nylatl was getting at her mind again.

Flipping in mid-air, it landed on its hind legs and sprang. She threw herself to one side. The claws caught in her sleeve, the creature swung around and went for her throat. The threads ripped, fortunately, and the blow missed by a whisker. As it landed she kicked it hard in the snout.

It struck the wall, fell and lay unmoving. Tiaan watched it, suspecting a ruse. A minute passed. She took a step towards it, blade down-hooked, then another. About to stab it, she saw its back legs tense.

She froze. The nylatl sprang but instead of going for her face, as she had expected, flew at her shin. Its teeth went though boot, trousers, sock, skin and flesh; she felt one tooth touch bone. She brought her other heel down hard on the join between head and body. The nylatl's teeth tore down her ankle before the jaws let go.

Tiaan tried to crush it beneath her boot heel. It gave a tortured wail; she felt something give. Its claws scratched the dirt floor and it flung itself sideways. She was in too much pain to think straight. All Tiaan wanted to do was hurt it as much as it had hurt her; to kill it before it killed her.

She must have done some damage for it now moved with a dragging motion of its hindquarters. Before it could gather itself for another attack she booted it. Its armour clanged on the side of the cauldron and the nylatl fell into the fire. Screeching hideously, it lurched out again. Tiaan, back-pedalling across the room, put her foot on a wooden mug and fell flat on her back. Her elbow struck the ground. The knife clattered away. Her whole arm began to go numb.

The fall had winded her; she could hardly move. The nylatl came at her, moving slowly now, and she smelt its singed, carrion-flesh odour. It eyed her warily. She expected it to take her hand off with a single lunge, but it stood just a pace from her face, staring.

Hungry!

Was it playing with her, or was it afraid now? She clutched the little blade in her other hand. She would have to strike across her body, a clumsy stroke, and the blade was the wrong way around.

The nylatl arched its back. Its eyes were mesmerising. It leaned toward her, opening its mouth, which was a gory red. The blue tongue began to roll up at the edges. She felt paralysed. Was it hypnotising her?

It was going to deluge her in venom then eat her face off at its leisure. She forced her arm to move. Clear liquid dripped from the tip of its tongue. Tiaan squeezed her eyes closed.

There came a meaty thump and the nylatl went flying. A death-like Fluuni swayed behind her, the bloody stone mallet hanging from her hand.

The nylatl whimpered, dragged itself across the floor and out through the curtain, leaving a trail of mauve blood. Fluuni collapsed onto her knees. Her unmarked face was fish-belly pale, but her whole front was red.

'Jiini?' she whispered.

'Outside,' Tiaan gasped. 'She's dead. I'm sorry.' She felt utterly useless.

Fluuni's eyes slid across to Lyssa. No need to ask about her.

'Where is Haani?' asked Tiaan.

One blood-spattered hand pointed towards the cellar. Tiaan hobbled over and lifted the trapdoor. In the furthest recesses, Haani cowered. Tiaan did not know what to say to her. Could anything make up for the horrors she had seen, or imagined? She threw a fur over Lyssa's middle.

'Haani, come out!' called Fluuni.

The child emerged warily into the light, then scuttled to Fluuni's arms. Fluuni allowed her to weep for a minute or two before she pushed her towards Tiaan.

'Tiaan mi. Tiaan mumu niss!' She looked up at Tiaan. 'Go with Tiaan. Tiaan iss mother now!'

Haani let out an awful wail and ran back.

'Tiaan mumu niss. Mi!' Fluuni gasped.

'But . . .' Tiaan was almost as bewildered as the child. 'Her family . . .'

'All dead!' Fluuni's arm swept the room. 'Tiaan iss Haani's mother now.' She looked up pleadingly.

Tiaan did not know what to say. 'Yes,' she whispered. 'I will be Haani's mother. I will take her with me.'

Fluuni gave a tiny grunt. Blood ran out of her nose and she fell sideways. Tiaan knew that she was dead but checked her anyway. There was no doubt of it; her whole belly had been torn open.

Leaving Haani clinging to her aunt, Tiaan found a pack, clothes and furs the child's size. She put in a wooden plate and other items Haani would need, and as much food as she could carry. Two furs had escaped the blood; Tiaan gathered them and a tiny canvas tent that was heavier than it looked. She could not have carried it had she been walking, but she could probably manage it skiing on flat ground.

There was nothing to be done for the women; the hut would not burn and there was no way to bury them in the frozen ground. She closed their eyes and dug the child out from beneath the furs. Haani screamed and burrowed back in. Pulling the covers away, Tiaan discovered that she had a small toy in one hand, a creature made from scraps of leather sewn together and stuffed with straw. It had a long body, small round ears, a duck bill and a flat, paddle-like tail. It looked like no animal Tiaan had ever heard of. Well, if it comforted her . . .

Tiaan led the child to the dead women, having her touch them and say goodbye. Then, hoisting up the pack, she took Haani's hand and led her outside.

Haani tied her boots into the bindings of the small skis. One boot was badly worn. Tiaan hacked a piece of leather from the bottom of the boat, added it to her overloaded pack, tied on her skis and, taking Haani's hand, set off down the river bank without looking back. Only much later did she realise that the child had not said goodbye to Jiini, her mother.

Not far away, the nylatl had found a burrow going down into the river bank, then up to a secure, dry and relatively warm home. A duck-billed creature dwelt inside. The nylatl had no trouble with it, or its helpless young.

When sated it curled up in the warmest spot and went into hibernation. It had many injuries to repair and that would take time. And when it finally woke, it would go on the hunt. The black-haired woman and the terrible, tantalising crystal could not hide. Wherever she took it, the nylatl would hunt it down. And then it would make the woman suffer for the torment of its existence.

FIFTY

The child said not a word that day, which was the most tragic part of the whole terrible affair. Haani skied to one side of Tiaan, or ahead, as if she wanted to get as far away as possible. She was an accomplished skier, better than Tiaan in these conditions. Her small round face, as pale as the snow, showed nothing but an icy bleakness. Tiaan felt culpable. She'd led the nylatl to them. If not for her, the creature would not exist. If not for her, their lives would never have been touched.

Her shin was excruciatingly painful but had not bled much, so she'd left it untreated. Getting well away, beyond the nylatl's reach, was more important. They went by a number of villages, at the first of which children were carrying water from a hole cut in the ice. Tiaan had not thought about that problem, but of course water would be hard won here in winter unless they had a well that did not freeze. The children stared but did not wave. Haani did not even look at them, just shushed past with Tiaan following in her tracks.

In the middle of the day she called out to Haani, skied off the river, sidestepped up a steep bank and settled on a log. The child followed, skiing round and round. Tiaan suspected that, had she not called, Haani would have kept going straight down the river until she dropped.

Tiaan was ready to drop right now. Her leg muscles had gone

wobbly. Taking off the skis, she massaged her thighs. It did not help. She felt weak and shivery. Not cold, for the day was mild and her exertions had made her sweat, but shuddering inside from the horror of the morning. The tragedy came directly from her aiding the enemy, and all the self-justification in the world, all the 'they made me do it', could make no difference. If only, she kept thinking. *If only . . .*

That was futile. Taking out a piece of fatty dried meat she began to cut slices from it. The meat resisted her blade, and only at the end did Tiaan realise that the child was still skiing round the log. Tiaan watched Haani go over a hump, down into a hollow where bare yellow twigs stuck out of the snow, between two trees that leaned towards each other to make an arch, across a smooth patch of snow and back over the hump. Her jaw was set; she kept doing the same movements over and again, but her mind was not there at all. It was back in the cabin with the dead women, and the nylatl.

'Haani?' Tiaan called. The child did not react. She called more loudly. Nothing. Tiaan stood up, shouting, 'Haani, come here!'

Haani jerked, gave her a vacant glare, but skied across to the log. Tiaan patted the space beside her. 'Sit down. Eat your lunch.'

She knew that the child understood a little of her language, though maybe not very much. Haani went to the end of the log, took off her pack and began nibbling on a piece of dried fish, staring into the emptiness between the trees. Tiaan had no idea what to do. She could hardly blame the child. It was a wonder she did not lie down and refuse to get up, or have a screaming fit. Perhaps it would be better if she did.

Tiaan ate her strips of leathery meat. After a lot of chewing, they released an overpoweringly strong flavour, like the smell of a male Hürn bear in the mating season. The taste did not appeal.

She washed the meat down with a swallow from her flask. 'Ready?' she said to the staring child.

Haani made not a sound but rose at once, tightened the bindings and put on her pack. Clearly she was used to travelling, and doing what she was told.

As she rose, Tiaan felt a stabbing ache in her calf and a cry of pain slipped out. Haani, who was already heading off, spun around on her skis. Perhaps she thought the nylatl was coming back.

Tiaan drew up her trouser leg, which was matted with blood. Her sock was stuck to the wound. It would have to wait until tonight.

As Tiaan struggled onto her skis, Haani glowered at her, sprang in the air, came down with her skis facing the other way and headed off at a pace Tiaan could not match. Perhaps she blamed Tiaan for not being killed, or taking on the role of her mother. Or the whole disaster.

Well, she was right to. Tiaan was to blame. And what was she supposed to do with an eight-year-old who had no relative left in the world? "Tiaan iss Haani's mother now," Fluuni had said. Tiaan had no idea how to be a mother to an eight-year-old, and there was no one she could model herself on. Most of the indentured children at the manufactory had families but she had not been to their homes. She had no idea what a home or a proper family was like. The only homes she'd been in were Joeyn's and the three women's. All dead because of her.

Haani was almost out of sight, skiing fast down the smooth ice and never looking back. Tiaan was about to yell at her but thought better of it. She increased her pace, pushing herself as fast as her injury would allow and knowing she would suffer tomorrow.

Around four in the afternoon, when the short day was rapidly closing, Tiaan skied around a bend in the river and saw Haani standing on the other side, staring into the forest. Tiaan stopped beside her.

'Time to find a camp, eh?'

The child sidestepped up the low bank and glided over soft snow into the trees. A few snowflakes drifted down. Tiaan went after her. It took an effort to climb the bank.

Haani's skis had left twin paths through the pristine white. Tiaan pushed through the silent forest and down into a dip with

500

an arc of trees around it. The child was taking her pack off. It was a good campsite – sheltered, plenty of firewood nearby, yet cleared land around so they could keep watch. The child was an experienced traveller, a necessary survival skill in these parts.

They built a fire on branches piled against a fallen log. Haani went about the camp chores silently: gathering wood, putting up the tent, filling the pot with packed snow. Tiaan prepared dinner.

Later, Haani sat across from the fire, staring at the flames unblinking. What was going on in the child's mind? Tiaan had seen no tears. Maybe she had blocked it right out. Tiaan wanted to comfort her but had no idea what to say.

Steam rose from the pot. Dipping out a wooden mug of water, she began to soak the bloody sock off her ankle. The scabs had stuck to the cloth and once it was free the wounds began to bleed.

There were deep tooth marks down her shin and ankle, the gouges torn and inflamed. It looked gruesome. After bathing the injury carefully, Tiaan squeezed honey over it, the only dressing she had, and bandaged it up. If it became badly infected she might as well lie down and die.

At one stage Tiaan looked up to see Haani's eyes on her and for the first time saw a spark of fellow-feeling there. Tiaan had suffered too.

Tiaan was in turmoil. Down at the coast she'd planned to find a boat going west, sail up as far as the sea of Milmillamel, then take another boat upriver in the direction of Tirthrax. How hard a journey would that be, and how long, with a child?

Minis had said that his people could last a year, at most. It had been late autumn when she'd left the manufactory, and winter as she'd reached Kalissin. Tiaan had lost track of time there but it must have been the best part of three months. So it was past mid-winter, though winter in these latitudes was long and maybe the worst of it was yet to come. She might get to the sea and find it frozen too.

Every prospect was gloomy. She could almost sense Minis's

despair. She was the last hope of his people and she was going to let him down. I've done my best, beloved, she thought. What more could I do? It did not help.

The child rose, stirred the pot with the knife and scooped out a mugful of stew. Haani ate listlessly, unaware of what she was eating.

There was a cold hollow in Tiaan's belly but she felt too depressed to eat. What kind of life would it be for the child, travelling month after month, having no home, never able to make friends with other children? And at the end, if they did reach Tirthrax, living in a cave in the mountains while Tiaan worked day and night to find her lover?

What on earth was she thinking? Of course she must take the child with her. She had to look after Haani until she had grown up. It was a sacred duty. But what about my life? Tiaan agonised. What about my lover?

Haani was still staring into the fire. There were bright red patches on each cheek, as if she had a fever. She had laid the mug aside and was rocking gently, her arms wrapped around herself.

Tiaan felt ashamed. The child had seen her mother and aunts brutally slain, her home debauched. The memories would never leave her. And all she, Tiaan, could think of was how her own life would be disrupted. How selfish she was.

Tears hovered on Haani's lashes. Tiaan moved down to her. The child tried to draw away but Tiaan put her arms around her and lifted Haani into her lap. Haani struggled but Tiaan held her more tightly and eventually the child began to weep.

Tiaan held her for an hour or more. Eventually Haani's head fell to one side; she was asleep. Putting her in the tent, in the fur-lined sleeping pouch, Tiaan went back to the fire.

She was afraid to sleep. Sleep led to dreams and she knew what she was going to dream about. Stamping her feet to warm them, Tiaan took half a mug of stew and found her thoughts wandering back to Minis. She felt a great flood of longing. She had to know if he was all right.

Taking out her devices she set them up and began to work

the beads. Nothing happened. It was as if Minis had never existed. Wrenching the helm off, she tossed it on the ground. She had failed him. The Aachim must be dead.

The amplimet looked dead too. It was cold, hardly glowing at all, and the little spark had disappeared. Useless thing! She gave the globe an angry kick, sending it rolling towards the fire. At the ice houses she might have escaped, had she tried a bit harder, but now it was too late. She could never go home. Yet if she no longer had her quest, she had nothing at all.

Tiaan paced around the fire. A walking disaster, she had caused the death of practically everyone she'd touched, starting with poor old Joeyn. She itemised them, human and lyrinx. All completely pointless. Better she drop the amplimet through a hole in the ice, and throw herself after it.

She had just taken off her boots to warm her feet at the fire when there came a cry from the tent. Tiaan was there in three bounds.

'Mumu!' Haani screamed. 'Mumu, im sklarrrr!'

'It's all right, Haani,' Tiaan said. 'I'm here now.'

The child retreated to the back of the tiny tent, holding her hands out. 'Mumu! Mumu!'

Tiaan tried to take the child in her arms. 'Haani, you're just having a bad dream. I'm here now.'

'Nya!' screamed the child, beating her off. 'Mumu nya!'

An elbow went into Tiaan's eye and she lost hold of the thrashing child. By the time she'd recovered, Haani was gone.

'Haani? Where are you?'

No answer. She could hear nothing but the wind in the treetops. Pulling a burning stick from the fire, Tiaan held it up. The flame went out. 'Haani?' she shouted, and running around the fire tripped on the globe. The amplimet was glowing now, though faintly. Holding it out, she followed the child's footprints in her socks. There was no time to put her boots on. It was snowing and if she lost Haani's tracks, the child would die.

The snow had a crust and in places there were no tracks at all. A dense overcast did not hint at moon or stars. Within minutes the night had swallowed up the firelight. Tiaan was no longer sure she could find her way back. She tramped harder, making sure she left tracks.

'Haani?'

No reply. How had the child gone so far, so quickly? Tiaan stopped within a windswept clearing. The stunted pines hardly broke the wind at all. The snow was packed hard. There were no footprints.

A blast blew through her unfastened coat. Pulling it tight, Tiaan looked around frantically. No sign; no sound. She held the amplimet up in fingers that were numb, and called more light from it. It waxed then waned, as if it was dying.

Hobbling across the clearing, she checked the patches of snow on the other side. No sign. She did a complete circle, came on her own marks, and despair crept like ice into her bones.

Backtracking, she found a single small print pointing left, before the clearing. It was under a tree. The child liked to climb trees. She looked up. 'Haani?'

'Haani,' she roared with all her might. All she heard was the whistling wind.

The light was dimming and Tiaan could not coax more from the crystal. She could hardly hold it, it was growing so cold. As she opened her mouth to yell, the cry of a wildcat came on the wind.

Haani screamed, to her left. Tiaan ran that way, her numb feet thudding the ground. Not far on, she stumbled on a bloody print, and another. Tiaan hoped it was just a cut foot. As she burst into another clearing, Haani was frantically trying to climb a tree. She kept slipping down the icy trunk.

Tiaan trod on a branch, which snapped loudly. Haani screamed and ran into the dark. Tiaan pounded after her. 'Haani, stop! It's me, Tiaan!'

Again came that wildcat cry. Haani shrieked, just ahead, and when Tiaan ran into the clearing the child came racing back the other way, looking over her shoulder, and crashed into her. Tiaan threw her arms around Haani, who screamed and screamed.

Squeezing her hard, Tiaan yelled, 'Haani, you're safe now!'

Haani went rigid, stayed that way for a minute then began to weep in great wracking sobs. Tiaan lifted her up. The child clung to her desperately. The foot injury was minor, though she was at risk of frostbite. Tiaan put Haani's feet in the pockets of her coat, wishing she could do the same for her own.

It was snowing hard now, the amplimet practically dead. Before she had gone far Tiaan lost her own tracks. She had no idea which way to go.

FIFTY-ONE

A week went by while Nish sat around in Tiksi, until he was completely fed up with idleness and his own company. Irisis and every other able-bodied person, apart from Ullii, had gone back to the manufactory days ago. Having heard nothing about his fate, he lived in fear of it. Fyn-Mah had given him access to her files on lyrinx flesh-forming. Nish read until his eyes ached, but found it difficult to concentrate.

Eight days after their arrival he was called to the master's mansion and ushered into the same chamber. Xervish Flydd lay back in the chair with his eyes closed, sucking on his beard.

'Good morning, scrutator!' said Nish politely.

The scrutator gave no reply. He simply ignored Nish. Nish cleared his throat several times, shuffled his feet and tapped on the table, wondering if the scrutator was asleep. He did not think so. Eventually Nish took a piece of paper out of his pocket and began sketching on it, considerations for improving the clanker javelards. He worked on that for an hour before the man sat up suddenly.

'I've been thinking to put you in the front-line, Cryl-Nish!'

The paper went one way, the pencil another. Nish bent down for them, trying to conceal his shock. He'd thought he had escaped that fate.

'And you could hardly appeal such a judgment, artificer, after the trouble you've caused. Even your own father's reports say so. Poor Jal-Nish. Well, it's up to me now. Have you anything to say for yourself?'

'I believe I've done some good since then,' Nish said weakly.

'Indeed? That's not what I heard from the plateau.'

'What did you hear, surr?' Nish had to force the words out, he was so afraid.

'I heard that you threatened Ky-Ara, which led to the destruction of his clanker.'

Nish looked around frantically, wanting to deny it but not daring to. There was no truth the scrutator could not dig out and the process would be most unpleasant.

'For the want of a clanker the artisan was lost. The crystal too! And a perquisitor maimed.'

'Ky-Ara should have resisted me,' Nish muttered.

'Indeed he should, and will be brought to account for his negligence. As will you.'

The scrutator glanced down at his bony hands. The fingers were gnarled and twisted as if they'd been broken in a torture chamber, then set by someone who knew nothing about bones. He flexed his fingers, which moved as awkwardly as the limbs of a crab. Nish shuddered and tried vainly to conceal it.

The cold eyes saw everything. 'On the other hand, you *have* shown courage, Cryl-Nish. And courage, I need not remind you, is an essential quality in the front-line soldier.'

'I may be more use to you at the manufactory as an artificer,' Nish said desperately.

'I doubt it! You're an indifferent artificer, Cryl-Nish, though you work hard at it.'

'I've done my best. Artificing was not my choice.'

'Indeed you have, but your best is not good enough.'

'What about my project for Fyn-Mah? To learn about the flesh-formers?'

'Have you done any good with it?'

'No, but I've only . . .'

'Leave it to her!'

'But . . .'

'No buts, artificer,' growled Flydd.

Nish stared at the floor in despair. He was doomed. Then inspiration struck. 'How have you gone with Ullii, surr?'

The scrutator's mouth curled down, and then suddenly he smiled. 'I see what you're about. You hope to prove useful in an endeavour that an old monster like me has failed at.'

'Well, er . . . the seeker is difficult to work with.'

'I found her not unusually so.'

Nish's mouth fell open. 'But . . .'

'People are not necessarily what they seem, boy. Sometimes we show others what they want us to see. You, for example, think of the scrutator as a bloody old bastard.'

Nish could hardly deny it, so he remained silent.

'I understand your friend Ullii very well. We got on famously and parted friends.'

Nish could not believe that, although the scrutator would hardly lie about something so easily checked. The piece of paper fluttered from Nish's hand. He watched it drift down but did not go after it. 'Then it's all over for me. I'm done for!'

Those eyes burned through him again.

'Perhaps I can use you after all, Cryl-Nish. I don't have the time to keep watch with Ullii. And why should I when you could do it for me? I think I *will* send you back to the manufactory. You can be a second-rate artificer by day. At night, when the seeker is not out hunting crystal in the mine, you will ensure that she keeps watch.'

'Watch for what?' Nish said stupidly.

'For people using the Secret Art. What else?'

'Oh!'

'Also for Tiaan. One day she will reappear and I want to know immediately. By skeet, and damn the expense! And then I want her found. This is the sole reason I have spared you, artificer. So you and the seeker can track down Tiaan and, more importantly, this rather interesting hedron she seems to have discovered. Don't fail me, boy, or you're lyrinx fodder!'

The following morning Nish and Ullii were on their way back to the manufactory with an escort of six foot-soldiers and a clanker.

Ullii was uncommonly cheerful. She did not say much, but when Nish mentioned the scrutator she said 'Xervish!' and smiled at some memory. There had to be more to the man than that unprepossessing exterior showed. No doubt there was – one did not rise to one of the most powerful positions in the land without having many talents.

Nish's father had recovered from his rages sufficiently to travel and had been sent home to Fassafarn by ship. Nish was delighted to see him go. His father the perquisitor was bad enough, but Jal-Nish the one-armed, mutilated failure was a terrible sight to see. The expedition had gone after Tiaan on his orders and it had been a disaster. The blame could fall nowhere else.

As they walked beside the clanker, Nish wondered what would happen to his father. Would he be quietly retired on grounds of injury? Was that what happened to important people who became incapable? They could hardly send *him* to the front-lines.

Nish could not see Jal-Nish settling calmly into domestic impotence. He would drive his mother out of her mind. Ranii was an ambitious, clever woman who, when she was at home, could stand no interference in the way it was run.

Well, Fassafarn was a long way away, thankfully. Nish was unlikely to see home in the next five years.

About a week later, Nish was helping to carry timber for the front doors when Ky-Ara's clanker rattled up the road. The machine was daubed here and there with mud and reeds, as if it had been hidden in a swamp. The plates were dented and streaked with rust.

The machine groaned to a stop. An elderly operator got out, removed his gloves and rubbed the small of his back. Two soldiers emerged. Turning toward the gate, they saluted smartly.

Nish set down his load, wondering what was going on. The scrutator stepped through the gate, signalling to a quartet of manufactory guards, who marched to the clanker and threw up the back hatch.

'Come out!' they ordered.

After a long interval, a dark-clad figure appeared in the opening, was hauled out and dragged across to the gate. Nish hardly recognised Ky-Ara. The once handsome young man was filthy, covered in sores and as thin as a crowbar. His operator's uniform was stained with mud, and in that tormented face his eyes looked as big as Ullii's.

There was no trial, since Ky-Ara had admitted his guilt. Nish had no idea what the punishment was going to be – execution, he presumed, in some horribly appropriate way. There was no point sending this man to the front-lines.

Ky-Ara was marched inside and bound to a stake between the artificer's workshop and the furnaces. The elderly operator drove the clanker through the rear gate and parked it beside Ky-Ara.

'Take the machine apart, piece by piece,' said the scrutator to the assembled artificers.

The artificers, including Nish, began to do just that. All the clanker operators, and their prentices, stood silently by. The manufactory's chronicler sat in a chair by the furnaces, recording everything. The teller being too sick to stand witness, another had been brought up from Tiksi. Her duty was to write the *Tale of Ky-Ara's Downfall and Ruin*, that it could be told in all sixty-seven manufactories of the south-east, and possibly across the known world.

Food and drink were laid out for him but Ky-Ara touched neither in the three days it took to reduce the clanker to the myriad parts from which it had been assembled. He hung from his ropes, staring with those bloody eyes, and every part removed was a thorn of metal being twisted in his flesh.

Nish was not much given to pity, but before the operation was over he did pity Ky-Ara. The man had withered before his eyes and Nish had never seen such suffering. He wished someone would put the fellow out of his agony, but Ky-Ara was guarded night and day. Justice must take its unforgiving course.

Then the real torment began. The entire manufactory lined up, from Eiryn Muss the halfwit to the scrutator himself, and even

Ullii. In stately tread, like pallbearers at a funeral, the greatest and the least went to the pile of clanker parts, selected one each, paced across to the open door of the furnace and hurled it in.

Ky-Ara screamed, and again for every succeeding part, until he no longer had the voice to make any sound at all. That process took many hours, and the line had gone round several times before they approached the end, the pair of cast-iron fly-wheels. Nish took hold of one, Overseer Tuniz the other. Far too heavy to lift, the flywheels were rolled across to the furnace door, where a dozen hands eased them up a sturdy plank and into the all-consuming blast.

The operator shrieked and fell unconscious. A bucket of water was hurled over him, for the trial was not finished yet. Crafter Irisis removed the controller that still hung about Ky-Ara's neck, took it apart piece by piece, after which she and the artisans and their prentices solemnly carried the pieces to the fire. Ky-Ara writhed as they went in, but made no sound.

Last of all the scrutator came forth, bearing a knife on a square metal plate. Placing the plate on a small table, beside the hedron from Ky-Ara's controller, he signalled to the guards. They slashed Ky-Ara's bonds.

The scrutator beckoned. Ky-Ara lurched to the table. He was a bilious yellow-green and watery blood ran down his chin from a much-bitten tongue. The scrutator indicated the hedron with his left hand, the knife with the right. Nish held his breath. Would the operator take the ritual suicide, the dishonourable way out, or would he pick up the hedron and carry it to the furnace, then await his fate? Or might he go berserk with the knife?

The operator's emaciated frame was wracked by a bone-wrenching shudder. His hand hovered over the knife, he looked up at the merciless face of the scrutator; then, strangely, he smiled and reached for the hedron instead.

The instant he touched the crystal Ky-Ara was transformed. He stood up straight and the anguish vanished. He seemed ennobled. Holding the hedron out in cupped hands, he bowed to the scrutator, to Overseer Tuniz and to Crafter Irisis, and finally to the mass of workers. Ky-Ara then spun on one boot-heel and marched to the furnace.

There his momentum failed. He made a half-hearted motion of his hands as if to hurl the hedron in, but could not go through with it. Ky-Ara turned back to the watchers, baring his teeth in agony. The scrutator said not a word.

Ky-Ara forced himself. Taking two steps up the plank, he darted his head forward. Nish gasped, thinking that the operator was going to throw himself in, but again Ky-Ara hesitated.

Rotating to face the manufactory, he steadily raised the hedron above his head. Against the blast from the furnace his body was just a dark shape, though the hedron, in front of the dark iron, shone brightly.

Ky-Ara was concentrating so hard that his hands shook. It was not until one of the prentice artisans collapsed, until Irisis cried out and held her temples, that Nish realised what the former operator was trying to do. He was calling power directly into the crystal, a deadly dangerous thing to do. Was he trying to destroy them all?

Nish ran forward but the scrutator caught his coat, dragging him back effortlessly. 'I can't afford to lose you, boy.'

The hedron began to glow, lighting up Ky-Ara's fingers red from behind. A tendril of steam rose from his hand, then the hedron flared so brightly that Nish had to cover his eyes. Ullii screamed and curled up into a ball.

When Nish looked again the hedron had gone dull and he realised that he had not seen steam at all, but smoke. The operator's whole body was smoking. His clothes were smouldering, and his hair. The crystal brightened again. Ky-Ara gave a shrill laugh which was cut off abruptly. Smoke wisped out of his mouth, his ears, and most gruesome of all, from his eyes. Steaming jelly oozed down his cheeks. Ky-Ara gasped, then slowly began to char from the forehead down. The burning garments fell off and he was like charcoal underneath.

The man was dead but he did not fall down. He became a spread-legged, carbonised statue, still holding the hedron above his head. Beside Nish, Ullii was screaming.

He bent down to put his hand over her nose. It did not calm her until, with a fizzing pop, the hedron burst, scattering fragments everywhere. The seeker's screams cut off instantly.

'A fitting end, anthracism,' the scrutator remarked. 'Cast the remains into the furnace!'

The remainder of the winter was a time of unending toil for everyone in the mine and the manufactory. Even though the people who'd fled from the raid were back at work, it took weeks to put the place back into operation. One of the furnaces was full of solidified iron and had to be partly demolished to get the residue out. It was not a happy time. Foreman Gryste, put in charge of the artificers after Tuniz's elevation, drove them like slaves, pouring out bile for the least infringement of his rules. Once Nish was flogged because he failed to ask permission to use the latrine. Gryste was driven by bitterness bordering on insanity, which they had to endure in silence.

Before they could begin building clankers they had to produce all the parts that went to make one up: metal plate, gears and driving rods, housings, nuts and bolts, pins, and a thousand other objects, to say nothing of controllers. The seeker laboured just as hard in the mine, for finding crystal proved more difficult than merely pointing to the rock. However, the crystals Ullii did locate were the best they'd ever had.

In their few free moments, Nish and every other able person laboured with stone and timber for the carpenters, the masons and the metalwrights as they worked to improve the defences of the manufactory. The new gates and strengthened walls were not impregnable, but they would resist attack by the small bands that had so damaged the place before. It would take a sizeable force now.

No one had time for leisure after the work was done – they simply fell into their beds in the middle of the night, knowing they would be dragged out again before dawn. And after all his work was done, Nish still had to visit Ullii and find out if she had *seen* anything, and if Tiaan had reappeared on her fans. The answer was always the same. *Nothing*.

Nish hardly saw Irisis from one week to the next, though each time he did she looked more and more stressed. They had not been lovers since leaving on the failed hunt for Tiaan. One night he went past her door at two in the morning and noticed that her light was still on. He knocked.

'Come in, Nish!'

She was sitting up in bed with a coat about her shoulders, staring at the wall. 'I'm not in the mood,' she said before he could open his mouth.

'Neither am I.'

'But . . .' She did not go on.

'I came because . . . are you all right, Irisis?'

She had drawn the coat sleeve across her face and was rubbing furiously at her eyes. 'It's started again.'

'What?'

'The sabotages. Another controller was damaged yesterday while we were out. Gryste has been making veiled threats.'

'Against you?' he said incredulously.

'The saboteur isn't *Tiaan!*' Irisis said with dripping sarcasm. 'After she went to the breeding factory I felt that it was the apothek, but he's dead. So who *is* it? I once suspected Muss the halfwit, but I don't know any more. Now I'm being blamed. Every time something has happened, I've been around. I have a record and I'm the obvious suspect. And if I *didn't* do it, Gryste is demanding to know why I haven't found out who did. I am in charge, after all.'

'Gryste is a bitter man,' said Nish. 'Is he out to get you, do you think? Have you ever had . . .?'

'He's not my kind of man.'

'Have you ever rejected him?' Nish asked delicately.

'Not knowingly. He's never asked. Besides, he goes for big, blowzy women. Artificers and other low types.'

He did not react to the provocation. She was not herself. 'Then why does he hate you so?'

'He was passed over for overseer, remember? Tuniz was way below him and promoted straight to the top. Her work is flawless so he's after me instead. He'd never have made overseer anyway,

514

and the scrutator blames him for not uncovering who the saboteur was last time. Gryste blames his troubles on me.'

The following day Nish was on his way to the water barrel when he heard two artificers gossiping.

'Reckon it is the crafter,' said one. 'You heard what she did to set up Artisan Tiaan?'

'Yeah! I've never liked Irisis, the stuck-up cow! About time the scrutator . . .'

They broke off as he approached, hurrying back to their benches. Nish heard a lot more of that in the next few days. The scrutator went about with a thunderous face and there were unannounced searches of many rooms in the manufactory, including those of Nish and Irisis.

Nothing was discovered, but a week later a hedron, one of the best, was found smashed on the crafter's bench. Within the hour Irisis was in the cells.

Nish was not allowed to visit; the way was blocked by a pair of the foreman's personal guard. He went looking for Gryste, but he was in conference with the overseer and scrutator. Collecting a plate of stew and rice from the refectory, Nish went to Ullii's room to ask his daily question.

'Have you seen any sign of Tiaan or the crystal?'

'No.' The seeker wrinkled up her nose, then slipped in her noseplugs.

He did not offer her any of his dinner, for she would not have been able to eat it. The stew was heavily spiced to disguise that it had been made a week ago and was well past its best. Ullii lived on fruit, vegetables and cereal, with an occasional piece of mild cheese, poached fish or boiled kid. She could not abide strong flavours of any kind, nor any sort of spice or condiment.

Nish sat on the floor, miserably eating his stew. It tasted even more horrible than usual.

'What's the matter, Nish?' The seeker crept up beside him.

'Irisis has been put in the dungeon.'

'That's nice.' She sighed.

'What?' he cried.

Ullii scuttled away from the miniature explosion. 'I was happy in the dungeon of Mancer Flammas.'

'Irisis will not be happy. And I can't even talk to her.'

The trial had gone badly from the first. A succession of guards testified that, at the time of the sabotages, the only person in the vicinity of the artisans' workshop had been Irisis. Foreman Gryste confirmed the evidence of his guards. Notes made previously by Gi-Had were read out. They contained Irisis's admissions about planting evidence against Tiaan and stealing her work. Lastly, the clerk read a statement by Jal-Nish, detailing his suspicions about Irisis and describing her 'unprovoked' attack on him by the frozen river. Witnesses were called to confirm the attack, including Nish.

Two chroniclers sat on the scrutator's right hand – the official historian of the manufactory, and a scribe recording the event for Irisis's family, to be sure the shameful scene was written correctly into the family Histories of the House of Stirm. The manufactory's teller was there too. When all was recorded the scrutator sat back in his chair, sucking on his whiskers. He stared at Irisis, at Nish and at each of the witnesses in turn. Irisis met his gaze defiantly. The others looked away.

'Well, Crafter Irisis, have you anything to say?'

'I have previously admitted to planting evidence against Tiaan and to stealing her work. It is true that I assaulted the perquisitor. The brute deserved it and I would do it again! I deny the sabotages and all the other charges.'

'She would!' cried Gryste. 'Scrutator, we must be rid of her for the good of the war.'

Xervish Flydd turned that gaunt face to him. 'Are you trying this case, foreman?' he said mildly.

'I just . . .'

Flydd waved his hand and the man fell silent. 'Clerk, would you read out the penalties for this series of crimes?'

The clerk, a tiny woman of advanced years and as wrinkled as a dried olive, squinted at a piece of parchment.

'On the charge of planting evidence, *admitted*, a month in the breeding factory.'

Nish was watching Irisis. As the penalty was read out, her face cracked. For an instant it looked as if she was going to scream, then she took control and he saw only a mask.

'On the charge of stealing Artisan Tiaan's work, *admitted*, three months in the breeding factory. On the charge of assaulting the perquisitor, *admitted*, two years in the breeding factory.' She paused to draw breath.

'On the charges of sabotage, *denied*, the penalties are public execution in each case, by any of the methods specified for the criminal's craft.' The clerk handed the parchment up to the scrutator for signature.

Xervish Flydd picked up a quill. 'Have you anything to say, Crafter Irisis, before I sign the warrants?'

'Only that the charges I have denied are false. I would never do anything to betray the cause I, and my family, have worked for over these past hundred and fifty years.'

'All traitors say that!'

'Once I am dead, you will still be looking for the real traitor and the sabotages will go on.'

'Hmn,' said the scrutator.

Nish put his head in his hands. He could not look at Irisis. The thought of attending the execution, as he would be required to do, was too ghastly to contemplate.

'Has any other witness anything to say?' said the scrutator.

Nish could think of nothing that would count as mitigation. No one else spoke either.

'Before I confirm the sentences,' the scrutator went on, 'which I am entitled to do on the evidence before me . . . Well, I like to be sure. I propose to call a witness, and carry out a test, of my own. Call the seeker!'

Nish sat up. It seemed irregular to say the least, and surely several of the sabotages had been carried out before Ullii arrived at the manufactory.

Ullii was led in, wearing her mask and earmuffs. She was trembling as she took her place beside the scrutator. He spoke softly to her and gave her his hand. As Ullii drew it to her nose, Nish felt a moment of jealous outrage. That was *his* role; surely the smell of that withered old man could not do the same for her?

The scrutator gave an imperceptible twitch of his snaky eyebrow. Nish, who was sitting up the back, heard the door-bolts click. The guards took their positions, two on either side of the door.

'I have here,' said the scrutator, holding up a chain and the broken remains of a pliance, and in the other hand a milky hedron, 'evidence which Overseer Gi-Had kept under special guard. It is the remains of Artisan Tiaan's pliance, destroyed when she tried to read one of the failed hedrons. The enemy felt this evidence so threatening that they attacked the manufactory to recover it. Fortunately they did not get it.' Reaching across, he put the objects by Ullii's hand.

'Seeker, Artisan Tiaan saw something in these artefacts. Can you read anything from them? Please stand so everyone can see you.'

Ullii stood up, shaking. For someone who avoided people at all times, this was the worst ordeal she could be put to. Holding the hedron out, she said something in an inaudible voice. Irisis, who had risen to her feet, sat down and the light faded from her eyes.

'Speak up, seeker!' rumbled Flydd. 'No one can hear you.'

In a voice that precisely imitated his, she said, 'It is dead. I can see nothing in it.' She laid the ruined pliance on the benchtop.

Among the crowd, someone let out a great sigh. 'And this crystal,' said the scrutator, 'which is the failed hedron from Disgraced Operator Ky-Ara's original controller?'

Ullii reached for the crystal but drew back at once. Emitting a single sharp scream, she began to curl up into a ball.

'Stop that!' the scrutator said sharply. 'Come back, seeker.'

Ullii froze, then slowly, gracefully uncurled.

'What do you see in the crystal, seeker?'

She gasped, clutched at his hand and said. 'A clawer! Spying on me.'

518

'Do you mean a lyrinx?'

'Yes,' she whispered.

'What else?'

'A man. The clawer is giving something to a man. White gold!'

'A man? The spy! Can you see his face?'

'No. His back is to me.'

'And that is *all* you can see?' Nish could read bitter disappointment in the scrutator's frame.

'Yes,' said Ullii.

'Very well. Have you anything to say, Artisan Irisis? Do you admit that this man is your paymaster?'

'Don't be absurd! My family is rich. I have more money than I can ever spend.'

'Doesn't mean you don't want more! Thank you, seeker. You may go down. Clerk, if you would be so good as to hand me the charge sheet, I will confirm . . .'

Suddenly something occurred to Nish and he sprang to his feet. 'Scrutator! scrutator!'

'Yes?' he snapped. 'It's too late for special pleading now, artificer. The trial is done.'

'It's new evidence,' he cried. 'Please, I beg leave to put a question to the seeker.'

'Oh? What question could you possibly ask that I haven't already thought of?'

Nish chose his words with particular care in case he insulted the scrutator. 'I know her better than anyone, surr. The seeker never volunteers, because it never occurs to her, and she only answers what she is asked. You asked the wrong question, surr. With great respect.'

'Respect is a commodity you've always been short of, boy, like your wretched father. Very well, put your question.'

'Ullii,' said Nish, his heart pounding, 'would you take up the crystal?'

Turning her masked eyes to him, she reached out, touching the hedron with one fingertip.

'No, take it in your hand, Ullii.'

She gave a little cry of anguish, or of terror. The scrutator clasped her other hand. Ullii took up the crystal.

'Look at the image of the man with his back to you. Do you recognise him?'

'No,' said Ullii.

'Bah! Damned nonsense,' came a voice from the crowd. 'I already know who the paymaster is.' Foreman Gryste stood. 'I've been doing *my* job, even if no one else has.'

'Are you suggesting that *I* haven't been doing my job?' the scrutator asked mildly.

Gryste faltered. 'No, surr. I'm sorry. I have the man in my cells, surr.'

'Oh?' said the scrutator. 'Which man, foreman?'

'The one who's always hanging around, sticking his fat nose into everyone's work, and doing none of his own. It's Muss, surr. Eiryn Muss.'

'The halfwit!' Flydd burst out laughing.

'He's no halfwit, surr. He's a cunning spy and he's fooled us all.'

'Even me, foreman?' Flydd said dangerously.

'I'm afraid so, surr.'

The scrutator gestured. 'Bring Muss here, and keep a firm hold of him. Don't let him see anything secret on the way.' He laughed at his joke.

It was like watching a corpse laugh; but Nish wondered, as he had once before, if Muss was more than he seemed.

The scrutator did not resume his questioning of Ullii. There was silence for a few minutes, then the guards came pounding in. 'Surr, surr!'

'What is it, man?' the scrutator inquired.

'The prisoner has fled, surr,' the leading guard cried.

'How?'

'The lock is burnt completely from the door. Sorcery!' He shivered.

Flydd did not look surprised.

'What did I tell you, surr,' said Gryste. 'This proves it.'

'It proves something, foreman, though I don't know what.'

Flydd turned to Nish. 'Go on with your questioning, artificer.'

Nish's confidence had taken a battering. There seemed little point in continuing. 'This man you saw in the crystal, Ullii, does he have a talent of any kind?'

'A very small talent,' she said softly. 'Tiny!'

'Then you should be able to see him in your lattice.'

Ullii shrugged.

'Search your lattice, Ullii. Is there anyone in it with the same kind of knot as that man's talent has?'

Irisis was on her feet, quivering with emotion. The scrutator stood as well.

Ullii folded up. 'Yes.' She looked down at the polished surface of the bench.

A buzz went through the crowd. One by one, everyone rose. 'It's Muss!' cried Gryste. 'After him, before it's too late!'

'Silence!' The scrutator held up his hand. 'The first person to make a noise goes to the front-lines.' No one moved.

'Is that man in the room, Ullii?' said Nish.

'Yes,' she whispered.

'Would you point to him?'

She pointed to the centre of the room. Slowly the crowd moved away until one man was standing all by himself.

'How dare you? You lying little slag!' roared Foreman Gryste, and launched himself at her.

He disappeared under a dozen bodies. They stood him up again, holding him tightly.

'Soldiers, search the foreman's room. Chronicler and teller, go with them. Ullii, you go too, and seek out anything that may be hidden. *Run!*'

They ran out. The agonising silence dragged on. The foreman stood as rigid as a post. The distinctive clove odour of nigah permeated the room.

Nish could not bear to hope. Finally he heard the clatter of running feet and the soldiers and recorders reappeared. Shortly after that, Ullii came in. Her light step made no sound at all.

'Well?' said Flydd.

'We found nothing,' said the first soldier.

'You witnessed this?' Xervish demanded of the recorders. 'The search was thorough?'

'It was just as they say . . .'

'Damn you all!' cried Gryste. 'I'll have reparation for this insult to my honour!'

'Indeed you will,' said the scrutator. 'If you prove to be innocent.'

'The soldiers found nothing,' snarled Gryste.

'And the seeker? *Did* she seek out what was hidden?'

'She did, surr,' said the recorders together.

'Come up, Ullii,' said Flydd. 'Did you find nothing at all?'

She crept up. 'Only this.' She took a sagging leather bag out of her shirt.

'It was under the floor, concealed by a charm,' said the chronicler.

The scrutator poured the contents onto the floor, a heap of ringing platinum. His eyes met those of the foreman, and such a look of contempt passed across his face that Nish's skin crawled. 'I wondered how you could support your nigah habit on foreman's wages,' said Flydd.

The foreman did not reply. His eyes darted this way and that.

'You're a failure of a man, aren't you, Gryste? You were a lousy foreman, a disastrous sergeant, and then a lousy foreman again.'

'Everyone was against me, surr. People are always trying to bring me down.'

'It's always someone else's fault, isn't it?'

'It is, it is!'

'Have you anything to say for yourself, Gryste?'

'The seeker is lying, surr. They're all lying. They've never liked me.'

'I don't like you either. And this is not your only crime, is it? *You* sabotaged Tiaan's crystals. *You* poisoned her with calluna. *You* killed the apothek to stop him talking.'

Gryste said nothing at all.

'Traitor Gryste, you will be executed tomorrow for grave treachery, by the method prescribed for your craft and rank. What is the method, clerk?'

She whispered something.

'How appropriate,' said Flydd with a death's-head smile. 'Traitor Gryste, you will be fed into the grinding mill. Take him down!'

The foreman was dragged off, wailing and screaming obscenities. 'Crafter Irisis,' Flydd continued, 'the unproven charges are dismissed. Sentence for the proven charges is suspended for one year. After that time, if you have met all your goals as crafter, they will be stricken from the record. This trial is ended.'

Nish went up to the bench. 'What about Muss, surr?' he said quietly as everyone was filing out. 'We can't afford – '

'Muss has been my prober here for seven years,' said Flydd, equally softly. 'And a damn good one. No one ever broke his cover. You could take a lesson there, boy. He won't be seen in this province again.'

FIFTY-TWO

After some six weeks of slave labour the work slackened. It had to, for everyone was so exhausted that they were making mistakes, and the toll of injured workers was horrific. They began to work six days a week and take a half day's rest on the seventh. On the second of those half days off, as Nish was sitting with Ullii in a darkened room, she sprang up. As usual, she wore nothing but spider-silk knickers and a sleeveless blouse. Her skin gleamed in the dim light.

'I can SEE her!'

'Ullii!' He leapt up to embrace her and she threw him against the wall. He'd forgotten how sensitive her skin was.

'I'm sorry!' He picked himself up. 'I was excited.'

'Your coat is like hooks dragging through my skin. Did I hurt you? I *am* trying hard, Nish.'

Ullii was much better now. She hardly ever used the mask these days, preferring goggles most of the time. Once or twice she had even been outside without earmuffs or plugs. It had been a tremendous ordeal but she had coped. Her brain could deal with one overloaded sense as long as the others were shielded. When she wore earmuffs, bright light did not hurt her so much. Only her sensitivity to smell had not changed. If anything it had grown more sensitive, as if to compensate. Often the tiniest of odours, that no one else could smell, would set her off. Outside her room she wore plugs in her nose.

Nish wondered how she had managed the changes in her life. Was it because he had befriended her, and Irisis defended her? Certainly she had seen more kindness and caring in the past months than in the rest of her life, and maybe that had helped. She had discovered that not everyone wanted to use her.

But of course I *do* want to use her, Nish thought. He was not blind to his own failings. He lusted after her small, sweet body every night; the soft, almost colourless hair, the baby-smooth skin, the small breasts and full thighs. He wanted nothing but to sate himself in her and to hear her cry out and wrap herself around him.

'I can *see* her,' Ullii reminded him, dragging him out of his unhealthy obsession.

'Where is she?'

She pointed south-west.

'Are you sure?' he said foolishly.

She continued to point.

'How far is it?' An equally foolish question.

'I don't know. A long way.'

'When did you first see her?'

'In the middle of the night. She hasn't been there for months, then last night she appeared, like a flower opening. Her crystal was so bright that I lost all the knots around her. I saw lakes and mountains too.'

That was not much help – to the south-west there were lakes and mountains for hundreds of leagues. 'I'd better find the scrutator.' He had been to the manufactory twice in the past month and was due to leave today.

She shrank back against the wall. 'Your friend, Xervish,' said Nish.

She slowly relaxed, then gave a tentative smile. After searching everywhere, Nish found the withered little man at the front gate.

'Yes?' Xervish said sharply. 'Make it snappy, artificer! The weather is closing in and I must be in Tiksi tonight. Another field has failed and we don't know why.'

'The seeker has seen Tiaan.'

The scrutator gave a great sigh. 'Which direction?' Anybody else would have said 'Where?'.

'South-west. A long way.'

The scrutator nodded, scribbled a note and handed it to the captain of his guard. The man saluted and turned down the path. Xervish came inside. He had the most peculiar, lurching walk, as if his bones had been dislocated in the torture chamber and not put back together properly.

'Let's see what we can find out. Not a word to anyone!'

Ullii greeted the scrutator cheerfully, but despite much urging and coaxing she could tell him no more than she had told Nish. Finally she became distressed, so they left her.

'What would I not give for one of the farspeakers of old,' said Xervish heavily.

'What were they?' Nish had never heard of such a thing.

'A way of talking from one side of Lauralin to the other. Golias the Mad invented them near three thousand years ago, using special crystals and wires.'

'What happened to them?'

'He was assassinated to get the secret, but the spark soon went out of the crystals and no one else could make them work, or find the source of them. Golias was a mancer and no doubt some great spell drove the farspeakers, but the spell and the secret died with him. If we had them now . . .'

'I don't see how it would help us,' said Nish.

'And you an artificer!' Xervish walked off in the direction of the refectory. Nish followed.

The scrutator selected baked vegetables, steamed millet and a small piece of poached fish from the trays, ladled the fiery red sauce called yalp over it, and carried it to a table. Nish took a small bowl of candied pears and another of rose-petal tea, since he'd already dined.

'If you would explain, surr,' Nish said tentatively, standing by the scrutator's table with his bowls.

'Sit down, lad!' Xervish ate quickly, using the old-fashioned eating sticks rather than fork and knife. His table manners made Nish cringe but he made allowances – his scribing days had taught him that what was ill-mannered in one place could be required behaviour in another. Besides, the scrutator was of another age, and he could decide Nish's fate with a snap of his fingers. And yet, Nish sensed that here was a man much more flexible than his father. A man always prepared to listen.

Xervish dipped his finger in the water at the bottom of the steamed millet. A few grains stuck to the twisted digit. On the tabletop he drew a series of arcs to show the coastline, a sweeping curve that was the line of the Great Mountains, the linked ovals of the inland seas of Tallallamel and Milmillamel and, between the seas and the mountains, the wilderness of lake and forest that made up the frigid lands of Tarralladell and Mirrilladell.

'We are here.' The scrutator stabbed a finger at the eastern end of the mountains. 'The seeker said south-west, which could mean anywhere along this line. But if . . . if we had a farspeaker, and could speak with another seeker a long way away . . .' his finger wandered across the seas to land on the other side, '. . . say, here, at Drow, and if that that seeker could find Tiaan, say, a little east of north . . .' He drew a line in that direction until it intersected the other line. 'There she is!'

Nish was stunned. The idea was so simple, so obvious, yet he had never thought of it. His respect for the man went up.

Xervish swept his hand across the surface, obliterating the marks. 'But of course we don't have farspeakers, and even if we did, how would we explain to the other seeker how to sense out Tiaan, one particular person in millions? It is, I'm afraid, quite impossible!' He stood up.

'If we were to move our seeker, it would serve the same purpose.'

Xervish sat again. 'Nice thought, boy, but how would we do it? She's got to travel a long way, quickly. The sight lines must cross at a large angle otherwise it's useless. We can't go fast enough, especially not at this time of year.'

'What if we put her on a ship?' Nish said excitedly. 'In a week we could be a hundred leagues down the coast, if the weather was with us.'

'But we'd be going away from Tiaan. By the time we got back she might have moved again. We'd still be months away from her.'

Nish sat with head in hands. There had to be a way. 'If only we could fly, like the lyrinx that carried her away.'

'We mancers have been searching for that secret for four thousand years,' said the scrutator. 'We've never even gotten close.'

'But the lyrinx . . .'

'They have *wings,* boy!' Xervish growled. 'And even their wings won't hold them up on our world without such expenditures of the Secret Art as few can maintain for an hour. Their wings were designed for the void. Trying to fly on Santhenar has killed more lyrinx than all our armies together.'

'Ullii could not speak for hours after the lyrinx flew away with Tiaan,' Nish said thoughtfully.

'Ullii was lucky. It must have been using such power, it's lucky her mind was not burned.'

'Could we make a wing flier, like the one they carried Tiaan away with?'

'I've had the best mechanicians working on that idea ever since you came back,' said Xervish. 'It was little more than a glider such as any school child might make. We can build one, though not strong enough to carry anyone bigger than you. We can launch it from a mountain, and maybe it will fly for five leagues, or ten. But what happens when it lands in the wilderness? The pilot dies because we can't find him. And it's fatal in any sort of wind. No, Nish, without some means of powering it, it won't work.'

'What about a special controller, like those used in clankers?'

'We've thought about that too. Clankers have legs; the controllers make them walk. How do we get your machine to fly? We can't walk on air.'

'Paddles?'

'Also tried. It was too heavy. It's a good idea, artificer, but beyond our skills.'

Nish spent the afternoon on his bed, thinking that there had to be a way. Only one flying device had ever been mentioned in the Histories – the famous construct Rulke the Charon had designed in his long imprisonment in the Nightland. But the construct had been destroyed after Maigraith used it to cross the Way between the Worlds to Aachan, taking Rulke's body home to his people, more than two hundred years ago. No mancer had ever seen inside the machine, and Rulke had left no description of it. Another secret that had died with its maker.

How *could* humans fly, without wings or a powered glider, or some incomprehensible force like the construct? He puzzled over that for the rest of the day; then, no closer to a solution, he decided to have an early night for once.

Nish roused toward the middle of the night with an answer. It came from a game he'd played with his brothers and sister when he was a child. They'd made bags out of scraps of paper glued together with flour and water paste, held them upside down over the fire and bet which one would fly up the chimney on the hot air and furthest across the yard.

Nish, being the youngest, had never won, but had kept making his models long after the other children lost interest. The primitive balloons were unstable, tipping over and falling back into the fire more often than they'd gone up the chimney. Then Nish hit on the idea of suspending a tiny weight on threads below the bag. His first balloon had floated straight up the chimney, across the backyard and landed in the next street.

Having succeeded, Nish had lost interest in balloons. Now he began to wonder. Leaping out of bed, he began to sketch furiously. Shortly he was banging on the scrutator's door.

'Surr, surr!' he cried.

After considerable muttering and cursing the door opened. The scrutator stood there, completely naked, in the light of a single candle. The rest of his body was as gnarled and twisted as his fingers, while scars criss-crossed a torso so lean that every bone could be counted, every sinew traced. What torture had the man suffered?

'What the hell do you want?' snapped Xervish.

'I have the answer, surr! A balloon powered by hot air!' He held out his sketches.

Xervish snatched them, muttering, 'Bloody fool!' He stared at the papers for a full minute, stepped back and slammed the door in Nish's face.

Nish shrugged. It was after midnight. He went back to bed. He'd done all he could.

FIFTY-THREE

On Tiaan hobbled, back to what she thought was the previous clearing, trusting to her instincts to carry her to the campfire.

They failed her. Shortly she encountered a gloomy copse that she had no memory of seeing before. Stopping at the edge, she reviewed her options. Without a fire she would probably die of exposure. Hanni certainly would. But she had nothing to make one with – flint and tinder were at the camp.

Holding up the amplimet awkwardly, for Haani was getting heavy, she tried to work out what to do. The first clearing, and her tracks, might be only a snowball's throw away, but which way? She dared not climb a tree to look for the fire, for fear the child would run away.

Haani moaned and shuddered. Setting her down, Tiaan took off her own coat, wrapped Haani in it, put her feet through the sleeves and tied the ends. With a piece of cord she made a sling around her neck and lifted the bundled child in. At least it left her hands free.

Leaning back against a tree, Tiaan tried to draw power into the crystal. It did not work. There was no field here. She could sense power deep in the earth, but only as the vaguest blur that was no use to her. It took a while to work out why, so sluggish was her thinking in the cold. With the helm and globe back at the fire, she had no way to focus the amplimet.

Pulling the child closer, she shut her eyes. There was some warmth between them, but not enough. Haani's teeth chattered. If only she'd thought to bring the helm. Tiaan could visualise it now. That was her unique ability, one of the reasons she had done so well as an artisan. She could look at an image any way she chose, rotate it, even turn it upside down. If it was of a working mechanism, like the gears of a clock, she could make it run and see any flaws at once.

As Tiaan idly rotated the helm in her mind, she felt a tiny pull to the right. She looked that way: the pull now seemed to come from straight ahead. Could the amplimet be calling to the helm, or the other way around? That seemed absurd. She mentally turned the helm and as its crystal came into view it glowed like the amplimet. The glow faded as the helm revolved away.

Maybe the helm's crystal *was* calling to the amplimet, and why not? Both had lain together in that underground cavity for an eternity. The Principle of Association told that the link must be maintained, even though they were separated by time or distance.

She turned the helm until its crystal faced her and the glow was at its brightest. Tiaan felt that pull again. She took a step towards it, then another. It was still there. Yes! she exulted. It can lead me home.

It led her somewhere, but after she had been walking for about as long as it had taken to find the child, Haani jerked, let out a wailing cry and the image vanished. By the time Tiaan calmed the child she could not get the helm's image back. She kept going, hoping she would end up at the fire. A faint hope. In the thickening snow she might miss it by fifty paces and never see it.

Her shin began to trouble her. It would be worse in the morning, if she lived to see it. She kept going, long past the point where the fire should be. Haani had not run all that far; certainly less than a thousand paces. Tiaan was wondering which direction to go, and how much further she *could* go on her frozen feet, when she caught a whiff of smoke.

She turned into the wind, testing the air like a dog. There it was again. She headed that way, tracking the elusive smell. It was sometimes there, sometimes not; now definitely stronger. Tiaan felt like cheering. Stumbling on, in a few minutes she saw, beyond the trees, the light of the fire. Tiaan ran the last distance, laid Haani down next to the coals and pulled her feet out of the sleeves. She expected to see the dull white of frostbite but to her joy the child's small feet, though deathly cold, were unmarked. She propped them close to the fire.

Tiaan's own feet were in worse condition, though at least she had been wearing socks. She put them near the warmth, then dipped a mug of stew each. Haani's hand came out of the coat and took her mug. The child did not look at her as she sipped. Tiaan did not know if she was angry or afraid. She did not care. Haani was safe. Nothing else mattered.

Soon the child began to droop. Tiaan put her in the sleeping pouch and got in with her. Haani lay rigidly in her arms. Finally she slept and, to Tiaan's relief, snuggled up and her cold hand took Tiaan's.

It was not the best night's sleep Tiaan had ever had. Dreams of lyrinx, nightmares about the nylatl, a reproachful, let-down Minis, all were mixed in with Haani's own fitful nightmares. Once more Haani woke screaming and thrashing, but with Tiaan's arms around her there was nowhere to go. Soon the child slept soundly.

In the morning Haani was better, though she still would not speak. There was nothing to be done about that but wait it out.

Tiaan's shin was little worse than before, though her muscles were very stiff. They ate a quick breakfast, got back on the river and skied all day, just going steadily. Haani seemed to need the activity – she was always first on her feet and last to sit down. It was all Tiaan could do to keep up with her.

Thinking about what had happened last night, Tiaan realised that the amplimet had been dull because she was too far from the node of Kalissin and there was no other node nearby. That was why she had been unable to contact Minis. He could still be alive.

The day passed and two more. It was the easiest skiing Tiaan had ever done – smooth ice covered with a thin layer of snow. They were making excellent progress, as much as seven leagues one day, by her estimate. They often passed villages but did not stop. Haani had no more interest in meeting strangers than Tiaan did. Maybe Haani was shy too. Probably was, living up there all alone.

Midway through the seventh day, the villages on the shore became more numerous and larger. They began to pass orchards and snow-covered market gardens. Late in the afternoon they reached the outskirts of a sizeable town.

Suddenly there were people everywhere. Hundreds of children played on the ice. Lines of porters skied to and from the smaller settlement on the other side, carrying huge loads on their backs, or sometimes their heads. Shabby little delivery boys mixed with well-dressed ladies and gentlemen gliding along the foreshores. The ice was their highway, a more convenient one than the frozen, rutted roads.

They continued until they reached a waterfront that appeared to be the centre of Ghysmel. After diligent enquiry Tiaan located the shipping offices. Going into the first, she asked about passage west down the sea. A tall, blond-haired woman came to the counter.

'You're in luck. We've had a thaw these last few weeks. The *Norwhal* is leaving tomorrow, and sailing all the way down the Milmillamel to Thryss and Flaha.'

'I don't know those places,' Tiaan said. Catching sight of a faded chart on the wall, she picked the name of a destination, since she would undoubtedly be asked. The war had not come this far south so she presumed there would be no restrictions on travel.

'I would like to purchase two tickets to Flaha.' It was a town on the north side of Milmillamel, a good two hundred leagues away.

'Cabin, hammock or steerage?' the blond woman asked.

'That would depend on the tariff,' Tiaan replied carefully.

The cabins turned out to be reasonably priced, one gold coin and two silver. Tiaan had more than enough, having not yet touched the contents of Joeyn's belt. The idea of living in a hammock for weeks, in a room with dozens of other people, probably dirty and smelly and prying into her business, could not be countenanced. She'd not shared a room since she became an artisan.

'Cabin, please.'

The clerk checked the gold and silver with her teeth, weighed it on a small pair of scales, then wrote out a ticket in beautiful handwriting full of swirls and flourishes. 'Where are you going?' she asked casually as she worked.

'What? Oh, Tatusti.' She named a town upstream from Flaha, unwilling to divulge her true destination.

'Tatusti?' The clerk sounded incredulous.

'The man I am betrothed to is there.' Tiaan flushed at the sound of those words, often thought about but never before uttered.

The clerk melted green wax onto the paper and stamped it with a seal.

'Thank you!' Tiaan took the ticket. 'What time is the tide tomorrow?'

'No tides in Tallallamel. Where is your home town? You must have come a long way.'

A common enough question. Tiaan had said 'Tiksi, over the mountains,' before she realised.

The clerk nodded. 'I thought so, from your speech, We see many travellers here, though few from that land. The *Norwhal* leaves at nine in the morning. Or ten. Or even eleven if the captain gets drunk again, which she usually does. Best be here at eight, to be certain.'

Tiaan thanked her, then turned back. 'Can you name a good inn, not too far away?'

'Go to The Mussel Gatherer, a few hundred steps back toward the town, that way. Ask for Pwym the porter. He's my little brother and he'll fix you up nicely.'

A most courteous young man, he did just that. In under an hour Tiaan and Haani were set up in a small but pleasant room

535

on the third floor, overlooking the waterfront. A metal bath was brought up and filled with buckets of hot water. They scrubbed away the grime of weeks.

In the evening they went to the markets, purchasing clothes for the journey. Haani looked like a hillbilly child in her dirty furs. Tiaan bought a needle, strong thread and various other things she might need on the journey, then spent an entirely unnatural amount of silver on a special outfit, the one she planned to wear when she met Minis.

In the morning they arrived early and were shown to their cabin. It was tiny, airless but clean and neat. The captain had stayed sober, evidently, for the boat unfurled her sails and left on the gong of nine.

The trip to Flaha took fifteen days. They did not stop for the first week, but after that visited one port after another, sometimes only sailing for half a day before docking again.

Tiaan and Haani kept to themselves, occasionally walking on the cramped deck, which was cold and windy. Haani was clinging now – she was shy in crowds and would not answer when people spoke to her. Tiaan understood that, though she found it confining.

On the third day, through a gap in the clouds, she glimpsed a familiar flying shape, just for a second. Was the lyrinx hunting her or was it just a coincidence? She could not think so. After that she kept to their cabin, busying herself in making a new pair of boots to replace Haani's worn-out ones. Tiaan enjoyed the work, using her artisan's skills for the first time in ages. It was helping to prepare her fingers for another job, one she planned to begin as soon as the boots were complete.

Whenever she needed a hand, Haani was there and seemed to know instinctively what to do. Tiaan appreciated that, though she would as soon have done it herself. She was so used to working alone that having to share a room made her feel uncomfortable. Besides, Haani was being helpful because she had been brought up that way. It did not mean the child liked her. Tiaan was sure she did not.

Haani never asked for anything. She hardly spoke apart from please, thank you, yes and no, and gave the briefest possible response to Tiaan's increasingly infrequent overtures. Tiaan felt guilty, but more and more she found the child a burden. Perhaps Haani realised that. When the boots were ready she said 'Thank you!' but continued wearing the old ones.

Tiaan's second job was a gift for Minis, a ring of woven silver and gold made from the precious metal in Joeyn's belt. First she formed the yellow metal, and the silver, into threads, tapping away with her little hammers for hours. She did not care how arduous the work was, or how long it took, as long as it was ready before she reached the mountain. It left less gold and silver than she would have liked, and that bothered her, for there was a long way to go. But she had to have a betrothal gift, even though every attempt to contact Minis had failed. More and more she felt that her journey was a fool's errand.

After the second day Haani grew bored, for there was nothing she could do to help with the ring. Tiaan began to teach the child her letters, using the copy of Nunar's treatise she had carried all this way. It was hard work. Haani did not see the point of reading and Tiaan discovered that as a teacher she had many inadequacies, not least of them being impatience. Haani proved to be a good listener though, picking up the language quickly. Each time she spoke the common language her accent was better and her command more fluent.

Accustomed to spending the daylight hours out of doors, the child was practically climbing the walls by the time they pulled up at the wharves of Flaha, a rambling, unattractive town built of grey timber.

Mount Tirthrax lay north of Flaha, another hundred and fifty leagues away. Tiaan had been prepared to spend what remained of the winter in Flaha, until she learned that, in this surprisingly well-populated land, it was possible to travel up the frozen rivers by iceboat if she left soon. The thaw was not far away.

'You want to go to Itsipitsi?' her informant asked. It was a good-sized town on the northern end of an extensive lake of the same name, little more than ten leagues from the great mountain. 'That's easy! There's an iceboat every third day, if the weather is good, and the winds usually blow from the south at this time of year. You can do ten leagues a day in good conditions; some days fifteen. But be prepared for a blizzard, and then you might not go anywhere for a week.'

Blizzards did hit more than once, though not for long. In three weeks they were disembarking in Itsipitsi, a frontier town built of logs chinked with mud. The place was bigger than Tiaan had expected though it had a temporary look. Thousands of prospectors would appear in the thaw to pan the rivers for sapphires and zircons washed down from the mountains, but in the winter there were few people on the dismal, windblown streets.

Tiaan's gold was exhausted but she still had silver enough to outfit them for the Great Mountains. Once at Tirthrax, she would be among the Aachim of Santhenar, those who had been brought here as slaves by Rulke the Charon, thousands of years ago, in the search for the Golden Flute. That was one of the Great Tales of the Histories.

It did not bother Tiaan that she was down to a few threads of silver by the time they were equipped and provisioned. The Aachim would provide. However, she thought of Joeyn every time she went to the belt. Poor Joeyn. His memory still brought tears to her eyes.

Of course, it would take time to find the Aachim. Tirthrax was enormous. But when she neared the mountain, surely a potent node, the amplimet would light up and she could call her lover. Minis would tell her where to go. If . . . if he was still alive. If he wasn't, she would never find the way in. The food would run out and she would be stuck up a mountain, a week from any place where she could get more.

FIFTY-FOUR

The range could not be seen from Itsipitsi, which lay in a valley with tall pines all around; however, Tiaan had caught glimpses from the iceboat. Even from this distance the Great Mountains were immense, a snow-and-ice-clad wall stretching from the eastern horizon to the west. Towering over all was the fang of Tirthrax, the highest peak on Santhenar. Highest on any of the Three Worlds, the Histories told. The repository of Tiaan's dreams for half a year was only days away.

They left at dawn, skiing upriver on snow-covered ice. The first day was hard work, though the slope was slight. They had done no skiing since Ghysmel and were carrying an enormous quantity of dried rations, enough to do them for three weeks. Tiaan did not go hard, though she wanted to. She dared not risk injury so close to her goal. In truth, she could not wait to turn into her sleeping pouch, for since their arrival in Itsipitsi she had dreamed of her lover every night, and each time more passionately. They had not yet consummated their love, in her dreams, though his caresses had driven her to such heights of ecstasy that Tiaan could think of nothing else.

The amplimet had been dull ever since she'd left the hut of the three women, its spark visible only in darkness. Now, each night when she unwrapped it the glow was brighter; she could feel its potential growing as they approached Tirthrax. She had tried three times to reach Minis, and sensed that he was there, but could never find him.

The weather was good; after the first day they made excellent time on the ice. The mountains swelled before them, vaster and more forbidding than Tiaan's most extravagant imaginings. Rivers of striped ice thrust forth between the peaks, and when the wind turned on the third morning she heard a monumental roaring and crashing. Once the glaciers had debouched onto an ice sheet covering all Mirrilladell, but it was long gone. Now they ended at precipices a thousand spans high, over which chunks of ice the size of hills would crack off and thunder to the plain. Below each icefall lay spreading mounds that waxed and waned with the seasons.

That afternoon they began to climb. The going now became extremely hard and they had to abandon the skis, which were too heavy to carry. Four days later they camped at the tree line and made a blazing fire, their last. There would be no wood from this point on. Tirthrax towered above them, so high that they had to crane their necks to see the tip, though it was mostly wreathed in cloud.

Tiaan was in her pouch by the fire the instant she finished her stew. Tomorrow they'd be on the mountain. She clutched the amplimet to her breast, its spark throbbing like her heartbeat. She always dreamed after using it, and having it near must enhance her dreams of Minis.

Haani was asleep. Tiaan could hear her gentle snores. But for Tiaan, neither sleep nor dreams would come. She had held back from using the amplimet, not wanting to arouse false hopes. And also, she was forced to admit to herself, because she wanted to present Minis with her triumph and see his reaction. Resigned to wakefulness, however, she put on the helm and began to work the globe.

It took a long time to find him. All she could see was smoke and bloody darkness. An hour must have gone by, Tiaan straining until her skull felt to be cracking apart, before finally there came the voice she had not heard for five months.

Tiaan! Can it be you?

'Yesss!' She exhaled a vast sigh. 'It's me, Minis, my love.'

I had given you up. We thought you must be dead.

'The amplimet is not strong enough to call you, except near nodes. I could not use it for months.'

Of course not. I should have realised.

'I've had trouble on the road, Minis. Terrible trouble. So many people have died . . .'

Then you've failed! Ah, Tiaan, they warned me that it was not possible . . .

'I have not let you down.'

What do you mean? he said hopelessly.

She wished she could see his face but the image was cloudy tonight, the voice in her head faint and crackly.

'I've done it!' she exulted. 'I've come five hundred leagues across Santhenar for you, Minis. I'm at the foot of Tirthrax now.'

Such a current passed through her that it made her black hair stand up on her head. She could sense his reaction in every nerve of her body.

Oh, Tiaan! She could almost feel the tears welling in his eyes. *Tirthrax is the greatest city the Aachim ever built. More than a thousand years they spent carving its chambers into the heart of the mountain. There is no city like it. Show me.*

Forcing her headache away, she got out of the pouch to walk barefoot around the fire and back to where she could see the immense horn of the mountain. There was no cloud. A bloody, mottled moon shone clear and full on its snow-clad flanks, the faces of layered rock, the spire reaching up beyond the air.

A gasp, a cry of pain and joy together. The scene grew smoky, then cleared. Minis ran through a doorway, his cry vibrating in her head, loud enough to wake the child in the tent.

Tirior, Luxor, Vithis foster-father! Come see! Tiaan has brought the amplimet to the very feet of Tirthrax mountain. Look, look!

Dimly she saw faces that she had seen months ago, while trapped in that icy bubble outside the battle cavern. They crowded around, jostling each other in their excitement. There were unfamiliar faces too, and on every one she saw desperate

541

hope, where for the past hundred years there had only been desperation.

Tiaan, said Minis, pushing through, *listen carefully. We have little time left. Maybe days; at most weeks. Already many of us have died. Can you hear me, Tiaan?*

'I can hear you.'

We're losing you. Tiaan, this is what you must do. You are days from the nearest entrance of Tirthrax, though not far from a hidden escape way. Go straight up the curving ridge you see before you. High up, the best part of a day's climb, you will come to a sheer face. From where you are standing, it has the shape of a four-sided diamond. Do you see it?

'I noted it as we camped today.'

At the lower point of the diamond you will encounter two folded bands of rock as red as rust, each a span or more thick. Between lies a thin yellow band. Follow them around the mountain in the direction of the double glacier; that would be to your right, I think?

'Left,' she said, though he gave no sign of having heard.

Go on some two thousand, one hundred steps. How tall are you, Tiaan?

'Eighty-two hundreds of a span,' she said. 'But our span may be shorter than yours.'

Are you short or tall for a human woman?

'Middling.'

Go on for two thousand, three hundred steps, more or less, and you will see a great faultline in the rocks that lifts the red and yellow bands up well above the ledge. Continue for another six hundred steps. You will come to what looks like a cave, very small. There may be water running from it. Crawl inside, and at the further end will be a blank wall. Smack your palm against the face, like this. He tapped out a complex beat and made her practise it until it was perfect.

The slab should go up to let you in. If not, you must find a way to force it. You will be in the very base of Tirthrax. Keep crawling along the tunnel. He described a series of passages to be negotiated and hidden doors to be opened. *Finally, take the stair up all the way to the top. It is very far. You will need to rest on the way.*

542

There you will find a gong made of glass. Strike it and the Aachim will come, if they have not already found you. Tell them your tale and give them the amplimet. Beware of using it inside Tirthrax. So close to the node, you risk your life, and the crystal, so do it only if you have no other choice. Is that clear, Tiaan?

'Yes,' she said softly. 'But . . .'

The Aachim will know what to do.

Tiaan explained to Haani what they were looking for. Minis's directions proved beautifully clear, though the distances were shorter than he'd estimated. They found the fault, and the opening beyond it, after the middle of the day. Tiaan had to take off her pack to get in, the entrance being nearly blocked with ice. At the other end the wall was also crusted with ice and a thin layer of white, crystallised from seepage through the rocks. She slapped the face in the rhythm Minis had taught her. Nothing happened. She did it again. Still nothing. Frowning, Tiaan sat back.

'Maybe the door is stuck,' said Haani.

'Of course! The edges are cemented up. Give me a hand, Haani.'

They tapped all around with pieces of rock, cracking the coating of ice and crystals off. The door still did not move and Tiaan had to clean out the gaps with a chisel from her toolkit. As soon as the last fragment fell, the door scraped up. Tiaan and Haani hurried through, in case it snapped down again. Light flared above them, coming from a glossy globe on the wall. Tiaan had not seen anything like it before, and it bothered her, though she had read about the clever Aachim in the Histories and knew their craft was greater than humankind's.

As they were donning their packs, Haani said, 'What's that?'

It was a dull clanging, far away. 'I don't know,' said Tiaan. 'Perhaps an alarm. Well, they'll certainly know we're coming.'

They were in a large tunnel with smooth walls of tormented schist. Mica sparkled here and there. They kept going, following Minis's instructions, and emerged through the final door into a cavern. Ahead, a stone stair wound up. Tiaan led the way. After the equivalent of five long flights, they came out in a stone-lined room.

'I don't see any glass gong,' said Haani. Tiaan had told her about that.

'We have to keep going up, I suppose.'

Outside, they trudged down a long corridor before emerging in a shell-shaped chamber, at least a hundred spans long, cut out of the twisted and knotted rock of Tirthrax. Tiaan just wanted the journey to end. Haani, though exhausted, plodded on without complaint.

To their left was another stair, a tight spiral of crystal treads held in place by wires. It looked too delicate to take their weight. 'This must be it,' Tiaan said doubtfully.

She put one foot on the lowest tread. It did not move; the stair was more solid than it looked. Lights came on above. Another alarm pealed, a higher note than the first, but there was no sign of life. No doubt they lived further up, since Minis had told her to go all that way.

The stairs kept going, floor after floor. There seemed no end to them and Tiaan was staggering long before the top. They rested on the wires, then continued, following the lights which went on above and off below. Other alarms sounded, pitched high and low, until the whole place echoed with them. The first stopped after an hour, so Tiaan supposed the others would, too.

It must have been three hours' climb before they found themselves at the low end of another enormous chamber. This one was egg-shaped, decorated with strange arts and furnished here and there, equally strangely. Before them stood the glass gong, twice Tiaan's height. A leather-coated wooden mallet sat beside it. Taking up the mallet, she struck the gong fair in the middle. It issued forth a low, trembly sound that she could feel vibrating in her bones.

A hundred alarms went off at once. Tiaan laid down the mallet and waited. And waited.

No one came. She struck the gong over and over. The result was the same. No one answered the call, not after an hour, or two hours, or four, or eight, or sixteen. Eventually the alarms stopped.

In the morning Tiaan struck the gong again and again. Haani did too. There was no response. Finally, in the middle of the night, after they had been in Tirthrax for a good thirty hours, Tiaan was forced to conclude that the Aachim, who had lived here for thousands of years, dwelt here no longer. The whole vast edifice of Tirthrax, the greatest city they had ever made, had been abandoned.

FIFTY-FIVE

The morning after his idea about the balloon, Nish was hauled into a meeting room to find every artificer and artisan in the manufactory there, as well as a short, plump woman Nish had never seen before. She had stringy hair, thinning on top; her clothes were distinctly shabby and not very clean. Nish wondered what a scrubwoman was doing at the meeting, for so he judged her to be. He prided himself on his own appearance.

'This is Mechanician M'lainte,' said the scrutator. 'I sent a skeet for her and she came in the night.'

Nish gaped, and immediately wished he hadn't, for Xervish Flydd was staring right at him. That this shabby creature could be the great mechanician was remarkable enough. That the scrutator had got her here so quickly was astounding. Even if a message had been sent to Tiksi by skeet straight away, it could hardly have found M'lainte before three in the morning. It was only eight now, so she must have travelled the road in the winter dark. That made her a lot braver than he was.

'M'lainte,' said the scrutator, 'please speak.'

'We are assembled to discuss an urgent new project,' said the mechanician. She held up a large drawing, clearly based on the sketches Nish had done last night. 'That is, to build an air floater, like an enormous child's balloon. One large enough to carry people through the air for . . .' She looked to Xervish.

'A hundred leagues, if necessary.'

'Just so! The balloon would be lifted by hot air from a stove.' M'lainte indicated a box hanging just below the inverted tear-drop of the balloon. Below that was suspended a wickerwork basket.

After a long silence, everyone spoke at once.

'It can't be done!' A loud voice from the back overrode the others.

'Oh?' said the mechanician coolly. 'Says who?'

'I am Porthis, senior artificer.'

'And noted jeremiah,' Nish muttered to Irisis. Porthis had made his life miserable since Nish had arrived here.

'What is your objection, Porthis?' asked the mechanician.

'The balloon would have to be enormous to lift such a weight. Maybe the height of the manufactory walls.'

'That's correct,' said M'lainte.

'The wind would tear it apart.'

'It's not fixed! The wind carries it. Besides, it would be built strongly.' She showed a drawing of the reinforcing – fine cables and strategically placed braces. 'If you judge this to be deficient, I challenge you to produce a better design.'

Porthis was not deflated. 'The hot air will go cold and the balloon will fall, killing everyone in it.'

'Thus the stove, which displaces the cooling air with more heat.'

'Will set fire to the balloon.'

'See here – I have marked in a protective flue.'

'In that case it will be too heavy.'

'Then, *Senior* Artificer Porthis, you will be in charge of making it lighter! And you will go on the first test flight, so make it strong and safe as well. Artificers all, I want to see a finished drawing for a trial balloon, tonight after dinner. I've already sent to Tiksi for materials. We'll begin making it in the morning.'

Three days after Ullii had first seen Tiaan, she lost her.

'I sensed her,' she said to the scrutator and Nish in the after-noon. They were in a dim room and Ullii was not wearing mask or goggles. The scrutator liked to see her eyes when he spoke to her. 'I saw her crystal more clearly than ever before. I could almost see her, and clawers, lots of them. They were flesh-forming. It was horrible! I saw a creature they made. It wanted to eat her.' Ullii sprang up and paced across the room.

Nish stared at her shapely bottom, until he realised that the scrutator was watching him. Flushing, Nish looked away.

'Go on,' said Flydd to Ullii.

'Tiaan was terrified. She made the hedron spit fire.'

'Fire?' cried the scrutator.

'Fire like a purple fan. The crystal became so bright that it hurt my head. I could not see the lattice at all. The fire burned holes in the wall and I lost her. I have not seen her since.'

'What wall?' said the scrutator urgently.

'A tower that is a mountain, with water all round.'

'What else do you know about that place, Ullii?'

'That's all. I only saw it once.'

Xervish lurched crabwise to the door, taking a map from his bag. 'A tower that is a mountain, south-west of here.' He traced her sighting line on the map. 'Of course, Lake Kalissi! It has a great spire in the middle, of natural iron. A very strange place. There have been rumours of lyrinx there!'

He paced back and forth. 'Then we won't need the balloon,' Nish said, disappointed that his idea would come to nothing after all.

'Of course we'll need the damned balloon! She may have escaped, since Ullii can no longer see her. If Kalissin is a base for their flesh-forming, we've got to find out *what* they're making. Fire coming out of a hedron, strong enough to burn holes in a wall! If somehow Tiaan has uncovered *real power*, we've got to have it *before the enemy does!*'

There were many trials over the next few weeks, not all successful. Two balloons crashed and caught fire. Another burned in mid-air, raining blazing debris and bodies down on the miners' village, including an unfortunate Porthis. Yet another balloon refused to take off at all; a leak was discovered. Two more, the third and the last, were moderately successful. The last rode up over the mountains, to be caught by the wind and driven for ten leagues in the direction of the plateau where the bloody battle with the lyrinx had occurred.

Ullii saw no more of Tiaan. She had vanished like an exploding star. Work on the final balloon continued. It was designed to lift ten people – Nish, Ullii and eight soldiers, to be led by Rustina – and all their gear. They were to capture Tiaan and bring her back on foot, since suitable winds for the return journey were unlikely. That was the problem with balloons.

The best part of two months had passed since the last sighting of Tiaan, and winter was almost over, by the time the balloon was assembled. It was made of tar-sealed silk stretched over a frame of light wood reinforced with tensioned wires. The structure was highly flammable but that could not be helped. Below the mouth sat a brazier built of wire mesh lined with furnace tiles. Below that hung a platform with basketweave sides, where they would eat, sleep and live. Fuel for the brazier would be stored there but they would have to replenish it on the way. They could not carry enough to take them to Kalissin, unless the winds proved particularly favourable.

The completed balloon, nearly fifteen spans high, not counting the basket, and ten wide, had used all the silk cloth in Tiksi. A valve at the top could be worked by a rope, to spill hot air and allow them to control where they landed.

The balloon's bracings kept it semi-rigid, so it looked as if it was ready to take off even when there was no hot air in it. It had been tested with different fuels while artificers measured the pull on springs attached to the ground, to see how much lift each fuel gave. Wood could be used if they had nothing better, though it had to be dry and took up a lot of space for the heat it gave out. Pitch or furnace coke were better, but pitch produced noxious black fumes and coke also required much space. Best of all was a clear liquid distilled from tar heated in an airless furnace, though it was dangerous to handle and liable to explode at the slightest spark.

One evening Irisis went to the scrutator and begged to be

allowed to go on the balloon. She could not stop thinking about Tiaan's crystal.

'What on earth for?' His single brow wrinkled into a series of furrows. 'What could you do that would justify the disruption your absence would cause here?'

Irisis had a carefully prepared rationale but before that cold stare it seemed childish. She dropped her gaze.

'You do want to be crafter here?' he said softly. 'The breeding factory is only a suspended sentence, remember.'

Irisis felt that he was peering inside her head, and that he knew, and had always known, what a fraud she was. Under her, the artisans were producing more and better controllers than ever, but no doubt he enjoyed having that hold over her.

'All I ever dreamed about was to be crafter.'

They still had a week's work to do when Ullii found Tiaan again. She was practically due west this time. 'Lakes and mountains,' said the seeker.

'As before?' Nish asked.

'No, big, big mountains.'

'Sounds like she's gone north from Kalissin,' said the scrutator. 'To the Great Mountains. She could be anywhere along a line a hundred leagues long. There's nothing for it, artificer. You'll have to leave at once.'

'The balloon isn't finished.'

'It will be. We'll work night and day to make sure of it. You'll go at dawn the day after tomorrow.'

Nish marked Ullii's direction on the map he was to take with him. On the last night the seeing was so strong that Ullii grew agitated. 'Fire and smoke, Nish!'

'A campfire?' Nish asked.

'Big fires. Fires coming out of the tops of mountains.'

The scrutator was alarmed. 'I don't understand. She's seeing *volcanoes*? There are no volcanoes in that land, or anywhere between the Great Mountains and the inland seas. Can her directions be completely wrong?' He cracked his crab-limb finger joints in agitation.

Further questioning revealed that the volcanoes were visions of Tiaan's, not what Ullii was actually seeing. The scrutator was not comforted.

'I don't like it. I wonder if I should come too?'

Nish did not care for that idea. There would be no credit in it for him if the scrutator led the expedition. 'Maybe better that I take a skeet to send word back,' he said carefully, 'and you remain here where you can act swiftly, should the need arise.'

Flydd gave him a knowing glance. 'There are arguments either way. I'll make my decision in the morning. Meantime, if I am to go, there's much I must record first. I also answer to unforgiving masters, artificer.'

Nish took the hint.

Dawn came and went. The wind blew in the right direction but the balloon was not ready, though everyone had worked through the night. Nish was utterly exhausted as he humped his pack out the front gate. He sat on it while the last checks were done.

Irisis was pacing round and round the basket. She wore full mountain gear, including down-filled jacket and pants. Was she planning to jump on at the last minute? Nish hoped not.

The scrutator was also dressed for the cold, though he was calm. 'Have you decided, surr?' Nish tried to conceal his nervousness.

'I believe I will come with you after all. There is much to be learned about this new means of transport.'

Nish's heart sank to his knees. 'That is wonderful, surr,' he lied.

The scrutator frowned. 'It's not a reward, artificer. This is a desperate venture. The chance of any of us getting there is slim. The hope of us coming back alive, with her, almost non-existent. You do realise this?'

Nish had been trying not to think about that but of course Flydd was right. This was not a bold mission but a suicidal one. What *would* they find at the destination? Most probably a lyrinx dining table.

'You can still back out,' the scrutator said quietly.

'And confirm your opinion of me, and my father's?'

'You don't know what my opinion of you is.'

Nish thought for a minute. He did not have to go, and all his life he'd taken as few risks as possible, never losing sight of his goal. He could stay behind, work hard at his craft and probably rise in it. The war offered many opportunities. And there was Irisis too.

He met the scrutator's eyes. On the other hand, if he did stay, who would take care of Ullii? In spite of his barely sublimated lust, no one cared for her as Nish did. Moreover, the balloon had been his idea and he wanted to follow it through. He wanted to redeem himself too. Staying here could never erase the stain on his record.

Most importantly, that the scrutator was prepared to risk his own life on this mission showed how vital it was. How could he refuse?

'I will go,' Nish said. His knee shook and he knew that the scrutator noted it. 'Even if there are a thousand lyrinx at the other end. How else are we to win the war?'

The man's eyes gleamed. Crab fingers gripped Nish's shoulder. 'Keep an eye out for anything of a flesh-forming nature.' The scrutator turned away.

At mid-morning the mechanician finally climbed down from the basket. 'It's ready. Fill it up!'

They began to inflate the balloon with hot air funnelled via a flexible pipe from a fire built nearby. They did not want to waste fuel getting the craft airborne. By the time it was inflated a strong wind was blowing. The structure strained at the guy ropes.

'Time to go,' said Flydd, examining the sky. It was midday. 'I don't like the look of the weather.'

Nish did not, either. Moreover, the late start meant that there was no chance of reaching their destination before dark. Setting down for the night in this wind would be perilous. By dinnertime he might be burnt to death, or fallen to his doom.

Ullii climbed in, crouching down in a padded basket specially made for her. A skeet was caged on the other side, to carry a message back. The cage was covered, skeets being notoriously vicious. Nish shook hands with the mechanician and Overseer Tuniz. Climbing up the rope ladder with wobbly knees, he went over the high side. Last came the soldiers and Rustina, whose gear had been stowed earlier.

Irisis was pacing more anxiously than before, practically running back and forth. What was she planning?

'Are you coming, surr?' Nish called down to Flydd.

The scrutator tugged the anchor cables. 'I just want to see how she lifts. Let go a few ropes and slacken off the others.'

Nish fetched him a salute. 'Cast off those ropes!' He gestured with a theatrical flourish that took all the braggadocio he could muster. 'Slacken the other tethers. Open the furnace damper!'

It was done but the balloon did not look like lifting. Nish was glad.

M'lainte frowned. 'I did wonder if it would take that much gear. Rustina, bring your troops down for a minute. We'll have to work this out again.'

Seven of the soldiers got out. The eighth began handing their gear down. He'd just lifted the second pack when a furious gust heeled the balloon over. It lifted sharply and all but one of the ropes ripped their stakes out. Everything not tied down, including Nish, fell against Ullii's basket. The skeet screeched. Ullii wailed. The brazier roared and flames licked up toward the tarred fabric. If it caught, the balloon would go up like a bonfire.

The mechanician shouted something. Nish could not tell what, with the wind in his ears. Irisis threw herself at one of the dangling ropes but was carried up into the air.

The balloon whirled on its remaining tether, down until it was in danger of smashing into the ground, then up again just as abruptly. Nish had to do something before it crashed and exploded. Whipping out his knife, he hacked clean through the remaining rope. Another gust lifted the balloon, which soared into the sky, righted itself and kept rising. Irisis wailed and let go.

Down below, the scrutator was shouting. The words did not

carry. A white-faced Irisis was staring up at him. She did not seem to be hurt.

'What else could I do?' Nish muttered, realising just what he had done. All but one of the soldiers were left behind. Everything was up to him now.

Ullii was moaning in her basket. The violent lurches would have terrified her. Nish's eyes met the soldier's and he forced himself to appear calm.

'I'm Cryl-Nish!' He held out his hand.

'S'lound.' The soldier crushed it. He was a tall veteran of maybe forty years, with thin grey hair and a white beard, rather stained about the lips.

They leaned on the rim of the basket, on opposite sites for balance, watching the manufactory recede until they could no longer see it. The balloon was climbing quickly.

'Cold up here,' said Nish.

'Ain't it!'

What he should have done, Nish realised, was to pull the release-valve rope. Too late now. They were travelling over rugged country where it would be risky to land.

They were drifting south-west. Nish was amazed at how fast the balloon was going. Landmarks below, that he had spent days labouring across, fled by in minutes. This was the way to travel! He began looking for the plateau where the battle had occurred.

Maybe an hour later, S'lound interrupted his thoughts. 'Looks like we're going down again.'

Nish had forgotten the brazier, which had died down to a thick layer of coals. The pitch burned hot but it also burned quickly. He climbed the rope ladder, swinging alarmingly in the wind, and fed the stove with more black slabs. It erupted greasy yellow and brown fumes. Nish got down hastily.

'Disgusting smell,' he said breathlessly as he regained the basket. The climb had been unusually hard work.

'Ain't it.'

A man with a small choice of words. Nish lifted the lid of Ullii's basket. 'Would you like to see . . .?' She snapped the lid down again.

Nish sighed. It was going to be a lonely journey.

They were now travelling so fast that they were past the plateau before he recognised it. Everything looked strange from above. By late afternoon they had crossed the first prong of the range and were moving rapidly towards the second. Beyond was the wilderness of Tarralladell, somewhere in the middle of which lay circular Lake Kalissi, where Ullii had *seen* Tiaan previously. But that had been months ago.

Nish tapped on the lid of the basket. 'Do you think you could come out now, Ullii? I need to talk to you.'

After a considerable interval her head emerged, swathed in a bag of spider-silk with a black hat crammed on top. 'What?' she said in the tiniest voice.

'Can you still *see* Tiaan?'

'Of course! That way.'

She was pointing west-north-west, by Nish's reckoning. He bent to his map. 'If we're now here, and she's seeing this way . .' The two lines intersected in Mirrilladell, a little way south of the Great Mountains. But the two sightings were close together, so the intersection would not be accurate.

S'lound interrupted his musings. 'It's not long to sundown. Were you planning to fly all night?'

'Definitely not! We might end up anywhere.' They were floating over the second prong of the range, though the flat lakelands of Faralladell were visible in the far distance. Nish pulled the valve rope and the balloon began to descend, rather too rapidly. He yanked the other rope, which closed it again. They drifted down toward a stony ridge.

'Do you think we can land there?' he fretted.

'Haven't a clue,' S'lound said cheerfully. 'Ain't been in a gasbag before.'

Nish eyed the vertical outcrops of slate. If they hit one, the balloon would tip over and probably be wrecked, or catch fire; or split open, dropping everything except Ullii's basket, which was tied down. Then, relieved of its load, it would be off again, carrying her. Nish imagined her shrieks dwindling away. He dared not risk it. Climbing up, he tossed more pitch into the brazier.

The further side of the slope was even worse – incredibly steep, with rocks and pointy trees everywhere. 'I thought flying was going to be the hard part,' he muttered. 'It's not a patch on landing.'

The valley bottom was hopeless, covered in trees, and the other side just as bad. It was nearly dark now. He spotted a bare area on the adjoining ridge. The balloon was drifting toward it. 'Let's try there.' Nish spilled air from the valve. They lurched in an updraft. Beyond, the trees loomed up like a jagged wall. He felt the panic of having no idea what to do. The wind was too strong, too gusty.

He jerked the valve closed. 'We won't make it! More fuel, S'lound!'

S'lound scampered up the ladder and crammed the brazier full of pitch, but Nish knew it was too late. It took ages for the stove to lift the balloon when it was already going down.

'We're going to hit the trees!'

A panting S'lound heaved something over the side.

'What was that?' said Nish.

'One of the soldiers' packs.'

Between them they sent the other packs after it, except for S'lound's. There was no pack for the scrutator. Had he been planning to come at all? Maybe it was another of his tests. If so, had Nish passed or failed?

The balloon slowly began to creep up. The treetops rushed towards them. 'Hang on,' yelled Nish.

The basket struck the top of a tree, drifted into another and snagged on a branch. The balloon tilted right over. Nish and S'lound threw their weight from side to side. The treetop bent, a strip of weave tore from the side of the basket and they were free.

'Close!' said S'lound.

'Ain't it,' Nish replied, gently mocking the soldier. 'We'll have to keep going now.'

They saw no other landing place before it grew dark. It was eerie, drifting along in black silence, having no idea whether they were mountain-high or just spans from the ground, or even which way the wind was taking them. The brazier cast odd-shaped patterns of light on their faces.

Ullii came creeping out of her basket, exclaiming at the strangeness of it all. S'lound grilled antelope steaks on the top of the brazier. They were delicious, though with a tarry flavour.

It became extremely cold. They climbed up and down to feed the fire, lingering there to warm themselves. In the early hours S'lound sprang into the basket, dusting his hands. 'All the fuel's gone. Anything else we can burn?'

'We've a couple of flasks of tar spirits but I daren't use it. The mechanician was designing pipework to feed it slowly into the brazier but it wasn't ready in time.'

'Might as well chuck it over, then.'

'It could be handy, if we can't find any dry wood.'

They drifted along for another hour, falling but having no idea how fast. 'Tarralladell is covered in forest,' Nish observed gloomily. 'We'll be wrecked in the trees.'

'And lakes,' S'lound replied. 'More likely we'll end up in a lake.'

'With luck a frozen one.' Nish stared into the darkness. 'I hope . . .'

'What?' said Ullii.

'I hope we haven't drifted as far as the sea. If we have, we're dead!'

No sooner had he spoken than they went smack into something. Water gushed in through the sides and bottom of the basket.

FIFTY-SIX

Despite Minis's warning, Tiaan had no choice but to use the amplimet and call him again. Haani looked on, fascinated. Previously Tiaan had waited until the child was asleep.

He was even slower to answer this time, and fainter, despite the undoubted power of the amplimet here. When Minis finally appeared, he looked drawn. His cheeks were dark with stubble, his face soot-stained.

Tiaan, he said after a long interval when he seemed to be looking for her but not seeing her. His voice was hoarse; it sounded as if it hurt to speak. *What's wrong?* he said in that strange, letter-by-letter way of speaking. *Can you not find the way?*

'I've been inside Tirthrax for a day and a half.' She visualised the vast oval hall for him. 'I've struck the gong a hundred times. All the alarms have gone off but no one came. Tirthrax is empty. What do I do now, my love?'

He threw his hands up around his face. His eyes were staring. *I don't know.* He disappeared.

'Who was that man?' asked Haani.

'What?' It took a while for her to realise that the child had spoken.

'I said, who was that man?'

Tiaan hugged her tightly. 'Did you see him too?'

'He was inside my head. He looked sad.'

The amplimet must be incredibly powerful here, if it could induce images in an ordinary mind. 'That is my lover, Minis.'

'Lover?' Haani sounded puzzled.

'He is the man I am going to bond with. We have come all this way to find him and help him, for he is in bad trouble. Is he not the most handsome man you ever saw?'

Politely, Haani did not answer that.

Minis was back, a little stronger now. *Tiaan, this is what you must do. Somewhere in Tirthrax there will be a room guarded by a triplet of sentinels, the little black devices like witches' hats that sound the alarm. It may even be on the level you are on. We don't know. None of us has seen it. All we have here are ancient records; very ancient! The room will have this kind of symbol on the door.*

He drew a swirling pattern in the air, with neither beginning nor end, inside nor outside. Fire followed his finger, reminding Tiaan of shapes she had seen on the hyperplane.

Touch the symbol with your crystal and you should see a mind-

map of the lock. Work it and the door will open. Inside will be devices of metal, wire, crystal and glass. Minis described a variety of objects the like of which she had never seen before.

You must take them apart and put them together into a larger device, like this. Minis put a plan into her mind, like a three-dimensional blueprint, rotating it so she could see exactly how it was structured.

When that is done you must test it, thus! What's that? He looked away.

It can't be done! came a harsh male voice. *She'll ruin the amplimet.*

No matter to us if we're extinct, Vithis, a woman replied. The voice was familiar though Tiaan had forgotten the name.

They moved out where Tiaan could see them. Vithis was tall,

long in the face but haggard-looking, with deep creases etched into his cheeks.

I say we face our fate on our own world. He bit off each word as if he wanted to spit it in their faces. *No good has ever come out of Santhenar. There is still a chance in the polar catacombs. I would take my clan there, even if we go alone!*

Then you will go alone, said Tirior, a handsome woman with black curly hair. *The Ten Clans are behind me, Vithis. Santhenar is our sole hope.*

I will not be bowed, he said.

There is no chance, Vithis, said Tirior. *Tell him, Luxor! You're the only one he'll listen to.*

Luxor could not be seen, though Tiaan remembered his dead voice.

Vithis, even in the catacombs the temperature is rising fast. The polar ice is melting; if you don't bake there, you'll drown. There's no way to keep the sea out. The gate is our only chance.

I would sooner take Clan Inthis to the Well of Echoes!

It has not come to that! cried Luxor, clearly shocked.

It is the noble way out.

Tirior appeared to relent. *Not that, Vithis. Inthis is, as you remind us, First Clan. I will humble myself. I beg you, come with us.*

Ha! cried Vithis. *I never thought I'd see it.*

He stalked back and forth for several minutes, whereupon he whirled and returned to the group. His face had set hard as congealed lava. *Very well. Clan Inthis will join the Ten; but only if I am leader.*

You, Vithis? cried Tirior. *But you have always been against this venture. Folly, you've called it from the first.*

Aye, I did, and still do. But if we are to take this path, I must lead the Clans.

Why? she said imperiously.

Because I do not believe. I always question. And because only I of all the clan leaders have truly thrown off the slave's mindset.

We were slaves for thousands of years, Vithis. It has changed us forever. We cannot go back to what we once were.

You still think *like slaves, though we gained our freedom near four hundred years ago. But I have a vision for the Aachim. If the Clans are to go to the new world I must lead.*

Come, said Luxor, urging them away. *Not in front . . .*

The image disappeared. Tiaan heard them talking but she could not make out what they were saying. After some minutes the image came back.

It is agreed, said Tirior. *You will lead us, Vithis. Clan Inthis may take the honour of first across, if the gate succeeds.*

You'd like us to take the risk, sneered Vithis. *Then if something goes wrong, you're rid of us! You've always resented Clan Inthis, Tirior.*

Don't be absurd, she replied.

I will be in the vanguard. I am prepared to take the risk for myself, as long as I see my clan safe. Clan Inthis will come last.

As you wish, she said equally coldly.

The risk is slight, said Luxor, *since the device is unlikely to work. How could an untrained human possibly assemble a working zyxibule, even with an amplimet? Even at the greatest of all nodes? She will surely fail.*

People do surprise, said Tirior, *and this human has done it over and again. But, if there is to be a chance, she must have the best preparation we can give her. Let us not waste time. Minis, continue the instruction as we have laid it out for you.*

'I don't understand what you're trying to do,' said Tiaan. They assumed too much.

Do you not? Minis sounded amazed. *But you spoke of it months ago, back in the ice sphere.*

'I have no idea what you're talking about,' she said.

You asked the original question!

'What question?'

You said, 'What if I tear open the wall between Santhenar and the hyperplane?' We assumed you knew. If it's done just right, you can create a wormhole that way.

Tiaan was beginning to feel really stupid. 'A wormhole?'

A passage that crosses a higher dimension between my world and yours. The hyperplane! You must have heard of gates, surely?

'Well, of course I've heard of *gates*!' she said. 'They're in the Histories. Why didn't you say that in the first place?'

We assumed . . . Perhaps we assumed too much, said Minis. *You seemed so knowledgeable. Never mind. Yes, we hope you can help us make a device to form a gate between your world and ours. We will, of course, control it from here. Listen carefully.*

He explained a complicated set of test procedures and the responses required. *When you have assembled the device, which we call a zyxibule, tested it according to our instructions, and all is working properly – AND NOT BEFORE, AT THE RISK OF YOUR LIFE – put your amplimet in the cavity at the centre and call again. Do you understand what I have told you?*

'I think so.' She asked enough questions to be quite sure. 'What will happen then?'

With luck, and if you can still contact me, and everything works perfectly after all this time, and the worlds are aligned, and you can channel enough power through the amplimet into the zyxibule, it will open a gate between Santhenar and Aachan and we will come through to our new world.

'Are there many of you?'

Some thousands . . .

Tiaan was relieved. Enough to help with the war but not so many as to cause problems.

We are prepared. A few lyrinx will not trouble us. Will you get ready now?

'I will.' She feasted on Minis for a few seconds more. Soon he would be here and they would be together, forever! 'But, Minis, what if I can't channel enough power, or something else goes wrong?'

He looked uncomfortable. *It could be that the gate won't open. Or it might open but close again before we can come through . . .* He trailed off.

'What else?' said Tiaan. 'There is something else, isn't there?'

Minis looked away, then was thrust aside and the hard face of Vithis appeared. *You know the risk of using the amplimet, artisan. It could happen that in channelling so much power you will be burnt from the inside out, or your mind destroyed but your body living on. The risk of that happening is considerable. Perhaps one in three or four.*

'Oh!' she whispered, sinking to her knees on the hard floor.

Another possibility is an explosion so colossal that the whole peak of Tirthrax mountain will be blown apart, and everything destroyed for twenty leagues around. We don't know, artisan. We never thought this plan would work. There was not enough time to properly design the zyxibule. We think we know how it will work but we can't be sure until we try it. Then, if it goes wrong, it will be too late.

Well? he snapped. *Are you still prepared to do this, to save what is left of the Aachim species? Do you have the courage? Do not raise our hopes falsely.*

What about *my* hopes? she thought desperately. Do *I* not matter? Clearly not to this bitter man. As an artisan, Tiaan had always lived with the threat of anthracism, though it had never happened in her manufactory. But this was an entirely different risk. She would have given up, but for Minis. Her death would be quick; his slow, painful and inevitable.

'I will do it,' she said in an almost inaudible voice, 'if you will just explain again what I must do.'

Vithis did so, for Minis had not come back. *Remember, when you have tested the device and put the crystal inside, call us. Be swift!* the hard man said, and faded away.

FIFTY-SEVEN

The room guarded by three sentinels took a deal of finding, for so far they had seen only a tiny part of the vastness of Tirthrax. Halls and chambers stretched in all directions, carved into the heart of the mountain, and there were countless other levels, above and below.

It was Haani who found the room, for she spent her time wandering the halls. There were a number of chambers guarded by triple sentinels, though only one had the swirling symbol on the door, like an image of infinity.

As Tiaan touched her crystal to it, a representation of the lock sprang into her mind. It was like no other lock she had ever encountered. How did it work? She imagined the orbital chambers revolving. At once the mechanism went *shuss* and the door opened to her touch. Tiaan went in with Haani trotting at her heels. The room was crammed with machines and devices great and small, though what function they performed no amount of examination could tell her.

One was enclosed in glass, like a bell jar the diameter of one of the roof pillars outside. Within sat a spongiform object of rough ceramic, rather like the fire bricks that lined the furnaces of the manufactory. From the myriad little holes protruded wire filaments or fine glass tubes, or sometimes both, the former inside the latter. The object was mounted on a rough-sawn slab of basalt with swirling patterns in copper fused to its polished top. A bundle of glass tubes came from a socket in the base. Some had threads of wire inside, not connected to anything.

Another was a single hexagonal prism of a dark-green mineral, striated down the sides, floating in a sealed glass dish of quick-silver. The crystal looked to be tourmaline, though more perfect than any Tiaan had ever seen. It would have filled a bucket.

There were many and various metal objects, some rough castings, others polished to the most brilliant lustre. Several objects had crystals or shaped pieces of smooth ceramic inset, or attached to protrusions, or connected by cables, wires or threads.

There were devices driven by a variety of mechanisms, some clockwork, though few of the cogs seemed to have a regular number of teeth and not all the gears were circular. Others had gears meshing with threaded rods, wheels driven by belts, or wound with wires, or mechanisms whose action was not apparent no matter how carefully Tiaan inspected them. In others, the workings were hidden inside cubes of crystal or onion layers of tinted glass.

Most seemed to have no input or output, which puzzled Tiaan mightily. She understood how a clock could be driven by a spring that eventually moved the hands, or how a mill powered by water could turn a grinding wheel. With these devices, she could find nothing to make them go in the first place, or what work they were supposed to do when they were going. And at the far end of the room, equally strange, was mounted an enormous metal slab, five spans high and three wide. It had no discernible function.

At least a day went by without Tiaan having catalogued the machines or worked out which ones she was to take parts from, or which connected to which. Tirthrax had few windows and the lightglasses stayed on whilever she was in the room, so she had little idea of the time.

Realising that it must be late, she looked around for Haani. The child was nowhere to be found and Tiaan could not re-member when she'd last seen her. Certainly it had been hours ago. She went to the door. Haani was not visible. Where could the wretched kid have gone?

Tiaan called her name but there was no reply. She wandered across the floor of that vast space, her boots echoing. The child could be in any of a thousand rooms. She might have become hopelessly lost, or fallen down a shaft. Her mind roved over the infinite possibilities for disaster.

'Bother!' she said aloud. 'I don't have time for this, Haani.'

A childish shriek, high up. Tiaan ran screaming, 'Haani? Where are you? What's the matter?' Why, *why* had she left her alone? Maybe some mountain predator lived in here. It was a perfect hideout. Now it had her and it was all Tiaan's fault.

Another shriek came floating down but this time she recognised it for what it was. Haani was shrieking with laughter. Where was she?

As she scanned back and forth a movement caught her eye, a flash through the hole, at least twenty spans above, where the spiral staircase went up through the ceiling to the next level.

'Haani!' she shouted, thinking that the child was falling.

Haani shot around in a spiral. She wasn't falling at all – the little wretch was riding the metal banister, swirling round and down like water going down a plughole. If she went off the edge . . .

But Haani did not. With a series of whoops and shrieks she slid the rail all the way down, shooting off the end and skidding across the smooth floor. 'Whee!'

Tiaan came running. She did not know what to say; she wanted to smack Haani, to yell at her to never do such a stupid thing again. Tiaan did neither, just stood with her arms hanging down and the terror frozen on her face.

Haani looked up at Tiaan's expression and the joy ran out of her. 'What's the matter?'

'I . . .' Tiaan gulped. 'I thought some wild beast was eating you. And then, when I saw you, I was sure you were going to fall and be killed. Oh, Haani, I was so afraid.'

'I was having fun. I wasn't going to get hurt. You just don't want . . .' She broke off.

566

Tiaan knew what she had been going to say. It saddened her because it was perfectly true. She cared for the child deeply but at the same time found her a burden, and resented her for it. What a selfish cow I am, she thought. She asks for so little, and even that I am incapable of giving her.

'Haani, I didn't want anything to happen to you. I love you too much.' It was true, though Tiaan only now realised it. She loved the child more than her own half-brothers and -sisters. More than her mother. More than anyone except Minis.

'You love me?' Haani whispered.

'Of course I do. Come here.' She held out her arms.

Haani stood unmoving. She took a step forward, stopped as if it could not possibly be true, took another step then flung herself into Tiaan's arms.

'I love you too,' she said in Tiaan's ear. 'You're not my mother though.'

'No.' Tiaan found tears in her own eyes. 'I can't be your mother, can I?'

'I had a mother, but the nylatl killed her.'

Silence.

'What would you like me to be, Haani? An aunt; a friend?'

'I had aunts. The nylatl killed them too. And . . .' She looked up at Tiaan. 'You're too old to be my friend.'

'How old do you think I am?'

Haani studied her. 'Really old. At least fifty.'

'Fifty? You little wretch! You need a good beating for even thinking such a wicked thing.'

Haani stepped well back, though she did not look alarmed. 'How old are you?'

'I'm twenty, as it happens. I'll be twenty-one very soon.'

'When is your birthday?'

Tiaan calculated. It had been two and a half weeks away when they left Itsipitsi, eleven days ago. 'It's not tomorrow, or the day after, or the three days after that, but the day after that. It's in six days' time.'

'Twenty-one.' Haani seemed to be weighing up the numbers. 'I could be your older sister.'

Haani considered that. 'I've always wanted a big sister.'

'Well, that's settled. I'll be your big sister.'

Tiaan gave her a sisterly hug; after a moment Haani pulled back, saying, 'I'm hungry.'

'So am I. Let's have our dinner. I don't suppose you found any water?'

'Way down there!' She pointed, then held out her hand. 'Come on! I'll show you.'

Tiaan took the hand. They ran and skipped across the chamber, where a room had implements recognisable as taps. Haani wound an S-shaped lever and water gushed from a spigot. She tried the other with the same result. Tiaan filled her pot. They sat on the floor, eating cheese, onion and very dry deer meat.

'I wish we had something different, for a change,' Tiaan said. 'We'll have to see if any food was left behind.' She was worried. They had enough for a week and a half, or two if they really stretched it, but what then? It was a long week's trek to Itsipitsi, and nothing to buy food with when they got there. If this place had been abandoned for years, perhaps centuries, there was probably nothing edible here either.

'I can look while you're doing your work,' the child said.

'All right, as long as you don't go too far. And don't do anything dangerous.'

'Of course I won't.'

They slept in one of the few rooms with a window, so they'd know when it was morning. That seemed to matter, somehow. At first light they breakfasted, went exploring but failed to find any food. On the way back, Haani put her head in through a doorway and said, 'What's this place?'

'A bathroom, I'd say. Want to try it?'

'What is a bathroom?' Haani asked.

Tiaan explained. It was a curious one, for when Haani wound the taps water sprayed out of the walls and ceiling. 'I think you're meant to stand under the water and wash yourself,' Tiaan said.

The water was not unpleasantly cold; better than they were used to. Haani was about to get out when she said 'Hey!' and put her hands out against the spray.

'What's the matter?'

'It's . . . getting hot.'

Tiaan eventually got the flow adjusted so that it was just perfect. What a luxury! Not even the breeding factory had hot water coming out of a tap. It was the ultimate mark of civilisation as far as Tiaan was concerned, far more impressive than the architecture outside, or the extraordinary machines.

The following day Haani was busy on some project that she carefully kept secret. A birthday present, Tiaan guessed. She went back to the room with the three sentinels and began dismantling the machines. She could recall each of the images Minis had shown her, and how she was to put everything together. Remembering was the easy part.

She made a start. Without proper tools, it was abominably difficult. By the end of the day she had not taken apart the first machine. At this rate it would take weeks. Minis would be dead by then, and so would they; of starvation.

She sat down, wiping her brow, for the room was warmer than the rest of Tirthrax. Haani came running in. 'Look what I found!'

She had in her arms a good-sized ham off some unidentified animal, completely encased in black wax. Tiaan's mouth watered.

'Better let me try it first. It might be no good after all this time.'

'Of course it will be good,' said Haani.

'Well, maybe not, if it's five hundred years old . . !' Tiaan peeled back the wax with her knife and carved a strip of meat off. Almost as hard as wood, it was the colour of coal, with a hot, spicy flavour. She tried a small piece. It was delicious, though it burned the tip of the tongue. She had some more. She was used to hot spices, and so was Haani.

They sat companionably, eating the meat and cooling their mouths with draughts of water. 'If only I had some tools,' said Tiaan. 'This work is so slow.'

'What kind of tools?'

'All sorts. Like those in my little toolkit, only bigger.'

'I found a whole room full of tools the other day,' said Haani.

'Why didn't you say so?'

'I didn't know you wanted them.'

With more tools at her disposal than she had names for, the work proceeded swiftly. Bored with her own company, Haani wanted to be part of the great project. The child proved to be surprisingly useful, fetching, carrying and steadying parts while Tiaan assembled them, or just being company, sometimes silent, sometimes chattering.

Tiaan now found that she missed Haani when she was out of the room. The child filled a void that had been there ever since Tiaan had left home. Haani had become family. A real family, like other people had. Soon Minis would complete it.

Her eyes rested on the child, who sat on the bench humming and swinging her legs as she screwed a tapered topaz crystal onto a threaded silver tube. Tiaan smiled. The child did feel like her little sister. Looking up, Haani caught her eye and smiled back. It warmed Tiaan from top to toe. They both deserved a little happiness. *And Minis.*

Within days the zyxibule was complete. Tiaan walked around the contraption. She could think of no words to describe it adequately. It was quite as bizarre as its name suggested. No, not bizarre – it had no symmetry at all, though when she stood back Tiaan could see a certain alien beauty in it. It rested on five slender legs made from a soft, lustrous rock that had the look of soapstone but the colour and translucency of amber. Each leg was carved in intricate, swirling patterns.

On the legs rested a thick plate, flat in the middle but dished at the perimeter, with a seven-lobed rim. It was made of no substance Tiaan had ever worked with before. It had the lustre of metal – a deep blue-black. It was light, hard and strong, but when she tapped it, it rang as if it was made of porcelain. An intensely blue glass, swirled with patterns that repeated at every scale, was fused to the underside.

She had constructed the zyxibule on top of that plate. It was framed by four doughnuts of clear glass, the largest two spans across, the smallest about half that. Wires ran through their walls here and there, terminating inside in little pieces of shiny foil. The doughnuts were arranged largest on the bottom, lying horizontally, up to smallest at the top, nearly two spans above. Each was set about with magnets so strong that when once Tiaan touched a spanner to one, she and Haani together could not pull it off. Tiaan had to set up a block and tackle to do so, and succeeded only after the most gruelling effort.

The third doughnut was fixed vertically, sitting inside the top and bottom ones and enclosing the smallest, which lay horizontally in the centre, not touching. Within that was another glass structure that Tiaan found difficult to describe, or even look at. It was a tube rolled and twisted back to join up with itself, but its inside seemed to become its outside then inside again. Tiaan could not see how it was made. Her eye found it hard to follow the curve of the thing, and kept sliding off it. Twisticon, Haani called it.

Within, around and above these structures was attached a profusion of wires, tightly wound metal coils, clusters of tubes and rods, mysterious constructions of wire and a host of the incomprehensible mechanisms she had spent so long studying on the third day. Everything was connected to everything else but nothing seemed to *do* anything.

'I'm sure that's it,' Tiaan said, stepping back. She had spent all day going through the test procedures. Each part worked as she had been told to expect. She had tried to contact Minis several times but there had been no response. She felt a chill of terror every time she thought about that.

'What is it for?' asked Haani, gnawing at a piece of green cheese.

'It is to bring my lover to me,' said Tiaan. 'Ah, but I'm tired. We'll begin in the morning.'

FIFTY-EIGHT

'Where the hell are we?' cried Nish, staring into the impenetrable darkness.

S'lound let out a mirthless chuckle. 'Not the sea, anyway. A bog, by the smell of it. And not a very deep one either.'

So it proved, when a cold day dawned some hours later. They had gone through thin ice into a waist-deep pond. There were reedy bogs all around, but little wind at ground level, so the balloon had stayed upright once the weight went off it. S'lound climbed up to the brazier, reporting nothing but mire in every direction. Ullii took one look at the place and retreated to her basket. Nish fed the skeet with a couple of half-frozen rats from a bin. The messenger bird screamed and tried to take his fingers instead.

'Now what?' said Nish as they ate bread and cheese for breakfast, washed down with swamp water.

'Gather reeds for fuel,' said S'lound. Nothing seemed to upset him. No doubt he'd had many worse days as a common soldier.

Nish picked a handful of reeds. 'No heat in these. We'll never get off the ground.'

'Soak 'em in tar spirits. That'll get us high enough that we can look for some wood.'

Nish doubted it. The expedition was turning into another disaster and this one was entirely his responsibility. Of course, they might not be able to walk out of this place at all. They might die here.

They spent the day gathering reeds. It was tedious work in the freezing water and sucking mud, and after labouring for about nine hours, all the daylight they had, the pile of fuel was depressingly small. Late in the afternoon Ullii came out of her basket and collected a bundle of reeds, handing it to Nish with the air of someone bestowing a great gift. It was, had Nish only realised it, but he was in no mood. He snapped at the seeker, who retreated to her basket, deeply hurt, and did not come out all night.

It was too late to take off that afternoon. The following morning, Nish's prediction proved correct – the damp, hollow reeds generated hardly any heat at all. The ones soaked in spirits of tar were better, exploding as soon as they were tossed in the brazier. The first time it happened Nish fell off the ladder into the water and emerged covered in smelly mud. Had it happened in the air, he would have been killed.

'Less spirits,' said the imperturbable S'lound, lifting him over the side all black and dripping.

It was nearly midday by the time they were ready to go but the balloon did not budge. The basket was stuck in the mud. They had to rock it free before it would lift, and then sluggishly. Once in the air they caught a breeze and drifted west over swamp, lake and yet more swamp. There was not a stick of wood to be seen.

S'lound leaned on the edge, cheerful as ever. Nish scrunched himself up in the corner next to Ullii's basket, pulled the coat over his head to keep the drifting flakes off, and felt a failure in every respect.

He was disturbed by a cold nose pushing against his cheek, an arm going over his shoulder. To his amazement it was Ullii.

'You are sad, Nish,' she said softly.

'We'll never get out of here. We'll never find her. I've failed again.'

She sat quietly beside him. Nish was touched. She cared about him.

'I can see trees!' called S'lound.

573

Nish jumped up. A scrubby patch of forest had appeared out of the foggy distance, and just as well. The reed bundles were exhausted.

It was almost dark when they landed by the forest. The following morning they chopped wood for several hours, and had a good bit stacked in the basket, when Ullii cried out.

'What's the matter?' yelled Nish.

'Someone coming.'

A tall man was advancing towards them, waving a wooden spear and shouting in an unknown dialect. There was a host of angry villagers behind him.

'Any idea what he's saying?' asked Nish.

'We're stealing his wood.'

'There's wood everywhere. It's rotting on the ground.'

'Nonetheless, it's his.' S'lound sprang up on the side and began shouting back, waving a menacing broadsword. 'Get the fire stoked up,' he said over his shoulder.

'We're ready to lift.'

'Untie the ropes.'

Nish climbed out. The balloon was already putting pressure on the knots. He got them undone but the balloon went up too fast. Afraid of being left behind, he gave a triple turn of the rope around his wrist. It tightened and jerked him up. A spear whizzed between his legs, close to parts he was particularly fond of.

Ullii gave a shrill scream. The rope felt as if it was going to tear right through his skin. If it came undone he was dead. They were already as high as the treetops.

He snatched and caught the rope with his left hand. It eased the strain a little. Then S'lound was leaning right out, hauling him up and grabbing his free hand to make sure he did not fall. Nish was pulled over the side and dumped on the floor. Ullii herself helped to bring him down, and when he lay there, gasping, she kissed him on the nose, an astonishing intimacy.

'I can see the sea,' S'lound said as the sun was setting.

Nish scrambled to his feet. 'We'd better put down. We can't afford to go over the water.'

'Then what?'

'We gather fuel and wait for a southerly to take us north to the mountains.'

'Shouldn't be too long a wait,' said S'lound. 'Feels like it's blowing from the South Pole right now.'

He was still saying that a week later. This time they'd gone to see the villagers and made an arrangement with them for fuel. Nish was canny enough to pay in coppers, which they were glad to have, and the villagers chopped and fetched a mountain of wood, enough to enable them to keep the brazier going the whole time. If the air in the balloon went cold it would take hours to fill it.

The wind blew from the west, the north and even the east, but never from the south. Nish fretted. What was Tiaan up to? Ullii had sensed great urgency the last time she'd *seen* her. They had, however, found out where they were, somewhere between the cities of Runcil and Tatusti. Ullii had managed a clear sighting on Tiaan. Assuming she had not moved, the intersection showed her to be near Mount Tirthrax.

Late on their eighth night in that place they were woken by a great buffet on the basket. The wind whistled through the ropes, a gale carrying not snow but stinging crystals of ice. It was a howling southerly that lifted the balloon with every blast.

'We'd better go,' said S'lound.

'I don't dare take it up in this.'

'It'll get worse! We'll lose it if we stay here.'

The wind screamed and flung the balloon right over. Nish thought it was going to smash against the ground. Before the craft could right itself another gust pushed it over again and the stakes on the windward side tore out.

'Cut the ropes,' S'lound roared, drawing his knife.

Nish did the same. Either way they were doomed. Before he could put his knife to the rope the other stakes tore free. The basket bumped along the ground. Flames belched out of the top of the brazier and he held his breath as they went close to the tarred fabric.

Bump, bump, then the basket struck an obstruction that

caved in the side but kicked them into the air. They drifted sideways, almost parallel to the ground. The wind eased and the balloon pulled the basket up.

Nish climbed the ladder, hanging by one hand while he stoked the fire with as much wood as he could cram in. 'I want to get as high as I can,' he said when he was safely down. 'That's where the winds are, and the further we're blown the less we'll have to walk.'

Soon the brazier was glowing red, the distant ground racing by faster than it ever had. The whole balloon was shuddering, as if the air up top was moving faster than at basket level. The moon reflected silver off a thousand lakes.

'How far to go?' S'lound asked.

'A hundred and twenty, maybe thirty leagues.' Nish was watching the procession of lakes and rivers go by, comparing them with his map and making constant amendments. 'This is a very poor chart,' he said, peering over the side. 'That huge lake down there isn't even marked, and the river turns west, not east.'

'Hard place to map, I'd reckon,' grunted S'lound. 'Bad maps are the soldier's biggest problem.'

'Except from a balloon!' He had an idea that might earn him credit with the scrutator. 'Hey, S'lound, what if we were to fly over all the lands where the soldiers were fighting and make proper maps from balloons?'

'Good idea! Guess that's why you're in the favour of the scrutator and I'm just an old soldier.'

'I'm not . . . *Really?*'

'So I hear.'

'That was before I cocked up this mission.'

'Ain't over yet. How long to go, do you think?'

'At this rate we should be pretty close by lunchtime. Ah, balloons are wonderful. This trip would take us months, through the snow.'

'If the wind lasts. And it takes us where *it* wants, not where we want to go.'

'Well, yes, but certainly closer.'

As the sun rose it reflected redly off the eastern flank of Tirthrax itself, a way to their left. They were no more than thirty leagues from the mountains, which thrust up in an east–west line from the hummocky plains.

'Oh, this is wonderful!' Nish cried. 'Come look, Ullii. You'll never see a sight like this again.'

She peeped out of the basket, earmuffed and begoggled, and even she gazed at the astounding spectacle with wonder.

'Can you still see Tiaan? Please say that you can, Ullii.'

'I can see her. Her crystal fills my mind.' She pointed to Tirthrax mountain, then darted back like a rabbit down a burrow.

'How close do you think we can get?' said Nish. The rugged foothills would be difficult country to walk in.

'The wind has turned more easterly,' said S'lound. 'It's carrying us in the right direction, at least.'

It was the first bit of good luck they'd had on the trip. 'And maybe it'll turn due east when it hits the mountains,' Nish replied.

'Or up and over, or fling itself at the cliffs. Might be an idea to set down sooner than later.'

'We'll keep going as long as we can. Most of those rivers look impassable.'

They drifted towards the mountains for another couple of hours. They were still east of Tirthrax, easily recognisable because it stood a good thousand spans above any of the other peaks. Great ice mounds covered the plain below the glacier falls.

Approaching the mountain wall, the winds did blow more from the east, carrying the balloon west towards their destination. They began to encounter turbulence, which grew worse the closer they approached, flinging the balloon about until they felt seasick. Nish could hear Ullii retching in her basket but she would not come out.

He let the fire die down. They were slowly losing height as Tirthrax loomed up before them. The buffeting diminished. Another hour passed. They crossed onto the middle flank of the mountain, the tree line a long way below them.

Nish called Ullii out, cleaned her up with a damp cloth, washed out her basket and asked her where Tiaan was now. Ullii pointed straight up the mountain, but as they drifted by her arm moved.

'We'd better put it down,' Nish said urgently. 'We'll get no closer than this.'

'There, ahead.'

It was a long slope stripped down to rock by ice falling from the hanging valley above. On the other side lay a great boulder field, beyond which was a clear space that looked safe, though it was rather small. More rough country extended beyond it. Making an instant decision, Nish pulled the rope to open the valve.

They drifted towards the boulders. 'Aren't we going down a bit fast?' yelled S'lound, who was hanging off the ladder near the stove.

Nish pulled the other rope. Nothing happened. 'The valve must have frozen open! Come down, quick!'

S'lound stayed where he was, fiddling with the brazier lid. 'Leave that!' Nish yelled. 'It won't make any difference.'

Nish kept trying the valve to the end. They were dropping too quickly and would smash into the rocks. The ground raced up at them but at the last moment a gust lifted them over the rocks, unfortunately carrying them beyond the clear area as well. They headed towards another cluster of boulders. Nish threw himself at the side of the basket, which swayed in the air, glanced off the side of a boulder, then another, and fell between them, thumping into the ground. S'lound cried out.

Nish was hurled off his feet, cracking his head against the corner of Ullii's basket. The slack went off the ropes; balloon and brazier seemed to be plunging straight at him. Momentarily he imagined the conflagration but the brazier stopped, resting on the rim of the basket. High above he heard a click that must have been the valve closing, for the balloon and brazier slowly drifted up until the ropes were taut.

The skeet let out shrill cries of rage. Nish picked himself up, bruised but unharmed. The basket was jammed between the boulders. He fixed the rope around a rock. 'Well, that's that. Are you all right, Ullii?'

'Yes,' she said softly.

Creeping out, goggles and muffs on, she surveyed the scene then slipped under Nish's arm. He gave her a gentle squeeze.

'Where is S'lound?' she said into Nish's armpit.

They found him around the other side, lying on his back with his head at a strange angle. He was dead. An unlucky landing had broken his neck.

Nish squatted beside him, head bowed. He'd never really come to know the soldier, but S'lound's company had been pleasant enough these past days. He'd provided a reliable solidity, a cheerful presence.

There was nothing to bury the man with, so they piled stones over him. At least, Nish did. Ullii had no concept of cooperative work. She sat watching while Nish laboured. At the end she picked up a small stone, studied it carefully, turned it around in her hands several times and placed it on the pile above S'lound's head.

Having done that, she slumped as if she'd done most of the work. Perhaps, for her, placing that small piece had been harder than Nish's labour. Who knew what went on in that strange, closed-over mind of hers?

'Let's eat,' said Nish, for it was well into the afternoon. 'Then I suggest we head up after Tiaan. What do you think, Ullii?' He did not expect much, but there was a mountainload on his shoulders and no one to help him carry it.

'I don't think anything.'

Nish sighed. The next few months, until they got back to the manufactory, were going to be harder than he had ever imagined. *If* they got back at all. He checked Ullii's pack, filled his purse with the scrutator's gold that would be needed for the return journey, and settled the sword on his hip. Lifting Ullii's pack on, he made sure the layers of padding under the straps were spread smoothly. They set off.

After about a hundred paces Ullii said, 'It hurts!' and threw the pack on the ground. By the time he'd fixed the straps the sun was low. Clearly they were going nowhere today.

Nish began to fret. Things were very different on foot. They had to find Tiaan quickly, for they could only carry so much food, and most was on his back. What was she doing here anyway? Presumably the lyrinx had brought her here because it was a place of great power. How could he possibly get her away from *them*? This mission was going to be a bigger failure than the last, he thought gloomily, and they would end up in a lyrinx's belly.

They camped among the rocks. Ullii, never comfortable out of doors, flung off the coat as soon as they stopped. The jerkin, blouse and spider-silk undershirt followed it. She rubbed at the red marks on her shoulders and the small of her back where the pack had chafed her, though she had only been carrying it for a few minutes.

Nish squatted by the tent roll, pegs in hand. He'd only ever seen her unclothed in a darkened room. Her figure was quite lovely. He could not take his eyes off her. He desired her more than he had wanted anyone in his life.

It was getting dark. He made a fire with bits of twisted shrub, since there were no trees this high. It would not last long, but hopefully long enough to cook their dinner. There was much to do and he had to do it by himself. But at least it kept the other thoughts at bay.

The flames leapt up. Ullii was sitting on a rock, staring at him, or through him into eternity – he could not tell. He wished she would put her shirt back on. The sight of her breasts, the nipples all puckered up with the cold . . . In suppressing the desire, Nish felt an overwhelming flood of anger at himself, and their predicament, and at her too.

'Are you going to sit there all night?' he said irritably. 'Do I have to do everything for you?'

Ullii reacted as if he had slapped her across the face. Her eyes screwed shut; then she cried out, hunching over and covering her face with her arms. She began rocking back and forth, mewling.

'Oh, Ullii, I'm sorry,' he whispered, careful not to alarm her further. After all, she had not asked to come. At his every step she twitched, much as he had done when the whip had been laid across his back months ago.

She hid her face. 'Don't beat me!' she said in the monotone of one who expects to be ignored.

'Of course I'm not going to beat you, Ullii. Have I *ever* hurt you?'

She did not answer. He rubbed one hand through his hair and slipped it under her nose. She went still as his forearm touched hers. Neither moved. Ullii gave a gentle sniff. Parting her forearms, she sniffed deeply. She sighed and he could feel the tension flowing out of her.

'I'm so afraid, Nish.' She spoke so softly he could barely hear her.

'Of me?'

'Not you.' Her hands pulled his palm against her nose.

'Then what?'

'I can see horrible things.'

'Is Tiaan one of them?'

'Tiaan is nice. I like her. But in the mountain . . . It's too much, Nish. Everything is so bright, I can't even see her crystal. There's some great . . .'

'Magic?'

'Some great magic there. It's not made yet, but already it's blinding me. It's awful. It's going to eat us, Nish.'

'Is it lyrinx?'

'I can't tell. There's too much light. Everywhere I look it's as bright as the sun. It hurts my mind. I can't shut it out.'

'Can you see anything else?'

She turned around, facing west. 'Nothing.' She rotated south and east, the way they had come. 'Nothing!' Ullii kept turning, and as she turned due east she cried, 'Clawers!' pointing up along the line of the mountains.

'What, flying? Or in the mountains?'

'I don't know. The Art is too strong.'

'Surely they are flying,' said Nish, 'otherwise they would not need to use the Art.'

She turned east–south-east, screamed and doubled over, protecting her face again. 'No!' She let out an ungodly shriek and began to rock furiously. The shriek came echoing back at them.

'Ullii? What is it?'

It took ages to coax her back this time. 'It . . . it's a black knot in my lattice. There's a pattern, a beautiful pattern, but I know if I tried to unravel it there's a monster hiding inside. Waiting to get me. It hates us.'

'Is it lyrinx?'

'No. It hates clawers too. It's a creeping, poisonous thing.' Her eyes sprang open. He saw himself reflected in them. 'It's hunting Tiaan!'

'Perhaps it's hunting her for the lyrinx.'

'No!' she shuddered and began rubbing her shoulder. The delicate skin was raised in red welts.

Nish went to his pack, found a flask of cooking oil and sat down beside her, lubricating his fingers. He slid his fingertips across the welts.

She stiffened, but the tension went out of her when his fingers slipped across the skin. 'That feels . . . nice.' Ullii slid off her perch onto the ground in front of him.

He worked the oil back and forth, ever so gently. The evening was cold but it did not seem to bother her. Finally, when all the marks were done, he let his hand slip away. He ached for her but was afraid to do anything.

'Don't stop!' she whispered. 'Oh, Nish, no one has ever touched me so gently. All my life people have hurt me. No one ever touched me but to cause me pain. Everyone wants to use me, except you. You are the kindest man in the world, Nish.'

If only you knew! Pouring oil into his palm, he smoothed it across her shoulders and down her back. Ullii sighed, and as he worked his fingers back and forth she began to talk about herself, as she had never done before.

'All my life I've wanted to be like other people. You can't imagine what it's like to grow up and never be touched, because you can't bear it. My brothers and sisters used to hug each other. My mother and father too. I wanted it so badly, but the feel of their clothes made me scream. My clothes did too. I screamed all the time and no one knew why.'

'Was it always like that?' He shaped her sides with his palms.

'It got really bad when I was two. After I lost my twin.'

'You had a twin sister?'

'No, I had a brother. I think he died. No one would ever tell me. I still miss him.' She gave a great shudder. 'Before that I don't remember. People have hard skin; their hands hurt me.'

He pulled up his sleeve, touching her with the soft skin on the inside of his arm.

She drew it across her cheek, wonderingly. 'You feel nice, Nish.'

'If I took my shirt off,' he said experimentally, 'you would see that underneath I have soft skin, just like yours.'

She did not respond, so he unfastened his shirt, laid it aside and pressed his chest against her back, very carefully. His fingers slid up to her ears.

She jerked away. 'Don't touch my ears,' she said sharply.

He pulled away, deflated.

She turned to see what the matter was. 'It makes a noise in my head like thunder, Nish.' She put his hands back on her shoulders.

He resumed, shortly feeling bold enough to run his fingers down her throat and onto her chest. When she did not react, he slid them all the way to the swell of her breast, and away again. She sighed and rubbed her cheek against his upper arm.

Nish circled her breast with a slippery finger, heading inwards. She sighed again. He continued, in and in, tracing the little bumps and up the peak of the nipple. Ullii sucked in her breath sharply and began to breathe very fast. She gasped. Her head drooped.

'That is . . . very nice,' she murmured.

At last he was getting somewhere. Nish lifted his finger. Her hand came up and put it back, pressing down hard. He took the nipple between finger and thumb, rolling it gently back and forth.

Then in an instant she had flung him backwards off the rock. She leapt to her feet.

'What have I done?' he cried.

She stood up on tiptoe, head forward, owl eyes searching the darkness. 'It's happening.'

'What, Ullii?' He rubbed the back of his head, which he had cracked on a stone.

'I don't know. It's like all the lights in the city went on at the same time, right in my eyes.' She turned until she faced the towering bulk of Tirthrax. 'It's coming from up there. *Inside the mountain!*'

FIFTY-NINE

Tiaan woke early in the night, aching for her lover. She had tried to contact him before going to bed but had failed. This time it had felt different, as if he was not there at all. As if he no longer existed.

You're just being silly, she told herself. He's too busy, or gone some place where you can't contact him, just as the amplimet only works near nodes. But he'd said to call when the device was tested. He would not have gone away at such a critical time. And that meant . . .

There was no possibility of going back to sleep so she rose quietly and went to the work chamber. The place seemed different now. Tiaan did not understand why until she'd gone out again and the light-glasses faded. The glass doughnuts were glowing. In the darkness they had a faint, unearthly shimmer.

She touched the wall lights to keep them off, closed the door and stood in the dark, staring at her contraption. It looked alive, ready to be used. The last step was to put the amplimet into it and call again. Hours mattered now – Minis had emphasised that.

She unwrapped the amplimet, which was glowing too brightly to look at, and carried it towards the zyxibule. Tiaan could feel rampant energy in the room. Her hair stirred; her clothes crackled and gave off little flashing discharges.

When she was still a few steps away, something went *click-thunk* inside the machine and the light drained out of the amplimet. The doughnuts flared. A low hum began and Tiaan felt a wave pass through her. For an instant the walls and ceiling seemed to curve inwards. She blinked and all was normal again, though the hum remained. The zyxibule had activated itself. What would happen when she put the amplimet inside?

Tiaan stopped, feeling as if something was not quite right. She compared the machine with the image in her mind. It was, as far as she could tell, perfect in every detail, so why did she have that troubled feeling? Perhaps it was the name. 'Zyxibule' resonated unpleasantly – it sounded alien and unfriendly. I'll call it 'port-all', she decided, and immediately felt better about it.

Tiaan spent the night checking and rechecking. Unable to identify any fault in the port-all, she ran though the tests yet again. Everything worked exactly as she had been told to expect. Worn out, she lay on the warm floor and snatched an hour's sleep.

Waking as dawn was breaking outside, she called Minis. She wanted to check that the machine was right before she put the amplimet in. He did not answer. At least it gave her time to get ready. She went to the bathing room, had a hot shower followed by a cold one and scrubbed herself until she was as clean as a baby. Today, if all went well, she would meet her lover. Tiaan was determined to look her best.

That was not something she knew much about. The most she had ever done was hack her hair short with a knife. Rather more was needed here.

Tiaan got out the special garments purchased months ago in Ghysmel. She had washed them a few days ago, to remove all trace of the musty smell from her pack. There was a set of pretty though wickedly scanty underwear, over which she put a short-sleeved blouse in a peach colour. It suited her honey complexion. Made of a fabric like silk, it clung to her breasts in a way that made her feel self-conscious. But then, she thought, Minis is my chosen lover, and why should he not admire my breasts? Soon he will be caressing them. A delicious thrill, that.

She recalled Matron in the breeding factory being rather

pleased with her breasts, though tempering her praise by pointing out that one was smaller than the other. Tiaan had made a point of inspecting other women in the bathhouse on board the *Norwhal*. She felt that she compared well.

With the blouse she had teamed umber pantaloons of the same fabric, tight around the waist and bottom, loose in the legs then gathered to show her slender ankles. Did the blouse clash with the pantaloons? She could not tell. Black sandals completed the outfit, though she worried that brown might have gone better. She wished her feet were smaller.

'You look nice,' said Haani, sitting up in the sleeping pouch.

'Thank you. I need to cut my hair. I don't suppose you've seen a pair of scissors anywhere?'

'What are scissors?'

Pulling out her sleeve, Tiaan made snipping motions with her fingers.

'Oh, *brawnies*? I saw some in a room on the next floor. I'll show you.'

She leapt out of bed. Tiaan followed more sedately, practising her walk, something between a sway and a glide. She thought it looked rather silly, but hoped Minis would find it alluring. 'And a mirror?'

Haani knew that word. There had been several on board ship. 'There's lots of mirrors. All the rooms up there have them.'

The room turned out to be a suite of chambers, someone's living quarters. The mirror was a large one of polished metal with a design etched around the edges. Tiaan wiped the dust off with a bedcover.

Her hair was dull, ragged and long, not having been cut since the stay in the breeding factory. Tiaan gave it a few hundred strokes with her brush, took up the offered scissors and laid them down in despair. She examined her face, which was wide, with fine, high cheekbones. How did one cut hair to suit?

Tiaan trimmed her fringe straight across, three fingers' width above her eyebrows. That was better. She managed to cut the sides straight, just below her ears, but eyed the ragged ends at the back in some alarm.

'Haani . . .'

'Yes?'

'Do you think you could cut my hair at the back? It would have to be very straight.'

'Of course,' Haani said with the confidence of the eight-year-old. She set to work. Tiaan's alarm grew as the thick swatches fell to the floor.

'Perhaps a little higher here, and here,' Tiaan said shortly.

'That's much better,' Haani said brightly as Tiaan stood up, brushing the loose hair away. 'You look beautiful, Tiaan.'

It was not *much* better, but it was better, though it looked more like a little girl's cut than a young woman meeting her lover for the first time. Well, nothing could be done about it.

'Ah, but will Minis think so?' she said to herself, not meaning Haani to overhear.

'Of course he will. If he doesn't he's a rude, nasty man and I won't like him at all.'

Tiaan had not considered that problem. What would Haani think of Minis? And how would he react to her? Tiaan fretted as she trimmed her nails and gave everything a last check. She did not look anything special. Tiaan felt panicky, then recalled a gift Marnie had once given in a futile attempt to make her daughter look feminine. A necklace of silver and amethyst, it seemed to suit.

Tiaan checked that her own gift, the woven gold and silver ring she had crafted so lovingly, was secure in her scrip. It was. She took a deep breath.

'Are you ready, Haani?'

'Of course.'

'What about your clean clothes?'

'They're by the bed. I'll get dressed in a minute.'

'Let's go down to breakfast. Then we'll brush our teeth. Make sure you do your hair, then we'll begin.'

Tiaan had another go at contacting Minis. Again she failed. Better get to work. Her worries about the machine had not gone away but it was too late now to do anything about them. She examined the amplimet carefully. It was dusty, with bits of fluff here and there, and a silver mark on one side where it had been pressed hard against the helm. She wiped it down with a clean pair of knickers, scrubbing at the mark until it came off.

'Well,' she said with a gulp and a fluttery feeling in her stomach, '*this is it!* Come on, Haani. Let's see what we can do.'

She marched into the room where the port-all stood, the amplimet held out in front of her. Tiaan looked like a maiden carrying tribute to one of the high temples of old. Haani skipped along behind, singing a child's rhyme. It was just another day to her.

Tiaan was pleased about that. She did not want to think what would happen if the machine went wrong: if it burnt her to a cinder, or left her body intact but her mind gone. She imagined Haani crouched over the body, bewildered . . .

Stop it! Probably nothing would happen anyway, since they had not taught her how to use it. Wrenching away from the morbid thoughts, she strode up to the port-all. The glass structures glowed as before. The hum was still there. When she approached, the glow intensified and a faint whine began. It rose in pitch. She stopped. The pitch stayed the same. She took another step. It rose again. The drifting spark inside the amplimet had brightened.

In the centre of the smallest glass doughnut, which enclosed the twisticon and was surrounded by the larger vertical one, hung a suspended basket made of the same amber soapstone that comprised the legs of the port-all. It mimicked the shape of the amplimet, with hinges that allowed it to be opened into two parts.

Tiaan stretched out and flicked the basket open. The doughnuts burst with light. The whine became a wail that tickled the insides of her ears. She felt pressure against her front, as if she was trying to push through a rubber sheet. The closer she came the more resistance she felt.

The light was now so bright that she had to squint. Her vision narrowed to a horizontal slit that showed only the central section of the port-all. Tiaan forced, and something pushed back just as hard. The amplimet did not budge. Minis had not told her about this.

She could not fail this close to her goal. There must be a way through. Tiaan turned the crystal so one of its pyramidal ends pointed to the basket, and heaved. The amplimet went a little way and stopped as if she was pushing against a solid wall. The other end did not work either.

There was only one thing left to do and she did it most reluctantly, remembering Minis's warning about using the amplimet here. Getting the wire globe from her pack, she placed the amplimet inside. The glow from the port-all disappeared. The whine was gone too. As soon as she put the helm on, the field sprang into view. It was different from other fields she had seen, consisting of multi-coloured billows and eddies radiating in all directions from the port-all. She felt she saw more than ever before, as if the swirls and whirlpools opened on a dimension she had previously been incapable of imagining.

The resistance proved as strong as ever. Tiaan went forward as far as she could go. Holding the globe straight out in one hand, she closed her eyes while manipulating the beads with the other. No matter how hard she tried, Tiaan could draw nothing from the field. She had no time to wonder why. She would have to try her fledgling geomancy again.

She sensed several sources of *that* kind of power. Great thrust faults lay below, where half a continent had been forced over another, pushing up these giant mountains. Such power was beyond the most powerful mancer's ability to tap or even survive.

But there was one source she might be able to use. Tiaan had seen them on the way here – the glaciers all around. They ended in icefalls, and the energy released by one tiny crack opening should be enough to force her way in.

She sought out and discarded many before finding a glacier that seemed just right. It was a little one, moving down a truncated valley on the other side of the mountain. She'd seen it as she was climbing up. But even a little glacier had awesome power to grind and crack and crush. She sensed out its structure, just above the icefall, and located a weakness along which coloured haloes danced in her mental image. It was ready to crack open. Tiaan waited.

'What are you doing, Tiaan? Why are you standing there like that?' came Haani's voice from behind.

'Shh!' Tiaan could not answer lest she lose her concentration. It was coming, *it was coming*! The crevasse cracked open. She drew power from it, clumsily. It had no perceptible effect on the glacier but Tiaan felt a surge of cold force stronger than anything she had handled before. It flowed into the amplimet, the spark lit up like a flash of lightning and Tiaan pushed hard.

The opposing force gave before her like a knife thrusting through a drum. She fell, almost crashing into the glass doughnuts. Regaining her balance, she slipped the amplimet from the globe, jammed it into the basket and banged the amber door.

The glow and the whine reappeared. The barrier came up so hard and fast that Tiaan was sent skidding twenty paces across the room. Fortunately there was nothing to crash into or she would have broken bones.

She lay dazed as Haani came screaming up. 'Tiaan, are you all right?'

Tiaan got up, with the child's help. 'I think so.' She dusted herself off, only to discover that the slide had torn a hole in the knee of her beautiful pantaloons. Not a large one, but it made her look like an urchin, rather than a beautiful woman rushing to meet her lover.

No time to change. The doughnuts were now dazzlingly bright, the amplimet glowed like a furnace through the walls of the basket, while tight beams of coloured light pulsed out of random parts of the device. The noises coming from it ranged from shrieks to barely audible rumbles. Every so often the whole machine vibrated as if to shake itself apart, and the twisticon was lit up by pulses of green light that formed standing waves inside.

'I've got to do it now, before it breaks.' Squatting down, Tiaan worked the beads in their orbits for what she hoped was the last time.

'Minis, Minis, where are you?' Blankness, struck through

591

with brilliant beams of light. 'Minis. Come to me. The port-all is built. It's ready to bring you to safety.'

Still nothing. She ran through her memories of all the times she'd contacted him before. Suddenly she smelt smoke.

'What are you doing, Haani?' She could not look or she would lose it all.

'Just sitting here,' came a small voice beside her.

'You're not burning anything?'

'Of course not!' the child said indignantly.

'It must be Aachan!' Tiaan said to herself. 'It has to be. *Minis!*' she roared, and there it was, a great dome of an island, upon which lava flows were advancing, boiling the sea to steam.

On the ash-layered top she saw people in their thousands, sheltering under steep roofs collapsing under the weight of ash and cinder. Others huddled in the mouths of caves. Jagged volcanic bombs rained from the sky, some bursting open to reveal liquid interiors. Everywhere people were screaming, weeping, dying. She caught a stinging whiff of brimstone.

Her viewpoint drifted up a slope. A tower appeared, made up of dozens of slender spires, the sides of which were clustered with shiny silver buttons, or domes, or bowl-shaped caps. They must have been huge, for around the spires a road spiralled its way to the very top. The road was suspended from the towers by cables that from this distance looked as thin as hairs. At the top stood a metal plate the twin of the one on the wall behind her.

What on earth was the structure? Could it be their end of the gate? It must be, though the winding road just ended at the top. 'Minis!' She did not know that she had screamed it aloud. 'Minis, tell me what to do!'

It's Tiaan!

Just a whisper, but it made her skin shiver. She was going to succeed after all. 'Minis, I've done it. I've made the port-all – the zyxibule.' That word felt unlucky. 'Tell me what to do.'

Why did you not call us, Tiaan?

She could not see him among the throng. How she wanted to. 'I called many times. You did not answer.'

No matter. It's too late. We can't open the gate, Tiaan. We're too weak now.

'There's power here. I can channel more if you need me to. Tell me how. I can make the gate from here.'

Voices were arguing; some she recognised. The harsh tones of Vithis, Minis's foster-father. The calm, resigned voice of Luxor, and Tirior urging them on, to seize the opportunity.

What have we to lose? said Luxor. *We're going to die anyway.*

I say we trust her, said Tirior. *Tiaan has taken on every challenge so far, and succeeded against our expectations.*

And if she fails? grated Vithis. *We don't die a noble death on beloved Aachan – we die trapped in the hideous void, to be eaten like carrion. Where is the dignity in that?*

Then stay behind! roared Luxor. *Go to the Well of Echoes and die with your precious dignity! I choose life for my clan.*

And I, said Tirior. *The Ten Clans have agreed on it.*

I don't like it, said Vithis. *To offer such a secret to an old human, and one who is barely out of childhood. What will she do with it?*

Time to worry about that if we survive, said Tirior.

Yes, said Vithis. *And we* will *worry, you can be sure.*

They voted and it was agreed. They would make the attempt. Minis came back and told Tiaan what to do.

Tiaan felt panicky to see the Aachim crammed there, dying. Their lives relied on her. She understood little about the deadly geomantic Art she would have to wield and get absolutely right the first time. If the great Aachim were afraid of the consequences, how could she hope to succeed?

But she had to. Her fingers worked desperately and Tiaan hurled her senses outward, skipping over the little glacier she'd used before. She needed a lot of power now. West she sped, to pick up the enormous glacier grinding down from the Tirthrax ice cap. It was the fastest of all – Tiaan imagined that she could hear it grinding in its bed. Yet even that pace was no faster than the creeping of a snail. The wait was agonising.

Where the glacier curved around the edge of the mountain toward the icefall, a fracture would open up from one side to the other. She could already see its field, like a concave lens. With desperate recklessness she seized upon the opening crevasse and took out every bit of power she could.

Ice screamed as it was torn apart and a paralysing cold rushed through her. Tiaan felt as if she had frozen solid. The whole port-all shuddered, exploding with light and sound. She thought it was going to tear itself apart.

The mountain shook. There came a noise like boulders being crushed and something went *boom*, so loud that her ears hurt. After that she heard nothing at all.

Haani was tugging desperately at her hand. 'Tiaan, say something!'

Tiaan picked herself up from the floor, feeling that a long time had passed. Her vision of Aachan had disappeared. Lightning forked from the amplimet basket to the metal plate on the back wall. The glass doughnuts went out. After an instant of utter darkness the glow reappeared. Aachan was back, too.

A monstrous curving lens flashed into being at the very top of the road winding up from those spiked towers. For an instant she saw Tirthrax reflected on the lens. It must have been a reflection, for it was a mirror image, the toe of the glacier falling off the wrong side of the mountain. Tirthrax was the other way around.

A star appeared in the centre of the reflection, then a hole blasted right through the lens. There were screams and hoarse cries as an avalanche of snow erupted through, to the incredulity of the Aachim. It was like a white umbrella that melted in the hot air and fell as blessed cold rain.

The gate! The gate is open! she heard the multitude cry.

Hurry! Before it closes again.

People raced to machines that looked like clankers. Briefly she saw Minis's face, and those others she had seen before – the ones who knew all about the gate.

Stop! Vithis cried. *The little fool has made the zyxibule the wrong way round. It's left-handed, not right. The gate may not work.*

Too late to worry about that now, screamed another.

Clan Inthis! Vithis ordered. *Stay back! It's not safe. You are to go last, after the Ten Clans! Let them risk all; this will restore us to our rightful place.*

Vithis ran to a complicated piece of machinery that vaguely resembled Tiaan's port-all. Hurling himself into a suspended seat, he began working a controlling arm in three dimensions. Ball lightning fizzed out in all directions.

The image of Aachan turned upside down and back to front. Tiann's lungs burned as if she had inhaled fire. Her control of the port-all was snatched away. A wormhole writhed across the ethyr like an electrified serpent.

No, Inthis! Vithis screamed, holding out his arms in entreaty as a squadron of blue-tinted constructs raced past. *Wait . . .*

They took no notice. Letting go the controlling arm, Vithis put his head in his hands and wept. A stampede of people and machines rushed up the spiral road towards the gate, but Tiaan lost them, and then she lost Aachan too.

On a mountaintop half a continent away, the tetrarch was observing the motions of the planets when, for an instant, they shook like jelly in a bowl. The field tied itself into knots. The globe-wide ethyr sobbed out a single note before returning to intangibility. Setting down his instruments, the tetrarch made a note on a slate.

Hundreds of leagues to the south, in a citadel on the frigid Island of Noom, a woman set down her quill, cocked her head to one side, and smiled. The long watch had borne its first fruit. She took up a lantern and headed down the Thousand Steps to her master.

SIXTY

'I saw *her*!' said Ullii. 'Tiaan was standing there with these big streamers of light going in all directions. The whole mountain was shaking. She had a little girl with her.'

'*A little girl?*'

'She had green hair.'

Another thing to wonder about. 'What was Tiaan doing?'

'I did not understand.' Ullii sagged. 'I have to sleep!' She ducked into the tent.

It was a dark night; too dark for climbing unknown mountains, though later on there would be a moon. Frustrated on several fronts, Nish tidied up the camp, stoked the fire and stared at the mountain. There was nothing to do but wait. Ullii was already asleep but that was not a possibility for him. He paced back and forth.

This was his big chance. If he could capture Tiaan and her crystal, and bring her back, it would make up for all his past failures. But what was going on up there?

'Nish!' Someone was shaking him by the shoulder. 'Nish, wake up!'

He'd gone to sleep against a rock, a rather lumpy one. Nish rubbed an aching neck. 'What's the matter, Ullii?'

'Come, come!'

'Where?' he said thickly.

'Up the mountain. Tiaan is starting.'

'Starting what?'

'What she came to do. I can see her, standing in a great chamber inside the mountain. She's using her crystal, Nish! She's going to bring them here.'

He flung himself out of his pouch, stuffed feet into boots, tied the laces. 'Bring who?'

'I don't know,' she wailed. 'I can't see them. *There's too many!* It's all dark and smoky.'

A shiver crept up his back and suddenly he did not want to go anywhere near that mountain. But he had to. Nish took her by the shoulders. Her huge eyes glistened in a stray moonbeam. 'What do you mean, too many?'

'Too, too many! You have to stop her, Nish.'

That *was* a transformation, Ullii urging a course of action. She must be really alarmed.

Nish hurled food into his little chest pack, strapped on sword and knife, gave Ullii another knife that he doubted she could use, and left everything else.

They climbed up the slope past the balloon, still jammed between the boulders and so deflated that its ribs and wires were clearly visible. Nish fed the skeet, made sure it had water, then followed Ullii, who could see perfectly in the moonlight and seemed to know exactly where she was going. She was on a trail, probably made by bears or goats. As they topped a rise, the setting moon reflected slantwise off the vast front of the glacier.

After going a little way Nish realised that the seeker was not following. She was sitting on the ground, staring numbly at the knife blade.

'Ullii,' he called. 'Come on.'

'Afraid,' she muttered, pulling her coat over her head.

He went back and, squatting down, took her hand. 'Ullii, we can't stay here. We've come all this way to find Tiaan. I've done my best for you. Now it's your turn. Please help me.'

Snatching her hand free, she thrust it inside her coat and began rocking furiously.

What was he to do? Nish did know what Ullii was going through but he was not going to let her weakness stop him now, so close to his goal. If he could just get Tiaan, and the crystal, it would make up for everything. He must, even if Ullii had to suffer.

'Then stay here by yourself!' he snapped. 'I'm going!'

He strode off as if she meant nothing to him. She let out a whimper. He did not look back, though Nish could practically feel her pain.

As he topped the rise, she gave a great wail of torment. 'Nish, don't leave me.'

He froze, one foot in the air, then hardened his heart and continued, heavy-footed.

Before he had gone another twenty steps she was beside him, running silently in her soft boots. He did not know what to expect, but suddenly Ullii was eager to please.

'I will show you the way, Nish,' she said, holding his hand so tightly that it hurt. 'Don't leave me alone again.'

'I won't,' he said, looking up the mountain.

By the time the sun rose they were high above the camp. Mist formed in the valley, pouring over the icefall and blurring the glacier into insignificance. Ullii stopped to put her goggles on. It was a hard climb on steeply dipping slate and sugary quartzite. The icy slate offered little grip for their boots. Nish's leg muscles were aching.

'Where now?' he asked as Ullii stopped on a ledge above which the face ran sheer.

For a moment she looked unsure. Ullii put her hand over the goggles, said 'Ah!' and headed off again.

Hours later they were level with the bottom of the ice. The rocks had changed to shiny laminated schists and then to contorted granite gneiss. They were going back and forth up the side of the mountain when there came an enormous crack and the grinding note of the glacier changed.

'What's that?' said Nish.

The attenuated rumble made by its weight rasping against the bottom and sides of the valley had altered to a sharper, higher note. A mound of ice had been forced up and was tearing at the fresh rock of the mountainside above them. It sounded as if boulders were being crushed to pieces. Rock began to fall. Nish watched it coming and didn't know which way to run.

Ullii screamed, caught his hand and jerked him to the right. She bolted up along the ledge that led away from the glacier. Nish fled after her. Rock roared and cracked above their heads.

This was no landslide but a chaotic fall of ice and rock plucked directly from the side of Tirthrax. A lump of mountain the size of his parents' mansion started to roll. It went straight for a few tumbles, split, and the larger half careered in their direction. Nish could see it out of the corner of his eye.

He ran so hard that blood began to drip from his nose. He was still running after the boulder passed by and thumped down the mountain towards the distant trees. The noise was cataclysmic.

Ullii was already out of sight, amazing for someone who never took any exercise. Nish gained a ridge that formed a natural divide and hurled himself over. He had to roll in the air to avoid landing on the seeker, who lay curled up on the ground with her hands over the earmuffs, desperately trying to block out the sound. Her mouth was open and she was screaming, though he could not hear a thing.

He found the earplugs in her pack, pushed them in and put the earmuffs back. Ullii sat up and said something. He had no idea what. The noise died away. They looked over the ridge. The fall of rock had stopped though the ice was pressing against the mountain right where Ullii had been leading them. The ground shook, several times.

With a roar that dwarfed the previous fall, a larger section of the mountain cracked off. There was another monumental fall of rock and ice. They watched it thunder down. A quarter of an hour later, when the glacier had resumed its normal note, Nish said, 'I wonder if it's safe now?'

Ullii must have thought so, for she began to head up the slope towards the fall. They came over the cusp of the ridge and stopped. Nish could see right inside the mountain. It was like a gash in the side of a termite mound, revealing the living cells within.

'A city inside the mountain!' He saw several levels and grand, highly decorated columns. 'So that's where she went! But why? Is it a lyrinx city?'

'I don't think so!' She shivered.

Dare he risk the rest of the mountain coming down? What of Ullii's other seeings: the flying lyrinx, and that unnamed horror?

'I can see her,' hissed Ullii.

He took no notice; she'd said that many times.

She shook him. 'I can see her, Nish. Up there!'

Following her arm he saw two figures at the entrance. They were too far away for his eyes, though he did not doubt Ullii. For all the difficulty of working with her, he had never known her to be wrong.

'Come on! We can take her!'

Whatever impulse had driven her this far now evaporated. Ullii curled up between two rocks. 'Too late. Too, too late!'

'Well, stay here!' he snapped. The opportunity, that he had never dared hope for, had come. Tiaan was alone but for the child. All he had to do was grab Tiaan, carry her to the balloon, fire it up with tar spirits and get away. It would make up for everything. He would be a hero. Nish ran.

As he approached the ragged tear in the mountain, which exposed three levels of the city inside, Nish began to see bright flashes of light. The figures disappeared.

Ullii screamed and came pelting up to him. 'Don't leave me!' she cried, flinging herself into his arms. 'It's coming!'

Nish did not ask her what. Such pronouncements seldom resulted in anything he could get a grip on. He kept on and she followed, treading on his heels.

They went in through the lower tear, found a spiral stair in reasonably good condition and crept up it. Up two flights, they came out on the level where Tiaan and the child had been. The floor, broken near the entrance, was strewn with mounds of rubble and ice, enough to fill a quarry.

The sight that met his eyes would live in Nish's mind until the day he died.

SIXTY-ONE

Haani was tugging at her arm. 'Tiaan, quickly!'
Tiaan got up, feeling frozen solid. A vast, crackling roar surrounded her. Blue icicles hung from the port-all. She smelt dust and vaguely recalled the sound of falling rubble.

Haani tugged her around. 'Look what's happened.'

The amplimet had gone dull but the twisticon was ablaze, colours chasing themselves around its surface, inside, then out, then inside again without any break. The vertical doughnut looked as if it was on fire. The annulus of light from it focussed to a point above Tiaan's head, then spread out again. It had torn a hole through the wall, and in the middle of the vast hall beyond, some hundreds of paces away, made another ring that stretched from floor to ceiling. Air shrieked through it. It must be the gate, but nothing had come out.

Something flashed into her mind, a fragment from the time she had been unconscious: screams, explosions of light and fire, and cries of utmost agony, as if people were being turned inside out. It vanished just as swiftly, but what had followed did not. A background wailing; thousands of souls in grief. Tiaan felt a chill of horror. What had happened to the Aachim in the gate? Where had they ended up?

Up the far end she saw light where there had been no light before. A tongue of blue-white ice had punched through the side of the mountain. Had she made a dreadful mistake? *'The little fool has made the zyxibule the wrong way round!'* Vithis had said. What had he meant?

'Do you think we should run away?' Haani clutched Tiaan's hand as the ice scraped and squealed towards them.

'I don't know.' The ice stopped moving. The floor shook twice, and with a rumble more of the mountain wall caved in. Rubble exploded everywhere. Part of the floor collapsed. Most of the ice and rubble slid back out.

They ran towards the opening. It was bitterly cold, for the great glacier that curved around the side of the mountain immediately below them had risen, pushed up against the wall, cracked it open and subsided again. The rock beneath had been ground off like the surface of a road.

Outside they could hear the crack of ice falling, the thunder of its landing far below. Tiaan shivered. Her blouse, pantaloons and sandals were quite inadequate here.

'Something's happening back there,' said Haani.

The great annulus had gone dark. Shadows danced on the wall opposite.

'He's coming!' cried Tiaan, embracing the child. 'Oh, he's coming, Haani!'

She ran forward. A hollow boom shook the floor. A dark shape appeared in the base of the doughnut-shaped gate. The shape pushed, concentric rainbows rippling around it as if it was held back by a transparent barrier.

'It can't get through,' said Haani.

There came a brilliant white flash, followed by thunder. Quakes shook the floor and a flat disc of mist condensed in the plane of the gate. The dark shape pushed through it and, as suddenly, the mist was sucked back the other way.

'What is it?' whispered Haani.

'I . . . don't know. Perhaps it's some kind of clanker.'

'What is a clanker?'

Of course the child would not know. There were no clankers in this land. The war had not come this far, yet. 'It is a cart that moves by itself, without horse or ox or deer to pull it.'

'Oh!'

It began to emerge, a long, tapering snout of shining blue-black metal, rising to a cockpit ringed about with circular rails, covered by a metal dome like a lid. Wisps of yellow smoke clung to it; fumes dragged out by its passage. The body was long and broad, with bulbous flares and inexplicable indentations and protrusions. The back was cut straight down. It looked like something made by a sculptor, but if so, the greatest genius in the world. It looked deadly, but it was a work of art too.

'It *is* like a clanker,' Tiaan said to herself, 'only larger. A dozen people could fit inside, and all their gear. How can they work metal so beautifully?' Beside it, the manufactory clankers would look like the work of a village blacksmith. She longed to see inside it and know how it was made.

'But it hasn't got any wheels,' said Haani.

There was nothing under it but a dusty, yellow-glowing blur, and it floated well above the floor. Moreover, it did not make the groaning rattle that alerted the whole world to the coming of a clanker. All she could hear was a low whine and an occasional hiss.

'It . . . It's a construct!' said Tiaan. 'It must be.'

The construct emerged from the gate, turned the other way, back towards them, and stopped. Another appeared behind it, followed by a third. Tiaan felt an indefinable foreboding. These vehicles seemed ominous rather than welcoming.

'Haani,' she hissed. 'Go behind me. Scuttle around into the ice and hide. Don't come out until I call you.'

'But Tiaan, what's the matter?'

'Do as you're told! *At once!*'

Haani sucked in her breath, gave a muffled sob and crept away. Out of the corner of her eye Tiaan saw her scuttle across the rubble-strewn floor to her left. Tiaan crouched down behind a fallen column.

She felt like weeping too. What must the child be thinking? That disaster was about to strike again? Not if she could stop it! Tiaan climbed onto the column.

The three constructs floated up the hall. More appeared from the gate, one after another. They were practically touching as they came out. Within minutes there were hundreds of them. All had the same overall shape but there were many variations in detail, and in size, from constructs that might hold fifty people to others that could scarcely have contained a family. Some had people running beside them, or clinging onto the outside.

The machines crept towards her, spreading out behind the first three until they formed a rank twenty wide in the vast hall, and a hundred deep. And still they came pouring from the gate. Two thousand already. If each held only a dozen, that was twenty-four thousand people. Minis had said a few thousand. Still, they were just a drop in the lake compared to the millions of humans. These Aachim with their amazing constructs would be a great help in the war.

Tiaan stood in the middle of the hall, completely alone. They came to within fifty paces, then stopped, every one, in the same instant. It was incredible. Eerie!

The central construct cracked open at the top, the dome tilting back to reveal a platform on which seven people stood. Most were dark-faced and near a head taller than their human equivalents. Not all, though. One, a woman with pale skin and red hair, was no taller than Tiaan. All were armed with bows, swords or other recognisable weapons. At the rear a man sat in a turret, behind a spring-fired weapon resembling the javelard of a clanker.

The construct to the left of the first came open, followed by the one on the right. Six Aachim stood on each platform. Tiaan scanned the faces for Minis but did not see him. They looked exhausted – bruised, battered and soot-stained – yet they had about them a lofty dignity. Despite their travails they were dressed richly. Tiaan glanced at her own finery and quailed. She was covered in dust, the hole in her knee gaped and she knew her hair was a mess.

A tall man pushed to the front of the platform of the central clanker. She recognised Vithis, though he looked haggard. His eyes were staring and he seemed to be having trouble mastering himself.

'Who are you,' he boomed in the common speech, 'who stand before the might of the Aachim?' His voice was richly resonant; a voice used to command. The accent was strange, the language stilted, and like Minis he pronounced every letter separately, giving his speech a sense of deliberation.

'I am Tiaan,' she shouted back. Her own voice sounded shrill, and timid. 'I made the device that brought you here to safety.'

'Awry!' he roared.

Tiaan took an involuntary step backwards.

'You made the zyxibule awry. You changed left for right. Everything is the mirror of its true order. Because of your stupidity, many of our number are lost in the void.' He choked back a sob. 'You utter fool. My clan has been wiped out.'

Horror shivered through her. 'I'm sorry,' she whispered, recalling the cries, the wails, the agony numbered ten thousand times. 'I'm dreadfully sorry. I made it exactly as was shown me!'

'You insult the memory of our dead. Dare not to make excuses for your incompetence!'

Tiaan caught her breath. 'I followed your instructions exactly. If left hand and right hand are different on your world, why did you not tell me?'

'You should have checked!' He was as bitter as venom.

She felt like a prentice before an angry master, but here there were twenty-four thousand of them. 'I called, as I was instructed. You did not answer, as you promised. Besides, you knew how the gate was before you left Aachan. I heard you say so. You snatched it out of my control to benefit your own clan. You made it go wrong.'

'How dare you challenge *me*! I am Vithis of Clan Inthis, First Clan of Aachan! Bow down when you speak to me. Do humans lack all respect for their betters?'

She bit back her angry words. The man was out of his mind with grief. She hoped the other Aachim were not all like him. She was not going to bow, though.

'Where is Minis, my lover?'

'Lover?' he said incredulously. 'Move out of my way.'

'I have saved your people,' she said, 'at no little cost to myself

605

and my own kind. Many of us died that you might live, and you show no gratitude. Is this the kind of people you are? *I would speak to Minis.*'

Another man, shorter and older, eased the first out of the way. 'We are indeed grateful, Tiaan,' said Luxor.

Tirior stood beside him. Luxor's hair was iron-grey. Tirior's was as black as Tiaan's, but curly, and her face was darker.

'I am Luxor,' said the man, 'of Clan Izmak.'

'And I, Tirior of Clan Nataz,' the woman said. 'We are clan leaders of the Aachim, on this excursion second only to Vithis. Do not take his bitter words to heart, Tiaan. He has just seen his clan extinguished – every child, every woman, every man. Please allow for his anguish.'

Tiaan bowed her head.

'Ask what reward you will,' said Luxor, 'and we will gladly pay it.'

'I ask for no reward,' Tiaan said. 'I did not aid you in hope of gain.' Apart from Minis.

'Nobly spoken,' said Tirior. 'You have done the Aachim a service that we will never forget. May we see the amplimet, Tiaan? Such a thing none of us have ever set eyes on.'

Did they plan to take it from her? They were armed for war and she could not stop them. Besides, she wanted to build bridges, not raise barriers.

'It's back there, in the room with the hole in the wall.' She pointed.

'Leave it!' growled Vithis. 'It is corrupted now and no use to anyone.'

'But . . .' said Tirior.

'Remember the accursed Mirror of Aachan!' he raged. 'This crystal will prove just as treacherous if ever we touch it.'

'I did so want to see it,' Tirior said wistfully. 'I have made a study of such things.'

'We must move swiftly!' Vithis rapped out. 'While we have the advantage.'

'But this is Tirthrax!' cried Tirior. 'It is the greatest city we ever made. My clan ancestors built this place.'

'They were enemies of First Clan!' snapped Vithis.

'That is a long time ago,' said Tirior. 'Most of our people are now dying on Aachan. Others have been lost in the void. We are all that remain of our kind and we cannot afford division. I have to see the city and learn why it has been abandoned.'

'There is no time! The mancers of this world must be shuddering at the power liberated here. Already they will be mobilising their forces. What if they are looking for us now? As leader of the Eleven Clans,' he choked back a cry of anguish, 'I say we go at once.'

'Very well,' said Tirior, 'but we will deal honourably with Tiaan first. Minis, come up.'

A young man climbed onto the platform of the central construct, the others drawing back to give him room. Tiaan feasted her eyes on him. Minis was tall, but not too tall; well built, though not extravagantly so. His dark hair fell in waves about his ears. His cheeks were thinner than she remembered, but his brow just as noble, his lips as ripe.

'Minis!' Tiaan called. 'I came as I promised. I have travelled halfway across the world to bring you here.' She threw out her arms to him.

He stared at her unmoving, as if he had no idea who she was. Tiaan went cold inside. But perhaps he was too reserved to show it before so many people.

'Minis. You said that you cared for me.' She dared not use the word 'love', not now. 'I have a gift for you.' Feeling in her scrip she drew the ring out. Running forward until she was just a few spans from the construct, she held it up. 'Minis, I made this ring with my own hands.'

She fell silent. It was a beautiful thing, but greater beauty lay all around, in the constructs and in Tirthrax. Everything the Aachim made was beautiful. She felt her own artisan's skills were meagre, her ring a rustic token that would embarrass him.

Minis smiled and put out his own arms. His fingers were remarkably long, an Aachim characteristic. The pupils of his eyes were oval.

'Tiaan, my love,' he cried, his voice as ringing as Vithis's, but warmer. 'For a minute I did not recognise you. Indeed I promised, and I keep my promises.'

'I've had enough of this nonsense!' cried Vithis, pushing through. 'Look what a shabby little wretch she is. This is not what I raised you for, foster-son. You are my sole heir now and I cannot allow it. Toss her a bag of platinum and be done with her.'

'But Vithis, foster-father – '

'We were slaves on our own world for thousands of years, foster-son. No sooner did we gain our freedom than our world died on us. History has used us ill. Never more will we be slaves! My clan died that we might stand here today, and if we are to take this world we cannot afford to lose *anyone*. Especially not *you*, Minis! You are all I have left. Together we must create Clan Inthis anew.'

Minis's extended fingers, which had touched the ring, drew back.

Tiaan's hand fell to her side. She could think of nothing to say. Had she given her all to be treated so badly?

'Tiaan!' cried Minis. 'We're not like that. Please believe me, Tiaan.' He tried to get down but Vithis held him back.

'Don't grovel, boy. We are Aachim and we have a world to make our own.'

'Please foster-father.'

Vithis tossed a bag to the floor. It clinked as it landed. 'A bag of platinum for your service, Tiaan.'

'Damn you!' she raged. 'You can't buy me.'

Minis had scrambled down the side of the construct and hung there, one foot on the rung, the other in the air. 'Tiaan – '

'Come back, boy,' grated Vithis. 'Put one foot on the floor and you are Aachim no longer.'

'But foster-father. Honour – '

'Honour demands that you stand by your own. We cannot do without anyone, but especially not you.'

Minis hesitated, and for the first time she realised that he was not strong at all. He wanted to please everybody.

'We're outnumbered a thousand to one,' Vithis said softly, 'We need you, Minis.'

Minis hung on the rung, his face anguished. Tiaan prayed. Surely he could not refuse her after all she'd done, and suffered, for him. Their eyes met. There was such terrible yearning in his. He did love her, she knew it. *He must!*

The moment stretched out to eternity. She felt uncounted eyes on her, weighing up her face, her ragged hair, the tattered clothes. She knew what they were thinking.

'Well, boy? Do you cleave to the wretch, abandoning your own people who hold such hopes in you? Is eternal exile what you want? She'll be dead in twenty or thirty years. If you live to be a thousand we'll not take you back.'

Minis looked up at them. 'What if she were to come with us?'

Vithis looked taken aback, but Luxor and Tirior spoke to him in urgent tones, evidently favouring this way out of the impasse. Vithis turned back.

'Not as your partner, Minis! She is not Aachim, and you know the sad fate of *blending* children.' He spoke with the others again. 'Very well. She has done us honourably, despite her blunder. You may bring her as your concubine, as long as precautions are taken.'

'Will you come with us, Tiaan?' Minis said with pleading eyes. 'As my lover?'

Tiaan was mortally insulted. That was not what she'd had in mind at all. Concubine was a transaction that reminded her of the breeding factory. But . . . would it not be better than to lose Minis? She hesitated.

Minis reached out an arm, let it fall, then raised it again. 'Tiaan . . !' He broke off at a movement in the shadows to Tiaan's left. Something flashed in and out of the rubble. Tiaan had forgotten Haani. What must the child be thinking, hearing all this?

'Don't leave me, Tiaan!' screamed Haani. 'Please don't go with him.'

Tiaan recognised the danger too late. 'No, Haani! Stay back!'

At the movement, the man in the turret swung his weapon around, aimed and released the lever. With deadly accuracy, it fired a club-headed projectile, meant to stun a warrior. As Haani emerged from the darkness the club struck her full in the chest, lifting her off her feet. She fell without a sound.

Tiaan dropped the ring and ran. 'Haani, Haani!' She fell to her knees beside the child, who lay on her back like a broken thing. Haani was trying to breathe but her chest was crushed. Liquid gurgled in her lungs.

Haani looked up at her. 'My chest hurts,' she gasped. 'Help me, Tiaan. Sister.'

'Of course I'll help you.' Tiaan could barely see for the tears dripping from her eyes.

'You won't leave me, will you?' Haani choked. 'Not like my mother and father and aunts did?' She managed to get a breath. The pain made her shudder.

'I'll never leave you, Haani. I'll be with you until the day I die.'

'I'm sorry!' wept Haani, trying vainly to reach into her pocket. 'I forgot . . .'

'What is it, little sister?'

'I forgot to give you your birthday present.' Tears poured down her cheeks.

Tiaan was having just as much trouble breathing. 'It doesn't matter, Haani.'

'It's today, and I forgot!' she gasped, struggling for breath. 'I'm sorry, Tiaan.' Haani fumbled out a folded piece of leather, the last of the piece Tiaan had cut from the bottom of the boat. Inside lay a bracelet made of plaited strips of leather, with flower patterns clumsily burnt into it. 'Tiaan, I love you,' it said.

Tears sprang to Tiaan's eyes as she slipped the bracelet on her left wrist. 'Thank you, little sister. You didn't forget at all. It's still my birthday.'

'I love you, Tiaan. You'll make me better, won't you?'

'I love you too, more than *anyone*.'

She kissed Haani all over her little face and did not stop until it was clear that she was dead. The club had driven the broken ribs into her lungs.

Tiaan lifted Haani in her arms, surprised at how light she was. Carrying her out, she stopped in front of the first construct, the child's little legs and arms hanging limp.

'She's dead!'

'I offer condolences,' said Vithis. 'An unfortunate accident.'

'She's dead!' Tiaan screamed. 'An eight-year-old girl. There's thousands of you and the greatest army on Santhenar, and you're so frightened you have to kill a child? Curse you, Vithis. The Aachim are not noble. You are the craven of the Three Worlds!'

Vithis swelled with rage. 'No one speaks to the Aachim like that, no matter what they have suffered. You are not worthy to be concubine. The offer is withdrawn.'

'Cowards!' spat Tiaan. 'Oath-breakers! Your word means nothing to you.'

Vithis tossed down another bag. 'Reparation for the child! Move out of the way, if you please.'

'You can't buy a child's life, any more than you can buy me!' She looked up at Minis. He was staring at her. She could still hope.

He put one foot on the floor.

'It's done and can't be undone,' growled Vithis, 'no matter how much we might regret it. Nothing you do can make any difference, foster-son. It's over. Take your place beside me.'

It would make all the difference in the world, Tiaan thought, if one of you actually *showed* you were sorry. Just you, Minis. Please.

Minis stared at the child. A tear ran from one eye, and he seemed to come to a decision. His eyes slid away and she knew she had lost everything.

'I am truly sorry, Tiaan.' He went back up the ladder to stand beside Vithis.

The constructs began to move, all in the same instant. She stood where she was, daring them to run her down and not caring if they did. Her eyes were fixed on Minis but he was staring straight ahead.

The front rank split and went around her. The succeeding ranks followed, heading down to the broken wall. They moved out onto the ramp of stone and ice, onto the glacier, and around the corner towards the lowlands.

'Curse you!' she screamed. Laying Haani's body down gently, Tiaan ran back, gathered up the bags of platinum and hurled them after Minis's construct. It did not help. Sitting beside the dead child she took the slender, bloodless hand in her lap. All for nothing. Less than nothing. She had bought their lives with Haani's. So many people had died that she might bring the amplimet to this place. Fluuni, Jiini, Lyssa, Joeyn; whole squads of soldiers and many lyrinx too. She saw the broken bodies and knew that the price was too high.

The constructs kept coming for an hour and a half. While they were still going around her she stood up, Haani's body in her arms.

'I swear by this dead child,' she whispered, 'that I will *never* love again! I curse you, Minis, and all your line, until eternity. I will be revenged on you who have so betrayed me. You will live to regret that you left me alive, *noble* Aachim!'

It made her feel no better. Staring blindly after them, she was roused by the crash and grind of metal. Three constructs, locked together, hung on the lip of the gate. Another nudged them over. They struck the floor and broke apart. Aachim scrambled out and leapt onto the sides of the other constructs. The procession continued, another twenty-two machines, and that was all.

Tiaan stumbled to the gate, carrying the child. Looking up inside she saw a long tunnel, a wormhole curving to infinity. There were hundreds more constructs in it but they could not get out.

The surface of the gate shimmered with colour and began to break up. Quite suddenly, it vanished. Again she heard that awful wailing and knew that another host of Aachim had been lost in the void.

The final twenty-two constructs formed a line. They flashed beams vertically at the ceiling; a signal, or a requiem. Then they turned and followed the others out of Tirthrax.

As Tiaan watched the last machine disappear through the side of the mountain, another horror struck her.

'We have a world to make our own,' Vithis had said. Such a force as was assembled here would have taken years to create.

All this must have been planned long ago. They had *used* her from the very beginning. Minis had not loved her at all. The Aachim had told him what to say and do, every word of it. She had betrayed her world, for nothing.

Nish, hiding in the shadows, stared at the rank after rank of black machines, standing hip-high above the floor. They looked vaguely like clankers though even from this distance he could tell how superior they were to the clankers he had worked on. A keen student of the Histories, Nish knew what they were.

They were constructs, made to the pattern of the one Rulke the Charon had built over two hundred years ago. Nish did not know who was inside them; he was too far away to tell. He assumed they were lyrinx, or their allies. However, it *was* clear that they represented the greatest threat Santhenar had ever faced, and that Tiaan had helped to bring them here. Traitorous bitch! His duty was self-evident. He must take her back for justice, no matter what it involved.

The constructs were moving again, going around Tiaan and heading towards the broken entrance. He pulled Ullii down the stairs until just their eyes peeped over.

Nish counted them past, noting how many there were, what size and how armed, and estimating the number of enemy that might be inside. The constructs numbered more than eleven thousand; the enemy a hundred and fifty thousand at the very least. That was priceless, strategic information, perhaps more important than capturing Tiaan. He must survive to get it home. Where had they come from? The armada was large and potent enough to deliver the final blow to humanity.

'What was that?' Ullii asked as the last construct went by.

Nish marked the direction on his chart. When he looked back towards the gate, it was gone. Tiaan was too.

'The end of humanity.'

THE END
OF VOLUME ONE

VOLUME TWO
TETRARCH

continues
THE WELL OF ECHOES TRILOGY

GLOSSARY

NAMES (MAIN CHARACTERS IN ITALICS)

Aachim: The human species native to Aachan, once conquered and enslaved by a small force of invading Charon (the Hundred). The Aachim are a clever people, great artisans and engineers, but melancholy or prone to arrogance and hubris. Many were brought to Santhenar by Rulke the Charon in search for the Golden Flute. The Aachim flourished on Santhenar, but were later betrayed by Rulke and ruined in the Clysm. They then withdrew from the world to their hidden mountain cities. The ones that remained on Aachan gained their freedom after the Forbidding was broken, when the surviving Charon went back to the void.

Arple: A battle-scarred sergeant and hero of the wars with the lyrinx.

Barkus: Deceased master crafter of controllers at the manufactory, uncle of Irisis.

Besant: A lyrinx matriarch (Wise Mother). She is a master of the Art, especially in relation to flying.

Coeland: Matriarch (Wise Mother) of the lyrinx in Kalissin.

Cryl-Nish Hlar: *A former scribe, a prober in secret and a reluctant artificer, generally known as Nish.*

Eiryn Muss: Halfwit; an air-moss grower and harmless pervert.

Faellem: A long-lived human species who have passed out of the Histories, though some may still dwell on Santhenar.

Fistila Tyr: A pregnant artisan in the manufactory.

Flammas: A mancer. Ullii spent years in his dungeon.

Fluuni: Older sister of Jiini; Haani's aunt.

Flyn: An irascible miner.

Fyn-Mah: *The querist at Tiksi. The chief of the municipal intelligence bureau.*

Gi-Had: *Overseer of the manufactory.*

Gol: A lazy sweeper boy.

Gryste: An angry foreman at the manufactory. He has a nigah habit.

Haani: *A girl of eight living near Lake Kalissi with her mother and aunts.*

Inthis: Vithis's clan of Aachim, first of the Eleven Clans.

Irisis Stirm: *A senior artisan at the manufactory; niece of Barkus.*

Jal-Nish Hlar: *The perquisitor (provincial inquisitor) for Einunar; Nish's father.*

Jiini: Haani's mother.

Joeyn (Joe): An old miner, adept at finding crystal. Tiaan's friend.

Ky-Ara: An overly emotional clanker operator.

Lex: The day guard at the crystal mine.

Liett: *A lyrinx with unarmoured skin and no chameleon ability; a talented flesh-former.*

Luxor: A conciliatory Aachim clan leader.

Lyrinx: Massive winged humanoids who came out of the void to Santhenar after the Forbidding was broken. Highly intelligent, they are able to use the Secret Art, most commonly for keeping their heavy bodies aloft. They have armoured skin and a chameleon-like ability to change their colours and patterns, often used for communication (skin speech). Some lyrinx are also flesh-formers; they can change small organisms into desired forms using the Secret Art. In the void they used a similar ability to pattern their unborn young so as to survive in that harsh environment. As a consequence, they are not entirely comfortable in their powerful but much changed bodies.

Lyssa: Jiini's younger sister; Haani's aunt.

Marnie: Tiaan's mother, a prize breeder of children.

Matron: The woman in charge of the breeding factory at Tiksi.

Minis: *A young Aachim man of high stature; foster-son of Vithis. Tiaan's dream lover.*

M'lainte: The renowned mechanician; in charge of balloon construction.

Mul-Lym: The apothek at the manufactory.

Myssu: A legendary, bare-breasted heroine of revolutionary times.

Nigah: A drug used by the army under extreme conditions to combat cold and fatigue. Also has medicinal uses as it induces lassitude, somnolence and indifference to pain. Made from the leaf of the nigah bush, it stains the gums yellow.

Nish: *Cryl-Nish's hated nickname, means 'pipsqueak'. (Even worse: Nish-Nash.)*

Nod: Doorman at the manufactory.

Nylatl, the: *A vicious and malicious creature created by Ryll and Liett's flesh-forming.*

Pur-Did: The shooter on Ky-Ara's clanker.

Rahnd: The shooter on Simmo's clanker.

Ranii Mhel: An examiner; formidable mother of Nish.

Rustina: A red-haired sergeant. An expert climber with a profound hatred of lyrinx.

Ruzia: The old, blind healer at the manufactory.

Ryll: *An ostracised wingless lyrinx; a talented flesh-former.*

Seeker: One who can sense use of the Secret Art, or people who have that talent, or even enchanted objects. Ullii is one.

Simmo: A clanker operator.

S'lound: A soldier who travels with Nish in the balloon.

Tiaan Liise-Mar: *A young artisan; a visual thinker and talented controller-maker.*

Tirior: An Aachim clan leader.

Tul-Kin: The healer at the manufactory; a drunk.

Tuniz: A senior artificer at the manufactory.

Ullii: *A seeker so hypersensitive that she is unable to go outside, or among people.*

Vithis: *Minis's foster-father; an Aachim from Aachan. The head of Inthis First Clan.*

Xervish Flydd: The scrutator (spymaster and master inquisitor) for Einunar.

MAJOR ARTEFACTS AND FORCES

Amplimet: An extremely rare *hedron* which, even in its natural state, can draw power from the force (the *field*) surrounding and permeating a node.

Anthracism: Human internal combustion due to a mancer or an artisan drawing more power than the body can handle. Invariably fatal (gruesomely).

Clanker (also armoped or thumpeter): An armoured mechanical war cart with six, eight or ten legs and an articulated body, driven by the Secret Art via a controller mechanism which is used by a trained operator. Armed with a rock-throwing catapult and a javelard (heavy spear thrower) which are fired by a shooter riding on top. Clankers are made under supervision of a mechanician, artisan and weapons artificer. Emergency power is stored in a pair of heavy spinning flywheels, in case the field is interrupted.

Construct: A vehicle powered by the Secret Art, based on some of the secrets of Rulke's legendary vehicle. Unlike Rulke's, those made by the Aachim cannot fly.

Controller: A mind-linked mechanical system of many flexible arms which draws power through a *hedron* and feeds it to the drive mechanisms of a *clanker*. A controller is attuned to a particular hedron, and the operator must be trained to use each controller, which takes time. Operators suffer withdrawal if removed from their machines for long periods, and inconsolable grief if their machines are destroyed, although this may be alleviated if the controller survives and can be installed in another clanker.

Crystal fever: A hallucinatory madness suffered by artisans and clanker operators, brought on by overuse of a *hedron*. Few recover from it. Mancers can suffer from related ailments.

Field: The diffuse (or weak) force surrounding and permeating (and presumably generated by) a *node*. It is the source of a mancer's *power*. Various stronger forces are also known to exist, although no one knows how to tap them safely (see *power*).

Flesh-forming: A branch of the Secret Art that only lyrinx can use. Developed to adapt themselves to the ever-mutable void where they came from, it now involves the slow transformation of a living creature, tailoring it to suit some particular purpose. It is painful for both creature and lyrinx, and can be employed only on small creatures.

Gate: A portal between one place (or one world) and another, connected by a shifting trans-dimensional 'wormhole'.

Geomancy: The most difficult and powerful of all the Secret Arts. An adept is able to draw upon the forces that move and shape the world. A most dangerous Art to the user.

Hedron: A natural or shaped crystal, formed deep in the earth from fluids that circulate through a natural *node*. Trained artisans can tune a hedron to draw power from the field surrounding a node, via the ethyr. Rutilated quartz, that is, quartz crystal containing dark needles of rutile, is commonly used. The artisan must first 'wake' the crystal using his or her *pliance*. Too far from a node, a hedron is unable to draw power and becomes useless. If a hedron is not used for long periods it may have to be rewoken by an artisan, though this can be hazardous.

Nodes: Rare places in the world where the Secret Art works better. Once identified, a *hedron* (or a mancer) can sometimes draw *power* from the node's *field* through the ethyr, though the amount diminishes with distance, not always regularly. A *clanker* operator must be alert for the loss and ready to draw on another node, if available. The field can be drained, in which case the node may not be usable for years, or even centuries. Mancers have long sought the secret of drawing on the far greater power of a node itself, but so far it has eluded them (or maybe those that succeeded did not live to tell about it).

There are also anti-nodes where the Art does not work at all, or is dangerously disrupted. Nodes and anti-nodes are frequently (though not always) associated with natural features or forces such as mountains, faults or hot spots.

Pliance: A device which enables an artisan to see the *field* and tune a *controller* to it.

Port-all: Tiaan's name for the device she makes in Tirthrax to open the gate (see *zyxibule*).

Power: A mancer of old, Nunar, codified the laws of mancing, noting how limited it was, mainly because of lack of power. She recognised that mancing was held back because:

- Power came from diffuse and poorly understood sources.
- It all went through the mancer first, causing aftersickness that grew greater the more powerful the source was. Eventually power, or aftersickness, would kill the mancer.
- The traditional way around this was to charge up an artefact (mirror, ring, whatever) with power over a long time, and to simply trigger it when needed. This had some advantages, though objects could be hard to control or become corrupted, and once discharged were essentially useless.
- Yet some of the ancients had used devices that held a charge, or perhaps replenished themselves. No one knew how, but it had to be so, else how could they maintain their power for hundreds if not thousands of years (for example, the Mirror of Aachan), or use quite prodigious amounts of power without becoming exhausted (Rulke's legendary construct)?

Nunar assembled a team of mancers utterly devoted to her project (no mean feat) and set out to answer these questions. Mancing was traditionally secretive – practitioners tried (often wasting their lives in dead ends) and usually failed alone. Only the desperate state of the war could have made them work together, sharing their discoveries, until the genius of Nunar put together the *Special Theory of Power* that described where the diffuse force came from and how a mancer actually tapped it, drawing not through the earthly elements but via the ultradimensional ethyr.

The ultimate goals of theoretical mancers are the *General Theory of Power*, which deals with how *nodes* work and how they might be tapped safely, and, beyond that, the *Unified Power Theory*, which reconciles all fields, weak and strong, in terms of a single force.

Secret Art: The use of magical or sorcerous powers (mancing).

Tirthrax: The principal city of the Aachim of Santhenar, constructed within Mt Tirthrax, in the Great Mountains, the tallest peak on the Three Worlds.

Well of Echoes, the: An Aachim concept to do with the reverberation of time, memory and the Histories. Sometimes a place of death and rebirth (to the same cycling fate). Also a sense of being trapped in history, of being helpless to change collective fate (of a family, clan or species). Origin sometimes thought to be a sacred well on Aachan, sometimes on Santhenar. The term has become part of Aachim folklore. 'I have looked in the Well of Echoes.' 'I heard it at the Well.' 'I will go to the Well.' Possibly also a source; a great *node*.

The Well is symbolised by the three-dimensional symbol of infinity, the universe and nothingness.

Zyxibule: An Aachim device, powered by an *amplimet*, to create a *gate*. Also called 'port-all' by Tiaan.

A SHADOW ON THE GLASS

Ian Irvine

Volume One of
THE VIEW FROM THE MIRROR

*Once there were three worlds, each with their own people.
Then, fleeing out of the void, on the edge of extinction,
came the Charon. And the balance changed forever.*

Karan, a sensitive with a troubled past,
is forced to steal an ancient relic in payment for a
debt. But she is not told that the relic is the Mirror of
Aachan, a twisted, deceitful thing that remembers
everything it has seen.

Llian, meanwhile, a brilliant chronicler, is expelled
from his college for uncovering a perilous mystery.

Thrown together by fate,
Karan and Llian are hunted across a world at war,
for the Mirror contains a secret of incredible power.

A Shadow on the Glass is the first volume in
a sweeping epic fantasy of magic and adventure
by a sensational new storyteller.

THE TOWER ON THE RIFT

Ian Irvine

Volume Two of
THE VIEW FROM THE MIRROR

As war rages across the land, Tensor,
the desperate leader of the Aachim people, flees into
the wilderness, taking with him the ancient Mirror of
Aachan and the chronicler Llian.

Only Karan can save the chronicler,
though she's not sure she can help herself. Tensor
wants her dead, the other powers are hunting her
for her sensitive talents, and Rulke the Charon
broods over them all from his Nightland prison.

The Twisted Mirror holds knowledge that
the world can only dream about. But its
power may yet betray them all.

'The complex cultures, detailed geography,
and the palpable weight of history provides a solid
background to an intense story . . . this stands out as
a worldbuilding labour of love with some truly
original touches' *Locus*

DARK IS THE MOON

Ian Irvine

Volume Three of
THE VIEW FROM THE MIRROR

Rulke the Great Betrayer is free at last to use
the deadly construct he has spent a thousand years
perfecting. To succeed he needs just one thing –
Karan's unique sensitive talent.

Karan and her love Llian are lost in the Nightland,
in an alien palace that is collapsing about them.
Only Rulke can open the gate and send them
home to Santhenar, but if the gate is not sealed
the world itself faces destruction.